Ends
of the
Earth

William Nester

Northwest Publishing, Inc.
Salt Lake City, Utah

Ends of the Earth

For information address: Northwest Publishing, Inc.
6906 South 300 West, Salt Lake City, Utah 84047
JC 1.6.96 / JP

PRINTING HISTORY
First Printing 1996

ISBN: 1-56901-904-5

NPI books are published by Northwest Publishing, Incorporated,
6906 South 300 West, Salt Lake City, Utah 84047.
The name "NPI" and the "NPI" logo are trademarks belonging to
Northwest Publishing, Incorporated.

PRINTED IN THE UNITED STATES OF AMERICA.
10 9 8 7 6 5 4 3 2 1

To all those
who explore the world and themselves
in search of something better.

One

The storm was well into its second night, pounding and saturating the earth, toppling trees, swelling creeks into rivers and rivers into seas. Ragged lightning ripped the pitch-black sky; thunder crackled and boomed—sometimes sharply, sometimes in slow, rumbling waves from west to east.

The Ohio River, clogged with huge uprooted trees, ran faster and faster, and rose silently up its steep banks. Several thousand people were scattered through Cincinnati's hundreds of frame and log homes, its score of taverns, and Fort Washington's barracks. Many huddled around fireplaces or candles, laughing and talking or silently waiting; others in bed stared into the dark, wondering about their pasts or presents or futures or nothing at all, and a few snored away the hours

1

dead asleep.

Blasts of wind and rain shook the Yates's home, whistled through the cracks, and sizzled down into the fireplace. The grandfather clock slowly ticked away beside the fireplace but no one noticed its long hand glide toward the top. Jake, as usual, was the center of attention. He used his big hands and long face as often as words to tell stories. "That giant mama bear charged me across that meadow, its cubs bawling and charging along behind her, set on tearing me to hell when they caught me…"

Pulling at his brown beard, Jake paused for effect, stared into the wide eyes of first Willie, who sat cross-legged on the floor wrapped in a red wool blanket, then Sarah bundled in her mother's arms. He sensed and then glanced up at their mother's frown. "Sorry, Jenny, I meant tear me to heck." He grinned over at his brother who continued to stare into the fireplace. Sam the stone married Jenny the hen, he sniffed. Damned fine pair!

"Where was Daddy?" Sarah demanded, interrupting Jake's mirth.

Willie glared at Sarah. Why wouldn't she just shut up and listen?

"As I was saying earlier, Sarah, I had no idea where your daddy was. I feared some godd…some darn Miami or Shawnee had butchered and scalped your daddy like they had darn near every man in St. Clair's army!"

Sam looked deeper into the red-hot coals, wishing he could plunge his head into them and sear away the mobile of memories from the three campaigns that forever whirred and twisted through his mind—the sudden screams and arrows flying at them out of nowhere; the blackened, rotting bodies of friends and neighbors; the mass rape of that fat squaw, her moans and later the thud of an ax in her head; the mad scramble of survivors, each trying to outrun the others, hoping the savages would be too busy torturing those behind to catch up; two different armies, first Hamar's in '90 then St. Clair's the next year, each almost completely wiped out; and then two more years of Indian raids and butchering and fear until finally "Mad" Anthony Wayne's victory at Fallen Timbers in '94 and the Treaty of Greenville that bought an uneasy peace since…

"So did you shoot the bear?" Willie asked impatiently.

"I didn't know what to do—and maybe you wouldn't have either, Willie. Ponder it. If I fired I might have killed the mama bear and then clubbed to death the cubs, but that rifle shot might have signaled the Injuns that was chasing me exactly where I was. Why, today my scalp might be fluttering from the wigwam of Little Turtle or Blue Jacket himself...but if I didn't shoot, that mama bear would be tearing me limb from limb within seconds."

Jake paused again, this time to reach over and pluck a smoldering stick from the fire and relight his long clay pipe. He sucked nosily at the pipe, his gaunt cheeks drawing deeper within his skull with each puff. Finally satisfied, he pointed the stem toward the children.

"I slowly leveled my rifle, gave that mama bear a few more steps, and then slowly squeezed the trigger...Click! I'll be darned if the flint didn't snap on damp powder and my rifle wasn't worth a damn.

"By now that bear was close enough to spit in my face if she'd a mind to. I turned heel and ran like all the devils of hell was after me with that mama bear just a handshake behind. I dropped my rifle and leapt for the branches of the first tree I reached and scrambled up as fast as I could but that bear just clawed itself up after me and soon I had run out of tree and had nothing but sky above..."

The clock began to strike seven. Jake looked up at it. Above the clock's face revolved a disk upon which a smiling sun and moon eternally chased each other in circles. In the background were tiny ships at sea, gusting clouds, and flying porpoises. "Wish I had me a tall clock like that," he commented. He sniffed, scratched his left armpit, and looked over the barrels of flour, nails, and gunpowder, and piles of cloth and deerskins stacked along one side of the room. It was good to work and live in the same house.

Willie leaned forward even farther. "So wadya do, Uncle Jake?"

"Uhmm...where was I?" Jake asked.

"The bear was chasing you up the tree," Willie quickly replied.

"That's right," Jake chuckled. "That bear'd caught up with me." He jerked a thumb toward the clock. "Unlike up thar where neither the sun nor moon catches the other and it ain't clear who's trailing who."

While Willie squirmed impatiently, Jake paused to puff again at his pipe. "Fortunately," he exclaimed suddenly, "I still had my skinning knife. I jerked it just as that bear sank its claws into my leg and started dragging me down." Jake lifted up his right pant-leg to reveal long red rows of scars down his calf. "I plunged my knife right into that bear's eye and ripped it out." Willie's eyes got wider.

"Yuck!" Sarah exclaimed and crinkled her face.

Jenny stroked Sarah's forehead. "It's just a story," she whispered. She frowned at Jake, relieved once again that she'd spurned him for his brother. She marveled at how Jake and Sam could be so different yet so close. Jake was a bad influence on Sam and the children, making them think about and do things they shouldn't think about or do. If only he had stayed in St. Louis, she huffed silently.

"The bear growled deep and began dragging me even harder. I kicked her in the face with my other leg and jabbed at her other eye, and hung on that tree for dear life with my left arm. Finally the bear lost its balance, crashed back down, and landed on its head, stunned. The cubs had been bawling all this time and bawled even louder when their mama landed in the middle of them. I wanted to jump down and scare off the cubs and sink my knife in the mama's neck but I felt weak and feared she would wake up just as I got to her. But the longer I stayed the more chance the Injuns would catch up to me so I slowly climbed down the tree cursing at the cubs and waving my knife at them. The smaller one ran off but I had to dig my knife between the big cub's ribs but not before he chewed up my arm something fierce." Jake rolled up a sleeve to reveal deep bear claw and teeth scars. "The mama was just coming to when I got to her. I stabbed her a dozen times before my arm gave out and I almost passed out, but reckoned I had a hundred miles of wilderness to thread with a pack of Injuns on my tail screaming for my scalp before I got back here to Cincinnati, so I just picked up my rifle and finally made it back in four days and maybe you can imagine how tickled I was to see your daddy drag himself into town a couple days later with a hundred other men that I had given up as all long dead."

"Well, Jake," Jenny said coldly. "I think you've given my children enough nightmares for one night." She set down Sarah and pulled at Willie. "Upstairs! Both of you! I'll be up soon to tuck you in."

"Ah, Mama, a little longer," they cried together.

"Hush and up with you!" She watched them turn and slowly climb the steep stairs. "Sam. Sam!" Her sharp voice jerked him from his lethargy. "It's about time we all turned in. You know we have to unload that flatboat tomorrow. You know how anxious I've been about those mirrors ever since we ordered them almost a year ago. Just think, Sam, if we can sell off those mirrors we'll be debt-free for the first time since we got here. Why it took that Philadelphia firm almost a year to send them after we sent our order I don't know, but thank God our mirrors survived those wagon roads from Philadelphia and the flatboat trip from Pittsburgh." Her voice softened. "Remember, Sam, it'll have been fifteen years ago in June that we made that same journey. Fifteen years! I hear the road hasn't improved much since." Sam nodded and stared back into the fire.

"Jake, you'd better get to sleep too, because tomorrow you'll have your work cut out for you doing something more around here than eat and smoke and drink and tell horrible stories." Jake smiled and rolled out his blanket near the fire. The storm began to howl louder.

"Damn glad I've got a roof over my head tonight."

"Sam, please!"

Sam glanced up at Jenny and then stared behind her. His eyes and mouth opened wide. "Oh, m-my God!" he stammered.

A stream of water snaked toward them across the floor and curled around Jenny's feet. Jenny screamed, "Sarah! Willie! Put on your shoes and come down! We've got to get to high ground!"

Sam leapt out of his chair and scrambled up the stairs. He grabbed a child under each arm, and carried them down to Jenny and Jake. "Jenny, take the children to the Cumberland's while Jake and I try to save the store!"

There was a loud thud on the back wall, then a slow scraping as whatever it was moved downriver. Everyone stopped to look, expecting to see the river burst through the wall and sweep them away at any second. Screams and shouts broke out from the other buildings fronting the river. Sarah began to cry, "My shoes aren't on!"

Jenny grabbed Sarah and shoved Willie toward the door. "Hurry! We'll get them later!" She yelled over her shoulder, "Sam take the clock and desk and everything else upstairs! Oh, and bring the Bible box!"

Jenny and Willie screamed as their feet plunged into the frigid ankle-deep water flowing through the street. Sarah whimpered in her mother's arms and Willie tugged hard at her dress, and together they groped through the darkness, the deep, cold mud sucking hard at their feet with each step.

Voices shouted to one another and lanterns bobbed through the darkness all around them as dozens of others scrambled away from the flood. Doors of homes opened ahead. Their owners stood framed in the light calling out "What's the matter? What's happening?" The rain poured down. Lightning flared.

"Oh Lord, why didn't I bring a lantern? Willie? Are we going the right way? Where's the Cumberland's?"

Willie paused and looked around. "I...dunno! I dunno!" Forked lightning flashed, revealing the two-story Buckhorn Inn ahead, ghost-like in the void. "That way, Mama! The Cumberland's are up ahead on the other side of the Buckhorn!"

"Where? Where Willie? I can't see where you're heading!"

• • •

The river flowed four blocks into Cincinnati, flooding those houses nearest the submerged bank waist-deep in water and those furthest knee-deep. Thin ice had spread across the shallows during the night after the storm surged on east. Now it slowly melted as the sun rose and hundreds of men crunched their way through, forming scores of human chains down to the half-flooded houses. The strongest men led the way, cursing and grunting as they dragged out such things as chests, beds, kettles, rocking chairs, and blankets. The goods were then passed on up the line from one shivering man to the next. Women waited anxiously at the end of each line, their breath steaming in the cold, fearing treasured bundles of letters or quilts or silverware had been washed away forever. The women and children sorted each item and stored it away in the neighbors' homes where they had sheltered for the night.

Sam and Jake worked alone in the Yates's home. Soaked and frozen, they strained to lift one barrel of store-goods after another into Jake's dugout.

"Hell, Sam, this flour barrel's more water than powder. Unless Jenny's planning to cook the world's biggest pancake, we best dump this and go after something lasting. The pirogue won't take much more anyway."

"Goddamn it, Jake, why can't you understand?" Sam groaned as they lifted the barrel over the gunwale. They held on to the dugout, gasping for air. Sam jabbed a finger toward the town.

"I owe...$512 to that son of a bitch...Cleaver...and another $78 to a half-dozen other creditors." Sam looked hard into Jake's eyes. "And every pound of gunpowder or flour I can dry and sell can keep a roof over my family's head a day longer."

Jake nodded. "St. Louis, Sam, St. Louis is the answer. Sell out, pull up stakes, and come on downriver to St. Louis and stay with me and Colette. You can get twice in St. Louis what you get here for goods, and when selling's slow you can come trading with me, like old days. The Injuns ain't as spoiled as around these parts. A twist of tobacco and a handful of beads'll fetch a pelt."

"Jenny'd never go for it. I promised her after we settled here that we'd move no more."

"Hell, Sam, that was then. Now that flatboat full of mirrors is at the bottom of the Ohio, your home's half underwater and you are drowning in debt. Cut loose. Women take longer to see sense than men, but Jenny'll come around."

"Well, Jake, listen now. You heard her yammering about those goddamn smashed mirrors. Now she wants to take the young'uns and go back to her mama in Philadelphia."

"You know women, Sam. She'll get over it. A man's gotta head forward rather than backward. Philadelphia's full of nothing but ghosts and Cincinnati's full of nothing but creditors. You can start fresh in St. Louis."

"What if trading don't work? How will we survive?"

"Land, Sam. Land's the real road to wealth and fame!" Jake grinned, his eyes flashed, and his words spilled out fast. He had been waiting for this moment since he arrived two weeks earlier. "I already told you I have 10,000 acres staked out along the Missouri River just thirty miles up from St. Charles and there are millions more across the territory free for the taking. Right now there are more French than Americans in the territory but Americans are gonna pour in now that word's out that Louisiana Territory was sold to the United States last autumn. Right now thousands of Americans are thinking of heading west to the territory and leaving their debts and worn-out farmland and spiteful neighbors behind to start fresh. If, of course, they aren't already heading West at this instance. We can make a fortune selling land to the newcomers! Why, we can do in Louisiana what the Scioto and Ohio companies did here in Ohio! We can be richer than Cleaver, richer than even Governor St. Clair himself! We—"

Sam held up his hands and hunched up his shoulders. "I'll think on it, Jake. Leave it be for now." Jake tried to calm down. He knew his elder brother always pondered a possibility for weeks until he made up his mind and the best thing to do was to sit tight and act as nonchalant as possible while he worked it through. For another hour they swore, shivered, and lifted more goods into the dugout until it threatened to sink under the weight.

"All right, Jake. I don't reckon she'll take anymore. Let's head for land."

"Why stop now, Sam? I was just starting to grow gills and enough scales to make me feel at home waist-deep in this damn near frozen river." Sam grinned as he untied the rope. Together they guided the dugout through the flooded streets, slipping at times in the mud. They passed a few groups of men still salvaging but most had gone to shore and now sat in homes, bundled in blankets before fires, pewter mugs of whiskey in their hands, thawing their frozen bodies.

Willie stood fidgeting on shore, hopping from one foot to another and blowing into his hands to keep warm. He muttered to himself,

"Why're they taking so long? Why don't they let me help? I hate being a young'un." He mimicked his father's slow, solemn voice, "No, Willie, you stay home with your mama and Sarah. You'll just get in the way."

Someone slogged behind him in the mud. He turned to face a huge Delaware Indian wrapped in a filthy blue blanket. "Chief! I was afraid you washed away." Chief's toothless mouth smiled wide across his pockmarked face.

"I no wash away. Willie, you got candy for Chief?"

His smile faded. "I ain't got nothing." He could almost hear his mother say, "Not 'ain't got nothing.' You 'don't have anything.'"

"Don't worry, Willie. You still got house. I see house from the hill."

"Yeah, but everything's flooded and the flatboat with the mirrors sank and my mama's been crying all morning."

The chief squinted and pointed toward the flooded streets. "There's papa. I go." He patted the boy's head and trudged away. They both knew Willie would get in trouble if Sam saw them together. "Stay away from that lice-ridden, thieving redskin!" Sam would thunder. For a moment he watched his father and uncle wading toward him, with the pirogue trailing behind them in the river. Then he turned and ran through the streets toward the Cumberland's to get help. He had almost reached the Cumberland's when a squeaky voice called out from a side street, "Whoa, Willie, where are you heading, lad?"

Startled, he turned to face two men: one short and skinny with a walrus mustache and whiskers, and the other tall, stout, and clean-shaven. "Mr. Cleaver, Sheriff Hackett, you got the jump on me."

"I repeat, Willie, where are you going?" Cleaver's voice hardened. He looked big to Willie but Hackett seemed to tower beside him.

"I was just gonna tell my mama that papa and Uncle Jake had fetched our dry goods and were headed back."

As Willie stared into Cleaver's small brown eyes he thought about the copperhead that he had caught down at Mill Creek last summer. He had grabbed the copperhead behind the neck as it was sunning on a rock; the snake had wrapped itself tightly around his arm as he carried it home. His mother screamed when she saw it, ordered him to toss it in the street, and then cut it in two with a hoe. Cleaver's eyes looked just like those of the copperhead.

"Well, now..." Cleaver continued while Hackett frowned at Willie. "I do hope they were able to salvage enough to meet expenses. Take us to them at once. We have business to attend to with your father." Cleaver struck his hickory walking stick into the mud for emphasis, and then struggled to pull it out.

Willie stood transfixed. How did Cleaver stay so clean walking through the muddy streets? Although his calfskin boots were mud-caked, his dark velvet overcoat, vest, and tan knee breeches were immaculate. The sheriff was draped in a long green wool coat that hung to his knees. Willie shivered as he remembered the times he had joined the crowds before Fort Washington to watch the sheriff whip thieves. The sheriff's smirk would widen just before each blow and scream. He had whipped one horse thief to death.

"Are you listening to me, Willie?" Cleaver's voice cracked. His eyes narrowed further. "Take us to him at once!"

Willie quickly calculated: Would they catch me if I ran? Where would I hide? Wouldn't they just find papa anyway? Would Hackett whip me like that horse thief? He stared down at Cleaver's boots.

"They just come to shore and are unloading."

"Lead on, lad!" Cleaver pointed his stick toward the river. The two men gingerly followed Willie through the muddy streets down to where Sam and Jake were busy emptying the dugout.

Jake nudged Sam. "Well, will you look at that?" Jake and Sam stopped and watched as the three approached.

"Willie, I told you to fetch mama and Mr. Cumberland when we pulled in, not these two," Sam said sternly.

Willie sniffed back tears. "They made me, Papa."

Sam leaned against the dugout. His breath slowly wheezed out between his teeth. This was no time for a fight, he reasoned. He nodded to Hackett, "Sheriff...what do you want Cleaver?" Sam added wearily.

Barely listening to Cleaver, Hackett carefully sized up Sam and Jake, wondering which was the toughest and how many gouges and kicks it would take to cut them down.

"Mr. Yates, I was so sorry to hear about the loss of your mirrors. You've been telling me for the past year that just as soon as you received and sold them you could retire your debt to me. What is your present scheme? You are well past due on your payments."

"I will pay you back, Mr. Cleaver, but my immediate concern is to feed and house my family."

Cleaver raised an eyebrow but managed to keep his voice level. The impertinent fool. Yates acts as if I forced him to borrow my money. "Of course, of course, Mr. Yates. I must deal with a score of families in the same unfortunate situation...but they must all bear the consequences of their decision to acquire debt." He turned to Hackett.

"Sheriff?" Hackett leaned back his head and stared down at Sam. He thought of the five percent collection fee Cleaver would pay him, and all the drinking and whoring he would do once he got it. "Yates," his voice was deep and stern, "you are well past due on your payments." Hackett pulled a large document from this coat pocket. "This is a summons to debtor's court. Either pay up or end up in jail."

Sam carefully read it. "March 27! That's next week! I'll be lucky if my goods dry out by then!"

"It's the law, Yates."

"Mr. Yates, let's be reasonable." Cleaver tried to sound sympathetic. "It is extremely unlikely that you will be able to pay the long past-due accumulated interest of $147, let alone the principal. Your home is a rotting, worthless wreck. It will cost a small fortune to fix it up. Now, as you know, I own extensive landholdings in Indiana Territory. Why not sell me your riverfront property and all your fixings and goods and I will credit you not only several hundred acres in Indiana, but the seed and equipment to farm it. I make you such a generous offer, Mr. Yates, despite your delinquency, only because your family is severely wanting."

"You want everything?" Sam asked incredulously. "Even our furniture?"

"Yes, of course, Mr. Yates, and even that will not cover what you owe me. I am losing hundreds of dollars on our deal because I trusted you to keep your word. I thought you were a man of honor. I was sadly mistaken. The least you can do is hand over what little you have to me."

"I've got a week to think on it, Cleaver. Now if you'll excuse us, we'll continue unloading."

Sam turned around and started to lift a small barrel of whiskey from the dugout. As Jake bent down to help, Sam glared into his eyes and murmured fiercely, "St. Louis!"

Willie stretched out his arm toward the branch but his feet slipped and he smashed face-first into the muddy slope. "Damn it!" he yelled, then looked around to see if anyone had overheard him. He relaxed as he realized that his voice was lost in the thick woods of ash, hickory, and beech budding in the early spring chill. For a moment, he watched bluejays and cardinals flitter through the trees and listened to a dove coo up ahead. Then he slowly picked himself up, almost slipping again, and continued plodding up the tall hill behind Ft. Washington. "Mama's gonna kill me!" he murmured as he tried to pick off mud globs from his green linen shirt and brown woolen pants.

Almost there, he smiled to himself. Soon he would be nestled in his lookout, scanning the forest for wolves and redskins, and gazing down at Cincinnati below. No one knew about his lookout at the top of the huge, decaying beech that had lodged against a branch of an even bigger oak. He had discovered it last spring during his wanderings and almost every day since had hiked to the hill's summit to shinny up the beech and chop out a bigger lookout at the top with a rusty hatchet he had found.

He picked up his pace as the slope leveled off toward the top, trying to forget that this was his last trip to the lookout. It would have been only another week or two until he had chopped out a hole large enough to squeeze in Sandra Cumberland. Willie daydreamed about Sandra's freckled face, long brown pigtails, and skinny legs. He worried over the words he would use to ask her. At least Sandra wasn't afraid of heights or snakes, like most girls.

"What?" He stopped and stared at the remnants of his lookout. The beech had slowly dried and cracked during the long winter, then the storm had soaked it to an immense dead weight until it had smashed through the oak branch and shattered on the forest floor below.

He clambered over the beech, carefully examining every knot and branch. The lookout had split off into four large fragments. He tried to lift one but it was too heavy. He looked up at the oak, and then began to climb, branch by branch. Briefly he paused at the huge stump whose branch had propped up the beech, and then climbed farther until he hugged the thin trunk at the top, swaying gently in the wind and sun.

Snatches of sound drifted up from Cincinnati—a blacksmith's steady hammering on a wagon wheel, the neighing of horses in the pastures along the Ohio, a drill sergeant's curses from inside the fort.

He stared down at the hundreds of tiny buildings in Cincinnati. Ant-sized people wandered the checkerboard streets or popped out of one building and then quickly disappeared into another. He picked out his home down by the river but he couldn't tell if the figures milling around it were his family. The church steeple poked out above the town. Every week his family entered the church in their Sunday best and sang hymns or listened to Preacher Taylor alternately mumble and shout his sermons at the packed congregation. "Hellfire and damnation ravings!" Uncle Jake called them.

Willie hoped there was no church in St. Louis. Downriver at the town's edge was the shantytown. "You stay away from the shantytown, Willie!" his mother had often warned. "Bad men and women live there!" He recalled the times he had slipped through the scattered huts and ramshackle cabins to watch the painted women beckon in the trappers and riverboat men, and the drunks lurching through the rutted streets; to listen to the coarse laughter, dirty songs, and an occasional bone-breaking brawl. He had dodged away when the women tried to hug him or men thrust tin cups of whiskey toward him. His gaze drifted back across the town upriver to Fort Washington's faded red walls.

He wondered if Chief was out front begging from passers-by, ignoring the curses and giving thanks for the occasional penny instead. A dozen keelboats lined the riverbank. Early tomorrow morning one of them would carry Willie and his family to St. Louis. "Damn near four weeks it took me to paddle that pirogue with almost two hundred pounds of pelts down the Mississippi and up the Ohio here to Cincinnati. I reckon it'll take the keelboat 'bout the same ta get back," Uncle Jake had said. Willie shinnied up a little farther and stared toward the west. The chilly wind cut into his face and through his clothes. How much beyond the horizon was St. Louis?

A rifle shot cracked to the north. Hunters? Shawnees? He shivered thinking about Uncle Jake's scalping tales and the thick forests that stretched away forever. A cold gust of wind arched back the trunk he was riding. The truck creaked sharply. Stomach fluttering, he quickly scrambled down to the ground. A fox barked somewhere nearby.

Willie peered through the naked trees trying to spot it, and caught a flash of burnt orange along the east slope. He turned and started down toward Cincinnati but suddenly stopped, a smile spreading across his face. He strode back to the beech and picked out a broad smooth section of bark. First he slowly chipped out a huge heart. Then he took even more care chipping out a "W" on one side and "S" on the other. He stepped back admiring his work. Trying to mimic a grown-up voice, he declared, "Sandra, someday after I learn how to write, I'll send you a love letter!"

Davie Cumberland was a short, pear-shaped fellow with a florid face and thinning red hair. He stooped to wrap his thick, hairy arms around a small crate of mildewed books in the Yates' bedroom. "They'll never pull this off," he muttered as he carried the crate out and down the stairs to the nearly empty ground floor where Jenny and Mary Cumberland were quickly packing clothes into a trunk. The room stank of rotting wood.

"Oh, sugar, let me help you with that!" Mary leapt up before Davie, almost colliding with him. Mary was half a head taller than Davie and as skinny as he was fat. "You could get a rupture with that load!"

"It's all right, dear. I've got it." For a moment they wrestled with it until they both tired and set it down. Jenny tried to remember the last time Sam had called her "dear."

Jake and Sam hurried through the front door just as Davie was about to lift the crate again. "Oh, hold on, Davie!" Sam tapped him lightly on the shoulder. Davie slowly straightened up. "We wrapped up the clock and desk in canvas and lashed them on the pirogue but with all the other chests and barrels piled on she's riding low and there's nary room for anything else. The rest we'll have to squeeze onto the keelboat."

Before Davie could open his mouth Jenny blurted out, "Sam, you said there would be enough room in the pirogue and you know Captain Henderson said the keelboat was already full. What are we going to do?"

Irritation reddened Sam's face. "Jenny, for a dollar or two the captain will find enough space and if not we'll leave what's left with the Cumberland's. They already have all our upstairs furniture—it won't matter to leave a few more odds and ends. Now hurry up with your packing and quit your yammering. Captain Henderson will cast off as soon as we're on and the pirogue is tied fast. I want to be downriver and out of shouting distance before Cleaver and Hackett get wind of our plans." He turned to Davie, "How much more upstairs?"

"This is it, Sam!" Davie smiled proudly, always glad to help.

During the Hamar massacre, Sam had cut an arrow out of Davie's shoulder and dragged him back to Cincinnati. Delirious from the pain and loss of blood, Davie would never have survived without Sam.

"All right, we'll load it in the wheelbarrow on top of that trunk." He jerked his head toward Jenny and Mary. "Are you ready?"

Willie burst in the door followed by Sarah and Sandra. "Papa! Papa! I saw Cleaver talking to the captain!"

"Goddamn it!" shouted Sam. "That son of a bitch better not stop me!" Everyone looked startled. Sarah's eyes started to tear. Sam glared angrily.

Jake spoke quietly and steadily, "Sam, I'll head on down to the keelboat and divert him and send Willie back to warn if he comes this way, and if he does, you can float the pirogue down to the keelboat while Davie takes Jenny and the young'uns toward the keelboat by Second Avenue while Cleaver heads this way up First. Don't wait for me, I'll meet you downriver."

"All right! All right! Good thinking, Jake," Sam said quickly. "Let's move!"

"Come on, Willie!" They hurried out the door and down the crowded avenue toward the keelboat tied up several hundred yards downstream. Willie's head topped off just about where Jake's chest began so he practically had to run to keep up. They dodged wagons and mules and cursing teamsters, women with baskets filled with food dangling from their arms, and children playing hopscotch in the dust.

"Willie! There they are, boy!" Willie craned his neck to see the captain and Cleaver on the keelboat's gangplank about fifty yards ahead. Although he could not make out their words, it was clear from their shouting and wild gestures that they were arguing. A half-dozen men on shore hoisted barrels and boxes to other men on the keelboat. "You stay here and watch my hand. If I touch my hat, run like hell and tell your daddy to cut loose."

Jake marched toward them, wondering just what he would say and how he could divert Cleaver. He reminded himself not to stare at the long red scar that sliced across Henderson's face from his chin to his drooping right eye.

"What the hell are you boys fighting about?" Jake winked at the captain and grinned in Cleaver's face as he turned toward him.

"Rumor has it, Mr. Yates," Cleaver shot out the words, "that you and your brother and his family are trying to weasel out of your debts by escaping downriver today in this keelboat. Is that true?"

Jake tugged at his beard. "Is that what the captain here says?"

"Jake," Henderson twisted his head and spat a stream of tobacco juice into the river, "I was just telling Cleaver that it warn't none of his goddamn business who or what I was carrying." The captain slowly ran a dirty forefinger along his scar.

"Well, that sounds like a reasonable answer to me. Don't you agree, Mr. Cleaver," Jake said mockingly.

"Watch out—we're headed up!" Two shirtless men had just rolled a large barrel of flour to the gangplank and attempted to push it up. "This here's the last one, Captain," one of them said.

Henderson nodded curtly to the men then barked, "Get outta my men's way, Cleaver, before either them or me carves ya up inta snapping turtle bait!"

Suddenly realizing that he was badly outnumbered, Cleaver quickly stepped aside. "As soon as I heard the rumor this morning, I sent word for the sheriff, and he will soon be here to settle this. You needn't threaten violence, Captain Henderson." Cleaver looked worried.

Now it was the captain's turn to be mocking. "Cleaver, ya told me earlier that the sheriff was out along the Little Miami pocketin' taxes and won't be back till evening."

Cleaver's confidence came back. "He'll be back at a gallop just as soon as he gets word about this nefarious attempt to defraud me! He's undoubtedly well on his way right now. You will all be imprisoned and whipped and fined—I guarantee it!"

"How much ya forkin' him, Cleaver?" the captain clenched his fists and angrily leaned into Cleaver's startled face. "Cut me some?"

Jake touched his greasy flop hat then took it off and waved it at the sun. Willie turned and ran back home as fast as possible. "Hotter than hell and clear as a bell today, is it not, Mr. Cleaver?" Jake's grin turned to a sneer. "Maybe you should get back to that dark little hole where you burrow as soon as possible. You could easily get dropped by a sunstroke on a day like today." Jake paused, "But, on second thought, I'll tell you what, Mr. Cleaver," Jake assumed the air of the Philadelphia gentleman he had once been, "if you will be so kind as to follow me to my brother's humble riverfront estate, I will prove to you beyond the shadow of a doubt that there is nothing amiss, and that my brother will see you in court tomorrow to fully pay what he owes you. Do follow me."

Jake turned and strode away up First Avenue. Cleaver hesitated and then scurried after him. The captain wrinkled his brow and frowned, then called out to his crew, "Get ready to cast off!"

Cradling their corncob dolls, Sandra and Sarah sat with their backs to the overloaded wheelbarrow outside the Yates home. Sandra scraped a circle in the dust with her bare foot. "Sarah, my daddy said St. Louis was far away. Can you and Willie come back and visit me?"

"Sure we will, Sandra, if my mama lets us."

"If you do, you better make Willie promise not to tease me anymore!" Sandra said solemnly.

"You mean like when he pushed you into the river when you asked him to dance?" Both girls burst into giggles.

Willie ran up panting. "Where's Papa?...We've gotta go! Papa!...Papa!"

Sam bolted out of the door and shouted back inside, "Let's go!"

Davie hurried out and began pushing the wheelbarrow across the street toward an ally which led to Second Avenue. Jenny grabbed Willie and Sarah's hands while Mary took Sandra's and they all began to follow Davie. Suddenly Jenny turned and shouted out, "Sam! No, I love our home! I don't want to leave." She began to weep.

Sam bit his lip. There was so much at stake. He wanted to slap and shake her. Instead, he walked over and gently took her in his arms. "We can stay if you want to visit me in debtor's jail."

"I know! I know!" She looked up at her little two-story frame home. The whitewashed walls were muddy waist-high and a front window was broken. "That...that...Cleaver is going to take it!"

"Well, if we hurry he won't take us! Jenny, please, we have to leave now!" Sam turned her toward the alley. "Hurry, Davie! I'll be there soon." Sam watched them disappear into the alley and then he turned, slipped past the house, quickly untied the dugout, and waded out into the Ohio River.

As they entered the Yates' home Cleaver turned to Jake and shouted, "Why, it's empty! You did trick me!" Jake hauled off and swung his fist at Cleaver as hard as he could, but Cleaver ducked and the blow glanced off his ear. Furious, Cleaver lashed his hickory cane toward Jake's knees but Jake dodged away out of reach. Each glared and panted at the other like two maddened rattlesnakes, wondering what to do next. Jake looked around the room for something to throw or strike with, but it was bare.

He turned and ran out the door, slamming it behind him and then held the knob tight with all his strength. A second later Cleaver was at the door, desperately trying to wrench it open. A crowd of passers-by began to gather in the street, laughing and cheering Jake on. Suddenly Jake's knob pulled off the door and Jake and Cleaver crashed back on either side. Jake scrambled to his feet and charged through the door just as Cleaver was getting up. The door smashed Cleaver in the face, throwing him back heavily against the floor.

Jake stared down at Cleaver's bloody face and still body, then stumbled back out the door, "One of you gawkers may want to fetch a doctor. It seems Mr. Cleaver just took a bad fall." The crowd burst into laughter and cheers. Most of them were in debt to Cleaver. "I'd do it myself, but I'm afraid I have a boat to catch!" Jake pushed his way through the crowd and then ran down toward the keelboat.

No one said anything as they marched down Second Avenue. Davie used the packed wheelbarrow to clear a way down the busy street while the others followed close behind. Whenever Willie got up enough courage to glance back at Sandra, she would give him a shy smile and then look down at his heels.

Mary chuckled. "Don't worry, Willie, you'll see Sandra again. Jenny, you will come back and visit, won't you?"

Jenny looked over her shoulder. "I already promised you a dozen times at least."

"I am going to dearly miss you all," Mary sighed as she imagined Sam's tall, hard body alongside Davie's squat figure plodding ahead.

They cut down an alley to the crowded wharf along First Avenue where a dozen keelboats were tied, and slowly pushed their way through the scores of gruff, scarred rivermen and teamsters loading or unloading, and stylishly-dressed merchants cutting deals. A wizened, old black man played Virginia reels on his fiddle as passers-by dropped pennies into his hat. Suddenly a half-dozen ragged boys streaked through the throng, drawing curses from all sides. One of them dangled a squawking red chicken by its feet.

The captain stood atop the cabin and began to shout and wave when he spotted the two families poke into the crowded avenue. Sam had just reached the boat himself and was busy tying up the dugout.

"There they are!" cried Davie.

"Chief!" Willie wrenched loose from his mother's tight grip and dodged over toward Chief who was leaning against a huge hogshead barrel stuffed with tobacco.

"Willie, come back!" Jenny's shriek was lost in the tumult. Chief grinned broadly as he ran up. "You go to St. Louis. Nobody gimme candy."

Willie pulled some rock candy out of his pocket and pressed it into Chief's grimy hand. The Delaware's grin faded as he stared up into the sky. He nodded and smiled down at the boy. "You go far, Willie! You don't know how far!"

Willie's face crinkled. "Whadya mean?" he asked, puzzled. Then Jenny caught up and yanked him away toward the keelboat. He twisted to glance at Chief.

Sam and Davie pulled the trunk and several crates on the keelboat while Jenny and Mary hugged and murmured promises into each other's ears. Willie and Sarah scampered up the gangplank and then began shouting goodbyes down at Sandra. Davie jumped down to the wharf and Sam lifted Jenny aboard.

"Cast off!" Henderson hollered.

Suddenly Jake appeared, dodging his way through the crowd. He climbed onboard, drenched in sweat and gasped to Sam, "I hope I didn't kill the bastard!"

On the narrow walkway on each side, a half-dozen powerfully built men began to carefully pole the keelboat away from shore and out into the main channel. Henderson stood in the stern, his hand on the tiller. He shouted out, "Care them sawyers boys! With the Ohio running this fast we'll be in St. Louis afore ya kin shoot, ifin we don't rip out our bottom first!"

The Yates huddled on the cabin roof. Jenny wept softly and everyone waved at the Cumberland's on shore. Willie stared at Sandra, wondering if he would ever see her again, then shifted his eyes to Chief, wrapped in his blue blanket, standing wooden on shore amidst the jostling crowd. His eyes wandered over the rapidly shrinking homes and warehouses fronting the river, the church steeple stretching to the sky, Fort Washington at one end of Cincinnati, the shantytown at the other, and the lookout hill and the other hills looming behind above everything.

"Are there hills in St. Louis, Uncle Jake?"

"Nope, nary even an anthill. But the woods around is thick with deer and bear waiting to be skinned and eaten and...Sam, look! There's the sheriff!"

A huge figure on a chestnut horse had appeared beside the Cumberland's.

They watched him lift himself higher in the saddle and wave madly at them until he shrank out of sight. Finally the keelboat flowed around a bend and Cincinnati disappeared into wilderness.

"I hope I didn't kill that bastard," Jake muttered again.

It was an easy ten day float down the Ohio. Occasionally they would surge past small villages or lonely cabins in stump-filled clearings, and they tied up at Louisville for half a day while Henderson bartered away a barrel of tobacco for a hundred pounds of furs. But mostly the hills on both banks were covered with thick, unbroken forest whose trees seemed to green a little more with each passing day.

On chilly or rainy days, Jenny and the children would wrap themselves in blankets and huddle inside the dark, musty cabin. Jenny would light a tallow candle and try to read them Bible stories. On warm days, they would lounge atop the cabin in the sun and count white-tailed deer feeding along shore. Meanwhile Jake and Sam would help the crew pole through the stretches where the current slowed but mostly they would trade stories with Henderson and the men or just gaze out at the wilderness. Sometimes the two brothers would stand in the prow and take turns firing shots at mallards or Canadian geese paddling ahead, and then Henderson would steer the keelboat over and one of the men would pluck the dead bird out of the river. The only danger was the stretches of rapids where everyone would hold on tight while

Henderson stood rigidly at the helm, scanning the white water ahead with his good eye and piloting the keelboat through. Despite Henderson's skill, the keelboat would sometimes scrape over or slam against a rock but the crew quickly smeared pitch over any leaks inside the hull. The pirogue tied up behind always made it through safely. Toward evening Henderson would search for a place to tie up for the night, either on small wooded islands or one of the banks. Tents were set up, fires were lit, a dinner of fowl, venison and pancakes was quickly gobbled down, and a guard was posted while everyone fell into a deep sleep. Mosquitoes buzzed around their ears all night and everyone awoke the next morning covered with bites.

The Mississippi was hell to pole up. Ten thousand times a day, from dawn to dusk, Sam, Jake, and the other men would simultaneously dig their poles into the riverbottom and slowly strain their way down toward the keelboat's stern. Then the two lines of men would trot back toward the prow and shove in their poles again. Henderson stood at the tiller, cussing encouragement to his men, fiercely searching the river for the best channel. Spring rains swelled the current until at times the keelboat seemed to stand still in midstream while the men struggled to inch it forward.

In places the Mississippi was clogged with trees that had to be either poled around or sawed through. Sometimes the keelboat ground to a halt against sandbars, or ran over holes so deep the poles could not reach bottom, so they had to float downstream a ways and try another route. The Mississippi often flowed in half-loops so that even when the keelboat made twenty miles on a good day, they might have advanced only five as a crow flew. Dry campsites were harder to find along the Mississippi bottomlands, and at night ,the mosquitoes seemed twice as thick. The camps were much quieter than on the Ohio. By now everyone had heard each other's stories several times over and usually the men were too exhausted to say more than a word or two at a time, and if they did, it was usually a profanity.

They tied up for half a day each at Cape Giradeau and Kaskaskia, and spent the night at St. Genevieve. In each village, Henderson bartered away more of his sugar, tobacco, and flour for beaver and deerskins while most of the crew headed for the nearest tavern, got drunk, laid the whores, and picked fights. Meanwhile the family would scatter. Jake usually joined the crew at one of the taverns; Sam would struck up conversations with the locals about farming or hunting or the price of goods; Jenny and Sarah poked through the dry goods shops or picked flowers at the edge of town; and Willie, after quickly wandering the few streets, headed for a nearby hill or climbed a tall tree and gazed out over the Mississippi Valley. Although Americans had been trickling into the territory for over a decade, most of the locals were still French.

Jake spoke French proficiently but was not usually around when Sam or Jenny needed someone to translate so they had to struggle with the few words or phrases Jake had taught them. His trading done, Henderson would fire his big flintlock pistol to signal that it was time to head upriver. The Yates quickly assembled back at the keelboat and most of the crew soon straggled in, but usually Henderson had to search the taverns for a few laggards and curse them back onboard.

The sun burned down hot and the river was sluggish. The poling was easy and the keelboat made good time. Jenny, Willie, and Sarah perched atop the cabin before Henderson at the tiller. The farther they got from Cincinnati, the more Jenny would tell Willie and Sarah stories about her life in Philadelphia. "We lived in a big, red brick home a block from Independence Hall where they wrote the Constitution. The home had green shutters and…"

"What's a consti…tution?" Willie demanded.

Jenny looked startled. "Why, it's the law of the land. It's the rules for our government and guarantee of our freedoms. And inside our home we had…"

"Who made the Constitution?"

"Politicians."

"Politicians like Governor St. Clair?" Willie pictured fat, pompous, white-haired St. Clair, so gouty he could no longer mount a horse and instead paraded through Cincinnati in a huge carriage led by two coal black horses. Papa called St. Clair an "old maid," for his prissy mannerisms, and cursed him for blocking Ohio's statehood for so many years while growing rich on bribes from those seeking offices and trading licenses.

"Why, no, Willie. Great men made the Constitution like Benjamin Franklin. Mr. Franklin often came to our home to visit your Grandfather. He used to sit in the parlor by the fire in a huge, yellow velvet wingback chair and tell funny stories about when he was ambassador in Paris…"

"An ambassador? Like a general? Was Mr. Franklin a general? Did he fight in the Revolution?"

Sarah dug her elbow into his ribs. "Willie, stop interrupting Mama!"

He shoved her back. "Shudup, Sarah!"

"Stop fighting!" Jenny screeched. "You're giving me a head-ache!"

The children fell silent and then glanced at each other. Sarah stuck her tongue out at him while he crossed his eyes and thumbed his nose back. Jenny slapped him. "Stop it, both of you, or you'll get a whipping! And, Willie, I told you your eyes would get stuck forever if you crossed them, then everyone will laugh at you the rest of your life."

For a moment they listened to the men's grunts and curses and the songbirds in the forest along shore. A fox barked somewhere to the east and Willie stared hard into the forest trying to glimpse it. Sarah's voice broke the silence, "Mama, how much longer? Captain Henderson said we would be in St. Louis today. I hate this keelboat!"

"Ifin I ain't mistaken, Sarah," Henderson's voice called out behind them, "St. Louis should be round the next bend!" All three turned to face Henderson who beamed back at them. "An' I'll be sorry to see ya all go! I sure enjoyed list'nin' to all your talk over the past month. I larned a hell...a heck of a lot from you, Mrs. Yates, and yer little Sarah reminds me of a little gal I used to have 'bout the same age, who died a' the pox with her mama, 'bout six years back. An' Willie reminds me a' when ah was his age."

Jenny began, "Captain Henderson, we are all deeply beholden to you for allowing us to accompany—"

"Willie! Look what's comin' downriver?" Henderson pointed a dirty finger ahead. "Pardon me, ma'am, but I know the boy'll wanna see this!"

They all scanned the river upstream and saw a large bleached object floating toward them. "What is it, Captain Henderson?" Willie asked excitedly.

"Buffala!"

Willie hopped down from the cabin and scampered up to the prow while Henderson steered the keelboat toward it. The men dug in their poles and held fast while the buffalo drifted past. Although it was half-submerged, the buffalo still loomed huge in the water, its body bloated and torn by branches and crows. He stared down at the buffalo's empty, bloody eye socket and the black horn that curved out of its head. "Where'd it come from, Captain Henderson?" he shouted.

"Lord knows, Willie. Probably drowned crossin' farther up the Mississippi, or maybe even floated down the Missouri from the Great Plains or even the Rocky Mountains a thousand miles away! All right, boys, you had a look! Now let's git ta St. Louis! Thar's smoke trails ahead and whar thar's smoke thar's fire! We're damn near thar!"

The men strained their poles against the river bottom and slowly pushed the keelboat through the current. It took another half-hour before they rounded the bend and could see the whitewashed houses of St. Louis in the distance. A dozen keelboats and pirogues were tied along the steep bank. On a small hill behind the town was a crumbling stone fort. From inside an American flag hung limply from a tall flagpole. The men craned their heads to see St. Louis, set up a scattered chorus of war whoops and hurrahs, then pushed on. Jenny and Sarah hugged each other and called down encouragement to Sam, Jake, and the crew.

As in other villages they approached, the people on shore stopped what they were doing and watched the keelboat come in. As the keelboat got closer Jake began shouting out in French or English to people he recognized and they would laugh and shout something back, usually a light-hearted insult. "Jean!" he called out to one of the small boys tending ox carts for hire atop the bank. Jean shot to his feet, cupped an ear at Jake's French commands, nodded, and dashed away. Jake winked at his brother. "Jean'll fetch Colette."

The keelboat was tied up, the plank lowered, and the men began unloading. Sam untied the dugout and guided it along to the shore while Jake hopped down to shake hands and slap the backs of a half-dozen acquaintances who gathered around to ask questions and laugh at his quips. After Jake introduced them to Sam and Jenny, they drifted back to their various pursuits. The brothers began carrying or pushing the heavier furniture or barrels up the steep bank, loading them into one of Jean's carts, while Jenny and the children struggled with the lighter fixings.

They had been working for more than an hour when Jake suddenly exclaimed, "Where the hell's my wife? I haven't been with her for almost three months and now she's disappeared." Jenny set down a butter churn in the dust with a thud.

Jake tried to be cheerful, "Don't worry, Jenny, you'll like Colette." Jenny wheezed for breath, stared hard at Jake, and said nothing. Jake looked at the gray streaks in Jenny's long brown hair, which as usual was tightly tied in a bun, and the web of wrinkles across her face. She'd been such a pretty, if serious, girl in Philadelphia, he thought wistfully. But that was long ago and Jenny had faded since, from frontier life and a stillborn child, shortly after they arrived in Cincinnati. Jake smiled, recalling how determined he and Sam had been to win Jenny's hand, and concluded it was a damn good thing Jenny had picked Sam's promises about wealth and respectability over his poetry and flowers.

Trailed by Jean, a slim, dark woman with long black hair, brown eyes and a wide smile, slid up behind Jake and flung her arms around him. "*Chéri! Tu m'a manqué!*"

Jake turned in her arms, let out a war whoop, and wrapped himself around her. They murmured endearments and pawed each other, while Sam and Jenny shifted uncomfortably nearby. "Ahem," Sam snorted.

Jake jerked his mouth up from Colette's. "Whoops, sorry," he muttered with a sheepish grin. "Sam, Jenny, this is Colette," he exclaimed proudly.

"Reckoned that, Jake," Sam croaked. "Pl-pleased to meet you, ma'am... Colette. Jake's told us a lot about you." Sam and Jenny stared at Colette, thinking it was bad enough that she was a French girl young enough to be Jake's daughter—but half-Indian! While Sam and Jenny struggled over what to say, Jake turned to Colette.

"What took you so long? I feared you'd run off to your pappy's in St. Charles...or high-tailed it to New Orleans with another beau!"

Colette's smile faded slightly. Before she could reply, Willie and Sarah ran up. "You young'uns greet your Aunt Colette," Jake demanded.

"This here's Sarah and that's Willie."

"Ah, what beautiful children!" Colette's smile widened. She knelt and hugged the children. Willie breathed in her sage-like scent, and marveled at her dimples and thick lips. "Their eyes, so pretty!" She said excitedly, "Sarah's eyes blue like summer sky and Willie's blue-gray like winter sky." She stroked Sarah's long walnut-colored hair and ran her slender fingers down Willie's cheek.

"How old you children?"

Willie stared down at his feet and mumbled, "I am seven and Sarah's six."

"Time's a-wastin', Colette," Jake urged. "You can visit later. We're damn near loaded and headed for home and there'd better be something to eat when we get there!"

Colette looked worried. "I see you there!" She turned and quickly disappeared.

"Well, whadya think?" Jake exclaimed proudly. "Ain't she the prettiest little gal you ever saw?"

Sam spoke slowly, "She's a looker, Jake, no doubt about it. You sure like 'em young."

Jake chuckled and winked at Sam. "Well, Sam, you know I've got enough fire in my belly for two men so I need a woman young enough to care for me proper! And Colette's got about as much fire as any woman I've ever known…Well, let's git. Three months…" He chuckled again. They soon loaded the rest of their belongings into the cart.

Jake pressed a bit into Jean's hand and told him they would not take long with the cart. Then they coaxed the ox through the muddy streets.

Sam and Jenny remarked upon the differences between St. Louis and Cincinnati. The buildings here were more scattered. There were fewer people and they seemed to be sitting or standing in groups chatting rather than tending to chores. Sights and smells of feces and an occasional rotting pig littered the streets while livestock wandered free. Most homes had high-pitched roofs, front porches, and small gardens surrounded by picket fences. Strangest of all seemed the French custom of placing the planks of their walls vertically rather than horizontally. The grandfather clock gonged everytime the cart hit a deep rut.

"Colette! Colette!" Jake hollered as they trudged up to his home at the village's edge. "Where the hell's she gone now?" A half-dozen scrawny yellow chickens scattered as Jake and Sam led the cart up to the front gate. Jake burst through the front door and hollered again, "Colette…well, maybe she went to the market." Sam and Jenny appeared in the doorway, while the children chased the chickens outside. "Well, let me show you what. There's a bedroom for you with a trundle bed beneath the big one. We can store everything in the parlor and dining room till you find a place of your own."

Jenny's eyes teared. She turned and yelled, "Stop tormenting those chickens! How would you like to be a chicken and have children run you to death?" Willie and Sarah stood and stared at their mother.

Then Willie tagged Sarah, shouted, "You're it!" and ran down the street, with Sarah in hot pursuit.

"Willie! Sarah!—"

Sam cut her short. "Damn it, Jenny, let 'em be! Now let's get that cart unloaded." Sam and Jake strode back to the cart, grabbed the walnut desk and carried it into the house while Jenny followed with a spinning wheel. Minutes later Colette appeared in the doorway carrying something heavy and bloody wrapped in cloth. The children followed.

"*Chéri, J'achète*…I buy the meat of cow."

"I wondered where you'd been. We haven't had beef since Louisville! Well, start cooking, sweetie. I have a hunger powerful enough to stuff down a whole bull, and that's just for startin'! And if that don't fill me, I'll gobble you down!"

The half-brothers could not have looked more different—Auguste was gray-haired, portly, solemn; Pierre was lean, dark-skinned, restless. Flop hats in hand, Sam and Jake stood before them on the Chouteau mansion's veranda.

Pierre shrugged his shoulders and raised his palms skyward, "Yes, Jacques, it's true! According to Captain Stoddard, your...our government will not..." he searched for the proper English word, "re...recognize?" He cocked an eyebrow at Jake, who nodded, "Recognize any land claims made between October first 1800 and the treaty. I am afraid all your land is no good. Even some Chouteau land is—"

"Disputed?"

"Yes, disputed!" Pierre had practiced his English intensely since last fall when word had reached St. Louis that Louisiana had been sold to the Americans. Spanish, French, American—it did not matter what flag flew over Louisiana as long as the Chouteau clan continued to dominate most of the region's land and fur trade! "You must work with us, Jacques, with the commitee to petition Governor Harrison when he arrives in autumn. If all the leading merchants and citizens of St. Louis stand together, perhaps we will convince him to change the law. Or perhaps the courts, Jacques. Perhaps we can make suit in the courts and win our land. But if not," he shrugged his shoulders, "it was nothing when you filed and it is nothing now."

"But I was planning to sell that land to settlers. I borrowed much money from you and your brother to purchase that land. How am I going to pay that off?"

Auguste understood more English than he let on. His eyes blinked when Jake wondered how he could pay his debts. "*Jacques, Jacques! Comme toujours vous pouvez faire des affaires avec les Fox et les Sac à la nord, ou remonter la Missouri! Il y a beaucoup des possibilités. Ne vous inquiétez pas, Jacques!*"

Jake began tugging at his beard. "*Oui, d'accord, mais...*"

"Auguste is right, Jacques. You continue your trade, and we will continue to credit you trade goods."

"But I promised Colette that we'd be rich and I wouldn't have to spend seasons up north. She's gonna be hotter than a polecat in hell when she hears our land's no good. And my brother, Sam, here, I promised him and his family that land sales would make them rich, too. What am I gonna do?"

Pierre shrugged his shoulders and raised his hands skyward once more. "Perhaps you can sell your land to new settlers after all. Many old settlers are selling and many new settlers are buying despite the risk. Prices may go up despite the restrictions! If not, the Fox and Sac, Jacques, or up the Missouri. We trust you, Jacques. We know you will pay us back."

Sam had stayed quiet since first shaking hands with the Chouteau brothers but the furrows across his forehead seemed to deepen throughout the talk. He touched Jake behind his elbow. "We best be going, Jake."

Jake jerked his head and stared into Sam's gray eyes, then turned back toward the Chouteau. "Well, we thank you both for your time."

"Of course, Jacques. But you better make your trade order as soon as possible." Pierre pointed toward Sam, "Our goods go fast with all these new settlers." Sam and Jake nodded, then began to walk out through the large vegetable garden which two burly black slaves were busy hoeing. "And Jacques," Pierre's words trailed after them, "give my best to Colette!" Jake cocked his head, paused, then continued walking.

With one last brisk sweep of her twig broom, Colette pushed the dust pile out the door, wishing she could sweep out Jake, Sam, and Jenny as easily; Jake so coarse and demanding, Sam so guarded, and Jenny such a proper American! If only Jake had stayed in Cincinnati.

But Willie and Sarah, what darlings! Colette gazed at Willie lying in the field across the rutted street; hands behind his head, he was watching clouds drift across the sky. "Willie! Willie!" Colette dropped her broom and strode across the yard and street toward him. He scrambled to his feet. Colette laughed and hugged him, "What do you see, Willie?"

He half-wanted to run, and half-wanted to stay buried against her warm, plump breasts. "I saw a buffalo," he muttered. She searched the sky. "It's gone now."

Colette pushed back the hair from his eyes. "Don't worry, Willie. You see more buffalo." She smiled. "What's wrong, Willie, you miss Cincinnati? Do you have a love in Cincinnati?" Colette giggled. "Is she pretty?"

He considered telling her about Sandra, but was afraid she would tell his mother. "I am just restless, that's all."

She sighed, "I wish I had a good boy like you, but Jake, he don't make me baby. He try and try. Too hard sometimes." Colette giggled again, "You learn someday."

"Colette!" Jenny called out from an upstairs window. "Colette!

What did I tell you?"

Colette released him and turned toward the house. "Your mama, she don't like me," she muttered.

"Willie, come in the house...now!"

He looked up at Colette but said nothing as he filed past. Suddenly he stopped and they both watched Sam and Jake stride rapidly down the street toward them. Colette ran up to Jake, "*Jacques! Tu m'a manqué! Nous devons parler!*"

"*Oui, sans doute!*" Jake's face was hard.

"*Qu'est-ce que c'est! Jacques, qu'est-ce que c'set! Ton visage...*"

"*Allons-y!*" Jake grabbed Colette by her arm and pulled her toward the woods behind their home. Colette began screaming, "*Qu'est-ce que c'est! Qu'est-que ce fait! Pourquoi? Pourquoi!*"

"Come on, son." Sam grabbed Willie behind his neck and led him toward the house.

"What happened, Papa? Why is everyone angry at Aunt Colette?"

"Never you mind, boy. Just get on inside."

Willie ran upstairs, followed by Sarah who had been playing with her dolls in the parlor. Trembling, they listened out the back window to Colette and Jake hollering at each other inside the woods, but it was all in French so they could not understand a thing. Meanwhile Jenny had gone downstairs and now whispered with Sam in the parlor. Finally the hollering stopped and Jake stumbled out of the woods and into the house. The woods were silent.

A chilly drizzle filled the night and drummed against the windows. Wrapped in blankets, Sam, Jake, and Jenny huddled in chairs near the fireplace. Jake prodded a log deeper into the fire. "Salt, Sam, salt's the answer."

"Salt! What are you talking about, Jake?"

"Salt from the Saline River below St. Genevieve. 'Bout fifty-sixty miles away as the crow flies."

"What's salt got to do with us?"

"It's the answer to our problems, Sam. You've just about sold off all the dry goods you brought from Cincinnati. My land's no good and I can't go trading with the Injuns till fall and it's barely May now. Meanwhile we can boil off enough salt to supply all of St. Louis and every new settler that comes through."

"Well, if it's that simple, why hasn't someone else already done that?"

"Many have and are and will, but only enough to supply their friends and neighbors. If we go steady for a month or so, we can boil enough salt to undercut everyone else's prices and make a small fortune! Salt's good as money out here."

"Well, now…"

Jenny drew in her breath and burst out, "What are you hesitating for, Sam? Jake's right! It's our only chance. And if you fail at salt-making, I am taking the children and going home to my mother's in Philadelphia. I can't take this wilderness much longer, Sam. There's nothing here but a village filled with crude foreigners, and I know you've told me a thousand times, Cincinnati, and even Philadelphia, started like this, but I can't take it anymore. I need someone to talk to about fashion and society and…ever since I met you, all you've talked about is unlimited opportunities to get rich, and how we'll be at the top of the heap in a new land, but we, or at least my family, were high society in Philadelphia, and how I ever fell starry-eyed for your dreams, I don't know, but that was over fifteen years ago, and where are we now…"

"All right, stop your yammering, for God's sake! We'll try our damnedest at salt-making and if it fails, I'll send you back to your mother's."

"And the children are coming with me!" Sam and Jenny's eyes burned into each other's.

"When do we start, Jake?"

"As soon as I get back."

"From where? Where the hell are you going? You just got me interested in salt-making and now…"

"Stop your yammering, Sam! I am headed to St. Charles to bring back Colette from her papa's. It's been over a week since she lit out and I am worried about her. She's lit out before after arguing, but never this long. Maybe she didn't dally with Chouteau after all, although those rumors I heard in the taverns after coming back and that son of a bitch's remark at his home that afternoon sure point to something, but I damn well hope she didn't dally with that rot-gutted bastard because if she did, I'd have ta kill him and somehow it don't set right for a man to kill his creditor."

Sam nodded. "When you heading to St. Charles?"

"Tomorrow, and I am taking Willie with me."

"What? You can't take Willie!" Jenny looked alarmed.

"I've got to, Jenny. Colette said she'd never see me again as long as she lived but she took a shine to the boy and I figure if she saw us together I might be able to sweet-talk her into coming back. Besides, it'll do the boy good to see a bit of the country."

• • •

It had rained off and on all day. The light was fading through the dark clouds as Jake and Willie guided the swaybacked, old bay onto the barge. Stiff and mud-splattered after the day's ride up from St. Louis, they stood waiting for several equally muddy, stiff farmers to amble down from the fields and clamber aboard. Jake pressed three pennies into the ferryman's callused hand.

"*Et les autres?*" said the short, skinny boatman, picking at one of his pimples. A farmer shook his head no. The boatman and three of the farmers grabbed poles, shoved them into the bank, and began pushing the barge toward St. Charles on the far shore. The fourth smiled complacently, happy there were only four poles.

Jake grinned down at Willie. "Well, Willie, what do you think of the Missouri?" The farmers and boatman stared at the Americans.

Willie grinned back. "It's something, Uncle Jake. How far west are the Great Plains?"

"I am told the Missouri heads west for a couple hundred miles then cuts northwest. 'Bout another hundred miles are the Plains. But as I was telling you, I've yet to make it that far. Someday though. There's some in St. Louis who've traded as far as the Mandan Injuns where the Missouri cuts west again to the Rockies. There's a heap of tribes in between—Osage, Kaws, Omaha, Otos, Poncas, Ioways, Arikaree, Sioux... Yup, I believe I named 'em all. And each tribe's got different customs and tongues and demands different goods. Colette's papa's been trading as far as the Omaha at the mouth of the Platte River four hundred miles upstream."

"Are any of the tribes dangerous?"

"I understand some of the Sioux can get ornery but generally they welcome us with open arms. Particularly the women." Jake's grin deepened.

"What's Aunt Colette?"

Jake's grin quickly disappeared. "Oh, Colette's part Osage, from west of here. I sure hope I can patch things up. Your Uncle Jake can be dumb as an ox sometimes." Jake glanced at the farmers and smiled. "Yup, Willie, sometimes I can be as dumb as these fellas look." Willie glanced at the squat, dark farmers and they both laughed.

The red brick and whitewashed frame buildings of St. Charles stretched for almost a mile along the Missouri. A low, grassy ridge rose behind the town. Five keelboats and a dozen pirogues were tied up along the bank.

"It looks smaller than St. Louis," Willie observed.

"It is, but it's a pretty little place." From one of the taverns came the sounds of drunken laughter and shouting, broken by a gunshot. A dozen people milled around outside. The noise got louder as they neared St. Charles. "Wonder what all the hollering's about? *Qu'est-ce qui se passe?*" Jake demanded of the boatman.

"Les voyageurs américains commencent demain!"

"Ah oui, d'accord! Willie! We've come at just the right time! Tomorrow that American expedition I was telling you about is heading out—heading all the way to the Pacific Ocean a couple thousand miles away! Damn, I sure wish I was going with them! Well, maybe if Colette don't come back with me, I'll join those boys!"

The barge ground ashore, was tied up, and everyone got off and scattered into the dark, including the boatman. Willie and Jake led the horse down the street toward the end of town. Few of the homes were lit inside. As they passed the tavern Jake poked his head in looking for Colette. Men and women shouted merrily at each other in English and French. Two men lay passed out in the mud outside. "I don't see her," he said as he rejoined Willie. "It ain't like Colette or her papa to miss a party. Where the hell is she?"

They plodded onward through the ankle-deep mud and finally stopped in front of a small frame home. "Well, here goes, Willie." Jake stepped up on the veranda and knocked on the door. *"Colette! François! C'est moi!"*

Jake entered and Willie heard him shouting inside. *"Colette! François! C'est moi, Jacques!"* Jake reappeared looking tired and sad. "No sign."

They tied up the horse and headed back into town. Jake ducked in the tavern once more then reappeared, smiling, "There're both over at Charles Tayong's! Appears François is heading upstream with the expedition. Charles is throwing a party for the leaders and guides. He'll let me in. He once joined me to trade with the Sac. He's not a bad one for being a Spaniard." They headed down toward the opposite end of town and stopped in front of a large brick home. They could see dozens of people through the window and hear the muffled sounds of their voices. "Come on, Willie."

A huge slave dressed in a long red coat and a tall black felt hat greeted them at the door. *"Monsieur?"*

"Dites M. Tayong que Jacques Yates est ici."

They waited impatiently. The door reopened. The slave and a short fat man with a pug nose and greasy black hair stood framed in the light.

"Jacques, how are you? Welcome." They shook hands and grinned at each other. "If I knew you come, I give you invitation. Come in! Come in! And the child?"

"My nephew," Jake said proudly. Jake and Willie stepped into the large entrance hall but hesitated to go farther, feeling foolish in their muddy clothes. "But, Charles, we ain't quite dressed for a party. I am looking for Colette."

Charles raised his eyes to the ceiling and gave a Gallic shrug. "I know Jacques, I know. Women! What can we do? Wait here. I'll get her," he said and disappeared into the huge, crowded parlor. Smells of roasted goose and venison drifted in from adjacent rooms with the sounds of loud talk and laughter.

"I am hungry, Uncle Jake, and tired too."

Jake patted Willie on the head. "I know. Me, too. We'll eat something soon."

Suddenly Colette drifted toward them across the entrance hall. She wore a long, flowing green dress, cut low across her breasts in the French style. Her eyes were filled with tears. "Jacques! Willie!"

Colette and Jake embraced. "*Je regrette!*" they said together, then laughed and stood awkwardly. "Come, Jake, Willie, come meet your countrymen!"

She led them into a room filled with elegantly dressed men and women talking together in small groups. Along one wall was a long table covered with large dishes filled with game and vegetables. Two slaves in red coats carrying large brown bottles of red wine wandered among the guests, occasionally refilling a glass. In the corner, Charles spoke animatedly with François, Auguste Chouteau, and two men dressed in American uniforms. All five sipped from glasses of red wine. François embraced Jake as they walked up and they murmured briefly in French.

"Jacques," Colette said. She turned and beamed toward the two American officers. "Let me introduce you to Captain Meri..." She giggled and spread her slender fingers on her breasts. "Meriwether Lewis and Captain William Clark."

"Pleased to meet you." Jake shook hands with them both. Clark was tall and stout with thinning red hair combed back from his large brow. Lewis was lanky and had large, piercing brown eyes and a sharply chiseled face framed by thick black hair.

"And who is this fine young man?" Lewis smiled down at Willie.

"My name's Willie."

"I am most happy to meet you, Willie. It's always a pleasure to meet a fellow countryman. There aren't many Americans in these parts yet, but don't worry. We'll soon fill up this territory with young men and women like you." Auguste took a deep gulp from his glass, cupped Clark by the elbow, and spoke into his ear. François, Charles, and Jake leaned forward, straining to listen.

"Are you really going to the Pacific Ocean?" Willie demanded. Colette sidled up to Lewis.

"We sure are, Willie. And we may be a long time getting there and back." Lewis turned and gazed down into Colette's eyes. "And I am afraid it will be a long time before I again enjoy the company of such a charming and beautiful woman."

Colette's dimples and smile deepened, but before she could speak, Clark touched Lewis's shoulder. "Meriwether, Mr. Yates here was just asking about President Jefferson's leadership abilities." Clark grinned. "Seeing you were his secretary, maybe you ought to answer him."

"Excuse me," Lewis smiled first to Colette and then Willie. He turned to address the men.

"Come, Willie, you are starved, no?" Colette took him over to the table and helped him pile a plate high.

Colette left Willie with two white-haired matriarchs who cooed over him while she slipped back between Jake and Lewis.

As the years drifted into decades, Willie's memories of the evening and the next day melted into a collage of images. "What was it like?" companions and strangers would demand when they learned Willie was present. "I remember Lewis's big smile and Clark's cold stare; my Aunt Colette's waist-long black hair shining in the candlelight; the grins and sharp laughter of Uncle Jake joking with his friends and the captains; the heavy perfume of those old French ladies damn near smothering me; riding back to Aunt Colette's home late that night on Uncle Jake's shoulders; then the next day, hundreds of villagers pushing and shoving along the landing; Lewis's speech about American destiny and the march to the Pacific; the gunshots, whooping, and hollering from the crowd as a score of rivermen pushed off the two keelboats and pirogue; the weather-beaten, blue-coated soldiers and hunters scattered across the three boats, waving and shouting goodbyes; Lewis and Clark standing like statues at the helm of the lead keelboat; and them all disappearing upriver in gusts of rain and dark clouds and warm wind."

Two

Willie dragged a log as thick as his leg and twice his height out of the thick brush onto the trail. Sweat dripped out of every pore, matting his clothes and hair against his grimy body. "Yuck!" He stopped to wipe a spider web from his face. "Ooh! No!" A large, hairy, brown spider scuttled down his neck. Dropping the log, he grabbed for the spider but it slipped down inside his shirt. "Aah! God!" he gasped as he tried to rip off his filthy linen shirt. He felt the spider dig its fangs into his chest near his right nipple. "Owww!" He finally pulled off his shirt and smashed the spider against his chest, leaving a smear of hair, legs, and brownish-yellow ooze behind. He grimaced and tears squeezed from his eyes as he tried to wipe the mess off with leaves.

"Poison ivy!" he suddenly discovered, dropped the leaves in horror, then ran down the trail crying, "Papa! Papa!" as tears streamed down his cheeks.

Sam heard him coming, dropped his saw and scrambled for his rifle. He cocked and raised it just as he burst into the clearing. "Papa! Papa!"

"What's wrong? What's wrong?" Sam shouted, his face flushed and strained.

"A spider! It bit me! Look!" He pointed to the smear and red welt on his chest.

"A spider? Goddamn it! What the hell are you yammering about a goddamned spider for? You scared the hell out of me! I thought you'd seen an Osage war party or a bear or something!" Sam swung his hand but Willie dodged aside. "What the hell's wrong with you? Why aren't you hauling logs like you're supposed to instead of yammering about a goddamned spider?" Willie's tears stopped. He glared at his father.

"Well, get back to work, boy. I want that wagon piled high and it and us at Saline Creek before nightfall. Your Uncle Jake's waiting on us."

Willie turned and strode back up the trail. Around a bend he cut down through the woods toward the creek and splashed into a deep hole. He scrubbed himself with sand then sat sunning himself on a rock. Cicadas buzzed through the thick midday air. A scarlet tanager dropped onto a nearby branch, blinked at him, then fluttered away. He started to cry again.

"Willie!" Sam's voice cut through the woods, "Willie!"

"I am in trouble now," Willie muttered. He scrambled up the bank and began running through the trees toward where he guessed his shirt and the log might be. He finally reached the trail and saw his father up ahead holding his shirt.

"Come here, Willie!" Sam called out.

Willie hesitated then marched up to Sam. He tried to encourage himself—Be brave! Take it like a man!—but felt his jaw start to quiver.

"It's all right, Willie. C'mere, boy." Sam held out his hand, his face concerned. "Let me see that bite. You gotta watch out for black widows. Remember when I showed you the black widows in that ol' warehouse in Cincinnati?" Willie nodded. "It don't look bad. Does it hurt?" Willie shook his head no then began to cry. "Now, son, don't cry. I know you've been working hard and you're still a young'un, but don't cry. You got to act grown up now. Big boys don't cry." Willie sniffed and rubbed his eyes. The crying stopped. "Maybe we can take a breather. We have enough wood for another day's boiling and I'm gonna sell off half our salt to a trader in St. Genevieve tomorrow while you and your Uncle Jake work the fires. So we'll grab a few more logs, saw 'em up, and head back to Saline Creek. All right?"

"Yes, sir."

The sun was hovering on the horizon as they reached Saline Creek. Pillars of smoke filled the shallow valley as a half-dozen parties fed fires beneath dozens of huge iron pots.

The Yates's camp was at the valley's far end. Willie and Sam could see Jake lounging beside the tall canvas tent and three big fires each with kettles steaming on top.

Jake was puffing at one of his long clay pipes. "Howdy, boys!" he shouted as they entered camp. "How far you'd go hunting wood today?"

"Howdy, Uncle Jake!" shouted Willie, always happy to see his uncle.

"Four or five miles north on the trail. Wood's getting mighty scarce," Sam said over his shoulder as he started unhitching the ox.

"You look beat as hell, Willie. Sit for a while." Willie stretched out on a blanket in front of the tent. "Well, Sam, I boiled off another half a sack. You fixing to sell off how many to Austin tomorrow? Fifty?"

"Yeah, like we were saying, dump fifty to Austin in St. Genevieve and take the rest back to St. Louis and pay off that order of dry goods."

Sam led the ox over to a grassy patch near where Jake's sway-backed bay and a young gray mule were grazing, and staked her out. "How many do you figure we'll carry out?"

"Well, if we leave in a day or so we'll carry maybe forty-four back to St. Louis. Add that to those twenty sacks we sold off in St. Louis in late June and it's a pretty good haul for over three month's work, enough to fetch a storeload of dry goods. Yup, Sam, look's like we're back on solid ground again."

Sam sat down cross-legged by the fire. "If we can get the store moving maybe we'll be able to build our own home in a year or two." He smiled, "Reckon you can put up with us that long, Jake?"

Jake chuckled, "Till whenever. Colette could use the company. I appreciate Jenny looking out for her while I'm away." Jake took a deep draw at his pipe and sighed. "Never thought I'd be a salt-maker. This is truly nigger work." Jake pointed his pipe toward the other parties scattered down the valley. "They all got slaves helping 'em 'cept us."

"It ain't right!" Sam looked disgusted. "How are we to compete when they use slaves?"

"Well, we'll just have to save up and buy some of our own." Jake grinned.

Sam shot Jake a scornful look. "I thought you didn't believe in slavery!"

Jake looked surprised. "Well, I don't, as a matter of principle. But, Sam, this ain't Philadelphia or Cincinnati. Slavery's legal here."

"I can't believe my ears. Why're you talking such nonsense? Jake, you were raised to believe otherwise, and to act as you believe."

"I know, Sam, and I wasn't seriously thinking of buying one, but now that you mention it, I've done some pondering 'bout slavery since I got here. Maybe it ain't all bad. Most of 'em don't live any worse than whites. And the French treat their slaves better than Americans. The Black Code says you can't kill or maim a slave or break up families or force 'em to work before sunrise or after sunset...and slaves can not only buy their own freedom, but they can even sue if their masters break the rules!"

"No man should own another under any circumstances! You once believed that. I am saddened you no longer do."

"I still believe it, Sam. It's just...things are different out here and a man's gotta bend with his surroundings. That's all."

"That's all is right! I don't wanna hear any more of your nonsense."

After gobbling down a venison and dumpling stew, the three stayed up another hour or so, slapping at mosquitoes and feeding the fires.

Sam and Jake remained silent toward each other. Jake, however, kept Willie chuckling or wide-eyed with a stream of stories about shady characters, bear hunting, and Indian fighting. Willie was tempted to ask Jake about slavery, but bit his tongue, fearing it would spark another argument. He felt his father's anger burning beside him like it would explode any second. But finally they all wrapped up in their blankets and drifted off to sleep.

The scream jerked Willie out of his deep sleep. He sat straight up, his mouth agape, but when he tried to holler, nothing came out. In the dark before him he saw his father thrashing and mumbling in his blanket and Jake trying to subdue him. "Sam! Sam! You all right? Sam!"

"Everybody's dead! Shawnees!" Sam shouted and started wrestling with Jake.

Willie was fully awake now. "Papa, it's me Willie!"

"Sam! Goddamn it, Sam, it's me—your brother, Jake. Settle down. You were just dreamin'. Everything's all right."

"What! Who's that!" Sam shouted. "Jake! Where's my rifle! Everybody's dead!" Sam suddenly stopped struggling and hugged

Jake. "Oh God, that dream again…Everybody was dead, Jake! Why?"

He started weeping, "I wanna climb in a hole, Jake! A deep dark hole an' pull in all the dirt behind me."

Sam halted the wagon on a low hill overlooking St. Genevieve. The town's fifty or so houses were scattered across a ridge about a mile from the Mississippi. Smoke wisped into the air from the wattle and daub chimneys. The church steeple stabbed the sky. Beyond was the long slope leading to the corn and wheat fields along the river. Sam imagined he caught whiffs of ham and apple pie baking. He smiled. God, it would be good to be in town again. People hurried through the crooked streets to join a crowd in front of the church. He prodded the ox forward. Must be an auction. Better hurry.

Almost all the town had turned out for the meeting: farmers and slaves just in from the fields; women in bonnets and homespun dresses; merchants with top hats and long cloaks; children standing on tip-toe or slipping through the throng for a better look; a dozen or so scarred, sun-darkened riverboatmen; trappers with long, greasy ponytails dangling down their buckskin clad backs; and three huge Osage watching silently at the crowd's fringe, wrapped in dark blue blankets, heads shaven except for scalp locks. Everyone jostled and talked loudly as they waited for the meeting to begin. Sam halted the ox at the crowd's edge then climbed atop the wagon for a better view.

Before them sat three men behind a long oak table in front of the church. One was short and plump with a round, troubled face framed by thick, graying hair. Hawk-like, his blue eyes nervously probed the crowd. The middle man slowly stood up, his huge belly overhanging the table, his fat, florid face staring. To his right sat a well-built man with thinning chestnut hair, who laughed and gestured to some friends before him. Two flintlock pistols and a skinning knife were thrust in his belt.

The fat man raised his heavy arms. "Ladies and gentlemen! Your attention please!" His deep bass voice, enunciating each word slowly, cut through the crowd and quickly silenced it. "We are gathered to debate the central issue of our time—our fate and our children's fate.

"As inhabitants of the new District of Louisiana…as citizens of the United States of America, how are we to be represented?" He paused, his brown eyes slowly sweeping the crowd for effect. "How are we to be represented? Who will represent us? And just what do we want our representatives to represent?" Again he paused. "These two gentlemen will attempt to provide answers. To my left…" he pointed to the plump man, "Moses Austin, a gentleman who settled here with his family almost a decade ago. A gentleman who, through boundless enterprise and ingenuity, has almost single-handedly revolutionized the most important industry of our territory. I speak, of course, of the lead mines of Mine à Breton. And finally, a gentleman, who, earlier this summer, received an appointment from Governor Harrison as one of five justices on the Court of Common Pleas and Quarter Sessions right here in St. Genevieve district."

The fat man waited patiently for the loud applause to die. "And to my right, John Smith T...the T, of course, standing for Tennessee, as Mr. Smith invariably points out." Smith and his cronies guffawed loudly. Austin frowned. "Mr. Smith T, a more recent arrival, is also a man of considerable enterprise, having acquired immense land tracts, conducted a flourishing trade in dry goods, and, I believe, has recently entered the lead mine industry himself...." The crowd murmured. It was common knowledge that Smith and his men were poaching lead from Austin's land.

"These two gentlemen will address the issues that I have laid before you. Issues that deeply affect all of us. Mr. Austin will speak first, followed by Mr. Smith T, and then we will open the discussion for general debate."

The fat man slowly sat down. Austin rose. A scattering of applause rippled across the crowd. "Thank you, Mr. Jenkins." Austin's voice was high pitched. He strained to project it across the crowd.

"Friends and neighbors!" Smith's cronies laughed loudly and dug elbows into each other's ribs. Smith's face was split by a toothy grin.

Austin frowned, his voice faltered then rose again. "My words will be brief, yet I hope you will carefully consider them. We are citizens of a great country led by great, well-intentioned men.

"But unfortunately, the representatives of Congress sometimes pass laws about areas of which they know little. The legislation regulating our land, what is now known as the District of Louisiana, is a case in point. The law nullifies all land claims made after October 1, 1800, and demands considerable proof, which is often unobtainable, for land grants made before that time. Such laws severely inhibit the natural flow of commerce and new settlers. Furthermore, it is rumored that slavery may be abolished and further immigration forbidden, and instead, the territory used as a dumping ground for the Indian tribes east of the Mississippi. Finally, we are ruled by a governor located far away, at Vincennes in Indiana Territory.

"If our territory is ever to be more than a distant, stagnant backwater of the American Republic, we must be allowed to freely buy and sell land and slaves, and our Eastern compatriots who desire to make a new home in our beautiful land should be allowed to freely settle here..."

Austin's voice was smothered by the crowd's cheers and clapping. Even some of Smith's supporters joined the enthusiasm. Austin smiled for the first time. "We must send a message to Washington, a message so powerful that Congress will clearly understand our needs and thus respond accordingly." More cheers and clapping.

"As many of you are aware, there is a cabal in St. Louis, the so-called Committee of Six..."

"Down with the French aristocrats!" someone shouted, sparking others to jeer. Jenkins slammed his fat fist on the table, glared at the hecklers, and demanded quiet.

"As I was saying, that cabal composed of the French pioneers Auguste and Pierre Chouteau, Bernard Pratte, Charles Gratiot, Peter Provenchere, and Louis Labeaume, have met several times and are planning to meet with Governor Harrison when he visits in October to petition him to redress their grievances. Those gentlemen..."

"Scoundrels is a better name for them!" someone hooted.

Austin nodded. "Those gentlemen, however, will represent only themselves and the other French inhabitants. Our needs, the needs of the American citizens of the District of Louisiana, who now make up more than two-thirds of its population, will go unrepresented unless we act. We must organize a committee of our own to meet with Governor Harrison and clearly articulate our perspectives concerning land, slavery, and the governance of this district. We must work together to set in motion the movement for the immediate transformation of our current status from district into a territory with the power to elect representatives to Congress. But the conversion of our status to that of territory should be only our most immediate and pressing goal. We must never lose sight of our ultimate goal, that of eventually achieving statehood! A goal years or, perhaps, decades away, but one which we must constantly keep before us. Thank you!" Austin sat down quickly amidst loud applause. Jenkins slowly rose and the noise gradually died.

"Thank you, Mr. Austin. And now, Mr. Smith T." Smith leapt to his feet as his crowd loudly cheered.

"Thankee, boys!" he nodded to his supporters. "My thanks to all," Smith spread his arms wide as if to embrace the entire crowd. "My thanks to all, including Mr. Austin for setting some of his cards on the table. We all agree that the land claims should be honored, that slavery is a God-given right that should not be denied, that our territory should be open to all those enterprising pioneers like ourselves who need elbow room to roam and fresh land to clear, and that we should be allowed to govern ourselves as soon as possible. Those cards Mr. Austin's showin' are fine and dandy." Smith paused and winked. "It's what he's got up his sleeve that's got me worried. What he's hiding, or at least trying to hide, though it's clear to anyone with a lick a horse sense that Mr. Austin ain't dealing straight." Smith slowly turned to glare at Austin who stiffened. "Yup, Mr. Austin!" Smith spat out the words, "is fixin' to shove the Committee of Six aside and hog-tie this territory to his own huge land and lead empire. He aims to shake all the riches out of the District of Louisiana into his own pockets!" Smith's crowd roared its agreement with the charges while the others looked worried. Jenkins banged his fist again shouting for silence.

"Mr. Austin criticizes the committee for being French. But after all, they first settled this country over seventy years ago and are entitled to have a say in its rule, as we all should. But you don't have to choose between the committee and Mr. Austin here. After all, Mr. Austin is as foreign as the committee. If you'll recall, he was born American and done turned his back on his country to jump the river and become a Spaniard and Catholic to boot. Now I don't know about all of you, but I am American and want to stay that way. I'll be damned if I'll let someone of mixed loyalties or a gang a Frenchies sew up this territory into their own pockets! I say any commitee elected to petition Governor Harrison should be all-American! And I'll be happy to lead the charge for all the changes necessary to make Louisiana a prosperous, self-governing territory and eventual state! Thankee, folks!" Smith shot the crowd a huge grin, waved his hands and sat down to loud cheering.

Jenkins's fist-banging temporarily silenced the crowd, but the open debate which followed was raucous and often bitter. Most Americans were split between supporting Austin or Smith. Understanding little, the few French in the crowd watched silently, afraid to speak out.

It took another hour before a motion was passed to vote for a St. Genevieve Committee of Five which would meet with Governor Harrison. Both Austin and Smith were elected to the commitee.

Throughout the debate Sam wanted to speak out against slavery, but knew that to do so would alienate almost everyone. Few would want to do business with a "nigger-lover." As the crowd dispersed, Sam headed toward Austin, who continued to discuss the issues with a half-dozen supporters. "Ah, Mr. Yates!" Austin called out when he noticed

Sam standing aside. "Thank you for your patience. Gentlemen, if you will excuse me, I must attend to some pressing business." He shook hands all around then approached Sam. "Let's escape this crowd," he said, grasping Sam's elbow. They strolled toward the town's edge. "Well, Mr. Yates, what did you think of our meeting? By the way, I noted and deeply appreciated your vote of confidence."

Sam smiled. "You have good eyes and a sharp memory, Mr. Austin."

"Actually, aside from those supporters in the front, you were the only one I could spot, and only because you were enthroned atop your small mountain of salt." Austin scratched at a louse beneath his blue cravat. "You and your brother are very enterprising and honest men. I am very impressed."

Beaming, Sam replied, "Thank you! We've fifty sacks here," he pointed to the cart, "and we'll take another forty-four back to St. Louis, in addition to twenty we sold off in late June."

"Very enterprising indeed, Mr. Yates! We need more Americans out here like you and less like Mr. Smith. The opportunities on the frontier are boundless but, unfortunately, they sometimes attract some very unscrupulous characters. Smith is currently squatting on my land and digging out a considerable volume of lead."

"I've heard tell. Why don't you drive him off?"

"Unfortunately, although I have the Spanish papers granting me the land, everything is in abeyance with the new government. It will be years before all the conflicting claims are untangled. In the meantime, outlaws like Smith are robbing law-abiding citizens like myself. My only recourse is to gather my men and force him and his gang out. But that would undoubtedly lead to bloodshed. And bloodshed is something I wish to avoid." Deep lines creased Austin's brow.

"As you know, I am new in these parts, but if there's anything I can do, Mr. Austin…"

"What are your plans, Mr. Yates? How will you invest the proceeds from your salt sales?"

"It all depends on whether you're going to pay in cash or in kind. Last time we talked you said you weren't sure."

"Mr. Yates, I have a proposal to make, and I hope you'll carefully consider it." Sam nodded. "But before I do so, I must have your word as a gentleman that you will guard what I am about to say in the strictest confidence."

"Let's shake on it, Mr. Austin." They looked each other in the eye and powerfully shook hands.

"My proposal concerns some new digs that my men recently opened on public lands. I hesitate to tell you exactly where these diggings are. Suffice it to say, that they are remote. The digs yielded traces of not only lead and iron ore, but…" Austin smiled deeply, "also silver. Whether the dig will ever yield silver in large quantities or not remains to be seen, but clearly we have uncovered a rich horde of lead. I need to get that claim established and production well under way before squatters like Smith catch wind of it. The trouble is that I am desperately short of hard working, honest men. Mr. Yates," Austin rested a hand on Sam's shoulder, "how would you and your brother like to buy into the mine, and oversee and safely transport its production back to St. Genevieve?"

The offer and Austin's hand on his shoulder made Sam feel uncomfortable. He resisted the urge to knock Austin's hand aside and step back.

"How much would it cost to buy in and what percentage of production would we get?"

"For your fifty salt sacks and services as overseers, I would give you five, no ten percent of all production." Sam looked hesitant.

Austin hastily added, "You understand, Mr. Yates, that I will provide all the equipment and undertake all the risks. All you and your brother would provide is your salt, your labor, and most importantly, your leadership!"

Sam spoke slowly. "That's a mighty fine offer, Mr. Austin. But one that I'll have to discuss at length with my brother."

"Of course, of course, Mr. Yates. But could you give me an idea of when I can expect an answer? I am anxious to commence and am considering several other possible candidates for this opportunity." Austin deeply smiled again and released his hand from Sam's shoulder, "You understand, Mr. Yates, the need for haste."

Sam pictured Smith and his henchmen, all heavily armed, riding into the mining camp. He shoved the fear aside by painfully recalling fifteen years of promising Jenny they'd soon be rich. A stark image of Jenny and the children boarding an east-bound keelboat flashed through his mind. What a fool I've been! This is my last chance! "Tomorrow evening?" Sam asked hesitantly, worried it would be too late.

"Tomorrow evening it is, Mr. Yates! Why don't you and your brother… oh, and your son's still with you, isn't he? Why don't you all come to my home, Durham Hall at Mine à Breton, for dinner? You can meet my wife and children, and some of my other associates…"

Sam smiled and quickly answered, "We'll be there, Mr. Austin!"

It took almost all the next day for the Yates to plod the ankle-deep dusty road through the thick forest from Saline Creek to Mine à Breton. They had lashed ten heavy salt packs each onto the mule and sway-backed bay, while the wagon was piled high with the other seventy-four plus their camp gear. The ox's tongue lolled and all three animals were sweat-soaked as Sam and Jake continually prodded them onward.

Although Willie's young body had hardened from a summer spent hauling logs, the humidity and long miles were wearing him down. He wanted to climb atop the salt sack mountain in the cart and fall asleep.

He flopped on his belly beside a small creek that cut across the road.

"Willie, don't drink that water!" Sam shouted. Willie's head jerked up. "Look at the color of that creek, boy. Clouds of brown, red, gray! That's metals washing down from mines upstream. You drink that, and you'll be sicker than a dog. Hang in there, boy. We're almost there. The woods are thinning fast from all the logging and look up ahead. See the smoke from all the smelters?"

They eventually emerged from the woods into a wide, almost treeless valley scattered with mines, gray slag heaps, and swaths of corn fields. The road ran alongside a dark brown creek. They passed several smelters belching black smoke, and a blacksmith shop, grist-mill, and distillery, each worked by a half-dozen or so men. Ahead, on a small bluff, was an immense two-story frame home with a half-dozen outbuildings. Across the creek was a village of twenty log cabins.

"That big white home is Durham Hall," Sam said admiringly.

Willie pointed, "Is that a cannon?" In front of the home stood a black man beside a three pounder. Spotting them, the slave lowered a long smoldering punk to the cannon. Boom!!! The charge echoed across the valley, causing the ox to halt bewildered and both the horse and mule to rear. The mule brayed shrilly. Sam and Jake dug in their heels, pulled hard on the halters, and finally managed to quiet the animals.

"If that's how they welcome friends, I fear ta think how they answer ta enemies!" Jake declared. A man, woman, and two children spilled out of the house and down to the gate while other people appeared in doorways and fields across the valley. All stared as the Yates trudged on to the mansion.

Austin smiled widely and extended his hand, "Gentlemen, wel-come to Durham Hall!" He shook hands with all three Yates. "Unfortunately, my associates have been delayed at our smelter and may not arrive until late tonight. Let me introduce my good wife, Marie," The short, plump, dark-haired woman smiled. "And my children, Stephen and Emily." The boy was taller; both were slender and brown-haired. "Marie, children, this is Mr. Sam and Mr. Jake Yates, and Sam's son, Willie. May I call you by your first names?"

Sam hesitated, "Certainly, Mr. Aus...Moses."

"Gentlemen," Marie apologized, "I know you'll want to discuss your affairs. If you'll excuse me, I must supervise the cooking."

"Of course." Sam nodded.

"And, children, I know you've been anxiously awaiting a playmate. Why don't you take Willie to the kitchen for some cider?" Marie suggested.

Emily smiled, dimples deepening at each corner of her mouth. "Come on, Willie! You look thirsty!" Willie followed Stephen and Emily behind the house. "How old are you?"

"I'll be eight in December."

Emily's thick hair hung to her waist. "I am nine and a half and Stephen's eleven," she said proudly. Willie wished that he was as big and old as they were. An enormous old black woman sat outside the red brick kitchen, methodically churning butter. "Annie, can we have some cider?"

"Sure thing, honey. Come on in." Annie slowly rose and led them inside. "Who's dis boy?" Annie asked as she began dipping cider from an oak barrel into three pewter mugs.

"This is Willie Yates." Stephen announced. "His papa and uncle are gonna work the new mine, the secret one."

"That a fact," she said lethargically. "Believe I'll have some cider maself." She handed each child a mug and began filling another.

The children thanked Annie. "Let's go sit down by the creek," Stephen suggested. "Aren't your papa and uncle afraid of Smith?"

Willie recalled last night's long campfire debate as papa and Uncle Jake carefully weighed whether or not to throw in with Austin. Smith was known to have killed a dozen men in duels, and neither Sam nor Jake wanted to tangle with him. To ally with Austin meant making Smith an enemy.

"My papa and uncle aren't afraid of anyone!" Willie declared. "Did you really get attacked by Indians?"

"We sure did!" Stephen stated proudly. "About thirty Osage attacked our home just two years ago. But papa and his men held them off and killed three of them!"

"Wow! I wish I was there. Were you scared?"

"Well, a little. Emily, me, Mama, and some other women and children had to hide in the cellar while papa and the men were shooting upstairs."

Stephen frowned across the creek. "And the French in the village didn't lift a finger to help. They're so lazy. They never helped us with anything. And they are always jumping our mining claims. Papa hates them!... Do you read?"

"Sure, I read some. My mama taught me how and I'm gonna go to school with the other American children when I get home."

"Do you wanna see our library?"

"All right. Did you use your cannon to fight off the Osage?"

"Nope. Papa dug that old Spanish cannon out of the ground and cleaned it up. Can you believe it! The Spanish just abandoned a cannon down near St. Genevieve for no reason. They're as lazy as the French!"

The children trooped into Durham Hall, glanced into the parlor where the three men, sipping from wine glasses, were negotiating, then headed into the library next door. "Wow!" Willie stared in wonder at three floor to ceiling cases full of books. "Where'd ya get 'em all?"

"Papa has the second biggest library in Upper Louisiana, after Chouteau," Emily stated proudly. "We've got everything here...history, philosophy, literature...Does your family have a library, Willie?"

He thought of the family Bible from which mama loved reading him and Sarah stories, and the dozen moldy books with tiny print. "Not like this." Willie pulled a book out of the stacks. "*Émile ou De l'Education*," he slowly read. "Jean-Jacques Rousseau." He opened it. "French! I have enough trouble with English...but French!"

"Stephen's going back to Connecticut to school. I'll be all alone." Emily sighed. "I wish you lived nearby, Willie."

"Maybe you can come to school in St. Louis with me, Emily," Willie said eagerly.

Emily was about to reply when a tall, skinny black man appeared at the door. He was dressed in a tan vest and knee britches. "Master Stephen. Miss Emily. You and your friend must wash up for dinner. You'll be eating shortly."

"Thank you, Jacob," Stephen said gravely.

"How many slaves do you have, Willie?" Emily asked.

"Well...we don't have any. My papa...my papa..."

Stephen gave Emily a dirty look. "I am sure Willie's family will get some if they strike it rich at the secret mine. I am starved. Let's hurry up and wash so we can eat."

Although the light was quickly fading outside, everyone glowed in the dining room under the glare of a half-dozen silver candelabra. The Austins sat at opposite ends of the long, polished chestnut table, with Jake near Marie, Sam near Moses, and Willie squeezed between Stephen and Emily on the other side. Austin arose holding up a glass of red wine.

His face was flushed and split by a broad smile. "I would like to propose a toast!" he cheerfully announced. "To my new associates and friends, Sam and Jake Yates. May the realities of our enterprise match our dreams of success and wealth!" The adults clinked wine glasses as Jacob and another slave began serving platters of baked ham, fried catfish, blood sausages, corn, gumbo, and squash. Everyone talked excitedly. Willie wondered what percentage they had cut with Austin. Jake had taught Willie percentages by cutting up apples. The Yates brothers had planned to ask for thirty-three percent then, if need be, slowly drop to thirty, twenty-five, and twenty, but they would break off negotiations if they could not get twenty percent minimum. He later told Willie that Austin had skillfully held them to twenty percent. "That Austin's one shrewd Yankee trader. I believe your papa and me met our match!" Jake said with a laugh.

Willie was starved and stuffed down food as fast as the slaves could serve it. A couple of times he caught his father's stern glance warning him to slow down. Meanwhile Stephen and Emily bombarded him with questions to which he replied with short answers. Emily's blue eyes and smiling dimples made him nervous and self-conscious. He imagined her coming to school in St. Louis. Jacob was offering him a choice of apple pie, watermelon, or cheese for dessert.

"What...oh, a little of each please," he said.

"Gosh, Willie, I never saw a boy eat as much as you," Emily declared.

"Well, I've been working at the salt camp all summer and my papa and Uncle Jake sure can't cook like this. I miss my mama's cooking."

Suddenly it seemed so long since he'd been with his mother and Sarah. He felt a tear well up in his eye. Don't cry in front of Emily! he silently ordered himself. Willie imagined his father calling him a crybaby. He gobbled down his dessert and asked for another piece of pie.

The men retired again to the parlor while Marie herded the children upstairs. Maybe I'll be in the middle, Willie thought hopefully.

He dreamt of snuggling up behind Emily and breathing deep the scent of her thick hair and warm body. They stopped in front of a door.

Marie kissed Stephen, Marie, and Willie goodnight, then walked back downstairs. "You all sleep tight!" she called over her shoulder.

"Goodnight, Stephen! Goodnight ,Willie!" Emily shouted as she disappeared into another room.

"Your sister sleeps alone?" Willie said astonished.

"Sure. We both have our own rooms. Don't you?"

"Sarah and I sleep together. I thought everyone did."

Although it was cozy beside Stephen in the big feather bed, Willie had trouble sleeping. The all-day hike under the hot sun, the huge meal, and thoughts of Emily kept him drifting on the edge of sleep all night. Strange color patterns and images of painted Osage warriors, crazed men brandishing huge carving knives, and Emily shrinking into nothing floated across his eyes. He finally fell into a deep sleep just as the morning bell rang for the field hands.

With the huge Yates's Bible resting in her lap, Jenny sat in Jake's large Creole chair with its split hickory seat.

Willie and Sarah sprawled on the oak floor before her. "Now, children, I haven't read you this story about how God created the world for a long time. So listen carefully." Jenny's voice was animated, a singsong. She loved reading to the children. "In the beginning, God created the Heaven and the earth..."

A gust of wind blew down the chimney and pushed against the windows. Willie tried imagining God making the whole world! And in six days! How do you make something from nothing? Staring dully at her mother, Sarah lay on her stomach, palms cupping her chin.

"...So God created man in his image..." Willie twisted over on his back and stared at the ceiling with his hands behind his head. God looks like a man? Like who? Uncle Jake? Auguste Chouteau? William Clark? Moses Austin? Papa? Sarah combed her corncob doll's hair.

"...Also in the midst of the garden, and the tree of good and evil..." Willie picked his nose. How could a tree be good and evil? All trees were good. Some were better climbing and some had prettier leaves. Sarah grimaced and started rubbing her feet which had fallen asleep.

"...And they were both naked, the man and his wife, and they were not ashamed..." Willie turned on his side and stared out the window at a maple tree's crimson leaves against the cobalt sky. He imagined Emily's smiling face at the window, beckoning him out to play. Sarah nodded off, her head on her crossed arms. Willie tickled Sarah's foot. Her foot jerked away and Sarah awoke making a face at him.

"...And the Lord God walking in the garden in the cool of the day:

and Adam and his wife hid themselves from the presence of the Lord God, amongst the trees of the garden. And the Lord God called unto Adam, and said unto him, Where art thou…" Willie smiled. God was playing hide-and-seek. If God really knew everything and was all-powerful, why didn't he know where they were hiding? Maybe God wasn't so smart after all.

From across St. Louis, the Catholic church bell gonged twelve times. Willie imagined Colette and the French talking excitedly as they spilled out of church. In good weather, every Sunday afternoon after church, the French would dance and sing in the square outside; in bad weather they pushed aside the chairs inside the church for their parties.

"…So he drove out the man: and he placed at the east of the garden of Eden, Cherubins, and a flaming sword, which turned every way, to keep the way of the tree of life." Jenny sighed and closed the Bible with a thud.

She beamed at Willie and Sarah. "Well, children. What did you think of that story?"

"Why didn't God want Adam and Eve to have knowledge?" Willie demanded.

Jenny's smile faded. "Well…God wanted them to be innocent like children, but after they tasted the fruit, they understood everything. So God was angry and sent them from the garden into the world. God is our parent. He made us. And he punishes us when we are bad, just like he did to Adam and Eve. So you should always be good and commit no sins!"

Willie was still confused. "But you want us to be smart. Why didn't God want Adam and Eve to have knowledge? If God made people, why is he always angry at them—?"

Sarah interrupted, "I'm a good girl, aren't I, Mama?"

Jenny placed the Bible on the floor. "Come here, sweetie." Sarah climbed upon Jenny's lap.

"Why did you marry papa?" Willie demanded. Jenny looked startled.

"Yeah, why did you marry papa?" echoed Sarah. The children had sometimes whispered the question to each other, but until then, neither had dared to ask.

"Well…Daddy—your grandfather—had lost his fortune during the Revolution and your father…" Jenny sounded uncertain. "We were in love. That's why people marry. Someday you'll both find someone you love and you'll marry and have children. That's what God wants us to do."

"Why did you love papa?" Sarah wondered.

"Well, he was handsome and strong and had many ideas and...hey! We're supposed to be talking about the creation story."

Sarah persisted. "When's papa coming home?"

"I told you before, Sarah. He'll be home for Christmas. You know he and Uncle Jake have to make the mine work. And then maybe we'll be rich and can live in our own home. Don't you want that?"

"I want my own room!" Willie stated. "Emily and Stephen Austin have their own rooms. And can I have a horse? Stephen has his own horse."

"And can I have French dolls?" Sarah added wistfully. "Willie said Emily has French dolls with velvet clothes."

Jenny set down Sarah and sighed again. "We'll see. It's a nice day. Why don't you both go out and play."

Willie and Sarah jumped up and ran out the door. Jenny sat staring into the ash-filled fireplace. If only Sam hadn't gone on those campaigns, she thought sadly. Those horrors had squeezed out what little humor and patience he had. Jenny slowly stood and crossed the room to the large oak table scattered with patches of material she was quilting.

"Let's go to the square, Willie!" Sarah shouted.

"I'll beat ya!" Willie ran past Sarah down the street.

"Wait for me!" she shouted.

They stopped to poke sticks at a bloated dead pig. Other pigs and dogs had gnawed at the carcass. The stench stung their noses. They heard singing and the whine of fiddles in the distance.

"Come on, Willie!" They dropped their sticks and ran toward the music.

The square was filled with people, laughing, singing, dancing. Two fiddlers, one black and one white, and a thickset old woman kneading a squeezebox, her head sporting a tan top hat, provided the music. A score of couples in their Sunday best twirled while three riverboat men, arms linked, danced a jig. Everywhere groups of young boys and girls giggled and flirted with one another. A squat young man with a wooden leg clumped through the crowd, hawking ribbons and earrings. At the crowd's edge, portly, gout-ridden Auguste Chouteau leaned on his cane while talking passionately with a half-dozen other leading citizens.

"Where's Aunt Colette? Do you see her?" Sarah asked.

"Nope." Willie pointed to a pretty little girl with a long blonde ponytail hanging on to her mother's hand across the square. "There's your friend Judy. Why don't you go play with her? I am gonna see those Indians!" He slipped through the crowd toward two Sac wrapped in red blankets silently watching the dance. Willie's eyes widened as he approached them. Blue and yellow paint streaked their scarred, pock-marked faces, red-dyed deer and horse hair roaches adorned their scalp locks, a dozen brass rings dangled from each ear, bear claw necklaces and medallions etched with Jefferson's profile draped their chests, and tomahawks and skinning knives their belts. The gray-haired Sac slowly waved a French fan. The younger Sac was missing all but the forefinger and thumb on his right hand. No one paid them much attention. Indian delegations were always passing through St. Louis to meet the gover-nor and receive presents in return for promises to stop raiding.

Willie stood to one side and stared. He wished he had something to trade. The older Sac impassively eyed him and then slowly returned his gaze to the dance. The younger one smiled. *"Tu es Américan ou Français?"* he asked with a thick accent.

"American. You're Sac, aren't you?" Willie had learned to distin-guish subtle differences in dress, hairstyle, and physique among the half-dozen tribes which regularly visited St. Louis. The Sac smiled and nodded.

"Do you know my uncle, Jake Yates? He sometimes trades with you."

The Sac looked surprised. "Jacques, with long brown beard and bear bites on arm and leg?"

"That's my uncle," Willie stated proudly.

The Sac raised an eyebrow and nodded. "Jacques fair trader." He stared into Willie's eyes and extended his mangled right hand. It looked like a huge, brown bird claw. Willie hesitated and then, trying not to shudder, grasped it. The bird claw briefly clamped then dropped his small hand. "Jacques strong man." The Sac smacked his chest with his bird claw. "Me Snapping Turtle strong, too!" he boasted. "Kill many Osage!"

The Sac's mouth drooped in disgust. "But Great Father Harrison tell Sac no more kill Osage. Promise many presents. No good! No good! Osage kill many Sac and friends Fox. Sac and Fox must take warpath! Kill scalp many Osage!"

"Tachawei." The older Sac said quietly to Snapping Turtle. The two Indians' eyes locked. The elder spoke softly. Understanding nothing, Willie strained to hear each musical syllable. Snapping Turtle nodded as the elder stopped talking, then replied, occasionally pointing toward Willie. The elder hesitated and stared down at the boy. Finally he nodded.

"Now we go home but...you know medicine? Sac very strong medicine. Most strong medicine of all Indians. Talking Crow," he pointed to the elder, "make very strong medicine. You, Jacques' boy. You good boy. Good heart. Someday you become very strong. Have strong medicine. Talking Crow know. He say. He show you medicine. You want see?"

Willie smiled. He loved magic. He remembered Chief pulling coins from his ear. Cincinnati seemed so far away. "Sure!"

"Here no good. We go woods. Come!"

Few noticed as the two Indians and little boy slipped away from the crowd and strode down the house-lined street toward the north end of town. In St. Louis, it was not unusual to see a boy leading Indians through the streets to different citizens' homes. The woods ahead blazed yellow, orange, and red against the sky. Willie inhaled a lung full of crisp air. Autumn was his favorite season. A quarter-mile down the rutted road leading from St. Louis, they turned off into the woods.

Their feet crunched through the thick bed of withered leaves until they reached a small grassy glade. They sat cross-legged in a circle facing each other. Eyes closed, the two Sac sat silent. Suddenly Willie felt afraid. He stared at them, wondering if they had ever killed any whites.

Talking Crow's wrinkled eyelids slit open. He slightly shook his head no, then his eyes languidly closed again. A fly buzzed the sunlight around them and somewhere far away an ax thudded steadily into wood. Meadowlarks sang and flitted through the trees. Willie closed his eyes. This was the day God rested. The sunlight wrapped him in a warm, airy blanket. His body seemed light enough to float away.

Something rustled beside him. Willie's eyes opened as Talking Crow pulled his pipe and a twist of tobacco from his pouch. Lying on a scrap of deerhide before him, was a motionless indigo bunting. Snapping Turtle sat still as a statue, his glazed eyes fixed on the bunting. Talking Crow pulled off a tobacco plug and packed it into the bowl. Then he struck a piece of steel on flint, loosening a shower of sparks on some tinder. He blew into the tinder, unleashing a small flame, then held it to his bowl while inhaling deeply. Rising, Talking Crow offered his pipe and puffs of smoke to heaven, earth, and the four directions. Then, his face held up to the sun, he chanted and sang. Sitting down, he inhaled deeply from the pipe and passed it to Snapping Turtle who did the same. Snapping Turtle looked into Talking Crow's eyes and nodded toward Willie. Talking Crow shook his head no and took back the pipe. He inhaled deeply again and blew the smoke toward the bunting.

Then, chanting and singing, Talking Crow gently stroked the still bird. Slowly the bunting's eyes cracked open and its legs twitched. Finally, the bird fluttered its wings, stared up at Talking Crow, and flew away.

Willie's mouth gaped open. With wide eyes he stared at first Talking Crow then Snapping Turtle who continued to silently pass the pipe between them. Finally, Talking Crow packed away the empty pipe, tobacco, and deer scrap. Snapping Turtle grinned at Willie. "You tell Jacques you see big medicine. Jacques good man, good heart. He come trade with Sac not Osage." Willie nodded. They rose and slipped through the woods to the road. After shaking Snapping Turtle's bird claw and Talking Crow's gnarled hand, Willie watched them stride north up the road until they disappeared.

Willie wandered the woods absent-mindedly kicking at patches of slush.

"Some Christmas present!" he grumbled. Papa'd said Austin had sent Emily back East to Kentucky for schooling too, rather than St. Louis. He envisioned the view from his Cincinnati lookout to the wooded hills beyond the Ohio.

Emily would have been the prettiest girl at Pringle's school. But all the older boys would have fallen over each other trying to make friends with her. Boys like Rene Goutard, who always teased the girls and bullied the smaller boys.

Willie seethed with anger again as he smelled the horseshit Rene had one day rubbed in his face just for fun. And Pringle had swatted them both for fighting. If only I was older, Willie thought miserably.

The snowball whizzed just past his ear and splattered against a tree. Willie jerked around. No one. He grabbed a pile of slush and packed it into an iceball. "Who threw that!" he called out. Silence.

Willie quietly slipped off through the trees to get around whoever had thrown it. He pretended he was stalking Shawnee. Hope it's not a trap! Twenty feet away, a face popped out from behind a tree, spotted him, then disappeared. Willie debated whether or not to charge. With a huge grin spread across it, the face appeared again. Willie hurled his iceball.

It splattered against the tree. Suddenly a madly grinning boy was running toward him, an iceball in each hand. Willie turned and ran wildly through the woods. He heard the boy running after him, quickly gaining.

"Ha!" the boy shouted, "ah got the drop on yer!" An iceball smacked Willie in the back. It stung bad. Willie stopped and turned, his fists up. The boy stopped, too. Both boys eyed each other, the breath steaming fast from their mouths. Grinning at Willie, the boy held his iceball ready to throw. "Yer give up!"

Willie remembered the words of John Paul Jones and smiled. "I have not yet begun to fight!"

"Well, guess there ain't no point then!" the boy said as he tossed his iceball aside. The boy was about Willie's height but leaner. He had a large hawk nose and his small brown eyes were as devilish as his grin.

"I've seen you before. Isn't your papa the blacksmith down by the landing? He's got long black hair and a big beard and a..."

"Limp?" the boy's grin faltered.

Willie's smile faded, too. "Yeah. I saw you hauling wood to the furnace. Why don't you go to school?"

"Ma Pa sez I don't hafta go ta school ifin ah don't wanna. Fulla foolish notions he sez. Can't say ahm partial ta smithin' or book larnin'. I'd like ta go ta meet the other fellas though."

"How'd your pa hurt his foot?"

"Dropped an anvil on it whilst he was drunk! Yer shoulda heard him cuss!" The boy chuckled, "The ol' man has trouble catching me these days." He extended his hand. "Name's Jess."

"Willie." They shook.

Giggling furtively, Willie and Jess huddled together on the back bench of the crowded, noisy schoolroom. Near the doorway, egged on by Rene and a half-dozen older boys, two seven-year-olds squared off, each daring the other to throw the first punch. Meanwhile, scattered in twos and threes across the benches, most of the other girls and boys jabbered or poked each other.

Sarah and Judy sat together on the front bench. Sarah had tried to strike up a conversation with Judy about some tiny kittens a neighbor's cat had just dropped, but Judy had hushed her and dutifully continued mouthing the words in her spelling book. Wondering why Judy took school so seriously, Sarah reluctantly stared down at her own book. Neither noticed a little tow-haired boy crouched right behind Judy, dropping spitballs down her back.

Some children nearby started giggling and Judy suddenly felt the spitballs against her back. She whirled angrily. The boy yanked her ponytail and scrambled over some benches. Judy burst into tears and, tightly holding her books, ran toward the door. Just before she reached the door, it burst open and slammed against the wall. Judy leapt back in horror as schoolmaster Pringle stood before her, his watery blue eyes glaring and his face reddening in anger. The boys scrambled toward the benches while the other children silently sat to attention.

"What is going on here!" the schoolmaster shrieked. "Judy! Where do you think you're going?"

Judy sobbed loudly and pointed behind her.

"Speak up, you ninny!" Judy tried to rush past him but he grabbed her by both shoulders and shoved her back. "Go sit down before I give you the spanking of your life!" Judy stumbled back and sat down at an empty place on the front bench. "And desist from that infernal whining immediately!"

The schoolmaster marched toward the front of the classroom. "And the rest of you! If I hear so much as one peep, I'll rap your behinds until you won't be able to sit down for a week!"

Willie peeped quietly. Several boys nearby snickered and he could feel Jess shaking beside him, trying to hold in his laughter.

"What's that laughing about back there! Bret! Stand up and account for your despicable actions!" At thirteen, Bret was the oldest boy in the school. He rose to his gangly height. "Well, Bret, just what is so funny? Do you think something is funny, Bret?"

Head bowed, Bret squinted through the long greasy hair that drooped over his eyes. "N-nothing, s-sir!" he stammered, as he recalled the sting of the schoolmaster's paddle.

"Then sit down and shut up!" Bret dropped back on the bench. "Idiots! The whole lot of you are idiots! There's not one among you who will ever amount to anything! None of you will become gentlemen or ladies! And why? Because you have no self-control, no ambition to rise above your vulgarities, your ignorance, your conceits. The only thing you understand is brute, naked punishment! The paddle!" Pringle attempted to jerk open his desk drawer but it would not budge. Willie tried hard to swallow a snicker as he felt Jess start to shake again.

"So that's it, is it!" Pringle shrieked again. His voice dropped to a harsh, loud whisper. "Playing games, are we? Naughty games? Naughty children? And we know what happens to naughty children, don't we?"

The schoolmaster gave the drawer a mighty jerk. The glue gave way and Pringle smiled as his paddle stared up at him from the drawer bottom.

"And I don't care how long it takes, but I will find out who the naughty child was who committed this naughty act." Both Willie and

Jess were shaking with suppressed laughter. The other children were astonished that one of them would be so bold as to glue Pringle's drawer shut.

Pringle reached for the paddle, but it would not budge. His face grew livid and his body shook with anger. He wrenched the paddle but the handle broke off in his hand. He brandished the handle at the children.

"So who did it?" he hissed. "Someone must have seen the culprit. Who is the culprit?" He began to move along the front bench, stopping before each child to repeat the question and shake the handle in their eyes. Judy and several other children wept quietly.

"Judy? You are always first to school. Did you see who did this?"

Judy sobbed and shook her head no. "Don't lie to me, Judy. I know you saw the culprit. Who was he?" He sharply rapped her knuckles. She screamed. Willie and Jess gave worried glances to each other. Could Judy or someone else have seen them? The raid had only taken a few minutes earlier that morning. They had squirmed up through the floor after loosening a board. Jess had glued the paddle and drawer while Willie quickly filed through one of Pringle's chair legs. They had hoped that Pringle would first try to sit down, the chair would collapse beneath him, and then, in his rage, he would try to open the drawer.

"I...I...saw..." her voice faltered in another sob.

"It's you or them, Judy. Who was it?"

Judy turned and looked back. Her eyes were red and her face streaked with tears. "I'm sorry," she murmured as she stared at Willie.

Pringle's dull eyes searched the boys' faces in the last row. "Who? Speak up, you ninny," he ordered as he prodded her with the handle.

"I saw Willie and Jess running from the school just as I got here," Judy exclaimed then burst into tears.

Willie's stomach felt like someone had knocked his wind out. "Run for it!" Jess muttered, then scrambled for the door.

"Stop them!" Pringle shouted.

Jess jerked open the door and darted outside while Willie stumbled after him. Just as he reached the door, he was tackled from behind and pinned to the floor. "You're gonna eat horseshit again, Yates," Rene whispered in his ear.

Pringle ran up shouting, "Good work, Rene! Good work!" Rene jerked Willie to his feet and pushed him toward Pringle. Willie trembled as Pringle dragged him toward the front of the class. Although Rene and some older boys were gloating, most of the other children were frightened. Judy and Sarah wept. Pringle spun him around to face the class.

"So this is one of the culprits!" he sneered. "And I'll soon have my hands on the other. Rene!" Pringle briefly considered, then dismissed, the idea of sending him after Jess. "Sit down, Rene...You will all see what happens to naughty little boys. Rene!" The bully stood to attention. "Go fetch a board from the woodpile." He slipped outside. "Yes, Willie, you will regret your decision to be naughty. And after today you will never be naughty again, will you?" Willie's body shook. "Will you?" Pringle gave Willie another jerk. "Speak up when spoken to or you'll get it twice as hard!"

Rene reappeared holding a short, thin split log. "Is this one about right, Mr. Pringle?"

Pringle grasped the log, weighed it in his hand, and leered. "Very good again, Rene. Yes, this is quite sufficient. Willie, bend over." Willie started to whimper but refused to bend over. Pringle poked him in the back. "Every time you refuse, you are going to get it worse. Now bend over!" Pringle growled. He hit Willie hard behind the knees, crumpling him to the floor. Then he grabbed him by his belt, jerked him to his feet, and started beating his ass with the log.

Willie howled and the tears streamed down his face. "You won't sit down for a week, you naughty child!" Pringle shouted. Finally Pringle released him. He continued to cry while rubbing his bottom.

"Now get out, Willie, and don't come back until you are ready to act like a civilized child!"

Willie bolted for the door. People turned to stare as he ran down the crowded streets for the woods greening in the spring air. Where's Jess? What'll mama do when she finds out? he wondered. Thank God papa's far away at the mine. Papa's paddlings hurt a lot worse than Pringle's!

Sweat-soaked, Willie hauled an armful of logs from the woodpile and shoved them into the furnace's mouth. Must be what hell's like, he thought as he stared into the roaring flames. He shuddered. Mama'd said the road of mischief was the road to hell. Indians don't believe in hell, he'd countered. Mama'd said that was because they were savages and didn't know better. For the thousandth time, Willie kicked himself for not planning the raid better. If only we'd sneaked in the night before, then Judy'd never have spotted us. Poor Judy! Must've said sorry a dozen times since. She couldn't have helped it. That Pringle was one mean bastard. Shame Judy's so bookish. She's sweet, though, and pretty. Shame she's plump and round-faced and pug-nosed and always nervously rubbing her hands and blinking her eyes. Maybe she'll curve like Colette someday. He tried imagining Judy as tall and shapely. He smiled. Even then, Judy'd still be serious, not fun-loving like Colette. Shame she spotted us. Today Jess and I'd be snickering together in the back of class, silently scheming even better pranks. Nope, not now. It's late June—school must be out for summer. I'd be stuck stoking this furnace anyway. Just as Jess'd be stoking his old man's furnace. Least he has a bellows.

"I don't blame you for staring—it is the finest smelter in Upper Louisiana and one of the finest in the country." Willie turned to see Major Hunt beaming down at him. He was only in his mid-thirties, but his potbelly, shuffling amble, graying brown hair, and sideburns that stretched to the corners of his mouth made him seem much older. Hunt's purchase of a thirty percent share of the partnership last November had made him the overseer. "Yup, Willie, were're all lucky to be working here. That Mr. Austin is truly a man of progress." Hunt prided himself on his engineering knowledge. "He single-handedly revolutionized the industry. Why, when Mr. Austin first came here a decade ago, the French were just digging shallow pits not more than ten feet deep. But Mr. Austin began sinking deep shafts. You know how deep ours is?" Hunt pointed a grimy finger to the mine across the creek valley. Several men stripped to the waist hauled buckets of earth and rock from the mine while a half-dozen others sifted out the ore into buckets and dragged them to the furnace. Willie shook his head. "Two hundred and thirty-seven feet and we're still digging," he stated proudly. "We may end up in China before the year's out." Hunt chuckled. His thick brown eyebrows arched everytime he made a new point. A smile tugged at Willie's mouth when he imagined Hunt's eyebrows were really brown woolybears crawling across his wrinkled forehead.

"And do you know why our smelter's the most productive in the territory?"

"Nope." Willie's legs felt heavy. He wanted to sit down.

"The French roast their diggings over an open fire. Just heap a couple thousand pounds of ore on a bonfire and keep feeding it for about twelve hours while the lead slowly seeps out and drains into a basin below. But the result's a mess—slag and rock mixed with lead. Now with this blast furnace of ours, we can concentrate the heat and then crush, wash, and filter the lead ash in a continuous process. Why, we can produce as much in two hours as the French smelt in twenty-four, and we extract twice as much out of the ore..." Willie's forehead crinkled. Hunt scratched a sideburn. "Well, you know fractions, don't you?" Willie nodded. "All right, another way of saying it is the French method extracts only thirty-five percent, or one-third, the weight of the ore in lead while we take out sixty percent, or almost two-thirds. Then we haul the remaining chunks to the ash furnace and melt out another fifteen percent. And we do it in one-twelfth the time. And now most of the French have abandoned their log hearths and come to us with their ore and wood and, in return, we take half of what they smelt and they're still better off." Hunt smiled. "You understand now, Willie?"

Willie smiled back. "Yup, that's real clear, Captain Hunt. You oughta be a school teacher. You'd sure be a far sight better than Pringle!"

Hunt chuckled again and patted the boy's head. "Well, it's nice of you to say that, Willie. Although I certainly regret the beating and expulsion you suffered, I get a kick every time I recall the prank you pulled on the schoolmaster. At least you got in the last lick. I wish I could've seen it when old man Pringle, puffed up with pride like a toad after expelling you, sat down and the chair collapsed beneath him and all the students roared with laughter."

Willie grinned. "Wish I could've seen it myself."

Hunt tried to repress his broad smile. "Keep up your studies while you're down here, Willie. I'll be happy to—"

"Riders!" A man splitting logs at the nearby woodpile called out.

They turned to see a dozen heavily-armed mounted men and a wagon pulled by four mules trotting up the road.

"Smith!" Hunt muttered. Across the valley the wood-splitters, haulers, and sifters dropped their work and stared as Smith's gang rode up.

"Major Hunt! Mightly fine day ain't it, though it's a trifle humid." Smith's words dripped with sarcasm.

Hunt's voice trembled slightly. "What do you want, Smith?"

"Just come to take possession of my land."

"Your land!" Hunt blurted. "What nonsense are you talking? This is our land and we have the deed to prove it!" Hunt's men began gathering around him. But none were armed. They had all left their weapons in their huts.

Smith unrolled a document. "Don't you remember selling me this floating concession a couple months back?"

Hunt peered at the document. "Yes, this is the floating concession of five hundred acres I sold you. But it's no good unless you've got a four-acre plot to anchor it to. And that's something you don't..."

"I wouldn't be so sure of that Major. You see..." Smith bared a huge grin, "your predecessor, Captain Stoddard, sold me a four-acre plot just a couple hundred yards up the valley, which I intend to mine."

Smith unrolled another document and handed it to Hunt. "I'll attach my floating concession to it." Smith's grin widened. "Looks like we're gonna be neighbors!"

"Impossible! You can't...it's forbidden to trade the old Spanish grants."

Smith's grin faded. "Major, surely you know Governor Harrison made a point of permitting us to work the grants until Congress decides one way or the other."

Hunt tried to remain outwardly calm while fervently wishing Sam and Jake hadn't taken that load to St. Genevieve. They wouldn't be back for several days. "As commander of the St. Genevieve District, I forbid you...in fact I have the power to remove you from all public lands."

"Power?" Smith asked silkily. "Power?" he glanced around at Hunt's dozen workers and Willie, then back at his men who began clicking back the hammers of their flintlocks. "Major Hunt," Smith mimicked the Eastern college graduate style of discourse, "I assume that when you speak of power, you mean governmental power. Well, remember my words. By the end of summer I'll have replaced Austin as a justice on the Bench of Common Pleas and Quarter Sessions, and will eventually take your position as commander of St. Genevieve. Until then, if you have anymore to say, you're welcome to visit me and my men at our diggings up the valley. Or you can talk to the new governor, although I don't believe General Wilkinson will provide a very sympathetic ear for your case. Good day." Smith grinned, tipped his flop hat, then he and his men spurred their horses up the valley, kicking up mud behind them.

The half-dozen men sat uneasily in Austin's parlor, sipping whiskey and puffing from long clay pipes, sending small clouds of smoke adrift in the humid air. "Smith took no time in digging his claws into the new governor," Hunt complained bitterly. "No time at all! Not only was General Wilkinson openly dismissive of my case, but then I find that he gave Smith my letter detailing my arguments against his squatting on public lands..."

"That's outrageous!" Judge Easton declared vehemently. "Communication from one officer to another should be as sacred as the faithfulness of one's wife!" Easton crossed his arms angrily over his ample belly.

Jake shifted nervously in his chair. "Couldn't agree more, Judge!"

"Well, read us the letter," Austin demanded.

Hunt pulled an envelope from one vest pocket and fumbled for his wire-rimmed glasses in the other. "Let me see here..." He held the letter away from him. The glasses were little help for his farsightedness.

"Well, after the usual opening platitudes, the general comes straight out and rebukes me for threatening to remove Smith. He states: 'The major may be deceived in point of fact, which will be most acceptable to me, because it is my warm wish that no occasion may occur to make it necessary to exert the arm of the law against an individual, much less one of Captain Smith's respectability...'"

"Respectability!" Easton's bland round face flushed; tiny sweat beads glistened across his bald dome. "Why, that—"

Austin hurriedly interrupted. "I understand that Smith played up the fact that his mother was a Wilkinson and that two of his brothers are serving in the army and another is a congressman from Georgia. And those are just the family connections he volunteered. There's no telling what else may have transpired..."

"Well, as I was telling you," Jake scratched his chin thoughtfully as he spoke, "Wilkinson was second in command to both St. Clair and Wayne. Now, neither Sam nor me ever got to know him personally, seeing we were just sergeants, and Wilkinson seemed brave enough when the bullets and arrows were flying, but we sure heard the rumors making the rounds 'bout him during his years in Cincinnati..."

"Is it true," Austin asked as he poured himself another glass of whiskey from the crystal decanter, "that Wilkinson was plotting with the Spaniards to detach the territory west of the Appalachians and create a new state with himself as dictator?"

Sam raised a finger. "Those are the rumors, but we'll never know for sure." He wrinkled his brow toward Jake. "But I don't agree with you, Jake, on Wilkinson's war record. Whether it was against Indians or the British during the Revolution, Wilkinson was always some general's aide, hiding well back from the fighting line." Sam glared fiercely at his companions. "Just because he's good at ass-kissing and wearing uniforms don't make him a fighting man!"

Jake shook his head in agreement. "You got a point there, Sam," he said quietly. "And it's rumored that General Wayne himself had clear evidence of Wilkinson's plot, but died before he could take him to court."

"How did a man like that become the ranking general of the

American army?" Easton asked incredulously.

"He plum ass-kissed every step of his way to the top," Sam declared disgustedly. "The fighting men get killed and the politicians..."

Sam hesitated, mouth open, as he realized that Austin, Hunt, and Easton fell into the same category.

"All right! All right!" Austin's face flushed with anger and whiskey. "So what's our strategy? We must reach a consensus. I am told Wilkinson's on the verge of deposing me and putting Smith in my place. And if that happens, I just may take my seat back by force of arms."

Easton clucked worriedly, "Moses! Moses! We must avoid violence at all costs, or even the talk of it! Someone must go to Washington and tell President Jefferson of the outrageous situation here. If the President only knew..."

"Agreed, Rufus, agreed!" Hunt added quickly, "But in the meantime, why don't we circulate a petition against Smith and, if Wilkinson does remove you from office, to restore you..."

"I may just challenge Smith to a duel, and then Wilkinson..." Austin glared down into his whiskey glass. "I'd derive great pleasure from putting bullets through both of them."

Sam lifted an eyebrow. "I don't know, Moses, Smith has killed at least a dozen men..."

"Yes, let the people decide!" Easton declared excitedly. "We must adhere to the democratic principles upon which our great nation..."

"Gentlemen?" a deep voice intoned at the door. Everyone twisted around to stare up at the house-slave, Jacob. "Dinner will be served shortly."

Mile-high thunderclouds drifted across the deep blue sky. Warm gusts of wind pushed through the woods, spreading ripples across the sluggish Mississippi current. Willie watched the stick-float on his line drift a dozen feet away.

He twitched his pole slightly. Not a bite. Jess had pulled in two catfish shortly after they arrived but neither had got so much as a nibble since.

Willie lifted his line from the water. The nightcrawler's remnants still covered the hook. He slowly lowered the line back into the brown current.

"I don't know how fish can see with water that muddy."

Jess scratched his long Roman nose. "Must smell 'em."

"You figure the hole's fished out?"

"Naw. Maybe we ain't fishing deep enough. Maybe ah got the little uns that the big uns pushed up top."

"Figure it'll rain?" They stared at the huge thunderclouds billowing above. "Those clouds seem to be piling up and they're getting darker. I bet we'll have a thunderstorm before evening. Maybe it's scaring the fish."

"Never know. Wanna try another spot?"

Willie stared downstream. The river was empty; St. Louis was invisible far around the bend. "Yeah. Let's head upstream."

After pulling in their lines and shouldering their poles and baskets, they began plodding up the narrow towline cutting the shore, stepping over the occasional broken bottle, worn out shoe, rotting plank. Jess suddenly turned and grinned. "Wouldn't mind going for a swim. You wanna forget fishing and jump in?"

Willie peered down at the two catfish lying listlessly in Jess's basket.

"I wanna take some cats home. My ma and pa're always saying I cut loose and don't do nothing."

"Ah'm surprised they let you go fishing instead of work on your house."

"I told 'em I'd be back 'round mid-afternoon." Willie's eyes drifted into the thick brush hedging the path, up into the leafy branches of tall sycamores overhanging the shore, then at the thunderclouds surging across the Mississippi. Shadows and sunshine swirled around him, alternately embracing him with cool and warm air. Cicadas buzzed and a red-tailed hawk circled overhead. He smiled. "I love days like this! We got the whole river to ourselves. Think we can make it to the Missouri and back before nightfall?"

Jess's grin deepened. "We kin try!"

They doubled their speed, stumbling over loose rocks and washed-out trees. Suddenly Jess stopped and held up his hand. "Listen!" he whispered. Ahead they dimly heard the sounds of boyish voices shouting and bodies splashing into water. "Let's stalk 'em." They quietly slipped along the shore. The voices got louder. Jess lifted his hand again and they crouched behind some bushes. "It's Goutard and Bret. We better not let 'em see us. No tellin' what they'd do." They watched the naked boys take turns swinging out from shore on a thick grapevine and then drop into the river.

"I'd sure like to get back at Goutard," Willie said fiercely.

"We wouldn't stand a chance in a fair fight."

"It's bad enough Goutard bullies young'uns smaller than him, but he fights dirty, kicking and biting..."

"Goutard makes me sick. Ah can just picture 'im nuzzlin' up to Pringle next week when we gotta go back to school."

"We gotta do something. Let's throw rocks at him and run. If we time it right, he'll never see us."

Jess shook his head thoughtfully. "Yeah, but ifin he ever catched us, he'd kill us!"

"Yeah," Willie reluctantly admitted, "you're right."

Goutard and Bret wrestled a huge log into the river and began pushing it into the current. They hung on to the log and kicked it out farther. Jess grinned. "Willie, ah got a plan!" A smile spread across Willie's face. Half the fun of being with Jess was scheming new pranks. "Goutard shamed you by smearing your face with horseshit. Well, reckon how shamed he'd be walkin' into town naked as Adam!" Goutard and Bret were still heading away from shore, splashing white water behind them.

Willie nodded and whispered excitedly, "Now's our chance before they turn around!" Keeping an eye on Goutard and Bret, they scrambled through the brush, grabbed the boys' pile of clothes and shoes, and then just as quickly disappeared. Willie and Jess grinned triumphantly at each other. "Come on," Willie motioned. "We better clear out before they notice. We gotta stay away from the river."

Jess raised an eyebrow. "You don't wanna watch their faces when they get back?"

Willie laughed. "You can stick around if you want, but Goutard's gonna be mad as a bull when he finds out and I wanna be far gone. I bet we'll hear him though. Let's get deep in the woods where they'll never find us. Then we can ditch their clothes and head back to town." They stuffed the clothes into the baskets and plunged into the thick brush and trees.

Suddenly Goutard's voice cut shrilly through the woods. "Hey! Hey, Bret! What happened to our clothes? Somebody took 'em! Who took our clothes? Hey, bring our clothes back! Come on, Bret ,we gotta find 'em!"

Willie and Jess laughed and poked each other. "Even if they find our path, they'll never catch up with all these stickers and poison ivy," Willie said. They pushed on with the curses of Goutard and Bret trailing behind them.

A half-hour's hard hiking later, Willie and Jess dumped the clothes into a deep ravine at the town's edge then strolled nonchalantly into the busy St. Louis streets. They halted just up from the blacksmith shop.

Inside, Jess's father alternately sang a dirty French song and cursed as he struck his hammer rhythmically on a wagon hoop. Jess shrugged. "Guess we'll hafta wait another day to reach the Missouri."

Willie frowned. "When! You gotta smith and I gotta work on the house every day till school starts."

Thunder cracked far away then rumbled across the thickly cloud-covered sky. The rhythmic hammering stopped. "Jesse!" A deep voice boomed joyfully behind them. "How was the fishing, boy?" Willie and Jess jerked their heads toward the blacksmith shop. Hank Baucus towered at the entrance, leaning on his good right foot, his long, black, tangled hair and beard streaming in the humid wind, hand clenching a hammer, huge grin splitting his blackened face.

The boys grinned back and walked up to Hank. Jess held up his basket. "Got two cats, Pa!"

Hank dropped his hammer, grabbed Jess's arm with one iron grip, rubbed his thick, greasy brown hair with the other, then released him.

"Ha, ah got the drop on yer!" Hank gave a deep belly laugh. "Thanks for the supper, but what're ye gonna eat?"

Jess darted away. "Ah'm hungry 'nuff ta eat these cats raw! Ah might save ya some bones though, Pa."

"Well, ifin you're fixin' ta eat the cats, ah'll just hafta eat me some real pussy and wash it down with wine!" Hank laughed even louder. "Thank the Lord that's something you boys gotta few years yet 'fore you pitch into."

Willie and Jess giggled knowingly. Shortly after they had began running around together Jess had taught Willie about fuckin'—"Just like dogs 'cept yer face the girl," Jess had explained.

"Didn't yer catch nothin', Willie? Yer musta been using the wrong pole." Hank laughed and the boys giggled again. "Well, now, yer bes' gitta working, Jesse. Ah'm havin' a helluva time with a wagon just come in. Man sez he needs it 'fore dark fer haulin' supplies up from a keelboat but it's got two busted wheels. So start workin' the bellows. Willie, yer kin help ifin yer gotta mind ta."

Willie shook his head. "I gotta go help on the house, and I'll probably get in trouble 'cause I didn't catch any cats."

They bid goodbyes and Willie headed to the new house on the south edge of town. He recalled his ma and pa arguing over the new house; Ma wanted their own home as soon as possible while Pa pushed her to wait a year. "I want my own home! Colette's driving me crazy!" Ma declared bitterly. "I do all the work while she's gallivanting around

St. Louis seeing Lord knows who. She's no wife for your brother—not that he deserves much better—and what kind of impression do you think she's making on our children—particularly Sarah. Do you want Sarah to become like Colette?" Pa finally gave in, and had grumbled ever since over the direct cost of the building material and labor and the indirect cost of receiving no percentage of the mine's earnings for every day he stayed away. Willie wondered how Pa could spend months pinching pennies then spend them all in one throw.

Thunder cracked and lightning flashed through the thick clouds surging above, sending people scurrying to shelter. Willie started a slow run through the emptying streets toward the town's south edge.

A handful of heavy rain splattered the dust around him. Hot gusts of wind battered him. In a wide field ahead he saw the skeleton of their home against the blackening sky. The house looked deserted, the piles of planks and cedar shingles around it like barricades. Willie figured everyone had gone back to Uncle Jake's. May as well wait out the storm inside, he decided, glad they'd finished the roof yesterday. Breathing heavily, he stopped outside to catch his breath. His heart jumped as he heard someone murmuring inside. He slipped behind a half-finished wall and strained to listen.

His father's voice spoke softly, "I just can't, Colette, you're my brother's wife...as pretty as I find you..." he added lamely. Willie felt paralyzed, unable to move or think, reminded of the dreams where something terrible is chasing him and he runs in slow-motion. Silence.

Did they spot me? Willie wondered wildly. Should I run? "Please, Sam." Colette's voice was husky, on the verge of tears. "I'm so lonely. Jake don't make me baby. I want beautiful babies, blue-eyed babies like your babies."

"My children..." Sam sounded bewildered. "I can't make a baby with you, Colette. It ain't right for anyone—Jenny, Jake, my children, you..."

"Kiss me again, Sam." Colette's French accent purred. "I am so lonely."

"Colette, no. No. Don't touch me there. Please. You're my brother's wife and I am married."

"It is long time since lovemaking, Sam?"

Sam sighed. Silence. "Colette...Colette, we're heading home." Sam said determinedly. "The rain's still holding off. And we're never gonna be alone together ever again. Do you understand?"

"Please, Sam!" Colette pleaded. "I wanna baby, wanna beautiful baby. I'm so lonely. Jake always away long times. Always trading or mining far away. And my mama dead three years and my papa upriver with Captain Lewis one year now. Maybe don't come back never. What can I do? And Jenny. She don't like me. Always angry with me. And now you tell me Austin no more judge, Wilkinson make Smith new judge. Maybe they make Louisiana independent country. Maybe they git you and Jake, too. Make you go away. Maybe Smith kill you. What can I do? Everything much change. I am so lonely. I wanna baby."

"We gotta go home now," Sam said tenderly. "Maybe we'll talk later. Come on."

Willie slipped behind the home and watched as Sam and Colette emerged from the front and began striding down the lane. Sam reached out for Colette's hand, quickly squeezed it, then walked faster. Thunder crackled. A gray curtain of rain suddenly engulfed St. Louis in the distance and slowly moved toward them, drenching everything in its path. Willie stared numbly as Sam and Colette ran forward, disappearing into the storm.

Three

1805–1808

All eyes were on Major Bruff as he paused to gulp down another mouthful of fiery rum. He wiped his mouth with the back of his hand, slowly circled the roomful of men with his eyes, and sighed. "Treason," he muttered. "I fear that treason is afoot."

"Just what did Wilkinson tell you?" Austin asked, his squeaky voice an octave higher from excitement.

"He talked in circles." Bruff shook his head in bewilderment. "Always circles, from that first odd meeting a half-dozen miles downriver when he first arrived over two months ago..." Bruff raised his battered pewter mug toward Willie. "Another laddie." Fascinated, Willie glanced into Bruff's ruddy face as he refilled his mug. With his fringe of thick gray beard, shaved upper lip, small brown eyes, and

67

heavy paunch, Bruff resembled some huge rodent that had just poked out of a hole. Willie wondered if all the questioning might scare him away.

"Maybe circles to you, Major," Hunt asserted, "but General Wilkinson shot straight at me at every encounter up till he relieved me of my command last month. Why, he—"

"Yes, yes, Seth, we're aware of all that," Austin interrupted impatiently. "Now, on with your story, Major."

Bruff blinked and nodded, "Yes, sir, odd from the first meeting, odd indeed." He paused again and stared at the ceiling, searching for all the details of Wilkinson's arrival. "July first was hotter than blazes and my men and horses were sweat-soaked and sullen all morning waiting for his keelboat to appear. The river was low and even after we spotted the boat it took a long time to come in. I lined the men up on horseback and we fired a volley as Wilkinson strode down the plank." Bruff took another gulp of rum.

"The governor was all business from the moment we saluted. 'Major, we have vital matters to discuss,' he said and motioned to the woods, and we started that way but the Chouteau brothers and some other Frenchies rode up at just that moment. Wilkinson damned them to their faces, not knowing who they were, and you should have heard him apologizing after I whispered that he'd just insulted the richest men in Louisiana!" Bruff chuckled and the others burst into laughter.

"How'd the Chouteaus take it?" Judge Easton asked as he mopped his sweaty bald dome with a dirty handkerchief.

"As you can imagine, Auguste was as impassive as ever while Pierre's face was doing somersaults with words he didn't dare say."

Everyone laughed again. "It wasn't till late that night after all the celebrations in town and the banquet at the governor's mansion that Wilkinson led me upstairs to the library. He locked the door and demanded I declare a solemn oath never to repeat anything that transpired." Bruff stared hard into the eyes of the half-dozen men circling him. "I consider myself a man of honor. I fought through the Revolution for the freedoms we all enjoy and if I didn't think that our beloved Republic itself was in danger, I would never be telling you all this."

"The oath of allegiance to one's country always supersedes any personal oath!" Austin declared vehemently while the others murmured their approval.

"The governor fired a volley of bizarre questions and assertions at me—'What sort of government would suit Louisiana?' he asked.

Without hesitation, I replied that a representative republic would meet both the wishes and expectations of the people. Wilkinson looked startled. 'I am surprised to hear that,' he says, 'for the French and Spanish speaking inhabitants of old Louisiana can't understand democratic principles, or be brought to attend elections…'"

"Maybe not brought, but certainly bought," Sam declared dryly; the others laughed loudly.

Bruff smiled knowingly then continued. "'…While the Americans,' he says, 'are a turbulent set, the mere emptyings of jails, or fugitives from justice, and don't deserve a free government…'"

"There might be some truth in that!" Jake cracked and the others chuckled nervously.

"Anyway, the general declared that Louisiana would be best ruled by a military government, and none other was contemplated. 'Democracy is no different from mob rule!' he asserted and denounced the Jefferson administration as 'a gang of radicals set to seize the property of the rich for their own pockets.' I started to protest but cut myself short when I realized that if I didn't shut up he'd never tell me his great secret. Finally Wilkinson lowered his voice and drew close. 'I am contemplating a grand scheme which if successful would make not just my fortune, but those of all concerned.' The general hesitated, waiting for me to express my desire to share his scheme for riches. I was speechless. He hinted at the grossest improprieties while never actually articulating them. When I continued to remain silent, he finally unlocked the parlor door and waved me off without another word."

"So what was the grand scheme, Major?" Austin demanded. "You never found out?"

"No, sir, I didn't. But, with former Vice President Burr arriving today, I thought I had better tell you gentlemen what I know and warn you to never let down your vigilance."

"Why didn't you speak up before, Major?" Easton asked eagerly.

"Well, I must confess, I was afraid that no one would believe me. But after Major Hunt was relieved of command and Judge Austin stripped of his position, and with all the rumors floating around that Wilkinson and Burr are planning to launch an expedition against Mexico or even declare the Mississippi Valley an independent country, I realized I could no longer remain silent."

"Well, gentlemen," Austin declared, "according to yesterday's express rider, Mr. Burr should be arriving around dusk, so, since it's getting late, I motion that we adjourn to join the mob…" Austin waited for the laughter to die, "at the dock. And to keep our eyes and ears as open as possible." The others quickly agreed, drained their mugs, and staggered out of Jake's home into the street.

Intrigued by all the talk of scheming and treason, Willie began carrying away the mugs to the kitchen. Gunshots and cheering erupted in the distance. Burr's here! he thought excitedly. I've got to see this! He barged out the door and began running toward the Mississippi.

Spotting the men striding ahead, he cut through back alleys and yards until he joined the crowd strung along the bluffs, everyone boisterously cheering Burr's kneelboat as it was poled to shore.

"Willie!" Jess shouted. "Come on up!"

He looked up and spotted Jess and a half-dozen other boys dangling their skinny legs from a warehouse's flat roof. He shinnied up a wooden drain pipe and squeezed between Jess and another boy just as the keelboat's plank was lowered. Waving to the crowd, Burr ambled down it to shake hands with Wilkinson, the Chouteau brothers, and Smith T. waiting on shore. A dozen soldiers in ragged blue uniforms fired a salute.

As the smoke drifted over the crowd, the five men squeezed into an open carriage led by four black horses. The soldiers cleared a way through the crowd, while the black driver cracked his whip and the carriage slowly followed them up the steep road to the top of the bluffs. There the carriage stopped and Wilkinson and Burr rose.

"Tweedle Dee and Tweedle Dum!" Willie exclaimed, and Jess and the other boys laughed loudly. Burr was somberly dressed in a black vest, and coat, tan knee breeches, and sported a tall beaver-felt hat, while Wilkinson wore his general's uniform, fringed with gold lapels and buttons; both men were short and rotund.

Wilkinson raised his arms appealing for silence. "Ladies and gentlemen, fellow Americans, as the governor of the District of Louisiana, it is my deep honor to present to you the distinguished Mr. Aaron Burr, the former Vice President of the United States…Mr. Burr!"

The crowd burst into loud cheers and applause; several hats and gunshots exploded into the air. "Good people of Louisiana, my words will be brief but—"

"Burr for President!" someone shouted loudly, and the crowd and Burr laughed.

"President?" Burr asked facetiously after the crowd quieted. "Perhaps someday!" The crowd cheered wildly. Some genuinely admired Burr for his Western sentiments, others because he had killed Alexander Hamilton in a duel, but most were simply excited to have a famous politician in their midst. "The Mississippi Valley is a very long way from Washington, and I fear Congress has neglected this region. It may not be fair, however, to blame this neglect entirely on Congress. Perhaps the country itself has simply become too large for effective rule. It may be years, nay decades, before you will have an opportunity to elect representatives to Congress.

"Who will look after your interests in the meantime? I ask you to think deeply about your interests and how they can best be realized. Holler your needs loud and hard to Congress, and if they don't listen, then perhaps the time will come for you to consider other political arrangements.

"Whatever happens, please do always remember that I will continue to hold your needs and dreams foremost in my mind. Thank you!" Deafening cheers, war whoops, and gunfire swept the crowd. The soldiers pushed through, his carriage close behind. Burr and Wilkinson beamed and waved.

"Jess, guess what?" Willie asked quietly.

"What?"

"I can't tell you here. Let's go!" The two boys dropped to the ground, dodged through the dispersing crowd and cut through back alleys until they reached the Chouteau mansion. A half-dozen carriages and a score of horses were tied out front and a line of men and women dressed in their Sunday best were slowly being greeted by Wilkinson and Burr on the front veranda. Other couples and groups of men showed their invitations to a sergeant as they strolled through the front gate. A soldier was posted on each side of the grounds to keep away anyone without an invitation.

"Sure like to be inside…" Willie panted.

"What's yer secret?"

"Burr and Wilkinson are gonna start a revolution!"

"What?" Jess frowned through his grin.

"Major Bruff said so."

"To you?" Jess asked incredulously.

"To my pa and Austin and the others. At Uncle Jake's house just before Burr come in."

"Why'd the major spill the beans? Ain't he beholden to Wilkinson?"

"Well, 'cause he's a patriot. That's why. And he'd know since he was governor of the district before Wilkinson and Wilkinson told him his plan when he came to replace him. Or at least partly."

"Well, what's his plan?"

"That ain't clear."

"Why not?"

"Cause Wilkinson never told the major directly. Just talked in circles."

Jess looked puzzled. "Now hold on. I don't git it. How could…"

"Take my word for it."

"Prove it."

"I can't prove it till they start the revolution."

"What if it don't happen?"

"If it don't happen, it don't happen."

"Talk about talkin' in circles!"

"All right. All right." Willie rubbed his chin. "Jess, I got a plan."

Jess grinned broadly. "Shoot!"

"I betcha after the reception they'll go back to the governor's and Wilkinson and Burr'll tell the others their plan. What'll ya betcha?"

"So? How're we gonna know?"

"Major Bruff said Wilkinson almost told him the plan in the upstairs library. How 'bout if we sneak up on top the veranda and listen in. It'll be pitch dark by then and everybody including the soldiers'll be drunk. It'll be a cinch to sneak in."

Jess poked Willie's ribs. "Good thinkin', Willie!"

They agreed to go home for dinner and then up to bed early, saying they weren't feeling good. When things quieted down they'd slip out and meet in the alley across from the governor's mansion.

Dinner was awkward, with Sam and Jake eager to talk but afraid to say too much in front of their wives and the children. Finally they excused themselves and headed out to Major Bruff's home where they would meet the others. Willie then feigned fatigue and was told to go up and get a good night's rest. He lay in bed impatiently waiting for Sarah to join him. It seemed like forever. Finally he heard the grandfather clock in the parlor below strike eight bells and Sarah reluctantly drag herself upstairs. She quietly opened the door and laid the candle on the dresser.

"Sarah…?"

"What?"

"You won't tell will you?" Willie hopped out of bed and put on his shoes.

"Tell what?"

"I hafta meet Jess."

"To do what?"

"It's a secret."

"Are you gonna get in trouble?"

"Not if you don't tell."

"What if you get caught?"

"We're too slick for that." Willie slid open the window and began to climb out on the porch roof.

Sarah giggled. "What about Pringle's paddle?"

"That was just...bad luck. Promise you don't tell?"

"I promise."

"See ya."

Sarah ran to the window. "See ya," she whispered into the dark, but he had already jumped down. There was no moon and he sometimes stumbled on a rut as he headed down the road into the silent town. Some of the homes were completely dark, but most still had candlelit rooms.

Whenever he heard someone coming on foot or horseback, he would hide behind a tree or shed and then tensely wait for them to pass. Finally he reached the alley leading to the side of the governor's mansion. Slowly he crept foward, hoping Jess would not try to get the drop on him. We've gotta be quiet as mice or else! he kept reminding himself.

A shadow crouched ahead. "Willie, is that you?" Jess whispered.

"Yeah." He slipped up beside Jess and they stared across the dark street at the mansion.

"What took you so long? I feared you got caught."

"Is the governor back?"

"Not yet. It'll be a cinch to sneak in. The guards are all gathered out front passing a bottle a' whiskey."

Willie sniffed the air. "What's that smell?"

"I slipped in horseshit."

Willie giggled. "That's great, Jess. They might not hear us but they'll catch us by smelling you. I hope they don't chase us with bloodhounds."

Jess struggled to stifle a laugh. Finally he said, "You ready?"

They heard the rhythm of horsehoofs and the squeak of carriage wheels from the front of the mansion. "You think that's him?"

"I betcha. Come on. Let's go." They slipped noiselessly across the street and quickly vaulted the picket fence surrounding the mansion.

Drunken laughter and voices sounded from the front of the mansion. First Willie, then Jess, climbed a tree beside the mansion, crawled out on a limb overhanging the veranda, and dropped atop the cedar shingled roof.

"Which room's the library?" Jess whispered softly.

"I don't know."

"You scared?"

"Yeah. Are you?"

"A little."

"When you get scared, just take a whiff of yourself."

Both boys trembled with suppressed laughter. Suddenly a room to their right was brightly lit by someone with a candelabra.

"Come on in, Aaron." Wilkinson's voice sounded faraway. "It's a little stuffy in here." Wilkinson opened the window. Willie and Jess stretched out flat on the roof. "There's no breeze tonight and it's hotter than hell." Wilkinson's slurred voice boomed into the dark. "Can you believe those soldiers lounging out front as if they were off duty? Soldiers just as lazy and unreliable as during the Revolution, huh, Aaron? America will never be known for its soldiers."

"Are you sure the grounds are secure, Jamie? Voices carry far on still nights like tonight. We can't be overheard." The smell of cigars suddenly drifted into the air.

"As we speak, those troops should be surrounding the house and searching the grounds. We have nothing to worry about."

Burr came to the window and stared into the darkness. "St. Louis," he sighed. "The edge of civilization. Edge? A tiny island in a vast wilderness. And yet, someday, this could be a cosmopolitan center of a great empire."

"New Orleans will be the capital. Brandy?"

"Thanks."

"We've come a long way since the Revolution, hey, Aaron? You—past Vice President. Me—past commanding general of the army."

"Indeed, we have. And yet, if our plan succeeds, it will make everything else we've done seem like child's play."

"When?"

Burr sighed. "A year. Maybe two. We must be patient."

"The British fleet, Aaron. The fleet's the key. We can get enough men but we need the fleet."

"Ambassador Merry assures me that London will cooperate. He didn't say when."

"And money. We'll need a vast sum to finance our expedition."

Burr laughed softly, "You're far more adept at fund-raising than me, Jamie. Are you still receiving both Spanish and British contributions?"

"Bastards!" Wilkinson growled. "Both are well behind in their payments." A lit cigar butt meteored out of the window into the dark below.

Willie shifted a little to see where it landed. A shingle tore loose and clattered loudly down the sloped roof and into the garden below.

"Did you hear that?" Wilkinson warned. Willie and Jess tensed.

"What?" Burr's voice was worried. He and Wilkinson hurried to the window. "Do you see anything?" Jess suddenly scrambled across the roof and leapt for the tree branch.

"Guards!" Wilkinson screamed. "Guards, stop them!" Willie ran down to the opposite end of the veranda roof and teetered on the edge.

"Guards!" Wilkinson called hysterically again. Soldiers charged through the garden below, cursing as they drunkenly tripped over shrubs and ripped their skin on rose thorns. Willie reached for a pillar and shinnied down.

A soldier stumbled past without spotting him. Terrified, Willie hit the ground running, and quickly scrambled over the picket fence into the street, while curses exploded and lanterns bobbed behind him in the dark garden.

He did not stop running until he reached the edge of town, then collapsed, gasping for breath in a field. Thousands of stars glimmered brightly down at him. An owl hooted twice nearby. Willie slowly inhaled a lung full of sweet-scented night air. Where's it all end, he wondered, stars, people, schemes…endless.

Finally calm, he strolled home and quietly shinnied up a pillar to the veranda roof. Exhausted, he couldn't wait to snuggle up to Sarah and drift asleep atop the thick cornhusk mattress. He quickly slipped through the open window and reached for the bed…

"Just where have you been!" his mother's voice cut through the dark.

Willie hollered, "Gosh, Mama, you scared me!"

"I repeat. Where have you been?"

"Out. Just out for a walk. Where's Sarah?"

"Asleep in my bed. What sort of mischief have you been up to?"

"Nothing, Mama, I swear!"

"You just wait until your father gets home!"

Jenny quickly wiped the sweat off her brow with the back of her hand, then carved off another thick slice of beef and carefully laid it atop the dozen other slices stacked on the platter. She glanced over at Colette, who was busy ladling carrots onto another platter. "Would you check the pies, Colette?" she asked hurriedly. "They must be done by now. Oh, and how's the ham doing? I want everything done at the same time."

Colette rolled her eyes and raised her arms, brandishing the ladle in her right hand. "You don't see?" she replied sarcastically. "I have only two hands!"

Jenny tried to sound conciliatory. "Oh, I am sorry, Colette. I know you're trying as hard as you can. It's just...well...you know how much this supper means to me and I want everything perfect...You're doing fine." Jenny placed the beef platter in front of the fireplace, then used hot pads to pull the pies out of the oven. "Perfect!" Jenny murmured as she placed the pies on the table. She smiled down at the browned, neatly crisscrossed strips of dough. "Just perfect!"

Colette rolled her eyes again as she retied the red ribbon on her ponytail.

Sarah shuffled into the kitchen. "I finished setting the table, Mama. When are we gonna eat? I am hungry."

"In just a few minutes, sweetie." Jenny lightly pinched Sarah's cheek.

Sarah giggled at Colette, making a face behind Jenny's back. Jenny laughed and twirled one of Sarah's long brown curls. "You're such a sweetie, Sarah. Isn't this exciting having our first dinner in our new house?" Sarah nodded. "Why don't you tell Willie to wash his hands and get to the table...and papa and Uncle Jake too."

Sarah skipped off through the house and onto the veranda where Sam and Jake sat on a oak bench silently watching the sun drop blood red through the autumn woods.

"Mama said to wash your hands," Sarah declared.

"All right, pumpkin," Sam smiled. "We'll be right there. Look at the sun. It seems to drop like a rock then hold back just before disappearing."

"I'd like to see it set over the plains," Jake said wistfully and took a deep puff on his long clay pipe. "That must be a sight."

"Someday, Jake, we'll have a big enough stake that we can take off and head West for a season's hunt. How'd you like that?" Sarah disappeared into the house.

Jake chuckled. "Sure, if Smith and Wilkinson don't drive us out first."

Jake slowly shook his head. "Don't look good, Sam. Don't look good at all. First Wilkinson kicks Austin out of the court and makes Smith judge. Then he dismisses Hunt. And all the while Smith's hard after our mine. Sooner or later Wilkinson and Smith'll be on our tail. Look's like we're on the losing side."

"Take heart, Jake. Once that petition reaches Washington, President Jefferson just may dismiss Wilkinson. If we had a straight-shooting governor we'd have nothing to worry about."

"That's a big if, Sam, but here's another. What if Wilkinson and Burr really do declare independence for the Mississippi Valley? Then they'd be dictators and no one would protect us. Then what'd we do?"

"All the more reason for the president to dismiss or even arrest both men as soon as possible. Anyway Burr's gone to New Orleans and I don't think even Wilkinson, that pompous, arrogant—would try something as crazy as that."

"Well, according to Willie," Jake chuckled. "That Willie, can you imagine him and Jess sneaking up on the governor's veranda to spy on Wilkinson and Burr themselves." Jake laughed and slapped his knee. "That boy's got spunk! Why didn't we think of that?"

"Those boys are damn lucky they didn't get caught!" Sam fumed. "And Willie's even luckier I didn't whip him till the cows come home…"

"Ah, Sam," Jake grinned and slowly shook his head. "You're too hard on the boy. We were just as wild."

"That don't make it right. What if he'd been caught…or shot?"

"Maybe so," Jake replied softly. "Sam, with all the cards stacked against us sometimes I wonder if we shouldn't—"

"Dinner's on the table!" Jenny's voice called from the parlor.

Jake sighed and knocked his pipe against the bench, spilling the ashes onto the veranda. Then both men slowly stretched and ambled inside.

Colette hurried into the room carrying platters of ham and beef. Colette and Sam's eyes nervously met then fled. Jenny appeared with platters of vegetables. "Where's Willie?" she said, irritated. "That boy is always wandering off. Would you call him, Sam?"

"That boy better not be down at the creek," Sam warned. From the front door he hollered, "Willie! Willie!"

"Comin'!" cried a distant voice from the woods.

Everyone was seated at the table busy forking food onto their plates when Willie burst into the parlor.

"Where have you been?" Jenny demanded. "Do you want to spoil our first supper in our new home?"

"Sorry," Willie murmured as he flopped into his chair and stabbed a piece of beef.

"Let me see your hands!" Jenny frowned.

Willie raised his palms. "I washed them in the creek."

"And that ain't all," Jake laughed at Willie's soaked pant legs. "What'd you do? Fall in?"

Trying to remain calm, Jenny shook her head. "Sam? Sam, would you make a toast?"

Sam gulped down a mouthful of beef. "Sure. Everyone have enough wine?" he asked, holding up the thick brown bottle.

"Please, Sam, I want some more." Colette held out her pewter mug. Willie's body tingled as he watched Colette gaze longingly at Sam. Sam refused to look at her as he quickly filled her mug.

"Jenny? Jake?" Sam demanded.

"Of course!" Jake drained his glass and held it toward Sam. "I don't know why we get the glasses and the ladies the mugs. A mug holds twice as much as a glass."

"Well..." Sam stood and raised his glass. "We've come a long way."

Sam looked thoughtful, faraway. Jenny beamed. Colette continued to gaze while the children ate silently. "A long way from Philadelphia, then Cincinnati, and then a long way since we first came here. It looks like, after fifteen years of struggle and difficulties, that we've finally made it! First of all, we're out of debt for the first time. And it was a great relief to send Cleaver what we owed him," Sam grinned down at Jake. "Though word has it Cleaver never did quite recover from that bump on his noggin you gave him!"

Jake chuckled. "I am glad I didn't kill that bas...kill him after all!"

"I am too, Jake. I often feared waking up with Hackett on our doorstep."

"That's behind us now," Jenny interrupted. "Finish your toast, Sam."

"Well, as I was saying..." Sam smiled gently at Jenny. "We're out of the woods, and well on the way to the wealth and security I always promised." His face flushed, Sam took a deep gulp and sat down.

Jake mumbled through a mouthful of food. "Wish I was as certain of our future, Sam."

Sam frowned. "Well, as we were saying out front, things ain't one hundred percent but—"

"I didn't have time to tell you my plan, Sam," Jake said as he belched and pulled absent-mindedly at his beard. Jenny stiffened. Sam glanced sideways at Jake. "As I was saying, with both Austin and Hunt down, and Smith hollering for our mine, and maybe Wilkinson and Burr tying us into an independent country, our turn's next. We already made a pile. Now's the time to cut a deal with Wilkinson and Smith."

"What?" Sam frowned angrily. "What are you saying?"

"Now don't get riled, Sam. I am just suggesting that we cut loose from Austin while we're ahead. Wilkinson and Smith'd welcome us with open arms. We never did nothing to them directly."

"I can't believe it!" Sam exploded. "Sell out Moses after all he's done for us!"

"Sam, please!" Jenny pleaded, "Let's not discuss this further. Don't spoil our supper, please." Fuming with hatred, Jenny stared at Jake. "Would you kindly stop infuriating my husband?"

"You drop that fool idea from your head, Jake!" Sam jabbed his finger toward him. "Drop it right now and never bring it up again!"

Jake shook his head in disgust. "I'll say anything I damn well please if it suits me!"

"Not in my house, you don't!" Sam shouted. "There's the door!"

Jenny started to sob. "Please, both of you, stop."

"Come on, Colette! Let's go!" Jake angrily pushed back his chair and stood up. Colette froze. "You heard me!" Jake shouted. "Let's go!"

Sarah suddenly started gagging and wheezing; her face reddening. "Oh, God! Help her!" Jenny cried. "Something's caught in her throat!"

Willie started slapping Sarah on the back while everyone else dashed around the table to help. Sam shoved Jake aside, jerked Sarah out of her chair, pulled her against his chest and began pounding her back while the others shouted directions or encouragement. Suddenly Sarah spit up a chewed chunk of beef and started crying.

"Oh! Thank God!" Jenny cried. "Let me take her." Sam placed Sarah in Jenny's arms. Everyone gathered around asking Sarah if she was all right. Sarah nodded through her sobs.

"Well, honey, I'm glad you're all right," Jake said softly as he gently patted Sarah's back. "Well, now," he nodded to Colette, "we best be going."

Sam looked strained. "No, stay. Let's finish dinner. Sit." He motioned Jake and Colette to their chairs.

Jake and Colette stared at each other then sat down. "I meant to tell you, Jenny," Jake tried to sound cheerful. "This is about the finest feast I've had in a long time!" He drained his glass and reached for the bottle. "Finest in a long time."

Willie kicked a pile of withered leaves into the air and watched them scatter with the wind. The leaves glided end over end and then scuttled across the frozen earth. A gust of cold wind rushed him, making him huddle in his long, navy, wool coat. He stumbled down the rutted road, images of the crackling fire ahead chasing the latest sting of Pringle's paddle. You can't trust anyone, he bitterly reminded himself. Pringle would never have known who blocked up the chimney if Judy hadn't started crying and told. He smiled as he recalled the coughs and watery eyes as everyone fled the smoke-filled classroom.

He frowned in disgust. What a fool I was to tell Sarah! I should've known she'd tell Judy. Ma will kill me when she finds out me and Jess were kicked out of school again. Willie gazed at the woods beyond the scattered houses and fields at the edge of town. Someday I'll head West and never come back, he promised.

"Willie!" Colette's voice cut through the wind behind him.

He turned to face her. "Wait for me, Willie!" Colette smiled broadly through her flushed, bronzed face. She was wrapped in a bright red blanket and rich laughter burst from her throat. "I've got something special to tell you and your family. A secret!"

"What secret?" he demanded.

Colette finally caught up and pushed his thick brown hair out of his eyes. "Your eyes are so pretty, Willie. But still, I don't tell you until we go home. But you will be very happy for me and Uncle Jake when I tell you." Colette laughed again.

Willie shivered. Once again, he remembered the day he had crouched outside their half-finished home, and again heard Colette pleading Pa for a blue-eyed baby.

He mumbled, "A baby?"

Colette's eyes widened. "Willie, how did you know?"

"I don't know," he stared down at his feet. "Are you really having a baby?"

"Yes!" she stated proudly.

"When?"

"Now is November. I will have baby in June, maybe July," Colette giggled. "Soon, I become bigger and bigger until this big!" She held a hand far out from her body. "Maybe I have two babies like you and Sarah. But, Willie," her voice lowered, "don't tell no one. I want to tell your mama and papa. They'll be surprised. Your father very surprised." Colette giggled again.

Jenny was knitting a green mitten and Sam was cleaning his flintlock rifle in the parlor when Colette and Willie pushed through the front door and slammed it behind them.

Jenny frowned. "Willie, why are you home from school so early? And Colette?"

Willie and Colette stood nervously before them. Sam fidgeted with his rifle then set it down on the table. "Did you get in trouble again, boy?" he asked solemnly, trying not to look at Colette.

Willie glanced at Colette, wondering which news would be worse— him getting kicked out of school or her getting pregnant. Could it really have been Pa? Colette looked at Sam, then Jenny, and started trembling.

"What's wrong? Where's Sarah?" Jenny demanded fearfully.

"Don't worry, Ma. She's at school. Aunt Colette..." Willie felt like running.

"I gonna have a baby," she blurted.

"What?" Sam's voice sounded incredulous. "Oh, God! You can't!"

Puzzled, Jenny stared first at Sam then Colette. "What? Why not?" she demanded. "Colette, do you...that's wonderful!" Jenny crossed the room and hugged her. "Sit down. You must be frozen. That's wonderful."

Colette hugged Jenny tight and started sobbing. "I am so happy, Jenny. You know I wanted baby long time."

"I know. I know, Colette," Jenny's voice was distant. "You just sit down and let me fix you some coffee."

Jenny glanced at Sam as she hurried into the kitchen. Colette sat down at the table. Desperately struggling for something to say, Willie and Sam stared at each other. "Pa..." Willie's voice faltered.

"I know," Sam sighed. "I know."

Willie gently placed the bark roof on the stick cabin and turned to the dozen scraggly children silently watching him. He smiled at Emily. She looked so pretty in her yellow linen dress. His eyes drifted beyond her to the scattered groups of men and women, dressed in their Sunday best, glasses in hand, gesturing animatedly in front of Durham Hall. Near the entrance sat the three-pounder in its two-wheeled carriage. Beside it, atop a tall pole, the American flag hung flacidly in the humid air. He grinned as he remembered Austin touching off the dawn salute and yet another later that morning when everyone had gathered to toast the fifteen-star flag as it was hauled to the top. Each charge had cracked loudly then echoed back across the shallow valley. Someday I'll fire a cannon, he promised himself.

"What're yer waiting for!" a child demanded.

Willie blinked. "Ya ready?" he asked eagerly.

Emily and the other children smiled and shouted, "Ready!"

"Stand back!" Willie warned and touched a smoldering punk to the short fuse snaking into the cabin. He leapt back as the fuse sparked then fizzled into the house. Boom!!! The cabin exploded into a shower of splintered sticks and bark.

"Owww!" a little boy wailed. Holding his cheek, he ran away crying.

"Are you all right?" Willie anxiously called after him. "Let me see it!"

"I'll take care of him, Willie!" Emily promised. "Come on, Sarah!" Emily and Sarah ran after the boy.

The other children laughed and nudged each other. "That was great!" they shouted. Willie smiled proudly, wishing he had another charge to blow.

Stephen sidled up to Willie. "You're lucky it didn't poke his eye out!" he solemnly admonished.

Willie looked startled. "Yeah, I reckon you're right."

"Willie!" his mother's voice cut through the children's shouts. "You come right here this instant!" Jenny and several other mothers stormed angrily toward him. Beyond them on Durham Hall's veranda, Emily, Sarah, and a tall woman huddled around the sobbing little boy. The groups of men and women stopped to watch the women stride toward Willie and the children.

Willie froze, debating whether or not to run for it. Too late, he groaned, as Jenny grabbed him tightly by the wrist. "Just who do you think you are setting off that charge?" The other mothers shot hard glances at him as they checked their children's safety. "You could have lost your fingers or an eye. And how would you feel if you blinded Jason or another little boy or girl? Our family would have had to live that down for the rest of our lives."

Willie stared at Jenny's feet and muttered, "Sorry. It was just a small charge."

"Come on!" Stephen called out to the children. "Let's go watch the militia!" The children tore loose from their mothers and ran after Stephen across the field, then splashed across the creek toward the town's edge where the militia drilled under the watchful eyes of its commander, Lieutenant Colonel Smith T.

Willie started to pull away. "No, sir!" Jenny intoned. "You're sticking close to me for the rest of the day. I am not letting you out of my sight."

"But, Ma, it's the Fourth of July!" he protested.

"Stop!" Jenny warned. "You'll do as you're told or your father'll whip you so hard you won't be able to sit for a week. You've already embarrassed me enough." She turned to the other mothers. "Were your children all right?"

"Yes," they answered and started back up the slight slope toward Durham Hall.

"You're going to apologize to Mrs. Bemis and Jason."

Willie grimaced and tugged his wrist free. "Are you gonna hold me all day?"

"Don't get sassy with me, mister. If your father wasn't talking business with Mr. Austin in the parlor, I'd march you to him right now. The nerve of you, embarrassing me like that in front of everyone."

"Willie!" Colette called out as she waddled toward them from the house. "What happened?"

"I just set off a charge, is all." He rolled his eyes in mock bewilderment. Look's like she's gonna drop her baby any second, he thought.

"This boy's determined to ruin the holiday!" Jenny sniffed. "This is one of my few opportunities to socialize with what few women of culture live west of the Mississippi and—"

"Jenny," Colette interrupted, "I think my baby's coming."

"Riders!" someone shouted, and everyone turned and stared as a half-dozen horsemen trotted across the bridge from Mine à Breton.

Austin and Sam appeared in the doorway of Durham Hall, then warily walked out to meet the horsemen. Ignoring Jenny's demands to stop, Willie sprinted toward the house and squeezed through the crowd gathering around the horsemen. The riders squirmed uneasily in their saddles as the crowd pressed around them. The lead horseman was tall and slender, with greasy brown hair and large porkchop sideburns that pointed to each corner of his mouth. Only the crow's-feet around his eyes revealed he was middle-aged rather than a young man.

He saluted as Austin approached.

Austin nodded curtly. "Welcome, Andrew. I'd like to think you've come to join our celebrations, but I sense that you're here either in your capacity as Judge Henry of St. Genevieve or Major Henry of its militia company."

"You're not gonna like this, Moses," Henry warned as he handed Austin a sealed letter. "I don't either, but there's nothing I can do about it. I am just following orders, is all," he added lamely.

Austin tore open the letter. His face contorted angrily as he read it. The crowd muttered and pressed closer. Voices asked nervously, "What happened? What is it?"

Austin crumpled the letter and threw it on the ground. "I'll be damned if I'll give up my cannon to that son of a…" he glanced at some

of the ladies nearby, "at that…that…That cannon is mine, not government property, and most decidedly not Smith's." Austin turned his
back on Henry and appealed to the crowd. "That letter," he pointed to
the wadded paper as if it were a rattlesnake, "is a summons from Smith
to give up my cannon, which as you all know I dug out of the mud years
ago. I'll be damned if I'll surrender my cannon to anyone, let alone
that…Smith!" The crowd broke into cheers and shouted angrily at the
riders to clear out. "If Smith wants it, he can come and try and take it
himself!" He turned to the riders. "And you, too, Andrew!" he shook
his fist at Henry, whose horse shied sharply, almost trampling Willie,
who stood nearby. Henry pulled tightly on his horse's reins. "I'll take
on you, too, Andrew, and any other man who joins Smith." Austin
glared at each rider. "Now clear off my property!" Henry rose his arms
for silence but the crowd shouted him down. Finally he motioned to his
escort and they turned and rode back through Mine à Breton to rejoin
the militia company waiting at ease at the edge of town.

"Gentlemen!" Austin shouted. "It appears that our feud with the
Smith-Wilkinson cabal is about to reach a climax. If it takes bloodshed
to rid our land of that corrupt, oppressive gang, then let it begin now!"
Most of the men set up a ragged cheer, but some men and the women
stood in silent, perplexed worry. "Men," he shouted, "gather your
weapons and I will provide arms to those without…"

"Moses, what about Stephen and the other children?" his wife
María implored. "They're watching the militia."

"Someone…" Austin looked wildly around, "who will save the
children?"

Several fathers immediately volunteered, but Willie called out, "I
will!" then bolted toward the creek.

"Wait! Willie, come back!" his mother screamed.

Willie dashed through the nearly deserted streets of Mine à Breton.
The American families were either at Durham Hall or the militia parade
while the French lounged in the shade around their homes. Panting
heavily, he ran up to Stephen and the other children, and gasped,
"You've gotta go back. There's gonna be a fight." The children
gathered around Willie, asking questions.

Nearby, Smith, Henry, and the other horsemen conferred, while
the militia company stood at attention in the hot noonday sun. Suddenly, Henry saluted and spurred his horse back toward Durham Hall.

Smith cantered over to the children who stood bewildered. "Isn't
that Willie Yates?" Smith demanded. "Come here, Willie. Tell me
what Mr. Austin said." Willie trembled in silence. "Cat got your

tongue, boy?" Smith asked disdainfully. He turned his pale blue eyes on Stephen. "Young master Stephen, you're the oldest boy. I will treat you like the young gentleman I know you are. You tell your father that I want that cannon for my parade, and, if he delivers it, then there will be no trouble," he paused dramatically. "But if he does not, then I am not responsible for what might ensue." Smith waved them away. "Now begone with you!" he ordered. Still puzzled, the children looked at each other then ran toward Durham Hall.

Winded, Willie slowed to a walk through Mine à Breton while the other children straggled ahead. He watched Austin and Henry gesture silently before the crowd at Durham Hall. Then Henry turned and galloped back through town, passed him with a glance, and headed out to the militia. The mothers shepherded their children inside the mansion while some of the men distributed rifles and pistols to the others. Jacob, the black slave, methodically loaded the cannon and stood by it with a long, smoking punk. Jenny and Sarah waited anxiously for Willie to stride up the hill. "Willie, you'll be the death of me yet!" Jenny exclaimed as she grabbed her two children's hands and dragged them toward the house.

Rifle in hand, Sam stood awkwardly with the other men. "You mind your mother!" he warned as they passed him.

Inside the mansion, children cried and mothers screeched as they crowded into the cellar. "There ain't no more room, missus. We're done packed in," a young house slave apologized as Jenny and the children reached the door. "They's plumb stacked up the stairs."

"Oh, God," Jenny wailed, "what are we going to do?"

"Well, missus, you can hide in our quarters out back." The black woman chuckled. "But it's a might crowded there, too, and not near as clean."

"Thank you. We'll rest here for now."

Suddenly a scream erupted from the cellar, then Colette's voice pleaded, "My baby coming! It hurts! My baby!" Other women's voices shouted for help, and some of the mothers and children stumbled out of the cellar to make way as María and another woman dragged Colette up the steps. Jenny met them at the top. Colette was sweat-soaked and left a trail of blood behind her.

"Into the parlor," María ordered. "Maggie! Hot water and towels, immediately." The slave hurried off.

Colette groaned loudly and clutched her stomach. "It hurts. It hurts," she cried. Willie and Sarah trembled as the four women disappeared into the parlor and slammed the door behind them.

"Is the baby hurt?" Sarah asked quietly.

"I don't know," Willie answered.

"Isn't Uncle Jake coming?"

"It's his turn at the mine. He won't be back till the end of the month. I'll get papa." Willie ran out the door. Rifles and pistols in hand, a score of men were scattered across the lawn. Other men, deserters from the militia, straggled up the slope toward them. Austin and Sam spoke earnestly together beside the cannon. Willie ran up to them, "Papa! Papa!"

"Goddamn it, Willie," Sam bellowed, "I told you to obey your mother!"

"Aunt Colette...her baby! It's coming!" Willie exclaimed.

"Hell of a time to pick..." Austin muttered.

Sam's tanned face blanched. "God! Is she all right?"

"I don't know. She's bleeding!"

Sam and Willie hurried into the house. Sarah stood petrified outside the parlor door, which muffled Colette's screams and groans. Sam tore open the door and they stared in horror inside. The three women variously held down and caressed Colette, who struggled and moaned on the couch. "Get out!" Jenny shouted. "Get out right now!"

"'Scuze me, master," Maggie called out from behind them, then squeezed by with a bucket of steaming water in one hand and a pile of cotton towels in the other hand. Sam stood aside to let her by, then shut the door behind her.

"Oh, God," Sam shook his head sorrowfully. "What now?"

"Is Aunt Colette gonna die, papa?" Sarah asked.

Sam shook his head in disbelief. "She's gonna have a baby."

Austin appeared at the door. "Everything all right?"

"I reckon," Sam declared dully.

Austin beamed. "About half the militia's deserted already. Keilor just came up and says Smith's on the edge of tossing it. Looks like we won the day. I knew if given a choice they'd abandon that windbag." Maggie reappeared and began wiping up the crimson trail with a rag. Austin declared grimly, "Reckon that'll be the only blood we see today," and rejoined his men outside.

"Go outside and play," Sam ordered.

Willie and Sarah ran out the door. Austin had gathered the men together. "Gentlemen," his voice cracked shrilly with excitement, "we appear to have won an important battle in our struggle with the Wilkinson-Smith cabal." The men cheered loudly and fired their rifles in the air. Austin waited for the clamor to subside.

"Jacob," Austin commanded, "point the cannon toward the woods!" Jacob impaled the ground with the smoldering punk and wheeled the cannon around. Austin grabbed the punk and waved it over his head like a sword. "But this is only the first victory of a long war," he declared solemnly. "We must stand together, ever vigilant, to resist that corrupt and oppressive faction that has so tragically splintered our community."

María appeared in the doorway. "Moses…!" she screamed. Austin dropped the punk to the touchhole. Boom!!! The ball smashed through the tree branches in the distant woods. The men set up a deafening cheer. María ran over to Austin and knocked the punk out of his hand.

"Colette's baby is coming and she's in desperate pain!" María screamed. "Leave her in peace!"

Austin looked startled, then turned to the men. "At ease, gentlemen. It appears the birth of our victory struggle is coinciding with quite a different birth—one that we must cheer in silence. Jacob, take the men out back and tap another keg of rum." A couple of men whooped again but were hushed by the others. Austin joined the crowd as they swaggered and joked their way noisily around the mansion while the mothers and children spilled outside to join them.

A half-dozen children gathered around Willie and Sarah, asking about Colette. "I don't know," Willie answered worriedly then brightened. "Let's go find that cannonball." He turned and ran toward the woods followed by the pack of children. They scrambled and poked through the undergrowth without luck. "It must be near here," he declared as he pointed up to the broken branches above. "There's where it smashed through…" he shouted excitedly. "There it is!" The children gathered around and stared at the ball imbedded about twenty feet up a huge oak tree. "I'm gonna get it," Willie declared, but there were no branches and the trunk was far too huge to shinny up. The children debated strategies for reaching the ball.

Suddenly Sam's voice cut through the children's chatter. "Willie, Sarah, come here." His face was a bitter mask. "You other young'uns, go back to your mothers." The children reluctantly trooped off through the woods toward the mansion. Sam kneeled and gathered Willie and Sarah in his arms.

"Your Aunt Colette…" his voice choked and a tear ran down his cheek, "and the baby…are dead."

After riding all night through the pitch-black forest, the horseman reached the diggings just before dawn, startling Jake out of a drunken sleep. Jake quickly mounted his swaybacked bay and rode hard through the steady drizzle. Mud-splattered and exhausted, he reached Durham Hall around noon.

Jacob greeted him at the door and ushered him into the parlor where the Yates and Austins solemnly talked in whispers. Without a word, Jake stood over to the large pine coffin resting on sawhorses in the middle of the room. Colette was dressed in her favorite red dress and the baby was swaddled and placed in her stiff arms. The humidity was quickly blackening and swelling both bodies; the rot smelled harshly. Jake gently stroked Colette's cheek and quietly said he'd like to be alone with her.

The others silently filed outside while Jake pried Colette's fingers loose from the baby and held it in his arms. "It was a boy," Jenny whispered as she passed and closed the door behind her. Jake sat down in a chair and began to cry bitterly over the tiny body.

An hour later, a soft knock on the door disturbed Jake's stony silence. Sam entered and placed a callused hand on Jake's shoulder. Jake stared vacantly up and asked, "Were you the father?"

Sam jerked his hand back. His mouth opened slightly but nothing came out. Finally he gurgled, "Jake?"

"I'm selling out, Sam," Jake declared quietly, "both my share of the diggings and my land along the Missouri. I'll head upriver with Manuel in the spring."

"Jake, wait."

"I been pondering it for a while now and decided on my ride up."

"I...Colette..."

"I know. I've been miss firing blanks all my life. I don't hold it against her or you." Jake exhaled a long hiss through his clenched teeth. "Better you than some other son of a bitch," he added bitterly, "like Pierre Chouteau." Jake's eyes hardened to slits. "Yup, I'd a' killed Chouteau, taken my skinning knife, and slit open his belly from his ass to that elegant mouth of his." Jake stared up at Sam. "I loved Colette."

Dotted with driftwood, the Mississippi current flowed fast and wide and lapped hard against the St. Louis wharves. Along a half-dozen thin gangplanks, chains of men passed boxes and rolled barrels from wagons on shore and stored them in the bowels of each keelboat. The men were mostly stripped to the waist and they cursed and their muscles strained with sweat under the warm spring sun. The usual melange of stylishly attired merchants and half-drunk, ragged idlers and Indians were scattered in small groups along the bluffs to see off the expedition.

Backs against a warehouse, Willie and Jake watched the loading below. "The best thing about being a partner is watchin' others do all the work," Jake declared with satisfaction as he tugged absent-mindedly at his long, tattered beard. "Yup, in about a year, if all goes well, I'll come home a rich man."

"I thought you were already rich, Uncle Jake," Willie wondered. "Why don't you just live off the money from your land and diggings?"

"Don't matter how much a man's got, he's gotta keep swimmin' with the tide or he'll get dragged under. Sooner or later, I'd a' drunk and ate up that eighty-five hundred dollars and then where'd I be? You always gotta keep movin', Willie. Stop movin' and you start to die."

"I'm not gonna have any grown-ups to talk to when you're gone," Willie said sadly.

"Well, I'm gonna miss you, too, Willie. But don't worry. When I come back, I'll teach you how to shoot and maybe even buy you your own rifle and take you hunting with me."

Willie smiled broadly. "Really?"

"Sure as I'm settin' here before you," Jake chuckled, "Yup, you're growing like a weed. You're ten now and you'll be a man before long. 'Bout time you learned how to shoot."

"Someday I wanna head up the Missouri with you," Willie declared eagerly.

"You can do anything you want, if you have a mind to. In the meantime, you gotta stay in school and learn your sums and reading. If you've got enough learning, you'll be rich and famous someday, a real leader. You've got the brains for it."

Willie frowned. "I'd stay in school if Pringle wouldn't keep kicking me out."

Jake laughed loudly. "Don't let that son of a bitch stand in your way. Or anyone else for that matter. What you can't move, you can move around."

"But what about—"

"Or someone else moves 'em for you. Like Jefferson out of the blue transferring Wilkinson down the Mississippi last August. Then in February, Burr gettin' arrested in Natchez for treason. And after all the talk the year before of Wilkinson and Burr taking over the Mississippi Valley and declaring independence...well, you overheard 'em yourself!" Jake guffawed and rumpled Willie's hair. "Sure wish I'd been with you and Jess on that roof! That took guts! I'll be damned if that didn't take guts! But ponder it, Willie. Sometimes when everything and everybody seems dead set against you and you've reached the end of the road, something happens and the way's cleared to move on again…although usually in a completely different direction…and," he paused and quietly added, "that's what I'm doing now."

"Yeah, but what about…"

"Manuel!" Jake hollered. "Over here!"

A stocky man with thick, curly black hair and a cherubic face ambled over to them. Jake and Willie scrambled to their feet to meet him.

"Jacques, is all ready?" he asked in a thick Spanish accent.

"We're gettin' that way. Meet my nephew, Willie."

They shook hands. "Nice to see you, Mr. Lisa," Willie declared. The Spaniard grunted curtly.

"Willie's gonna come upriver with us someday," Jake stated proudly.

Lisa grunted again. "We need as many good men as possible. I want to leave before noon." The three squinted up at the morning sun.

Jake grinned. "We'll be off well before then, Manuel. 'Bout an hour I reckon." Jake rubbed his hands together. "Can't wait to get upriver."

Lisa pursed his lips and nodded. "Good! Come get me at the Gray Horse when all is ready," Lisa chuckled. "I make business. You wanna come? No white women upriver, Jacques." Both men laughed sharply and Jake slapped Lisa on the shoulder.

"I done spent all last night finishing up my business. If Allison's around, grab her. I reckon she's the best the Gray Horse's got to offer. She's the only one that hasn't tried lifting my wad. She just keeps shooting it." Both men laughed sharply again.

"Last chance, Jacques."

"Maybe someday we'll pack white women upriver for a little variety but, for the next year, it's all plump little squaws for me." Lisa winked and ambled back into town. Jake poked Willie's ribs. "Someday you'll be sporting with the best of 'em, Willie! Till then…" Jake grinned and looked upriver.

Willie envisioned Colette with her long, shining black hair, soft French accent, and giggle; her musky smell and the feel of her warm, heavy breasts when she hugged him. Now she and the baby were rotting together deep under the St. Genevieve clay, probably already skeletons.

"Uncle Jake?"

"What?"

"Nothing."

"What're you looking so glum about? Come on, I'll introduce you to some of the boys." For the next couple of hours, they scrambled over the keelboats—Jake slapping backs, joking with everyone, and occasionally breaking up a fight; Willie eagerly asking questions about Indians and trading but mostly breathing in the scores of scarred, tattooed rivermen and trappers, their curses and tall tales, and the volatile cauldron of hopes, hatreds, and fears bubbling near the surface of them all. Finally, with loading almost complete, Jake sent a runner to Lisa.

A huge crowd of family, relatives, and sweethearts had joined the merchants and riffraff along the bluffs. Jake and Willie stood near a gangplank.

Jake chuckled. "Well, Willie, I hope you don't get in too much trouble for skipping school to see me off." His smile faded. "Do give your pa my best next time he comes up from the diggings. And little Sarah…and your ma." Willie nodded.

Lisa and a few other men stumbled drunkenly down the slope. Lisa slapped Jake on the shoulder and winked as he stumbled up the gangplank.

"Allison, she very good!" The men laughed loudly. The crowd along the bluffs began to cheer.

"You take care, Willie." Jake pressed the boy's shoulder with his big hand, smiled into his eyes, then turned and strode up the gangplank.

The gangplanks were pulled up onboard and Lisa ordered the swivel gun at the prow of each keelboat to fire. Boom!!! Boom!!! The crowd's cheers were deafening. Gunshots were fired and hats thrown into the air as a score of men on each keelboat dug their poles into the Mississippi bottom and slowly pushed off upstream. Willie joined a smaller crowd of mostly boys and young men who ran along the bank, waving and shouting encouragement to the expedition. Finally tired out, he climbed a tall tree and, tears in his eyes, watched the keelboats push slowly out of sight around the bend.

Everything droned lazily in the humid air: Pringle endlessly mumbling Scene III of *Hamlet* before the packed classroom, the hundreds of cicadas buzzing loudly outside, the hoofbeats and squeak of wagons plodding past the schoolhouse. Willie wiped the sweat off his face and glanced around at the thirty other children, aged six to fourteen, crowding the narrow benches; they either dozed or stared.

With the dunce cap on his head, Jess sat on a tall stool beside

Pringle.

Willie smiled as he recalled Judy's expression and screams when Jess had dropped that frog down her blouse. After Pringle enthroned Jess as class dunce for the day and began reading *Hamlet*, Willie had made a variety of faces at Jess, trying to get him to crack up. At first Jess had grinned and starting shaking with repressed laughter, but finally he shut his eyes and calmed down. Now Jess's head was nodding and his eyes struggled to open...

Suddenly Jess crashed to the floor and then sprang, dazed, to his feet. The class burst into laughter. Pringle's face reddened in anger. He slammed his hand down on the lectern. "Silence!" he shouted. The children immediately swallowed their laughter and smiles. No one wanted Pringle to demand, "What's so funny?"

"I'm sorry, Mr. Pringle," Jess blurted in confusion. "Ah reckon I kinda lost ma balance. I didn't mean nothin' by it. I swear!"

Pringle stared coldly at Jess. "Well, Jessie, you truly are a dunce!" Jess shrugged his shoulders and slightly tossed his head in mock humility. A grin tugged at the corners of his mouth. "Was the significance of the passage I was reading that overwhelming? Hmmm?"

"Yup, that was it, Mr. Pringle," Jess agreed enthusiastically. "Old Bill Shakespeare sure can sling the words."

"True. Very true, Jessie, although I might not have put it quite as rustically. Now then, just what was the passage saying?"

"Well, ah, it was a might over my head, Mr. Pringle."

"You couldn't be more wrong, Jessie. Couldn't be more wrong at all!" Pringle pointed to the passage. "You read this aloud to the class." Jess swallowed and glanced around the classroom at the expectant faces. The grin tugged again at his mouth when he spotted Willie's cross-eyes and fish mouth. "Read it, boy!" Pringle ordered. Gunshots and cheering broke out in the distance.

Jess took a deep breath and slowly began to read, occasionally stumbling over a difficult word: "'To be or not to be, that is the question—Whether 'tis nobler in the mind to suffer the slings and arrows of outrageous fortune, or to take up arms against a sea of trouble, And by opposing end them. To die, to sleep—No more; and by a sleep to say we end the heart ache and the thousand natural shocks that flesh is heir to—'"

"That's enough, Jessie," Pringle interrupted. "Now what is Hamlet saying, or I should say, what is Shakespeare telling us through Hamlet?"

"Well," Jess stammered, "with all the talk a' arrows and taking up arms and dying, I reckon Hamlet's got a heck of a fight on his hands."

"Jessie, you are quite correct. But what kind of fight is it? Who is he fighting?"

"Ah, well now, you was saying Hamlet was Danish so I reckon he might a' bin fighting…" The tumult in the distance grew louder. The class stirred in curiosity.

"No, Jessie! Hamlet was not fighting another nation, and although he had conflicts with almost everyone around him, he was really fighting only one person…" Pringle looked hard into the children's faces as he paused for effect. "Hamlet was fighting himself! Listen to his words: 'To be or not to be, that is the question.' Hamlet is trying to decide whether or not to kill himself!" Pringle's face reddened further and his voice rose shrilly. "Have any of you thought of killing yourselves? Yes, you may be young, but everyone faces death, and on this infernal frontier, death can come at any moment, whether by the hands of others or oneself. That is the choice Hamlet faces! That is the choice we all face!"

"What's happening?" someone shouted. "What's all the ruckus about?"

"Lisa's back!" someone else shouted.

Willie sprang to his feet then ran for the door. "Willie!" Pringle shouted. "Stop!"

As he ran, Willie dodged through knots of townspeople hurrying toward the wharf. Ahead he could see the weather-beaten trappers and boatmen crowding into the taverns or guzzling bottles of rum and whiskey in the streets.

Gunshots and war whoops shattered the humid air. Suddenly a long-bearded trapper, swigging deeply from a jug, staggered across the street before him.

Willie tugged at his greasy, tattered shirt. "Where's Jake Yates?" he demanded. The trapper turned and blindly swung his fist at his imagined assailant, then toppled over face first in the dust and lay still. Willie jumped over him and continued running toward the wharf. He spotted Lisa passing a bottle with four other trappers before the Gray Horse Tavern.

"Mr. Lisa! Mr. Lisa!" Willie shouted. "Where's my uncle Jake?"

Lisa and the others stared up mirthfully. "Jacques Yates?" Lisa asked drunkenly. "Good man! Damn good man!"

"Jake your uncle, boy?" demanded one of the trappers. Willie nodded.

"Jake's gone, boy. Left camp one day high on the Yellowstone to check his traps and never come back. We looked damn near everywhere for him but the Blackfeet was thick as ticks on a hound's back and put a dozen of us under over the past year. Never seen hide nor hair of Jake since." The trapper sighed, "Jake was a damn good man!" Willie stared in disbelief. "He's gone, boy!" the trapper repeated angrily. "Maybe the Blackfeet put him under. Maybe the earth swallowed him up. Or maybe Jake sprouted wings and flew off to California, from way up the Yellowstone."

Four

1812–1814

Laughing and cursing loudly, a crowd of red-faced, swaying men jostled around the table, thrust their empty mugs at Willie, and demanded more whiskey. Willie tilted the jug rapidly into one mug after another, spilling as much as he filled. Most of the men then staggered off and others took their place; some gulped down the whiskey and demanded more. When the jug was empty, Willie quickly turned to the barrel behind him and pulled the lever releasing more whiskey into the jug, ignoring the men's gibes to hurry before they died of thirst.

"Fill 'er up, Willie! I've a powerful thirst that's bin trailing me for days!" a wiry, elfin man with a goatee and battered top hat shouted above the din.

"Mr. Gerber!" Willie shouted back as he slopped whiskey into the man's mug. "Do you think my pa can win?"

"It's a toss up, Willie. The whiskey's flowing free and fast on both sides! Rumor has it Peterson's gonna use his speech to shovel a load of mud on your pa!"

Willie's brow furrowed. What could Peterson have on Pa? he wondered. "How?" Willie demanded.

Suddenly a black bearded, barrel-chested man, towering above anyone present, shoved and elbowed his way through the crowd and knocked Gerber aside. "Whiskey!" he roared.

"Owww!" hollered Gerber. "You son of a bitch! Get the hell off my foot!"

The giant snarled and slashed his pewter mug across Gerber's face, breaking his nose and knocking him against the crowd. The crowd shoved Gerber back toward the giant who kneed him in the groin and turned back toward Willie. "Whiskey!" he roared again as Gerber sank to his knees. Mouth agape, Willie stared up in disbelief at the giant. "Whiskey, goddamn it!" the giant snatched the jug out of Willie's hands, tipped it to his lips, and began gulping. His face bloodied and contorted in pain, Gerber slowly struggled to his feet. He reached under his tattered brown coat, pulled a skinning knife and thrust it deep into the giant's side then slowly tore it around to his navel. "Awwwhhh!!!" the giant choked and puked out a stomachful of whiskey, bile, and half-digested food onto Willie, Gerber, and others nearby; blood spurted through his torn shirt. The giant shattered the jug against Gerber's head, smashing him back to the ground. Bellowing curses, the giant savagely kicked in Gerber's teeth as a half-dozen men tried to pull him back. Willie wiped the puke off his face, grabbed an empty jug, and scrambled up on the table. The giant struggled to wrench free of the men as he continued to kick Gerber. Willie swung the jug against the giant's head. Enraged, the giant screamed and twisted around toward Willie. A half-dozen men still tried to hold the giant back while the crowd of several hundred men surged toward the fight. Willie swung the jug again, shattering it against the giant's face, then leapt back off the table. The giant howled with pain, staggered back, and collapsed, heavily pinning several men beneath him.

Several pistol shots exploded through the din while Judge Easton, Sam, and Peterson, a thickset man with silver hair and a ruddy face, stood on a small stage shouting, "Back! Back! Give 'em air!" The crowd finally quieted and began to break up in small groups.

Many shoved and shouted their way toward Peterson's whiskey

stand. Willie trembled as he pushed through the crowd toward the bodies, over which a half-dozen men knelt.

"Gerber's dead!" someone shouted. Holding his side, the giant wheezed and choked out curses; blood oozed through his thick fingers. "Maddox's leaking a barrelful!" someone else shouted. "Fetch some needle and thread and I'll sew 'im up!" A wagon was pulled through the crowd. Gerber's tiny body was easily tossed inside but the men struggled hard to drag Maddox into the back. Finally loaded, the wagon was driven away toward Doc Sach's home.

Several more pistol shots were fired. "Gentlemen! Gentlemen! May I have your attention please!" shouted Judge Easton from atop the stage. Sam and Peterson stood tensely behind him. The large crowd gathered before the stage; most of the men waited impatiently, while some continued to talk and laugh loudly.

Easton gestured toward the crowd and someone handed him a flintlock pistol.

He cocked, raised, and fired the pistol into the air, then handed it back to its owner. "Gentlemen! Gentlemen!" Easton pleaded again. "Please be silent and allow our candidates to speak!" Willie squeezed his way through the crowd until he stood before the stage. He tried to smile encouragement at his father, but Sam ignored him as he sternly swept the crowd with his eyes.

Willie's stomach churned and his knees trembled; he felt like crying.

Easton's voice boomed, "Each candidate will *briefly*," Easton emphasized the word "briefly" as he glanced at Peterson, "make a few concluding remarks as his last opportunity to make a public address in the long campaign that has preceded our present gathering, to be followed by a general vote. Mr. Yates will speak first, followed by Mr. Peterson!"

Sam stepped to the front of the stage and stiffly raised his arms. Loud cheers drowned out the catcalls. "Gentlemen! Gentlemen!" he hoarsely shouted. The crowd quieted. "The year 1812 has indeed been momentous...Congress has finally granted our repeated pleas for territorial status, and I am deeply honored to be allowed to address you today as a candidate for the House of Representatives of Missouri!" Cheers and war whoops erupted.

Sam stiffly waited for the clamor to subside. "But our most important step on the road to statehood has occurred simultaneously with Congress's declaration of war against England!" Booes and curses filled the air.

Sam held up his hand for silence. "Therefore, we, as a territory, face tremendous challenges. Not only must we organize and lead a government responsive to the needs of the people, but we must defend it against the depre…" Sam stumbled over the word, "depredations of the British and their Indian allies. At this very moment, British agents are distributing presents and addressing the council houses of the tribes of the upper Mississippi and Missouri valleys, attempting to buy and excite them into an alliance designed to sweep away our civilization. We must not allow that to happen!" The crowd erupted with loud cheers.

Someone shouted, "What are you gonna do about it?"

Sam glared at the heckler. "I'm glad you asked that," he stated fiercely, once the cheers had died. "As you are all aware, I am a veteran of the three Ohio campaigns against the Shawnee and Miami alliance, and I am pleased to note that several fellow veterans of those campaigns are among us today." Sam's eyes searched out several weather-beaten woodsmen in the crowd. "It took years of long, hard struggling to defeat those Indians—and defeat them we finally did! Not only did we win peace for the frontier, but we opened the entire Northwest Territory to settlement by our enterprising people. Tragically, the British and their Indian allies have shattered that peace and threatened the advance of our nation. I promise no easy solution to our present peril, but I do promise you this…If you elect me, I will work as hard as possible to ensure that the defense of our homes and communities is our territory's highest priority, and that all necessary resources are available to overcome this terrible threat. Our fight will be long and difficult, but in the end, we will triumph in a glorious victory to be remembered for all time! Thank you."

Sam stepped back as the crowd cheered wildly. Easton waited for it to subside, then gestured to Peterson who stepped heavily forward, smoothed a hand over his silver mane, and grinned broadly. "Fellow Missourians!"

Peterson's voice was deep and loud. "The moment we have long awaited is before us! In little more time than you can shake a stick at, we'll be voting for the first time as a territory, and voting for the candidate who can best lead Missouri out of its present danger. Reckon hard the choice before you. As you are well aware, I've lived in this territory for over a decade. I've worked as hard as any man to turn the vast forest land I claimed into what is now a highly prosperous plantation worked by twenty-seven slaves! I've been dedicated to public service, both for our fine town of St. Louis, and the territory at large. Those who know me will vouch for my character. I stand before you ready to lead our St. Louis district and Missouri to victory in our war against Britain and prosperity into the decades ahead!" Some in the crowd cheered loudly.

"Contrast me, if you will, with Mr. Yates," Peterson gestured dismissively toward Sam. "Few doubt his enterprise as a successful merchant and miner. But just which district will he represent? His dry goods store here in St. Louis, or his mining interests in Mine à Breton? How many of you are merchants or miners? Almost all of you are farmers. Just how well do you think Mr. Yates will represent your interests? It takes a farmer to lead farmers!" Peterson cocked a thick silver eyebrow. "And Mr. Yates's views against slavery are well-known. Would Mr. Yates work to limit or even abolish slavery?" Some in the crowd cheered, most booed. "And what's to stop Mr. Yates from simply using his position to further line his own pockets, rather than work for the common good?" The cheers and booes grew louder. Sam stiffened and stared fiercely at Peterson.

"And as for character..." Peterson lifted his head and gazed down his nose at the audience. "Many of you may recall the rumors that swept St. Louis five years ago and have dragged at Mr. Yates's heels ever since..." The crowd stirred expectantly. Sam's eyes narrowed to slits, his face flushed, and his fists clenched tightly. Willie's knees trembled; he felt himself pulled apart by the maelstrom of the crowd's clamor, Peterson's booming voice and flamboyant gestures, and Pa's tension.

"The rumors of Mr. Yates and his brother's half-breed wife..." Peterson jabbed his finger toward Sam. Some of the crowd shouted, cheered or booed; most murmured darkly. Sam stepped toward Peterson, shook off Easton's fat hand on his shoulder, and shoved Peterson hard. Peterson turned and swung his fist, hitting Sam in the ear, then both men started punching wildly as Easton tried to break them up. The crowd's roar was deafening; some were rooting for Sam, others were for Peterson. Willie and some men scrambled on stage. They strained to pull Sam and Peterson apart.

Panting heavily, Sam and Peterson glared at each other.

"A duel, Peterson!" Sam spit out the words. "Bloody Island tomorrow morning, you son of a bitch, and we'll settle this man to man!"

"Gentlemen, please..." Easton pleaded.

"I'll be there, Yates!" Peterson spat back. "Just make sure you show."

Sam strained against the men who held him back from attacking

Peterson. "I'll be there to blow your brains out!" he shouted.

"Escort the candidates back to their respective whiskey stands and we'll conduct the vote." Easton ordered as he mopped his bald head with a handkerchief.

"Don't worry, Pa!" Willie shouted as he joined the group pulling Sam off the stage. "You'll kill him!" The group pushed through the crowd toward Sam's whiskey stand as Easton shouted for order. Several pistol shots exploded through the din.

Willie pulled hard against the current, trying to focus on the sound of his oars rhythmically sweeping then breaking the water. Sam sat tensely in the stern; his right eye twitched uncontrollably and he rubbed his temples with trembling fingertips. He and Willie stared down at the space between them; neither dared to glance at the other, or to break the silence, question the other's thoughts. In the prow, Easton peered through the mist. He shifted heavily and grunted, "Blast this fog! Can barely make out the island...Steady pulling to your right, Willie!" he ordered. "We'll be there in a minute. Yup, there's a pirogue and four men ashore. Peterson and his cronies." Easton tapped the polished walnut dueling case on his lap. "Won't be long now, Sam!" he warned. Sam nodded grimly. "Pull hard straight ahead, Willie, and we'll come right alongside her."

Cotton-mouthed and biceps aching, Willie strained numbly against the oars; sweat mingled with the cold mist across his face. A kaleidoscope of images swirled through his mind: Peterson's pompous face and gestures; Gerber ripping open the giant's side with a skinning knife; Pa's clenched fists and eyes; Colette and the baby rotting into the red clay.

This can't be real, he muttered silently, repeatedly. Why? The rowboat grated sharply against the bottom then stopped abruptly.

"Far as she goes," Easton observed and stepped gingerly into the shallow water, followed by Willie and Sam. They dragged the rowboat on shore, then turned to face Peterson and his three associates. "Gentlemen," Easton greeted the four men, who nodded back.

Willie gazed through the mist at the huge, ghostly oaks lining the shore and the cramped meadow beyond. Silently he screamed, "Stop!" as he imagined grabbing the pistols from the box to shoot down Peterson, then shoving Pa back into the rowboat, and cutting loose downstream. His knees shook uncontrollably and he swallowed hard from his dry mouth.

Sam stared savagely at Peterson while he grinned malevolently back.

"Second thoughts, Mr. Yates?" Peterson chided.

"Just on whether to put a ball into your brain or belly," Sam snarled. His right eye twitched and his hands trembled.

Peterson chuckled confidently. He was a crack shot and had killed a man in a previous duel. "You won the election by a handful, Mr. Yates. But you will soon lose the most important race of all—life."

"Gentlemen, please," Easton implored. "Let's finish this terrible business as expeditiously and with as little rancor as possible."

"Shall we?" Peterson bowed slightly and extended a hand toward the meadow.

"After you," Easton declared. Peterson and his men trudged into the meadow followed by Easton, Sam, and Willie. The two groups faced each other.

"Pa?" Willie's voice cracked.

"Wait till we're set up, Willie," Sam replied grimly.

Easton exhaled slowly. "Mr. Peterson, you still have no objections to me acting as referee?"

"Not a one, Judge," Peterson replied cheerfully.

"Allow me to check your pistols," Easton quietly ordered. Peterson nodded to a short, swarthy man with a walrus mustache, who opened a large polished box. Easton pulled out each pistol and checked its priming.

"Looks sufficient," Easton declared. "Gentlemen?" Easton glanced at first Peterson then Sam. "Any last declarations before we commence?" Peterson smiled broadly as he shook his head no.

"I want to talk to my boy," Sam declared, and guided Willie by the elbow to the meadow's edge just out of earshot.

"Don't do it, Pa!" Willie pleaded. Tears welled up in his eyes and rolled slowly down his cheeks.

"No choice, son," Sam grimly stated. "A man's gotta do what's right, and right what he's done wrong."

"But—"

Sam cut him short. "I wish I'd been a better father to you, son. I been awful hard on you. I shoulda been more like your uncle Jake."

"You…" Willie's voice choked. All the whippings, curses, and indifference suddenly seemed insignificant. "You're the only father I got," he sobbed.

Sam tightly gripped his son's shoulder, "You gotta take care of your mama and little Sarah. Rufus," he nodded toward Easton, "will execute my will and manage the estate till you've come of age. He'll invest some of the mine earnings into the store and the others into new enterprises. You and your mama and Sarah will live comfortably all your days."

"Pa, don't talk like that," he implored. "You're gonna live."

"You're right, son. I'm just talking in case worst comes to worst. I ain't a bad shot myself," Sam sighed heavily. "I'd a' like to have seen what you made of yourself, Willie. Fourteen years old. 'Nother year or so and you'll be as tall as me," Sam grinned. "Yup, if you stay outta trouble long enough, you just may make me damn proud of you someday." Sam hugged Willie hard.

"Come on now, let's get this over," he said gently. They rejoined the others.

"Gentlemen, your pistols," Easton commanded. "Watch your priming in this mist." Each man pulled a heavy flintlock out of his case. "You others to the side please." Willie joined the other four men at the meadow's edge. "Position." Sam and Peterson stood back to back. Each held up his pistol. Peterson was medium-sized like Sam, but stout; he stood relaxed, confident. Sam stared stonily into the woods, his hands shook slightly. Willie's knees shook uncontrollably; his mother's and Sarah's bitter tears and repeated pleas to his father last night and this morning echoed through his mind. "I'll count off the paces. At ten, turn and fire."

Easton paused. The river gurgled beyond the misty woods. An owl hooted once nearby. "Are you ready?" Easton's voice cracked. Both men nodded.

"One! Two! Three! Four! Five!" Each man rhythmically stepped forward through the trampled wet grass and weeds. Willie's heart pounded, his breath gasped in short bursts. "Six! Seven! Eight! Nine!" Both men were almost at the glade's end; each hesitated as they waited for the last command. "Ten!"

"Pa!" Willie shouted. Sam and Peterson turned and fired simultaneously.

Peterson screamed as the ball shattered his knee, knocking him to the ground. Sam stood and stared, uncomprehending, as Peterson thrashed and groaned in the thick grass. Peterson's supporters dashed over and stood around wondering what to do while Willie and Easton hurried over to Sam. "You did it, Pa!" Willie smiled broadly as he and Easton slapped Sam's back.

"I—" Suddenly Sam's head jerked back, his eyes bulged and his open mouth gurgled.

"Pa!" Willie screamed as Sam toppled over on his back. "Pa!

What's wrong? What happened?" Sam's head and left side twitched powerfully, then suddenly he lay still.

Snow spiraled crazily, silently down, and tumbled across frozen rooftops and fields, drifted high into the corners of buildings and against picket fences, and lashed the reddened faces and hands of those few plodding the streets. Inside the general storeroom of their home, Willie, Sarah, and Sam sat in reed-bottomed chairs by the fireplace. Their breath steamed in the cold room, despite the roaring fire. Wind gusted and howled against the frosted windows, prompting Willie and Sarah to occasionally glance out at the blizzard. Barrels of flour, gunpowder, and nails; boxes of multicolored ribbon, cloth, and thread; and tables of blankets, hats, and clothes were piled high around them. Three small wooden cradles, a spinning wheel, and a plow crammed one corner; eleven packs of beaver skins reached the ceiling in another; and large glass and ceramic jars filled with spices and pickled fruits were behind the counter.

Sarah got up and draped a blanket around her father who stared before him. "There, Papa. Do you feel better?" she asked as she gently patted his head. She sighed tensely. "Do you think he understands anything?"

Willie shifted nervously in his chair as he looked painfully at his father. "I dunno," he said in exasperation. "He eats and messes, but don't walk or talk or even move his eyes."

Sarah nodded sadly. "Do you think Papa will ever get better?"

Willie's breath hissed through his clenched teeth. "I dunno." He shrugged his shoulders. "Don't ask me. It's been over a year and he hasn't changed a bit." His eyes returned to the first canto of Byron's Childe Harold cradled in his lap.

Sarah sat down, sharpened the nib of her long goose quill with a penknife, then dipped it into the ink well. Her tongue lodged firmly against her left cheek, she began slowly, carefully, to finish a sketch of their home, adding a smoking chimney and curtains in the windows. Satisfied, she proudly held it up. "Do you like it?"

Willie glanced at Sarah's sketch then back down at his book. "It's all right," he muttered impatiently. "Listen to this, Sarah. 'So deemed the childe, as o'er the mountains he did take his way in solitary guise: Sweet was the scene, yet soon he thought to flee, more restless than the swallow in the sky.' Don't you ever feel like that?" he asked excitedly. "That you enjoy something beautiful that stirs your blood but after a while you just wanna move on 'cause you know there's something even better over the next hill? Wouldn't you love to wander the world like Childe Harold from one adventure to another? 'Solitary guise!' All by himself with no one tellin' him what to do or what not to do. That's how I wanna spend my days!"

"Nope! Not me! I love our home and don't wanna move anymore," Sarah pouted, "and you didn't even look at my sketch. You never pay attention to anything I do."

"That's 'cause you're a girl," Willie said with disgust.

"Well, if you don't like girls, then you wouldn't like to live like Childe Harold, 'cause he's always chasing beautiful women." Sarah smiled triumphantly.

He blushed. "If there were women like that around here, maybe I would." He stared intently at his book, trying to concentrate on the next stanza.

"Judy says she likes you," Sarah smiled sweetly. "Do you think she's pretty?"

"She's all right," he said, frowning.

"Why don't you court her?" Sarah asked eagerly.

His frown deepened. "She's too young. Leave me alone, I'm reading."

"You're just shy. She's sixteen and you're seventeen. Lotsa boys been courting her, but she's turned them all down." Annoyed, Sarah crinkled her nose as Willie continued to savor each line of his book. "I heard Rene Goutard's interested," she whispered conspiratorially. "And Judy thinks he's strong and handsome. Would you like to lose Judy to Rene?" she added mockingly.

Willie glanced sharply at Sarah. "That Rene—" The front door suddenly opened, letting in a gust of frigid wind and flurries. Willie and Sarah jumped. They stared as a girl wrapped in a large gray capote struggled to push the door shut against the wind, then clumped through the narrow aisles of the cluttered room toward them.

"I'm damn near frozen stiff," her words chattered as she pushed past them, dropped a heavy sack with a thud, and held her hands and shivering body before the fire. Mouths slightly open, Willie and Sarah stared up at her.

The girl glanced down at her feet and lifted a heel to reveal a ragged hole in the sole of her boot. "These are plumb worn out."

Puzzled, Sarah asked, "Who are you? I've never seen you before."

"Name's Sharon," she pulled back her hood and shook her long black hair like a wild horse tossing its mane. "We just settled here a couple weeks back. Come up from Frankfort." She rubbed her hands briskly together. "God, it's freezin'. Do you have any whiskey?" Willie and Sarah's eyes widened further.

Sharon giggled. "Not for me. For my pa. He kicks me out for more every time his jug runs dry—even in weather like this. Usually go to that store out the pike, but it's closed."

Willie sprang to his feet. "I'll get you some. Is that your jug?" He pointed to the sack.

"Yup." Sharon pulled a chipped brown jug out of the canvas.

"Lucky I didn't bust it when I dropped it. Pa'd killed me." Willie grabbed the jug, walked over to a huge whiskey barrel behind the counter, and pulled the lever over the jug's mouth.

"How old are you?" Sarah asked.

"How old do I look?" Sharon smiled slightly.

"'Bout Willie's age." Both girls smiled at Willie as he returned and handed Sharon the jug.

Sharon pulled the cork, lifted the jug to her full lips, and took a large gulp. "Damn sight warmer than the fire," she sighed contentedly as she wiped her mouth with the back of her hand. "Want some?" With the cold driven from her, Sharon's voice was throaty, velvety.

Willie's body tingled as his eyes locked with Sharon's. Her eyes were large and light brown. They seemed to change in intensity with each moment. "Never seen a girl drink whiskey before," he declared incredulously as he took the jug and raised it slowly to his lips. He tried hard not to gag as the whiskey burned down his throat.

Sharon stepped in front of Sam and peered into his dull gray eyes and deep wrinkles furrowing his face. Sarah and Willie frowned.

"So that's your pa? Heard he ain't spoke for over a year. Just sits silent as a stone."

"What's it to you?" Sarah demanded indignantly. "What do you think he is, some kind of good on display? If you think so, get out right now."

"Sorry," Sharon said sheepishly. "I didn't mean nothin' by it. I was just curious. Wish my pa was like that," she added thoughtfully. "He's a real son of a bitch."

"Why? What's he do?" Willie wondered.

"Oh, things," Sharon paused, then quickly added, "he ain't ma real Pa. Ma real Pa run off when I was a baby then ma mama took up with this'n. Mama died a' fever back at our home outside a' Frankfort and after we buried her we pulled up stakes an' set out for here. Pa was all fired to cut loose outta there. Never could figure out why till we got here. Got three older step-brothers," Sharon sighed. "There many our age in St. Louis? I've barely come to town since we arrived. Pa and my brothers keep me busy cooking, cleaning, and fixin' up the house. We bought the Fleming place a few miles south of here. Ya know it?"

Willie and Sarah nodded in amazement. "Some say it's haunted. You seen or heard anything?" Willie asked eagerly.

"Not really," Sharon giggled, "but I gotta wild family. Likely no spook'd wanna stick around after a night or two with us."

"Jess and I—Jess is a friend of mine—you'd like him," he added eagerly, "we been through the Fleming place many times and never saw nothin' directly, but heard some queersome knockings. There's cold spots in the cellar. You felt 'em?"

"Yeah, I have. I don't like going down there alone."

"Why'd your family buy the Fleming place?" Sarah asked. "It's so run down and all the stories keep folks clear of it."

"Pa said," Sharon lowered her voice to mimic him, "'forty acres that cheap that near town. Man'd be a fool not ta take it.' So we bought it."

"Hardly anyone's gone near it, let alone considered buying it, since old man Fleming axed his wife and six young'uns, then blew out his brains with a shotgun a couple years back." There was admiration in Willie's voice.

Sarah giggled. "Except Willie and Jess. They're always pulling pranks and getting into trouble."

"Oh yeah?" Sharon cocked her head, smiled slightly, and raised an eyebrow. "What kinda trouble?"

"I reckon we're the best prank-pullers in St. Louis," Willie stated proudly. "Been few pranks we ain't pulled."

"Oh, yeah? Name one," Sharon eagerly demanded.

"Well…" Willie frowned. She's got me there, he thought. "I can't let on, less we lose our surprise advantage. But keep your ears open and you'll learn of them directly. Do you like pranks?"

"Yup," Sharon grinned. "And I've pulled a few of my own in my time."

Willie cocked his head. "Yeah, well, maybe we'll let you in on a few."

"I'll be waitin'," Sharon replied coquettishly, then sighed as she glanced out at the blizzard. "I better go now, or Pa'll tan my rear. Temperature's dropping steady as a rock and the snow'll just get deeper the longer I wait."

Willie's heart pounded. God, she's pretty, he thought. Like a wild mare. "Wait!" he blurted. Sharon gazed at him expectantly. A smile tugged at the corners of her mouth. "Uh…" Willie stared blindly down at Sharon's shoes. "I'll…I'll walk you home," he stammered.

Sharon's dimples deepened with her smile as she nodded her head yes.

"Willie!" Sarah's voice was concerned. "Almost three miles there and then back again in weather like this! You'll freeze solid."

He shrugged his shoulders helplessly. "I ain't got nothin' better to do," his voice quavered. He pulled several wool blankets off a table and thrust two into Sharon's arms. "These'll keep us warm. Tell ma not ta worry. I'll be back directly." He looked shyly out of the corner of his eye at Sharon. "Ready?"

"Wait a second, Willie," Sarah demanded. "Aren't you gonna make her pay?"

"Oh, yeah," he mumbled, "you got two bits?"

Sharon dug two coins out of her pocket and pressed them into his palm. "You'd be an easy mark." She chuckled and smiled mockingly into Willie's eyes. She dropped the jug in her sack and slung it over her shoulder. "This'll keep us warm if the blankets don't." She turned and filed through the store with Willie following closely at her heels.

The cold cut deeply through them as they stepped outside and slammed the door behind them. Willie pulled an otter fur hat over his ears.

"We'd be warmer if we shared," Sharon tried to sound coquettish but her teeth were already chattering.

"Reckon yer right," he mumbled. They wrapped the blankets tightly around their bodies. An arctic gust of wind plowed into their backs pushing them down the path.

Both were shivering by the time they had stumbled through the drifts to the road. Breath steaming, arms tightly around each other, they huddled within the blankets and peered south through the swirling snow. Sharon twisted around to face Willie. He felt his groin tingle as she pressed her warm body and breasts against him. "This is crazy." The words slowly chattered from his mouth. "Storm's gettin' worse. We'll never make it." Sharon began shivering uncontrollably. She locked her eyes into Willie's, silently pleading. "We gotta turn back. You'll hafta spend the night till the storm dies." Sharon nodded. They wrapped the blankets even tighter around themselves and stumbled through the drifts and spiraling snow back toward the house.

Not much longer, Willie thought for the twelfth time that hour as he glanced at the grandfather clock ticking loudly in the corner.

His body tingled and a taut smile spread his lips as he envisioned Sharon in her faded yellow cotton dress that fit her body so tightly, her plump breasts wiggling and her hips swaying and her long black hair tossing when she visited town. Men and boys would cast eager glances or stare openly at her. Some son of a bitch'll steal her from me sure enough, he thought morosely. He slowly shook his head. What's there to steal? She ain't mine. I haven't even tried to kiss her, even when she seems to hint she wants it. He clenched his teeth and nodded. Today's the day! Down by the creek near her home. Today or never! The clock chimed the half-hour. He glanced up. Five-thirty. 'Nother half-hour and I'm a free man. He jutted his face into a hand mirror and peered closely at a white-capped pimple on his chin. He probed it with a dirty fingernail. "Damn spots," he muttered. Willie grimaced as he slowly pinched it between his forefinger and thumb, then wiped off the white pus dribbling down his chin with the back of his hand.

"Must you do that in the storeroom?" Jenny hissed while nodding toward a mother and her young daughter nearby examining a multicolored pile of cloth.

Willie frowned, "I can't help it."

"You certainly can help it," she whispered each syllable slowly, clearly. "You do that in the kitchen. What will our customers think of such uncouth behavior? Would you like to shop in a store where the proprietors engage in such disgusting practices? And if you would wash properly…"

"Ah, leave me alone," he exclaimed angrily. "I don't give a damn what they think." The woman and little girl looked up in surprise, then the mother motioned the daughter to follow her outside. Willie and Jenny watched as they closed the door behind them and disappeared down the street.

"Willie!" Jenny cried. "Now look what you've done. You know how pinched we are and then you scare off customers. What is wrong with you?"

"I didn't do a damn thing!" he shouted back.

"And such impudence. You wouldn't do that if your father were still…"

They glanced in alarm at Sam, who was, as always, hunched in an armchair before the fireplace. Jenny began to weep softly. "Why do you have to act that way? I try so hard to make ends meet and provide a good home for you and Sarah," she sobbed loudly, "and you're always getting into trouble and running off and staying out at night doing God knows what."

Shame dissolving his anger, Willie reached out his fingers toward his mother but did not touch her. "I am sorry, Ma," he said grudgingly. "You don't hafta cry."

"What else can I do?" she sniffed, dabbing her eyes with a handkerchief. "Judge Easton gambled and lost all our mine shares in that Illinois canal scheme this winter. Everybody's in debt. Nobody's buying on account of this war. I just can't stand all this strain. Why can't you act like a grown-up and support me?"

Willie clenched his body in anger, recalling the cheery words Easton had used to talk his mother into agreeing to speculate their small fortune in the venture, and the solemn words he had used to console her several months later after word of the fraud had broke. "That son of a bitch!" he shouted.

"Stop that foul language in this home!" Jenny shouted back. "You know the judge lost as much money as we did to those thieves."

He glared out the window at distant naked trees swaying in a chilly spring breeze. God, how I'd like to bust outta here, he thought grimly. "Well, what can I do?" he exclaimed. "Do you think I wanna work this store the rest of my life?"

"The rest of your life!" Jenny said in surprise. "Why, you're still just a boy. Willie, sometimes you say the strangest things."

"Whadya mean strange? What's strange about not wanting to spend my life as some store clerk."

"Willie, you won't be just some 'clerk.' You'll own this store someday. But, in the meantime, we must all pitch in and work hard, so we can slowly pay off our debts and regain our respectability."

"Respectability!" he exclaimed in disgust. "Is worrying what the neighbors think all there is in life?"

"And just what else do you aim to do? How many times have I tried to encourage you to think of studying law when you're older? With your fine mind, you'd make a great lawyer, but when I bring it up, all you say is 'the only thing about law I am interested in is how to break it without getting caught.' Now just what would make you say such a strange thing?"

Willie frowned. "I am just fooling when I say stuff like that. But you know darn well the biggest thieves around are those damn lawyers and judges that line their pockets from other people's problems. 'Best justice money can buy,'" he said mockingly, "and you want me to be like them? Humph!"

"And just what else can you do? Farming?" she said disdainfully.

"No, not farming. I dunno," he muttered. He envisioned himself and Sharon floating down the Mississippi in a flatboat. "I just wanna go someplace. Get outta here."

"Well, so do I! If we weren't in debt, I'd take us all back to Philadelphia. Good Lord," Jenny groaned as she carefully folded her linen handkerchief, "why did we ever leave? It would take months to get back. Philadelphia's on the other side of the world. Anyway, we have to stay here and work hard and pay off our creditors. I won't have it said that the Yates ran away from their responsibilities."

"We did in Cincinnati."

"And I was firmly opposed to our leaving like thieves in the night but your father wouldn't listen to me. He never did." She looked at Sam in anger. "And he still doesn't!"

The front door creaked open then shut with a bang. Jenny and Willie turned to see Jess grinning at them. "Come on, Willie," Jess urged as he waved a battered shotgun over his head. "Heard tell from a farmer that jus' come in that there's a flock a' turkeys roostin' a few miles out the west road. Gotta couple hours 'fore dark to knock some outta the trees."

That's all I need, Willie thought darkly. Now Jess'll wanna know why I can't go with him and, if he finds out, he'll tag along to Sharon's just to fun me. "Thanks, Jessie," Willie tried to hide his aggravation. "Got things to do 'round here. Some other time."

"Oh, go, Willie," Jenny waved a hand toward him as if to whisk him out the door. "I can take care of anyone else who comes in. Besides, we haven't had turkey for a while."

"But, Ma," Willie stammered.

"Time's a wastin', boy," Jess waved his shotgun again. "Grab your iron and let's go!"

"Awh...awh..." Mouth open, he stared from Jess to Jenny and back again.

"It's all right, Willie," Jenny said soothingly. "We'll finish our talk later. You go along."

"Yeah! Let's git!" Jess pointed out the window. "Sun's settin' fast and we gotta move faster."

"I can't, Jess," he blurted in exasperation. "I got things to do."

"What's more important than..." Jess's grin widened. He nodded in understanding. "Willie! You're gonna go courtin' Sharon, ain't ya? Ain't ya?" Willie rolled his eyes and ran his fingers through his hair. "Well, now, Willie, I s'pose you'll be needin' your trusted copain to see ya mind yer manners and don't do nothin' shameful like! Yes, sir! The two of us'll hafta pasture turkey shootin' for a while 'cause tonight's courtin' night!"

"Willie," Jenny said sharply, "you're not seeing that wild girl who spent the night a month back, are you?"

Willie spread his palms wide, stared at the ceiling, and muttered, "Why me, Lord?"

The door creaked open again. Sarah and Judy stood in the doorway trying to slip past Jess. "S'cuse me," Judy muttered.

"Squeeze you," Jess said in mock surprise then grabbed Judy in a bear hug. "Thought you'd never ask, Judy."

"Stop it, Jess," Judy shouted as she tried to squirm free. Her long, thick, blonde hair shook free of its bun and cascaded down her back. "Leave me be. I don't have any time for your foolishness."

Jess released her. "Well, if ya don't have time for my foolishness, whose do ya have time for?" Jess said puzzled.

"Willie's!" Sarah said triumphantly.

"Why, Willie's done spoken for," Jess pointed out. "But you ladies are welcome to join us when we go courtin' Sharon this evening."

"What?" Judy's mouth gapped open. She and Sarah looked at Willie with disgust. "Sharon Reims? That wild girl who moved into…"

"Yes! Yes!" Willie exhaled sharply. "That's the one. Now I'm gettin' outta here and you all leave me be." He grabbed his brown wool coat and headed for the door. "An' that means you, too, Jess," he warned as he pushed by the three of them. At the door he turned and one by one stared each of the four in the eyes. "Just leave me be!" He slammed the door behind him then stomped out of the yard toward the south.

He hiked the three miles down the rutted road to the Reims place as fast as he could. Sweat beaded his face and soaked his armpits despite the chilly evening air. At first he threw quick glances behind to make sure Jess was not tailing him. But the sounds of birds flittering and singing through the trees and smell of wet earth and foliage slowly relaxed him. He nodded absent-mindedly to the occasional farmer trudging wearily in from the fields as he debated just what words to use then just how to kiss Sharon. "Stick your tongue down her. She'll love it!" Jess had advised. Willie tried imagining what it would feel like.

Suddenly he stopped and ran his fingers through his greasy brown hair. What if she laughs at me and runs off? Then tells her pa and he comes after me with his old fowling piece? He sighed deeply. What the hell am I doing? Maybe I oughta court Judy. But she's too prissy—just a girl. Sharon's a woman! With a deep breath, he strode on.

Might as well die trying! he thought grimly. All a man can do!

He paused at the edge of a newly plowed field and stared at the ramshackle two-story house set several hundred yards from the road. Pigs and chickens rooted in the yard. Old man Reims and his three sons were just stumbling in from the corn field. Each carried an ax and one of the boys led two mules. Willie had hoped Sharon would be in the yard so he could wave her to join him. He hated being around her old man or step-brothers. They were always punching each other and cutting up, but they mostly just stared hard at Willie like they resented his presence. Smoke drifted up from the stone chimney. Reckon Sharon's fixin' dinner. He imagined her bent over some kettle on the fireplace.

His stomach grumbled. God, I'm hungry! he suddenly realized. Maybe they'll feed me, he thought hopefully as he headed toward the house.

Suddenly two yellow curs jumped up from where they had been dozing under the porch and, barking wildly, charged him. Willie froze for a second, then glanced at the woods along the creek. Too far! They'll tear me apart halfway there! He picked up a rock in each hand and posed to throw the one in his right hand. Barking shrilly, the dogs pulled up a half-dozen feet from him.

Sharon joined her father and brothers on the porch. They stared at the dogs and Willie. "Gran! Rat!" Sharon cried out, then ran toward Willie. "Stop it! C'mere!" She grabbed one by its neck and dragged it back while she kicked at the other. "Goddamn it! Stop it!" Growling at Willie, the dogs stood guard in front of Sharon. She gently stroked each of them. "That's it, boys! He ain't gonna hurt'cha! Jus' settle down." One of them licked her face. She giggled then looked up at him. "Ya sure know how ta stir things up, Willie. You can toss them rocks. They won't hurt'cha."

Willie shook slightly. "Hope you're right." He dropped the rocks. The top three buttons of Sharon's yellow dress had pulled undone when she had ran out to him. He felt his groin tighten as he stared at her deep cleavage.

She noticed him staring and smiled mischievously as she slowly buttoned her dress. "You 'member, Willie. Now you boys be nice to him. Go head, Willie. Pet 'em. They jus' gotta get ta know ya agin."

Squatting, he told himself, can't show the dogs or Sharon fear. He held his hand out. "C'mere. I don't mean no harm. C'mere." The dogs stopped growling but eyed him carefully.

"What'd ya call 'em? Rat?"

"Yep." She rubbed the smaller dog's throat. "Rat's a ratter.

Better'n any cat. Likes ta catch a rat and shake it apart. And Gran here,"
she pulled at the other dog's ears, "minds me a' my ol' granny who use
ta mostly sit 'round sewing, but was always watchin' and waitin' ta
jump on anybody who crossed her. She died a' the same fever that took
my ma," Sharon said sadly. "Damn fine dogs, ain't they?" she added
quickly.

"Yeah…I s'pose," Willie sighed. "You wanna walk some? Down
by the creek?"

"Sharon!" her father hollered from the doorway. "Come on, girl!
We're fixin' to bust from hunger!"

Sharon frowned as she turned around. "Comin', Pa!"

"Maybe I should…"

"Ya et supper yet?"

"Well, I, ah…" Willie stammered.

"I reckon we got 'nuff ta go 'round. But I'll hafta ask Pa. Then
maybe we kin go for a walk after dinner…it'll be dark then," she added
demurely.

The dogs continued to hug her as they walked back to the house,
then curled under the porch as Sharon and Willie went inside. The room
smelled of bacon, sweat, and whiskey. The four Reims men sat around
the table noisily debating whether to dig or blow out a huge oak stump
in a woods they were clearing. Reims nodded grudgingly when Sharon
asked if Willie could join them for supper. He uncorked a jug, took a
deep gulp, then passed it to the oldest son. Willie sat on an overturned
pine bucket at the table. Sharon pumped Willie for all the latest town
gossip as she hurried to ladle ham and hominy onto everyone's plate.
His voice cracked twice as he stammered answers to Sharon's questions.

He glanced nervously at old man Reims and her step-brothers as
they noisily gobbled their food. The old man had a monkey-like face
with steel-colored greasy hair combed straight back from his brown,
wrinkled forehead. His forearms were thick and hairy; his taut body
and bark-like laughs made him seem ready to explode. The three sons
looked like younger, leaner versions. God, I'll be glad when this is
over, Willie kept telling himself.

Finally the plates were scraped clean and everyone leaned back.
Old man Reims belched loudly as he reached for the jug. He tipped the
jug to his mouth, swallowed hard, then leaned across the table toward
Willie.

"Hear tell your pappy's done busted his brain. Don't say nor do
nothin'. That a fact, boy?" The Reims boys cackled loudly.

Willie squirmed on the bucket, and looked warily from Reims to Sharon. He debated telling the old man it was none of his business.

"Daddy, that ain't nice ta say!" Sharon demanded indignantly. "Leave Willie be!"

"Ya shush, girl! I was jus' wondering if his pappy done busted his brain from thinking too hard." The boys snickered.

"I think I better leave," Willie said quietly as he rose.

"Willie, wait!" Sharon jumped up from the log she was sitting on. "I'll walk you out."

"You ain't going nowhere, girl!" Reims shouted menacingly.

Sharon glared at her father. "I'm walking Willie to the road whether ya like it or not."

Reims lowered his head and shook it slowly. "You'll get it tonight, girl."

Sharon's face paled as she turned toward the door. "Come on, Willie," she said quietly. Laughter exploded as she banged the door shut and they stepped off the porch. "Stay!" Sharon ordered as the two dogs rose and stretched. "Don't move a muscle!" The dogs eyed them. The sun's last rays were turning streams of clouds into kaleidoscopes of pink and orange.

Sharon slipped her hand into Willie's as they walked quickly toward the road. She looked into his eyes, "I ain't stayin' there tonight."

"What's yer pa gonna do?" Willie asked warily.

"Things." She bit her lip. "But no more."

They reached the road and looked back at the house being swallowed in the dusk. Wisps of mist were rising from the damp fields.

A dove cooed from the woods. Sharon turned to Willie, slipped her arms behind his back, and reached her mouth up to his. Willie's eyes opened wide then closed tight as he felt her full lips on his. She sucked on his lower lip then slipped her tongue in his mouth. He felt himself sucking on her tongue and caressing her back with his fingertips. Suddenly she giggled.

"Why, Willie," she murmured as she pulled her body hard against his erect penis, "don't take you long ta git excited." Willie felt like he was floating in a warm cloud. Am I dreaming, he wondered. "Not here. Come on," she urged, then, arms around each other, they were strolling toward town.

"You're awful sweet, ya know that, Willie?" She stopped him and they kissed long and hard. Finally, Sharon pulled away. "We gotta git," she said softly.

Willie struggled to speak. "Where?" he whispered.

"I can't go back." She buried her face on his neck. "I gotta stay with you and your folks. Please, Willie," she pleaded.

Everything—the road, woods, sky, even Sharon—was fading into dark. He imagined the stern faces and words of his mother and Sarah if he took Sharon home. "But—"

"Willie, please. You're all I got. My step-Pa…" She started quietly whimpering. He felt her warm tears roll down his neck as she hugged him tighter. "Please."

"All right, but…" She kissed him and they started walking again.

Each was wrapped in his own thoughts as they stumbled down the rutted road back to St. Louis. Willie wrestled with the fear that her father did something worse than hit her. If he did I can't let her go back, he concluded. But Ma won't let her stay. What the hell am I gonna do? He imagined her father and brothers, faces ablaze with anger, rifles in their callused hands at the Yates's front door, demanding Sharon's return.

The Yates home was dark, except for the glow of tallow candles and the fireplace behind the parlor's flour sack curtains.

"Sharon…" his voice faded. How could he tell her she would not be welcome? She brushed his cheek with her lips and nestled against him. He let out his breath in a long hiss. "Won't be safe here," he whispered. "This is the first place your pa'll look. My ma can't…If my pa and uncle were…I can't…"

Sharon gripped Willie tight. "What're we gonna do?"

"Jess!" he said quickly. "Maybe Jess's Pa will let you. Come on." They hurried into the silent town.

All morning Willie's stomach heaved and churned; his mouth spilled belches and yawns; his fingers drummed the counter and frayed long red ribbons into threads. Although he welcomed the occasional customer, he could barely nod or croak out a word to their questions and small talk. Sometimes he stood sentinel at one of the windows and stared out at the steady drizzle that soaked the roads into quagmires, leaving the few travelers drenched and mud-caked. He repeatedly checked the priming of his father's battered flintlock rifle or absent-mindedly weighed it from one sweaty palm to the other. Stay home out of the rain, Old Man, he silently pleaded. Leave me and Sharon alone! He bit his lip, worrying what to do if all four Reims rode up, armed and mad as hell. Shoot down the old man? Would the three sons run off or charge the house? And what if they only wanted to talk? His eyes widened and he started shaking.

I'd be hung for murder! He pictured his mama sewing and papa staring vacantly in the parlor. What about my folks? What would Mama say? I gotta warn Mama, he kept telling himself. But he did nothing.

The grandfather clock slowly chimed ten times. Willie shivered and tried shoving aside his worries with memories of Sharon's juicy mouth and probing tongue, her plump, soft breasts and thin waist. He chuckled at Jess's astonishment and wide grin when they appeared on his doorstep last night. Old man Baucus limped to the door then tugged thoughtfully at his long, tangled hair and beard as Willie breathlessly urged that they hide Sharon.

"My Pa does worse than beat me," Sharon added quietly as she stared at the dust. "I can't take it no more." Baucus hurried them inside and they all perched on barrels near the fireplace, pondering choices. "'Fraid ya can't stay here, girl, and you're both too young for marriage... 'less a' course, ya be in the family way!" Willie's head jerked up in horror; Sharon sighed and shook her head no. Then Baucus slapped his good leg and shouted, "St. Ursula's! Your old man can't fetch ye home from a nunnery." Everyone laughed hard at the thought of Sharon in a convent.

"But I ain't Catholic," Sharon protested.

"Well, girl, it's either yer vows or back to yer papa! Yer can break 'em when yer old 'nuff ta be on yer own."

They stumbled the dark streets across town to the convent and banged on the huge oak door. An old, wizened nun, clad in black, finally appeared.

She held her candle alarmingly close to Baucus's beard as he struggled to explain with his limited and mostly profane French.

"*Un moment, s'il vous plaît, monsieur,*" the nun commented softly and closed the door in their face. After a long wait, another nun appeared and motioned Sharon inside. Sharon stepped in and cast Willie a sad glance as the door was shut firmly behind her. Willie stared in disbelief at the door. Baucus slapped him hard on the shoulder. "Easy come, easy go, Willie." He laughed sharply. "Time we all be in bed, though it looks like you'll be sleeping lonesome tonight, boy!"

The front door creaked open and Willie jumped in fear. "Judy!" he blurted. "Thank God it's you!"

Judy pulled back the hood of her white capote, and shook her thick, damp, blonde hair. She smiled. "Why, Willie, you've never thanked God before for my presence. Are you feeling all right?"

"Why su-sure..." he stammered as he stumbled from behind the counter toward her. "Where's Sarah?"

"She's coming. Pringle made her stay after for whispering and she told me to wait for her here." Judy sighed. "Did you have a good time last night?"

"Ah...well...I...reckon..." he mumbled as he glanced into Judy's light blue eyes then looked away.

Judy's smile widened. "You don't sound so certain. What's wrong, Willie, cat got your tongue?" He shrugged, debating whether to tell her.

Suddenly she frowned. "Are you in trouble, Willie?" She placed her hand on his shoulder. He noticed how long and slender her fingers were. "Don't worry. You can tell me," she said quietly.

Willie looked down into Judy's blue eyes. She's so different from Sharon, at once nervous and gentle. He debated whether he'd call her pretty. Hips slightly wider than her breasts, a waist thicker than Sharon's, and her round face and pug nose. But her eyes were gorgeous. "I...ya promise you won't tell?"

Judy smiled again as she pulled back her hand. "I promise," she said eagerly.

"Well, Sharon's..." The door opened with a bang, startling them. "It's him!" Willie shouted.

Reims seemed to fill the doorway. Water streamed down his slouch hat and the dirty brown blanket wrapped around his shoulders. His cold gray eyes locked into Willie's. "Where's she, boy?" he asked warily.

"Who is he, Willie?" Judy demanded worriedly. She began to tremble. Willie's mouth opened wordlessly. It seemed like a nightmare in which he was frozen before some monster.

He finally managed to blurt out, "She ain't here, Mr. Reims."

"Well, where's she, boy?" Reims pulled off his blanket and flapped it sharply, sending water flying. A pistol and butcher knife were thrust in his belt.

Willie glanced over at the rifle lying on the counter, then back at Reims. He damned himself. Out of reach. "She's at the convent," he said nervously.

"Take me there," Reims demanded.

Judy nervously glanced from Reims to Willie and back again. "Willie's not leaving here," she said, shaking.

Reims ignored Judy and continued to bore his eyes into Willie's. He placed a gnarled hand atop the butt of his pistol. "Let's go, boy. Time's a wastin'."

"What're you gonna do?" Willie asked warily.

"Nobody's gonna get hurt. I jus' want ma girl back. Now you take me to that convent."

"If Willie takes you to the convent," Judy exclaimed, "then I am going with him."

"Suit yourself," Reims snorted gruffly and nodded toward the door. "Let's git this over with."

Willie and Judy looked at each other in alarm. "You can't," he blurted. "He's…"

Judy whispered behind her hand into his ear. "Don't worry, Willie, there's safety in numbers. I'll stick with you," he nodded reluctantly.

"Time's a wastin'!" Reims ordered. "Come along now!"

"Your mother?" Judy asked as Willie pulled on his coat. He shook his head no.

Rain soaked and mud sucking down their ankles, the three silently trudged the empty streets to the north end of St. Louis.

Willie offered his hand to Judy for help through the deep puddles and mud, while whispering snatches of what happened to Sharon. Finally the convent loomed ahead through the mist, looking like a castle with its high stone walls and steep slate roof. Willie gestured. "There it is."

Reims stopped and stared anxiously at the convent. His lip curled in anger as he turned on Willie. "You got 'er into it, boy, now you get 'er outta it!"

"Are you coming?" Willie asked.

Reims hesitated. "I'll wait here."

Willie put his arm around Judy's waist. "Come on." They stumbled up the road to the convent.

"What are you going to do?" she asked, her brow wrinkled in worry.

He sucked in a deep breath. "I don't know."

They stopped before the convent door and looked back. Reims had followed and now stood half-hidden behind a huge, budding maple tree twenty feet away. "He looks ashamed," she whispered. "Maybe if Sharon goes back he won't hurt her anymore."

"Don't bet on it," he said grimly. "He's a real bastard."

Reims pointed angrily toward the convent. Willie banged loudly on the door. A young robed and hooded nun opened the door. She smiled, "*Bonjour monsieur, mademoiselle.*"

"*Bonjour…*" Willie hesitated. Hmmm, he thought to himself, if nuns are both virgins and brides of Christ, should I address her as mademoiselle or madam?

"You are American?" the nun asked in a slight French accent. Willie and Judy nodded. "I speak English. How can I help you?"

The nun's cheerful face grew taut as Willie hurriedly explained. She peaked out the door toward Reims who ducked behind the tree.

"Come inside," she beckoned, then barred the door behind them as they stepped into the entrance hall. "Wait here." She disappeared down a corridor.

They waited silently. How do I get in fixes like this? Willie repeatedly asked himself. Is being with Sharon worth all this? Being with her! He mocked himself. Hell, Sharon being hidden away in a convent is as bad as being with her old man. Either way, I just get glimpses of her.

Finally the young nun, two older nuns of last night, and Sharon appeared before them. Willie stifled a smile at Sharon's black habit and hood. She smiled wanly at him then looked suspiciously at Judy. The old wizened nun asked him in French to bring in Reims. He nodded, opened the door, and waved. "Mr. Reims, they want to talk to you." Reims poked his head out from behind the tree and glared intensely. Willie suddenly felt anger burn within him. What right did that son of a bitch have in harassing me or anyone?

"It's your choice, Mr. Reims, you can talk or you can hide," he mocked. "Why not face it…" He stopped short of saying, "like a man." Better not press it too hard, he told himself. Reims slowly moved toward him. Each tried to stare the other down. Willie opened the door wide for Reims, who hesitated, then stepped inside.

"Sharon," Reims barked angrily. "Why the he—" he shot glances at each nun, "why'd ye run off like that?"

Sharon's face was strained, her eyes teary. "I couldn't take it no more, Pa."

"Did ye," Reims lowered his voice and glanced at the nuns warily. "Did ye tell…" Sharon nodded. Reims's face reddened; he balled his fists and glared madly at Sharon who looked down at his feet.

"Ye goddamned…" The nuns and Judy gasped; Willie steeled himself to tackle Reims.

"Mr. Reims," the young nun implored, "no man is without sin. We all live our lives in shame and regret. But we can choose to atone for our sins, our mistakes…"

"Don't give me that god—that Catholic hogwash!" Reims spat bitterly. "I want ma girl back and I want 'er now!"

"Sharon is now a sacred member of this community," the nun

calmly explained. "She can only leave of her own will."

"I'm 'er pappy and she'll do as I tell 'er!" Reims shouted.

"Mr. Reims," Willie struggled to control the tremor in his voice, "you push this and the word will be all over St. Louis about what you did to Sharon and you'll be lucky if the only thing the men will do is tar and feather you, then run you out of town!"

Trembling in rage, Reims clenched his fists in Willie's face. "Goddamn you!" he shouted, then glared around the hall. "Goddamn you all!"

He lowered his voice and screwed up his face. "I'll get ye fer this, boy," he leered. "I'll get ye." Reims strode outside slamming the door behind.

Soft and smooth as velvet, Willie thought as he stooped and ran his fingers over the shiny green moss. He stuck a dirty forefinger into the deer hoof print and glanced around at the thick woods dripping from an earlier shower. Fresh. Can't be far off, he thought hopefully. Maybe it's a giant buck—five, no, six points! My first deer! 'Nuff venison to feed the family for a month. He checked the priming on his father's rifle. Dry. Gotta track and kill it. Granddaddy of every buck in creation! Boy, Jess'll be sore when I drag it into camp. Hope he ain't hard on the trail of his own deer. Wonder how far off he is. Maybe sighting one now. Gotta move. Gotta be first. Be dark soon.

He slipped slowly through the trees and undergrowth, thankful that the rain-soaked leaves made no sound beneath his feet. His body was sore from the third night on the ground. The clouds were thick and low; the woods were shrouded in the dark mist. Sudden gusts of sultry wind brushed the treetops, sending showers of drops below. Walking into what wind there was, he reasoned, I'll get the drop on that buck. He yawned. Damn mosquitoes buzzing and biting all night. Why would a loving God make mosquitoes? Or poison ivy? Don't make no sense. Miss my cornhusk filled mattress at home. And Ma's cooking. Sick of biscuits and squirrel stew, though. Nobody's buying or selling on account a' that damn war! Reckon the whole country's living off credit, but there ain't much to live on. He slapped a mosquito digging its quill into one of the thick blue veins ridging his right hand. "Goddamn mosquitoes!"

Why didn't we bring a canvas? Why'd we pick these flatland forests to hunt? We shoulda ridden a couple days farther west. Two days outta St. Louis ain't 'nuff. Gets rockier and hillier farther west. Coulda found a rock overhang to keep off the rain. 'Course the meat'd spoil 'fore we got home. Everyone says hunting's better farther west.

Everything's better farther west. Osage country. Willie suddenly felt afraid. He froze and slowly peered through the woods around him. Osage had been friendly mostly. Didn't join in with Tecumseh's confederacy and the British. He thought of the two scraggly bays tethered back at camp. Osage might be stealin' our horses this very instant! He debated going back. Naw, odds are 'gainst it. Osage villages are another week's ride west and we're camped a couple miles off the trace. But ya never...Black beans! Willie smiled down at the scattered piles of deer droppings. He probed a pile with his fingers and looked up.

Just dropped! That ol' buck must be just ahead! Willie pulled back the hammer of his rifle and, hunched over, slowly crept forward. Maybe it's an elk! Say, there's still a few elk 'round. Uncle Jake musta killed plenty of elk way up the Missouri before he went under. He suddenly felt his heart tighten.

Why did Uncle Jake hafta go? Almost six years now. Uncle Jake always promised he'd take me hunting someday. And Pa...Pa never promised anything—just ordered. And now he just sits there staring day in and day out. Uncle Jake always treated me proper. Told me stories and listened and laughed. He shook his head sadly. Why couldn't Pa have been like him? And now he don't say nothing. Notta thing. He shuddered and rolled his neck to stretch the tightness. God, it's good to be away. Maybe we oughta forget everything and just keep headin' west. Up the Missouri! All the way to the Pacific Ocean! God, I'd love to see the ocean with its saltwater and waves tall as a man, and giant trees bleached white tossed on shore! Lewis and Clark made it. Why not me and Jess? 'Course Lewis and Clark had thirty or more men with them but still.

And Lewis dead—some say murdered, others whisper by his own hand. Willie pictured Lewis's thick, curly black hair and lively brown eyes. He was nice to me. He remembered me when he passed through St. Louis on the way back east. Men die in their prime. Or wither up like Pa. He frowned bitterly. Why's a loving God allow that?

Something tawny moved through the trees ahead. It's him! he silently shouted. The granddaddy buck! Gotta get closer. Gotta move slow and quiet as a snail. His body taut, his heart thumping, he gently, repeatedly placed one foot then the other forward. He slipped from tree to tree until he was at the edge of a series of small grassy glades broken by clumps of trees. He sucked in his breath sharply.

A deer stood about fifty feet away, its head bent into the tall grass.

There's my buck! He slowly raised his rifle and squinted down the barrel. Gotta be calm. Gotta aim right above the shoulder and gently squeeze. The deer jerked up its head and stared toward him. Where's its rack? A doe? I want a buck for my first kill.

Can't brag on a doe for my first kill. Should I let it go and hunt elsewhere? Didn't see any other sign. Guess it's gotta be a doe. His finger curled around the trigger. Suddenly a spotted fawn pranced out from behind some bushes and reached up its nose toward its mother. The doe bent its head to sniff the fawn then, satisfied, buried its head in the tall grass.

That fawn'll die if I kill the mama. But I gotta feed my family. Credit's tight! Sick a' squirrels and biscuits. Damn war! He felt his hands start to tremble slightly. He pulled down the rifle. The doe and fawn continued to graze. Family's gotta eat. I'm the man a' the family now. Gotta take care of them. Won't tell anyone 'bout the fawn.

Willie raised the rifle again and squinted toward the doe. Everything seemed blurred. Gotta kill it. I'll get a buck next time. Maybe tomorrow. Gotta kill some venison. For the family. He jerked the trigger. Kerboom!!! The rifle kicked back against his shoulder and a dirty yellow powder cloud drifted across his eyes. Willie straightened up and peered into the glade as the doe and fawn crashed away through the woods. He stumbled forward to where the doe had been grazing then brushed his fingers against the gnawed clumps of grass. He frowned as he noticed dark scattered drops.

Blood! He peered into the woods where the deer had run. How bad did I wound her? How am I gonna track her with dusk coming on? She could run for miles before she weakens.

"Willie!" Jess's faint shout cut through the thick forest. "Hey, Willie! Where are yer?"

"Over here!" he shouted back then, suddenly exhausted, sat down in the damp grass. They called to each other several times before Jess ambled up.

"So where's yer buck?" Jess asked mockingly as he dropped down alongside and leaned his rifle against a rotten tree stump.

Willie jerked a thumb behind him. "Missed."

"How many points?" Jess asked eagerly.

"It was a doe. With a fawn." He slowly shredded a dead hickory leaf.

"Oh."

"See anything?"

"Plenty a' sign."

"Hey, Jess…"

Jess glanced sideways at him. "Yeah?"

"Aaa…"

"What's on yer mind?"

He took a deep breath and looked away. "You ever miss your ma?"

Jess jerked his head back and opened his mouth but did not say anything.

"Sorry, Jessie, I don't mean to pry. I was jus' wonderin'."

Jess pulled up his knees to his chin and wrapped his arms around them. "That's all right," he said glumly.

"It's jus' I was thinkin' a my pa and uncle Jake and wonderin'…"

"Ya think of 'em often?"

"Can't help but think of my pa being he's right there. Maybe it's better your ma being…"

"Dead?" Jess asked. Willie nodded. Both were silent for a while.

"Willie?"

"Yeah?"

"My ma ain't dead."

"What!" Willie's mouth dropped open. "But I thought the pox took her when you was seven back in Nashville."

"That was…" Jess searched for the proper words, "a matter a speaking." Willie frowned in puzzlement. "Promise you'll never tell nobody?" Willie nodded. "Jus' 'tween us." He nodded again. Jess took a deep breath and let it slowly hiss through his teeth. "Fact is…my ma…" Jess looked Willie in the eye then rested his chin on his knees. "Fact is my ma done run off with another man." Willie's eyes widened. "Kneelboat captain bound for New Orleans." Jess swallowed hard and sniffed. "Yup. All the way from Nashville down the Cumberland and Ohio and all the way down the Mississippi to New Orleans. Pa said Ma always talked a' wandering but he never reckoned she'd stray that far."

"You never heard from her?"

"Couldn't write far's I 'member. Never heard from her."

"Figure she's still down there?"

"Hell if I know. Hear there ain't much after New Orleans but swamp till the Mississippi hits the ocean. Maybe she's still there. Ain't nowhere else ta go."

Willie began shredding another hickory leaf. "I always wanted to go to New Orleans."

"Me, too," Jess said quietly.

Willie glanced up at the thickening dusk. "We better get back to camp," he said as he scrambled to his feet.

Jess hugged his knees hard. "Yeah, reckon yer right."

"Welp, let's go."

"Willie?" A grin tugged at Jess's mouth.

"What?"

"Where's camp?" Willie jerked his head around at the forest then looked worriedly back at Jess. Then they both burst into gales of laughter.

Willie took another gulp then set down the jug with a thump in the dust. The whiskey burned down his throat into his stomach. Cicadas buzzed noisily the thick woods. He smiled at a monarch floating on the splintered sunlight above the morning glories entangling the creekbank. He chuckled softly and lay his head back in the dirt. His eyes wandered the cirrus clouds drifting across the azure sky. My mind's as light as that butterfly. I wanna fly away and ride those clouds!

"Where's your manners, boy?" Jess's deep voice boomed. "Pass that jug over here."

Sharon giggled as she reached across Willie's chest for the jug. "Ladies first!" She tipped back the jug and swallowed hard. Some whiskey dribbled down her chin into her blouse. Jess grinned hungrily at her deep cleavage. Sharon set the jug down on Willie's stomach. He groaned as he grabbed the jug. "Wake up, Willie! We're s'posed ta be celebratin' my freedom. Ain't ever 'day I kin cut loose a' the convent."

Jess laughed sharply. "What's it like bein' a nun?"

Sharon giggled, took another deep gulp, wiped her mouth with the back of her hand, and handed the jug to Jess. "I ain't no nun!"

Jess tipped back the jug, gulped hard twice, and belched loudly. Sharon giggled again. "Yer disgustin', Jess!"

Jess lowered the jug and grinned broadly. "Why thankee, Sharon. Yer sure are loose with yer compliments."

"That ain't all I'm loose with," Sharon purred and shoved Willie, who smiled bashfully.

Jess's grin widened further. "So I hear tell." He belched again, "Now, then…" He shook his head vigorously, "Wahhh…that whiskey kicks like a mule! Where was I…Oh yeah, what's it like bein' a nun?"

"Jessie! I already told you I ain't no nun!" Sharon replied with mock indignity. "They jus' look after me is all. It ain't easy. There's other girls like me and they work us hard and watch us like hawks. It's like prison. They're learnin' me readin' and figurin' though, and the vittles is better than at my home…" Sharon suddenly fell pensive.

"How long ye fixin' to stay? Will ye ever go back home?" Jess asked quietly.

"I ain't got nowheres ta go," she said sadly. "Nowheres. I git stir crazy in that convent, but I can't go home. I ain't really gotta home. My real home's back in Frankfort but ma mama's dead. I wanna cut loose outta here but I don't know where ta go. Maybe I'll head downriver."

Willie winked at Jess. "New Orleans?"

Sharon smiled. "Yeah, New Orleans." Willie laid his head back and smiled contentedly. "Maybe I'll go with you," he said slowly.

"Oh, Willie!" Sharon said excitedly. "Ye mean it? What're we waitin' for? Le's go! Now's as good as later." Willie frowned at the sky. Is now as good as later? he wondered.

"What do ye see in them clouds, Willie?" Sharon asked. "What're ye ponderin'?"

With a laugh, he admitted, "I was just thinking a' riding those clouds all around the world. Ya wanna come?"

"Ya sure are a dreamer, Willie." Sharon's words were slurred. She squinted up at the sky. "It's hotter 'an blazes down here. Those clouds are too close ta the sun." She dipped her foot in the sluggish creek. "I'd rather go swimming. Ya boys coming?"

Willie and Jess stared drunkenly at each other. "Skinny-dipping?" Willie asked incredulously.

Sharon cocked an eyebrow and tossed her head back. "Don't wanna git our clothes wet now, do we?"

"You bet!" Jess said eagerly as he stripped off his shirt.

Willie pushed up on his elbows. Why'd I ask Jess along, he condemned himself. If only I were alone with Sharon! This could a' been my chance! Sharon rose languidly and smiled down at Willie. "Ya coming?"

Willie scrambled clumsily to his feet. "Ah...well," he blurted nervously.

Jess's enthusiasm suddenly ebbed. His fingers played with the buttons on his pants. "Come on, Willie! What're yer waitin fer?"

"I...ah...well...what're ya in such an all fired hurry for?" he asked sheepishly.

Sharon slowly unbuttoned her blouse and pulled it off. Willie and Jess felt their groins stir as they stared at her plump breasts and erect nipples. She stepped out of her faded blue cotton skirt as it dropped to the ground. "See ya in the water, boys," Sharon said as she stepped gingerly into the creek. "Hope there ain't no snapping turtles 'round." She giggled as she looked back over her shoulder. "You boys better watch where ya drag them poles a' yourn. May come in handy someday." Wide-eyed, penises erect, Willie and Jess gazed at Sharon as she waded into the creek. They savored each of Sharon's unsteady steps forward as the muddy water rose up her legs to her crotch then soaked the bottom of her thick, waist-length black hair.

"Jess," Willie whispered, "she's my girl. Ya mind...?"

Jess nodded. "Sure, Willie, I'll slip off." He took a deep breath. "But ya mind if I watch some?"

"Ya boys gonna stare and whisper all day or ya comin' in?" Sharon called out from mid-stream where she treaded water.

"Ah...we...I'm coming," Willie called back as he stripped off his shirt and began unbuttoning his pants.

"Whew-yee!" A voice shouted behind them causing Willie and Jess to jump. "Will ya look at that! Ain't that a sight!"

Rene! Willie frowned. That son of a bitch! And he gets bigger every time I run into him. Must be over six foot and couple hundred pounds a' muscle.

"What...what're you doing here?" Willie stammered.

"What's it ta ya, Yates?" Goutard scowled at Willie as he ambled up. "Free country, ain't it?"

"Ain't ya boys gonna introduce me?" Sharon demanded. "Why, ya boys got 'bout the worst manners a' anyone I ever seen."

"Pleased ta meet ya, miss," he called out cheerfully. "Name's Goutard, Rene Goutard. Ya kin call me Rene. Water looks mighty invitin'."

"Sure is! Come on in. Those other boys wanna stand in the sun all day."

"Buck naked and willin'!" Goutard whispered gleefully as he hurriedly pulled off his clothes. "Jus' how ah like ma wimmen."

"She ain't your woman!" Willie said fiercely.

Goutard turned and spit a stream of tobacco juice at Willie's feet. "Maybe not yet, Yates, maybe not yet." He waded out into the creek toward Sharon.

"Come on," Willie said as he desperately peeled his pants.

Sharon's sudden giggles caused Willie to freeze. He stared out at Rene wading toward Sharon in mid-stream then glanced at Jess standing naked beside him. Willie felt himself shrivel with humiliation.

"Got no choice, Willie," Jess said as he stepped into the creek. "We gotta protect your girl." Dazed, Willie followed and they waded out toward Sharon and Rene.

"Where'd ye git them muscles?" Sharon asked Goutard admiringly.

"I load and unload keelboats all day," he replied proudly.

He flexed a bicep. "Feel it," he demanded.

"Whoee!" Sharon exclaimed. "Hard as a rock."

Rene grinned wickedly. "Whole body's like that." He scowled at Willie and Jess. "Why don't ye boys be on yer way?"

"Willie and Jess're ma friends," Sharon said indignantly. "We stick together."

"Why don't you be on your way, Goutard?" Willie's voice quavered. "Nobody invited you to join us."

"Free country, ain't it, Yates!" Goutard snarled. "I'll stay here if I damn well please! And if ye don't like it, I'll break ye in two. And ye too, Baucus."

"No need ta be threatenin', now, Goutard," Jess said nervously. "We ain't lookin' for a fight. We jus' wanna be left alone, is all."

Goutard jabbed a finger toward Sharon. "She invited me so mind yer own business. Didn't ye?" he demanded.

"Well, ah reckon ah did, but had no idea it'd 'cause sech a stir." Sharon looked worriedly at Willie and Jess. "Maybe we oughta head on back."

Anger and fear tore at Willie as he debated fighting or fleeing. Everything seemed a blurred nightmare. He tried to focus on Sharon's beautiful brown eyes. "Sun's still high and you don't hafta be back till sundown. But the water's starting to turn foul. Maybe we oughta find another spot."

Jess tried to sound confident. "Yup, Willie, Sharon, le's head on elsewhere. Come on." He turned and started wading back to shore. Willie and Sharon followed.

"You little bastard!" Goutard shouted and leapt on Willie, shoving him deep under water. He choked as the water poured into his mouth. He tried to struggle but Goutard's powerful arms held him under. I'm gonna drown! he silently screamed. Suddenly Goutard released his grip as Jess hit him from behind. Willie burst to the surface, gasping and choking. He turned to helplessly watch Goutard battering Jess with his fists. Sharon reached down in the waist-deep water, pulled up a large rock, and smashed it hard against Goutard's ear, knocking him sideways. Goutard reeled, stunned. Jess unleashed a flurry of punches to Goutard's face while Willie jumped on his back and dragged him down, savagely punching and kicking him.

"Stop it, Willie!" Sharon screamed as she tried to pull him off Goutard. "He's done!"

Willie pushed off from Goutard, who moaned and slowly dragged himself to shore. He lay on the bank groaning and holding his ear. Willie and Jess panted heavily. "I bes' be goin'," Sharon said quietly as she waded out of the creek and quickly pulled on her clothes over her glistening body. Jess looked at Willie and jerked his head toward the bank. Willie nodded and they waded ashore.

Willie shook slightly as he stood over Goutard debating whether to kick in his teeth. Goutard groaned loudly and looked up at him. "Goutard, you ever trouble me or Sharon again and I'll kill you," he said quietly.

"Men!" Sharon shouted angrily. "All ye ever wanna do is fight and fu...there's not a hair's width difference 'tween ya!"

Dazed, quivering, Willie stared at Sharon as she stomped down the trail toward St. Louis until the woods swallowed her up. He looked from Jess to Goutard to his own pale, naked body, shuddered, and slowly pulled on his pants.

His back against a split rail fence, Willie gazed at the crescent moon hanging low on the eastern horizon. "Where the hell is she?" he muttered as he brushed at a mosquito whining in his ear. He shook his head in disgust. Darn that Sharon! he silently cursed. At ten bells she'd promised to slip out of the convent, but it's long past that now. Must be going on eleven. He peered through the dark at the convent's ghostly, gray stone walls. He glanced around nervously. Quiet as a grave. Hope there ain't no spirits around! Least no humans'd spot me here. My butternut shirt and pants make me invisible in this dark. If only I could be invisible all the time. Yeah, he smiled, and if I could fly and go through walls! I'd be invincible! I could go anywhere and do anything and no one could catch me or even know it was me. Boy! I'd raise some hell! Jus' like God.

Bible says God's always dropping out of the sky scaring the hell out of folks. Like Job. Poor Job! Can't do nothing right in God's eyes. Ma says we've all gotta be like Job. No matter how hard we try and bad it gets, Mama says we can't give up or lose faith. He pictured his silent father, slowly drying up in his chair before the fireplace. Eating and shitting's all he does, he thought grimly. 'Course it's all anyone does when ya come down to it. Why's God always testing folks? Why can't he leave 'em alone? He scratched at a mosquito bite on his ankle. Where is she? he fretted. Maybe little ol' dried up Sister Marie nabbed her. He grinned. First-class bitch, Sharon had called her.

The convent door squeaked sharply open and shut. A dark form stumbled out into the road. "Willie?" Sharon whispered loudly. "Are ye there?"

He scrambled to his feet. "Over here. Where you been?" he asked impatiently.

"Shhhh!" Sharon whispered harshly. She glided over and slipped her arms around him. Their lips met awkwardly then passionately. Willie felt his irritation melt and his body stir. "There now, better?" Sharon purred in his ear. He nodded and sighed contentedly. Sharon grabbed his hand and tugged, "Come on. We gotta slip off lessen they heard me." They hurried down the road toward the river.

"Where you wanna go?" Willie asked.

Sharon chuckled. "You'll see! But let's find a grassy spot on the riverbank for now." She stumbled in a rut. "Damn it! Darker 'en pitch out here!"

"Have any trouble sneaking out?"

"Those nuns keep a sharp watch on us girls. Sister Marie caught me twice headin' to the door but I just pretended I was sick and heading to the privy in the courtyard. Women's curse, I told her. Shame those courtyard walls are so high. It ain't easy slippin' out the front. I tried waitin' till I figured everyone was sleepin'. Think they heard me?"

"I sure did. How you gonna get back in?"

Sharon giggled. "This!" she said proudly as she held up something.

"What's that?"

"Front door key. I swiped it from Sister Marie's room when she was scoldin' me the other day."

"You're something, Sharon!"

They stopped beside a split rail fence. "River's on the other side of the pasture, just past them trees," he said as he helped Sharon over the fence. "I don't see any cows, but watch your step." They quickly crossed the pasture and slipped through the trees fringing the river. They sat down on a patch of grass at the river's edge.

The moon reflected weakly off the silently flowing river. Sharon sighed. "Pretty, ain't it?"

"Sure is. I—"

"We'll talk later," Sharon whispered as she wrapped her arms around Willie and pulled him on top of her. They sucked hard at each other's mouths.

Sharon's body and lips seemed to burn into him; she smelled of new-cut grass and sweat. He reached his hand under her shirt and slowly began kneading her breasts. He felt himself floating, happily lost. This is heaven! he thought to himself.

Sharon lightly bit his lip then whispered, "Willie?"

"Yeah?" he panted.

"Do ya love me?"

He jerked his head back in surprise. "Well...I...awwhh..."

"I love ya, Willie," she said softly.

"You do?"

"Ya surprised?"

"Well, I...I just never had a girl before...so you caught me off guard."

Sharon slowly brushed her fingers up and down his back. "Well...do ya love me?"

He nodded. "I reckon I do, Sharon. I think of you night and day."

"Yer always in my thoughts, too." They kissed passionately. Sharon spread her legs then wrapped them around him. Wonder if I'm gonna do it tonight, he thought excitedly. His hard-on felt like it was going to rip his pants. If I do, I just gotta remember to pull out in time, he warned himself.

"Willie, do ya want me?" Sharon whispered. He grunted. "Lift up," she demanded. He did and felt her fumbling with his pants' buttons. Finally she pulled down his pants to his knees. "Take me!" she urged.

Willie yanked up her skirt and pushed his loins between her legs. He felt his penis slip up inside her wet vagina. It seemed bigger than he expected. He thrust wildly inside her. "Oh, God!" he gasped as he came. He let out a deep breath and gingerly pulled out his penis. "God!" he panted again then lay down beside her.

Sharon nestled her head on his chest and sighed. "I love ya, Willie."

"I love ya, too," he replied wearily. He waved off a mosquito biting his hand. "Wish we had a blanket."

"Wish we had our own house, don't you?"

A wave of fear suddenly tore through him. "Oh, God! I forgot to pull out! What if you have a baby?"

"Well, now, settle down, Willie," Sharon said softly as she massaged his chest. "Odds are it ain't the right time of month."

"What's the right time of month?" he demanded fearfully.

"Well, ah, I ain't quite certain."

He shook his head in bewilderment. "This better not be it!"

"Willie, don't worry," Sharon cooed soothingly. "We got nothin' to worry 'bout. And if I have a baby, we'll just get married."

"Married! But we're only seventeen! We can't get married."

"I thought ya said we was heading down the Mississippi to New

Orleans together?"

"Well...I said...I said I'd think 'bout it."

"Ye said ya would!" Anger quivered in her voice. "Ya tricked me! Ya jus' wanted..." She sat up and hugged her legs to her chest.

Willie felt bewildered. "Hold on, Sharon," he blurted. "I...you...everything's happening too fast. One instant we're watchin' the moon and the next we're...you gotta give me time to think."

"I thought ya loved me," she sniffed. "I don't have nobody but ya."

"Well, I...I do love you," he grudgingly admitted again.

"I can't stand that convent any longer," she said bitterly. "I'm leavin' soon as I got the chance. And if ya ain't interested in me, I'll run off with someone else...like Rene."

"Rene!" Willie shouted angrily. "Why that son of a bitch tried to kill me and you're thinking...I'll blow that bastard's brains out before I let him have you!"

"Well, then prove ya love me!" Sharon demanded. "Ya think I'd let just anyone do to me what we jus' done? I told ya I loved ya and let ya do that..." She started sobbing.

A wave of regret submerged his anger about Goutard. He sat up and wrapped his arms around her. "There. Come on now, Sharon," he said softly, "I'm sorry. I didn't mean to make you sad. We...I just need some time to think things through is all." He lightly kissed her neck and cheek. "You forgive me?"

Sharon turned and kissed him passionately. "'Course I do, Willie. 'Course I do," she whispered softly. "We jus' need time." Then she reached between his legs.

"I'll get to it in a while, Pa," Jess hollered inside the blacksmith shop. "Jus' gotta finish talkin'...talkin' business." He winked at Willie and they laughed.

"Business!" Baucus hollered over the clanging of his hammer. "What sort a business ye talkin, robbin' or rapin'?"

"We're talkin' love here, Pa!" Jess exclaimed. "The love of Willie's life!"

Willie rolled his eyes and drew up his knees to his chin. Jesus, Jess, not so loud, he silently screamed as he nervously watched two mud-smeared farmers snicker at the exchange.

"Well, after ye boys done lovin'," Baucus hollered back, "then git ta work, ye hear?"

"All right!" Jess chuckled and slapped him on the back. "Willie! First time! Damn proud of ye, boy! Surprised ye ain't crawlin' after tangling with a wildcat like Sharon!"

He wanly smiled. "But what am I gonna do?"

Jess frowned. "What are ye gonna do! What the hell kinda question is that! Yer gonna do it again and again, and keep on doing it till yer pizen falls off!"

Willie shook his head and laughed. "But what if I get her in the family way?"

"Well, like I was tellin ye, Willie, ye jus' gotta pull out 'fore ye fire, is all."

"I planned on it but it happened so fast that I kinda forgot," He shrugged helplessly. "Well, I didn't forget but I jus' didn't remember till it was over."

"Uh huh." He cocked an eyebrow, his grin widened. "Willie?"

"What?"

Lowering his voice, Jess asked, "Was she a moaner?"

Willie kicked at a stone in the dirt. "Well, I...ah..."

"Come on, now." Jess poked him in the ribs. "Ol' Sharon was prob'ly moaning loud 'nuff to wake the dead. Folks prob'ly heard her in Nashville and thought a thunderstorm was brewin'."

Willie sighed and glanced around. Several little girls with red ribbons tied to their pigtails skipped down the street. An old, bent woman shuffled the other direction; two live chickens dangled from her belt. "Fact is, Jess," he lowered his voice conspiratorially, "this is just 'tween us." Jess suppressed a grin and nodded. "It all happened so quick I don't imagine she felt much."

Jess nodded again. "Yup. I know jus' what ye mean. Same thing happened to me first time I done it..." he chuckled, "and more than a few times after that. 'Course, whores don't seem ta mind. Fact is they kinda want ye ta finish and skedaddle."

"And ye never got the clap?"

"Not far as I kin tell." Their heads jerked up in surprise as a brown stallion trotted past pursued by a stout, red-faced boy with a bridle in his hand.

"Fact is, Jess," he said sadly, "she was no moaner. Least not with me."

"Ah, don' worry 'bout it, Willie. Ye jus' need more practice, is all. Pa sez a man's gotta do it a hundred times or more afore he gets it right. Jus' think a' all the fun ye'll have practicin'." They both laughed.

"Yeah, but what'll I do about her wanting us to run off to New Orleans together? I don't wanna get tied down. I mean I lo...I'm mighty partial to her. But I wanna wander. I sure don't want any young'uns. And I gotta take care of my folks. I don't know what to do…about anything. I sure as hell don't wanna be a store clerk the rest of my life. I wanna head up the Missouri, cross the Rockies and make it all the way to the Pacific."

Jess nodded to several greasy, bearded men sauntering by, armed with flintlocks. He frowned, "I thought we was headin' to New Orleans together."

He rubbed his face with both hands. "Yeah, I know."

"Yup, jus' the three of us! Can't wait. We kin take turns. Hell, she'll prob'ly still wear us ragged."

Stay calm, he warned himself. Jess is just funnin'. I hope. "Yup, I can't wait," he mumbled. "But what're we gonna do in New Orleans?"

Jess shook his head sadly. "Willie, sometimes I wonder 'bout ye, boy. What're we gonna do in New Orleans?" Suddenly he jumped to his feet, waved his arms wildly, and hollered, "Why we're gonna turn that town inside out! We're gonna raise so much hell that they'll be talkin' 'bout it fer years, centuries even! Why they'll erect monuments and hold parades and declare holidays to honor all our hell-raising." Jess shoved his face right in front of Willie's. "That's what we're gonna do in New Orleans," he added quietly.

Willie laughed and shoved Jess away, "Yup, I reckon we will. But I'm trying to figure out the details…" Jess frowned. "Raising hell's the easy part. We're experts at that." Jess smiled proudly. "What I am pondering is," Willie counted off each point with a finger, "how're we gonna get there. How're we gonna make a pile while we're there. How long we're gonna stay. And how're we gonna get back."

Jess pointed his right index finger skyward, "Willie, I bin ponderin' this a while an' got it all figured out. When ye hear this ye'll agree it's a stroke a' genius. Ye ready, now." Willie nodded. "Here's the plan. War's knocked the bottom outta fur prices, ain't it? Traders is sitting on their packs waitin till the war's over. Ain't nobody buyin' nor sellin' much a' anything. Ye got more 'en fifteen packs of beaver sitting in yer storehouse, don't ye? Well, now, 'stead a waitin' fer the war ta quit and those rich buyers from back east or New Orleans ta come ta ye, why don' ye and me take them furs ta New Orleans? Rivermen say beaver's fetchin' four dollars a pound in New Orleans compared to two dollars here. We sell there, make a pile, buy trade goods cheap, and bring 'em back here ta St. Louis. Now what're ye think a' that?"

"Jessie, you're right. That plan's ingenious! We just gotta find room on the next keelboat heading down the Mississippi."

"Nope! We're not takin' a keelboat. We're headin' south in our own pirogue."

"Pirogue?"

"Yup, if we hop a keelboat we'll arrive the same time as all the other traders on that boat and those New Orleans wolves'll play us off 'gainst each other and cut down the prices. But if we take a pirogue we kin get there faster and play the sharpies off 'gainst each other!"

Willie's smile broadened. "Ingenious!"

"Of course! Did ye 'spect anythin' less?"

"No, as a matter...Hey, hold on," he exclaimed worriedly. "What about Sharon?"

"We'll make room in the pirogue. We'll could use another poler." Jess laughed sharply and slapped Willie on the shoulder, "After all we'll be poling her day and night!"

Glancing up at the thunderclouds drifting the sky, he implored, Why me, Lord? "You think my ma'd go along with it?"

"Only one way ta find out. Come on," he jerked a thumb toward Willie's end of town. "We'll be back directly, Pa!" Jess hollered inside.

"Don't git caught, whatever ye do!" Baucus hollered back. Willie and Jess grinned then disappeared down the crowded street.

They burst excitedly into the store, startling Sarah and Judy, who were playing checkers behind the counter. "Ladies!" Jess intoned in his deepest voice as he spread his arms wide as if to embrace them. The girls giggled.

"Who you boys on the run from?" Judy asked as she tossed her blonde hair.

"Not from, but to. We're running to the most beautiful ladies in St. Louis!" he replied. The girls giggled again.

"Where's Ma?" Willie asked nervously.

"In the parlor feeding Papa," Sarah replied. "Why? What're you two fixing to do?"

"Nothin'..." Willie mumbled.

"We're headin' to New Orleans!" Jess exclaimed. "You girls wanna come?"

"New Orleans!" the girls cried in unison.

"Yup! And we're gonna strike it rich, too. Why, with our profits, we'll cloak ye beauties in velvet and pearls, bathe ye in the finest scents of the Orient, pop sweets in yer mouth with one hand, and fan ye with the other, we'll..."

Willie poked Jess in the ribs. "Jessie!"

"Huh?" Jess replied, puzzled.

"I was hoping we could slip outta town quiet-like. You tell these gossips and all St. Louis will know about it within hours."

"Willie!" the girls protested.

"Willie, why would you say such a nasty thing about us?" Sarah exclaimed indignantly.

"Yeah, Willie," Judy added demurely, "and maybe we'll join you. I always wanted to visit New Orleans." She suddenly grew worried. "You boys aren't going to move there permanent, are you?"

"Like I was sayin'," Jess began.

"All right," Willie interrupted. "You tell 'em all our secrets while I talk to Ma." Willie heard Jess excitedly continue his story as he closed the door behind him.

"I thought I heard you out there, Willie," his mother called out from the table where she was sewing together pieces of a quilt. "Who were you with? It wasn't that Jess, was it?"

"Yeah, it's Jess."

Jenny tried to keep back a frown, "Look, Willie." She proudly held up the fragment of the quilt. "Do you like it? I am making it for you. That old quilt of yours is getting ratty and it'll be getting cold soon."

"Yeah, that's pretty, Ma. Thank you." He moved over in front of his father sitting at the table and stared into his vacant eyes.

"Lord Almighty, I try," Jenny complained, "but he seems to get skinnier everyday."

"Ain't he eating?"

"Isn't he eating!" she corrected then sighed. "I just do not know what to do. It is such a strain." She dabbed at a tear.

"Ma?" Willie began hesitantly. "I've got something to talk to you about."

"What?" Jenny exclaimed worriedly as she sat down. "What have you done?"

"Oh, nothing, Ma," Willie said quickly. "Don't worry. I am not in trouble." Jenny breathed a deep sigh of relief. "It's just. Well, Jess and I have a great plan to get…" he rejected using the word rich, "get respectable again."

"You sound like your father," Jenny said with ill-concealed bitterness.

"Mama, if we can pull this off, we'll be sitting pretty for years."

"I am listening." Willie hurriedly explained their plan, leaving out any mention of Sharon. Jenny's face grew tauter as she listened.

"Willie," she said quietly as he finished, "I am happy and proud that you are trying to ameliorate our situation. But have you considered the dangers of your plan? You've heard of the river pirates and Indians haunting the Mississippi between here and New Orleans. And what of the river itself? You boys don't know anything about the twists and turns of the Mississippi. You say it will take a month down and three months back. Do you honestly think that you could make it all the way to New Orleans past all those dangers with your lives and the furs intact, sell them to a scrupulous merchant, buy adequate supplies, and then somehow pole up that powerful current back home?"

"Well…there are a few settlements along the way. And we'd both have our rifles and a pistol or two. And…" he suddenly noticed how gray his mother had become. "Are you all right, Mama?" he asked worriedly.

"I am just feeling worn out," she replied wearily. "All our financial troubles, your father, and now this…this scheme of yours. It's all too much."

"But, Ma, this could change everything!" Willie pleaded.

"Willie, the answer is no," she said determinedly.

"But, Ma…"

"No! And that's final."

Five

Willie and Jess clung to branches high in an elm overhanging a steep Mississippi bluff. Gusts of wind tugged at them and tousled their hair as they gazed out at the huge clouds billowing across the deep blue sky, at the collage of scarlet, yellow, and orange blazing in the woods on either bank, at the storm-swelled current surging below.

"Getting a mite chilly," Jess said as he huddled within his buckskin coat. "Betcha there'll be frost again tonight."

"Frost…that's certain," Willie said softly. Colder and colder, he reflected. Yup, Sharon's got more distant ever since I told her I couldn't take her downriver to New Orleans. Haven't made love since and barely kiss. Don't slip out during the week like she used to and only go walking after church on Sunday. What's she want from me?

"Gonna be a damn cold winter, I am a-thinkin'," Jess added.

"Where is she?" he demanded, annoyed.

"Huh? Hell, hold yer horses, Willie!" Jess cautioned. "Sharon'll be 'long directly. Can't be more 'an a bell or so past noon. Ain't a woman alive that knows how ta keep hours. They jus' see time different from men, is all. Kinda like Injuns in that way. Injuns think a' life as seasons not hours. Wimmin're much the same," he added. "And it don't do no good ta hurry 'em. Jus' fires 'em up."

"Maybe I shoulda tagged 'long to church after her."

Jess grimaced in amusement. "Damn, boy. Ye are one lovesick pup, ain't ye? Anybody who'd wanna slip inta church on account a' some girl's gotta be drownin' in love. And ye ain't even Catholic. Anyways, those nuns won't let those girls outta their sight and if any man pokes along those nuns'll charge him like a mother goose after a dog sniffing at her goslings."

"So where is she?"

"Hell, I don't know. I'm a mite surprised that Sharon'd pass up a chance of us lettin' her in on the hell raisin' we got planned fer devil's night. Maybe she ain't feelin' well counta wimmen sickness or maybe she couldn't slip away from the other girls or maybe she jus' forgot that she's s'posed ta meet us here. Could be anything."

"Yeah, and what if she's found some beau to walk and sweet-talk her?" He scrambled down the elm.

"Where ye headin'?"

"Back to town," he said decisively. "Ya coming?"

"Might as well," Jess said as he quickly climbed down. "Gettin' damn cold out here." He dropped the last half-dozen feet. "Hey, Willie?" Willie impatiently raised an eyebrow. "What're ye say we stop by yer store and sneak out some corn-squeezin's? Don' know why we didn't think a' that afore."

"We gotta find Sharon first," Willie stated as he slipped through the trees, crunching loudly through the thick fallen leaves and branches. "Come on."

They quickly slipped through the woods and past the farms dotting the outskirts of St. Louis then dodged through the crowded, muddy streets until they finally reached the Catholic church. Jess chuckled as Willie peeked into the deserted church. "Wadya think she's still prayin'?" he demanded.

"Nobody's there. Where could she be?"

"Maybe she turned into an angel and floated off ta heaven."

"We'll try there later," Willie asserted as he pushed his way through a half-dozen brown cattle being driven past the church by a little boy brandishing a long willow switch.

"Heaven'll be harder 'an hell ta git inta," Jess called after him and laughed. "Partic'ly fer us. Where ye headin' in the meantime?"

"To the market down at the levy," he said over his shoulder. "Come on."

Jess caught up with him. "Looks like the market's bustin' up," he observed. Farmers drove horse-drawn carts filled with corn or pigs or chickens past them. Women strolled by, chatting to each other as they embraced armloads of candles or shoes or sacks of flour. Playing "catch," muddy, ragged children darted through the traffic. The boys finally reached the levy as the last wagons were pulling out and stalls being dismantled.

"Do ya see her?" Willie asked anxiously.

"Nope, not Sharon," Jess exclaimed, "but there's Sarah and Judy 'cross the way." He waved and hollered. "Hey, girls! Over here!" The girls jerked their heads around, giggled and whispered in each other's ears, then waited as the boys dodged their way toward them through the scattering crowd.

"Ladies!" Jess greeted them merrily. "The gods have smiled upon me today to allow me the pleasure of your company," he said in an affected gentleman's accent and demeanor. "And indeed how lovely you both look. "

The girls giggled. "Yes, Willie, here are at least two angels who have not floated off to heaven."

Willie and Judy smiled sheepishly at each other. He breathed in her dimples and thick, long, blonde hair and icy blue eyes and full figure beneath her maroon capote. God, she's pretty, he marveled.

"Why, Jessie," Sarah remarked impishly, "I didn't know you could be so poetic. Where did you learn how?"

"Couple of things," he said proudly. "Reading Willie's Lord Byron and listening to the merchants when they come into the shop. But I only talk fancy for special occasions, like being with you ladies."

"What brings you boys to market?" Judy asked, as she toyed with a long, golden curl in her hair. "We figured you'd be running around out in the woods or planning mischief someplace."

Jess grinned. "Matter a' fact, Judy, we was doing both till not so long ago. But Willie feared the love of his life had done skedaddled off with another man and so we had to run plumb all the way inta town ta track her down." The smiles quickly vanished from the girls' faces.

"Something wrong?" Willie asked worriedly. "Did you see

Sharon?"

Mouths parted slightly in surprise, Judy and Sarah looked at each other, then at him. "You saw her, didn't you?" he demanded. "Who was she with?"

Sarah touched his arm. "Sharon…" She looked helplessly at Judy. "Sharon was walking…Now, Willie, you gotta promise you don't get all riled up."

"Tell me!"

"Willie!" Judy pleaded, "Please calm down. I understand how hurt you must feel…"

He shook off Sarah's hand. "Who?"

Sarah stared past him. "Rene Goutard," she said softly.

The image of Sharon and Rene together twisted Willie's mind into knots. "What?" he gasped in disbelief. "Goutard? Where are they?"

"Willie," Jess said with quiet firmness, "I know what ye wanna do, but we gotta think this through afore we act. Don't worry. We'll get the son of a bitch. But we gotta figure out the best way. We can't jus' go chargin' after him."

The anger and shame shriveled Willie with first heat, then cold. He desperately longed to dissolve into nothing until he was not even a memory.

"Willie?" Judy asked, her forehead creased with worry. "Are you all right?"

He looked into the anxious faces of Judy, Sarah, and Jess. Their stares seemed to cut through him. He shivered and opened his mouth, but nothing came out. He held up a hand, turned his back on them and walked away into the blur.

Sarah and Judy looked at each other and in low voices debated joining him. "Nope, bes' not," Jess said softly. "Times Willie likes to crawl off ta lick his wounds. Gotta leave 'im be for now. I'll trail 'im ta make sure he don't do nothing crazy."

Willie blindly zigzagged the town's streets. Fiendish revenge plots and images of Sharon's thick lips and earthy smell and husky laughter churned through his mind. "I'm gonna kill that son of a bitch," he periodically muttered. He imagined himself and Goutard stripped to the waist, fists flailing each other, with Sharon impatiently waiting for the victor to walk off with her. He felt himself trembling.

Goutard'll kill me in a stand-up fight! he admitted fearfully. How can I win? Suddenly an image flashed of his father at Bloody Island. A duel! I'll have an even chance with pistols! Suddenly a cruel smile tugged at his lips. I'll blow out his brains…or his balls!

"Willie!" Jess's deep voice cut through his daze. Wide-eyed, Willie swirled around. "Ye all right, brother?" Jess asked.

"Ye–yeah!" he sputtered. "Damn it, Jess, this is no time to get the drop on me."

"What're ye figurin' on doing?"

"Duel," he asserted quietly.

Jess nodded. "Reckon that's yer bes' chance. But maybe ye oughta parley with Sharon first. Whole thing might be a misunderstanding."

"What's to misunderstand! She left me hangin' for Goutard."

Jess cocked a thick, brown eyebrow. "Well, have ye bin ta the nunnery yet?"

Willie looked away nervously. "I been pondering it."

"Well, time's a wastin', boy, le's go!"

"Whoa!" Willie held up his palms. "I ain't quite ready yet."

Jess grinned. "Ye mean yer ready to march off ten paces with Goutard, but ain't ready ta wrassle with Sharon?"

"All right," he admitted helplessly. "Let's go." Each lost in their thoughts, they quickly headed off through the muddy streets toward the convent.

"Gettin' colder 'en hell," Jess observed, "Hardly anyone out now. Be dark in an hour or so. I wonder…" He grabbed Willie's wool coat and pointed to a figure about one hundred paces away trudging toward them, "Look who's comin'." Goutard noticed them at the same time and stopped abruptly.

They stared at each other. "What's yer plan?" Jess whispered.

Willie glanced around at the sun splayed, stubbled fields beyond the split rail fences lining the road and the convent beyond Goutard. "I dunno," he muttered. Goutard started walking slowly toward them. "What do ya think?"

"He can't take both of us," Jess said defiantly.

Willie glanced up at Jess. He was about as tall as Goutard, but lean, while the bully was stout. Willie and Jess stared warily at Goutard. "Gotta stand our ground," Willie said grimly. "Wish I spent all day loading keelboats like him."

Goutard stopped a half-dozen feet away. He pulled off his slouch hat and ran a grimy hand over his short-cropped, black hair. A cruel grin split his flushed, beefy face. "That Sharon, she sure kin kiss, now can't she, Yates?" he sneered. Willie felt his body tense and fists tighten. "Yup, Yates, ye done lost out to a real man, boy. Sharon's all mine now! What're ye gonna do 'bout it?"

"Blow yer brains out," Willie heard himself threaten.

Goutard spat a stream of tobacco juice toward Willie's feet. "With what?" he snarled. "Why, I'll tear ye in two afore ya can shit! And ye too, Baucus," he warned as he raised both fists. "I'll kick yer ass 'cross the Mississippi if ye try anything!"

"Don' be so sure, Goutard," Jess said fiercely as he stepped forward. "Ye've no 'cause ta..."

Suddenly Goutard charged them. Jess dodged to the side while Willie hurled himself at Goutard. They punched wildly at each other; Willie watched blood spurt from Goutard's nose then felt a fist slam twice against his cheek and another against his stomach, doubling him over in pain. Goutard grabbed Willie, rammed a knee into his groin, then madly began battering him with his fists. Willie dropped to the ground, moaning and grasping for breath. Jess threw himself at Goutard and smashed him into the mud. He shoved his knee into Goutard's backbone, locked a powerful forearm across Goutard's throat, and pulled up. Goutard's face reddened, eyes bulged, and arms flailed as he tried desperately to shake Jess off. Then he gripped his huge, powerful hands on Jess's arm and slowly began to pry it loose.

Willie slowly raised himself on his hands and knees. "Don' let 'im go!" he gasped.

Jess felt the strength quickly draining from his body. "Help!" he hollered. "I can't hold on..."

Willie struggled to his feet, "All right, let 'im go!" he cried hoarsely. "I'll take the son of a bitch!" He swayed and started gagging.

"He'll kill us!" Jess shouted, "Goddamn it! Kick his teeth in!" A surge of desperate power suddenly swept through Jess. "You bastard, Goutard!" he raged as he dug his knee harder into Goutard's backbone and pressed his forearm tighter against his neck, "Give in, goddamn it!" Goutard's fingers weakened and mouth gurgled then his body suddenly grew limp. Jess felt his forearm savagely jerk up Goutard's neck; felt it snap against his chest.

"Oh, God!" Jess hollered as he sprang to his feet. "What've ah done!"

"Is he dead?" Willie groaned as he sank to his knees and started retching.

"Ah don' know!" Jess cried. "He ain't movin'. Ah think ah busted his neck!" He shot glances up and down the road. "What're we gonna do? What if somebody saw us or comes?"

Willie stared. "Goutard's dead?"

"What're we gonna do?" Jess demanded again desperately.

"I don' know. We gotta hide 'im."

"Where?"

"I don' know. Behind the fence."

"They'll hang us!" Jess cried.

Willie's eyes widened. "Hang…" A image flashed through his mind of a black-hooded hangman tightening a noose around his neck and someone shouting, Let him drop! "No! We gotta run!"

"Where?" Jess demanded.

"I don' know. Downriver. New Orleans. Come on!" Willie shouted as he grabbed one of the bully's arms and Jess the other, and they began dragging him through the mud toward the fence. They struggled to lift Goutard over then dropped him on the other side. Panting, muddy, Willie and Jess stared down at his still body.

"Ah didn't mean ta kill 'im!" Jess's voice trembled. "It all happened so fast. Ah didn't mean ta kill 'im!"

Willie put his hand on Jess's shoulder. "I know. We'll get outta this somehow." Anger suddenly fired Willie, "Goddamn it!" he wailed. "Why'd Sharon hafta leave me and run off with Goutard? Why'd we hafta run into the son of a bitch! Why'd he hafta die! It don't make no sense!"

Willie gazed at the flames dancing and devouring the logs piled in the fireplace. The fire and rum tingled warmth throughout his body and dissolved his thoughts into tiny, drifting clouds. He slowly brought the mug to his lips and swallowed. The mouthful of rum burned down his throat and into his stomach. He sighed heavily and slowly turned his head toward Hank and Jess sitting solemnly in battered hickory chairs beside him. They seemed far away, like in a dream. He felt oddly secure.

The wind whispered outside and pushed against the door, reminding him of the nightmare in the field north of town.

Hank slowly shook his head. "Ye boys done got yerselves in a fix this time. Yer jus' lucky nobody saw ye. Damn lucky. But somebody'll spot his body tomorrow and put two and two together and then…You boys gotta be downriver afore daybreak," he quietly asserted. "New Orleans is yer bes' bet. Ifin ye kin slip off with a pirogue and paddle like hell fer a month then sign on a ship at New Orleans for the far ends of the earth…"

"Ah didn't mean ta kill him," Jess said softly as he stared into the flames.

"New Orleans," Willie whispered. "Ends of the earth." He felt himself rise and heard himself say, "I gotta see my folks first."

Hank tugged at his beard and nodded. "Hurry back, Willie. You boys gotta long road ahead a' ye."

Willie stumbled through the cold dark streets. Gusts of frigid wind cut into his face and swirled around his body. Shivering, he paused to marvel at the Milky Way glowing across the black sky. A meteor streaked briefly from the west. "Ends of the earth," he muttered sadly, then trudged on.

He hesitated outside the parlor window, listening to the murmur of his mother and Sarah talking within. What am I gonna tell 'em, he wondered.

He imagined his mother's anger, shame, and bitter denunciations. Then images of Sharon's coquetry and Goutard's still, muddy body flashed through his mind. What a fool I've been, he lamented.

He slowly extended his hand to the front door, turned it, then opened the door with a creak.

His mother and Sarah gasped. "Willie!" Sarah cried as he stood staring at them from the open door. "You scared us! Well, close the door and come inside before we catch the death of cold!"

"Where have you been, Willie!" his mother admonished as he closed the door and walked over to the fireplace. "We ate long ago and your supper's cold. And what happened to your cheek? It's all bruised. Have you been fighting?"

His father sat, as always, in his maple armchair before the fire. Someone had wrapped a quilt around him. Drool trickled from a corner of his mouth. "Mama, there's something I gotta tell you," he said quietly as he looked into his father's vacant gray eyes.

"Oh, Willie," she pleaded, "what now?"

He turned to them. "Mama...Sarah..." They stared anxiously at him. "I'm leaving tonight. I gotta get downriver."

"What did you do?" his mother cried as she rose and hurried to him. "What are you saying?"

"I...Jess...We got in a fight," he muttered and looked away.

"With Goutard?" Sarah asked hurriedly.

"Yes."

"But why do you have to leave?" his mother's voice was heavy with dread.

"He's..."

Sarah's mouth dropped open. "Did you kill him?"

He shook his head no and raised his hands in exasperation. "No...I didn't...but we gotta leave. I gotta grab some things and get downriver fast as possible."

"Why?" his mother cried. "What shame have you brought upon us now?"

"Nothing. It was a fair fight is all I'm saying." He suddenly felt exhausted. He sat down on the oak floor and hugged his knees. "Can't you just help me for a change?" he asked wearily.

Jenny shook her head in bewilderment, "Well, where are you going? How are you getting there? How long are you going to stay? And what are you going to do when you get there?" she said as rationally as possible.

"We're going to New Orleans by pirogue but I don't know for how long or what we'll do. I gotta get some things."

"If your mind's made up, Willie, so be it," his mother said with heavy resignation, "Now you rest and Sarah and I will gather your belongings. Sarah, you wrap up the rest of that ham while I tend to his clothes and blankets."

Sarah nodded. "Don't worry, Willie," she said quietly. "Everything will be all right." They lit candles and hurried off.

Willie stared up into his father's eyes which seemed almost buried inside his gaunt face. "You understand what's happening, Pa?" he demanded. "I'm leaving. Maybe for good." A spasm of anger shook him.

"I never was good enough for you, was I, Pa? I always fell short in your eyes, didn't I?" He jabbed the air with his fist in front of his father's nose. "Well, now you can't even see or hear...or if you can, you're not letting on." Tears filled his eyes. He hugged his father's feet and began to sob, "Oh, God, why are you so silent?"

Sarah quietly walked over to him and put her arm around his shoulder. "Willie, what really happened?" The sobs and cries heaved within his body. He turned to her and they hugged each other tight. Sarah gently rubbed his back, "It's all right, Willie. Don't worry. Everything'll be all right." Jenny entered the room and set down an armload of blankets and clothing. Perplexed, she frowned at her children. How grown they look, she thought, and how childish they are. Noticing his mother, Willie quickly wiped off his tears and struggled to his feet. "Take five of the beaver packs," she stated coldly. "It'll be a gamble but if you can sell them you might be able to retrieve some of our fortune, if not our honor." He nodded. "Well, you need to take the wagon."

He nodded again, grabbed the rifle, powder horn, and shot bag out of the corner, and hurried out to the barn. Jenny and Sarah pulled on their heavy wool coats, picked up the ham, clothing, and blankets, and followed him. Speaking little, they quickly hitched up the ox then dragged five one hundred pound beaver packs out of the storeroom and onto the wagon. Exhausted, their breath steaming in the cold air, they leaned against the wagon.

"Sarah, I'm just too worn out to accompany you," Jenny said. "Do you think you can bring back the wagon from the levy by yourself?"

"Don't worry, I can, Mama," Sarah replied.

"I best be going, Ma," Willie stated.

Jenny nodded. "Give me a hug." They embraced gingerly then he and Sarah climbed up into the wagon seat. "Stay out of trouble, Willie," Jenny demanded wearily. "And try to come back soon. We need you."

"I will," he said quietly. "Goodbye, Mama." He prodded the ox with a stick and they slowly rolled off. Jenny watched them a moment then slowly shuffled back into the house. "Ma sure looks old, doesn't she?" he declared sadly.

"I'm worried about her," Sarah whispered as she huddled against him.

"Sarah…"

"He's really dead, isn't he?" she asked quietly.

"I didn't do it," he replied desperately, "it was an accident."

"I hated Goutard as much as you did, Willie," Sarah stated grimly. "Everyone hated him. I'm glad he's dead…But when can you come home?" she pleaded.

"I don't know, Sarah," he replied. "Maybe not for a long time." She began to weep quietly.

An occasional dog barked as the wagon creaked through the deserted streets. The church bells struck nine as they finally reached the blacksmith shop. Willie jumped down and knocked softly at the door. "Who's there!" Hank demanded from inside.

"It's me. Hurry!"

Hank opened the door and he and Jess stood there peering out into the darkness. "Willie," Jess said excitedly, "he ain't there!"

"What?"

"We went out to bury him after you left, but he ain't there. Somebody musta carted him off. They may already be lookin' fer us!"

"Well, hurry then!"

Coats already on, Hank and Jess carried out provisions and loaded them into the wagon. Hank, as he squeezed his shoulder, said, "Good luck, son. Ye take care of yerself. Ye, too, Willie. Jessie, ye write me to the Yates's house and Sarah'll read yer letters to me, won't ye, Sarah?"

"I promise, Mr. Baucus," Sarah replied.

"Well, hurry now," Hank warned. "Surprised we ain't heard any doings account a' the body being found."

Willie prodded the ox and the wagon slowly rolled off toward the river. They got out atop the levy and the boys strained against the wooden hand brake as the ox skidded down the steep, muddy slope. A dozen keelboats and half-dozen pirogues were tied up along the deserted wharf.

"Looks like we got our pick," Jess whispered. "Bes' grab the biggest to haul all these pelts. How 'bout this one?"

"Looks like the longest," Willie replied. "But it's hard to tell. Night's darker 'an pitch."

Jess jumped in the prow and scrambled down to the stern. "Dry as a bone," he observed, "and there's already poles and paddles in it. We kin use the ones I brought fer extras." They strained to load their provisions and pelts into the pirogue while Sarah tended the ox. "Colder 'an hell," Jess complained as they dragged in the last beaver pack. "We're gonna freeze our asses off on that river."

"Not gonna be half as cold as swinging from a gallows," Willie replied.

Jess chuckled. "Ye gotta point there, Willie. You push off and I'll take the stern. Take care yerself, Sarah."

"Bye, Jess. You, too," she replied quietly.

"Well, Sarah..." Willie said sadly.

She hugged him tight.

"When can I see you again?" she sobbed.

"I'll write. I'll...you take care of yourself and Mama."

Sarah sniffed back her tears. "I will," she promised.

He untied the rope bonding the pirogue to the wharf, hopped into the prow, grabbed a pole, and digging it into the soft river bottom, he pushed off into the current. "Sarah?" he called as he turned the pirogue parallel to shore.

"Yes, Willie?"

"Tell Judy..." he hesitated as he fumbled to exchange the pole for a paddle. Sarah and the ox and wagon were shadows against the dark bank. "Tell Judy that I'll come back to her, too, someday."

Sarah's giggles erupted from the void. "I promise. I love you, Willie. 'Bye."

The boys dipped their paddles deep into the Mississippi and pulled hard toward midstream. Willie glanced back over his shoulder toward St. Louis but Sarah, the wharf, and town had already dissolved into the moonless night.

"Think we'll make it, Willie?" Jess's deep voice cut through the darkness behind him.

Willie twisted around and peered over the beaver packs at Jess's black form silhouetted against the star-strewn sky. The pirogue glided and rocked gently with the powerful current. He tried to sound brave but his voice croaked hoarsely, "Or die trying!"

The Mississippi was crowded from St. Louis to the Ohio River. The boys hailed passing keelboats, traded shots of whiskey with local toughs at hamlet taverns, tied up at farms for buttermilk and biscuits, and listened nervously to tales of river pirates and scalp-hunting Chickasaws haunting the lower Mississippi. Beyond the Ohio, fewer homesteads appeared around each bend until there was nothing but endless wilderness. The river got wilder, cutting immense horseshoe loops through the forest, submerging it into swamps and low, wooded islands. Days of steady paddling stretched into weeks; aching muscles hardened; skin toughened against cold drizzle and mist; eyes sharpened to pick out sawyers and sandbars; fears dissolved into the river's rhythm, into boisterous horseplay and the thrill of escape, into shared dreams of far-off lands and buxom coquettes and pockets bulging with silver; nights broken by occasional pangs of homesickness or savage nightmares. They found sandy beaches to fill their kettle with mallards, catfish, turkey, and venison, then lay their exhausted bodies.

Autumn lingered then became late summer, frosty nights, balmy; colored leaves a waxy green; mosquitoes reemerged to buzz their ears and prick their flesh at night. Days passed with the boys feeling as if they were the last humans on earth. Then a keelboat would grow from a speck downriver and slowly loom larger until the boys shot past it as the rivermen's curses and groans filled the air. One hot afternoon they passed a burned-out flatboat stranded on a beach littered with naked, blackening bodies. The bodies were too far off to tell whether they were ripped by arrows or rifle balls, and the boys were too frightened to go closer.

The following day they paddled silently around a bend and almost rammed a canoe from which three startled Indians dragged fishing nets. Willie and Jess hastily grabbed and aimed their rifles while the Indians paddled furiously for shore. "If they were painted, we'd a' shot 'em!" the boys later maintained.

Then one day they spotted a smoke column drifting into the sky far downstream, and whooped and hollered when it turned out to be from a chimney rather than a campfire. Beaming and babbling about "homecooking," they tied up the pirogue and hurried across the stump-filled clearing toward the shack. Suddenly, in the doorway appeared a wizened dwarf cradling a shotgun. In a high-pitched voice he shouted angrily at them in a language they had never heard. Perplexed, they stopped and stared, then turned and ran when he fired over their heads. Downstream they passed other farms that, with endless muscle and sweat, had been carved out of the forest; they did not stop unless someone waved them in.

Natchez was as bawdy, violent, and seductive as tales had told. From the distance Natchez seemed like St. Louis. Whitewashed homes and warehouses lined the banks and bluff top. A score of keel and flatboats crowded the wharf. Scores of men hauled boxes or rolled barrels. Wagons and teams of mules waited patiently or were driven through the throng. Curses exploded in a dozen languages. A well-dressed crowd of men surrounded the slave block where a tall, skinny gentleman in a rust-colored top hat and tails solicited bids for the huge, surly Negro beside him. Urchins darted through the crowd trying to steal what they could.

As soon as Willie and Jess leaped ashore and tied up the pirogue, they were charged by a dozen men—white, mulatto, and half-breed—wearing patched clothes and slicked-back hair, who elbowed and shoved each other to trumpet the pleasures of the rickety whorehouses they represented across the street from the wharf. Bewildered by the jostling onslaught, the boys scrambled back into their pirogue, fearing to leave it, lest someone lift their beaver. Warehouse prices were high, they learned, five silver dollars a day for the packs and an extra dollar to watch the pirogue—money the boys had planned for a tavern bed, whiskey, and maybe a painted lady. They waved off the pimps and played two warehouse clerks against each other until one agreed to store the packs and watch the pirogue for three dollars a day.

After storing their gear, the boys sauntered through the crowd and into a tavern where they bought a bottle of whiskey and four helpings each of greasy pork and dumplings, while cardsharps and whores tried to hustle them.

Stuffed, slightly drunk, Willie reached for his pouch to pay the bill and realized in horror that it had been picked. "I've been robbed!" he gasped, and grabbed tightly by the wrist the fat whore who had been running her hands over his body. "Where is it?" Willie shouted. "That was all the money I've got!"

Jess struggled drunkenly to his feet. "What? What?" he blurted, "the whore lifted yer wad?"

The bouncer was six and a half feet of mostly muscle, and his assistant was only slightly smaller. Willie released the whore's wrist as they towered before him.

"There's the door!" the bouncer commanded, pointing a huge arm toward the entrance.

"But she stole my money!" Willie pleaded. "It's all I got!"

The bouncer grinned down into Willie's face. "A fool and his money are soon parted, boy. Now git!"

The boys looked helplessly at each other, shrugged, and shuffled toward the door as laughter echoed behind them. "What're we gonna do?" Willie demanded angrily as they emerged into the crowded street. "We shoulda brought our rifles. They wouldn't a' robbed us if we had our rifles."

"I don't know, Willie," Jess shook his head in frustration. "That crowd'd a' robbed a regiment of regulars blind. Ain't nothing we could a' done. I got seven dollars and we still got the packs. Let's sell one here stead a' waiting fer New Orleans."

"What!" Willie said incredulously, "You heard what packs're fetching here. Three hundred fifty dollars when we might get four hundred and fifty in New Orleans."

"Hell, Willie, it's a hundred better here than in St. Louis and we still got another week a' paddling 'head a' us. 'Sides, you heard 'em talking a' rumors the British was gonna try ta take New Orleans. Price a' beaver'll drop like a rock if it be true."

"Maybe yer right," he conceded bitterly, "but my ma told me I gotta send back a fortune and I can't do it if I sell out at the first asking price."

"And another thing," Jess said quietly. "If the British is gonna attack New Orleans, we can't ship out. We'll be trapped like rats in a barrel if the law's on our trail."

The thought was sobering. "Well…" Willie pondered the choices. "If New Orleans is captured, we'll just hafta buy horses and ride the trace to Tennessee then maybe head on east. Be like a needle in a haystack for the law to find us even if they knew which direction we went. But maybe you're right. Maybe we should sell at least a pack now…" He looked at Jess's greasy, torn clothes and short, scraggly brown beard then down at his own.

He chuckled, "Least we can do is get a bath and shave."

They spent the rest of the afternoon haggling with merchants over a beaver pack, and finally settled with a Spaniard for three hundred dollars worth of calico, paints, hairbrushes, nails, gunpowder, lace, and rum, and sixty silver dollars. By chance they literally stumbled over an old, grizzled keelboat captain named Beasly they recognized from St. Louis, who had curled up behind some flour barrels on the wharf. He blinked and cursed when they woke him, then spent almost an hour spitting tobacco juice into the Mississippi and telling river tales before agreeing to take on the shipment for forty silver dollars.

Then the boys, Captain Beasly, and several of his boatmen celebrated the deal with a bottle of whiskey at a tavern. Late that night, drunk and exhausted, the boys finally staggered off to find a bed.

The inns were all overcrowded with rivermen and merchants, but they finally found a dilapidated house where, for one dollar each, they could climb wearily into bed on either side of a garishly tattooed mulatto who was missing his left ear. The mulatto snored away the night in a drunken stupor, his rhythmic grunts only temporarily broken by the frequent elbows Willie and Jess jabbed into his ribs. Red-eyed, hungover, and cotton-mouthed, the boys stumbled out into the already busy streets early the next morning.

Retrieving their pirogue, packs, and gear from the warehouse, they quickly paddled downriver, swearing hell would freeze over before they ever returned to Natchez.

The boys marveled at the vast cotton, corn, and cattle plantations spread along each river bank from Natchez to New Orleans. Most people they stopped to talk to were friendly, but the rumors of an impending British invasion grew more alarming the farther down-stream they paddled.

"Turn around and head back before it's too late!" people warned while mournfully shaking their heads. "The British'll be in New Orleans before Christmas, and they'll burn it to the ground like they did Washington!"

"We'll take our chances," the boys would mutter nervously before returning to the pirogue. "Trouble ahead, trouble behind," Jess often declared. "Can't seem ta shake it." As much from fear as sport, the boys sometimes fired at huge alligators and snapping turtles basking on the muddy shores. But at night the reptile monsters and hordes of redcoats mingled with Rene and black-hooded hangmen to crawl after them in their dreams.

Around noon on the sixth day after leaving Natchez, they paddled around a bend to gaze dumbstruck at New Orleans's wide skyline poking above the long levy. At least fifty boats of all kinds crowded the shore, including a steamboat, the first they had ever seen, while hundreds of stevedores and soldiers labored or strolled on shore among thousands of cotton bales, and hogsheads of sugar, tobacco, molasses, wine, and whiskey. Clouds of seagulls swooped and squealed over garbage drifting on the river. After eagerly tying up the pirogue at a wharf piling they charged up the levy and stared wide-eyed beyond at the crowded streets and brick houses with lace iron balconies. They shouted excitedly and pounded each other's backs in disbelief at having paddled through a thousand miles of mostly wilderness to a city more beautiful and wondrous than their wildest fantasies. Reluctantly, Jess returned to guard the pirogue while Willie asked his way to the warehouse whose owners Captain Beasly had sworn might not cheat them. Willie and one of the partners, Kyle Macintosh, a short, skinny Irishman with a bulbous nose, pockmarked face, orange ponytail and handlebar mustache, and gold earrings, slipped back along the crowded wharves to the pirogue. They haggled for over an hour, with Macintosh repeatedly dismissing the "bloody moth-eaten pelts" as "damn near worthless," and warning that prices had shot sky-high and beaver well-deep with a British fleet in the Gulf.

"Goddamn it!" Willie muttered as he angrily shook Macintosh's hand. "We coulda done better in Natchez."

"Deal's sealed now, Willie," Jess muttered back as he smiled wanly at Macintosh and slapped him on the back.

"You're getting the best price possible, laddie," Macintosh clucked soothingly, "fifteen hundred dollars worth of supplies and a hundred dollars in silver! Four hundred dollars for each hundred pound pack a' poor pelts! I must be bloody mad to pay such prices." He grinned. "Ye lads are tough bargainers."

Willie glared down at Macintosh, "But the amount of supplies is really only half what we got a year ago for the same price! It's like you got two packs for nothing!"

Macintosh's face flushed and fists tightened, "Did I send that British fleet to the Mississippi and army a' bastard lobsterbacks toward New Orleans!" he angrily demanded. "Huh? Well, laddie, speak up! Now did I?"

Willie shrugged his shoulders. "Reckon not," he reluctantly admitted.

"I've gotta sit on these bloody pelts till Jackson sends that pack a' English dogs yelping back to Britain with their tails up their arses! And if he don't and the English army marches in, they may steal me blind like they did me mother country!" Macintosh glared fiercely at each of them. "Ye lads can run back to ye mothers in St. Louis! Where kin ah run? Huh? Ye ever think a' that? Why…" he pondered, "ah oughta jus' fergit the whole notion a' trading with ye." He nodded his head slowly, "Jus' fergit it."

"No, wait!" Willie exclaimed. "We done shook on it."

Macintosh squinted up at Willie. "All right now, ahm a' man a his word. Deal's a deal and it's done." He wagged a finger in Willie's face, "But no more a' ye foolishness, laddie."

"Sorry," Willie said sheepishly as he extended his hand to Macintosh, who clasped it vigorously. "Just disappointed at the price is all. I understand your situation and 'preciate your dealing with us."

Willie glanced nervously at Jess. "Ain't no ships at all sailing out, Kyle?" he asked nonchalantly.

"None since late November. Come on, lads, we'll draw the papers and ye supplies." He leered impishly. "Then celebrate with a bottle a' whiskey or two."

Less than an hour later, jostled by mostly drunken American backwoods and river men, the three were trading shots at the crowded counter of the Mississippi Bottom tavern.

Macintosh's pink face glowed more with each shot. He laughed sharply. "Ye lads better enjoy it while ye can. Rumor has it General Jackson's gonna declare martial law and herd up every last jack, lad to granpappie, into the militia." He pulled a folded sheet of paper from his coat pocket and waved it in their faces. "General Jackson issued this proclamation this morning. Where was that line?" His eyes scanned the tiny type on the paper. "If the general can fight as hard as he writes, he'll knock the British all the way back ta England. Ah, here it is!" He cleared his throat. "Jus' listen ta this: 'The safety of the district entrusted to the protection of the general must and will be maintained with the best blood of the country; and he is confident that all good citizens will be found at their posts, with their arms in their hands, determined to dispute every inch of ground with the enemy…the general…will separate our enemies from our friends—those who are not for us are against us, and will be dealt with accordingly.' Well, laddies, ye'll be soon hearing British balls whizzing past yer ears and feel British steel twisting in yer guts!"

Jess snorted, "Yeah, well what about ya? Ya gonna hole up in that warehouse of yers?"

Macintosh's slouched, skinny body snapped straight. He jutted his face into Jess's. "Watch ye tongue, laddie! I'll be marching off with the rest of the lads a' the Louisiana Blues. They's mostly Irishmen," he stated proudly, then added, "the whole town's turned out to fight under the colors of the Battalion of New Orleans. Everybody's joined their own, the Creoles with the Dragoons, Carabinier, Chauseur, and Volunteer Rifle companies. Them lads 'ere tougher 'en they look. Even got some a' Napoleon's veterans amongst 'em. Then the free niggers is formed into the Battalion a' Free Men a' Color."

Willie whistled imagining the different reactions of Pa and Uncle Jake to the news. "Ye think they'll fight?"

Macintosh nodded grimly. "Fought already few years back. Helped put down a slave rising."

"Nigras fighting Nigras?" Jess asked incredulously.

"They'll fight like the rest a' us," Macintosh noted grimly. "Quarter a' New Orleans is free niggers." The boys stared in wonder.

Willie turned to Jess. "Reckon we oughta fight," he stated. Jess nodded. "Ain't no Missouri companies here, is there?"

Macintosh took another shot and belched. "Naw, but there's two regular regiment's, the 44th and 7th, that 'ere begging fer cannon fodder."

"We don' wanna be in nothing permanent," Jess explained. "We jus' wanna git inta the fight and out quick as possible."

"Well, then, lads, there's Coffee's Tennesseans. Ye kin ask them ta take ye in, and if they don' want ye, I kin maybe talk the Blues inta taking ye, even though ye ain't Irish or even from New Orleans," Macintosh chuckled merrily, "or Lafitte's pirates may let ye take a hand at their batteries, or maybe the Choctaws'll let ye raise a scalping knife aside 'em! And there's other companies forming in town and coming in from the country. Don' worry, lads, ye'll have plenty chance ta fight when the time comes!" Macintosh glanced out the dirty tavern window at the darkening street. "Good Lord, lads! I gotta be runnin'!" He leered up at them. "Gotta Creole beauty from a rich family ah bin courting, and ah gotta elbow aside me rivals if ah want half a chance. Could be parta high society someday, lads. Bin dreaming a' having me own coach and a big nigger driver to carry me 'bout the city to all the soirees and quadrilles. And the Quadroon Ball!" He breathed in deeply and sighed. "All beautiful women with a touch a' nigger in 'em jus' falling all over ye ta make 'em ye wife or mistress! Now that's living, lads, and it ain't far off fer me. Ye rest awhiles in the city and if ye wits last, and ye brains ain't blown out by a lobsterback or jealous husband, ye'll git yer share a' money and beauties. Till Jackson's army strolled inta town there was more wimmen than men, and the pickings were easy. It'll be easy pickings again once those boys go home." Macintosh smiled broadly and vigorously shook each boy's hand. "I'll see ye lads at the warehouse tomorrow. Stay out late as ye want. The nigger watchman Baptiste'll let ye in. Good huntin'!" he winked then turned and slipped out through the crowd.

Jess clapped Willie on the back. "Ya 'eard 'im, Willie. We're young, the night's young, and there are hundreds a' beautiful women out there jus' waitin ta fall inta our arms! Le's git!" They pushed their way into the dark, muddy street. "Which way?" Jess demanded.

"Tonight or tomorrow?" Willie asked anxiously. "I know we've pondered this day and night since we lit out, but do you still reckon the odds are no one would be trailing us? Ye really think we oughta stay in New Orleans and join up for the fight?"

"I don' hanker paddling up current ta Natchez ta the trace then back East, even if Goutard's kin weren't followin' us and ifin they was, they'd pick us off the river. And like Kyle said, the redcoats may take Mobile, so that route's probably cut off. If an' when Ol' Hickory beats the British, the sea'll be open and then we'll hop a ship an' be free men sailing ta the far ends of the earth! And if we help Jackson lick the British, we'll be heroes! And the wimmen everywhere'll swoon inta our arms and men'll buy us round after round, an' we'll live the life a' Byron like we always said we would."

"Reckon yer right," Willie said thoughtfully, then brightened. "Welp, the way tonight is straight into the heart of the city and the heart of a couple a' beautiful, willing women!" They stumbled through the rutted streets past knots of crowded, drunken sailors or soldiers singing or shouting, rows of brick houses with floor length, shuttered windows and grilled balconies, beggars pleading with grimy arms outstretched, some rotten with leprosy, crowded noisy cafes, and an occasional streetlight smokily burning whale oil. The odors of excrement and spicy gumbo mingled in the air.

"Where we headin'?" Jess suddenly asked. "Ladies or whores?"

"Hmmm...where we gonna meet ladies this time a' night?"

"Whores it is then," Jess replied cheerfully. "We're rich. Least kinda rich. And if fate's waitin' 'round the corner fer us with a musket ball or rope, we might as drop inta hell with smiles on our faces."

"Well, then," Willie chuckled, "we might as well dip our wicks at the best whorehouse in town. Wherever that is."

"Don' hurt ta ask. But the soldiers and wharf rats'll jus' send us ta the cheapest places. Gotta find a rich man ta ask."

"Ye think a rich man'd tell us? We sure don' look rich and maybe they jus' take older fellas. We shoulda asked Kyle."

"Too late now. Maybe we oughta jus' go ta the first whorehouse we come…"

Jess stepped in front of two men in long overcoats walking past them. "Pardon me, sirs, but my friend and I…"

"Yes, dearie," one of the men lisped. "How can we help you?" Both men giggled.

Jess looked helplessly over at Willie. "We're looking for a wh…we're looking…"

"We'd like ta meet some ladies," Willie added quickly.

"Ladies," the man repeated disdainfully. "We can't help you there. You boys are recent arrivals, aren't you? Do you need a place to stay?" he asked hopefully. "The city is so frightfully crowded and…"

"That's right nice of ye, mister," Jess replied, "but we've gotta place ta stay. We're jus' hankering fer some female companionship, ifin ye know what we mean."

"High class!" Willie added.

"Well, well now," the man sniffed. The other man giggled. "Justin, send them to *Le Cercle des Hommes*." They both giggled.

"Oh, I shouldn't, Claude. The dearies seem so innocent."

"We're not as innocent as you think," Willie asserted.

"Yes, quite…well, well, what to do. I really don't know about such things, but if you really must…Claude's brother," he linked his arm with that of the other man, "frequents *La Maison du Soleil Levant* down this side street. On the sign there's the most lovely yellow sun peeking its head up from behind green hills. Claude, don't you just love that sign? Anyway, it's…on the right…or perhaps the left…Claude?"

"I do believe the left," Claude replied impatiently. "You boys run along now. Scoot. Come along, love." Arms still linked, the men resumed their gingerly stroll down the dark street. "And if you don't like *Le Soleil*," Justin called back to them, "then by all means attend *Le Cercle des Hommes* just down the street. It has the most adorable girls in the city!" The men's giggles erupted from the dark.

"Something mighty queersome 'bout those two," Jess reflected.

"Yeah. Never heard no one talk like that before. Maybe they were English."

"Ifin they're English, what're they doing here?"

"Hell if I know. Do ye think Lord Byron talks like that?"

"Not how I pictured him." Jess affected their accent. "Come along, love, the whores are awaiting." Both laughed and trudged down the side street. After peering at the dark signboards of several cafes, they finally reached *La Maison du Soleil Levant*. They paused outside, listening to the sounds of laughter and piano music behind the thick curtains blocking the windows. "Welp, time's a wastin'!" Jess declared as his hand reached for the door knob.

"Hold on!" Willie exclaimed. "What if we git the clap!"

"Well, hmmm…" Jess pondered. "Times ah went to Lucy's down by the landing ah never got it, but…hmmm…with all the French around, chances are prob'ly a lot worse here. Well, ah heard it don' hurt much and sometimes clears out completely after a while. Kinda like gettin' a bad fever for a spell. An maybe these girls'll be clean."

"Yeah, but how do ye know?"

"Well, ahhh, hmmm…I don' rightly know," Jess said perplexed. They reflected silently for a moment.

"Jess, I never been to a…what'll…how do ye…ye know?"

Jess chuckled. "Jus' like with Sharon 'cept ye hafta pay. Wimmin's wimmen, whether they're whores or ladies."

Willie shrugged. "All right," he said reluctantly, "le's do it." He reached for the door.

"Hold on!" Jess cautioned. "We better get slicked up first." They quickly tucked in their shirttails, brushed their long hair out of their eyes, and rubbed their shoe soles on the iron mud scrapper beside the door. Jess grinned. "Glad we shaved and washed after signing the papers. Ready for love?" he demanded heartily. Willie nodded.

They stumbled into the entrance hall and stood astonished, blinking in the light of a half-dozen candelabras on tables and a chandelier hanging from the tall ceiling, at the oriental rugs, salmon-colored walls adorned with paintings of naked women sprawled across beds or bathing in streams, and the tall staircase and polished walnut banister. The music and laughter loudly seeped out from closed rooms on either side of the hall. They watched a huge man with a walrus mustache rise from a wingbacked chair and stride toward them.

The bouncer towered over them. "Gentlemen?" he demanded sternly.

The boys glanced sheepishly at each other, both feeling ashamed of their tattered clothes and youth, and wishing they had never entered. Jess sucked in his breath. "Well, we…we just come…came downriver and sold five beaver packs and we'll probably join up tomorrow and we was…were wondering…that is we heard…"

"This is a respectable establishment open to all gentlemen," the bouncer intoned gravely. "You are gentlemen, aren't you?"

Willie and Jess felt smiles tug at their mouths. Usually they would answer such a question with mock indignity—"What did you call us! Take it back!" Instead Willie replied, "Well, of course, sir. We are men of affairs from respectable families."

"The club membership fee is five silver dollars, and of course drinks and entertainment are extra." The bouncer slowly extended his palm. "Gentlemen?"

Willie reached for his pouch while Jess demanded, "How much for the drinks and entertainment?"

"Drinks are a dollar each, and the ladies will explain the entertainment fee."

Willie fished out ten silver dollars and extended his palm. The man quickly snatched and pocketed the money then ushered them into a parlor behind the staircase. A half-dozen stylishly attired middle-aged men lounged on sofas and chairs as a heavyset woman joked with them. They all looked up as the boys entered and the bouncer closed the door behind them.

The woman smiled broadly and opened her arms wide as she approached them. She was dressed in a thin, sky blue dress, cut low across her huge breasts. A string of pearls surrounded her neck and smaller strings dangled from her ears. Her hair was a deep chestnut and her plump face gaudily made up. She laughed sharply. "Come in, boys. I am Catherine, the proprietor of this establishment. Do rest your lovely bodies." She pointed them toward an empty sofa near the fireplace. "Can I get you something to drink?"

"Whiskey. Two please, ma'am," Jess muttered. Catherine hurried to the bar as the boys sat down and the men laughed at some remark. The boys squirmed nervously. Two more ladies entered and sauntered over to the men. One woman whispered something into a man's ear. He grinned, rose, and hand in hand they strolled out the door. The remaining lady began tantalizing the others with double-entendres and jokes.

"There's somethin' 'bout her, Willie," Jess whispered as Catherine returned with a large drink in each hand. Willie glanced from Jess to Catherine as she bent before them and softly caressed their thighs.

"Our establishment is quite crowded tonight. But fear not, gentlemen, one of the girls will soon be attending you."

"Are we behind them all?" Willie asked.

Catherine laughed. "No, sugar, some of the men are just here for the fine conversation."

"Do you…" Jess stammered.

Catherine stared into Jess's eyes and looked him up and down. She said thoughtfully, "Not anymore. Well, only for extremely privileged guests…I haven't seen you boys before. You're not from New Orleans, are you?"

"St…St. Louis," Willie replied as he swallowed a large gulp of whiskey.

"I was born in Nashville," Jess said warily, watching for Catherine's reaction. Catherine's smile faded and she drew back her hands from their thighs. "Nashville…" she said softly.

"Have you ever been there?" Willie asked.

Catherine's eyes narrowed as she searched Jess's face. "And just what might be you boys' names?" Stony faced, Jess stared down into his lap.

"My name's Willie and this is…" He glanced at Jess then hesitated. Jess placed his drink on an end table and struggled to his feet.

"I think…Willie…we bes' be going."

"Yes," Catherine's face tightened as she stepped back. "Yes, I believe you should."

Jess hurried to the door. Confused, Willie followed him out and into the entrance hall. The bouncer rose and barred their path. "Leaving so soon, gentlemen?" he demanded.

Catherine's voice cut behind them. "It's all right, Henry, let them go."

The boys pushed open the door and stumbled out into the dark street. Jess stopped and looked back at the mansion.

"Jessie," Willie asked softly. "Do you think…?"

Jess shook his head slowly. He stared at Willie. "It's been ten years…She looks…and she acted…"

"Was Catherine yer mother's name?"

"Yeah," Jess said sadly, "it was."

"Maybe it's a coincidence."

"Yeah, but what if…"

"Ye wanna ask?"

"What happens if she is?"

"She acted awful funny, like she knew ya."

"She don't wanna see me again. I'm like a ghost to her. Haunting her."

Willie poked Jess with a grimy finger. "You ain't no ghost."

Jess tried to smile. "Le's go get finished gittin' drunk."

"Show the way."

"Maybe we oughta leave New Orleans after all."

"Le's figure it out in the morning."

They trudged down the street. Groups of drunk men stumbled nosily past them and painted women called out from balconies, but they paid them no heed.

"I don' feel like gettin' laid no more," Jess admitted.

"Yeah, me neither."

Jess glanced up at a dimly lit balcony above a raucous cafe from which hung a huge purple and green striped banner. He stopped abruptly and grinned. "There's our battle flag."

Willie laughed. "How ye gonna git it?"

"Jus' hafta mosey inta the cafe and creep upstairs. Sounds like all hell's breakin' loose inside. Anyways, I am a ghost. They'll never notice."

"Hey, that's *Le Cercle des Hommes* that those fellas was tellin' us 'bout."

Three men barged out of the cafe and, arms linked, sang their way down the street. "Those fellas said we'd see the purtiest girls in town here." Jess chuckled and lightly punched Willie's shoulder. "Come on, boy, time's a-wastin'. Maybe we'll git laid after all." They pushed confidently through the door then stared in amazement at the crowd of burly stevedores, effete gentlemen, long-haired woodsmen, swarthy Spaniards, and heavily made-up women in gaudy dresses shouting, laughing, toasting and hanging all over each other.

"Wagh! Everybody's in town here!"

Willie shouted above the din. "They might not be the prettiest but they sure are the biggest wimmen in town!"

Jess laughed. "Don' worry, Willie. Yer man enough for 'em. Come on." They pushed their way through the crowd. Jess stopped to tap his finger on the backs of two tall women before him. "S'cuse us, ladies, we gotta git through." The ladies turned around. One of them had a mustache.

"*Allez-y, chéri,*" he cooed at them and stepped aside. Jess and Willie shot past.

"Jess, hold on!" Willie shouted in Jess's ear. "Somethin's mighty queersome 'bout this place."

"Yeah, ah know what ye mean! We gotta git upstairs outta this crowd. We're almost to the stairs!"

Suddenly, Willie felt someone pinch his buttocks hard. He turned to face two huge stevedores leaning against each other with sleeves rolled up over their immense, tattooed biceps, mugs of beer in their beefy hands. They laughed down in Willie's face and one of them pinched his cheek. "There's a nice little morsel for you, Jeffrey. Hey, boy, wanna join us in the orgy room!"

"Orgy?" Willie repeated, puzzled.

"Yeah, come on, boy!"

Willie jumped back from the huge hand reaching toward him and collided with someone behind him.

"Oh, goodness!" a thin elderly gentleman in knee breeches and a powdered wig screeched. "Just look what you've done to my blouse! You made me spill wine all over it. You ninny! I'll never get it out!"

"Sorry, he's after me!" Willie apologized. The stevedore's hand clamped down on his shoulder and spun him around. "Lemme go!" he shouted as he forced off the stevedore's hand, shoved the gentleman toward them, and darted after Jess. The stevedore's laughter was lost in the crowd's din.

Jess was waiting before the staircase. "Le's git outta here!" Willie shouted as he struggled free of the crowd.

"We are! Come on!" Jess turned and threaded his way up the steps past male couples embracing or talking furtively. Face grim and body tense, Willie followed. The upstairs hall was filled with groups of men drinking and laughing and waiting impatiently outside of closed doors. Jess reached the door facing the balcony and glanced nervously past Willie down the crowded hall. Several men stared at them as Jess opened the door and they both slipped outside. They both paused to breathe in the chilly night air.

"I heard tell a' men like that, but never seed 'em afore now, have ye?" Jess asked. Willie shuddered and shook his head.

"Makes ye feel kinda sick, don' it?" Jess asked. Willie nodded yes. Jess exhaled sharply and began untying one of the knots binding the flag to the grill.

"Hurry!" Willie urged as he fumbled with the other knot. Suddenly they were flooded with light as the door opened behind them.

The boys jerked fearfully around. Standing in the doorway, two greasy, bearded woodsmen grinned and peered out at them. One of them chuckled, "We saw ye boys go past and was jus' wonderin' ifin ye'd like ta join us in one a' the rooms." The boys glanced nervously at each other.

"No...thanks...we jus' wanna be left be," Jess's voice cracked as he replied.

The man chuckled again. "All right then, but ifin ye change yer minds, we'll be right down the hall in room nineteen." They closed the door and Jess immediately turned and started pulling up his side of the flag.

"My side's done. Hurry up!"

Willie fumbled with the knot. "You do it!"

Jess pulled his knife out of his sheath and cut the knot. "Don' know why ah didn't think of that before." He quickly balled up the large flag and tried stuffing it under his shirt.

Willie laughed. "Ye look like one a' 'em got ya pregnant!"

Jess grinned and peered down into the dark street. "Trouble ahead, trouble behind. Long drop," Jess pondered. "I know! One of us'll go down and the other'll throw it down ta him!"

"What!" Willie said in astonishment. "I ain't staying here alone or going down alone!"

Jess nodded. "Yeah. Know what ye mean." He slipped down the narrow balcony to its end. "Here's our escape!" he said triumphantly as he reached out his arm, grabbed a tree branch, and pulled it. "Seems strong 'nuff." He swung out, locked his legs around the branch, and began shinnying down toward the trunk. The balcony door opened and three men stumbled noisily out into the half-dark. Willie jumped for the branch and scrambled down the tree to join Jess below. Jess slapped Willie on the back. "We did it!" he shouted.

Willie laughed. "Yeah, they can drape that over yer casket at yer funeral."

Jess's grin faded. "Yeah, we gotta git."

"Where?" Willie asked wearily.

"The warehouse fer now."

Willie felt a boot prod his back. "Up an' at 'em, lads!" Macintosh's voice cut loudly into his ear. He groaned and turned over. His head felt like it was being pounded by thousands of tiny hammers.

"What..." Willie's parched throat cracked. Why'd I hafta finish that bottle with Jess and the Negro watchman last night, he silently wailed as he squinted up at Macintosh's cherubic, grinning face.

Macintosh lightly poked Jess with his boot. He held up a sheet of paper in the half-light. "Gotta special greeting to ye lads from Ol' Hickory himself."

Jess's head swayed as he struggled to sit up. "Can't this wait till a decent hour?" He massaged his temples. "I'll never drink rum agin."

Macintosh chuckled. "Ye lads do look a bit under the weather, but after ye hear the great general's latest proclamation, ye'll be bloody glad ye tied on one last drunk last night." Macintosh cleared his throat.

"Here's the long and short of it, lads. I quote: 'No persons shall be permitted to leave the city...Street lamps shall be extinguished at the hour of nine at night, after which time persons of every description found in the streets, or not in their respective houses...shall be apprehended as spies.' It's martial law, lads, jus' like I was tellin ye. Ye better join up soon as possible."

"Wouldn't want ta see ye lads swinging from a lamppost in the *Place d'armes*." The boys stared at each other and shrugged.

Shivering slightly and trying to fight off another wave of home-sickness, Willie hugged his knees to his chest and gazed across the sodden, misty fields to the British camp several hundred yards away. This was not the war he expected. Byron wrote of duels and fields of honor, not enduring continuous rain or drizzle for almost a week, or the ankle-deep mud churned up by several thousand cursing, feverish men. He wrote of castles perched atop pinnacles, not defending a chest-high mud levy behind a shallow, fetid canal. He wrote of boisterous banquets and gallant toasts, not the salt pork and wormy biscuits they daily forced down. He wrote of heroes bedecked with velvet and plumes, not the lice-ridden, tattered, grimy specters they had become.

It had started out grand enough. Willie smiled grimly as he recalled the three of them slipping through the crowded New Orleans streets to the Louisiana Blues headquarters on Dumont Street; trembling slightly before stout, triple chinned, Captain Maunsel White, who sternly looked them up and down before curtly dismissing them with a, "They'll do"; strutting the streets in their short blue jackets and black caps, winking at lovely girls in balconies and carriages; toasting each other, Old Hickory, New Orleans, America, Ireland, beautiful women of all lands and times, and virtually anything and anyone else of importance. But above all else, on December 18, two days after enlisting, the thrill of standing on tiptoes in the *Place d'armes* among the five hundred men of the Battalion of Orleans Volunteers and several thousand spectators as General Jackson, his staff, and Governor Claiborne stood in review before the cathedral.

Jackson was truly a hero worthy of Byron's pen—erect, defiant, emaciated, clad in a simple, threadbare blue uniform; his gaunt face framed by iron gray hair and a jutting jaw, sliced by a thick white scar left by a British saber thrust when he was a boy; his shoulder stiff where a pistol ball remained embedded from the last of his three duels; the victor of brilliant, ruthless campaigns against the Creeks, the deliverer of New Orleans, the vowed eternal enemy of England; a man to follow to the earth's far ends, to victory or death! As an aide read stirring addresses in French, Spanish, and English, Jackson's fierce eyes swept slowly over the ranks, seemingly trying to burn into the soul of each man to determine how brave or cowardly they were. Willie vowed to fight to his dying breath as his eyes left Jackson and drifted up the cathedral spires pointing deep into the overcast sky. Redemption! A chance to rise above all the past mistakes and foolishness and misspent enthusiasms.

He glanced at Jess, who stared listlessly at the opaque canal waters below. If only Jess hadn't heard that officer boasting of poking all the whores at *La Maison du Soleil Levant*, including Catherine. He recalled standing frozen as Jess squared off with the officer, angrily shoved him, and then both were swinging wildly. Willie and others finally managed to pull Jess and the officer apart, but, bloody, sweaty, chests heaving, they continued to curse and lunge at each other. The officer swore to press charges while Willie and Macintosh apologized profusely. Captain White finally pushed through the crowd, heard the stories, calmed the officer, and sternly rebuked Jess. He then had Jess stripped of his uniform and banished from the company. Willie quickly shed his uniform and an hour later they stood timidly before General Coffee who allowed them to join Company F of his Tennesseans. But the battle-hardened men either poked fun or ignored the "boys." Fate seemed determined to keep them outsiders.

His mind drifted back to Jackson's review. The exhilaration quickly turned to wistfulness as Jackson and the other leaders turned their backs and filed away and the review slowly broke up. Willie could have forever soaked in Jackson's silent, sublime power, the impassioned speeches, the massed, expectant bodies, the band gaily playing quadrilles, and the soaring cathedral. It all seemed over so quickly.

Then afterward, as they slipped through the milling crowd, Jess clapped him on the shoulder and merrily shouted, "Hell of a birthday celebration the ginral threw fer ye!" Celebrate? The word churned up a tangle of conflicts within Willie. Exactly eighteen years on earth. What have I done worth celebrating? Would I ever achieve greatness? Happiness? Escape? How much time was left? Would I be struck dead by a musket ball tonight or tomorrow? Die quietly in sleep sixty years hence? What's the point of it all? Suddenly the night of carousing they had planned after the review seemed absurd. An overwhelming desire surged through Willie to fly away to the most distant wilderness and wander alone there for all time.

He glanced back at Jess and said softly, "Think we'll ever truly escape?"

Puzzled, Jess frowned. "Whadya mean?"

"We're hemmed in from all sides. But even if we could sail away to the earth's far ends, it seems like something'll always be trailing us, breathing down our necks."

"Ye mean guilt? Fear?"

"That and other things."

"Yeah. See what ye mean. If only…" Jess shuddered as he recalled Goutard's limp body beneath him. "Ye git metals fer killing while defending yer country, but ye git hung fer killing while defending yerself," he lamented. "Don't make no sense."

"Even if Goutard hadn't died. If we were safe and sound back in St. Louis. Seems like somethin'd be chasing us, hangin' on our heels. Maybe the only escape is death."

Jess pondered Willie's words for a while and replied quietly, "Ye thinkin' a' callin' it quits? Like Lewis?"

Willie felt again a sliver of the numbing shock that engulfed him a half-dozen years ago when the word reached St. Louis that Meriwether Lewis, who with Clark had led an expedition to the Pacific Ocean and back and then served as governor of Missouri Territory, was dead of a seemingly self-inflicted gunshot in a lonely cabin on the Natchez Trace. It must have been murder! Why would a great hero kill himself? Once again, the soiree at Tayong's mansion on the great expedition's eve whirled through his mind.

Lewis had taken an immediate liking to Willie and displayed all the kindness and attention void in his father, and all the elegance and sophistication lacking in Jake. Willie's mind jumped two and a half years later to the thrill of joining the boisterous crowd in welcoming back the expedition as it tied up at the St. Louis wharf. Willie had whooped and Lewis winked back recognition as the crowd swept him, Clark, and the other adventurers past toward the governor's mansion. So long ago.

"No. Not like Lewis. But somehow."

"Maybe yer right," Jess replied defiantly. "Maybe the only escape is death. But at least we kin choose to die heroes 'stead a' condemned fugitives. There's somethin' in that."

"We'll die someday regardless." But when? Willie peered through the mist at the McCarty mansion several hundred yards down the line where Jackson had his headquarters. He could barely distinguish a group of officers on the balcony gazing toward the British lines. What would Jackson do? Rumors continually buzzed from one soldier to the next up and down the muddy line. Jackson would retreat his small army and burn New Orleans. Jackson would attack the enemy advance guard that night before the rest of the British army arrived. Jackson would simply wait and let the redcoats assault the Americans' massed rifles. Jackson...

The answer came that evening. Coffee and other commanders along the line assembled their men, ensured that their rifles were cleaned and primed, then led them slowly, quietly down the dark, muddy roads toward the British campfires. Company F was the last in line and the boys were sent to trudge along at the column's rear. Most men were confident, eager, relieved the uncertainty had ended. The officers ordered, "Quiet in the ranks! Close up! Close up!"

Willie tightly hugged his rifle and glanced nervously at the dark mass of men shuffling before him. He never felt more awake. Death waited ahead. It could strike anyone down. Dozens, perhaps hundreds, would die, most in lingering, terrifying torture. Shells and balls would shatter human limbs and bodies. Suddenly everything seemed precious, fleeting.

The resignation he felt that afternoon gave way to a fierce desire to live. He ached to be with his family, in their secure, snug home. Visions of Sharon and Judy spiraled through his mind. St. Louis seemed so far away, on the other side of the world, at the beginning of time. He brushed away the tears filling his eyes. Will I fight or run? he wondered. It would be so easy to slip off into the dark once the firing began. He wanted to share his fears with Jess but feared more the anger of Captain Raskin trotting alongside the column a dozen feet ahead and the contempt of the other men. Instead he kept silently repeating what Jess muttered as they marched off: "This is where we stop running!"

At exactly seven-thirty, the American sloop *Carolina* opened fire on the British lines. Screams and shouts erupted from the British camps as the shells tore through their ranks. Coffee halted the column but his men stirred restlessly. "Looks like this is it, Jessie," Willie muttered. Jess nodded.

"Steady, men, steady," Captain Raskin whispered loudly. "Quiet. Wait for the signal." Willie peered at Raskin's dark form, picturing his tall, skinny body, jutting Adam's apple, sloping forehead, and thinning blond hair. Raskin had been a Knoxville lawyer before joining Coffee's volunteers, and was elected captain by the power of his eloquence. But some men muttered that Raskin whined too much about the harshness of army life and worried too much about keeping his uniform immaculate. He didn't duck fire though, the men admitted, and was fair enough when resolving disputes in the ranks. My fate's in his hands as much as anybody's, Willie reminded himself, and resolved to stay as close to Raskin as possible. Just be a good soldier and follow the captain's orders, he warned himself. If anything goes wrong, I can just blame Raskin.

A half-hour later, white, blue, and red rockets flared into the night from Jackson's headquarters. The *Carolina*'s cannon abruptly silenced. "That's the signal, boys," Coffee yelled from the dark ahead. "Le's go!" The column trotted forward. Men cursed as they slipped and stumbled. Muskets fired sporadically ahead and in the darkness on either side. The British began firing volleys at the flashes in the dark. Bullets whistled past. Someone screamed from the column's front rank and was dragged off the road. Suddenly Coffee's men surged forward—shouting, cheering, and firing—then spread out as they smashed into massed British troops. The Americans and British screamed curses, fired point-blank at each other, then swung muskets and fists. Willie and Jess held their fire as they pushed through to the chaotic front line. Some of Coffee's men turned and fled to the rear. "To the front, goddamn it! To the front!" Raskin yelled. Willie tried to distinguish friend from foe admidst the men struggling before him, but the smoldering campfires, musket flashes, and accented curses revealed little. More British than Americans began fleeing until suddenly there were none left who had not been killed or captured. "After 'em, boys!" officers shouted. "Push 'em into the Mississippi!" Willie charged on behind a score of Coffee's men. He tripped over a still body and his rifle discharged into the sky as he fell.

"Damn it!" Willie hollered as he struggled to his feet and tried reloading.

Raskin prodded him. "No straggling, soldier! After 'em!"

Willie stumbled over the collapsed tents, smashed muskets and drums, and groaning, thrashing bodies littering the camp. A volley of musket fire tore through the night ahead. A dozen Tennesseans surged past him. "Fight, damn it. Turn and fight!" Raskin shouted and he and a half-dozen others rallied around him and desperately tried to reload. Willie reached for his bullet pouch but it had been torn off earlier. Ahead a British officer cried, "Forward!" and Willie could barely make out a dark mass moving slowly toward them. Willie raised his rifle by the barrel and fiercely awaited the British charge. This is the end, he thought grimly. Firing continued in the darkness all around.

More Americans staggered past. "Hold your ground, you goddamned cowards!" Raskin screamed. "All right, boys!" he called to the few men remaining. "Aim low at those bastards and fire!" Three rifles exploded but the black mass continued advancing. "Run for it!" Raskin yelled and Willie and the others turned and fled.

A quarter-hour later, he reached the American lines and joined a dozen men huddled around someone who was trying to spark a damp pile of wood. Some of the men boasted of the attack and their feats, most sat dazed.

I lived, Willie thought wearily, joylessly. I stood or charged when others ran. He suddenly began to shiver. Where was Jess? Officers pushed through the encampment, ordering men to rejoin their companies. Voices called out their company names from the darkness. He pushed his way through the throng toward Company F. Campfires began flickering along the line. Captains called roll. Willie reported to Captain Raskin and asked Jess's whereabouts.

"Not in yet," Raskin admitted. "Get some rest, boy," he ordered. But instead Willie wandered along the embankment and watched the men straggle into camp.

Some were limping, bleeding. He stared out toward the British lines where muskets sporadically popped and flashed, debating whether to search for Jess. Was he slowly bleeding to death from an arm or leg shattered by a lead slug or gut twisted by a bayonet? Was he already dead? Captured? Frost was forming on the grass and a thin crescent moon peeped behind clouds. His shivering worsened. I'll never find him in that pitch-black, he concluded. Probably get shot by our own pickets.

Exhausted, he stumbled back into camp, found his blanket roll, and curled up near a smoldering fire. An image of Judy smiling and waving seductively flashed through his mind as he began sinking into a deep well of sleep.

Seemingly minutes later, someone shouted, "Look at that boy run!" and men began whooping. Muskets cracked in the distance. Willie blinked in the dawn light then struggled to his feet. Groggy and stiff, he gazed at the hundreds of men littering the ground along the line, slumbering or slowly stirring, frost on their blankets. A score of soldiers cheered nearby atop the embankment. Willie scrambled atop the wall and stared in amazement toward the British lines. A couple hundred yards away, Jess was dodging his way toward them, pursued by eight redcoats. "Come on, boys!" a Tennessean hollered, "le's help him!" and they jumped down and splashed across the ditch and into the misty fields between the two armies. The British stopped abruptly, then turned and fled.

Gasping for breath, Jess stumbled into their midst. The men gathered around laughing and shouting. "Thankee boys," he wheezed as he bent over and dropped his rifle. His forehead was bruised and caked with dry blood.

Willie slapped Jess on the back. "Where the hell ya bin! I feared ya went under!"

Still panting, Jess grinned as he looked up. "Was a prisoner...till I run...for it."

"What happened to yer head?"

He gingerly touched his forehead. "Some son of a bitch...cracked me."

The men laughed and they all sauntered back into camp. Captain Raskin met them. "Baucus," he asked, "were you in the British camp?"

"Yup," Jess replied gamely. "Hospitality warn't too good, so I bid 'em goodbye." The men laughed and nudged each other.

"Come with me," Raskin ordered. "You other men, back to your posts."

The men slowly scattered. "We'll get your wound bandaged and your stomach filled first, but you must describe everything you saw and heard to General Jackson."

Jess blinked in astonishment. "Yes, sir!"

"Can I come, too, Captain? Please?" Willie pleaded.

Raskin smiled, thinking it wouldn't be long before his sons were that age. "Oh, very well, Yates. But mind yer manners in front of the general."

A half-hour later the three were marching up to the McCarty mansion, a whitewashed, two-story building with verandas surrounding the house on each floor. A half-dozen horses were staked out front. Conical tents sprouted in the yard among huge cypress trees with Spanish moss hanging low. Blue-coated soldiers lazed around smoky campfires. The two guards standing at the double mahogany doors stiffened as the three clumped up onto the veranda.

"I am Captain Raskin of General Coffee's Tennesseans. I have important information for General Jackson."

"Yes, sir!" one of them saluted and disappeared inside. A minute later he returned. "The ginral can see ye now, sir." He pointed inside. "Jus' up them stairs in the front bedroom."

The boys glanced nervously at each other as they entered the mansion and followed Raskin up the huge winding staircase. Laughter and cigar smoke drifted through the heavy air. Suddenly the boys were peeping around Raskin into a room filled with officers sitting around a huge table. The officers stared at them expectantly.

Jackson beckoned to them. "Yes, come in, Captain. Come in."

"What!" General Coffee exclaimed as he pulled a thick cigar from his mouth. "Now what'd those boys do? I feared they might be trouble when I signed 'em up." He turned to Jackson. "Signed 'em up here in New Orleans after they got thrown out of the volunteers for fighting."

"Ah, yes, General," Major Plauche, a short, swarthy, barrel-chested man with chestnut hair and long sideburns said excitedly. "Captain White gave me the full report. They attacked an officer and a gentleman of my battalion without provocation."

Jackson glared at the boys. He looked like a hawk that was about to pounce. "Why, that," he said slowly, "could be a capital offense."

Captain Raskin held up his hands. "No. Hold on, General. It's not like that at all. In fact this boy," he pointed to Jess, "is a hero. He just hightailed it from the British lines this morning after being captured last night."

Jackson's eyes bored into Jess. "Your story, soldier."

"Well, I…ahhh," Jess stammered, "I was…well…last night…"

Jackson's face softened. "Relax, boy. Just tell us what happened and what you saw."

"Well, Sir, General," Jess began slowly, his voice trembling slightly. "The fighting was mighty fierce. It was all confusion. It was hard to tell who was fighting who. We done licked the redcoats and they run off, but then a while later, they come back. I fired off a few rounds but I don't know if I hit anyone. It was all confusion. When they pitched inta us, somebody cracked my skull hard and knocked me flat. I musta bin out for a while 'cause when I come to, the fightin' was over and the redcoats were cleaning up their camp and some of 'em were wandering round with torches checking the bodies. I played 'possum when one of 'em peered over me. They dragged off some wounded from both sides that had been groaning and cursing nearby and when they left, I crawled into some bushes and musta passed out ag'in, 'cause when I opened my eyes ag'in it was gettin' light." Jess paused and massaged the bandage binding his forehead. "Sorry, Ginral. I am feelin' a mite…"

Jackson motioned, "Have a seat, son."

"Thankee, Ginral," Jess said wearily as he pulled up an adjacent chair. "Like I was saying, I woke up in the bushes to find myself smack-dab in the middle of the British camp. Most was sleeping but some was sitting around campfires. Nobody was paying much mind to our lines and I figured I bes' make a break for it afore everybody was up for breakfast. I was just about to light out when some ginral and his aides rode up and began talking to the officers of the regiment…"

"What regiment?" Jackson snapped. "And what general?"

"Ah, well, Ginral," Jess said hesitantly. "I don' rightly know. I was tryin' ta keep low and warn't paying much attention. I jus' wanted to git back to our lines."

Jackson winced and began massaging his stiff shoulder. "And what condition were they in?" he replied impatiently. "Did you note their casualties? Morale? Any reinforcements? How many cannon?"

"Well, Ginral. Lookin' cross those fields, it was kinda hard tellin' who was sleepin' fer the night and who fer eternity." Some of the officers and Willie snickered. Jackson shot them a steely glance. "But there was some bodies lined up nearby that was stone dead and I reckon there was twice more redcoats as our boys 'mong 'em."

"That's all you found out?" Jackson asked. Jess nodded. "Well," he demanded wearily, "tell us how you escaped."

"Well, now," Jess became more animated, "when I saw that ginral and his staff ride inta camp, I was mighty sore, 'cause I figured he'd rouse the whole army and I'd 'ventually be discovered, but suddenly he rode off and I tells myself this is my chance 'cause I figured the sentries and anybody else awake would be eyeing the ginral and might not see me skedaddle. Sure 'nuff that's what happened. Most was watchin' the ginral ride off and the others was talkin' among themselves so I took off my bluecoat and moseyed real calm-like through camp toward our lines."

Jackson squinted at Jess. "Were you scared?"

Jess exhaled sharply. "You bet, Ginral. I never bin more scared in my life. I figured any moment some redcoat'd put a ball or bayonet in me. I was steppin' around men snoring away in their blankets and past small groups of men sitting 'round campfires and I felt like a ghost, 'cause no one paid more than a glance at me, jus' figurin' I was one of them, and it wasn't till I started out between the lines that a sentry challenged me." Jess paused for effect and glanced around the room into the eyes of Jackson and his officers.

"Well, what happened?" General Coffee asked eagerly.

"The sentry shouts, 'Hold there! Where are you going?' I turned 'round an' saw other sentries down the line, holdin' their muskets ready, and some men 'round the campfires get up and stare," he paused again briefly. "Now or never, I told myself, an' took off running, zig-zagging cross that field toward our line while they opened fire and started chasing me. I don' know whether I'd a' made back on my own or not, but Willie here and some other Tennesseans jumped down from our wall and run off the redcoats," he grinned broadly. "And here I am."

"That was quite an escape, soldier," Jackson exclaimed with admiration.

"Yes, that surely was," Coffee added with a smile. "Sorry I expected the worst when you boys came in."

"Oh, that's all right, Ginral. No harm in that. Willie an' me's used ta such reactions," Jess winked at Willie, who smirked back, "ain't we?"

"Well, you boys, go get some rest," Jackson said gently. "You'll need it soon enough. Our scouts and British deserters report that General Pakenham and the rest of his army are moving into line. In fact," he added indignantly, "one deserter claimed Pakenham intended to sit down to Christmas dinner in New Orleans. Well, if so," Jackson's eyes flashed, "he'll find me at the head of the table! Don't you worry, the British'll never take New Orleans no matter how many men they bring up. Not with the likes of you boys and several thousand others like you. Those damn British will bleed thousands of men before our lines and the remnants will scurry back to that devilish country England where they belong! You mark my words." Jackson was now scowling. "Dismissed!"

Jess, Willie, and Raskin saluted briskly, turned, and quickly departed.

Willie playfully punched Jess's shoulder as they walked back to their camp. "Jessie, you're a genuine American hero! Congratulations!"

Jess chuckled and replied cheerfully, "Jus' gittin' warmed up, Willie. Ye ain't seen nothing yet."

For two weeks neither side did little more than harass the other, and the boys, and most of each army, were getting restless. Each day Willie and Jess would wander along the line, marveling at all the different faces, colors, uniforms, and languages manning the American army. On the right flank along the Mississippi, were the two regular regiments dressed in regulation blue and armed with muskets, and local units including the Battalion of New Orleans Volunteers, Lacoste and Daquin's-colored battalions, and Beale's Rifles, each of which had its own uniforms, weapons, and position in society. The frontier regiments of Carroll's Tennesseans, Adair's Kentuckians, and Coffee's Tennesseans, with their greasy, buckskin hunting shirts, tomahawks, and long rifles, lined the center and left. The hundred Choctaws were relegated to the mournful cypress swamp filled with alligators and water moccasins, but they did not seem to mind. There were seven two- or three-gun batteries along the line manned mostly by Lafitte's bearded and gaily dressed pirates. Altogether Jackson had roughly forty-four hundred men along his half-mile line between the Mississippi and the swamp.

Pakenham commanded twice as many troops, most tough veterans of the Napoleonic wars, and no one could understand why he was delaying an attack.

On different days, British artillery bombardments did succeed in blowing up the *Carolina* resting at anchor in the Mississippi and forcing the schooner *Louisiana* to retreat upstream, igniting some of the cotton bales protecting the American guns, stampeding the army's full-dress New Year's Day parade, exploding two artillery cassions packed with powder with an enormous blast that startled everyone for miles around, and riddling the roof and some of the walls of Jackson's headquarters with shot. But mostly the British cannon balls plopped deep in the mud without hitting anyone while their Congreve rockets whizzed spectacularly but harmlessly overhead. No more than a score of Americans were killed and twice as many wounded during the bombardments, while Jackson and his staff suffered not a nick. Meanwhile the British army had rested in their camps ever since an advance one morning by General Keene's three regiments along the river and Colonel Rennie's regiment through the swamp was ravaged by American cannon and rifle fire and forced to retreat. Each night more British sentries were picked off by Choctaws and Tennesseans creeping through their lines. Each day the British delayed their attack meant more of their men down from fever or snipers or cannon shot while the American ranks swelled with reinforcements and their defense line strengthened.

Willie had yet to fire a shot at the enemy. The boys went on three "'coon hunts" with groups of Tennesseans, but were always ordered to hold their fire should the British counterattack while the sharpshooters were reloading. But those British pickets that survived the initial fire always fled in terror. Willie loved the thrill of stalking the soaked fields and clumps of woods between the lines, and war whooping and catcalling the beleaguered British. But otherwise there was not much to do. The boys risked arrest several afternoons by slipping into the city, strolling the streets, and drinking in the cafes. But they could neither bring themselves to pay for a few fervent minutes of passion from the tavern wenches, nor could they could find any unattached girls for sweethearts.

Army life was mostly very frustrating and boring, with long periods of tedium broken by a patrol or artillery duel or smile of a pretty girl from a balcony. The officers tried to keep everyone busy drilling or widening the canal and raising the wall, but mostly the boys lounged around the campfires with the other men, trading stories or dozing on their damp cotton beds. British deserters continually warned of impending attacks and the boys spent most nights huddled in their blankets at the wall with the others.

The camp and water filled steadily with filth, and dysentery and yellow fever began striking dozens. Jess managed to stay healthy, but Willie spent much of each day squatting with his backside to the canal. They ate well though, once Jackson organized a supply system, with a steady stream of beef, eggs, coffee, bacon, and vegetables traveling from the city into the pots of their company and all others along the line. They received new pants and blanket cloaks out of thousands made for the army by the ladies of New Orleans.

One night Willie was dozing when suddenly voices and laughter erupted farther down the line. "Jackson's coming!" voices nearby exclaimed excitedly. Men began struggling to their feet. The half-moon and smoldering campfires cast a dull light along the line. Jackson's voice cut through the night, cajoling, questioning, and encouraging each group of men he met. Someone threw wood on their fire and it flared brightly.

Jackson and two aides stepped up to the fire and warmed their hands at the flames. Grinning in excitement, Willie, Jess, and other men crowded around. The General peered sharply from one face to the next and nodded. "Howdy, boys. Always good to see some familiar faces from home. Fine chance we'll see some action tomorrow. You boys ready to fight?" The men boasted loudly and graphically of their eagerness for the British attack. "Everything all right? Eating enough? Any complaints?"

"Just wanna see them redcoats in buckrange," someone replied.

Jackson smiled and nodded slowly. "You there, Baucus. Private Baucus." Jess stiffened to attention. "Wouldn't you rather be with your sweetheart back in St. Louis?"

"Not by a damn sight, Ginral," he replied gamely, "though I wouldn't mind my sweetheart spending a little time here." Jackson and the men chuckled merrily. Jess had become a favorite with the company.

"Well, son, the harder you fight, the sooner you'll be back with your sweetheart." He motioned to his aides and they strode on down the line. The men stood around talking softly to each other then drifted back to their posts.

Willie smiled broadly. "Why, Jess! Ye done bin holding out on me.

Who's that sweetheart back in St. Louis ye bin talking 'bout?"

Jess grinned back. "Your sister!" Willie giggled nervously.

Neither of them could sleep after Jackson's visit. They reminisced in low voices of their past escapades in St. Louis, down the Mississippi, and in New Orleans, and rechewed the arguments about whether after the war to catch the first ship to sea, head overland back East, or stay in New Orleans.

Suddenly the cathedral bells began ringing loudly, summoning the believers to mass. The boys paused to listen. "Dark's fading fast. Be dawn soon," Jess remarked. Two rockets whizzed into the sky above the British lines.

Bugles blew, drums rattled, and bagpipes wailed in the distance. "By God, they're coming," Jess shouted. Raskin and other officers along the line began yelling orders. The men scrambled to their feet and crowded along the parapet.

Jess rested his battered rifle on the wall and squinted down it into the misty half-light. "How we gonna see ta shoot?"

"Damned if I know," Willie muttered. His stomach felt queasy and his knees weak. He wanted to just lie down and sleep. Why'd they come now, he cursed silently. We bin up all night. He trembled slightly. What's it like to kill a man, he wondered once again. Just like hunting deer, the Tennesseans had repeatedly declared when he asked them. Besides, they added, with all the smoke and confusion, you'll probably never know if you hit anyone or not.

The British bugles, fifes, bagpipes, and drums sounded steadily closer. Suddenly through the wispy fog, masses of men appeared marching forward, led by standard-bearers holding their regimental and British flags high and officers waving swords. Three cannon shots cracked from the center of the American line and tore gaps, screams, and curses through a British column. The redcoats' closer ranks marched on. British officers called out commands and their troops trotted forward, huzzahing wildly. Mounted on a huge chestnut horse, General Coffee cantered by behind his troops, shouting, "Hold your fire, boys! Hold your fire till you get the word!" The men anxiously aimed their rifles at the British columns. Other American batteries opened fire, tearing apart dozens, then scores, of men. Thick yellow smoke drifted slowly over the line. Musket fire rattled off to the right.

"Ready along the line!" Coffee screamed. The artillery and musket fire elsewhere was becoming deafening. "Aim!" The Tennesseans cocked their rifles and picked out targets among the British columns which were now less than fifty yards away. Willie's trembling wors-

ened. Damn buck fever! he cursed himself as he tried to aim. "Fire!"
The massed rifles roared, cutting down scores of British.

Willie pulled the trigger and the hammer fell, but his rifle did not
kick or smoke. He angrily jerked back his hammer and frizzen, and
checked his priming. "Damn it!" he screamed.

"What's wrong?" Jess shouted as he rammed down another ball.

"Powder's wet!" Willie cursed and watched impotently as volley
after volley cut the British columns to pieces and redcoats littered the
ground in squirming heaps. Handfuls of British soldiers rushed forward and fired up at the wall but it was too high to scale and they were
quickly shot down.

The remnants of the British regiments milled in confusion then
either broke and fled, tossing away their muskets and knapsacks, or
raised their hands in surrender.

Cheering broke out along the line. Some Tennesseans leaped atop
the wall for a few last shots while others shook their rifles in rage and
shouted, "After them! Kill all those bastards!" But the officers called
them down and hollered, "Reload and hold ready!"

Willie's ears were ringing. He felt dazed, as if in a dream. The
smoke slowly drifted away. He stared from Jess to the hundreds of still,
thrashing, crawling, limping, moaning, screaming, silent bodies in the
field before him. Some Tennesseans jumped down and scrambled
across the field to take the swords of officers and round up prisoners.
"What happened?" Willie shouted.

"Biggest turkey shoot I ever seen," Jess choked as tears rolled
down his face.

Paper and quill in hand, Willie sat cross-legged atop the levy,
watching the brown waters of the Mississippi swirl away to the sea.
Seagulls screeched and dove at flotsam. The sun was disappearing and
its last rays turned scattered clouds crimson and lavender. The smell of
rotting bodies hung heavily in the air. God, to escape that smell, those
horrors! He shuddered as he recalled hauling and burying the countless
shattered bodies and limbs during the truce the day after the attack. The
graves were shallow and the rains soon washed away the thin soil. The
fields between the lines were perforated with rows of earth mounds
upon which hundreds of crows and buzzards perched, pecking at the
exposed flesh of the corpses. God, to sear from my mind the screams
of the wounded, their pleas and their curses as their legs and arms were
hacked off and dumped in piles.

Willie stretched out along the grass and propped up his head with his hand, recalling the last three weeks since the attack on January 8. The British remained encamped, neither retreating nor attacking. Each night deserters trickled into the American lines. They spoke of the British army's broken spirit, the mutinous mutterings among the ranks, the hundreds of additional lingering deaths from dysentery and wounds, and the rationed, rotting food. Then one morning the British camp was empty. During the night they had hastily packed up, marched back to the Gulf, and boarded their transports for home. A week later, word arrived that a peace treaty had been signed in Ghent on Christmas Eve! All the fighting and dying, all the fear and tortured bodies and destruction was for nothing.

Willie grimaced bitterly. And I never got off a shot the whole time. Should I feel remorse or pride? Was I a hero or a fool? To kill in self-defense is just. So should I have killed? For my country? For me?

The victory parade at the *Place d'armes* later that month seemed hollow, despite, or perhaps because of, all the gaiety and pageantry. The New Orleans officials invited only Jackson, the other generals, and Plauche's volunteers. The rest of the army remained encamped along the wall. Willie and Jess had to sneak away from Coffee's regiment, slip past the guards patrolling the city streets, and squeeze through the crowd at the square. The show was magnificent. A triumphal arch atop six Greek pillars and covered with flowers was erected in the square's center. On each side of the arch stood a beautiful maiden—one representing liberty and the other representing justice. Holding crowns of laurel, two little girls stood on pedestals beneath the arch while two lines of pretty girls stood between the arch and the cathedral doors, each representing a different state or territory, each cloaked with white dresses and blue veils, and holding a basket of flowers in one hand and a small American flag in the other. Plauche's Volunteers, resplendent in their rainbow of glittering uniforms, were massed by company around the arch, while thousands of spectators eagerly pressed in from all sides. Jackson and his entourage strode the street from the river to the arch, saluted by cannon shot and a band playing "Yankee Doodle." He paused beneath the arch as the two children crowned him with laurel, then marched slowly, solemnly up to the cathedral doors as the other maidens tossed flowers in his path. At the door, Miss Louisiana curtsied and the abbé greeted him. Jackson made a short speech, noting his and America's deep appreciation for all the sacrifices made by the people of New Orleans. Then, while a chorus sang a "Te Deum" and the cathedral bells rang and cannon roared, the abbé accompanied him inside for mass.

The war's over! Most everyone else who hasn't headed home soon will. Except us. He dipped his quill in an ink bottle and wrote: "With no one to touch despite all my mind's might." Jess strolled up and plopped down beside him. "Where's Kyle?" Willie asked.

"He'll be 'long directly. I ran into him this morning and told him to meet us here at sunset for a last bottle 'long the Mississippi." Jess pulled up his knees to his chest. "Ya all set for tomorrow?" he said gravely.

"Reckon." He thought of the merchantman they had signed up with as crew members, bound to West Africa for a hull full of slaves. He imagined his father exploding at the idea. Liberty? Justice? "Shouldn't we wait for another ship? I don't fancy slaving."

"We'll jump ship someplace long before Africa. Prob'ly the West Indies. Jus' hope the British navy don't try to press us. That'd be somethin', wouldn't it?"

"Outta the frying pan and inta the fire. Seems ta be how we do things."

Jess shrugged and glanced down at Willie's paper. "Writin' a letter?"

Embarrassed, he folded up the paper and put it in his cloak pocket. "Naw."

"Looked like a poem."

"'Twas."

Jess looked disappointed. "Ye know I like poetry. Ye ain't gonna share it?"

"Well…it ain't any good. Jus' come to me quick and I wrote it quick. The meter's all wrong."

"If that's how ye feel. But I'd really like to hear it."

Willie squinted at Jess through the half-light. The city lights twinkled behind him while the evening star glimmered bright through the glow in the western sky. "Time's fadin'. All right." He pulled out the paper and cleared his throat.

> *How many sunsets have I watched alone*
> *The wind whispering by with a subtle moan*
> *The kaleidoscope sky an ever changing hue*
> *Each color of the rainbow for anyone's view*
> *A wine-filled bubble the earth will consume*
> *Enjoy it now before its ultimate doom*
> *But one piece lacks this glorious scene*
> *A beautiful girl who on me will lean*
> *Her tender full lips brushing my ear*

Telling me she will always be near.
But the light fades as day turns to night
With no one to touch despite all my mind's might.

Jess frowned pensively. "That was good, Willie. Real good. Ye thinkin' a Sharon?"

"Think of her all the time," he confessed. "And Judy, too. Odds are I'll never see either of 'em again."

Jess exhaled slowly. "Sure got ourselves in a mess."

The sound of scuffling feet and then Macintosh's voice cut through the dark. "Jessie! Willie! Where are you, lads!"

"Up here, Kyle!" Jess hollered.

Macintosh scrambled up the levy and sat beside them. "This is a fine spot ye chose to celebrate." He pulled a bottle of wine from his coat pocket and pulled the cork. He chuckled merrily. "Outside a' the city here. No tellin' who ye might run inta. Here's to ye, lads." He raised the bottle to his mouth, took a deep swallow, then passed it to Jess. He chuckled again. "Yeah, lads, ye never know who ye'll run inta or what kinda company ye truly keep." After guzzling deeply, Jess passed the bottle to Willie. "Why, take ye lads here. Innocence itself it would seem. Yet..." he paused for effect. "Why, ye lads could be notorious murderers on the run."

Willie choked on the wine he was drinking and started coughing. Wide-eyed, Jess straightened up and stared hard at Macintosh. "Whadya saying, Kyle?"

The Irishman chuckled again and slapped his knee. "I was jus' saying now that how do ye truly know someone. Why ye lads...well, perish the thought!"

Willie pointed his finger at Kyle and started choking again. "Ye heard somethin' 'bout us now, didn't ye?" Jess stated angrily. "Well, whadya hear? Quit toyin' with us like a cat with a mouse."

"Well, now, lads, it seems Captain Beasly made it to St. Louis and delivered the supplies to Willie's mother and word arrived today at me warehouse from another keelboat captain that, well..."

"What!" Willie growled. "Damn it, Kyle, talk straight!"

"To make a long story short, ye never did kill that lad after all. Seems he just passed out was all," Macintosh laughed. "Now why didn't ye tell me ye lads was on the run?"

"Goutard's not dead?" Jess asked incredulously. "Ya mean we kin go home?"

Macintosh pulled two envelopes from his coat pocket. "The full story's undoubtedly in these letters to Willie."

Willie grabbed them eagerly, held them up to the twilight, and squinted at the handwriting. "One looks like my mother's writing and...I can't tell the other's." His heart thrilled. What if it was Sharon's? But Sharon barely knows how to write. He ripped open the letter. "Can't hardly make out anything in the dark." He turned over the page and barely made out the signature. "Judy!"

"Damn, Willie! We kin go home," Jess shouted and slapped Willie on the back. "Ye mean there ain't no charges 'gainst us?"

Macintosh's toothy smile flashed in the dark. "Ye lads are free men."

Willie smiled. "Free," he said quietly. "I still ain't sure what that means." He jumped to his feet. "But let's celebrate anyway! Come on!"

They stumbled along the levy back toward New Orleans, whooping and passing the bottle. They later paused as Willie tossed the empty bottle far out into the Mississippi and strained to hear the splash. Willie unbuttoned his fly and urinated into the river. He laughed. "Least somethin' of me'll reach the ocean!"

Six

1821–1822

Will smeared the sweat dribbling down his face and neck then angrily cuffed a mosquito whining in his ear. "Damn it," he muttered as he squinted down again through the smoldering candle light at a particularly tedious passage on torts from Blackstone's *Commentary on Law*. Crickets and cicadas trilled endlessly in the black night. Voices murmured from the front porch. He felt suffocated in the sultry air and cursed the hellish Missouri summers.

"Why don't you go to bed?" his mother droned wearily from a rocking chair where she was patching some trousers. "You've been studying for three hours."

"You're the one who wants me to make something of myself," he indignantly replied, and immediately regretted his anger. In recent

181

years, her body seemed to dry up daily while wrinkles deeply etched her face. Little things seemed to set her off and he had to tiptoe around her, like she was some fierce dog dozing before a door.

"Don't you?" she asked.

"Yeah," he admitted. "I suppose."

"You keep claiming you want to be another Thomas Hart Benton."

"I'll never match his eloquence or ideas."

"You're barely a man. You will someday if you're determined enough. You have the smarts for it."

"Politicians are rich and we aren't."

Jenny sighed. "Your father won on our modest holdings."

They both fell into a silence as thick as the summer night. Will thought of his father's simple headstone and grassy mound in a shady corner of the graveyard. Where would he be without the stroke that cut him down, or the duel that prompted it? Where would they all be? Squinting into the candle flame, he said quietly. "Everything's linked to everything else. Things happen and build up in long, endless chains. We're all tied down by thousands of those chains, chained to the past, to things we did, or things that happened to us, or things we failed to do, that we barely understood at the time—if at all. Most people don't think about them, or try to make sense of them or are even aware that they exist. But we're all tangled up in them like a fly in a web."

"Until we're devoured by a spider," Jenny replied with a bored tone.

He nodded. "Death. It's always waiting nearby."

"Is that what Blackstone says?"

"That's just horse sense. Don't you ponder such things?"

Jenny slowly shook her head. "I used to. Not anymore. There's no point. It just makes you feel more helpless." Sarah giggled loudly from the front porch. "I better bring that girl in. Just how sweet do you think she is on Jess?" she demanded. Will shrugged. "What you both see in that smart aleck is beyond me." She set aside her sewing and struggled to her feet. "Why doesn't she get serious about Davie Mossbach or even Josh Winthrop? Those are good boys from good families. Not a wild boy with an even wilder father," she sniffed. "And why aren't you thinking of making Judy an honest woman?"

"That's between me and her," he sharply replied. "I don't wanna get saddled with a wife and young'uns anytime soon."

"Well, she wants marriage—with you! I know that from talking with her," she snapped. "And I want to hold grandchildren in my arms before my time's up. When's that going to happen?"

"Ask Sarah."

Jenny scoffed. "Any offspring of Jess would be a hellion. You children are so selfish. All you think about is yourselves and your pleasures."

Jumping to his feet, he sputtered, "I've had enough of this! All Sarah and I do all day is mind the store or haul goods from the river or weed the garden or mend fences or cut wood or fetch water or…Me—selfish! What do you want from me!"

"All right, all right!" Jenny hissed. "Will you quiet down? What will the neighbors think?"

"The neighbors?" he bellowed. "Is that all you think about? I don't give a damn about the neighbors." The front door squeaked open and Sarah and Jess nervously peeked in. Jenny shot them a bitter glance then glared back at Will.

"And that's why you'll never achieve anything, because you not only don't care what others think, you openly defy them. And me. You openly defy me! You have no respect for your own mother!"

"Why should I care what anyone thinks?" He waved angrily toward town. "People'll just entangle you in their own chains for their own purposes. I am nobody's slave," Jess grinned and winked. Sarah's mouth was half-open but she dared not interrupt.

"Well, Mr. Know-it-all," Jenny mocked, "you know everything, don't you? Even as a little boy you had to be different, running off and getting into Lord knows what kind of trouble and sullying our good name. You were always different, but you've become increasingly insufferable ever since you got back from New Orleans a half-dozen years ago."

"I only know what's best for me. Everyone else can do what they will. They can all hang themselves for all I care."

"That's just it!" Jenny shrieked.

Sarah ran to Jenny's side and put her hand on her arm, "Mother, please."

Jenny shook her arm free. "You'll both do as I tell you."

"Why?" Will replied.

"Because I am your mother," Jenny said vehemently. Sarah began to cry.

"I am getting out of here." As he brushed past Jess, he muttered, "Come on."

Jess was torn between comforting Sarah and following Will. "I'll see ya later, Sarah," he said quietly. She nodded as she wiped away her tears. Jess caught up to Will striding down the dark road. "What was that all about?" he asked.

Will suddenly stopped and turned toward him. "Did you ever sleep with my sister?"

"Well...uh...I...hmmm...not really...I mean she never let me...completely." Jess paused in confusion. "Would ya mind if I did?"

"Well," he said hesitantly, "no. I suppose not. Better you than somebody else."

"Thankee, Will," Jess laughed and slapped him on the back. "Always knew I could count on ya."

"What're friends for?" Will asked with a bewildered tone.

Jess grinned and jabbed his finger into his shoulder, "Ya still never poked Judy?"

Will laughed nervously. "I...ah...whelp. Yup," he said proudly, "number a' times. We sneak out to her barn at night with a blanket."

"Why didn't ya tell me!" he laughed. "Boy, if her daddy ever caught you, he'd skin ya alive!" Images of burly, slow talking, quick-fused Seth Morgan flashed through their minds. He once broke a man's leg and collar bone by throwing him down a flight of tavern steps. Seth claimed the man cheated him in a three card monte game. "Ain't ya feared of knocking her up?"

"We try doing it before or after the ah...woman's time."

"How was she, Will?" Jess asked eagerly. "Was she like Sharon?"

"Different," he said quietly. "We take our time, and it's real soft and tender like."

"Ye ain't fixin' ta git hitched now, are ye?"

"'Course not."

"She know that?"

"Well...ah...I reckon. But she keeps hinting of wedding bells. Strange thing is, after waiting five years to bundle, now that we do it regular, I just don't feel as excited about her anymore."

"Now that's somethin'. Boy, you were some love-sick pup for a few years there, writin' poetry and pining away when she was outta sight."

"She had a power, a spell over me before. Not anymore. But now she wants to get hitched more than ever. I sure don't, but we've been courting so long, it's like we're already married. I half want and half don't wanna shake her. I guess I love her. I don't know what I want."

"Whew, boy! Yer in a fix. I knew we shoulda headed upriver with the Missouri Fur Company this spring. Whada we doing here in St. Louis?" he asked indignantly. "We haven't had an adventure since New Orleans 'cept some hunting trips to the Gasconade River Valley.

We're like rocks in a stream. Everybody's passin' us by and headin' West."

Will stared up at the silvery clouds drifting across the stars and a yellowish half-moon low on the horizon. "Yeah. Know what ya mean," he said sadly.

"Well, what're we gonna do 'bout it?"

"Don't know. Don't know what to do."

"Ye really fixin' ta be a lawyer?"

"Hell, I don't know," he said with a trace of disgust. "Better 'an running that damn store. But all those damn torts and other nonsense bore me to tears. We oughta go upriver. To the Rockies and become beaver men."

"Yeah!" Jess said excitedly. "Now yer talkin'. When?"

"Hafta be next spring. All the parties done left up the Missouri."

"That's nine months from now. I'm so restless, I don't know if I kin wait that long."

"Know what ya mean."

"What're we gonna do in the meantime? Smithin' and storin'?"

Will shrugged.

"So we're headin' upriver next spring?"

"Yup. Le's do it!"

"Deal's a deal. Le's seal it with a shot a' whiskey or two."

"Now yer talkin'." They headed into town through the silent streets.

Will shifted nervously against the wall. He tried concentrating on his Blackstone, but Benton's voice resonated through the thin walls and door before him. The rhythmic clang of presses printing hundreds of copies of Benton's biweekly newspaper, the *St. Louis Inquirer*, seeped up from the first floor. He looked at the half-dozen other supplicants lounging down the hall. I'm next, he thought with relief. Been here couple hours at least.

He tried rehearsing just what he would say. Gotta make a good impression, he kept warning himself. First impressions are the most important.

Suddenly the door jerked open and a French farmer with a thick accent repeatedly thanked the senator and bowed lightly as he backed out. As the man shuffled down the hall, Will jumped to his feet, stepped into the room, and closed the door behind him.

"Sir...Senator?" he asked meekly.

"Welcome! Welcome, young man!" Benton boomed as he stepped up to Will and vigorously pumped his hand. "Whom do I have the pleasure of addressing?"

"I'm...I'm William Yates of St. Louis, sir," he stammered as he stared up past Benton's bearlike body to his intense gray eyes, his flabby, reddened face framed by a double chin and black hair streaked with gray. "I wondered if I could possibly spare...or if you could possibly spare a moment of my...your time."

"Certainly, Mr. Yates! Certainly. Have a seat. What can I do for you?"

Benton slipped behind a desk cluttered with piles of papers and books, and settled into a huge, green leather armchair as Will sat down in a hard walnut chair before him.

"I am studying for the bar and..."

"Excellent! Excellent!" Benton chuckled. "I see Blackstone accompanying you. Your constant companion?"

"Well, I—"

"A most excellent first friend, but you'll need an assembly of other noble thinkers to join you. Aristotle. Tacitus. Locke. Montesquieu. Hume. Coke. Jefferson. *The Federalist Papers.* For a start. Then all the classics of history. You must become a well-rounded man. A man of the renaissance and enlightenment. A man of the American renaissance and enlightenment! A man of a nation of enterprising and daring men that will eventually spread to the Pacific and beyond!" his voice rose to a powerful crescendo as he slowly shook his fist for emphasis.

"Your present occupation, Mr. Yates?"

"I tend my mother's store."

"Times are hard, are they not, with the economy's present collapse. Almost one-third of the nation's population is struggling at the brink of survival. In Washington City, the fair capital of our young republic, the homeless and shiftless crowd the streets. Crime—thefts, shootings, fraud—is rampant. And the Congress of which I am a part—at times a proud and at other times an ashamed part—fiddles, while the country burns! These are indeed perilous times. Think, my boy, of how prices rose exorbitantly after the war. Why, when I first arrived here in 1815 you could buy a town lot for thirty dollars. Four years later the price was two thousand dollars! Can you imagine!"

Benton shook his massive head sorrowfully. "If I had several thousand dollars when I arrived I could be worth a hundred times that now! But," he wagged a finger at Will, "the key is knowing when to sell. Perhaps we should have anticipated the inevitable burst of that titanic bubble of land and credit speculation a mere four years later. But we became prisoners of greed—of the avaricious belief that the price of our land and other ventures would forever rise," Benton harrumphed. "A quaint notion! Today this great nation is awash in a sea of paper money—money not worth the paper on which it is printed. Your family, as store owners, is undoubtedly the reluctant holder of a considerable amount of such notes, is it not?" Will nodded. "Young man, this country needs a great many things and one of the most basic is a sound banking system!

"But!" he arched a thick black eyebrow, "where are we to obtain the silver for our financial system?" Will helplessly shrugged his shoulders and shifted nervously in his chair. "Mexico!" Benton intoned solemnly and pointed to a framed map of North America hanging on the wall. "Mexico. At this very moment, the valiant and steadfast Mexican people are revolting against their Spanish oppressors. And we, the United States of America, should be helping them in their noble struggle. Think my boy! Think! A free Mexico will throw off the shackles of Spanish mercantilism and open its wealth of mines and plantations to the outside world. And we, Missouri, sit at Mexico's backdoor! Our great state can benefit the most from these exciting developments. But whether we as a state succeed or fail to capitalize on Mexican independence depends," he cocked a beefy finger toward Will, "on fine young enterprising men like yourself. Rumor has it that some parties are already contemplating setting forth to Santa Fe to open a trade stream that will eventually become a mighty river uniting two great nations! And from there our merchant army and fleet will expand to all the markets of Asia!

"But what stands in our way? Our government's own shortsightedness! Outrageous are the 1819 treaties with Spain which keep us from rightfully acquiring Texas and with Britain which forces us jointly to occupy Oregon when we are the rightful owners! Our peoples and commerce should be flowing up the Missouri and down the Columbia, and then conveyed to all the ports of Asia. When I return to Washington this autumn, you can rest assured that I will ceaselessly and tirelessly champion all these and other great crusades that I have set before you. I defy all those who oppose me and will crush every assailant on the ground with as much ease as a giant would crush an eggshell!" Suddenly Benton lowered his voice to a conspiratorial whisper. "Do you recall, my boy, the great words of Tacitus?"

Will strained to think but realized he had never read or even seen anything of Tacitus. His voice cracked, "Which ones?"

"I refer to Tacitus's immortal statement on the purpose of life." Benton rose to his feet and intoned, "'Every man should aim at doing something worthy of being written, or at writing something worthy of being done.'" Benton arched his eyebrow, "Need I say more?"

"N-No."

"Well, then, my boy," Benton circled the desk while Will jumped up and found his hand once more being pumped by Benton's. "Go forth and do great things. I will be watching and waiting."

Will stumbled back, yanked open the door, and bowed slightly as he stepped outside. "I will, Senator," he mumbled, "I will."

Soaked with sweat and flush faced, he dashed into the blacksmith shop startling Jess and a short, wiry black man who were straining to lift a wagon onto a block. "I saw him! I talked to him!" Will said breathlessly.

"Damn it, Will," Jess groaned, "give us a hand!" Will nodded and put his shoulder under the wagon with them. "Hold on!" Jess ordered as he let go, grabbed a four foot tall block, and slipped it under the axle. "All right, let her down!" Panting, the three straightened. "Whew! Welp, won't take long to get this wheel off and fixed up," Jess chuckled. "Musta bin some mule that could smash those spokes in!"

The black man solemnly shook his head and wiped the perspiration off his face with a red bandanna. "Yes, sir! That's some mule ah got." He jerked a finger toward two mules munching hay in a stable. "That one on the left there's the mean one. Ma other mule's sweet as kin be. Last month that mean one kicked down part a ma fence. Last year kicked down the barn door. Highest, hardest kickin' mule in Missouri!"

"Ever kick you?" Will asked.

"No, sir. Ah know better and he know better. Ah know he might kill me if he did and he know ah'd kill him if he didn't. It's a standoff. He don' kick me but he kicks down everythin' else."

Jess turned to Will. "Gentleman's name's Israel. From out West. Franklin."

Will smiled and nodded. "You're a long way from home."

Israel frowned bitterly. "Missouri's no longer ma home."

The friends glanced nervously at each other. "Reckon becoming a state warn't good for everybody," Jess said sympathetically.

Israel sighed. "Not for freemen, it warn't."

"I'm sorry," Will said sheepishly. "It ain't right."

"Ah'll find a new home back East. Massachusetts is good for freemen. A freeman kin even vote there, same as a white man."

"It's a long way. You got yer papers?" Jess asked.

Israel tapped a shirt pocket. "Never leaves ma body. I kin lose everythin' else," he gestured toward a pile of wooden boxes and clothes in the corner, "but if ah lose ma papers, ah lose maself. Somebody'll come and make me a slave agin."

"Ain't right," Will muttered.

"So who'd ye see that yer all fired up about?" Jess demanded.

Will suddenly felt deflated. He recalled Benton's impassioned support for making Missouri a slave state and driving out the free Negroes. He glanced at Israel. "Well, I…I don't support everything he says and believes," he said apologetically.

"Benton?" Jess asked. "Ya talked to him?" Israel looked away.

"I'm studying for the bar," Will explained to Israel, "and I went to him for advice."

Israel shrugged. "Well, sir, ta tell ye the truth, folks don' think much a' him and the junta back where ahm from. But ahm sure he done give ya good advice."

"Will's father here done run aginst the junta back in 1812," Jess said proudly. "He's no friend a' the Chouteau brothers, Pratte, Hempstead and that crowd that rule St. Louis and most of the state. Are ya, Will?"

"No, not the Chouteau junta," he replied emphatically, "and I'm no friend of the other faction either. The junta crushed Pa's life, and the other gambled away my family's fortune," he fumed bitterly. "I stand alone. I rely on nobody but myself. Ya can't trust anyone farther than ye can puke."

He glanced at Jess. "Well, almost anyone." Israel nodded approvingly.

"So? What he tell ya?" Jess asked.

"Well, when ya come down to it," Will admitted, "not much more than his speeches and newspaper articles. Kept talking 'bout America's destiny and then he challenged me to live up to something Tacitus said," he frowned. "Something 'bout doing and writing great things. Can't quite remember. But he told me to have adventures and be enterprising."

"Adventure?" Jess said disgustedly. "Look's like we're stuck here till next spring." He explained to Israel, "We wanna head up the Missouri and trap beaver in the Rockies!"

"Ifin ya gentlemen's looking fer venture, ya oughta look up Mr. Becknell of Franklin. He's fixin' ta head out on the Plains for a hunt. Some sez he's really fixin' ta go to Santa Fe."

"Santa Fe!" Will said excitedly. "Benton said the Mexicans are revolting and, if they win, they'll open up trade with the United States!

First man across with a wagon of goods could be rich!"

"When's this friend a' yers fixin' ta set out?" Jess asked.

Israel walked over to his belongings and pulled out a stack of newspapers from a chest. "Don' know him maself but ah heard the talk and later read 'bout it in the *Franklin Intelligencer* last week. Let me see. Dis one." He pulled open a newspaper, scanned the headlines, and handed it to Jess. "Notice on bottom of page three."

"Lookee this, Will!" Jess said excitedly. "'An article for the government of a company of men destined to the westward for the purpose of trading horses and mules, and catching wild animals of every description—'"

Will interrupted with his own reading, "'Every man will fit himself for the trip with a horse, a good rifle, and as much ammunition as the company may think necessary for a two- or three-month trip.' We got all that!"

"Lookee this," Jess pointed to the bottom of the notice. "'Signers to the amount of seventy will be received until the 4th of August, when every man wishing to go is requested to meet at Ezekiel William's on the Missouri, about five miles above Franklin.' Le's go, Will!"

"All right. What's today?"

"July 7," Jess noted. "'Bout four weeks. We gotta get upriver fast before they leave or before the company's filled up. Why I bet every man left in Missouri'll be in Franklin before us."

"Will?" The three men turned to see Judy standing before them. Her eyes were red and she twisted her fingers in her hands.

"Judy!" Will exclaimed. "What're you doing here? I haven't seen you for a while," he admitted nervously then stated proudly. "We headin' out West. To the Plains."

"Will, I've got to talk to you," she replied meekly. "Alone." Will suddenly felt like he was floating in a bad dream. Oh, God, he repeated to himself, not that! Not that! "Be back later, Jess. Good luck ta ya, Israel." He shook hands with the black man and hurried out into the crowded street beside Judy.

"What's wrong?"

"Not here," she replied and they marched silently, hand in hand to the fields west of town. Finally Judy stopped and sat demurely in the shade of a huge chestnut tree. She was wearing a thin, faded yellow cotton dress which clung tightly to her sweaty body. Her long blonde hair was tied back in a ponytail. He sat down beside her and, fearing the worst, began shredding a leaf he had plucked from a tree.

"Willie, do you love me?" Judy demanded.

He sighed in relief and glanced at Judy out of the corner of his eye. "Is that all you wanted to tell me?" he asked hopefully.

"No."

"I've told you before," he admitted reluctantly.

"Only when you were on top of me," she replied disdainfully. "We've been sweethearts ever since you got back from New Orleans. Doesn't that mean anything to you?"

"Of course," he said, wishing her dimples would appear with a smile.

She looked down at her lap and said quietly, "Willie...I think I'm..."

"No...Judy...What makes you think...?"

"It's been two months."

Tears started rolling down her cheeks. He wrapped his arms around her and held her tight. "All right, all right. Don't worry. Everything'll be all right."

She started sobbing and her heavy breasts heaved against him. He felt himself stirring. "I guess we'll hafta get married," he said quietly.

Judy turned her face up toward his. "Really?" she said and smiled broadly.

With a slight smile, he replied, "Don't see what else we can do." She pushed her lips into his, kissed him passionately then laughed.

"Oh, Willie, we've got so many things to decide. When to have our wedding, and who to invite and, well...I suppose we'd live at your home."

"Ah, Judy, I suppose we'll hafta get married but I was thinking..."

"What?"

"Well, it just kinda struck me that the baby's not due for another seven months, which means it won't be here until at least February and I was thinking...well, did you hear what Jess and I were planning?"

"Something about heading West...to Franklin?" she asked hesitantly.

"There's a party led by a man named Becknell going onto the plains to hunt and trade horses," he said eagerly.

"Will Yates!" she demanded, "how could you think of going out there and exposing yourself to all those dangers when you'll soon be a newlywed and a father?"

"The notice said they'd only be gone a few months and...well, we could make a small fortune if we trade goods with the Indians or even in Santa Fe..."

"What!" Her frown deepened. "Santa Fe!"

He nodded excitedly. "And we could use the money to buy our own house. I don't wanna live with you in the same house as my mother and Sarah."

"But what if something happens to you?"

"Nothing'll happen to me. I'll be with seventy other men. That's a small army."

"Isn't that what your Uncle Jake thought before he went to the mountains?"

A cloud passed through his mind. "Well, I'll try to be careful and not go off alone. That's what happened to my Uncle Jake. They never found him. He could still be alive out there somewhere."

"Do you really believe that ,Will?" she asked, her voice filled with skepticism.

He shrugged. "Anything's possible."

Judy pouted. "It'd be your choice if we weren't going to have a baby but…"

"Judy," he pleaded, "if we hafta get married, this could be my last chance to see the Rockies and Santa Fe. My last adventure. I work hard. You know that. Someday I hope to get into politics and rise high in society. You've told me there's nothing I can't do if I set my mind to it. But I've gotta experience all sides of life first. Don't you understand that?"

Judy sucked in a deep breath then let it out in a long hiss. "We'll see."

A week later, the Yates, Morgans, and several score friends and relatives crowded the tiny Methodist church on Elm Street. Will stood stiff and unsmiling in front of the altar while Jess grinned beside him. They both stared up the aisle toward Judy and Seth waiting impatiently at the church doors.

"Like looking down a rifle barrel," Will muttered.

Jess snickered. "Shotgun," he corrected in a loud whisper.

A smile tugged at Will's mouth. "You really pay Preacher Dick to leave town? It's 'bout the only hope I got left."

"Only had 'nuff coin ta pay him ta be late. Musta got carried away by that funeral of the boy that drowned in the Mississippi he was preachin' at this mornin'. Or maybe the second coming's today, the dead are rising from the earth, and Preacher Dick's tryin' ta talk 'em all inta joinin' his congregation. Life kin be mighty queersome."

Will chuckled. He glanced at his mother and Sarah smiling gently up at him from the front pew and frowned. This is what they want, he thought angrily. "How'd I get inta this?" he spate. "Ain't what I had in mind."

"That's what pokin' kin do to a man," Jess replied philosophically. "Least ya finally talked Judy inta letting ya off the hook for the Plains." He glanced down at Will's trousers and snickered. "Glad ye changed britches. That other pair was plumb wore out from all the time ya spent on ye knees pleadin' ye case."

"Warn't easy," Will muttered as he rubbed a handkerchief over the beads of sweat dripping down his face. "Dark wool suits in July. Feels like I took a soakin' in the river, too. Everything's crazy."

There was a commotion at the door and Preacher Evans brushed past Judy and Seth then, as if suddenly recognizing them, stopped abruptly and shook hands.

"I am so sorry, so very sorry to be late," he apologized in his loud, squeaky voice. "I had to comfort the bereaved. Tragic just tragic. Life is filled with utter tragedy. Oh, the Lord's ways can be so mysterious," he lamented. He turned his back on them and hurried down the aisle, the folds of his black robes swishing and his steps creaking the floor. Mumbling apologies, he shook hands with Will and Jess, then fumbled inside a pocket, extracted his wire rim glasses, and twisted the frames over his large, protruding ears.

Looks like an old bloodhound sniffing after sinners, Will thought as he examined the preacher's tall, skinny body, drooping jowls, puffy bags under sad red eyes, and thinning gray hair. Evans flipped nervously through a ceremonial book, found the page he was looking for, and loudly cleared his throat. "Will Mr. Seth Morgan bring his daughter forward?" he squeaked. The murmuring in the church died and all turned to watch Judy and Seth glide slowly down the aisle, her left hand gently cupping his bent elbow. She smiled radiently as she gazed into Will's eyes. He inhaled deeply and smiled back. She is pretty, he thought happily, marveling at her sleek, white cotton dress, dimples, full lips, and long golden hair. He thought of the life stirring within her thickening waist. I'll try to be a kind, easy father, he promised himself—like Uncle Jake or Hank Baucus, not Pa.

As Judy stepped beside him, Will took her hand and turned to face the preacher, with Jess and Seth flanking them. Evans cleared his throat once more.

"We are gathered to join William Yates and Judith Morgan in holy matrimony..." Evans jumped into the liturgy but he seemed distracted, sometimes losing his place or repeating some words. Will reckoned the boy's death had really rattled him. He tried to concentrate on the words and their meaning, but his mind wandered and he sometimes felt overwhelmed by a feeling of panic.

Suddenly Evans was saying, "and do you, William Yates, take this woman, Judith Morgan, to have and to hold from this day forward, to love and to cherish, for richer, for poorer, in sickness and in health, until death do you part?"

The collective weight of Judy and the crowd staring at him, waiting eagerly for his reply nearly overwhelmed him. He felt like dashing madly for the door and disappearing forever. Too late now, he admitted reluctantly.

"I do," he mumbled.

Judy squeezed his hand tightly and smiled up at him as Evans asked her the same. "I do," she said with deep feeling.

"I now pronounce..."

"Preacher," Will hissed in annoyance, "the ring!"

Evans looked startled. "Ah yes...the ring." He impatiently waved his hand toward Will, who quickly slipped a gold ring over Judy's finger. Her smiled deepened as she spread her fingers in wonder.

"I now pronounce you man and wife. You may kiss the bride," the preacher ordered. The newlyweds pecked each other lightly on the lips and turned to face the audience, which broke into boisterous applause and cheers.

They strolled slowly down the aisle as everyone crowded around them to shake hands or kiss them on the cheek. Will laughed and traded quips with the well-wishers. Like running the gauntlet, he joked silently.

They finally broke free from the dark church into the bright sunlight and stepped into a buggy while the rest of the wedding party piled into wagons or strolled after them toward the Morgan farm three miles west of town. Passersby tipped their hats and shouted congratulations, and some joined the procession.

The sun boiled down relentlessly from a cloudless sky and everyone was sweat-soaked and dusty by the time they stumbled into the farmyard. They crowded up to long tables covered with stacks of plates, platters of meats, vegetables, bread, and fruit pies, and jugs of hard cider and whiskey. Several farm wives, who had spent a hectic morning preparing everything, hovered behind the tables, swishing away flies, carving slices of roast beef and pork onto eagerly presented plates, and demanding why it took everyone so long to get there. A fiddler and banjo player started playing "Turkey in the Straw" and couples were soon whirling in the yard. Children darted through the throng, playing tag and snatching food.

Will and Judy were pulled apart by the crowd. Juggling a plate piled with food in one hand and a mug of cider in the other, Will joked with Jess and a half-dozen male friends and acquaintances who surrounded him and winked as they offered advice for the wedding night and extolled Judy's charms. Will and Jess talked excitedly of their trip onto the Plains and the others expressed their disappointment at not being able to come along.

A gunshot exploded. Startled, everyone turned to face Seth swaying atop a wooden chair. He tossed down his still-smoking flintlock pistol and raised a mug. His short, pear-shaped wife, Betty, beamed below as she tried desperately to prop him up. "Where's my daughter and son-in-law?" he bellowed cheerfully. "And the rest of my children! All five of them! And Jenny and Sarah! You all come up here, too!" Will, Judy, and the others squeezed through the crowd toward Seth. "Gather 'round everbody and hear this. Hush now!" he commanded and the crowd silenced. "I got some important words to say!" Seth thrust his mug toward Judy and Will and some whiskey slopped down on Betty's head. She giggled loudly. "To my daughter and new son-in-law! May they live in happiness to a ripe old age and give us many grandchildren in the meantime!" Everyone whooped and hollered as they lifted mugs high then tipped them back to their lips and guzzled.

"Kiss!" someone shouted and the couple kissed eagerly and everyone cheered. The fiddler and banjo player struck up a Virginia reel. Judy grabbed Will's hands and merrily shouted, "Let's dance!" They promenaded through the crowd's laughter and raised mugs while other couples joined and followed.

The last drunks did not collapse or shuffle home until past two in the morning. Betty had promised the couple that they could have the girl's room all to themselves for their wedding night. But although Judy's sister Mary slept in their parents' room, Will had to drag two men into the hall who had passed out on the bed. He staggered back into the room, quietly shut the door, and propped a chair beneath the knob. Judy had already kicked off her shoes and curled up on the bed. Her eyes were half-slits and her thick lips were slightly parted. "Not tonight," she mumbled. Will nodded wearily and crawled into bed beside her.

They had been riding all morning, lulled into a doze as their mounts and the packhorses ambled on. The horses' hoofs sucked and slopped rhythmically in mud up to their fetlocks. Cicadas buzzed loudly and songbirds whistled and flitted through the thick, steaming woods. They passed an occasional cornfield and cabin, and nodded to the sweaty, filthy farmers who leaned briefly on their hoes and stared back.

Will kept yawning and nodding and a few times almost fell off his horse. Images of Judy whirled before his eyes then vanished before he could seize her. Soaked and sticky from the showers and humidity, he longed to stretch out on Judy's cornhusk mattress and spoon his body and arms around her.

Why did I ever leave her, he rebuked himself. He savored the feeling of Judy hugging him tightly, silently, as they rode through town to the St. Charles road. They dismounted beneath the huge chestnut tree where she had first told him of her pregnancy. The road was deserted and a misty rain began to fall. He tried to sound cheerful as he repeatedly told her not to worry, that he would be safe, rich, and back in her arms before she knew it. But his heart felt leaden and his mind torn over whether to leave. She tried to be brave, blinking back tears and sobs, then pressed an envelope in his hand as they kissed passionately goodbye and he trotted off. She shrank a little more each time he twisted in the saddle to snatch a glimpse and wave until finally the woods swallowed her tiny blue-clad body. He jerked his horse to a stop and tore open the envelope. There was a lock of her golden hair and a note proclaiming her eternal love, faith, and hope for their future. He resisted the urge to gallop back, wrap his arms around her, and promise he would never again leave her.

Instead he stuffed the envelope in his shirt and kicked his horse forward into a canter as his eyes blurred and his throat choked with cries. A couple of hours later, he rejoined Jess, who had been waiting impatiently at the St. Charles landing, and they rode west along the muddy road to Franklin.

"Wettest summer I kin remember," Jess commented with a sigh. He glanced at Will. "What're ya looking so hangdog 'bout?" He nodded toward a half-dozen men scything a pasture. "Look at those boys try to get in that hay before the next cloudburst. It'll all rot anyway. Jus' think, we could be working for a livin' 'stead a' being footloose and fancy-free."

"True," Will admitted grimly. "Old man Morgan had me harvesting the corn crop or chopping wood dawn till dusk for the two weeks I spent at their place. I'll never farm again! But now I just wanna get a good night's sleep for a change. Eight straight nights a' rain since we left and that canvas tent ain't worth a damn. We can't make any time wading this stream folks here call a road and Becknell'll probably have left by the time we get to Franklin."

"Welp," Jess replied cheerfully, "if that farmboy we passed a ways back was talkin' straight, we'll find out in a couple of hours. But if they left we can always catch up." He prodded his horse and tugged on the lead to his packhorse. "Cum on, gal!"

They rode on in silence. Their minds wandered and dozed until finally they topped a rise to stare down at several score of buildings and fields alongside the Missouri River.

"Must be Franklin," Jess observed. "Ezekiel Williams's place is supposed to be five miles upriver. Hope there's a trace."

They got directions in town and plodded on for another hour along the river road which cut through thick woods broken by farms. William's place was a large cabin with a sagging roof surrounded by a stump-filled corn field. Smoke drifted out of the chimney and the odor of ham and manure hung heavily. A score of horses and a half-dozen tents were staked out around the cabin. Men lounged on the porch cleaning rifles or whittling. Chickens and pigs rooted amidst the squalor.

"Riders," someone shouted and other men gathered before the cabin to stare. Will and Jess nodded as they rode up, then wearily dismounted.

"What kin we do for ye boys?" asked an wizened man with a week-old gray beard and no teeth. He slowly chewed a wad in his cheek.

Jess smiled and nodded. "Lookin' for Mr. William Becknell. We're fixin' to join his party to the Plains."

The man spat a stream of tobacco juice and slowly patted it into the mud with his boot. "Ye come ta the right place. The captain's in town tending to some...business," the man laughed hoarsely. "I'm Zeke Williams," he said, extending a gnarled hand. Will and Jess introduced themselves and shook hands with the others.

"Is this all?" Will asked. "We figured if you hadn't already left, that there'd be at least seventy men here, and you might not have room to take us."

Zeke's hoarse laugh turned into a hacking cough. "Goddamn if my guts ain't rottin' out," he shook his head angrily. "This is it, boys. Everbody else who could git aways done gone upriver. Rest is tied ta thar farms. Captain's got business ta tend. Could be 'nother week or more afore he leaves, if t'all. Seems half the county's suing him to git their loans back."

Zeke giggled merrily. "Owes more 'en eleven hundurt dollars. But don't worry, boys, you'll be out on the plains soon 'nuff, if the captain don't get jailed. 'Course if he don't raise a helluva stake out thar," Zeke gestured toward the West, "then he better not come back." He giggled again. Jess and Will glanced nervously at each other. "But whar's ma manners? Ye boys look mighty ragged. Ye want some grub? Ye kin rest ye fixins on the porch here till ye git situated."

Will and Jess quickly pulled the saddles and packs from their horses then rushed into the cabin. Eager to hear news from back East, a dozen men crowded around them as they gobbled down platefuls of ham and hominy. Jess as usual did most of the talking, regaling them with stories as he shoveled food into his mouth. They lazed the rest of the afternoon, trading tales and swigging applejack. Showers rattled the roof and in places dripped through the cedar shingles. Tobacco and wood smoke fouled the air.

The other men were mostly young, in their twenties and thirties, and from the surrounding countryside. None had been on the Plains before and all listened eagerly to Zeke's tales of his own adventures across to the Shining Mountains and back. Zeke had journeyed with Champlain's 1811 and 1812 trapping parties across the Plains along the Rockies' front range to the Arkansas headwaters. The first party was successful but all of the second were killed by Indians or captured and imprisoned by the Spanish except Zeke who escaped down the Arkansas and finally trudged back to St. Louis. Undaunted he returned two years later with the Philibert party to raise the furs and goods the Champlain party had cached on the upper Arkansas. Zeke and a few companions then returned to Missouri with their loot while the rest pushed on to the Rockies. Word eventually drifted back that Philibert and his men had been captured and imprisoned by the Spanish.

It was about dusk and Zeke was in the midst of a buffalo hunt story when they heard a rider trot up outside. Everyone paused expectantly then nodded or greeted Becknell as he strode through the open door. He was lean and of average height, had high cheekbones and green eyes, and slicked his greasy black hair behind his ears. He dropped a huge sack of flour heavily on the floor. "Son of a bitch is soaked through!" he said in disgust.

Zeke laughed hoarsely. "Figured ye was in jail, Bill."

Becknell peeled off his muddy linen shirt and wrung it tightly. "We'll see," he muttered. His eyes focused sharply on Will and Jess. He nodded. "Ya boys headin' West with us?"

"Hope to," Will replied. "Just when are you fixing on leaving? Paper said August fourth. That's today."

"Well," Becknell admitted wearily, "there's been a change of plans." He glanced around the room at the men's expectant faces. "Boys...looks like it'll be a few weeks yet. September first at the latest." The men groaned and cursed.

Will frowned bitterly, thinking of three more weeks he could have spent with Judy. He recalled again her soft body sobbing in his arms the night before he left. Was I really as selfish and uncaring as she claimed? he wondered. Only a couple weeks together after the wedding. But wasn't I doing this for both of us, for the baby? Old man Seth and her brothers seemed to understand, but her mother and sister got colder as the departure date neared. Judy tried to be cheerful, but her fears and the morning sickness dragged her into deep depressions.

He stared angrily around the noisy room crowded with dirty backwoodsmen and piles of trade goods. Another month in this scum hole, he cursed silently. "Got half a mind to head home," he muttered.

Jess chuckled and poked him in the ribs. "Now don't ya fret, boy. Ya'll be back with yer woman in a few months and then can settle down for the rest of yer days, bouncing children and grandchildren and great-grandchildren on yer knees. Till then just enjoy all the fine company we found ourselves among and all the adventures from here to maybe even Santa Fe and back. 'Sides, don't ya think Childe Harold ever had mixed feelings afore he set out to wander the world? Or what about Odysseus leaving Roxanne for twenty years to fight Trojans and be serenaded by sirens and 'scape from blind Cyclopses and such? Hell, we'll be lucky to even face a scalping knife or Mexican prison."

Will smiled. "How do I let you talk me into harebrained schemes like this?"

Jess grinned back. "What're friends for?"

Will sat cross-legged with his back to Fort Osage's rotting log wall. His eyes wandered the fluffy clouds drifting the turquoise sky to the lumpy green blanket covering the horizon and finally the diamonds sparkling through the trees on the Missouri River below. A dozen men were milling about a keelboat at the landing. Horses grazed nearby in the meadow. A teamster cracked his whip and mules yanked a canvas covered wagon forward up the steep slope to the fort. Will dipped his quill in an ink bottle and scratched it across the paper on his knees. "It will be fall soon and I will greatly miss the golden and red leaves as there will be few trees where we're heading," he wrote, then gazed beyond the river where huge shadows surged across the forest.

His mind drifted through the collage of memories he had collected since leaving St. Louis over seven weeks earlier. Although he suffered waves of guilt and depression since his tearful goodbye with Judy, his bouts of anguish slowly subsided in intensity and frequency. Life at Zeke's farm hadn't been bad, what with hunting the woods for deer and riding into town for provisions and whiskey at the local taverns. Only seventeen men had answered Becknell's call. Though they chaffed at the delay, the men got along well enough. They staged frequent shooting contests to hone their skills, then drinking contests afterwards to celebrate. Finally, on September 1, 1821, with cheers and rifle shots splitting the air, they rode off to the ferry at Arrow Rock.

Will shuddered as he recalled the Missouri crossing. The crossing was easy, but he and the others were haunted by a severely "touched" teenage boy who was chained to a cabin porch on the south bank. He had a small, round head atop an immense mountain of fat. His vast, protruding belly, and arms and legs swollen twice that of a man, all jiggled when he moved. He was bug-eyed, saliva drooled from his gaping mouth, and his pudgy face and naked arms were covered with welts, scabs, and open sores. As they rode past he giggled, babbled incoherently, and pranced toward them until his leash jerked him back.

He swayed stupidly then burst into a shrill howl and jabbed his hands toward them. "Die! Die! Die!" he chanted maniacally as the men spurred their horses into a canter. They rode in strained silence for a while until someone suggested riding back "ta put that creature outta its misery." "Kain't kill that demon," Jess replied. "Ye kin kill its body but its ghost'll chase ye ta the ends of the earth." Most of the men were superstitious and feared the boy foresaw their deaths. Their spirits dampened further over the next five days as they shivered from chilling rains as they plodded through rolling tall grass prairie and woods until they reached Fort Osage.

"Fear not, my dearest," he scratched, "we are a small but powerful party, well armed and provisioned, and no Indians will impede our journey to Santa Fe and triumphant return with saddle bags full of silver." He frowned at the line wishing he had not written it. Wouldn't do to get her hopes too high about getting rich, he reasoned. 'Course she did maintain repeatedly that she prayed only for my safe return and didn't care even if I was penniless. Still...

He tapped the turkey feather against his forehead. Oh, well. He dipped his pen again and wrote, "We leave at dawn tomorrow and I must tend to many chores in the meantime so I will close now. Forever Yours, Will." He carefully folded then addressed the letter's blank backside. Wonder if I'll ever see her again, he thought as he slipped it into a shirt pocket, plugged the ink bottle, and rose to his feet.

He strolled around to the fort's front gate and paused as a half-dozen Osage spilled out, their arms filled with blankets, copper kettles, paints, hatchets, and beads. The men's skulls were shaved except for long scalp locks, brass rings pierced their ears and noses, and their arms and naked chests were tattooed with sweeping swirls and patterns. Most were taller than Will and glanced contemptuously at him as they pushed past. If these were friendly Indians, what were the Plains Indians like, he wondered. He shuddered slightly as he imagined himself alone on the endless plains with a war party riding hard after him, howling and shaking scalping knives.

He nodded to a private cradling a musket beside the gate. "They ever give ye any trouble?"

He spit a stream of tobacco juice. "Not 'round here they don't, but they'll strip and beat within a hair's width a' death any independent traders who reach their villages. 'Course Chouteau's men got free passage. Hear tell, though, the politicians in Washington may do away with these government forts and special traders like Chouteau and let anyone trade with the savages. Don't know what the Osage'll do then."

Will smiled. "Then you'll be out of a job."

"Naw," he shook his head sorrowfully, "they'll jus' ship us somewhere else. Don't know why I ever joined up in the first place. Wish I was free to go as I please like you boys. Got another year and five months till I am out."

"Well, good luck to you," Will nodded then picked his way across the crowded parade ground. A score of Osage and Kaw gathered around several bearded traders hawking trinkets, while other Indians passed in and out of the trade house. Half-breed children shouted and chased each other. Fat mongrel dogs dozed or scratched at fleas. Soldiers in threadbare, faded blue uniforms lounged atop the four corner blockhouses and either stared below or toward the meadows outside the fort. Two plump Indian women giggled and gestured lewdly to a half-dozen of Becknell's men, and then they all strolled toward one of the cabins. Becknell and the Factor, George Sibley, sat and talked earnestly on a pile of buffalo rugs before the trade house. They stopped and looked up as Will walked hesitantly up to them. "Begging you gentlemen's pardon," he said as he handed Sibley the letter. "Excuse me, sir, but could you please forward this to my wife in St. Louis? I didn't have any wax to seal it."

Sibley was a slight man with a bald head and watery brown eyes. He smiled gently up at Will. "Certainly, son, we'll get it sealed and on a keelboat tomorrow or the next day. As I was telling the captain here," he laid a callused hand on Becknell's shoulder, "you boys can tell your loved ones to fear not. You'll have no trouble getting across and back as long as the Mexican Revolution succeeds. But just be hard as nails with the Osage," he glanced warily at three Indians squatting nearby, "and any other tribes you encounter. Hard, but fair. And make damn sure your horses are staked close to camp and sentinels are eyeballing them all night or they'll be long gone the next morning when you wake up. And if you run into Chouteau and his men, don't give them the time of day. Chouteau seems to think his exclusive license to trade with the Osage makes his clan king of the territory and he's not above encouraging the Osage to steal your horses or provisions."

Becknell chuckled. "We'll make it," he declared confidently, "and put a ball through any nigger that stands in our way, be he white or red. Ain't that right, Will?"

Will smiled slightly and nodded. "Anybody," he replied softly.

The horses plopped slowly over the soaked earth, sidestepping prairie dog and rattlesnake holes. Their riders stared across the short grass prairie stretching before them to the horizon. The sky was broken with shafts of bright sunlight and dark, heavy clouds trailing gray curtains. The only sounds were the sucking of hoofs in sod, the men's staccato coughing and sniffing of phlegm, and an occasional curse at some discomfort, a sore throat, an aching back, a fever. It had rained nearly every day of a week from Fort Osage and some men were muttering a desire to turn back. All day they scanned the horizon for buffalo but the immense herds that earlier wanderers had marveled at seemed to have been swept off the earth, leaving only their whitened dung and bones behind.

Will and Jess rode alongside Becknell at the column's head. Becknell could barely write and read, and kept them close to enjoy the tales they told of Byron and Scott. But the last several days Becknell rode silently with a body hunched and face bitter from flu. He spared his words mostly for curt orders to halt and dry out the trade goods and graze the horses.

"Wish ol' Zeke was with us," Becknell suddenly mumbled.

Will recalled Zeke grinning toothlessly at them from his cabin porch as they rode off to Arrow Rock ferry. "See ya in hell if not sooner," he had hollered after them. Everyone had laughed but now the laughter seemed foolish.

"Ol' Zeke's a character if ah ever met one," Jess stated cheerfully. "We'll have a few tales ta tell him when we return."

"What's that to the left?" someone shouted and they all strained to make out brown dots against the tawny plains a couple miles off. Buffalo? they all wondered hopefully. "They're movin'," someone observed.

Becknell grunted. "Who wants to run 'em?"

Will, Jess, and a half-dozen men volunteered and tossed the reins of their packhorses to the others.

"Save yer horses till yer within spitting distance," Becknell warned as the hunters rode off.

Will's fatigue melted. A smile broke across his face as he dug his heels into his horse's side and it broke into a canter. Finally, he thought happily, buffalo! The image of that bleached buffalo floating past on the Mississippi so long ago suddenly flashed in his mind. He sometimes dreamed of its bloody eye socket and curled horn rising on the current and then drifting away. The more distant the memories he tried to retrieve, the more unreal they seemed, like hazy dreams. Was his family's flight from Cincinnati to St. Louis from his life or someone else's? "Get that silver dollar and jug a' whiskey ready, Will," Jess shouted as he rode alongside. "The payoff's finally coming."

"We'll see who'll drop the first buffalo," Will replied with a laugh, remembering the bet they had made years ago.

"Hold up," someone hollered, "I gotta check my priming." They reined in their horses and everyone hastily clicked open their pans.

"Anybody ever hunted buffalo?" someone asked. They searched each other's faces but no one answered.

"Gotta aim low. Just above the shoulder," Jess maintained.

"Maybe we oughta scatter out so we don't get in each other's way," Will suggested. "And let's approach 'em at a walk till they run. And remember what Zeke said about shooting cows rather than bulls. Lucky the wind's in our faces." The others nodded. They spread out and slowly advanced toward the brown dots.

"Keep clear of them horns, Will," Jess called, and the others hushed him into silence.

Will chuckled nervously. He tried imagining how he could ride at a full gallop, aim, and shoot at the same time.

It was a small herd of about one hundred. A couple of lean wolves sat on their haunches just out of charging distance and stared hungrily at the shaggy beasts. The wolves noticed the riders first and loped away while the buffalo continued browsing. Suddenly, when the riders were about one hundred yards away, a bull on the herd's fringe snorted and the buffalos' heads raised up and sniffed the air. A few buffalo broke into a run and then the rest of the herd stampeded after them. One of the men fired his rifle but missed. The riders yelled with excitement and kicked their horses into a gallop.

Will's horse was fast and soon caught up to the herd. He gripped his reins and rifle tightly as he guided his horse alongside a fat cow with a calf trailing behind. A couple of shots exploded nearby admidst the thundering hoofs, but he barely noticed. The herd was starting to scatter and the cow suddenly lurched away, but Will jerked his horse alongside again. He exalted in the terror and thrill of galloping among a score of buffalo, shuddered at the image of his horse stumbling and throwing him before those horns, hoofs, and huge, lumbering bodies. He slipped the reins between his teeth and pointed his rifle at the buffalo's chest. His rifle jolted with his galloping horse over the rough ground. He slowly squeezed the trigger as the sight passed over the beast's shoulder. The buffalo disappeared in yellow smoke. His horse dodged at the shot and Will almost fell. He grabbed the reins out of his teeth and slowly eased his horse into a canter as a half-dozen buffalo tore around him.

He twisted in his saddle and looked back. The herd and riders had scattered in all directions. A rifle shot cracked. One man had dismounted, tied his horse's reins to the horns of a dead buffalo, and was already cutting through the fur. With its calf nuzzling its flank, the cow he shot limped slowly, painfully, a hundred feet off. Will reined in his horse and reloaded, then trotted his horse after the cow. The cow tried to run but stumbled and fell. The calf sniffed its mother's face. "Git," he yelled as he rode up.

The calf ran off a short distance then stood staring. Will grimaced as he pointed his rifle at the buffalo's head. The buffalo's chest was heaving and blood spurted from its nose and throat. He glanced back at the calf. One of the wolves was running up behind it. "Look out!" he hollered just as the wolf sunk its teeth into the calf's throat and flung it to the ground. The calf struggled and bawled a few times, then lay silent. The wolf glared at Will then warily began tearing at the calf's rump. Will shuddered and stared back at the buffalo. It gasped heavily. Must have hit a lung, he thought grimly. He aimed again but then thought better of it. Gotta guard my shot, he reasoned. He dismounted, dropped the reins, and walked slowly over toward the buffalo. Its visible eye was half-closed. He stood over the buffalo and pulled out his skinning knife. This ain't the garden of Eden, he reminded himself. Here everything eats everything else. He plunged his knife into the buffalo's neck and pulled down, unleashing a stream of blood. The buffalo lay still.

Will propped his rifle against the buffalo and slowly turned in a circle. The thunderclouds and sun threw strange racing patterns of shadow and light across the endless plains. His horse grazed nearby and the wolf tore greedily at the calf a hundred feet away. Four men and their horses had gathered around the other buffalo a quarter mile off. Jess was galloping toward him. He whooped and waved his rifle then pulled up hard. The wolf darted off to a knoll and stared back. Grinning madly, Jess jumped down and pumped Will's hand. "Ya did it, by God, ya did it!" he shouted excitedly. "My shot kicked up nothing but dust. I'll fetch yer jug and dollar in Santa Fe!"

Will smiled weakly. "Just help me carve this up. A man's gotta live."

They hit the Arkansas River a few days later. The river was several hundred yards wide and flowed sluggishly around long, thin islands. Its muddy waters were shallow, at most waist deep, but obscured treacherous patches of quicksand that could suck down a man or beast in seconds. The banks were barren except for an occasional cottonwood or ash tree. Huge herds of buffalo wallowed the river's holes or grazed the short grasses alongside. At night, the guards threw stones to drive the shaggy beasts away from camp. The men feared a thunderstorm or Indians would stampede a herd through their tents as they slept. Hunting was easy. They lived off buffalo meat which they cut up in big chunks and roasted over buffalo dung fires on their ramrod tips. Rattlesnakes seemed as numerous. They sunned themselves by the dozens on flat slate rocks and rattled furiously as the party rode slowly by. Wolves and coyotes howled eerily at night and trailed them just out of rifle shot during the day.

The men trudged around twenty miles a day, and the air seemed sharper the farther west they rode. The plague of flu and colds slowly died and the men's spirits rose as steadily. But though they rested often, their mounts were breaking down from the pace and thin grass, and they abandoned several lame horses to the wolves. They crossed an occasional trail of unshod ponies and cold ashes of fires but saw no Indians.

After almost a month along the Arkansas, they turned southwest up the Purgatoire River. A couple of days later they heard a distant rifle shot, but feared sending out scouts to investigate. With each day of travel, the cliffs along the river rose higher, and the river narrowed and rushed through the shallow canyon. The nights grew colder and they often woke with frost on their tents. As they rode they scattered fewer buffalo, then none at all, but mule deer, elk, and big horn sheep grew more numerous and fell to their rifles. A rider sometimes pointed out huge grizzly tracks but the bear were as invisible as the Indians. After six days of hard riding up the Purgatoire, the canyon boxed them in on three sides. For two days the men cut away a trail to the canyon rim, rolling away huge boulders and shoveling the rock-hard earth. It took another day to coax the horses with their baggage up the cliffs. One horse stumbled and was crushed on the rocks below. They rode across a flat plain for two days until they hit the upper canyon of the Canadian River and spent a half-day crossing to the west side. Game and wood became scarce after they left the Purgatoire and the weather more bitter. One day fierce winds and snow flurries blasted them. Their horses stumbled only a dozen rugged miles daily. The men grew haggard and short-fused. But they finally emerged onto rolling, grassy plains where they spotted cattle and sheep tracks and herds of wild horses. Beyond the plains stretched the dark green jagged wall of the Sangre de Christo Mountains. They cheered at their first sight of the Rockies.

It took two more hard days' rides to reach the mountains' base. Then they turned southwest, skirting huge mesas that jutted out from the Sangre de Christo and each night camping in cottonwood groves alongside clear flowing streams.

Will grew more exalted the farther west they rode. He reveled in the vast rolling plains, the dark, moving masses of buffalo, the skittish antelope, the black strings of geese high above honking their way south, the wolves always lurking furtively nearby. His mind drifted through the swirling waters of the Arkansas and Purgatoire, flitted through the golden leaves of the cottonwoods rustling in the piercing autumn air, or glided past red canyon cliffs and mesas sculpted weirdly by eons of wind and rain and up across the snow-capped Rockies. He and the other men seemed the last on earth, and despite occasional squabbles and accusations, there was a security, a warmth in their circle as they rode all day, crouched wearily around campfires, and snored away the long dark nights. At times Will felt like whooping with joy.

He envied God. He strained to soar into the turquoise sky and expand a million times so he could be everywhere at once. He wanted to embrace all the earth with his spirit and eavesdrop on every living creature.

One chilly morning a week after struggling out of Purgatoire Canyon and a day after starting up between the juniper- and piñon-pine-covered walls of Pecos Canyon that cut across the southern end of the Sangre de Christo, they finally saw riders. The men cocked their rifles and rested them across the their saddle pommels as a dozen men cantered toward them. Looking more savage than white, they wore ragged Spanish uniforms covered with sleeveless leather jackets, broad sombreros, and carried lances or short muskets. Gourd water jugs, rolled rainbow-colored serapes, and bull-hide shields dangled from their saddles. They pulled up a hundred yards off. Their commander walked his horse forward.

"This is it, boys," Becknell stated grimly as he looked around at his men. The hard trail had turned his face gaunt and body stooped. "Either riches or war. Me an' Will'll go parley with 'em. They look peaceful 'nuff, but cut 'em down if they try something. C'mon, Will." They kicked their horses into a trot. "Least they's smilin'," Becknell observed.

Will's body tingled and his mind raced. Will they politely warn us away, or is it a ruse to capture us and drag us off in chains? Or will they proudly escort us to the silver and dark beauties of Santa Fe? He regretted mentioning that he had picked up some Spanish phrases along the St. Louis wharf. The captain's relying on me, he worried. I can't let him and the others down.

They reined in their horses a half-dozen feet from the Mexicans. Their commander was short and plump. His legs barely seemed to reach the stirrups. A thick silver handlebar mustache curled across a face as wrinkled and dark as a walnut. His saddle and bridle were studded with silver. He bowed slightly and tipped his sombrero. "*Buenos días, Señors,*" he intoned gravely. "*Bienvenedos a la República de México. Estoy enteramente a su disposición.*"

The Americans nodded and lifted their slouch hats. "*Buenos días,*" Will replied. "*Nosotros somos americanos. Este hombre es mi comandante,*" he pointed to Becknell. "*Deseo...*" He searched his mind for "trade." He glanced at Becknell whose mouth was stretched in a taut smile. "*Deseo...plata.*" The commander's head jerked back slightly. He smiled and spoke rapidly.

"What's he sayin'?" Becknell demanded.

"Sorry, Captain. Can't make out a word. He's speaking too fast and my Spanish is too limited."

The commander spoke several words in a questioning tone. Will shrugged. The commander shook his head in bewilderment. He pointed to the Americans and then waved them toward his detachment.

"Looks like he wants us ta join him," Becknell remarked.

"Think it's a trick?"

Becknell sighed. "Only one way ta find out now, ain't there." He nodded to the commander then twisted in the saddle. "C'mon, boys. Uncock yer rifles unless we run inta more of 'em. And smile. We're outta the wilderness and inta the land a' milk and honey. We're gonna get rich." Some of the men whooped and the commander looked alarmed. "*Amigo*," Will pointed to Becknell and the other men. "*Nosotros somos sus amigos*." The commander smiled and extended his hand.

They rode northwest together then camped for the night, communicating through smiles, nods, shared provisions, and Will's smattering of Spanish.

The next day they reached the village of San Miguel far up Pecos Canyon. The Mexicans surged out of their adobe huts and milled about, laughing and talking excitedly around the grimy, bearded riders. By luck, living in the village was a Frenchman named Claude Dupuis, who agreed to ride with them to Santa Fe and serve as interpreter. A half-dozen miles farther they paused to marvel at the jumbled stone ruins of an ancient village atop a small, juniper-covered mesa. Dupuis swore that even the Pueblos had no memory of its habitation.

Late the following afternoon, two and a half months after leaving Franklin, they rode over the pass and gazed in wonder at the broad Rio Grande Valley before them. The piñon and juniper stretched down the slopes for miles until it faded away into sagebrush. They could not see the Rio Grande, they could only make out a distant dark crevice snaking among the small mesas scattered across the valley's floor. Fifty miles to the west was a long, snow-capped mountain range that paralleled the valley. Huge thunderclouds drifted through the cobalt sky. The men cheered and marveled at the promised land's splendor.

It was not until dusk that they finally emerged from the piñon and juniper forest and rode past scattered adobe huts and corn and wheat stubbled fields and small herds of cattle and sheep into Santa Fe's plaza. The comandante disappeared into the governor's mansion while, chattering merrily, a crowd gathered around the Americans. Tears streamed down the smiling faces of some of Becknell's men in relief at the friendly welcome after the hardships of the long journey and uncertainty over whether they would be greeted with a prison cell or open arms. The men were particularly smitten by the pretty Mexican girls who flirted boldly. The comandante finally emerged with permission to house the men and their packs in an empty warehouse across the square and herd their horses into a nearby corral.

That night, Becknell's men and several Mexican officers and prominent merchants celebrated their arrival with thick slices of roast beef, chicken, and mutton wrapped in tortillas, and washed down with fiery aguadiente.

With Dupuis translating, the men toasted one another, American and Mexican independence, and the beginning of an eternal and prosperous friendship between their two countries.

Will stuffed himself with food and drink, and joked heartily with the others. It all seemed a dream and he feared awakening huddled in his blanket back on the frozen plains. The beguiling smiles of the Mexican girls in the plaza kept swirling through his mind, and he guiltily tried to expel them. But whenever he tried to focus on Judy, she faded away and those doe-eyed girls with their eager faces and low-cut blouses came rushing back.

Jess poked him in the ribs. "What'd turned ya into a pumpkin all of a sudden?"

Will shrugged. "I was jus' thinking that Judy's probably fearing I'm nothing but a pile of bleached bones out on the prairie and here I am getting drunk and wishing I spoke enough Spanish to court them Mexican gals."

Jess chuckled. "What Judy don't know won't hurt her. Hell, she's probably doing the same." Will's eyes widened. "Yup, she's prob'ly run off with another man, prob'ly with Rene. Ye know what a ladies' man Rene—"

"Shut yer trap!" Will replied, half-annoyed and half-amused.

"Enjoy it while ya kin," he urged, "ya never know when yer time's up." Will shrugged. Jess glanced furtively around and said in a voice barely audible above the drunken clamor around them, "We oughta git the jump on these other boys, rise bright and early tomorrow morning, and stretch our legs out on the square amongst all those beauties. Between yer Spanish and ma dazzling good looks we oughta be able ta stroll off with a half-dozen on each arm." Jess gulped down a mouthful of aguadiente and belched loudly. "By God, Will, did ya see them gals!" he said excitedly. "They was runnin' their fingers across our arms and eyeballing us head ta toe and lingerin' over the bulges between our legs! Those gals are as juiced as bitches in heat!"

Will nodded and sighed. "I know. It's like a dream. But ya'll hafta fend for yourself with the ladies tomorrow morning. I've gotta go with the captain to meet the governor." He lowered his voice. "A couple nights back the captain proposed an 'association' where I'd send goods to him in Franklin and he takes 'em out here." His eyes and smile widened. "We could make a fortune if we financed and supplied Becknell like Stone, Bostwick, and Company does the Missouri Fur Company! How's this sound?" He raised his hands like he was framing a picture. "Yates, Baucus, and Company!"

Jess nodded approvingly. "Mighty fine ring to it, Will, mighty fine." He leaned closer, winked, and said in a low voice. "But why do we need the captain? After all, he was none too pleased back in Franklin that we had our own trade goods and didn't hafta rely on his like the others. And now he's asking for an association? Don't git me wrong, the captain's fair as he is hard. But we owe him nothing. What if we took the goods across direct ourselves?"

Will smiled broadly and glanced around the room crowded with flush-faced men cramming their gullets with food and drink or talking loudly. "Could be a helluva foot race."

Becknell, Will, and Dupuis doffed their hats as the comandante ushered them into the governor's office. Governor Facundo Melgares stood from behind his desk and bowed slightly as they entered. From the austere whitewashed wall behind the governor hung the hide painting of an emaciated saint gazing mournfully at eternity. Melgares was as short and plump as the comandante. He was dressed in an elegant mustard waistcoat, chalk knee breeches, and a huge white silk cravat. His thinning iron-gray hair was greased straight back from a sloped brow. He had high cheekbones, bright brown eyes, and a small, pursed mouth. He tilted his head back slightly and peered unblinkingly at them as they stood awkwardly before him. *"Bienvenedos a la República de México,"* he finally intoned gravely. *"Estoy enteramente a su disposición."* Melgares smiled, then, with exquisite politeness, began interrogating them, waiting patiently as Dupuis translated. He asked first about their intentions, background, and the route of their journey, what savages, beasts, and other perils they had encountered, and finally the population, wealth, power, and ambitions of the United States.

He then picked up and read from a document that he had received from the national government several months earlier which declared, among other things, that henceforth "with respect to foreign nations, we shall maintain harmony with all, commercial relations, and whatever else may be appropriate." Then, somewhat apologetically, he admitted Mexico's sparse and unenterprising population, and encouraged them and any other Americans to emigrate.

The governor motioned them to a heavy oak table upon which rested a wine decanter and a half-dozen long-stemmed glasses. After he poured them each a glass, Melgares raised his and eloquently proclaimed the commercial and social marriage of two great and powerful republics.

While they sipped their wine, Melgares spoke of the province's unending material needs and the failure of Mexico to supply them. Gunpowder in particular was in perennial shortage. Commanches, Utes, Navaho, and Apache raided the province's villages with impunity—murdering, raping, enslaving, and pillaging—then traded their booty in Santa Fe or Taos. There were only a couple hundred Mexican troops to patrol the vast province, equipped only with threadbare uniforms, broken muskets, and even bows and arrows. The Indians were often better armed and frequently defeated the pursuing Mexican troops.

Would Mr. Becknell be interested in returning with a large supply of gunpowder and rifles? Becknell enthusiastically agreed. Melgares promised they would meet again before the Americans returned home, and then dismissed them with the hope that they would enjoy a profitable and happy visit.

They emerged, blinking, into the plaza's bright sunlight and chilly morning air. The rest of the men and much of Santa Fe's population waited outside, they cheered loudly when Becknell assured them of the governor's warm welcome and intentions. The men then hauled out their trade goods and spread them on blankets on the plaza among grim-faced Indians from distant pueblos who had brought in their own blankets, pottery, bone flutes, and piles of blue corn, pumpkins, and squash for trade. Will had to pry Jess loose from several pretty señoritas who had gathered around him, chattering and gesturing provocatively. Jess's grin was never wider. He reluctantly returned with Will to the warehouse and helped drag their goods into the square.

The Mexicans crowded around, bidding against each other for the wealth of knifes, awls, calico, mirrors, lead, gunpowder, linen shirts, and bells before them. They had no concept of goods' value in the United States. All they knew was the goods were either scarce or nonexistent while they had a plentiful supply of silver Mexican pesos, and were willing to pay prices ten or fifteen times what they cost in St. Louis. Dupuis wandered through the throng, helping negotiate deals in return for a small commission. By late morning, the Americans had sold off virtually all of their goods and some were buying serapes and woolen clothes from the Pueblos. The Mexicans drifted away for siesta until the Americans and Pueblos were left to pack up their remaining goods.

"We could be home for New Year's," Will exclaimed excitedly as he counted pesos into a large sack.

"Ya thinking of leavin' when we jus' got here? What's wrong with ya, boy?" Jess gave him a playful shove.

"Gotta baby coming, that's what's wrong. And after your cut, I got over six hundred dollars to carry home. I can pay off some debts and buy some more goods for next year."

"Most of the boys is talking of trapping the winter and returning next spring. With a hundred pounds a' beaver fetching five hundred dollars we could take twice as much wealth outta the mountains."

Will sighed and rubbed his forehead. "Yeah, I know," he said quietly. "I sure wish things'd turned out different with Judy. I'm in a real fix. All my dreams of wandering the world are lost. I'd just like to ride up into those mountains and never come back."

"Well, ya also dreamed a' wealth and power, too. Least yer on the road to riches."

"I wanted both."

Jess winked. "And don't forgit them señoritas. Ya ain't gonna let marriage cheat ya outta chasing pretty wimmen now, are ya? C'mon! Le's git this loot back ta the warehouse and start courtin' some beauties. They'll be all rested up after their naps and ready for the fandango! Can't wait to stretch my legs ta some fast fiddle and guitar picking."

The warehouse was filled with sweaty, twirling couples, whooping spectators, smoke, laughter, and the frenzied strumming of Spanish guitars. Couples collided and stumbled drunkenly, but no one seemed to mind. Some of the couples were openly kissing while others slipped through the crowd and out into the cold night. Hungry men and women crowded around a long table covered with platters of mutton, beef, stacks of tortillas, chiles, onions, and pitchers of wine.

Will leaned heavily against a wall, trying to focus on the dancers. The heat and wine flushed his face and tingled his body. He laughed loudly as he watched Jess fling a plump Mexican girl from one arm to the next while pulling her through the other dancers. Someone tugged at his sleeve. He turned to face a tall, slender women with long curled eyelashes, wide nostrils, and thick lips. She giggled in his face and spoke softly.

"Sorry," Will smiled and threw up his hands. "I've given up Spanish. No one seems ta understand me and I don't understand anyone else."

The woman pointed to herself. "María," she said, then pointed to him.

"Will," he said slowly with a smile. "Ain't quite sure who ahm tonight." She giggled again and tried to pull him onto the dance floor. With a laugh, he gave in. "Well, if you insist." Trying to bow gallantly, he pitched forward onto the dirt floor. María giggled as she helped him up.

"Think ah done drank too much," he mumbled cheerfully as he clung to her, "gotta lot ta celebrate." He struggled to focus on María's face. "You're mighty purty, ya know that...*usted es muy bonita*!" María pulled his face to hers and kissed him fiercely. Her lips were plump and wet and nibbled softly at his. They pulled each other tight and slowly rubbed their sweaty bodies against each other. María giggled as she felt him harden.

Suddenly someone slugged Will in the side, pried away the woman, and shouted angrily in Spanish. Will crumpled to his knees and watched a stout Mexican drag María away. "You son of a bitch," he hollered as he staggered forward, swung the Mexican around, and punched him in the mouth. María screamed as the two men flailed their fists at each other. The music and chatter stopped as everyone gathered around. The Mexican pulled a knife and lunged.

Will pulled away but the blade sliced across his ribs. Someone tackled the Mexican from behind.

"Goddamn it, Yates!" Becknell shouted as he pushed his way through the crowd, "What the hell ya doing? Tryin' ta get us all thrown in prison?"

"Well...I..." Will stammered. He suddenly felt foolish and deflated. How'd that happen, he wondered in amazement. "I'm sorry, Captain."

Becknell jerked a thumb toward the Mexican, who glared angrily at them both. "Tell him," he ordered.

Will walked up to the Mexican with his hand outstretched. "Perdone," he muttered. The Mexican stared at his hand briefly, nodded, and clasped it. Then he grabbed María's hand and pulled her outside.

Becknell bowed toward the Mexican officers and merchants. "My deepest apologies. Forgive us." The comandante bowed and ordered the musicians to play. Couples hesitated, then joined and began dancing. Drunken conversations resumed. Men stuffed food and drink down their throats. With Dupuis translating, Becknell and the comandante spoke and gestured animatedly.

Jess slipped up beside Will and chuckled. "Can't leave ya outta ma sight without ya gittin' inta trouble."

"Don't know what happened," Will said in bewilderment. "One minute I'm minding my own business enjoying the fandango, the next some whore's sticking her tongue down my throat, and then some son of a bitch greaser sticks me with his toothpick. Don't make no sense t'all."

"Gotta hand it to ya, Will. Ya sure have a way with wimmen."

"Yeah, well, what happened to yer lady?"

"Dancing with another'n. Fear not, amigo, there's more where she come from. I'm jus' gettin' warmed up. Fore ya start mindin' yer own business agin, ya might wanna take care a' that scratch there. That shirt a' yers is more red than brown now. If ya ain't careful, all that blood'll clean away the filth ya bin collecting for a couple months now."

Will stared down at his bloody shirt and felt for the wound with his fingers. Suddenly he felt faint and slowly sat down. Jess pulled him to his feet and guided him over to a corner. Will turned his head and vomited harshly. While he pulled off his shirt Jess brought over a mug of aguadiente and splashed it across his wound. "Damn it!" Will hollered, "Ya coulda given me some warning!"

"What are ya cryin' fer? Ain't more than a scratch. Don't even hafta sew it. Jus' need a clean dressing is all, though ah don't know where ya'll find anything clean amongst us." Will pressed on the wound to stop the bleeding but some continued seeping through his hands.

"Can't wait ta see the look on Judy's face when ya explain how ya got it."

He shook his head in exasperation. "How do I get in situations like this?"

"Yup, Will, ya'll have quite a few tales ta tell yer grandchildren. If ya live long enough ta have any."

His eyes and hearing blurred as he slowly slid down the corner. "Help," he murmured as he blacked out.

Becknell's group slowly broke up over the next few weeks. Restless and seeking more riches, about half the men drifted off to the beaver streams of the Sangre de Christo while the others lounged around town drinking and carousing. Though he could trade shots with the best of them, Becknell was mostly business, and met frequently with Governor Melgares and other leading merchants to cut future deals. On December first, another group of Americans straggled into town to unroll their blankets alongside Becknell's men in the warehouse and earn a similar welcome and profit on the plaza.

Jess planned to winter in the mountains. He swore that "any day now" he would gather a half-dozen other men and trap his way north up the Rockies' front range until spring when they would head home across the plains loaded with beaver pelts. But meanwhile he would disappear for hours and sometimes days, with a buxom fourteen year old named Luísa. When asked about the liaison he would grin and claim she was just his Spanish teacher. No one was betting that Jess would soon break free of Luísa's warm embrace.

Will's wound healed quickly but the blur of that night's kiss and knife thrust haunted him. He frequently lifted his shirt and picked at the thin crusty scab. It had all happened so fast, with one wild passion consuming the other, he told himself. If the knife had sliced between my ribs it would have punctured my lung and I'd have spent a hellish minute drowning in my own blood, leaving my widow and future child with the stigma of my unfaithfulness that led to my brutal murder. And if a jealous lover had not intervened, would I now spend my days and nights entangled with María's musky body?

He grew more anxious as the departure date with Becknell neared. Just two men would return with Becknell, Will and Jim Harrison, a lanky farmer from Franklin who had signed on as a lark and had pined for his family ever since. He worried about three men surviving a seven hundred mile ride across vast, frozen plains traversed by murderous Comanche, Kiowa, Arapaho, Pawnee, Osage, and Kaw.

He tried to dismiss his fears as he carefully prepared himself for the long journey home. He fattened his bones with enormous meals, cut back his drinking, and replaced his tattered clothes with Mexican woolens. At night he slept warmly in four brightly-colored blankets, and during the chilly days, he squeezed his head through two serapes that fell to his ankles.

With all his goods sold off, he had nothing but free time. Some days he spent wandering the streets or sitting in the churches, squares, and cafes. He reveled in the brown adobe buildings with their tiny blue framed doors and windows, at the blood-colored strings of peppers dangling from rooftops, at the constant smell of piñon smoke. But the Mexicans fascinated him most. What a mixed-up people, he thought— neither Indian nor white. They could be either the laziest or hardest working, the most puritanical or licentious, the most Catholic or pagan, and the most dignified or volatile people imaginable! He wished he could stay long enough to master their language and solve the paradox of their lives. Though sorely tempted, he waved away any women who approached him and avoided their smiles. Likewise, he dismissed Jess's attempts to fix him up with Luísa's sisters and friends.

"Gotta live with myself," he would quietly admit.

Many days he joyfully rode the surrounding plains and canyons, where he would occasionally discover the ruins of some ancient village. Then he would tether his horse and spend hours exploring or just sitting on some high point and letting his eyes and mind wander. Purity, he thought repeatedly as his gaze slowly drifted the horizon. The snow-capped mountains against the brilliant blue sky looked at once enticing and forbidding. Hawks and eagles soared the thermals far above. Deer and elk wandered in and out of rifle shot. Winter silenced the songbirds and insects. The cold wind gusted but mostly lay still. Somewhere to the west was the Rio Grande, which flowed from the Rockies far in the north all the way to the Gulf of Mexico, a thousand miles away. He imagined paddling downstream in a pirogue until he finally met the endless ocean. Then where?

But just when he disappeared in the complete happiness of endless vistas and possibilities, his mind would jerk him back to Judy and St. Louis. He imagined Judy's endless hours at the spinning wheel or fireplace, her belly swelling daily, tormented by the fear he would never return. What a fool I've been, he lamented, so selfish, so irresponsible, so much a prisoner of my passions. He recalled all the pressure he put on Judy over the years to lay with him. If only I knew then what I know now, I'd have been celibate as a priest, at least with Judy. But now it was too late. He was married with a baby due soon. He would be yoked to Judy and the baby for the rest of his life, a burden he could never lighten. He longed to fly to Judy's bed, hold her tightly, beg forgiveness for the pain he had caused, and promise he would make everything right. If only there were two of me— one for Judy and one for me!

The night before they planned to depart, Will awoke with his body aflame and guts torn by convulsions. He spent the night retching and defecating violently into a bucket, then lay delirious and sweating. No one knew how to help him. He was carried to Luísa's family, whose women took turns forcing corn mush between his lips. Becknell was anything but sympathetic and cursed the journey's delay. Two mornings later when Will still failed to improve, Becknell announced that, "There's no point in waiting for him ta die," and he and Harrison rode off, trailing seven heavily laden mules.

His illness slowly lifted. A week later he was completely lucid and could shuffle around, although dizzy spells frequently forced him to lie back down. Another week and I'll be strong enough to ride home, he kept telling himself. He was desperate to get back to Judy, but greatly feared embarking on that long journey alone. Zeke Williams had spent months, and John Colter and Daniel Boone years, alone in the wilderness and lived to tell about it, he repeatedly reminded himself. And if they can do it, so can I! But self-doubt and fear gnawed at his resolve.

Jess repeatedly tried to dissuade him from leaving. "Yer fever was a blessing in disguise," he'd argue. "Ya gotta be crazy ta set off ta St. Louis now when ya could join our trapping party and then return ta St. Louis next spring with twice the wealth."

Will was torn over what to do. He had feverishly told Becknell to pass on word that he would set off as soon as he was able. Judy was already heartsick and she would assume he was dead if he spent the winter trapping. Yet he might not make it back on his own.

Jess's plan did not seem much more encouraging. So far the trapping party consisted of himself and two other men. Joe Turnhill was a wizened little man with hollow cheeks, a pockmarked face, and a fringe of long gray hair surrounding his bald dome. He was tough; he had spent four years upriver with the Missouri Fur Company, and could put a ball through a silver dollar at fifty paces. "Damn near killed as many Indians as beaver," he'd remark when asked about his time on the Upper Missouri. "Hard ta make a living with savages crawling the woods like fleas on a hound's back." Two Blackfoot scalps fluttered on the front of his filthy elk-skin hunting shirt. The trouble was Joe was as touchy, unpredictable, and venomous as a rattlesnake, and the others gave him a wide berth. And then there was Hank Moss, mentally and emotionally frozen at the age of nine, when he was kicked in the head by a horse. He was of medium height and build, and had a cherubic, beardless face marred by a smashed nose, which whistled slightly when he was out of breath. He tried so hard to be liked, cheerfully letting people touch the indentation above his ear from the kick, and cackling incessantly at anything anyone said. But some people took offense or were unnerved by his presence, and Hank was frequently beat up. He took it all in stride though. "Jus' like ma Pa and brothers," he'd later giggle after he stopped crying. When his father had heard of Becknell's expedition, he had marched Hank to Williams's place. "Don't come back unless you're rich," Old man Moss warned as he strode off. Just seventeen, Hank could shoot square and did as he was told without complaint. Strangely, Joe took a liking to Hank and looked after him. "Boy's like ma own son," he would declare as he put his arm around his shoulders and Hank would beam with delight. When Jess was not with Luísa, he was gambling and drinking with Joe and Hank.

When Jess pressed him for a decision, Will could only reply, "I'll think on it."

Will toured the town for the first day since his illness. Though he rested frequently, he rejoiced in the energy flowing through his veins. In a few days I'll be physically and emotionally strong enough to ride back alone, he thought as he briskly hiked the narrow streets, nodding alike to peasants, merchants, and the occasional American.

At twilight he returned to Luísa's home for supper. To celebrate his recovery and the family's kindness, he carried two chickens and a jug of wine. To his disappointment, Jess was gone and no one knew where he was.

The family was happy at his contribution and the women spirited the chickens to the beehive fireplace in the corner, where they were plucked, seasoned, and roasted. Will's stomach churned as savory smells wafted from the oven. He could never get used to the meals. He would sit cross-legged with Luísa's father, uncle, and sometimes Jess on a wool rug around a low table. The three pretty sisters would dash over with stacks of tortillas, chiles, onions and thin slices of chicken or beef, then return to the oven where they would gossip as they ate with the mother and grandmother. He longed for their presence. They had clucked so lovingly over him during his illness, gently feeding him, and wiping the sweat off his feverish body. Now that he was stronger, they would tilt their heads coquettishly and smile, then giggle some comment to each other. The three men ate greedily, packing a tortilla, shoving it into their mouths, then washing it down with gulps of wine. A tallow candle sputtered on the table, casting dull shadows. The brothers spoke fitfully between bites, occasionally raising a toast to Will.

Hoofs suddenly clattered outside. The front door creaked open and the cold and Jess rushed in. He swiftly slammed the door behind him and peered hesitantly at the three men who cheerfully greeted him. Luísa skipped across the room and hugged him. Jess smiled and murmured some words to her, but they seemed forced. She lightly touched a large bruise on his forehead and questioned him but Jess just shrugged and sat down at the table.

"Will," he said softly as he grabbed the wine jug, "don't get riled, but we gotta get outta town quick as lightning."

"What happened?" he replied as calmly as possible. The brothers sensed something was wrong and stared. Luísa and the other women watched anxiously from across the room.

Jess sighed. "Little difference between Joe and a greaser over a dice roll. Greaser's dead. Joe and Hank are waiting for us on the San Miguel road. If ye was still planning to set off fer home on yer own, ye got company now."

Will grimaced and shook his head. "Witnesses?"

"Room full of 'em," Jess grinned. "Helluva fight getting out. Weren't followed and had no trouble saddling up, but the word's out and I reckon the soldiers'll be after us directly."

Cold fear surged through Will. "*We're just gonna dance right outta here?*"

"No choice," Jess replied as he rose and walked over to a corner where he had piled his belongings. He opened the pan of his rifle and checked the priming.

Luísa hurried over. "*Qué pasa? Qué pasa?*" she demanded. Jess hugged her and murmured words in her ear while Will began gathering his own belongings.

The family crowded around asking questions. Will and Jess hauled their gear outside and packed it on their mules.

Will climbed into the saddle then reached down and pressed some silver coins in the father's hand. "*Muchas gracias, señor,*" he said with a trembling voice. He looked down into the puzzled faces. "*Muchas gracias,*" he repeated hollowly.

Jess and Luísa were entwined in the doorway. She was sobbing. Finally he pulled free and clambered atop his horse. "*Te amo,*" he whispered as she hugged his leg. "Le's git," he said as he dug his heels into his horse's side. They trotted down the dark street trailing their mules. Jess glanced back over his shoulder and said mournfully, "I'm gonna miss that little girl a' mine."

For the next few days they rode swiftly, resting little until they were well onto the rolling plains beyond Pecos Canyon. Fears of pursuit gradually faded and they slowed their pace. For several days they retraced their route along the Sangre de Christo then angled east to avoid the now snowbound mountains and canyons they had struggled across only a month before. The grasslands thinned to parched, rocky earth. Water and game were scarce. The mules endured but the horses steadily weakened.

A week from Santa Fe, they camped in the shadow of a lone twin humped mountain. They found a shallow water hole in a sandy creek bed and staked their horses nearby. A clump of cottonwoods yielded enough logs for a large fire over which they warmed their hands and the remnants of an antelope Joe had shot the day before. They huddled in their blankets and stared into the flames as the twilight faded into black. A balmy wind blew from the southwest, occasionally stirring the embers. They bedded down just as a full moon rose on the horizon.

Will felt anxious for the first time in days. Judy hovered and spinned through his mind, beseeching, silently pleading. He trembled and moved closer to the dying coals. God, how I wish I were home now, he lamented repeatedly. I'll never leave you again, Judy, he promised. A coyote howled plaintively nearby. He peered at the still shadows of his companions, trying to imagine wandering these vast plains alone. He finally fell into a shallow, troubled sleep.

Some time later he awoke, smothered with dread. He gasped for breath, strained to rise, but felt staked to the earth. He tried to call out but his tongue lay frozen in his open mouth. Finally, he wrenched himself free from the terror and stared madly around him. The full moon was high overhead, bathing everything in an eerie light. Hank's nose whistled softly. Jess mumbled something and turned over. Their horses and mules noisily munched grass at the end of their tethers. The twin humps gleamed in the distance. Will wondered how far across the plains he could see from the snowy summits. He took some deep breaths then rose. The night was chilly, but there was no frost. Rifle in hand, he stepped quietly out of the circle of men and crunched softly up the dry creek bed. The walking calmed him. He paused several hundred yards from camp and stared at the mountain. Two more months and I'll be home, he reasoned.

He sat down with his back to a cottonwood. The wind had died. There was no sound. He pulled his serape tightly around him and dozed off.

The mule's braying woke him. The moon was low in the west. There was a gray tinge across the southeast sky. He scrambled to his feet and peered through the dusk. There seemed to be figures moving among the animals and others running toward the camp. "Indians!" he yelled as he sprinted down the creek bed. "Stop them! They're stealing our mules!" The Comanches whooped and screamed. Two rifle shots exploded. Joe cursed loudly. Then another shot.

Some Comanches had mounted the animals and were riding off. Jess and Joe were desperately reloading their rifles. An arrow through his throat, Hank was groaning and thrashing on the ground. A Comanche dragged himself away. Three others charged into camp. An arrow slammed into Joe's thigh, and cursing violently, he pulled frenziedly at it. Jess fired and one of the Comanches toppled over, then limped off. A deep wail burst from Will. Startled, the two Comanches turned toward him. One pointed a bow at him and an arrow whizzed by his face. Will halted, brought his rifle to his shoulder, aimed at the Comanche, and pulled the trigger. When the smoke cleared, the Comanche was lying on his back, and the other dashed off toward the fleeing raiders.

Will ran into camp and crouched among the others. Joe was pulling at the arrow in his leg. Jess was reloading. Hank lay still with his hands on his neck.

"Well, goddamn it, Yates," Joe cursed, "don't jus' stand there, reload! And reload Hank's rifle! Those hounds a' hell kin rush us again."

"They got all our animals," Jess declared angrily. "Ever' damn one!" Will and Jess reloaded then piled their belongings and dragged some logs around them.

"Hank's dead," Will announced as he hovered over Hank's limp body. Hank's mouth gaped in a silent scream and his eyes stared skyward. Blood streamed from both ends of the arrow. He recalled Hank's giggles and constant attempts to help others with saddling or hauling. The boy had wanted so badly to be accepted.

"Bastards!" Joe fumed. "I oughta kill ever' last one of them. Get this goddamned arrow outta ma leg!" Will held Joe down while Jess pulled on the arrow—it would not budge. Joe cursed through the excruciating pain. "Push it, goddamn it, push it through." Jess pushed hard but the arrow broke in his bloody hands. "You goddamned fool," Joe screamed. Jess and Will glanced nervously at each other, wondering what to do. Joe lay back and gasped heavily for a while, then propped himself up on his elbows and glared at the surrounding low plains. A dozen Comanche on horseback watched from atop a low hill just out of rifleshot. They carried bows and coup sticks. "Sun'll rise soon. Bastards won't rush us till nightfall if t' all. We got water. Ye gotta git me a mule. Either that or carry me to St. Louis. I ain't staying here."

He stared at the dead Comanche lying twenty feet away. "How the hell'd we only kill one of them? That your shot?" he demanded to Will, who nodded. "Well, fetch his scalp, boy!"

Skinning knife in hand, Will stumbled toward the Comanche who lay sprawled on his back.

He was barrel-chested and dressed in greasy buckskins. His bow and two arrows lay nearby. A bear claw necklace and crucifix hung from his neck and two eagle feathers were tied to his long black hair. The ball had smashed through his right eyebrow and blew out the back of his head. Blood oozed from the eyebrow and a puddle framed his head.

Will stared down at the Comanche's broad face and closed eyes. He felt like he was swimming in a fog. He tried to grasp what had happened but he could form no thought other than, why?

"Rip his scalp, boy," Joe yelled, "rip it!"

Will hesitated, trying to recall how others had gustily described the procedure. Finally he placed the knife point on the Comanche's skull, grabbed a handful of bloody hair with his left hand, sliced a circle on his skull, and jerked. The top of the Comanche's skull came off in his hands. He stood back and stared at the mangled gray brains spilling from the Comanche's head, then fell to his knees and retched violently. He vaguely heard Joe cackling in delight behind him.

Seven

Will shivered uncontrollably as the frigid wind, like slender icy daggers, sliced his flesh in a thousand places. *Not much farther*, he repeated as he stumbled through St. Louis's nearly deserted streets. Breath steaming, he hugged his rifle and pack to his chest and drew the buffalo robe closer around him. Rasping a rabbit-skin mitten against his whiskers, he cursed the days of not being able to bathe or shave since the cold snap began. He smiled. *Poke, poke, poke, Judy'll complain with a mischievous smirk when I kiss her. Then she'll melodramatically hold her nose at my stench. What a sweetheart!*

Just outside of town a gust of wind halted him in midstride and almost blew off his badger-skin cap. He stiffly turned his head in hopes of finding shelter, but there was only the frosty stubble of cornfields along both sides of the road. *Maybe I shoulda warmed my hands at*

Jess's fireplace instead of heading straight to Judy's from the landing. Too late now. Gotta push on.

Eight months of separation seems like eight years! Judy don't know if I'm alive or dead. If only I was there when the baby came. Judy'll be resting up now after the trauma, cuddling the baby in her arms, smiling gently down at it. Boy or a girl? Don't matter. I'm a papa! Gotta get to Judy as soon as possible, he commanded himself, pushing into the wind.

'Nother mile to go. Damn this cold! What am I complaining about? He recalled the desperate days just after the Comanche attack. They had no shovel to dig a grave for Hank and simply pried loose rocks from the hard earth and piled them over him. Futile gesture. Comanches must have pulled off the rocks and scalped and mutilated Hank as soon as we stumbled eastward a couple days later. Today Hank's bones'll be strewn around the campsite while that dead Comanche's hanging in a cottonwood, wrapped snug in a buffalo robe.

With Will and Jess dragging Joe between them, they limped northeast across the plains. For a few days the Comanches followed just out of rifle shot but made no attempt to rush them. Then one day they were gone! But the Comanches haunted their nightmares long after. Each day Joe grew more feverish as his leg festered with gangrene. Saw it off, he pleaded repeatedly, but they had nothing more than skinning knives. Neither Will nor Jess voiced their common thought of abandoning Joe. Without him they just might make it, but with him they could only cover a dozen miles a day at most. Their burden grew heavier daily. The long days of dragging themselves across the plains, longer nights taking turns staring intensely into the dark, hearts pounding and adrenaline surging at every moving shadow, tore apart their minds and bodies.

Water holes in the creek beds were few and far between and usually fouled with buffalo dung. They shot an occasional prairie hen or rabbit and devoured it greedily around a buffalo chip fire. But antelope and buffalo were always specks on the horizon. They left their cooking fires behind and spent the frosty nights in darkness.

The biblical stricture about a rich man having about as much chance of getting into heaven as a camel passing through a needle's eye spun frequently through Will's mind as the heavy sack of silver coins with the necessities in his blanket roll dug into his back. He debated abandoning it along with Joe, but he continued to cling to both. Jesus fasted forty days and nights in the wilderness, but he never faced any Comanches. Oh, Satan, you can keep all your riches and power—just whisk me away to Judy's warm bed and my soul's yours forever!

Then one day they woke up and Joe was dead. They did not mourn his passing. His bitter curses and threats were now silenced. Will stuffed his Comanche scalp inside Joe's hunting shirt and they left his putrefying body there stripped of his rifle, powder, balls, and silver. Onward they pushed across the frozen, empty earth. Their leather shoes wore out and they wrapped their feet with strips of blanket until, one day, Jess shot a doe and for several weeks they fashioned crude moccasins from the buckskin. They reached the Arkansas a week after Joe died and followed it northeast until it began to bend south again. There they left it and headed straight across the plains. Immense herds of buffalo shuffled before them and they ate well, though they lived in constant dread of a stampede that would pulverize them. They holed up in an arroyo for three days while a blizzard blanketed the plains with a foot of snow. Then they burrowed out and slowly took turns trampling a path through the snow. To prevent blindness they masked their eyes with bandannas and peered out through the slits at the glistening white.

Nine weeks after fleeing Santa Fe, they stumbled into Fort Osage. They wept unashamedly as George Sibley patiently heard their story. They had to wait another week before a keelboat set off downstream but, in the meantime, they gorged themselves and traded stories with the other traders and soldiers. Becknell and Anderson had passed through a month earlier and the captain was said to already be organizing another expedition to set off for Santa Fe in March or April. Laden with stacks of buffalo robes and beaver packs, the keelboat left amidst a cold snap that clogged the Missouri with ice floes. The river was swift though, and with short stops at Franklin and St. Charles, it finally docked in St. Louis six days later.

Will smiled as the Morgan home appeared in the distance, smoke curling from the chimney. Tears filled his eyes as he pushed rapidly forward. Gotta get it out now, he warned himself. Can't let Seth and the boys see me cry. A hound ran barking toward him as he walked into the yard, then wagged its tail as he called its name and bent to pet it.

The front door cracked open and Seth's florid face appeared, but he said nothing. Will smiled broadly as he hurried up to the porch and pushed inside. Seth put one massive hand on his shoulder and raised a fat finger to his lips. "Quiet now, she's restin'. Where the hell ye bin?" he demanded sternly. "We done figured ye was dead. Ma girl's been through hell."

Will's eyes widened and his stomach churned. "What happened?" he whispered as he set down his pack and rifle.

"Fever took the baby and almost her." He pointed a finger to his temple. "Made her touched. Spends all day rockin' by the fire. Sometimes she's clear's a bell, but mostly she don't hear nothing."

Will leaned back against the door and rubbed his face with his hands. "What?" he muttered incredulously. He looked up wearily. "Can I see her?"

Seth exhaled sharply. "Suppose. Might jolt her outta it."

The parlor door opened and Mary stood there. "Will!" she exclaimed happily.

"Hush!" Seth ordered.

Betty appeared beside Mary. "Come in, Will," she said coldly. Judy was rocking slowly near the fireplace. Betty hurried over to her and said quietly, "Look who's here, sweetie. Will's home." Judy continued to rock and stare into the flames. She was emaciated and dark circles blotched the pale skin under her eyes.

Stunned, Will fell to his knees beside her and took her hand in his. "Judy?" he asked quietly. My baby's dead and my woman's mind's gone, he agonized. "Judy?" he asked again. He shifted between her and the fire. Her blue eyes were feverish. "Please talk to me, Judy. I love you."

Judy stopped rocking and struggled to focus. "Will?" she mumbled, "is that really you?"

He forced a smile as tears ran down his cheeks. "It's me, sweetheart. I'm home and won't leave you again."

"The baby..." She burst into tears.

He embraced her awkwardly, wishing the Morgans were not crowding around them.

"I know," he said softly, as he stroked her long blonde hair, "it's all right. Everything's all right now." But he felt something alive and powerful within him draining away.

Will lay in bed with Judy stiffly beside him. The roosters had been crowing for hours and the sun was creeping over the newly planted corn field. Smells of hominy and bacon and the murmur of voices wafted from the kitchen. It was long past time to rise, but his veins and brain seemed filled with lead. Although he had slept fitfully, if at all, since his return, it was more than just the lack of sleep. He glanced at Judy. Her eyes were tightly closed and she breathed shallowly, feigning sleep. She would not rise until after he had dressed and left for town. Something had clearly snapped inside.

Her moods swung wildly. At times she would rock before the

fireplace and stare unblinkingly into the flames. Then she would be gripped by manic bursts of energy when she would clean, sew, or churn for hours, all the while chattering incessantly. There was no middle ground, and the affectionate, caring Judy seemed lost forever. It had been over two months and she still allowed Will nothing more than an occasional awkward embrace. At first he had cooed to her lovingly, thinking tenderness would pull her from her grief. But Judy was mired in pain and fear far deeper and darker than Will could comprehend; he had given up reaching her.

He hated going downstairs. Seth and Betty said nothing, but barely hid their bitterness. He had violated their daughter and now their home. You broke my little girl! The unspoken indictment echoed through his mind, conveyed through their silence and occasional harsh words. Judy's younger brothers Tom, Silas, and Evan were more openly cutting. They were burly farmboys and more than once seemed on the verge of squaring off with him. Will did not relish tangling with any of them. Although he was older, they were bigger and tougher. And even Mary, who had once been so supportive, increasingly shunned his presence.

They even despised his apprenticeship to Jameson. "Lawyers ain't interested in the truth," Seth once said as he and the boys headed into the fields, "ain't interested in right or wrong. They jus' wanna line their pockets. A man works with his hands, not his mouth. Lawyers are nothin' but slack-wrists."

Will had resisted grabbing a hoe, silently following them, and turning the earth until he dropped dead from exhaustion.

What did a man need to do to prove he was a man? How many hundreds of miles did he have to skulk through savage and beast-filled wilderness? How many scalps did he have to rip? How much bone-freezing cold and frying-pan heat and gut-twisting hunger and thirst did he have to endure? How much silver did he have to jingle in his pocket? Or, failing that, how many seasons did he have to spend yoked to a plow, dawn to dusk, year after endless year of back-breaking, mind-numbing planting, weeding, and harvesting? Seth's words still burned his ears. He's right, Will admitted. It's all sophism! Webs of fancy, convoluted words to ensnare gullible jurors. Slick, puffed-up lawyers, saying and doing anything to stoke their pride, power, and wealth. There's little justice in the courts. The side that can dispense the most pretty words to the jury or coin to the judge wins. Do I want to be like that? But what else can I do? What do they want from me?

He had performed his social and moral duty. He married Judy after impregnating her. Now they were bound for life. But what kind of life were they sharing? No one was happy. Would slipping away make things better? The Morgans might not miss him, but they would always condemn him. If he fled St. Louis, his past would forever imprison him, the guilt dragging at his heels wherever he went. But what am I guilty of? he continually demanded. Everyone blames me, but for what? Sometimes babies die at birth. Sometimes tragedies irreparably split a mind. Was I responsible for either happening to Judy?

At times he toyed with a pistol, wondering whether death was better than a lifetime of a bitter, inescapable trap. Was there really a heaven or hell? Or was there simply nothing, the same nothing that had preceded his birth? Either way, he would find out eventually. Maybe it was better to die now than later. After all, he was already living life in a coffin.

His mind hovered to the tiny earthen mound next to his father's. Catherine Elizabeth Yates, they had finally decided to carve on her headstone—the name for a daughter he had never seen. He tried to imagine her reddened and squirming and bawling like other babies. But she was stillborn and had been buried deep in the frozen earth while he fled Comanches, frostbite, and starvation a thousand miles away. Why had he had lived while she died?

Will glanced at Judy; she stared back at him, cold and bitter.

Will and Jameson tied their horses to a thin maple tree and slumped down on a fallen log beside the trail. Even in the forest's shade the humidity drenched them with sweat. Cicadas buzzed shrilly and mosquitoes hovered.

Jameson slowly wiped his red face and thick white hair with a dirty handkerchief. "I am getting too old for this," he said wearily. "I cannot afford any delays at this time of my life."

"Socrates must have paused occasionally," Will replied with a faint smile, "even in his older years." Jameson modeled his speaking style and discourse after that ancient Greek, and his oratory was renowned throughout Missouri.

"Laurels are no place to rest for even the greatest of men. Remember that, William. We must all aspire to greatness, and our efforts to that noble end must be relentless."

Will sighed. Greatness? Defending chicken thieves and embezzlers? Was it great being the biggest frog in a puddle? "What is a great man, Mr. Jameson?"

"Why, William," Jameson replied, flustered. "That should be self-evident to all who study history or," he straightened proudly, "have the honor to fall under a great man's shadow."

Will stared down morosely at lines of ants marching to and from a tiny mound. He nodded toward them. "Those ants are riding their own circuit. I wonder if any of them are great."

"You compare men to ants?" Jameson replied in disgust. He pressed his boot heavily on the anthill then lifted it. A half-dozen ants lay pressed still or struggled in the flat-topped mound while others scurried in confusion.

Startled, Will replied hastily, "I suppose you're right, sir." He was too hot and tired for debate. He glanced at the late afternoon sun. "We should be in Boonville before nightfall."

"Our esteemed colleagues will already be trading toasts in the local tavern," Jameson replied with a trace of resentment.

"We got a late start," Will reminded him. He thought of Jameson nursing his hangover that morning in an inn at St. Charles long after the judge and other lawyers departed. "The circuit'll wait on us," he said, trying to be encouraging.

Jameson pulled a silver flask from a pocket of his coat and offered it. "No, thank you, Mr. Jameson. It's a mite too hot for whiskey."

Jameson nodded, tipped the flask to his thin lips, and swallowed deeply. "Life's elixir," he exclaimed sourly as he massaged his broad belly.

"Are you sure...?"

"Sure about what?" Jameson demanded.

"Well...I was just a little worried...with your chest pains and all...you're looking a little peaked, sir."

Jameson's annoyance softened with reflection. "Well, son," he replied with a gentle voice, "I appreciate your concern." His wide forehead crinkled with inner debate. "William," he said finally, "I am an old man. You must forgive my conceits, my vanity, and yes, my illusions." He glanced down with remorse at the flattened anthill. "Sometimes my weaknesses get the better of me. You questioned greatness, and rightfully so. What have I accomplished in my life? How will I be remembered? I have spent a lifetime uttering fine phrases, defending the innocent and guilty alike. But all those countless torrents of words and gestures delivered with such flourish were undoubtedly forgotten soon after. History will not record my petty deeds. And I have no progeny to carry on my name. You know of my loss..." Tears filled his eyes with memories of his six year old son, his neck broken in a fall from their home's roof. "Over thirty years have passed and I still wonder what would have become of my only child." He dabbed at his tears with his handkerchief.

Will brushed away his own tears as his mind filled with the image of a daughter he had never seen. He wanted to embrace Jameson and weep deeply in his arms. Instead, he said, "I better get that shoe back on," as he rose and walked over to his horse. He lifted the horse's back hoof and inspected the nail holes. "Wish we had a hammer," he said, scanning the rutted trail for a suitable rock.

"William," Jameson called after him. "A lawyer's life is not always courtroom eloquence and drama. I realize that you must get discouraged at times with the profession's drudgery and sometimes outright deceit. Greatness? I look to great things from you, William. Yes, at times your spoken words are uncertain and, at other times, your passion gets the better of you. But those defects can be remedied by diligent study, reflection, and experience. And your written words reveal a mind of subtlety and power." Will nodded as he placed a nail in the shoe and set it over the hoof.

"William," Jameson asked quietly. "Forgive me for asking but…are things all right between you and Judith?"

Embarrassed, Will shrugged. "What makes you ask?" he finally said.

"People talk."

One by one the men jumped off and helped the women down from the wagon. Seth handed the switch and reins to a Negro man they had hired for the occasion. "Ye keep a good watch, Elias, ye hear?" he warned as he hurried off to join the others. Everyone, the Morgan family and Will, walked eagerly toward the clearing through the dozens of wagons and horses tied along the rutted road.

The summer heat was slowly dying with the dusk. Fireflies flickered through the darkening fields and woods. Mosquitoes whined. Ahead, torches bobbed in sweaty hands or hung from trees. Small groups of people knelt alongside the road, reading from Bibles, singing hymns, or listening to someone preaching. Couples slipped off furtively into the woods. A half-dozen young toughs swaggered drunkenly through the throng, mocking the worshippers.

Judy babbled excitedly and linked arms with Will, who smiled back at her. He had not seen her so relaxed and animated since he left for Santa Fe. He lightly kissed her cheek and she smiled shyly. Maybe this is what she needed, he thought hopefully. Maybe things'll be different now, the way they used to be.

"I can smell the gates of heaven before us," Seth said repeatedly as he inhaled deeply and playfully scuffed and shoved his three stocky sons.

"Oh, go on, Seth," Betty exclaimed as she waddled behind him.

"I can feel the power of Jesus within me already," he replied cheerfully. "Yes, sir, it won't take more than a lamb's shake for Preacher Caples to set off the Lord's passion! I'm a powder keg primed to blow!"

In the clearing several hundred people pressed around an empty pine platform with stairs at the back leading down to a large, closed tent. The Morgans and Will pressed into the boisterous crowd and stood on tiptoes watching impatiently.

Will glanced at the Morgans' flushed and grinning faces. They're more accepting now, he thought with relief. Maybe the storm's blown over. It's been one long miserable half-year, he grimly reminded himself. He gingerly put an arm around Judy, who stiffened slightly but did not pull away. "Won't be long now," he whispered in her ear. She nodded eagerly. He wished she were thinking of their love-making again rather than the revival.

Preacher Caples's power frightened Will. He feared getting carried away by his spirit. Most of St. Louis had been abuzz for the last week since word arrived that Caples would preach three afternoon sermons and an evening revival the following Sunday west of town. Caples had preached for years elsewhere on the frontier but had never been to Missouri. Will recalled stories of Caples healing the sick and coaxing folks to speak in tongues. His mind drifted back to that sultry afternoon long ago in his childhood when he sat in a clearing with the two Sac warriors, and one breathed life back into a sparrow. Did Caples have the same power over life and death?

Suddenly the tent's flap was pulled aside and a giant stepped out and up onto the platform. Roger Caples was tall and broad shouldered; his thick, chestnut-colored mane swept back from his forehead; caterpillar-like eyebrows lifted and fell above his dark eyes; he worn a black frock coat and pants, and a white linen shirt. He spread his arms wide and swept the crowd with his glare. The crowd was stunned into silence. "Most of you," he thrust both arms wide as if to encompass the crowd, "are condemned to an eternity in hell!" He let the accusation hang heavily for several long moments. "You are all sinners! Of what sins do I speak? It is not merely murderers and violators who burn in eternity!" He counted off on his fingers. "Fornication! Card playing! The reading of novels and poetry! Swearing! Gambling! Sabbath-breaking! Scandal mongering! Gossiping! Drunkenness!..."

A smile tugged at Will's lips. God's gonna be mighty sore with me, he mused. And anyway, as he loved pointing out to revivalists, wasn't Jesus' first miracle to turn water into wine? And didn't Jesus lay his head and drink among prostitutes and drunkards and the poor? And what about the rich having as much chance of getting into heaven as a camel through a needle's eye?

"...Who among thee is not a sinner! The Bible is clear! The Bible is our only guide! Our only education for life! Jesus is the only path to salvation. All other paths lead to hell, to an eternity in molten fire..."

Surely not all Indians or Jews or Mohammedans are evil, Will reasoned. Why would God cast them into hell? Is it their fault if they never got the Word? And if God is love, why does he condemn a novel reader or gossip to burn forever alongside the truly wicked?

"...There is a pass high in the Rocky Mountains from which two streams flow, mingling with other streams until the one eventually flows into the Gulf of Mexico and the other into the Pacific Ocean. And there is a rock hanging above those two tiny streams high in that Rocky Mountain pass. And from that rock is suspended a dewdrop. You are that dewdrop. A wind can blow you either way! Into heaven or into hell! Death stalks our lives and eventually wins us! We can never know when our hour is gone! When the last grains of sand in our glass disappear..."

Will wished he could fly away to that pass and then soar high above and embrace the world within his mind.

"...Are you ready to meet your maker? Have you repented? Have you accepted Jesus into your heart and soul?" Tears dripped down Preacher Caples's cheeks as he shouted "Come, sinners, come! Jesus is our compass! He is the way—the only way—through a wilderness of sin and pain. Don't grovel before sin! Break free of its fetters and chains! It's not too late! You're not dead yet, thank God! Come! God calls on you! Fly! Death is stalking you! It's hot on your heels and breathing down your neck! You're perched on the steps of hell! Don't be dragged into the abyss! Come to Christ! Come now!"

People dropped to their knees weeping, wildly confessing horrible sins, and exhorting God to enter them. Some jerked uncontrollably, eyes white in their sockets, frothing at the mouth, shrieking, groaning.

Caples pushed through the throng, demanding repentance and obedience to God's word. The believers crowded around him, beseeching him for forgiveness and tugging at his coat. He laid his hands across their heads, shoulders, and breasts, demanding obedience to God's word. Seth and his boys screamed, "I believe! The Lord's spirit's burning within me!" And Betty, Judy, and Mary wept and hugged each other.

Will trembled slightly. He felt suffocated and longed to flee the madness and passion. Suddenly the preacher was before them, laying hands on the Morgans as they tearfully embraced him. He turned quickly and shouted down into Will's face, "Do you believe? Are you washed in the blood of the Lamb?"

"I...I..." Will stammered. "Can you bring the dead back to life?" he blurted.

"Only God can bring life to the dead and living alike! Now son," he boomed down at Will, "do you believe that Jesus is the only way to salvation?"

He heard Judy, the Morgans, and crowd urging him to give himself to Jesus. Shrieks and strange words filled the air as the spirit entered Seth. "The Indians...have their own way...there may be many ways...or even no way!" he shouted back.

The preacher's face twisted in disbelief. Judy tugged at Will's arm and cried for him to repent while others crowded around, cursing his blasphemy.

The preacher encompassed Will's head with his huge hands and drew him close. His breath was hot and foul. He pressed his fingers hard into his skull and shouted, "Repent! Repent! Cast out thy evil. Or you will burn in hell for your doubts and blasphemy!"

"It's not that simple," Will shouted back and struggled to break free of the preacher's crushing grip.

"Repent! Repent, ye servant of Beelzebub!" the preacher shouted and the Morgans and others took up the cry.

Will felt swallowed up by the din and crush of bodies. He stomped his foot into the preacher's instep and yanked himself free, then twisted around and pushed through the crowd while some struck or shoved him. He finally pulled free of the mob and dashed toward the road. Preacher Caples's voice cut through the clamor after him, "Begone, ye servant of hell!"

"This is so ridiculous," Jenny blurted angrily. "My hands are so knotted and swollen I can't do anything for myself anymore."

"I'll thread it for you, Mama," Will said as he dutifully set down the account ledger and reached across the table for the offered needle and thread. "How's your eyes, Mama?" he asked as he stared into her slightly clouded irises.

"Everything's fading," she moaned. "Someday I'll wake up and there'll be nothing but dark. How did I become like this?"

He sighed heavily as he glanced at her. Mama had aged so rapidly; her body had thinned and sagged, her joints knotted with rheumatism, her face was etched with wrinkles, and her once-tawny hair was iron-gray. She was all shriveled up! "I'll always read to you, Mama," he said, trying to sound hopeful.

Jenny pursed her lips. "When are you going back to Judy?" she demanded. "People are talking. It isn't proper for you two to be apart. It's well past time for a reconciliation."

Will inwardly groaned. "Mama, I've tried to explain many times before," he said, trying to tame his irritation, "that things just haven't been the same since the...birth."

"Well," she sniffed, "maybe if you had been by her side, rather than gallivanting in Santa Fe, things might have turned out differently."

His forehead knotted with anger but, before he could reply, the door slammed open and Sarah angrily charged into the shop. She stopped abruptly and glared at Will. "Some friend you have. I don't know why I've wasted my time on him for all these years."

"What's wrong, sweetheart," Jenny cooed. Sarah burst into tears and ran to her mother's arms. "There, tell me your troubles."

"Jess..." she sobbed. "I saw him holding hands...with Suzy Cotrane."

Will rolled his eyes. Darn that Jess! Why'd he have to go and do a thing like that!

"I always told you that Jess was no good," Jenny harrumphed. "Maybe you'll listen to your mother next time. And think of all the beaus you've lost in the meantime."

Sarah dabbed at her eyes with a handkerchief. "I don't know what I ever saw in him," she said, trying to regain control.

"I'm sorry, Sarah," he said sheepishly. "I'll have a talk with him."

"You didn't know he was seeing Suzy behind my back?" Sarah said accusingly.

"Honest, Sarah," he said, vigorously shaking his head. "I wouldn't let him get away with seeing Suzy on the side. Jess..." Someone rapped loudly at the door. "It's open," he hollered. "Can't he read the sign?" he muttered as he reached the door. He pulled it open and stepped back in surprise as Seth stood awkwardly before him.

They stared at each other for a moment until Seth said, "Son, we've gotta talk."

Will nodded and stepped outside. "Mind if we walk?" he asked quietly.

"Suits me fine," Seth replied, and they strolled out of the yard and down the busy street, occasionally nodding to passersby and side-stepping wagons and carriages. They had walked a hundred yards before Seth broke the silence. "Ye gotta mend things with Judy," he said sadly. "That girl spends most of her days rocking and sewing. Me and her mother've tried everything, hard and soft words, threats, promises, reading the Good Book, prayer...nothing'll snap that spell!"

Seth stopped and turned toward Will. "Son, I know it warn't easy on ye being with her, without her...responding. It ain't natural and that's a fact. But that's my little girl and somebody's gotta mend her and maybe only you can do it." Will nodded. "We're different, you and me. We differ in a lot a' ways and sometimes that household's tense as two tomcats in a bag. And the revival," he paused, trying to control his anger. "How ye could challenge Preacher Caples is beyond my understanding! Why, that was pure arrogance! Disrespectful," he sputtered, "to a man of the cloth!"

Will held up his hands. "Hold it right there, Seth," he said in a slightly trembling voice. "Don't start. There's no point. You yourself said we were different. I take your way of thinking as good enough for you. Why can't you take my way of thinking as good enough for me?"

"All right, all right," Seth said, more bewildered than angry. "But it's my house. Ye hear my family asking such questions? They're all good, God-fearing Christians, every one. Think what ye want, but why can't you keep your doubts to yourself and jus' go along with things? Ye'll never get anywhere if ye fight everything and everybody."

"Listen, Seth," he said, trying to keep the edge off his words, "I care deeply about Judy and want the best for her. But like you say, there's no telling if there is a best for her. We were half a year together since I got back and..." he shook his head sorrowfully. "Nothing really changed."

"Yer her husband. Yer studying the law. Ye know damn well that legally and morally yer beholden ta her till death do ye part. And that's a fact!"

Will's emotions reached a boiling point. "You're right, Seth, that is a fact," he said sarcastically, waving a finger in Seth's face. "And here's another. You don't need to lecture me about morality or the law. If you want me to come back, you're gonna have to treat me with the respect I try to show you. Man to man! I ain't your family. You boss them all you want, but you don't boss me. You hear?"

Seth glared at Will's finger, looking like he wanted to break it off.

"All right," he finally said through clenched teeth. "Fetch yer bags." Seth turned and stomped away through the thick dust.

The steady clanging from the blacksmith barn emptied into the crowded street. Will peeped around the corner and watched Jess hammer a horseshoe into shape. Jess suddenly looked up from behind the anvil. "Will!" he exclaimed, "you're a sight for sore eyes." Will trudged into the barn and dropped a huge gunny sack beside his feet. Jess pointed his hammer at the sack. "Running away from home?" he grinned.

"Just running," he admitted wearily.

Jess cocked his head. "From what?"

"I'll let you know soon as I find out."

"A dozen more shoes and I'm done. Wanna go fishing?"

"We gotta talk."

Jess's grin faded. "'Bout what?" he asked warily.

"You been poking 'sweet' Suzy?"

Jess exhaled sharply. "What makes ye say that?"

"Sarah saw you two walking hand-in-hand this morning."

Jess shook his head sorrowfully. "Jus' whad she see?"

"Enough."

"Reckon I'll hafta talk ta her."

"Jess, why'd ye do it? You broke my sister's heart."

"Well…you know how it gets. Sarah kept talking a' tying the knot. What's a man ta do?"

Will nodded sympathetically. "Yeah, well…you didn't think Sarah'd find out?"

"I didn't think…I didn't mean…she jus' saw us hand-holding?"

"Far as she tells. When'd it start with Suzy?"

"Not long. Couple weeks."

"Why didn't ye let Sarah down easy?"

"I don't wanna lose her. I jus' need to breathe free for a while. I need some time ta ponder."

"Why didn't you tell her?"

"I was planning on it but jus' kept putting it off."

"You made a helluva mess."

"I know, I know. Things got away from me is all."

"How you gonna set things straight?"

"I'll talk ta her tonight. Will ye soften her up for me? I hate it when she cries."

"Damn it, Jess. I am on my way to Judy's."

Jess eyes widened. "I thought ye was done with her. What made ye change yer mind?"

"Seth come by today. Called me back. I'll try once more for Judy."

"Ye really going back?"

"Suppose." He stared down at the hard-packed earth. "It ain't so bad when I'm riding circuit."

"That ain't more than a few months a year. Whadya gonna do the rest of the time?"

"Survive," Will said angrily.

Jess chuckled. "Sure wish I was there when ye lit out from Preacher Caples's revival."

A smile tugged at his mouth. "You shoulda seen the look on Caples's face when I said there might not be any way to heaven at all. His face puffed up like a toad's and I feared he was gonna explode and blow us both into hell."

They both laughed loudly. "We never have time ta run off these days," Jess observed ruefully.

"Yeah, obligations," Will frowned. "How's your old man?"

Jess looked worried. "Got the shakes again."

"Thought he was taking that powdered bark from South America. What's it called?"

"Quinine. Whole town's dry."

"Don't whiskey help?"

"Only if he passes out."

"Shame. Your father's a good man." He picked up his bag. "Well...I best be going."

"Ye ain't gonna talk ta Sarah for me?" Jess pleaded.

Will shook his head. "Not less you can talk to Judy for me."

Jess grinned. "It's a deal! Come on! Le's head ta the Morgans! I'll straighten Judy out in no time."

He started for the open barn door. "I knew I shoulda kept my mouth shut," he said over his shoulder. "I'll try ta slip off this Sunday. Ye wanna go fishing then?"

"Yeah, if either of us is alive." They both laughed uneasily.

"Snow!" Will exclaimed as he bolted from his chair to the window. "First of the year!" He watched the flakes swirl and dance beyond the frosted panes. "Think it'll stick?"

Jameson chuckled. "You sound like a little boy." Will straightened, sighed, then slipped reluctantly back behind his desk cluttered with books and piles of papers. "Have you finished my brief?"

"Almost," Will said quietly as he shuffled through the pages. "I've dug out quotes from everyone from Aristotle to Madison. No horse thief will have ever been more philosophically defended." Jameson beamed. "Do you think he'll hang?"

"His guilt has yet to be established," Jameson replied shortly.

"He'll leave a wife and five children. And his neighbors swear he never stole anything before, let alone a horse. Ain't right to hang him," Will said sadly.

"You're a good boy, William," Jameson said softly. "Diligent yet spirited. Hard as nails amidst the wilderness and savages, yet compassionate toward those less fortunate." He reached for a decanter and two glasses on the serving board beside his desk. "The winter chill is upon us," he said heartily. "Stoke up those flames and draw the curtains. We'll drink a toast to our horse thief, and the cow he has delivered unto us for payment. May that fine bovine's milk never go dry!" Will did as he was told. "Come, William," Jameson beckoned silkily from the settee to which he had moved. "Come sit beside me before the fire. We have many important matters to discuss."

Will took the proffered glass and sat down. "It looks like an open and shut case. You'll have to work some mighty powerful magic on those jurors to get an acquittal," he said, shaking his head mournfully. He sipped thoughtfully at the brandy and stared into the flames.

"Magic words it will be, with your help of course. Our client's woes are tragic indeed. But in our profession, we must distance ourselves as much as possible from such vicissitudes," Jameson paused then asked soothingly, "and how are things with your life, William?"

With a harsh laugh, Will replied, "Least I don't face hanging."

"Judy's condition and the family's resentment remain unchanged?"

"The family tolerates me. We don't have much to say to each other. Judy?...sometimes she seems to really want to break loose of her...demons," he struggled to find a better word but that was all he could think of. "You can see her straining to be nice and affectionate. But she never quite escapes from her hole. The demons drag her back from the edge."

"That is indeed a tragedy. Perhaps someday medicine will have advanced to the point where such cases can be treated. Until then, they can only elicit our pity." He refilled their glasses to the rim. "You know, William, I often see my son in you." Will took a gulp from his glass and, wondering how to respond, gazed into the flames. "Richard was such a precocious lad. Bright, yet torn by pangs of melancholy. What seized him to climb up on that roof I know not. He often spoke of wanting to fly away like a bird."

"At least you still have Anne," he said, trying to sound positive.

Jameson pursed his lips. "Anne, yes, she keeps an orderly home for which I am thankful, but we've never been close."

Startled, Will asked. "Even before the marriage? Was it...like mine?"

"No," Jameson chuckled. "Nothing like that. Our conjugal relations began long after our wedding, were limited before Richard's arrival, and have been nonexistent since."

Will's eyes widened. "I am sorry, Mr. Jameson. I hear tell some women are like that."

"Oh, Anne, no not her," he chuckled deeply again. "She was quite willing. It was me...I...I frankly find the very thought of bedding a woman unbearable."

Perplexed, Will frowned. "Even pretty ones?"

"Yes," Jameson admitted, "even pretty ones. My father was like me. We were so close, so loving until his death. His love made me what I am. But I dared not experience such love again until the birth of my son."

His smile faded and tears welled in his eyes. "And with Richard's death, I have poured all my emotions and energies into my practice. Discipline! I have locked my inner soul in unbreakable chains. But I always hoped that someone would come into my life to unleash me."

Will felt increasingly uneasy, but could not quite understand why. He took another gulp of brandy and rose to toss a log on the fire.

"Then one day..." Jameson paused long in inner debate. "And then one day you walked through that door," he said quietly, "and I knew my prayers had been answered." Will shot a confused glance at Jameson who stared intently back. "Don't be frightened, William. I mean no harm. I often struggled over whether or not to ever reveal myself to you, and will never again speak of such matters if you so desire."

Suddenly Will understood. "Plato's *Symposium*!" he blurted. "And the ideal love that Socrates proclaimed. So that's why you gave your copy to me!"

Jameson nodded slightly. "My deep affinity with Socrates is more than cerebral."

Will backed up slowly and bumped against his desk. "Mr. Jameson, I best be going," he said hurriedly. He grabbed his coat off a wall peg and put it on.

"Wait!" Jameson said, rising. "Pray, wait! You mustn't go yet. Hear me out!" Will stared warily at Jameson. "You've another sixteen months of your apprenticeship. Do not throw it away. You will make a brilliant lawyer someday. Forgive my shared secret. It was but words, nothing else. Cast from your mind all those words and let us resume our great work together as if they were never uttered."

"I...I can't forget! I can never think of you the same, never feel comfortable around you again. I'm sorry, but I just can't."

"William," he replied gently, "forgive an old man a single indiscretion which will never be repeated. I promise. Think carefully about your decision. But if you decide to leave your apprenticeship here, pray never reveal to anyone what has passed between us. Will you promise that? Please, William, they were merely words. My legacy will be ruined. My entire life has been such a torment and public knowledge of my inner world would destroy me. Feel for me the compassion you feel for our horse thief. My life is a daily hanging without end."

Will nodded. "I won't tell anyone," he said quietly. "If I don't return, I'll try to cover my tracks so they don't lead to you. I'll think of something. I wouldn't hurt you. You've been very kind and taught me so much. I'm so sorry that your life has been so unhappy. But I best be going. Goodbye." He quickly slipped out the door and into the bitter cold street.

"The Dirty Cock," Jess exclaimed as he spread his arms wide in mock embrace. "Home sweet home!" They gazed up at the faded sign of a mud-splattered rooster hanging from the tavern's gable, then Will yanked open the door and they peered into the smoke-fouled dark. The drunken shouting and laughter died at the intruding light, then resumed. They pushed their way through the throng and sat down at a rickety table. "A truly distinguished clientele," Jess remarked cheerfully as his eyes squinted at the burly, greasy farmers, trappers, and rivermen crowding the room. The floor was stained a slick brown from endless streams of tobacco juice and an occasional puddle of puke; the walls and low ceiling blackened by years of pipe and wood smoke. "The perfect shelter from a cold, wet, winter afternoon. Why the finest clubs of London or Philadelphia or New York could not compare to the heights of civilization and culture found here. Ain't that right?" Will nodded sullenly.

They waited impatiently as Wayne the owner joked and bantered his way from one crowded table or knot of drunken men to the next, slopping whiskey from a jug into their mugs and, with a sharp laugh, snatching a coin or promise from each. Wayne was of average height but twice the girth of most men.

He waddled up to them and wiped the sweat off his red face with the back of his hand. "Ye boys shoulda got here sooner," he admonished with a deep chuckle, "outta mugs. Long swallow each'll cost ye a bit," Jess nodded and pushed a coin into Wayne's grimy hand in exchange for the jug. Jess held the jug under his nose and inhaled sharply. Wayne cackled loudly.

"Gotta charge ye extra if ye wanna snort it."

Jess grinned. "Well, now, Mr. Connan, if in ye'd traveled the world like Will and me to the likes a' New Orleans or Santa Fe, ye'd know that a true appreciator of the spirits savors the smell afore the taste."

Wayne cocked a heavy brown eyebrow. "Santa Fe ye say? No foolin'?"

"There with Becknell," Jess stated proudly, "back jus' the two of us."

"Why didn't ye tell me all the other times ye was in here?"

"Jus' modest, I reckon."

Wayne nodded. "Two free on the house for the experience." Jess swallowed hard from the jug and passed it to Will who took a deep gulp.

Jess shivered happily, "Now that's fine sippin' squeezins."

Wayne scanned the room until his eyes caught sight of a slight gray-haired woman perched on a barrel in the corner. She puffed moodily at a corn cob pipe and wore a patched gingham dress. "Karen!" he bellowed.

"What the hell do you want?" she shouted back.

"Come on over here, girl, got something ta show ye!"

Karen glared then stomped into a back room, slamming the door behind her. "That woman's gonna drive me to an early grave," Wayne said wearily. "All we ever do is fight like wildcats. Jus' wanted her to meet you boys. I'd like to do some tradin' in Mexico. Gotta talk her inta takin' care a' things while I'm gone. You boys catch any silver down yonder?"

Jess leaned back in his chair. "Nuff ta drink steady in yer place for a lifetime," he said confidently.

"Whiskey!" someone shouted and others took up the cry.

Wayne nodded. "Gotta make the rounds. Take a few more quick ones." Jess and Will took turns gulping eagerly from the jug. "Stop by when it ain't so crowded. I wanna pick you boys' brains in exchange for a few more free shots." He winked and waddled off.

"Now that's what I call hospitality," Jess exclaimed. "Well, now, Will, ye jus' gonna sit there all day silent as a stone or ye gonna say something?"

"Ain't much to say about anything," he replied.

"How's Judy?" Jess asked quietly.

"Same." He picked at the scarred table. "Same." He shook his head sadly and leaned forward. "Jess, what am I gonna do?"

Jess shrugged. "When's the last time...?" his voice trailed off.

Will snorted irritably and shook his head. "Night 'fore we left for Franklin." Jess whistled softly.

"Ye still love her?"

"Like a sister."

"Man ain't supposed ta marry his sister."

"Didn't start out that way."

"Been little more than a year since we got back from Santa Fe. Spring's round the corner. Ain't it 'bout time fer 'nother adventure? Why not head upriver?" Jess demanded eagerly.

"Time's long past. Wish I could be there now."

"What's stoppin' ye?"

"You know. 'Nother year under Jameson and I can sit the judge's exam and, if all goes well, get a law license. It's my only way out."

"Only way?" Jess scoffed. "What's a year in a lifetime? The mountains beckon."

"Believe me, I'd give anything to be a thousand miles from here."

Jess leered. "Jameson still chasing you round the desk?"

"Shhh!" Will frowned. "Like I told you before, neither of us has said anything that about for the last three months. He can't help being what he is and thank God he's kept it to himself. But if word leaked he'd be ruined."

"And ye with him. He may have driven his boy to try to fly away," Jess said grimly. "Hope ye got wings when ye jump."

At the next table, a huge balding man pleaded, "I didn't mean it, Johnny," to a wiry man with a handlebar mustache and long, matted brown hair sitting beside him. Johnny shouted, "Greer, ya bastard!" and smashed a bottle of rum across his face. Stunned, Greer held his hand against his face as blood oozed out between his fingers, then suddenly threw himself at Johnny, knocked him to the floor, and began pummeling him with his fists. Johnny swore, sunk his teeth into Greer's nose and ripped off the tip.

Greer reared back and howled in agony. Wayne shoved his way through the crowd gathered round and pulled the two men apart. Greer sat down heavily, moaning and holding his bleeding face with his two meaty hands.

Wayne snarled in disgust, kicked Johnny hard in the groin, and dragged him to the door. "Pardon me, mister," he nodded to a tall, lean man with a white ruffled shirt and fresh buckskin breeches who stood in the low doorway. The man tipped his broadbrim hat and stepped aside. Wayne pushed Johnny out into the muddy street. "Come back when ye learn some manners."

"Trouble?" the man asked sympathetically.

Wayne's barrel-chest heaved and sweat dribbled down his face and soaked his shirt. "That Johnny's a hellcat ifin there ever was one. Sometimes I gotta bring him ta his senses." He shook his head sorrowfully. "How's Greer?" he hollered at the crowd.

Greer had a dirty shirt wrapped around his face and held his nose tip in his grimy hand as he was steered out the door by a couple of men. "We'll fetch him to a doctor," one of them replied. The other patrons resumed their drinking and storytelling as if nothing had happened. Will and Jess retrieved Greer's and Johnny's glasses then slipped through the crowd.

Wayne nodded to them and turned to the man. "Name yer poison," he demanded.

"Nothing right now, thank you," the man replied. "But, sir, if I could just have a word with you?" Wayne arched an eyebrow. "I am General William Ashley's clerk and the general has asked me to recruit for his expedition to the upper Missouri."

"That a fact," Wayne said with interest.

"I've watched your advertisements in the *St. Louis Inquirer* for the past month," Will interrupted. "No luck recruiting?"

"Well…" the clerk replied tentatively.

Jess frowned at Will. "Why didn't ye tell me 'bout the advertisements?" He turned to the clerk. "Upper Missouri ye say? When're yer headed upriver?"

"A fortnight. Are you interested, Mr…?"

"Baucus," Jess thrust out his hand. "Jess Baucus. And this here's Will Yates. We was jus' speakin' a' such a possibility. Ask and ye shall receive as the Good Book says! Ain't that right Will?"

"I could use some salvation," Will admitted with a weak smile.

The man nodded. "Jim Clyman." He shook hands with all three men, then turned to Wayne and motioned to the crowded tavern. "May I?" he asked.

"Suit yerself," Wayne replied. "No tellin ifin they'll listen or not."

Clyman loudly cleared his throat. "Gentlemen!" the word shot out in a deep bass, the kind that immediately grabs attention. Heads raised. "Hear these words!" He paused dramatically. "I speak of the future.

Your country's future! Missouri's future! Your future!" Clyman enunciated each word powerfully and distinctly. The tumult died. All eyes fixed drunkenly on the speaker. "I am here to gather enterprising, courageous men interested in gathering the riches of the upper Missouri tributaries. In two weeks, General Ashley will lead an expedition up the Missouri to join his partner Colonel Andrew Henry and one hundred of America's finest who have been trapping the richest beaver streams known to man!" With stirring words, Clyman described the easy wealth of beaver greater than the silver mines of Peru, the world's greatest hunting with herds of buffalo that stretched for days across the prairies, the sublime beauty of the mountains and valleys, and the company of men united in a noble adventure.

But when asked, Clyman admitted that he had never been west of St. Louis and that, while last year's trappers had been allowed to keep half their catch, as a result of unforeseen circumstances, Henry and Ashley could now only offer annual wages of two hundred dollars— but that in advance! "Could make ten times that or more back in Santa Fe," Will mumbled. "Them's slave wages." After Clyman finished his pitch, a dozen men crowded round him demanding more answers or where to sign up.

Jess nodded in mock gravity. "This is it, Will. Divine intervention. Can't defy the Lord's doings. Bes' enlist afore the miracle disappears in smoke."

"When'd you get so God-fearing?" Will asked in amusement.

"Hell's being in one place so long yer whiskers turn ta moss. Heaven's damn near any place else. God lets us choose. Simple as that."

"Jessie," Will replied cheerfully, "ye got the makings of being a true theologian."

Jess grinned broadly. "We headed upriver or not?"

Straining, sweating, stripped to the waist, twenty men on each cordelle stumbled and slipped through the mud, water, and thick brush along the Missouri. Day after day, from dawn to dusk, for two and a half months, they cursed, slapped at mosquitoes, and dragged each huge keelboat packed with ten thousand dollars' worth of trade goods up the surging spring current. A thousand times daily onboard each boat a score of other men jabbed their poles into the river bottom, pushed their way to the stern, then, reaching their poles' length, jogged to the bow to repeat the task. The current wandered continually from one bank to the other and the cordelle men crossed across the river in the skiffs a dozen times daily to keep the keelboats in midstream. They got little respite from the harsh routine. A day's whoring and drinking at Franklin, and half a day each to sport the Kaw and Osage women at Fort Osage, the Omaha and Oto at Fort Atkinson, and the Poncas at their village. On rare days the wind blew steadily behind them and the men could huddle wearily onboard while the sails were hoisted and the wind dragged them upstream. Inevitably though, the wind would die or the current would surge, and the men would have to haul out the cordelle and poles and fight the river once again.

They hardly noticed late winter turn to spring. The thick woods along the lower Missouri had thinned the farther west and north they pushed until there were only scattered clumps of cottonwood and scrub oak, but their tangled branches budded then burst into shiny new leaves. The days of frigid winds were increasingly broken by cool or even warm days until finally the sun burned down steadily and the men longed for showers to soothe their reddened bodies.

The once cold, silent air now trilled with songbirds and cicadas. Snapping turtles and water snakes slid off logs into the muddy waters swirling before the first man on the first cordelle. Wild flowers blossomed in bursts of red, yellow, blue, and orange amidst the tall prairie grass. But eventually the grasses thinned and shortened until only dull buffalo grass and prickly pear covered the hard earth. They saw no buffalo though, and only glimpsed mule deer and elk bounding away from the riverbanks.

Will stubbed his big toe on a bleached log as he attempted to drag his naked foot over it. Gritting his teeth and cursing silently, he yanked impotently on the cordelle then limped forward. The water and rocky ground had callused and whitened his feet; the constant pulling had thickened his muscles; the patches of stinging nettle, buckthorn, and wild rose had furrowed webs of thin, bloody scratches across his legs, arms, and chest; sores glistened from wood tick and mosquito bites.

He shook his head in irritation. Two hundred dollars a year! Could've made that in an afternoon haggling in Santa Fe's plaza! The scents of piñon smoke, baked tortillas, and sizzling beef, onions, and chiles mingled again in his mind. He squeezed off those memories and imagined instead the expedition's half-dozen hunters who ranged far ahead and occasionally left a gutted deer hanging from a cottonwood like some offering to the gods. How he envied their freedom! He glanced back at the keelboat trailing twenty-five yards downstream, his eyes angrily hunting out Ashley who stood grim-faced at the tiller behind stacks of red trade blankets. Damn that salt pork and moldy hardtack he rations us four times daily! And damn his mad race upriver against the Missouri and French fur companies! Must be a month ahead of any rivals!

He resumed his inner debate over whether or not to desert. Several dozen men had already slipped off in twos and threes into the dark over the past few weeks, while everyone muttered darkly of doing the same. He was on watch that night. He imagined waiting until the campfires burned low and the men snored away in deep exhaustion before slipping back into camp, quietly gathering up his blanket and bag, and heading downriver. Should he tell the other guards of his plans? Would they let him disappear just like that? Would they join him? Or would they thrust a rifle barrel in his gut and march him back to Ashley and Clyman?

And what about Jess? He leaned sideways to peer around the half-dozen men on the line before him to spot Jess near the front. Jess jokingly dismissed his complaints, no matter how tedious and exhausting the trek got. How did he endure? Beats smithin', he proclaimed repeatedly. But how much was he just afraid of letting on—we'd be better off in Santa Fe with our own goods than slaves to Ashley?

Damn me! Will thought bitterly. Why'd I go along like some dumb sheep? He imagined sitting through trials at the courthouse and preparing briefs for Jameson. Suddenly he sneered as scenes of cases won or lost by money changing hands or drunk jurors or somnolent judges or appeals to emotion rather than reason streamed before his eyes. Justice? Rarely. And only then by chance. System's rotten from top to bottom. He sighed. Least in court I can use my mind. I'm losing it out here!

And what about Judy? She was resigned to me leaving this time. A few silent tears was all when I first told her and a few more a week later when I pecked her cheek goodbye. Her mother and sister were just as subdued. Seth and the boys were all in favor. They probably hoped some Blackfoot would raise my scalp way up the Missouri. Of course, leaving Seth the two hundred dollars sure helped. "You're a good boy, Will," Seth exclaimed as he quickly pocketed the silver with one hand and slapped him hard on the shoulder with his other.

Judy! He imagined her staring moodily into the fireplace. A lifetime together? That's no life at all. Sometimes I wish she was...No, I can't think that!

It's too late now! I can't abandon Jess and scurry back to St. Louis with my tail between my legs. 'Course the women'd be relieved, but other people'd snicker behind my back, or even to my face. I could never hold my head up again and my desertion'd be thrown back in my face if I ever raised heading West again. And old man Morgan'd never get over it. Particularly when I had to pay back most of the two hundred dollars. Jess might understand and forgive, but something'd be lost between us, probably forever.

"Pirogue!" someone shouted from the keelboat, and everyone stopped and stared at a tiny speck approaching them from upstream. "Tie 'em up!" Ashley hollered and the men at each cordelle found a suitable rock or log. Ashley hurried toward the keelboat's prow and eagerly strained to identify the man.

The pirogue grew as its sole inhabitant, a grave bearded man, paddled it toward them. "Mr. Smith!" Ashley shouted triumphantly and waved his top hat. Smith paddled his pirogue alongside the keelboat, tossed a line to one of the men, and scrambled onboard. Ashley and Smith shook hands then retired immediately to Ashley's cabin.

"One of Henry's men?" Will incredulously asked the others. "Did he paddle all the way down from the Yellowstone by himself?" Everyone shrugged. He felt a jab in his side and turned to face Jess.

"Well, ,Will, ya think that Mr. Smith was deserting?" Jess asked impishly. "Don't know why anyone'd wanna desert now that the fun's just beginning, do you?"

Will's brow crinkled as he shook his head slowly. "Jess…sometimes I just don't know what to make of you."

The keelboats were anchored midstream, just in range of the stockaded Arikara villages. The men crowded the decks watching anxiously as Ashley, Smith, and Edward Rose, the half-breed interpreter, rowed a skiff toward shore to barter for safe passage and horses. Hundreds of Arikaras watched silently between the upthrust logs of the palisade or from atop the earthen mound homes within. The warriors brandished lances, bows and arrows, or muskets while the squaws hugged their children tight.

"Think they's white?" Will asked, pointing to the scalps fluttering from poles in the center of the lower Arikara village.

"Ah reckon," Jess answered solemnly. "Probably those Missouri Fur Company boys they kilt earlier this summer. Ashley may drive us like slaves but he's got a hell of a lotta guts going inta the village with jus' Smith and Rose."

"I wouldn't trust Rose farther than I could spit," Will replied, shaking his head. "Said to have sold out the Astorians a decade back.

And I wouldn't wanna get on his bad side either. Heard that when he was living amongst the Crow they called him Five Scalps for killing five Assiniboine with just a tomahawk."

"Well, Ashley must not trust him much either. Hear tell he shrugged off Rose's warning to anchor over near the bar on the other side of the river."

"Ya blame him with all those Rees skulking behind that breast-work they got on the bar? Could be Rose's trick ta get us all massacred and add our scalps to his collection."

"Wagh!" Jess grunted. "It'd take more'n Rose and a couple Ree villages ta put all us under."

"That's right," Aaron Stephens piped in. He was a large, powerful man with sandy hair and a chiseled face who liked to brag loudly of his winning ways with ladies and whores. "It'll be no different with the Rees than with any other tribe up or down the Missouri. They all like ta strut and shake their coup sticks afore our eyes. Three years I was soldierin' at Fort Atkinson I seen a dozen tribes pass through. Red niggers is all the same." He laughed loudly. "Keep yer pizens dry, boys. We'll be dipping our wicks inta Ree girls tonight."

Will glanced at Stephens, admiring his bulk and womanizing but, as always, felt uneasy in his presence. Maybe Jess and Stephens were right. Maybe they would trade and whore peacefully with the Arikara like they had the Poncas, Otos, and Omaha in previous weeks. He scanned the narrow channel with the Arikara villages on the west bank and the breastwork across the large sand bar on the east. His eyes drifted across the endless undulating plains beyond both river banks. "The Rees are different," he finally replied. "Way I hear it the Rees've been trading horses and robes from the upper Missouri and Plains tribes for guns and powder from the lower Missouri tribes and American traders. They ain't likely ta be happy 'bout us undercutting their business by pushing past 'em and trading direct up the Missouri and cross the Plains."

Stephens hooted in exasperation. "Damn ye, Yates! Ye jus' ain't bin listen ta what ah bin tellin ye! Americans bin trading past the Rees far up the Missouri since Lewis and Clark, and the Spanish and French were there long before. Ashley and Henry had no trouble when they passed through last year, trading for horses and robes, and they ain't gonna have trouble this year doin' the same."

"Then why'd the Rees raid the Sioux down south and even attack the Missouri Company's Cedar Fort if they weren't trying to regain their position as middlemen of the Plains? And they'll be hot for vengeance since the son of their chief, Gray Eyes, was killed in the attack. They ain't gonna care whether or not we're a different company. We're Americans all the same to them. And if the Rees don't take kindly to our visit, just how do ye figure we can fight our way up that channel and round that horseshoe right under their noses?"

Jess pondered a moment. "Nightfall," he stated decisively. "We jus' pole on past in the middle of the night. Maybe give 'em a barrel or two a' whiskey and get 'em good and drunk so they can't see straight 'nuff to piss, let lone shoot."

"That current's mighty strong. Might hafta use the towline. Ye wanna be ashore dragging those keelboats upstream with hundreds of Rees charging us like fiends outta hell?"

Stephens snorted. "Yates, ye worry too much 'bout nothin'."

"May not come ta that," Jess said quietly. They watched Ashley, Smith, and Rose step ashore, unroll blankets filled with awls, mirrors, and ribbons, and, with hands held high in greeting, call on the chiefs to come forth and parley. The village buzzed with debate. Finally two chiefs approached the shore and shook hands with the whites. Jess nodded in satisfaction.

"They seems friendly 'nuff."

It was late afternoon the day after they dropped anchor below the villages. Forty men lounged around a half-dozen tents and piles of trade goods scattered across the beach. The men had spent the afternoon cleaning their rifles, scrounging for driftwood, or just watching Ashley, Smith, and Rose bartering with the Arikaras a hundred yards up the beach. The wind gusted and the sky thickened with dark thunderclouds. The men frequently shot worried glances toward the sky and the Arikara stockade a couple hundred yards upstream.

"Gonna be a wet night," Jess declared. "Don't know how we're gonna all fit inside that tent."

Will looked up from his battered copy of Blackstone and smiled. "I don't mind a little rain. I just can't wait ta see the last of the Missouri. Feels good to be ashore without that damn towline between my hands. We was lucky to be amongst those chosen to go across."

"Gonna be a long walk," Jess replied as he glanced at the dozen horses staked out before their camp. "Got 'nuff horses ta carry our provisions but not 'nuff for anybody ta ride."

"By cutting due west cross the Plains we can be on the Yellowstone long 'fore the keelboats. And we can trade for horses from other tribes 'long the way. We'll be riding soon enough," Will replied confidently.

"Party's over," someone declared, and everyone's head turned to stare up the beach. Ashley was being rowed to his keelboat while Smith and Rose, pulling three ponies each, approached camp.

"Gentlemen, a word," Smith declared as he and Rose finished staking out the ponies. The men scrambled to their feet and gathered around. Tall, lean, and grave, Smith looked like an Old Testament prophet. The men marveled that he read the Bible daily, and never smoked, swore, drank, or fornicated. Smith absent-mindedly stroked his long, brown beard as he carefully chose his words.

"We're heading out at dawn tomorrow. The Arikara will trade no more unless we accept their demand of a gun, one hundred rounds, and a knife for each horse. General Ashley has steadfastly refused to do this. The Arikara are in a foul mood and we must take every precaution to ensure there is no…trouble. You have your assignments. Let no man shirk in his duty. Are there any questions?"

"Rees gonna attack us, Cap'in?" someone asked.

Smith sighed deeply. "Mr. Rose, what is your assessment?"

Of African, Cherokee, and white ancestry, Rose was short and swarthy, and his muscles were rock-hard. He had a wispy mustache which ran down the sides of his mouth, had lost his nose tip in a fight, and an *X* had been branded on his forehead—but he never revealed why and no one dared to ask. His murky brown eyes were furtive, and seemed to alternate flashes of murderous anger and merry abandon. He wore buckskins and a blood-red bandanna over his graying hair. "Hard ta say. Lower village a' Gray Eyes is talkin' war. The upper village of Little Soldier is talkin' peace." He shot a stream of chewing tobacco before his moccasins. "Could go either way."

"Can't we visit the villages?" someone else demanded. "We got some trading of our own ta do!" Nervous laughter rippled across the group.

"You are well advised to stay as close to camp as possible," Smith replied. "The Arikara are hostile and unpredictable. Whether their rules of hospitality to strangers in their midst can hold back those who advocate war, I cannot say. General Ashley, Mr. Rose, and myself have visited both camps with no harm. And the Arikara, like other Indians, are emboldened by their enemies' fear and restrained by their fortitude. Perhaps it would be wise to act as naturally and fearlessly as possible." He shook his head wearily. "We are caught in a dilemma for which I have no answers."

He looked hard into the eyes of the men around him. "If there are no more questions…?" he paused. "That is all." Smith retired to his tent and the men scattered to their campfires.

With his hands behind his head, Stephens was stretched out on his blanket.

"You boys interested in doing a little sportin'?"

Jess grinned. "You thinkin' a' visitin' the village?"

"Don't know why not. Smith says we're supposed to...how'd he put it...act natural? Well, I don't know anything more natural than bedding down with a plump little squaw now do you? Why there mus' be hundreds of Ree girls jus' drippin' for us ta drop atop 'em." Stephens slowly rose and stretched. "Any ye boys wanna join me?" he demanded to the dozen men nearby as he stuffed some calico and bells in his hunting shirt. "Last chance ta dip yer wicks till the Yellowstone."

Most of the men looked away or laughed nervously. "Ye gotta be crazy, Stephens," one responded. "Those Rees are madder than hornets for Ashley cutting 'em short. Ye'll end up with yer scalp waving from one a' them poles."

"Think so do ye?" Stephens replied haughtily. "Well, once those niggers see the size a' ma pole they'll drop to their knees and pass me ever' virgin in camp." Stephens squinted down at Jess. "Baucus? What kinda man be ye?"

"Man enough," Jess replied gamely. "Believe I will tag 'long Stephens. Besides, the Rees're unlikely ta kill a few of us if they aim ta kill all of us. Will?"

"What kinda man?" Will mused aloud. "Don't believe anyone can answer that with certainty." He shrugged fatalistically. "Reckon I'll join ye. Been wondering what the insides of that Ree village'd be like."

"Anybody else?" Stephens demanded loudly.

"Those Rees jus' may skin ye boys alive," someone remarked with disgust, then spat for emphasis.

Rose ambled over and chuckled deeply. "Well, well, Stephens, ifin yer headin' inta the village, ye'll be needin' an interpreter I'm a-thinkin'."

Will and Jess glanced nervously at each other as they grabbed some bundles of trade goods. "Ye think we'll be safe?" Will asked meekly.

Rose's face split with a twisted grin. "Safe as ifin ye was a babe in yer mother's arms." He raised a palm high, "I promise."

The four men strolled up the beach toward the palisade. At a narrow opening in the wall they joined a ragged procession of Arikara women and children straggling in from the corn, pumpkin, and squash fields. Rose and Stephens cackled and gestured lewdly at the women while Will and Jess smiled wanly. A dozen scowling warriors quickly gathered around the Americans. Rose threw up his hand, smiled broadly, and spoke rapidly in their tongue. They parted sullenly. Rose nodded to his companions. "Come on, boys. We gotta pay our respects ta Gray Eyes afore we spread any legs." The word of their arrival was excitedly shouted and the Arikara poured from their earthmound dwellings as the Americans filed through the village.

Will smiled and nodded to the Arikara as he walked swiftly past. Everything seemed like a dream. The deepening dusk. The hot gusts of wind and surging thunderclouds. The Ree warriors with the tattooed swirls across their faces and arms, huge pendants dangling from their ears, bearclaw necklaces draping their chests, eagle feathers knotted in their long braids or loose hair; most warriors shook war clubs and jeered the Americans; others stared silently, with expressions of fear, curiosity, or contempt varying from one brown face to the next. The array of buckskinned women, some comely, others toothless, gray hags. Naked children and scrawny dogs darting through the throng. The din of shouting, yelps, ululations, shrill whirling of bull whistles, beating of skin drums, and bawling babies. The mingled stench of rotting offal, dung, and rinds. The ponies with flattened ears staked before the scattered earthlodges.

Will muttered over Jess's shoulder. "Feel like we're canoeing a river full a' gators and snapping turtles. My blood's tingling with the thrill of the ride and fear a' tipping over."

Jess laughed. "Know what ye mean."

"What do you figure'd happened without Rose along?"

"Prob'ly be gutted and roasted by now," Jess replied grimly. "May come ta that yet. Too late ta back out now."

They halted in front of Gray Eyes's lodge, the crowd pushing tightly around them. Rose spoke loudly through the opening, then stooped and stepped inside. Relieved to leave the din and crowd behind, the other three followed.

Beneath the smokehole in the center, they sat down before a small fire over which a buffalo gut pot hung from a wooden tripod. Gray Eyes and a half-dozen chiefs peered at them from the other side while a squaw shoveled stew from the pot into gourd bowls and pushed it into the Americans' hands. Rose inhaled deeply from his bowl then plucked out a chunk of meat and popped it in his mouth. "You boys're in fer a treat," he said between bits as he nodded to Gray Eyes. "Dog meat. Ain't everybody git such an honor." Rose and Gray Eyes began talking loudly and gesturing to each other.

Will tried not to grimace as he gingerly put a small piece between his lips. He chewed it delicately. "Hmmm. Ain't bad," he declared and Jess and Stephens grunted consent. "Mus' be what living in a beaver den's like," he remarked as his eyes struggled to focus in the dim light.

The earth lodge was large, over forty feet in diameter, and was supported by four thick upright cottonwood logs and scores of criss-crossed branches. The earth floor was covered with buffalo robes, piles of pumpkins and squash, and parfleches. Bows and quivers of arrows, muskets, garishly painted shields, tomahawks, and a coup stick with its spine sprouting a dozen eagle feathers were propped against the walls. Three long, black scalps dangled from a stump on one of the pillars. Long strips of buffalo and elk meat dried from racks. A half-dozen ponies were staked near the entrance. Women and children crouched in the shadows, watching silently. Several of the women cooed at babies in cradleboards. Flies buzzed, fleas bit, lice crawled.

Gray Eyes raised a long pipe toward the smokehole and muttered a prayer. Lowering the pipe, he pulled an ember from the fire and touched it to the redstone bowl while sucking deeply at the stem. He handed the pipe to the chief on his right, who puffed deeply and passed it on. Everyone sat silent, tense, as the pipe made its way around the circle. The blue smoke hung heavily in the stale air. When it returned to Gray Eyes, he spoke forcefully and at length.

Rose nodded in cadence to Gray Eyes's speech, then, once the chief lapsed into a sullen silence, spoke slowly and clearly, occasionally striking his chest, or chopping the air with his hand. Still speaking, he untied his bundle and spread it before the chief. He handed a twist of tobacco to Gray Eyes and handfuls of beads to the other chiefs.

Then he picked up a jew's-harp, set the end in his mouth, and twanged out a ditty. Smiles broke across several of the chiefs' faces. Rose handed the jew's-harp to Gray Eyes who twanged away at it for a while then laughed in delight. Gray Eyes lit another pipe and, as it was passed around, spoke animatedly with Rose. Other chiefs occasionally interrupted with a question or boast. Finally Gray Eyes put his pipe away carefully in a parfleche.

"That's it, boys," Rose said cheerfully as he motioned them to rise. "We done come at jus' the right time. Ol' Gray Eyes and the others were debating the wisdom of the deal they struck with the Ginral this afternoon. Our presence eased Gray Eyes's mind over his son killed down at Fort Cedar. We might jus' make it upriver after all." Rose winked and hooked a finger toward one of the chiefs who had sidled up to them. The Arikara was squat, plump, and missing three of the fingers on his right hand. "And best of all, Yellow Horse here has offered ta share his wives with us." Yellow Horse spoke loudly to Rose, grinned lewdly at the other Americans, then ducked out of the lodge. The Americans followed, with Rose and Stephens boasting of their sexual prowess.

It was pitch dark now as they stumbled the deserted village paths. Heat lightning flashed and thunder rumbled across the black western sky. Will inhaled deeply and savored the energy surging through his body. "What a night," he whispered to Jess. "All hell's gonna break loose soon."

"That's what I'm afeared of," Jess whispered back.

They slipped into a lodge and joined a dozen Arikara lounging around a bed of coals. Yellow Horse spoke quietly first with the Arikara then with Rose.

"Well, boys, a bell or mirror'll get ye a poke," Rose exclaimed. "Jus' pay Yella Horse."

"How do we know what we're gittin'?" Jess asked.

Rose conferred with Yellow Horse who then called into the darkness. Two blanket-clad figures approached the fire. Yellow Horse tossed some dried dung on the coals and blew steadily on it until it burst into flame. He called gently to the two figures and they approached the flames. Both were as short and plump as their husband.

"I told ye I don't want his wives," Stephens said harshly. "I wanna virgin."

"Damn, Stephens, that all ye think of?" Rose replied. "And I done told ye before, a virgin'll cost ye a horse." He laughed sharply. "Sides, ifin yer as big as ye tell, ye'll be making her moan like she was a virgin."

Stephens hastily dug into his bundle, pulled out a mirror, and thrust it into Yellow Horse's hand. "I'll make her moan all right." He grabbed the wrist of the prettier squaw. "Come on, girl!"

"Hold on, Stephens," Rose said malevolently. "That's the one I fancied."

Stephens released his grip on the girl and turned to tower over Rose. "Was my idea on the beach fer a whore and it's my pay now." Rose stared up into Stephens's eyes while his hand curled around the knife handle in his belt. "I told ye I fancied her, Stephens, and I aim ta git her," he said slowly, forcefully.

"You gentlemen forgetting where we are?" Will said as calmly as possible. "This ain't St. Louis."

"Yeah, boys," Jess added. "Let's compromise. I'll take the pretty one and ye two fight over the other."

Rose continued to stare up at Stephens. "If it warn't fer me, Stephens, those Rees'd bashed yer thick skull in. Now stand aside and take the other. Ye kin have mine after I'm done with her." Stephens stepped back and grabbed the wrist of the other squaw. "All right, Rose," he leered. "She'll git it twice as hard." He motioned into the darkness.

The squaw glanced at Yellow Horse who stoically nodded. The squaw led Stephens into the dark. Rose gently slipped his arm around the other squaw and murmured softly into her ear, then they disappeared toward another side of the lodge. Jess whistled softly, "Stephens is one crazy son of a bitch."

"Ye still want yer poke?" Will asked quietly.

"Don't know how those boys kin get it up under the circumstances. I sure lost my charge," he admitted ruefully.

"Let's get outta here. I seen what I came to see."

A shriek and tearful female pleading shattered the silence. Elsewhere Rose cried out, "What the hell ye doing, Stephens!"

Yellow Horse and several men rushed into the darkness. Thuds, the girl's shrieks, and Stephens's curses filled the air. Then Stephens groaned and screamed for help.

Will and Jess stood petrified, debating whether to run or help Stephens.

Hastily tying up his buckskin pants, Rose shouted, "Stephens, ye dumb bastard," pushed past them and fled toward the lodge entrance.

"Come on," Will urged and they tore after him. Outside they could barely see Rose sprinting in the dark before them. The wind gusted with bursts of light rain. War cries erupted dimly behind them. Someone stepped in front of Rose and was knocked aside. The Arikara sprang to his feet and, whooping at the top of his lungs, chased after Rose. Will and Jess charged along just behind him. Other Arikara stepped out into the dark and took up the pursuit.

The rain was slickening the hard-packed earth and everyone ran gingerly as fast as they could. Ahead was the black opening in the bleached logs of the palisade. Rose tore through it with the Arikara and Will and Jess hard on his heels. A few seconds later a dozen other warriors spilled out of the village. Campfires flickered down the beach. Jess caught up to the Arikara and shoved him hard. The Arikara stumbled and fell. Gasping for breath, Will leapt over him. Ahead the campfires were being kicked apart or smothered with sand. Men were shouting fearfully. Dim figures crouched in a ragged line. The ponies were being pulled inside the camp. One by one the Arikara gave up the pursuit.

A hundred yards from the camp, Rose shouted, "Don't shoot! Don't shoot! It's Rose!" Will and Jess gasped out their own names. Chests heaving, the three men stumbled into the camp and collapsed.

A score of heavily armed men gathered tightly around them. Smith's voice cut loudly through the dark. "To your positions, men! I'll attend to this." He stooped over Rose and demanded, "What happened?"

"Stephens...dead," Rose blurted between gasps.

"How?"

"Dallied...with a Ree girl."

"Did you kill or injure any Rees?" Smith asked quietly.

"No...happened too quick."

"Yates? Baucus? Are you all right?"

"Barely," Jess replied.

"That was close," Will added. God was that close, he repeated in wonder to himself.

Smith nodded. "Mr. Clyman!" he called out. "Take word to General Ashley." Without a word, Clyman trotted to a skiff on the shore and pushed it into the Missouri.

"Gentlemen," Smith said softly. "I fear it will be a long night."

The storm broke and drenched everyone with pounding rain and wind. Some men huddled in the tents, trying to keep them from blowing away. Will, Jess, and others spent the night straining at the ropes on the horses to prevent them from running off. Everyone watched tensely through the black at the beach and prairie. They debated whether to move the horses and themselves across the river as soon as the storm passed or to wait until light. Toward dawn the wind and rain died. Ashley sent word that they would hold tight and demand the return of Stephens's body.

Will curled in a shallow hole in the sand he had scooped with his skinning knife. His shirt and blanket were spread nearby to dry. The damp sand and air made his body gritty and sticky. His hair was plastered against his head. The long night of struggling with the horses had exhausted him but the dregs of adrenaline racing through his body would not let him sleep. He watched the gray light broaden across the eastern sky. Suddenly fear gripped him as he imagined hundreds of Rees creeping stealthily toward camp. He yanked up his head and stared down the empty shore at the still darkened palisade a couple hundred yards away. He let out his pent up breath in a long whisper, then stood, stretched stiffly, and slowly turned. Men, half-hidden beneath the sand, were scattered in a line across the beach. Most were motionless, silent. Others talked quietly or puffed their pipes. Jess snored away in the next hole. Have we all dug our own graves, he wondered? Fuming bitterly, he tried once again to pull the soaked charge in his battered rifle but it would not budge. He drew out his ramrod and resisted breaking it over his knee. Just like New Orleans! He began to shiver uncontrollably as he heard again the fifes, drums, and bagpipes looming closer through the mist; saw again the massed British soldiers torn to shreds by musket and grapeshot; Redcoat screams and curses echoed brutally through his mind. He wiped away the tears burning down his cheeks.

What am I doing here, he silently screamed. I've spent my life running from one failure to the next. I should be back tending Judy and writing briefs for Jameson. This is madness!

War whoops suddenly burst from the village. Will thrust out his rifle and aimed toward the palisade from which hundreds of Arikara poked muskets and arrows. As the sun rose up from the prairie, Yellow Horse walked slowly down the beach toward them until he was a hundred yards from camp.

Rose warily walked out to meet him but Yellow Horse refused to take his hand. The two argued heatedly.

Smith stood up in his hole and hollered, "Mr. Rose! What is he saying?"

"Wants a horse fer Stephens!" Rose shouted back.

Smith pondered the demand then answered, "No trade!"

Rose and Yellow Horse continued arguing. Finally Yellow Horse yelled and gestured wildly at Rose, then marched angrily to the village. The Arikara brandished their weapons and screamed war whoops and taunts. Rose trotted back to camp.

"What did he say, Mr. Rose?" Smith asked.

"Well, Cap'n…" Rose began with a grin.

"You may retain the expletives." Rose looked perplexed. "Curse words."

Rose nodded in understanding. "He said he'd return Stephens's body."

The screaming from the village rose higher. "That's him," some-one hollered. Several Arikara stood at the village entrance, carrying a headless, naked body bruised and torn by dozens of blows. Suddenly they tossed the body down the slope where it tumbled then stopped at the river's edge. Yellow Horse appeared waving Stephens's scalped and bashed head by the ear. He hurled it high in the air. It hit the ground and rolled erratically until it stopped.

A shot was fired from the palisade and then a long volley. Bullets and arrows whizzed by or thudded in horses or men. A few men fired back but there were no clear targets. Most men burrowed deeper in their holes. Some screamed curses or pleas to God. A man ran for the river and was shot down. Ripped by dozens of balls and arrows, most horses lay still while others kicked, neighed shrilly, and struggled to rise.

"We gotta git ta the keelboat," Jess hollered above the incessant firing as he desperately reloaded.

"They got us pinned down," Will yelled back as he peered out toward the river. "Ashley'll have to come to us!" On both keelboats men cowered behind the long cabin in the center while Ashley stood at the helm of the lead boat, exhorting them to pole toward shore. A few men were lowering a skiff into the water. On the beach men screamed for help. Two dashed for the water. One was gunned down but the other dove in and flailed madly toward the keelboats as bullets splashed the water around him.

"We gotta run fer it," Jess urged.

"Not less they rush us or the boats come," Will replied firmly as he gingerly reached out for his blanket and shirt and stuffed them in his haversack.

Jess pointed. "Here they come!"

Three skiffs were skimming the water toward shore. Suddenly the rowers in the lead skiff were knocked down and the skiff drifted downstream. A half-dozen men from shore rushed into the river and splashed toward the skiffs.

Jess's face was flushed and sweaty. "Now or never! Come on, Will, yer gonna git kilt!" They grabbed up their rifles and haversacks and sprinted past dead men and horses, scattered equipment, and shredded tents toward the river. Other men ran, crawled, or limped along with them. Some were shot down.

The frigid spring current shocked Will as he plunged in and the weight of his rifle, blanket, and haversack dragged him deep under. The silence, near invisibility, and slow motion beneath the surface felt like a languid dream. He was tempted to suck the river into his lungs and drift away with the current. A body floated by through the brown liquid, its face bloated, eyes bulging, and arms stretched upward. Will shuddered and kicked toward the surface to gasp for breath in an air filled with screams and gunshots. The water frothed with the crazed efforts of a score of men.

"Will, I'm hit," Jess hollered nearby.

He turned and watched Jess sink below the current. Pushing away his rifle and haversack, he swam toward him. I just lost my old man's rifle, he realized as he caught Jess's arm and pulled him to the surface. And my Blackstone and the mittens Judy knitted me and…Jess choked hoarsely. Will struggled to keep their heads above water. A skiff shot alongside and a bearded man reached down to help. Suddenly his jaw was shot away and he screamed as he fell into the river. Will grabbed the gunwale and someone inside helped drag him and Jess into the boat. Three other men splashed over and tipped the boat perilously as they pulled themselves over the side. They all lay exhausted and terrified in the bottom as the skiff drifted downstream. Balls whizzed past. One splintered the skiff at the waterline and the river seeped in.

Breathing heavily, Will peeked over the gunwale. Survivors were being pulled into the keelboats and the other skiff. The beach was littered with dead men and horses. A few bodies floated downstream. The palisade belched puffs of smoke as the Arikara continued firing. Some Arikara skulked along both banks but they kept to cover. With the last men aboard, the moorings were cut and the keelboats drifted downriver. Will grabbed an oar and used it as a tiller to keep the skiff in midstream. After bitterly tongue-lashing them, he finally shamed the other men into rowing while he bound the bloody hole in Jess's thigh.

"Did it go through?" Jess asked weakly. Will shook his head no. "Hope my dancing days ain't over."

"We'll find out soon enough," Will replied. "We're heading home."

Eight

1823

The men shuffled and blinked as the sun rose swiftly above the low, parched hills on the far horizon. Before them, searching for words, Ashley rubbed the brim of his top hat between his fingers and stared down at the two fresh earth-mounds at his feet. He looked almost comically frail with his massive head towering above his short, slender body, his thinning brown hair, receded chin, large bulbous nose, and tiny brown eyes. Smith, Clyman, and Rose stood awkwardly nearby.

Will tightly gripped the new flintlock in his hands and brushed the powder horn with his elbow for reassurance. He craned his neck to look up and down the ragged line of eighty men. Their faces were tense, exhausted, uncertain. He glanced back at the two keelboats tied close to shore. A half-dozen armed boatmen walked the decks and nervously scanned the banks and surrounding hills. He shuddered as he recalled descending the steep steps into the hull of the *Yellowstone* shortly after dawn. He had gagged uncontrollably on the mingled stench of urine, excrement, and whiskey, and cringed before the groans, curses, and prayers of the wounded. He marveled at Jess's spirit. Although he was barely conscious, Jess had mustered enough gumption to mumble gratitude over not getting hit in his third leg. The doctor said Jess'd make it if gangrene didn't claim him.

Will stared at the two graves before them. Delirious, ranting, the men died during the night and had just been buried. Smith had led them in prayer. Will trembled as yesterday's screams and gunshots on the beach ricocheted through his mind. Once again he huddled in that sand pit as bullets and arrows tore up the ground and men and horses all around him, dashed madly with the others into the river and sank gratefully deep into its cold silence, then burst above the surface into that bedlam of men flailing desperately toward the keelboats and pirogues. He tried to quell his surging terror by clinging to Smith's words: "Though I walk through the valley of the shadow of death, I shall fear no evil, for thou art with me." Will glanced again at the men around him and thanked God he was not marooned out there alone.

"Gentlemen," Ashley said quietly then paused long in inner debate. "Gentlemen!" he repeated, loudly this time, and squinted into the faces before him. "We have suffered a severe and unexpected setback. Our dead," he pointed to the graves, "now number fifteen and our boats are filled with another dozen wounded. Our spirits lie heavy with grief for our fallen comrades and fear for the future." He puffed up his sunken chest with a deep breath and cocked back his head. "We must bury our fear with our dead," he intoned loudly. "My officers and I have debated throughout the night our options and have concluded," he paused to emphasize the next word, "unanimously, that our only course is to go forward up the Missouri..." Protests and curses erupted from the ranks. Ashley winced then glared back.

"We're with ya, Ginral," someone shouted and others took up the cry. Ashley threw up his hands and waited for silence. Not wanting to appear afraid, Will kept his mouth shut, but he prayed the men would force Ashley to return to St. Louis.

"We can't let the Rees get away with this!" Ashley shouted excitedly once the ranks settled. "Those savages," he snarled the words, "will prey on anyone who ascends the Missouri! No one will be safe from their depredations! Major Henry and over one hundred men stranded on the Yellowstone desperately await our arrival with fresh supplies and reinforcements! We can't abandon them! We must run past those Ree villages by stealth or fight." Grumbles rippled through the ranks. "A fortune is at stake!" Ashley blustered. "You must do your duty! I have paid you each two hundred dollars for a year's labor…"

"You kin have it back," someone shouted, and others piped in. Other men tried to shout down the dissenters. The ranks broke up as men squared off in groups and argued bitterly.

"Order!" Ashley shouted. "Order!"

A score of men approached Ashley and pleaded with him to head downstream. Will joined them and to his surprise, suddenly hollered, "Let's vote on it, General!" Others began shouting for a vote while Smith, Clyman, and Rose conferred earnestly with Ashley.

Finally Ashley raised his hands. "Silence!" he ordered. "We will vote!" The tumult died as all eyes targeted Ashley. "Now form ranks!" The men shuffled back into line. Knowing the vote would go against him, Ashley hesitated. He angrily chewed his thin lips and silently cursed their cowardice. "All right!" he finally growled. "We'll see who among you are men of courage, perseverance, and character, and who," he glared contemptuously, "are base cowards. If the vote is nay, the cowards can take one keelboat and scurry back to St. Louis, whimpering like a pack of dogs with their tails between their legs. Meanwhile, I, and any men of honor among you, will ascend the Missouri in the other keelboat. If you vote for fulfilling our mission and your contracts, I will tolerate no desertions and we will all head upriver tomorrow. Is that understood!"

Some men nodded but most stared sullenly. Will debated what to do. It was madness to push again up the Missouri. It would be impossible to pole their keelboats around that horseshoe at night under the nose of those stockades. The Rees would get wind of it and murder them. But Ashley was right, arguing that a retreat would embolden the Rees and other hostile tribes to close the river indefinitely to any traders. The fur trade was St. Louis's lifeblood. Without it, commerce and all their lives would wither.

"All in favor of fulfilling your contracts and reaping a fortune on the upper Missouri," Ashley commanded, "join me!" A few men strode forward and stood defiantly behind Ashley. The others hung back, sheepish and uncertain. Ashley glared fiercely at the holdouts. "Are these the only true men among you?" he mocked as he pointed to those behind him. A dozen other men trickled hesitantly forward. Will was torn in indecision.

"What will you tell your family and neighbors upon your return?

That you lacked the courage and honor to follow where hundreds of your countrymen from Lewis and Clark to Henry have already trod?" In twos and threes others stepped forward. Reasoning that the majority would probably know best, Will waited to see whether most men would join Ashley. The trickle of men ended and both sides stared tensely at each other. At least two-thirds refused to stand with Ashley. Will felt both guilty and relieved. "So be it," Ashley said bitterly. "Mr. Clyman, take the names of all the deserters. There'll be hell to pay upon our return to St. Louis!" He stalked off toward the horizon.

Jess winced and fiercely gripped the cottonwood crutch under his armpit.

Will reached out to steady him but Jess bitterly shook his head. "Damn this leg," he fumed. "What have ye decided?" he demanded.

"I don't know. Most are heading back."

"If most jumped off a cliff, would ye?"

Will chuckled. "You sound like my mother. Besides," he added morosely, "I lost my Pa's rifle."

Jess softened. "Yeah, that was one fine shooting iron."

"Been with us down the Mississippi to New Orleans. And a half-dozen hunting trips across Missouri. And all the way to Santa Fe and back."

Jess grinned. "Those were some times."

Will shook his head sadly. "Promised Pa I'd guard it with my life. Course, he was silent and still as a pumpkin when I told him. But I think somehow he understood."

"Your pa warn't easy to set with afore or after his stroke."

"He was a bastard at times," Will said bitterly. "Always hollering at us, particularly me. Nothing I did was ever good enough for him."

"How'd he git like that."

"As my uncle Jake told it, Pa never was one for lightheartedness. Then surviving the Hamar and St. Clair massacres hurt him deep, but he never let on or talked 'bout it. Licking the Shawnee and Miami with Wayne at Fallen Timbers didn't help. Something burned away deep in his guts all those years. He was a brave man. Carried his rifle all the way through. Probably killed a lot of men with it, but he never let on."

"You kilt a Comanche with it," Jess observed warily. "Your pa'd been proud of that."

Will shrugged helplessly. "Don't know if he would or not. I think he hated watching people die as much as he hated people in general. Frontier trapped him into killing or being killed. Something drove him north with the army those three times."

"Fear a being called yellow?"

"Might of been pride. Conviction. Both. I don't know. I just know it wasn't love of killing." He scratched a circle in the dirt with a twig.

"He entrusted that rifle to me and I threw it away. Now it's rotting and rusting deep in the Missouri mud."

Jess nodded. "Yup, see what yer mean." A twinge of pain jolted him. "Damn it," he sniffed irritably. "If it warn't for this leg I'da joined Smith and that Frenchie to take word upstream to Henry."

"Smith's the bravest man I ever met," Will marveled.

"And I sure as hell wouldn't be headed home," Jess added.

"I'm amazed you're on your feet again after only a week."

"Ain't fair sending back all the wounded."

"Ashley's short so many men he can't spare any to look after you."

"Why don't we both stay and ye can look after me till I heal up, then we'll trap every stream in the Rockies and take a fortune in beaver."

Will chuckled. "I think you're just afraid of facing Sarah again."

"I jus' had my heart set on the Rockies, is all. 'Sides, I wouldn't a' figured ye was all fired anxious ta git back with Judy."

"A man's got obligations."

"That a reason or an excuse?" Jess demanded. "Ye gonna run back to St. Louis like a wet hen?"

"I told you I ain't decided yet," Will replied angrily. "We could sit on this island all summer and not have the army or other fur companies join us against the Rees. What'd be the point of that? Besides," he added, "I ain't too all-fired anxious to try my luck again. A few steps slower and we'd a' ended up like Stephens."

They lapsed into silence and watched the boatmen load equipment on the *Yellowstone*. A harsh, high-pitched voice exploded nearby. "Brown, yer a yellow sack a' shit. Ye running back to yer momma's skirts, ain't ye?" Isaac Slade was of medium height and sinewy build and had a narrow face with a broken nose and missing eyebrow. Will had pegged him a bully since the expedition left St. Louis in the spring and gave him a wide berth. Brown was slender and blond-haired. He held up his hands and backed away.

"Leave me alone, Slade," he struggled to sound brave, but his voice and hands trembled. "Ah don' want no trouble."

"Brown's gonna get it," Jess said, half in sympathy, half in contempt. Brown had no real friends among the men. He always weaseled out of work and slipped behind the others whenever danger reared. Most of the men barely tolerated him. "He shoulda stayed in St.

Charles," Jess declared.

Slade poked Brown in the ribs. "Come on, little boy. Take yer bes' shot." A few other men gathered around and jeered Brown.

"Leave me alone," Brown's voice cracked. He seemed on the verge of tears.

Slade shoved Brown hard and he stumbled over a powder keg. Brown jumped to his feet and swung a fist. Slade ducked easily and kicked the boy in the groin. Brown doubled over gasping. Slade tackled him, sunk his teeth into an ear, and ripped. Brown's screams startled everyone and they ran over to the fight.

Will pushed through the crowd and leapt on Slade's back. "Leave him alone, Slade," he yelled as he jerked back Slade's head.

Slade jabbed an elbow into his stomach. Will released his grip. Slade twisted and wrestled him onto his back.

"Yer turn, Yates!" Slade snarled and lunged his mouth toward his nose. Will slammed his forehead against Slade's cheek as someone grabbed Slade's hair and jerked back his head.

"Fun's over, Slade," Clyman warned as he twisted Slade's right arm behind his back and dragged him to his feet.

Will sprang up and glared at Slade. Someone caught his arm as it shot toward Slade's face. "That's enough, Mr. Yates," Smith said quietly as he gripped his arm. Will relaxed and nodded.

"Ye'll get yers, Yates!" Slade shouted then laughed at Brown who blubbered and held his ear delicately between his fingers. Ashley pushed through the crowd and fired his flintlock pistol into the air. "Save your fighting for the Rees and any other savages in our way," he hollered. "The boats are loaded. This is the last chance for all who're running!"

Jess hobbled up beside Will and laid a hand on his shoulder. "You'd a' looked a mite funny without a nose," he grinned. Will nodded and started trembling slightly. "Bes' be going," Jess said quietly, and hobbled toward the *Yellowstone* along with the others. Will followed. "Ye ain't fetching yer fixin's?" Jess asked at the gangplank.

Will shrugged his shoulders and scowled. "I don't know what the hell to do."

Whimpering, Brown pushed by and stumbled up the gangplank. Will and Jess stared at him. "No guts, no glory," Jess mocked gently.

Will sniffed irritably. "Glory? Not much glory in pulling a towline all day. Or getting my nose torn off. Or dodging Ree arrows."

"Least ye gotta choice," Jess said bitterly. "Ye kin finish what ye started."

"Don't know where it'll end."

"That's the beauty of it."

Will's brow furrowed. "Damn it, Jess. Wrong one of us two's been pursuing law all this time. You gotta answer for everything."

"So what're ye gonna do 'bout it?"

With a wry smile, Will replied, "Reckon I'll stay and see what happens."

Jess grinned broadly. "Knew ye'd 'ventually see it my way. I'll be back soon as this leg mends," he promised. They shook and Jess hobbled up the gangplank. A dozen men shoved on after Jess. The thirty men remaining crowded the shore and gazed either resentfully or wistfully as the boatmen dug their poles into the mud and pushed off.

"Will!" Jess waved from the deck and shouted, "I'll see ye in hell if not sooner!"

Will nodded and waved back. That just might be, he admitted.

The August sun burned down, oven-hot and merciless. A couple hundred Sioux on ponies trotted ahead in small groups across the prairie. Naked but for loincloths, armed with coup sticks, bows, and muskets, the Sioux and their ponies were garishly painted and feathered for war. With a half-dozen chiefs rode Ashley, Henry, Colonel Leavenworth, Joshua Pilcher—the head of the Missouri Fur Company, and Rose. Ashley and Henry's engagés trailed behind them, followed by Leavenworth's six companies of two hundred thirty blue-coated infantry. Several hundred unmounted Sioux warriors, women, pony-drawn travois, mangy dogs, and children straggled along each column's flank. Far away down the river, five keelboats loaded with supplies, two six-pounders, and Pilcher's forty trappers were being slowly poled upstream.

Will felt proud and slightly out of place marching alongside Smith and Clyman at the head of Ashley's men. To Will, Jedediah Smith was a flesh and blood Byronic hero—fearless, noble, and aloof. Smith's feats of trekking alone through endless savage and beast-filled wilderness were legendary among the trappers. Will doubted if he could ever be as unflinchingly brave and resourceful. And Smith's piety intrigued him. What great truths had Smith discovered? And why didn't he share them? Smith tightly held his beliefs, along with his passions and past, deep within him. Will longed to pry Smith open and explore all his secrets.

He glanced back at the long, ragged column of men strung out across the plains. Like everyone, he was eager to avenge the massacre, but his stomach and his body churned with nervous energy.

The chance for revenge had been an excruciatingly long and demoralizing time coming. After the *Yellowstone* departed they holed up on that island at the Cheyenne River mouth for over a month. Although there were plenty of deer and elk visible on either shore, Ashley had permitted only a few trusted men to cross and hunt, fearing anyone else would desert. Plagued by homesickness, boils, diarrhea, and swarms of mosquitoes, they could only sit out the monotony.

In early July, Smith, Henry, and fifty of his men moored their keelboat and pirogues at the island. Ashley had planned to head back upstream as soon as these reinforcements arrived, but abandoned the hope after Henry admitted his men had no stomach to fight. The Blackfoot had killed four of his trappers and forced the rest to abandon over two hundred traps in the streams and flee to their fort at the Yellowstone and Missouri. It was there that Smith had found them after an epic overland trek. Henry and his men had embarked and poled swiftly down the Missouri to the Cheyenne in less than in two weeks. A half-dozen miles above the Arikara villages they waited anxiously until dark, then glided silently past in the dead of night. Ashley and Henry decided to descend the river to friendly Sioux camps to trade for horses and enlist their warriors as allies against the Arikara. But the Sioux claimed they could spare no horses, and the refugees continued downstream to the Missouri Fur Company post of Fort Kiowa where they received word that Leavenworth and Pilcher were preparing a relief expedition. The "Missouri Legion," as they proudly called themselves, arrived at Fort Kiowa on July 30, and together they ascended the river.

The lead groups of Sioux peaked a low ridge, broke into piercing war cries, and charged down the other side. Brandishing their weapons and screaming, the other mounted and unmounted Sioux rushed after them.

Ashley turned in the saddle and waved his top hat. "Come on," he urged, and the Missouri Legion broke into a trot.

Incessant screaming and sporadic shots cracked beyond the ridge. "Hope it ain't all over by the time we get there," Will blurted as he puffed up the slope.

Smith glanced at him. "You'll have your chance, Mr. Yates," he said with a slight smile.

Atop the ridge the commanders rested their horses and debated tactics. As the column trotted up Ashley turned and hollered, "Captain

Smith, take the men to the right flank and form a line!"

Ashley's men topped the ridge to stare at the melee of Sioux and Arikara swirling madly around each other on the plain before the villages. The warriors thrust lances, swung clubs, and twanged arrows, all the while screeching war cries and taunts, their ponies kicking up little clouds of sod and dust. "Like a swarm of bees," Will remarked. Within minutes it was over. The Rees rushed back to their villages with some of the Sioux thundering close on their ponies' hoofs. The Sioux reined in their ponies as Ree inside the palisade fired a ragged volley, then jerked their ponies' heads and galloped away. On the plain, the Sioux warriors and women hacked away at the Ree dead. Screaming, the Sioux cut off and triumphantly waved bloody feet, hands, penises, testicles, and scalps. A lone Arikara dashed out of the palisade and, war club in hand, stood taunting the Sioux. A Sioux warrior kicked his pony into a gallop and charged the Arikara, who fled back into the village. The Ree lining the palisade inside fired at least fifty shots as the Sioux galloped past. The yellow smoke drifted away as the Sioux, unscathed, galloped out of gunshot.

Dressed in a grizzly bearskin, another Sioux crawled forward on all fours toward an Arikara, who lay wheezing with an arrow through his lung a couple hundred yards from the palisade. The other Sioux continued to hack away at the dead Rees and avoided looking at the grizzly warrior. The Sioux chiefs rode up to the officers and, with Rose translating, pleaded with them not to watch the grizzly warrior or he would lose his medicine.

Leavenworth ordered the soldiers and trappers to avert their eyes but the men stared in fascination and horror anyway. Growling and snarling, the grizzly warrior continued to lumber forward. He occasionally rose up on his hind legs and sniffed the air, then dropped back to all fours. He crawled slowly up to the dying man and sniffed him as sporadic Arikara shots kicked up dust all around. Suddenly the grizzly bent his head to the Ree's stomach and began tearing off chunks of his quivering flesh and entrails. The Ree's hands twitched and he gave a gurgled scream before lying silent. The Sioux reached his hand up into the cavity, ripped out the man's heart, and tore it apart with his teeth.

"Savages," Will muttered in disgust.

"It's easy to make a savage of a civilized man, but impossible to make a civilized man out of a savage," Clyman quietly replied.

Smith nodded. "I fear the beast is within us all."

"You think we're all capable of that?" Will asked incredulously.

"Under the right circumstances we're all capable of anything—the greatest good and greatest evil," Smith answered.

General Ashley rode along the ranks. "Rest easy men," he called out. "Colonel Leavenworth's awaiting the guns."

"When we gonna pitch into 'em, General?" Will asked warily.

"Don't worry, Mr. Yates," Ashley declared confidently. "We'll slaughter those Rees and burn their villages to the ground before sunset."

"You think the keelboats'll be up before dark?"

Ashley stretched to his height in the stirrups and squinted downriver. "Don't see 'em." He glared fiercely down at Will. "They'll be here, if I hafta ride down and drag 'em up myself!" Ashley kicked his horse into a canter toward Leavenworth and Pilcher.

Will shuddered as he stared at the palisade a half-mile away. Arikara covered the mound lodges and poked their weapons through the palisade's upthrust logs. Cannon balls might smash holes through the wall and kill some Rees, he reasoned, but there'd be plenty left to resist an assault. What if we're all pinned down before that stockade like we'd been on the beach? There'd be no chance of digging holes in that hard earth. He wanted to convey his dread to Ashley or Smith, but feared being branded a coward. Instead he said to Smith, "Ah, Captain? We've got a lot more men than we had two and a half months back, and cannon and spirit and position. You think the Rees'll give us much of a fight?"

"Those are their homes," Smith replied grimly. "I'd be mighty surprised if they didn't fight like demons and die to a man."

Will nodded. He imagined dodging Arikara balls and arrows amidst a mass of charging Sioux and frontiersmen. He stared out at the plain. The Sioux were trickling away from the mutilated bodies toward the corn, pumpkin, and squash fields west of the villages. The infantry sprawled in a long line west along the ridge. Dangling strings of empty canteens, some of the bluecoats and trappers walked toward the river.

"May be a helluva fight," Will said quietly.

There was no more fighting that day. After pillaging the crops, the Sioux withdrew a mile west of the villages and raised their teepees. The Missouri Legion marched across the plain and encamped just out of rifleshot of the first palisade. The sun had begun to ripen the mangled bodies of the Arikara and several horses. Gagging and puking, the men dragged the remnants several hundred yards away, but the stench slowly thickened over their camp.

The sun was sinking fast when the keelboats were tied up.

Leavenworth had decided to encircle the two villages to cut off escape, and bombard the Rees into submission the next day. After the supplies and two six-pounders were unloaded, Leavenworth marched his infantry, guns, and Pilcher's men through the dusk to a low rise west of the villages.

Ashley allowed no fires after sunset. The trappers were deployed a half-dozen feet apart in a long oval before the palisade. The horses were staked and hobbled within their ranks. The sun and day's march had exhausted the men. They lay still and talked quietly or chewed salt pork and biscuits. Although they were supposed to watch in shifts, no one got much sleep. All night, mourners wailed from behind the palisade while the Sioux held a scalp dance and their distant drums and war cries reverberated across the plains.

Silence emerged like fog just before dawn, granting the trappers an hour or two of troubled sleep before light spread again across the earth. Then a distant bugle blared reveille. Cursing, the bewildered men stiffly rose, stretched, massaged their knotted muscles, and stared at the bleached palisade walls. Pilcher rode over to mull strategy with Ashley, Henry, and Smith. The sun burned more intensely as it rose. There was no breeze.

Startling everyone, the first cannon shot boomed an hour after sunrise. The shot screamed over the lower village and splashed into the river beyond. The men scrambled into line and watched eagerly. Several minutes later, the second cannon boomed, and the shot plopped in the sand on the river's far shore. The infantry formed ranks behind the guns. Dozens of Sioux appeared on the far horizon, racing their ponies toward the cannon-fire. Another shot boomed and splashed in the river.

"Goddamn it!" Pilcher shouted to Ashley. "What the hell they doing? Fishing?" Pilcher was ruddy-faced, bald, large and stout. His mouth was always twisted in a scowl. He was as short-fused as he looked. "I'm gonna tell those blue-bellied bastards ta lower their sights." He waited impatiently for Ashley and Henry to saddle their horses and then the three galloped the quarter-mile to the army camp.

Despite Pilcher's protests, the gunners were unable to improve their aim. Every five minutes a cannon roared, but the shots were erratic. Some arched far over the village; others dropped to smash a large hole in one of the earth lodges or splinter logs in the palisade. Bored and disappointed with the impotent fire, the Sioux began drifting back to their village. Leavenworth allowed the infantry and trappers to break ranks and rest up for the assault.

There were no tents or trees under which to cower from the relentless sun. The trappers erected crude shelters with their blankets and rifles, and went in shifts to swim in the river. The rotting stench of yesterday's dead thickened in the still oven-like heat. A cannonball smashed down a pole in the village center from which a dozen scalps fluttered. A few soldiers and trappers cheered, but most had not noticed.

"Gonna take more'n that to level that village," Will remarked.

Smith nodded. "The army won't have enough shot." He frowned slightly. "Look's like we're going to have to charge that village as it is. It might not be as bad as it seems. The Rees may be short on ammunition."

The cannon stopped firing around noon. Ashley and Henry galloped back to their men. "Into ranks!" they cried. "We're going in!" The men hastily assembled and checked the priming in their rifles. They were all nervous. Some chattered maniacally while most just stared at the village. The two commanders rode along the ranks. "The plan is this," Ashley hollered. "Colonel Leavenworth has ordered Mr. Pilcher and Captain Riley's companies to assault the upper village with their riflemen while his other five infantry companies provide covering fire. After reaching the wall, Mr. Pilcher and Captain Riley will determine whether a general assault can be successful. Meanwhile, we will pin down the lower village." Ashley twisted in the saddle and pointed toward the palisade. "While Major Henry's men fire, my men will charge forward and seize the ravine near the walls and shoot down any Ree in the village who shows his head between the logs. Is that clear? Are there any questions?"

A few men nodded. No one spoke. In the distance they could see the infantry marching toward the upper village. Hundreds of Sioux had gathered to watch. The palisade bristled with musket barrels and arrows.

"All right!" Ashley shouted fiercely. "Mr. Smith! Take our men to the right and get ready to run like hell for that ravine when you hear the cannon shot. Major Henry! Advance and prepare to fire!"

Will stumbled along with Ashley's men toward the river. His stomach and mind churned with images of massed British redcoats being torn apart by volleys of rifles and cannon balls at New Orleans. It won't be like that, he kept telling himself. The Rees are short of ammunition and have no cannon. He tried to keep close to Smith and Clyman.

"Don't bunch up," Smith loudly warned the men. "Spread out

some! Crouch low when we run till we reach the ravine!"

They halted in a ragged line about two hundred yards from the village. Several shots whistled overhead. With each shot, a puff of smoke would appear between the logs and hang in the still air before dissolving. War cries erupted from behind the walls. Ashley's men were silent, absorbed in their fears. The sun blazed down through the cloudless sky.

Will trembled slightly and his breath surged in shallow bursts. Damn my body! How am I gonna shoot straight? As he fought to control himself, he suddenly felt the urge to urinate.

A cannon boomed. Henry's men fired a staccato volley. "Charge!" Smith hollered. The men sprinted across the plain of buffalo grass and prickly pear.

Balls and arrows whizzed by or plowed the earth at their feet. As Ashley's men ran, some of them whooped and cursed the Rees. The palisade blurred larger before them. The ravine's eroded lip appeared snaking near the village. Suddenly the trappers were jumping down into its shallow trench and hugging the bottom as arrows sliced the air all around. Everyone was sweat-drenched, panting, and red-faced. A few men poked their heads above the earth. A shot exploded from the ravine, then another. In the distance, Henry and Pilcher's men fired sporadically at the village.

Like most of the men, Will lay curled and gasping for air and silently pleading for God to whisk him home to St. Louis. He watched as beside him Smith crept the half-dozen feet up the ravine's slope. "Don't squeeze till you've got a clear target," Smith yelled. He slowly pushed his rifle forward and aimed carefully down the sights. Bang! Smith crouched down and fumbled with his powder horn plug. He stared briefly into Will's eyes. "Do your part, Mr. Yates," he said calmly as he tipped his powder horn to his rifle barrel.

Shamed, Will slowly straightened along the ravine's wall. Someone slapped him on the shoulder. He turned. Clyman's flushed, grim face was a nose away. "Now's our turn to do some killing, Will! Vengeance is ours!"

"Yeah," Will mumbled, but all he could think of was the Comanche's mangled head.

Clyman jumped to his feet, thrust out his rifle, and searched for a target. Shots cracked from the village. He slowly squeezed the trigger then quickly dropped down to reload.

Will glanced left and right along the ravine. Some men were reloading or aiming, but most still crouched low. He took a deep breath, then gingerly raised his head above the surface. Brown faces and bodies flitted between the gaps of the cottonwood log walls, occasionally pausing to fire or scream a taunt. He leveled his rifle and squinted down the barrel, waiting for brown flesh to appear between two large logs. His finger curled around the trigger. The slender curved metal felt delicate and cool to his touch. His trembling stopped. A face jerked into view, then disappeared just as Will fired. He peered through the drifting smoke at the wall. His shot had splintered a log an inch from where the Ree's head had appeared. An arrow tore into the ground near his elbow and he quickly ducked below the ravine's rim.

Although most of the men were now firing and reloading, a few still cowered at the ravine's bottom. One man was weeping hysterically. "Everyone take a shot!" Smith hollered. He angrily glared at the laggards, then raised himself above the surface and patiently waited for a target.

Determined to join him, Will hurriedly yanked his ramrod out of the barrel and primed the pan. Smith fired just as he leapt up beside him. "Hit him?" Will shouted above the gunfire.

"Couldn't tell," Smith replied.

Will searched for a shot. "They seem to be keeping low!" he observed.

"Must be outta ammunition," Clyman said as he crawled up alongside him.

He found a target and fired. "Damn it! Missed!"

Will fired at a glimpse of brown flesh but again splintered wood. "Maybe they're more scared than we are," he wondered aloud as he slid down the gritty slope. "Why's Leavenworth holding us back?"

Smith shook his head. "I've no idea. If Colonel Leavenworth sent us all charging in at once, we'd overrun the village."

Poking his head above the ravine, Will stared at the palisade. The Arikara had vanished. He assumed most of them were crouching in the shallow trench just behind the wall. He turned to view the surrounding plains. Henry's trappers had stopped firing and now sprawled across the plain. To the west the infantry and artillery men stood at ease just out of gunshot. Nearby, Leavenworth, the fur company leaders, several Sioux chiefs, and a half-dozen mounted officers conferred and passed around a telescope. The Sioux continued to drift away from the battlefield to their village beyond the horizon. Desultory shots from Pilcher and Riley's men popped north of the villages. Suddenly Ashley kicked his horse into a gallop toward his men. "Something's happening," Will exclaimed. Other men in the ravine turned and stared at

Ashley.

"Keep your eyes peeled on that village," Smith warned, then fired at an Arikara's face which suddenly appeared. The shot thudded into a nearby log.

"Captain Smith!" Ashley shouted in the distance. "Have your men fire then fall back!"

Everyone looked startled and some protested the order. "You heard General Ashley!" Smith said loud enough for all to hear. "Don't fire at once! Choose your target carefully then retire!" Gunshots exploded and several men scrambled out of the ravine and ran back toward the other trappers. Other men fled without firing. Most waited eagerly for one sure last shot, but few Arikara exposed themselves and the glimpses were fleeting. An occasional shot cracked and then a man would sprint to the rear.

Will was determined to be the last man to retreat and equally determined to kill a Ree with his last shot. He crouched and watched the gaps between the log walls. He shuddered, recalling that mad dash with Rose and Jess through the dark, rain-slickened village with a dozen Rees on their heels, and then the slaughter on the beach the next morning. The Rees had butchered his friends and almost himself. They deserve to die, he thought bitterly.

Clyman fired and shook his head wearily. "Just haven't had much luck today," he exclaimed as he reloaded. "Well, boys," he nodded to those nearby. "See ya all back in camp." He pulled himself out of the ravine and trotted away.

A half-hour later, Will, Smith, and only a half-dozen men remained in the ravine. "That's it, gentlemen," Smith announced. "No point in waiting longer. You may retire. I'll cover you." The other men nodded gratefully and scrambled to safety. "Go ahead, Mr. Yates," Smith urged.

"I'll wait with you, Captain."

Smith smiled. "As you wish." He fixed his eyes again on the palisade then suddenly raised his rifle and fired. "Now!" he warned as he pulled himself up the ravine's slope. "Hurry!"

"Go ahead!" Will shouted as he aimed toward the village. "I'll pin 'em down for you!"

Smith crouched at the ravine's edge and extended a hand to Will. "Come on!" he shouted.

A face and musket appeared between the logs. Will swung his rifle toward it and fired. The shot tore out a chunk of log beside the Arikara. "Damn it," he yelled angrily. He turned, grasped Smith's hand, and was pulled out of the ravine. Together they dodged across the field toward the hundred cheering trappers. A gunshot cracked behind them. Three arrows zipped by, inches away. They finally ran beyond rifle range of the village and into the horde of trappers who swarmed around them, slapping their backs and war whooping.

Ashley pushed through the crowd toward Smith and Will. "That was quite a run, boys!" he exclaimed. "Mr. Yates, you've gotten into a nasty habit of escaping those Rees by the skin of your teeth!"

Will grinned. "It's a habit I'd sure like to break, General." Ashley and the men chuckled.

"Why'd we pull back, General?" Smith asked. "The Rees had ceased firing."

"I know, I know," Ashley scowled. "Leavenworth's orders. Riley and Pilcher failed to breach the north village walls and now Leavenworth's marching them back to the lower village. I just don't understand it! Leavenworth may have won honors fighting against those redcoat bastards back East in the last war but he ain't worth a tinker's damn out here against savages. By God I wish I was regular army rather than just a militia general. I'd have taken those villages at sunrise!" He scratched angrily at his huge red nose. "And then," he sputtered, "Leavenworth warned the Sioux we were pulling back and told them 'to save their stragglers from the tomahawks of the Arikara!' Those were his exact words! Can you believe it? The Sioux have lost all faith in us. Pilcher was near bursting with rage. I thought he was going to shoot the Colonel. Come on Mr. Smith," Ashley said bitterly, "let's go try to talk some sense into Leavenworth." He and Smith started to walk away when Ashley suddenly turned.

"Oh, Mr. Yates," he added. "Why don't you come, too? You've been in the village and seen its defenses. Maybe together we can put some backbone into that spineless son of a bitch!"

Will beamed with the honor. "Thank you, General!"

With Ashley leading his horse, the three men strode toward the army position. Firing had ceased. A dozen Sioux and Arikara conferred before the upper village. "Look at 'em," Ashley declared angrily. "Rose said some Sioux were talking of uniting with the Rees against us."

"Look, General," Will said pointing to two men cantering their horses toward the gathering. "There go Pilcher and Rose."

"Lord knows what'll happen!" Ashley muttered. While keeping an eye on the negotiations they marched rapidly up to Leavenworth, the Sioux chiefs, and the officers.

"General Ashley," Leavenworth exclaimed heartily. Although stocky, he sat ramrod straight in his saddle. His hair was flecked with gray, his cheeks were pouchy, and his eyes bloodshot and puffy from lack of sleep.

"Your men performed admirably! Casualties?"

"None," Ashley replied.

"Very good, very good," Leavenworth turned and trained his telescope on the men before the village. "Captain Riley had only two men slightly wounded. Mr. Pilcher none. I'd give my commission to finish this campaign with no losses."

Ashley grimaced. "Like we've been trying to tell you, Colonel," he stated forcefully, "the campaign won't end until those Rees are thoroughly whipped! Anything less and they'll be saucy as ever and robbing and murdering everyone up and down the Missouri!"

"I believe the Arikara want peace just as badly as we do, General," Leavenworth responded softly. "Look there!" he said excitedly. "Here they all come! We can ask them ourselves!"

Trotting their horses, Rose and Pilcher led the Sioux and Arikara delegations back toward Leavenworth. The Rees slouched timidly and their eyes were tear-filled as they rode up. Smiling broadly, Leavenworth shook hands with all the Indians. Everyone dismounted and sat cross-legged on buffalo robes in a circle. The head chief of the upper village, Little Soldier, spoke loudly, nervously, to the colonel. Rose translated. "Sez Gray Eyes of the lower village is dead. Cannon ball cut 'im in two...Attack was all Gray Eyes's idea account a' his son being kilt on that raid on Cedar Fort and Stephens's dallying with that squaw...Jus' wanted vengeance was all...Upper village always bin fer peace and now even the warriors in the lower villages got no stomach ta fight...Many children have no fathers and wives have no husbands... begs ye ta fight no more...ta love 'em..." Rose snickered. "Oh, great white father, he calls ye."

Leavenworth nodded gravely. "We have come not to make war, but to make peace. Our hearts are good. If Little Soldier and his people wish to make peace, we will do so happily with our hearts singing." Pilcher rolled his eyes and shook his head in disgust. "But first," Leavenworth pointed a finger skyward, "you must restore all of General Ashley's property, including his horses and robes. Second, you must hand over five hostages until the agreement is fulfilled," He paused. "Finally, you must promise never again to war on your white brothers."

After hearing the translation, Little Soldier nodded and spoke eagerly. "Sez he'll fight no more. His lodge is always open to his white father and brothers...but the Sioux done stole or kilt all his horses...Promises ta hand back what property he kin find...Sez he'll give up five hostages...Wants ta smoke then shake on it."

Leavenworth nodded. "That sounds perfectly reasonable..."

"Now hold on thar, Colonel," Pilcher interrupted. "Ye can't trust these skunks farther than ye kin piss. Soon as we leave, the Rees'll be back on the warpath. Only thing they understand is fire and lead. We need ta march in thar, take all that belongs ta us, then burn those villages ta the ground."

Leavenworth glared at Pilcher and held up a hand in silence. "The agreement has been made, Mr. Pilcher, and a just agreement it is." He turned to Ashley. "General, do you have any objections?"

Ashley frowned. "I don't have time to quibble over details as long as those red niggers return our horses and equipment. I've gotta get my men to the Rockies for the fall trapping."

"Thank you, General," Leavenworth said with relief. "Now then, if there are no reasonable objections, we will smoke and shake on the agreement. Mr. Rose, convey our satisfaction to Little Soldier." Rose spoke rapidly in Arikara. Little Soldier and the other Rees smiled happily. Little Soldier pulled a long pipe from his parfleche and raised it to heaven and earth, then to the four directions. He packed the bowl with tobacco, sparked it with flint and steel, and inhaled deeply at the stem. He handed the pipe across to Leavenworth who gingerly puffed at it then passed it on.

When the pipe reached Pilcher, he disdainfully refused to touch it. Jumping to his feet, he shook his fist in the Chief's face and he shrank back in alarm. "If you red bastards ever again attack my operations, I'll bring back my men and slaughter every last one of you!" He then angrily stormed out.

Leavenworth was noticeably embarrassed by Pilcher's outburst. "Forgive my white brother," he pleaded with the Arikara, "his anger will cool with the prairie winds and his heart will grow warm toward his Arikara brothers."

After the pipe completed the circle, Leavenworth rose, walked over to Little Soldier, and warmly embraced him. "From this day, let us forever have peace and happiness between your people and mine across the prairies to the shining mountains beyond."

During the night, the Sioux quietly packed up and left, taking with them six government mules and seven of Ashley's horses. Ashley exploded in anger when the theft was reported shortly after daybreak. "Goddamn it!" he screeched. "I'll trail those bastards to hell to get back my horses!"

After calming, he dispatched Rose, Smith, and Will to the lower village to receive the stolen horses and equipment. Little Soldier and a half-dozen chiefs met them outside the village and spread buffalo robes for a smoke. Rose asked the whereabouts of the stolen goods. "Soon," Little Soldier replied as he passed the pipe. Through the gaps in the palisade they observed the Rees busily piling bundles outside their lodges or tying them on travois. "They's fixing ta leave," Rose observed. "Dead of night they'll slip out, cross the river, and be long gone fore mornin'."

"What'll we do?" Will asked.

"It all depends on how many horses they return to us," Smith replied.

The Americans sat impatiently in the hot sun with the Arikara for over an hour while Little Soldier nervously repeated his love for the whites and hopes for peace. Finally, an old squaw led out a sway-backed horse upon which was strapped three rifles and sixteen buffalo robes.

"Is that all?" Smith demanded incredulously. Rose did not need to translate. Little Soldier nodded slightly. Smith leapt to his feet and snatched the reins from the woman. "Come on," he ordered and stalked away toward the army camp.

Will and Rose followed. Alarmed, Little Soldier trailed behind them, pleading for understanding. The other chiefs hurried back into the village. Leavenworth, Ashley, and the other leaders watched the group advancing toward them. "This is it, General," Smith announced as he got within earshot.

Ashley glared at Leavenworth. "What do you say to that, Colonel?" he demanded.

Leavenworth looked startled. Before he could speak, Little Soldier grabbed his stirrup and pleaded with him to understand that his people had nothing more to give. Then, to everyone's disgust, Little Soldier begged to be given refuge in the American camp if the soldiers attacked and went so far as to point out the weak points in the lower village walls. "Sez ta aim your cannon lower, Colonel," Rose chuckled merrily, then added, "Ye might wanna take his advice."

Captain Riley spoke up heatedly. "Colonel, I entirely agree with Mr. Rose. We've gotta bloody these Rees so bad they'll never think twice of killing any whites again. For three years we've been sitting on our asses at Fort Atkinson doing little more than eat pumpkins. This is our chance to win glory and promotion and, if we don't take it now, we'll be stuck out here for the rest of our lives."

"Our duty, Captain Riley," Leavenworth replied testily, "is to keep the peace for our country and not provoke a bloodbath for the utterly selfish reason of desiring promotions or glory." He sighed heavily. "Little Soldier has used every effort to induce his people to comply with the treaty, but all his efforts have been for naught. Our choice is clear, we can either assault the village and cause yet more destruction and loss of life. Or we accept the reality that nothing more can be done. I am confident that the Arikara have been sufficiently humbled to convince them fully of our ability to punish any injury which they might do to us, and that they will behave well in the future if we leave them undisturbed in their villages. General Ashley, the government will reimburse you fully for your losses. I have therefore determined to abandon that article of the treaty requiring them to make good on their former depredations."

Ashley swore loudly and argued with the colonel. "The government can pay me twice what I lost to the Rees and Sioux but promises won't carry me to the Rockies!"

"General Ashley," Leavenworth replied, "I sympathize totally with your plight. Your enterprise has been victimized by outrageous circumstances. But I refused to countenance any further loss of life."

Ashley coldly stared into Leavenworth's eyes. "I need a dozen horses, Colonel. And if you can't provide them, I'll have no choice but to lead my men against that village ourselves and retake what is rightfully ours."

"Count me in on that, Bill," Pilcher declared. "Fact, my boys'n me may burn those villages even if ye git yer horses."

Ashley nodded to Pilcher. "Knew I could rely on you, Josh." He turned toward Leavenworth. "Dozen horses or we attack, Colonel." Leavenworth pursed his lips.

"You know what you are saying is blackmail, don't you?"

Ashley shrugged. "If the government's going to repay me, it might as well start now."

"General," Leavenworth remonstrated, "please reconsider. You know that I have only a dozen horses and mules left myself."

Ashley frowned and glanced at Henry. "Andrew?"

"We gotta cross the plains somehow, Bill," Henry replied.

Ashley's face twisted in inner debate. "Make it a half-dozen and it's a deal," he finally demanded.

"Done!" Leavenworth declared. "Although my regiment cannot afford the loss, I will have my quartermaster sign over to you a half-dozen horses and mules." Leavenworth glanced up at the sun. "Now let there be no more talk of fighting and burning."

Pilcher snorted. "I'll burn those Rees in hell 'fore morning!" he warned.

Leavenworth pretended not to notice. "Mr. Rose, if you will, convey my decision to Little Soldier so he can tell his people there is no reason to abandon their homes." After Rose finished speaking, Little Soldier's face cracked with a huge smile. He jumped to his feet and hugged Leavenworth.

"There," the Colonel said as he gingerly patted Little Soldier's sweat-drenched back then squirmed away. "That should conclude the campaign," he noted with a slight smile.

Despite the agreement, the Arikara fled during the night. Only Leavenworth was surprised the next morning to find the villages abandoned. Grim-faced, he and his commanders inspected the lower village. The colonel was appalled by the damage inflicted by his cannonade, the thirty-one fresh graves, the whimpering, mongrel dogs tied to posts, the bloated, stiffened horses, and the pervasive stench, offal, and filth. Gray Eyes's ancient mother was found barely alive beside his grave in his lodge. Leavenworth knelt beside her, gently stroked her hair, and had Rose explain that no harm would befall her. He then issued strict orders that the villages would remain unmolested.

Will was allowed to trail along behind the officers and fur company leaders. He initially felt exhilarated to walk amidst the squalor and destruction. Pausing before the fallen lodgepole from which a dozen scalps had once fluttered, the adrenaline surged through his body as he recalled that sprint with Jess and Rose through the mist-filled dark a step ahead of a half-dozen howling Rees. One stumble and he would have been fiendishly tortured to death and his scalp hung high over the village. "I wish there were more of them," Will angrily remarked when an officer reported the total number of graves. His companions nodded their approval.

But later, in Gray Eyes's lodge, when he saw his bereaved mother, tears filled Will's eyes as he thought of his own withered mother so far away. How many years does my mother have left? he wondered. He longed to fly to his mother and apologize for all the anxiety he had caused her over the years. She'd never really been happy. Until Pa's death, she had always tried to sigh away his seriousness and penny-pinching. Her face only lit up when she spoke wistfully of her younger years in Philadelphia. Will pushed through the other men and stooped out of the lodge into the dazzling sunlight. What if I never see my mother or Sarah again, he mourned. He swiftly wiped away his tears as the others stepped outside beside him.

Leavenworth gave the orders to break camp. By noon the rivermen were poling the keelboats downstream and the trappers and soldiers had begun the long march south along the riverbank. A few miles from the villages someone pointed to smoke billowing behind them. Everyone turned to see the villages engulfed in flames. Leavenworth shouted, "I'll have the perpetrators of that crime court-martialed!" A roll call revealed that two of Pilcher's men were missing. Leavenworth angrily ordered Pilcher and his entire command dishonorably discharged from the Missouri Legion. Swearing vengeance, Pilcher crowded his men into their keelboat and they poled rapidly away on the current.

Ashley's company marched with Leavenworth's troops as far as Fort Kiowa, two hundred forty miles downstream. There, Ashley refitted his company and tried to recover their own horses and buy others from the nearby Sioux villages. But most of the Sioux had already departed for the central plains to hunt buffalo, and those remaining had no horses to sell. Skeptical that the venture would ever get off the ground, and fearful that if it did another massacre awaited them in the Rockies, dozens of men deserted in twos and threes. In early September, Henry departed for the Yellowstone with thirty men and six horses. It was another month before Ashley could equip Smith and the fifteen remaining men with seven packhorses he bought from the French Fur Company. Ashley had borrowed his men's money to pay for the horses. He also promised the men that they were now free trappers and could sell their catches to the highest bidder. His business complete, Ashley returned with a keelboat bound for St. Louis to resume his duties as Missouri's lieutenant governor and revamp his trapping enterprise.

Once again, Will was torn between returning to St. Louis or heading to the Rockies. Three letters had awaited him at Fort Kiowa. Jenny wrote several pages about the store's meager sales and ended by admonishing him to be careful. Sarah filled him in on the latest gossip and explained how she had nursed Jess back to health, although he still hobbled around with a crutch. Judy's letter tugged the hardest on his heart. She apologized profusely for her emotional swings and admitted that she still loved him dearly and wanted their marriage to be happy again. But she warned him not to return so long as the need for wilderness captured his spirit. "I can't continue to stay with you and always wonder when you'll next leave," she wrote.

Until the day before Ashley's keelboat departed, Will swung between boarding it and heading West. It was a hunting trip with Smith that decided the issue. They rode a dozen miles out on the rolling plains. Thunderclouds drifted across the sky. Here and there a few cottonwood and ash shaded stretches of the dry creeks. There was a chill in the air. They spooked no deer or elk from the hollows and saw only a few antelope galloping away far in the distance. They rode mostly in silence, each mulling his own memories and emotions, or basking in the surrounding grandeur.

"This land's pretty well hunted out," Smith commented. Like most of the others he had shaved his beard shortly after they arrived at Fort Kiowa and now daily scraped away the stubble. He had thick sandy hair, blue eyes, a long gaunt face, and stood six foot. He rarely smiled and always seemed to be contemplating something important. Will had to remind himself that Smith was actually two years his junior.

"Sky's so blue out here," Will exclaimed happily, "bluer than in St. Louis. A rich deep blue. And the air's so pure. Summers back east drag a man down with all the humidity. Summer winds here lift a man up. You wanna fly away on the clouds."

A smile flickered across Smith's face. "You've a poetic side to you, Mr. Yates."

Will looked away, embarrassed. "I sometimes scribble some verse. Lost a ledger full at the Ree fight I'd been writing up the Missouri. Mighty discouraging. Written some new ones since, but when I try to recall the old, all I get are fragments."

Smith nodded sadly. "Memory's like that. Longer you live a life, the more of it seems to slip away from you."

"I've scribbled a poem or two about that," Will admitted with a smile.

"Poetry inspires me," Smith said eagerly. "If you would be willing, I'd very much like to read your verse sometime."

"Well, I...all right. Back at camp. But they're no good. It's mostly what I'm feeling or seeing. Things boil up inside me then I empty 'em on paper. Writing calms me."

"I can't think of a better reason to write. What's important is they're true for you."

"You seem so old for your years, Captain," he observed gingerly. "My impression's that you must've had a hard life."

Smith shrugged. "Hard as most I suppose," he said softly. He pointed his rifle. "Let's follow that ridgeline. We may scare up something on the other side." They kicked their horses into a canter. Atop the ridge they let their horses crop the stunted prairie grass while they scanned the horizons.

"Not a sign," Smith observed. "Are you sailing with the keelboat tomorrow?"

"I haven't decided yet. My wife...I just don't know what to do." To his surprise Will found himself confessing the loss of his daughter, Judy's condition, and his conflicting feelings of guilt and release at being away.

"Without Judy I couldn't live in St. Louis any longer. I know that town inside and out. There's nothing more to see or do. I've got family and friends and mostly good memories to go back to, but I can only stay for short stretches. I've gotta keep moving. When I stand still too long I start to shrivel. Something deep inside's always tugging me elsewhere. Life's so short and uncertain. The world's so vast and filled with interesting characters and fantastic sights. I wanna see as much of it as I can before my time's up."

Smith nodded sympathetically. "I know exactly how you feel. I am the same way." He paused then added, "I am truly sorry to learn of the tragic loss of your baby and Mrs. Yates's troubled mind."

"You know the Bible," Will said bitterly. "God seems as much against us as for us. He's as wrathful and capricious and unjust as any man. Why would a God who's made us in his image and supposedly loves us allow such things to happen?"

"I've asked myself that same question all my life," Smith admitted. "I've read and reread the Book of Job. Paradox...the truth lies within or beyond such paradoxes. There are some questions that can't be satisfactorily answered. Faith. I have faith that God's will is just, that the world's injustices and paradoxes will be resolved after our deaths."

"You really believe that?"

Smith sighed. "Without faith the world falls apart." He kicked his horse into a trot. "Let's scout that coulee over there." They rode in a troubled silence until they could stare down into the shallow valley. "Nothing," Smith grimaced then locked his eyes into Will's. "Seek and ye shall find, Mr. Yates. The Bible's full of seekers. They always found something. They just didn't always find what they were looking for, and what they found was often in unexpected places. Jesus found truth in the wilderness." Smith glanced at the sun low in the western sky. "It'll be dark soon. Better head back."

On September's last day Will and fifteen other trappers trudged due west. Each man was equipped with a rifle, skinning knife, toma-hawk, full powder horn, fifty shiny lead balls, strings of moccasins, and buffalo robes or blankets. Other necessities—bullet molds, small kegs of powder, rifle worms, kettles, flints, horseshoes, fifty-three beaver traps, ax, shovel, tent, and small sacks of flour, nails, beads, mirrors, fish hooks, awls, and paints—were strapped high on the seven horses which the men took turns leading.

A day after they set out they reached the White River and hiked for days along the low, sun-baked ridges flanking its meandering course. The riverbed was dry and the occasional waterhole, usually fouled or alkaline. Treeless, the White yielded no shelter from the broiling sun or chilly nights. Rattlesnakes coiled in crevices everywhere and rattled angrily as the men stepped gingerly past them. Prickly pear was often so thick that the men had to dig it out with their knives before they could stretch out to sleep at night.

Though sun-blistered and parched, they found foraging easy enough. Ravines were often entangled with patches of wild plums or chokecherries. The men would then halt and greedily pluck the sour fruit into their mouths until there was no more. Deer were also plentiful. Several were killed daily and the steaks broiled over sagebrush fires. But to their disappointment they saw no buffalo, only the trampled earth where huge herds had once ranged. Wolves trailed behind the men just beyond rifle shot, fed off the deer carcasses, and howled mornfully at night.

Though they crossed no Indian sign, Smith took no chances. The men took turns peering into the darkness after they bedded down at night. The Arikara had vanished after the midnight flight from their villages, and the men fearfully imagined them huddled just beyond each distant ridge, plotting revenge. Back at Fort Kiowa, rumors of their whereabouts drifted in with the occasional trapper or Sioux hunting party. Some claimed the Rees had joined the Mandan and Hidatsa higher up on the Missouri. Others swore they'd heard that the Rees had fled to their Pawnee cousins down on the Platte. The Rees could be anywhere. A party of hideously painted warriors could be stalking the party now and, waiting for just the right moment to thunder into camp, screaming and firing.

A week out of Fort Kiowa, the White River began to curve toward the southwest through a valley edged by weirdly sculpted badlands. After mulling their options, the men agreed to leave the White and continue due west in hopes of finding a river valley with water and grass. For almost two days they hiked without water. The men stretched out over several miles, each pushing on at his own pace. Smith trailed at the rear, encouraging the laggards. Late on the second day, Clyman and Will found a waterhole in a creek bed. Clyman fired his rifle to signal the others, then both men plunged into the waist-deep pool. Most of the men trickled in soon thereafter but Smith did not appear until dusk. After drinking to his full and resting briefly, he started back with water and horses for two men who had collapsed several miles away. He had buried them in sand up to their necks to preserve their remaining moisture. It was almost morning before he brought them into camp.

The party rested up by the waterhole another day and then headed west once again. By mid-afternoon they reached the Cheyenne River, and rejoiced in its clear flowing water and the cottonwoods scattered along its banks. Toward dusk the following day they spotted teepees scattered a half-mile ahead along the river. They nervously waited in a ravine while Rose strolled fearlessly into the camp. The Indians gathered excitedly around the breed who spoke briefly with them then signaled the party forward. It was a band of Brule Sioux. The party camped with the Brule for several days and traded for a half-dozen ponies. The men's spirits lifted with the Sioux's hospitality and tales of beaver-filled streams in the Black Hills farther west. They prayed that the worst was behind them.

They left the Cheyenne and filed across the plains, scattering small herds of buffalo and occasionally shooting a fat cow. Far away to the west, the Black Hills rose above tawny plains. They hurried onward toward a V cut in the range's southern end and, reaching it, up into the low mountains of clear streams, flower-covered meadows, towering ponderosa, and aspens blazing golden on the slopes. They tarried several days, trapping and lolling under the pines, then pushed impatiently onward.

The terrain grew more rugged across the divide. Carrying the supplies and leading the horses, they slipped and struggled down through a deep, narrow canyon whose eroded, silent cliffs rose hundreds of feet high and were barren of water, grass, or game. Despairing of ever getting out, they filed through it for several days, climbing over landslides and boulders. The canyon echoed with the erratic clatter of horseshoes and an occasional curse. Ribs began to show on the horses and men. On the third day, a misty rain fell and balled the clay on the men's feet and the horses' hoofs, dragging their procession to an exhausted, slippery crawl.

Through the weeks of grinding hardship and setback, Will wrestled constantly with whether he had made the right choice. His mind often drifted back to hot pies baking in the fireplace, fishing with Jess on the Mississippi, spooning with Judy under the quilt on their soft, warm, cornhusk mattress, Sarah's cheerful chatter, even his mother's nagging. I've gotta be crazy stomping through this wilderness, he rebuked himself repeatedly. And to what end? To be gutshot or tortured and have my bones strewn across the earth? On the third evening in the canyon, he stumbled blindly off into a side ravine a half-mile or so from camp and broke down in tears and sobs.

Homesickness was bad enough, but the strain of constantly struggling to keep up with the other men was at times overwhelming. Will longed to be a leader—to be a man apart and above all others. Yet, though he was physically and emotionally tougher than most, a few others had a clear edge. Images of his betters flashed through his mind—Smith, Rose, Clyman, Bill Sublette, Tom Fitzpatrick. How could he ever rival their carefree ability to thread wilderness or crack a joke when everyone else was bone-tired? He tried to picture them crying or despairing but saw only their grim, hardened faces. If fear or pain ever gripped them, they buried it deep within themselves.

They finally emerged, exhausted and frazzled onto the rolling plains. Five horses and three men were so broken down that Smith decided to let them rest up while the main party slowly trekked onward. Smith sent Rose ahead to search for the Crow.

On the morning of the fifth day from the Black Hills, the party hiked down a long, dry creek bed lined by thick patches of brush and an occasional cottonwood. At the front, Will limped alongside Smith and eagerly recounted his trek to Santa Fe and back while silently cursing the inflamed knee tendons that made every step an agony. Smith had questioned him closely about the route, attitudes of the Mexican officials, habits and resources of the populace, and a dozen other details. He filed away each bit of information without comment then softly probed for another answer.

"Ever consider studying law, Captain?" Will asked. "You sure can wrap yourself around a subject and squeeze it to death. You'd make a great lawyer."

Smith scanned a low ridgeline a hundred yards off. "I've a notion something's up there."

Will nervously stared at the ridge. "Indians?"

Smith shook his head. "Man or beast...I don't know. Just a feeling.

Probably nothing."

"Want me to take a look?" Will asked, not sure whether he wanted Smith to reply yes or no.

"Probably nothing. Anyway we're out of bowshot and there's good cover along this creek bed." Smith scanned both sides of the shallow valley. "Yes, I did once consider the law."

"What made you drop it?" Will replied, trying to squeeze off the tension welling within him. He glanced again at the ridge.

"Just didn't seem right for me," Smith replied thoughtfully. "My mother was disappointed. I suppose she wanted to make amends..." Startled at his own words, Smith frowned at Will. "It's you who should follow the law, Mr. Yates. You certainly know how to pry open a man."

"Amends?"

Smith glanced back at the dozen men scattered a hundred yards behind them then quickened his pace.

"I'm sorry, Captain," Will said soothingly. "I didn't mean to touch a sore spot. I couldn't help asking."

"That's quite all right, Mr. Yates," Smith said thoughtfully. "You've been a trustworthy companion." He sighed softly then said, "When I was a young boy my father was accused of passing counterfeit coin. We abandoned our home in the Susquehanna Valley and headed west toward the Lake Erie shore. My mother always mourned the loss of our home and our once friendly neighbors. My father grew silent and moody after that. My brothers, sisters, and I were hushed to never tell why we had left, but somehow the word followed us. Word always gets out. Nothing was the same with our family ever again."

"Every family has its secrets," Will replied, wondering whether to tell Smith about his father and Colette.

"Confession, it's said, is good for the soul. But there are some things that one can confess only to our Maker and then beg forgiveness."

"You lead such a clean life. I can't imagine you having anything to confess."

"The Bible tells us that thinking sin is as evil as committing it."

"I've never understood that," Will replied in irritation. "Just don't seem right. Some thoughts are beyond our control but as long as we keep 'em buried, they don't hurt anyone."

"Perhaps not others," Smith replied sorrowfully. "But evil thoughts can gnaw away at our own souls. We try to flee them, but they trail right behind us, snapping at our heels. We can no more sever them than we can our own shadows."

An image of Sharon's soft, musky body hovered in Will's mind. He smiled sadly. "Lustful thoughts are natural. They may drive a man to distraction but they seem harmless enough. Not much we can do about them. No sense feeling guilty about them." Suddenly he thought of Jameson and glanced warily at Smith. "Unless…"

As if reading his mind, Smith abruptly changed the subject. "Dr. Simons was my mentor, a kindly man who immersed himself in his books and family and caring for others. I've never known a more giving or learned man. He saw something in me. Something my father didn't see. He encouraged me to find my own path. Knowing my love of the forest, it was Dr. Simons who gave me a copy of Lewis and Clark's narrative. That was my calling! To explore the wilds and then guide others to new lands and wonders." Smith searched at the ridgeline again. "Something's up there. I'm certain of it."

They stopped to scan the ridgeline. Strung out along the creek, the other men did likewise. Meadowlarks twittered. The still air was cool. The sun glowed distant behind a veil of clouds.

A huge, ash-colored furry head poked above the brush along the ridgeline then disappeared. A few men saw it and pointed excitedly. "Grizzly," someone shouted.

His heart pounding, Will stepped up on a fallen cottonwood to get a better look. If the grizzly charged, he debated whether to try a long-shot or wait until it was close enough to shoot in its open mouth. His flintlock was only a .36 caliber. He recalled an old trapper at Fort Kiowa scoffing when Will asked him whether it would bring down a grizzly. "Hit it with that sling-shot a' yours, son, and ye'll jus' rile 'im hotter 'en hell! Only way ta bring down a griz is ta shove that barrel in his mouth an' blow his brains out." The trapper cackled cheerfully. "Course ifin ye miss, he'll tear ye ta shreds."

A deep ravine angled from the ridge down toward the creek. Suddenly the brush above the ravine crackled and shook. Smith jumped up beside Will. They glimpsed the grizzly as it smashed through the brush and disappeared into the ravine. Rocks clattered and sage-brush snapped as the grizzly loped down the fissure. Catching wind of the bear, a horse neighed and reared. "Mr. Sublette!" Smith yelled, "get those horses away before they're spooked!" Sublette and the other wranglers jerked their reins and urged the packhorses back down the creek. "Don't shoot till you've got a clear target!" Smith warned the other men. The grizzly charged out into the creek bed. The men scattered into the brush. The beast reared up to its nearly seven-foot height and stood blinking its nearsighted eyes and snorting. A shot exploded from down the creek. The grizzly turned and grunted angrily.

All the men between Will and the grizzly fifty feet away had fled. Hoping he could stun it, Will took careful aim at the back of the giant bear's head. He tried to quell a slight trembling then slowly squeezed the trigger. The shot tore a long bloody furrow alongside the bear's massive skull. The grizzly growled harshly, dropped to all four legs, and charged.

Will stood dumbfounded as the beast bore down on him. It was like a nightmare. He felt nailed to the earth. "Run!" Smith yelled as he pushed Will off the log then jumped off beside him.

Will stumbled off a dozen feet into the brush then tripped and sprawled. "Oh, God!" he hollered, "it's gonna get me!" He struggled to rise and stared back at the creek bed in terror.

Smith stood unflinching as the grizzly charged up to him and reared. He aimed his rifle toward the bear's heart and pulled the trigger. The hammer snapped on damp powder. The beast crashed down atop Smith and chomped its huge jaws around Smith's head. Smith screamed and struggled to pull his skinning knife. Other men came running and shouting. Will scrambled to his feet, charged the grizzly, and repeatedly smashed his rifle down on its shoulder.

The beast released its hold on Smith's head, growled deeply, and turned on Will. "Watch out, Yates," Fitzpatrick hollered as he thrust his rifle-barrel into the grizzly's side and fired. The grizzly twisted toward Fitzpatrick then sat back on its haunches and panted heavily. Blood oozed from its side, mouth, and head. It stared, uncomprehending, at Fitzpatrick. Smith lay bleeding and moaning beside the beast. Will tried to reload but he had broken the lock on his rifle. Clyman aimed carefully into the grizzly's gaping mouth and fired. The ball exploded into its brain and the grizzly toppled over dead.

The men gathered anxiously around Smith. "Think he'll live?" Fitzpatrick asked quietly as he bent over and touched Smith's ripped face. Blood dribbled from a dozen jagged gashes. Smith winced. "I'll live," he gasped. "Get me...some water." Clyman ordered two men to continue down the dry creek bed until they found enough water to fill their canteens and return.

Smith tried to sit up then collapsed in agony. "Ribs broke," he muttered. He slowly moved his hands to the side of his head and softly probed the wounds. He bit his lip and blinked back his pain. "Mr. Clyman," he groaned. "Needle and thread...sew me up."

Clyman blanched. "I'll do what I can, Captain," he replied nervously, "but..." Someone pressed needle and thread into Clyman's hand and he slowly began knitting Smith's face back together. Smith winced and trembled and grasped tightly the hands of Will and Fitzpatrick who knelt beside him.

Twenty tortured minutes later, Clyman said softly, "Captain, I closed the wounds around your head and face, but your ear, it's hanging by a few scraps of flesh. Looks like you're gonna lose it."

"Oh, you must save my ear," Smith pleaded.

Clyman shook his head helplessly. "I don't know, Captain. I'm no surgeon." He knelt back and sighed deeply. "Gimmee a fishhook, Bill," he said to Sublette. "Smallest you can find. This needle ain't worth a damn for sewing an ear." Sublette rummaged through a sack on one of the packhorses and drew out a fishhook. Clyman threaded it and gingerly began sewing the tattered ear onto Smith's head. Finally he muttered, "Best I can do, Captain."

Smith nodded slightly. "Gotta get water…Help me on a horse." With Smith grimacing in agony, Will and Fitzpatrick pulled him slowly to his feet and led him to the gentlest of the packhorses. Sublette unstrapped the pack from the horse and tightened the saddle cinch. Smith grasped the horn and gingerly climbed up into the saddle. His eyes closed briefly as he struggled to stay conscious. "I'm afraid," he said in a barely audible voice, "I may need some support." Will and Fitzpatrick stepped alongside each stirrup.

Smith stared over at the grizzly and shuddered. He glanced at the men crowded expectantly, fearfully, around him. "I thank God…that we have all survived…the attack of that beast." Smith gasped as waves of excruciating pain shot through his skull. Will raised up his hands to steady him. The pain briefly subsided. "With God's will…" Smith murmured, "we will persevere."

Nine

1823–24

They found a spring-fed water hole a mile up the creek and pitched their sole tent beside it. Smith trembled and moaned as Will and Fitzpatrick helped him off his horse and guided him to a pile of buffalo robes within the canvas. The men gathered around solemn and pensive until Clyman waved them away.

Smith winced and blurted, "It'll be awhile...before I can travel." He closely his eyes tightly and bit back the pain.

"Don't talk, Captain," Will said softly. "You need rest."

Smith gasped. Tears welled in his eyes; he tried to blink them away. "I'll hold you back...leave me...push on."

Will and Clyman squirmed and glanced uncomfortably at each other. "Can't do it, Captain," Clyman said as cheerfully as he could.

"We're in this together."

For ten days the men waited impatiently beside the spring, scraping hides, sewing patches on tattered clothes, or just gazing wistfully at the horizons. They took turns riding far out into the plains to hunt and explore. Four days after they arrived, the three men and their horses that had been left behind in the canyon wandered into camp. But after the stragglers came in, there was no sign of Rose or any other human, red or white.

Each day it seemed the wind's bite grew colder and the morning frost grew thicker on their blankets. From a nearby hilltop they could just make out the Bighorn Mountains, ninety miles to the west. Somewhere beyond were the Crow and a warm village in which to winter. Behind them, thirty miles to the east, rose the high, undulating back of the Black Hills. The men marveled that the mountains could look so soft and serene in the distance, yet hold so many terrors and hardships.

Smith gradually strengthened. In ones and twos, most of the men would slip into his tent to chat, read Bible passages, or bring him curiosities, like pieces of petrified wood or arrowheads. But a few others resentfully stayed away and beneath their breath harshly cursed Smith's wounds and piety. All winced inwardly at the sight of his sunken cheeks and the jagged red scars ribbed with black thread crisscrossing his face.

One day Sublette dragged in a huge mastodon femur he found in a nearby gully. "Reckon the critter's kin's still kicking in these parts?" he chuckled as he dropped the fossil before Smith. Will and the others nervously scanned the distant hills.

"Genesis speaks of behemoths," Smith croaked. "Giants that once stalked the earth. But no more."

"What killed 'em off?" Will asked in hushed awe.

Sublette hooted. "Same thing that'll rub out all the beaver someday. Man." The men glanced curiously at each other. Then they drifted off to lose themselves in repairs, naps, or long walks across the dry prairie.

Each day the scars slowly sank deeper beneath Smith's thickening strawberry blond stubble. On the eighth day he crawled painfully out of the tent and used his rifle to struggle to his feet. The men stopped and stared uneasily as he swayed before them. "Gentlemen," he said quietly. "Please bear with me. I'll soon be ready to resume our journey."

On the tenth day he climbed unaided into his saddle and signaled them forward. The men cheered and fired a round into the air.

A few days later, on the Powder River, they crossed the trail of a large band of Indians. By the marks of the travois, women- and child-sized moccasin tracks, and large pony herd, they knew it was not a war party so they followed it south. They caught up to the band in late afternoon after a hard two days' hike.

When the Indians spotted the whites, shouts and screams erupted. The warriors grabbed their bows and lances and raced their ponies toward the Americans while the women, elderly, and children hurried away.

Smith ordered his men to stand ready. Metal clicked in the still air as the men pulled back their rifle hammers and checked their priming.

Arikara? they all wondered. Smith stared briefly at the charging, screaming horde, sighed, then walked his horse forward, Clyman and Will alongside him. The three men raised their right hands high and gripped their rifles tightly with their left. A score or more Indians reined in their horses a dozen feet away followed by dozens of others who massed behind them. Arrows were fitted on bows; war clubs brandished.

Will felt weak-kneed and lightheaded. He worried whether he could muster the energy to raise his rifle and pull the trigger. Won't matter anyway, he reasoned. If killing starts, I'll be as stuck with arrows as a pin cushion before I can squeeze off a shot.

"Cheyenne," Smith whispered as he nudged his horse forward and extended his hand toward the warriors.

A chief rode forward to grasp Smith's hand. His long braids were streaked with gray and his face was cracked with countless wrinkles. He carried a long, curled coup stick wrapped with otter skin, from which a dozen eagle feathers fluttered. The chief and Smith signed for several minutes, then shook hands in agreement.

Smith turned and waved on his men. "This is Yellow Wolf of the Hair Rope band of Cheyenne," he explained as his men gathered nervously around. "They've been hunting buffalo ten sleeps north on the Tongue and Little Bighorn rivers and are now returning to their winterlands on the Platte. Yellow Wolf's invited us to join them. They welcome our rifles against their enemies, the Sioux and Crow. I didn't tell Yellow Wolf that it's the Crow we're trying to join. We're just trappers passing through who need horses. Yellow Wolf said he was willing to trade." Smith paused and his scarred face slightly reddened.

"Oh, and one more thing, gentlemen. Cheyenne women are...extremely chaste. Let there be no incident." He turned his horse and rode up beside Yellow Wolf.

The late afternoon sun burned warmly from a cloudless sky and the air was still. Yellow Wolf passed the pipe to Smith, who puffed at it then handed it on. The pipe was puffed and passed along the circle of a dozen Cheyenne chiefs, Smith, Will, Clyman, Fitzpatrick, and Sublette. They sat on buffalo robes while the other Americans and warriors lounged all around.

Beyond the council, women were raising the teepees in a loose circle, little boys herded the ponies down into a grassy creek bottom, and young women scattered across the prairie to dig out wild turnips and prickly pear, or gather dried buffalo dung. The pipe returned to Yellow Wolf. He drew the tobacco smoke deep into his lungs then pointed the stem to heaven, earth, and the four directions.

The chief began to sign. Smith translated. "He welcomes his white brothers and bids them stay for as long as they wish. He notes our ragged appearance and promises to fatten our bones and provide us warm beds on which to rest our heads. His people have sometimes suffered harshly at the hands of their enemies and the seasons, and always try to help those in need. He notes my scars and asks how I received them, and the journey that brought us into his camp."

Smith signed for almost an hour, explaining all of his adventures since he had first left St. Louis two years before, and sometimes pointing to one of his men to cite a brave deed. Will felt a rush of pride every time Smith gestured toward him. Yellow Wolf and the chiefs occasionally uttered a "Hah!" of approval. Smith finished. Yellow Wolf nodded gravely and began to sign. "He sympathizes deeply with the struggles we have endured on our journey. His band is leaving the Powder River country forever and is heading to the Arkansas for a new life, and hopes the other Cheyenne bands will follow. He complains bitterly that the Sioux have driven his people and the other Cheyenne bands away from their homes around the Black Hills. Yellow Wolf has counted many coup against the Sioux but they have become as many and relentless as locusts and it is time for his people to move on.

"It was at the Cheyenne's holy mountain, Bear Butte, on the plains just northeast of the Black Hills, that Sweet Medicine, one of their great warriors of many generations past, received the Sacred Arrows from Maiyun, the Great Spirit. Two of these arrows have power over men and two over buffalo and, as long as the Cheyenne have them, they will defeat all the attacks of their enemies and the buffalo will cover the earth. He bids us to join his band and the sacred spirit that protects them, and promises us we will take many buffalo robes from the upper Arkansas River and beaver pelts from the nearby Rockies."

Smith glanced at his men. "Gentlemen, I am not sure how this will go over, but I suppose we'd better level with Yellow Wolf that we're heading into the Bighorn River country, though I'll leave out our hoped-for rendezvous with the Crow." Smith signed and Yellow Wolf and the chiefs glanced in surprise at each other. Yellow Wolf responded. "He warns us that the Bighorn River is the Crow heartland and they will murder us and steal our horses. He implores us to stay with his people and he will care for us as a father tends his children.

"I'm thanking him profusely for his kind offer," Smith explained as he signed, "and am telling him that the Cheyenne people are truly great, and their hearts are as big and good as the world itself. Alas, we can only travel with him for several days, and then must bid farewell to our friends and brothers and head west toward the setting sun."

Yellow Wolf signed again. "He begs us not to decide yet, but only after enjoying his people's hospitality."

Smith signed and explained, "I profusely thank him again for his hospitality and promise him that my men and I will consider carefully his words before we decide."

The chief nodded and began the pipe ritual once again. A couple hundred yards away, the women were returning from gathering roots and dung. They suddenly burst into a high-pitched song. In twos and threes, the young Cheyenne men nudged each other, grinned, and sprinted off to the nearest ponies. Even some of the chiefs had faint smiles and glanced around restlessly as the pipe was being slowly smoked and passed. The warriors cantered out toward the women, and as they approached, the women began pelting them with dung. The council broke up in laughter and everyone dashed out to watch. All the Cheyenne were shouting taunts and war cries. The warriors circled the women and tried to ride in and snatch at the robes filled with roots. When a warrior was hit, he dropped out of the game. Finally, an intrepid warrior managed to dodge a volley of dung, ward off blows by the women, grab a handful of turnips, and ride away to a hillside. The other men quickly gathered around him, eating the roots and hurling catcalls at the women. Yellow Wolf and the other chiefs ran out to join them. The women gathered up the roots, prickly pear, and dung, then marched into camp, giggling and singing a song denigrating the warriors' manhood.

Will and the other Americans were amused and mystified by the mock battle. "Never heard of such doings," he remarked to Sublette. "Have you?"

Sublette chuckled and ran a greasy hand through his thinning sandy hair. He was tall and lean, had a thin florid face and aquiline nose, and was in his early twenties. "Reckon if them Cheyenne's legs is as tightly shut as the captain sez, then that's 'bout as much blow-off as they's allowed. The way I hear it, those girls is virgins till they tie the knot and then, after they drop a kid, the happy couple sometimes waits fourteen years till they try fer another. I'm surprised they's airy Cheyenne left if sparkin' spooks 'em so. They ain't the Injun wimmen I signed on fer. We jus' got here and this child's ready to ride day and night fer the Crow country. I ain't had a tumble since we left that Brule village on the Cheyenne River. Now those Sioux gals know how ta tumble!" He licked his lips, rubbed his belly, and elbowed Will in the ribs. "When's the last time you dipped yers, Yates?"

Will gave Sublette a playful shove. "Too long to remember. I am turning Cheyenne."

They burst into exaggerated laughter then stared hungrily at the young women filing past. Still singing, most of the women strolled by as if the bedraggled trappers did not exist. A few of the women glanced shyly at the men. Sublette poked Will in the ribs again and nodded toward a girl dragging a heavy bundle about to pass before them. "Whoa, Yates, lookee there. Now there's a fine young filly I'd like ta break in. That little gal kain't be more'n a child but with that slim waist and long legs and the way her teats are pushing out she'd make this nigger stay home at night, she would at that!"

As the girl glided past, she looked into Will's eyes and smiled faintly. He felt his heart jump and body burn and tried to remember to smile back but she had already passed by.

"Yes, sir, Yates, now that there's prime beaver! I aim ta trap me some a' that!"

Will turned and watched her until she disappeared into a teepee painted with figures of scalped Indians lying on their backs, horses, a crescent moon, buffalo, an eagle, Indians fighting with knives and spears, and above all, a yellow wolf.

"Well, now, Yates, by the sign I do believe that may be Yellow Wolf's daughter."

"Knowing my luck," he replied glumly, "she's probably one of his wives."

• • •

Judy picked flowers on a hillside when a dozen Rees appeared on the ridge and galloped toward her but she didn't see them and Will yelled and waved his arms and sprinted toward her but she didn't hear him and the Rees surrounded her and taunted her and poked her with their lances and one dragged her on his horse and disappeared into dust while the others turned on Will and thundered toward him and he turned and ran but seemed to run in air and a Ree grabbed his shirt and dragged him backward and the others leapt off their horses and struck him repeatedly with their war clubs and a huge, fat Ree grabbed a hunk of Will's long brown hair and held a scalping knife to his skull and Will tried to struggle free but his arms waved helplessly like they were lead-filled and the Ree turned into Rene Goutard and he laughed cruelly and ripped off Will's scalp and Will screamed and felt someone shaking him just as he glimpsed Sharon smiling and beckoning sphinx-like on the horizon.

"Will!" Fitzpatrick said firmly in his Irish brogue as he shook him, "Wake up, damn ye, ye scared me witless with your hollering! Ye tryin' ta wake the dead?"

Will sat up abruptly and gasped for breath. There was a slight glow from the buffalo dung fire, a hard rain beat steadily off the teepee, and figures huddled all around in the shadows. One of the figures chuckled and murmured something in Cheyenne and the others laughed loudly then laid back down. Trembling slightly, he scolded, "Damn it, Fitz! Why'd you have ta wake me?"

"Sounded like ye was being bloody murdered, that's why!" Fitzpatrick whispered loudly, half-amused, half-irritated. "Besides, it might not sit too well with our hosts to startle them in the middle of the night. They might well forget their rules of etiquette and cast ye out into that storm. I was tempted to do it myself. Well, was ye being murdered or what?"

"I was, but I saw Sharon!"

"Who? And pipe down, will ye?"

"A long-lost love," he whispered sadly. "She was floating in the distance. Sharon always had the most beguiling smile. She seemed to mock you and invite you at the same time. I haven't dreamt of her in ages."

Will massaged his forehead. "And the Rees…stole my wife and scalped me and…" Suddenly his whisper hardened, "It was Goutard who took her. That bastard! He's still haunting me after all these years. I gotta get back to Judy. She's in danger. What the hell am I doing here a thousand miles from home?" He groped for his rifle.

"Steady, lad," Fitzpatrick warned quietly as he tightly squeezed his shoulder. "Let's talk on it tomorrow. Even if that rain don't turn ta snow, it's gonna be a long miserable day a-ridin'." Will strained briefly against Fitzpatrick's iron grip and then relaxed.

"All right," he said softly. He laid back down and wrapped his blanket tightly around himself. The rain drummed off the teepee and the moisture seeped through the robe beneath him. He shivered and felt like crying. A world away from Judy and every step was a step farther. Why'd he abandon her? He'd promised a God in whom he had trouble believing that he would stay with Judy until death tore them asunder. God or no God, wasn't he man enough to carry the burden of a woman whose stormy moods shifted with the wind? He'd cast himself from her and into a wilderness where any second some beast or savage could rip him to shreds. And if he turned tail and ran back to her, what then? Wouldn't he just be running back to one fear from another? Would he return to rediscover his passionate young bride, or the cold, embittered, evasive creature that she had become?

"Yates," Fitzpatrick whispered, "ye awake?"

"Yeah."

"I knew a lass in Ireland before I left," he confessed dreamily, "Brenda was 'er name. She had chestnut-colored hair that flowed down to her backside and she'd toss it like a spirited horse does its mane and her face was a creamy white and her eyes the color of the sky and lips so thick and soft looking, jus' made for kissing…Sometimes Brenda blesses me with herself in a dream, and I reach for her, but she disappears and I awaken alone in the dark. Is your Sharon anything like that?"

"Yeah," Will said sadly, "a lot. Why'd ye leave her?"

"Brenda was never mine to leave. She was married to the miller and he kept her in finery and was said to 'ave been quite the man to her. I've been smitten with her since I was just a wee lad, but from then till I was seventeen and left for America, I never so much as bid her good day. She'd smile at me when we passed in the village lanes and I longed to open my heart to her, but never did. There'd 'ave been no point regardless," Fitzpatrick sighed. "I hope ye had better luck with your lassie than I with mine."

"Not sure I did. She left me for another. Goutard," he said bitterly. "I lo…loved her. But like you, I was young and she was…too much, too strong and spirited. I couldn't hold her. Maybe no man can."

"Well, Yates, if that be so, then maybe we're both better off out here."

Will smiled and turned over in his damp robe.

"Hard ta say." He closed his eyes and listened to the rain drumming all around him.

The storm passed before dawn and left the earth soaked and shining in the early light. Will stooped out of the teepee and stretched just as a dozen Cheyenne rode away to the east to hunt buffalo. He watched them disappear over a ridge and longed to hop atop a pony and gallop after them. He smiled, remembering that he'd be riding a pony of his own by afternoon if the trading went well between Smith and Yellow Wolf.

He strolled through the village, breathing it in with all his senses. Smoke wisped from the tops of teepees and voices murmured within. Cheyenne women were scraping hides, sewing, or hanging strips of meat while the men lounged around in twos and threes, talking or mending weapons. Will nodded to them as he passed by, but they paid him no heed. The dozens of mongrel curs, though, eyed him suspiciously and trotted over to sniff him.

"If only I was as invisible to the dogs," he mumbled. He held out his hand gingerly and, to his relief, they did not snarl or bite. Several little boys stopped playing and gathered around him, shouting and counting coup on him with their toy bows. He signed for them to leave him alone but they jeered him all the more. He looked around helplessly. The adults watched but no one scolded the children. Then he saw Clyman emerge from a nearby tent. "Jim!" he called. "Help!" Clyman laughed and shook his head.

Will pointed toward Clyman and signed the children that he would give them a knife. The children dashed off toward Clyman, who ducked back into the teepee. Mindful of not alarming the dogs, he slipped behind a line of teepees and headed toward the thick sagebrush and cottonwood along the creek. He slipped behind a tree and peeped back. The children were chasing another trapper through the village.

He sat with his back to the cottonwood and savored the privacy. A magpie flittered through the branches of trees across the creek. How nice to be able to just fly away from everything. A baby began crying from the village and the wails got louder. Someone's carrying it this way, he cursed. He carefully glanced around the tree and thrilled at the sight of the girl he saw yesterday carrying a squalling papoose into the brush farther up the creek. He quietly trailed her. After a couple hundred yards, she stopped and hung the cradleboard high on a broken tree branch. Red-faced and squirming, the baby bawled.

She sang it a song and then, to Will's amazement, turned and glided away.

He rose from behind a clump of sagebrush and called out, "Wait! Your baby!" She stared at him cautiously. He pointed at the infant and signed danger. She smiled demurely and walked away. He slipped through the brush and took the cradleboard down. He sat down cross-legged and cooed softly at the baby, rocking it gently in his arms. It suddenly stopped crying and stared up at him. He marveled at its plump, delicate face, shiny, big brown eyes, and black fuzz covering its head.

A brightly quilled turtle amulet dangled from the cradleboard and Will knew that the baby's umbilical cord lay inside. It was a good custom, he reasoned, carrying through life that link with one's mother and all that passed before. He wondered about the fate of his own cord. Tossed to the hogs, he guessed, just after he struggled out into the world. Tears dribbled down his cheeks as a melange of memories of his family and Judy tore through his mind.

He wiped a fallen tear off the baby's forehead and smiled down at it. "Why'd your mama abandon you?" he asked softly and gently rocked the baby in his arms.

Slim brown arms reached down for the baby. Startled, Will instinctively pulled the cradleboard away. The girl smiled down at him and talked softly.

He reluctantly handed over the baby and she turned and walked back toward the village. "Wa...wait," he called, feeling confused, aroused.

The girl turned, glanced at his eyes, then looked toward his feet. A slight smile tugged at her lips. "Why leave baby?" he signed.

She crinkled her brow and giggled as she signed. "Baby cry. Whites no leave cry baby?"

Astonished, he signed, "You leave cry baby forever?"

She giggled again. "Come back after baby stop cry. Baby fast learn no cry or lonely."

"Oh!" he said, relieved, then tensed again. "Your baby?"

"Sister."

"You Yellow Wolf's wife?"

"Daughter."

"That's a relief," he mumbled. "You're about the prettiest girl I've ever seen, white or red." He sniffed morosely. "Not that it does me any good."

Her brow furrowed slightly. He hesitated then nervously signed,

"You very beautiful!" She averted her eyes. A smile pulled at her thick lips. He feared she would flee. He signed quickly, "Your name?" She glanced at him and hesitated.

"Little Antelope," she signed. They stared briefly, intensely, into each others eyes. The girl lowered hers.

"Have man?" he signed hesitantly.

Little Antelope shook her head no. "I good girl," she signed, then turned and walked away through the brush toward the village.

"Wait!" he called urgently. She took another half-step then turned. Will dug into his pouch and fished out a dozen elk teeth. He cupped them in his hands so she could see them, then laid them at the cottonwood's base.

"Present," he signed. Then he hiked up the creek away from the village. Everything seemed such a blur, he felt he would dissolve. Don't look back, he warned himself repeatedly. He finally twisted around at a bend in the creek. In the distance he saw her stepping into the circle of teepees.

After half a day of patient trading, Smith acquired a pony for each man and enough others to carry their equipment. Some of the ponies remained half-wild so the best riders had to break them. In late afternoon, the entire band gathered around the trappers as they prepared to mount. Smith and his leaders heartily shook hands with Yellow Wolf and the other chiefs. Yellow Wolf continued to implore them to stay, at least for the winter. Smith promised that they would return to hunt with the Cheyenne on the upper Arkansas at their first chance.

Will slipped through the crowd toward Yellow Wolf, worrying that somehow the chief had heard of the encounter with his daughter. Yellow Wolf's eyes narrowed with mirth as Will stepped before him. He shook Will's hand and began to sign. "Your chief say you good warrior. Fight strong against Arikara. Now you ride many sleeps to the west." The mirth disappeared from his eyes. "Take many Crow horses and scalps," he ordered.

He spread his arms wide and slowly scanned the village. "Return to Cheyenne people. We wait for you on the upper Arkansas River." Yellow Wolf grinned broadly. "You need many horses and coups to be Cheyenne." Will smiled then looked around for a glimpse of Little Antelope but was hemmed in by warriors. The trappers were mounting their ponies and kicking them into a trot toward the west.

Sublette hollered, "Come on, Yates! Them Crow gals are dripping fer us. Don't waste yer time with one of them Cheyenne nuns!" The other trappers burst into a chorus of similar catcalls.

Will grimaced, cursing himself for earlier admitting to Sublette of his fondness for the girl. He stared into Yellow Wolf's eyes. "I return," he signed, "I promise." He pushed through the throng toward his pony, pulled the stake, grabbed a handful of mane, and slipped onto its back. The pony pranced and tugged at the rein. He kicked its ribs lightly and the pony cantered forward. He scanned the crowd for a last glimpse of Little Antelope. Finally, he spotted her standing motionless before Yellow Wolf's teepee. The elk teeth dangled from her deerskin dress. He smiled slightly then urged his pony into a gallop to catch up to the others.

It took six hard days of riding before they crossed the broken hills at the southern end of the Bighorn Mountains to the river beyond. They rested a day, recruiting their horses, then slowly trapped their way up the Bighorn into the Wind River Valley.

Daily the cold grew more bitter; flurries sporadically tumbled from the leaden skies. Beaver were scarce. Fists settled disputes over the most promising stretches of the side creeks. The men huddled away the long nights beneath crude shelters of cottonwood branches and sage. Most of the men were edgy.

A few openly despaired of ever finding the Crow and cursed the decision to leave the Cheyenne camp, or muttered about turning back to the Missouri before they froze to death or were massacred. The worst bully and malcontent was Slade. Smith talked or stared down Slade and his followers, but they still savaged him behind his back.

Like the other men, Will was always cold and sometimes frostbitten. He had only eight pelts to show for weeks of effort. Gasping, shivering, he waded the icy streams to set his traps while trying to conjure up memories and ambitions to ward off the numbing cold. Most often he tried to focus on Little Antelope, imagining them alone and naked beneath thick robes in a fire-lit teepee. But those images only seemed to draw the cold deeper within him and freeze the tears on his cheeks.

One day, just after he began working his trapline, the temperature plunged. Soon he could not stop shivering. Ice crystals seared his lungs; his lower legs and feet ached from the frigid waters. The cold even froze through his rabbit-skin mittens, buffalo robe capote, and beaver cap. The sun shone dimly through patches of dark gray clouds dumping trails of snow. He lifted his last trap with his pole and stared at its empty jaws then plunged it back in the stream and quickly waded onto land. The pain from his frostbitten feet pushed a deep moan through his lips. He pulled two pairs of moccasins onto his feet and rubbed them vigorously. Then he grabbed his rifle and lurched through the brush toward his pony a hundred yards away, all the while imagining Sublette or Clyman slowly chopping off his toes with a butcher knife. The pony slowly turned his head as Will approached.

Ignoring his pony, he dropped to his knees before a pile of twigs and tinder he had gathered earlier. He pulled off a mitten with his teeth and groped for the flint and steel in his pouch. But his swollen hand trembled so violently that he could not grasp them. He wailed loudly, pushed himself to his feet, and turned to his pony. "Thata boy, don't spook," he mumbled as he slowly reached toward the horsehair rope that tied the pony to a cottonwood.

He pulled himself along the rope until he could grasp the mane and stiffly drag himself on the pony's back. He drew his knife and cut the rope then kicked his pony into a trot. The ride was agonizing. The frigid winds seemed to cut straight through him. He tried to focus his mind on the fires smoldering in camp several miles away but all he could do was weep and curse. He hugged the pony's neck. "God, oh God," he sobbed repeatedly, "guide me through this."

The camp was in a cottonwood grove along a stream. A half-dozen fires blazed high in a circle and the men huddled close within it. When he saw Will, Smith rose and approached him. "Mr. Yates," Smith asked urgently, "have you seen Mr. Fitzpatrick? He's still missing." Will shook his head. Smith nodded, grabbed the halter, and pulled the pony into the circle of campfires. "Mr. Clyman," he called, "would you bring Mr. Yates's robes?" Smith helped him off his pony and Clyman wrapped two buffalo robes around him.

"Thank you," Will muttered and blinked back tears as he crouched before a blazing fire. He rubbed his feet and hands rhythmically; they slowly thawed. Gusts of warm and cold air swirled within the fires. The men were silent, some sullen, others at peace. Along the creek the ponies stamped the hard ground and strained at their pickets. He stared into the crackling, dancing flames and savored the warmth creeping through his body.

A string of geese passed honking high above. He glanced up and watched them wing themselves south toward the jagged snow-capped peaks of the southern range. "Bound for Santa Fe," he muttered to himself and unleashed a covy of memories of his journey there and back which dissolved into visions of his mother and sister. His eyes misted over and he began trembling slightly. "So far away. Everywhere's so far away."

He turned his back to the fire. His eyes wandered across the red capstoned mesas scattered across the valley to the northern mountains.

"Beautiful," he murmured. Suddenly the camp sounds faded to nothing and something vital within Will melted then burst out in scores of rays across his world of sight and memory and he sensed he was hovering on the edge of something infinite. But just as he was settling into a deep peace, a monologue gurgled through his mind as he tried to understand and snapped him back to the desolate cold. Seconds later, all that remained was a diminishing warmth and a hunger to once more be everywhere at once.

A rifle barrel poked him in the back. "Off yer raggedy ass, Yates," Slade's voice growled low. "Draw was done when ye was gone. That Bible-hugging bastard," he jerked a thumb toward Smith at another fire, "done rigged the game aginst me. I want to kill before twilight, an' ifin it ain't meat ye'll do."

Will turned and tried to stare down Slade but his body began to tremble and he glanced away. "We'll see who kills what," he said quietly. He had managed to dodge Slade's shadow since he pulled the bully off that boy on the island. He had dreaded the inevitable time that they would be alone together. This would be it.

They mounted their ponies and rode side by side into a long twisting canyon. The frosty sage was belly-high to their ponies. The creek bed was dry and rocky. What few tracks or dung they spotted was weeks old.

Slade's face reddened deeper with rage as he cursed the cold, Smith, his pony, savages, and God himself. His grumbles soon turned to loud threats.

He leveled his cocked rifle over his saddle pommel so it was pointing straight at Will. "Yates, ye cowardly little sack a' shit, maybe I oughta jus' blow out yer brains an' gut ye. Ye like that?" He scowled and thrust his rifle toward his face. "Blow off yer jaw so ye won't need ta worry 'bout eatin' no more. Ye like that, Yates?" His finger curled around the trigger.

"Save yer shot, Slade, you won't get much meat off this carcass." His hands began to tremble on the reins.

Slade snorted. "Oh, I ain't gonna kill ye fer the meat, Yates, jus' fer the fun of it."

Will struggled to remain calm. Slade's a mad dog, he warned himself, and any sign of fear would invite an attack. "Slade? Jus' what makes you so damn mean?"

Slade looked puzzled. No one had asked him that before. He sniffed and rubbed his runny nose. "Don't like pretty boys," he declared quietly. "All there is to it."

"And just what did those pretty boys ever do to you?"

Slade's face contorted with anger. "Evil things they done me when ah was jus' inta britches! Spillin' seed in barren places," he intoned harshly. "Like ta smash their pretty faces. Break their pretty bodies. Jus' like what ah done ta that boy on the Missoura." He laughed hoarsely. "I'm long pass due fer another stompin'."

"I've done nothing to you, Slade."

"Yer livin', Yates. Ain't that 'nuff? It was 'nuff fer those pretty boys ta do evil ta me."

Will stared down the rifle cradled in Slade's arms. His shivering worsened.

"Ease up, Slade." It was more a plea than an order.

"Yer feared ain't ye, Yates? Ye know I mean it. Ye know jus' one little tug a' my finger'll blow off yer jaw." He hooted. "Justa huntin' accident I'll tell 'em and they'll be none the wiser. 'Bout time ye bes' beg fer mercy, Yates. Judgment day's here at last!"

Will felt limp with helplessness.

"I ain't ready to die yet, Slade. How 'bout tomorrow?" was all he could think to say.

"Now, Yates," Slade sniffed loudly, "I done told ye judgment day's settin' right before ye..."

Suddenly Will squinted ahead into the dusk then craned his neck to see better. "Elk!" he whispered harshly. Slade pulled his rifle to his shoulder and pointed it up the canyon.

"Where?" he hissed.

Will swung his rifle his down onto Slade's which fired. Both ponies reared and Slade tumbled off his horse. "Ye bastard, I'll kill ye, Yates," he screamed.

He hung on desperately as his pony broke into a gallop up the canyon.

"Turn, damn it, turn," he hollered as he tried to neck rein his pony around toward camp. He imagined Slade coolly loading and blasting a ball into his back. He slowed his pony to a canter and wheeled it back down the narrow canyon.

A couple hundred yards away, Slade was stalking his pony which had stopped to graze. Will jerked his pony to a halt.

Slade turned toward him. "Ye cowardly bastard, Yates!" he

screamed. He quickly began to reload.

Will's mind whirled over the possibilities. He could try to shoot Slade or his pony or Slade's pony might spook at the shot and he'd outdistance Slade but could only flee up the box canyon and Slade might trail and murder him but he could ambush Slade and Slade the lazy son of a bitch would probably tire of the stalk and head back to camp and dismiss the incident as a joke.

Slade raised his rifle and Will ducked behind his pony's neck. Slade fired and the ball whined overhead. The pony bucked, hurled Will to the ground, and kicked into a gallop down the canyon. The other pony joined him and they galloped out of sight around a bend. Will crouched behind some sage and peered through the brush across the canyon floor. Slade had disappeared. His eyes darted frantically around searching for Slade, better cover, a way back to camp, friends, for any escape from the nightmare. He found nothing.

The wind picked up and he started shivering violently. He imagined Slade crawling slowly toward him, lusting to murder. He tried not to panic.

Be dark soon, he reasoned, gotta find cover. He checked his priming then squirmed through the sage toward the sandstone canyon slope. He paused occasionally to listen and peer carefully through the sage but the canyon was silent and revealed nothing. He crawled between some boulders and trembled against the cold stone. He watched the canyon fill with twilight and then dark. He imagined Slade huddled and frozen down canyon. He'll be no more riled for a fight than me. If I stay here without a fire I'll be dead before morning. Gotta get my blood moving. Get back to the fires. Take your chance with Slade. He can't get a bead on you in this dark. Die on your feet!

He crawled stiffly out from the boulders and began stumbling down canyon. The sage crackled loudly as he pushed through it but he did not care. In his mind he fixed that circle of campfires and struggled toward it. He paused once to listen but heard nothing but the wind whistling through the piñon on the canyon walls. The canyon seemed to meander endlessly. His feet were numb and his body spent. He fought against the urge to lie down and drift off to death. Finally he emerged into the valley. A distant glow hovered in the dark. He trudged toward it, stumbling over the broken, rocky ground.

A rifle cracked then a voice hollered far ahead. "Mr. Yates!"

"Here!" Will's voice cracked hoarsely. "Here!" He squeezed the trigger and his rifle exploded loudly. He summoned his remaining strength and trotted forward.

"Mr. Yates," Smith's shout was closer. "Where are you?"

"Here," he yelled back. He saw movement through the dark. "Over here!" A horse and rider materialized through the black. They looked like ghosts.

"You're safe now, Mr. Yates," Smith reached down his arm and pulled him up behind him. Another rider appeared.

"You all right, Will?" Clyman said softly.

"Yeah," he said weakly.

Will held onto Smith tightly as the horse wheeled and cantered back toward camp. He began to sob. "Slade...tried to...kill me."

Smith nodded. "I assumed as much. He claims you attacked him and drove off the ponies. Don't worry. We'll take care of Slade."

A quarter-hour later, they rode into the fire circle. Clyman helped Will down and cloaked him in robes.

"Yates!" Slade screeched from one of the fires. "Ye cowardly murderin' son of a bitch. He tried ta kill me! He smashed my rifle and tried to shoot me! Let me at 'im!" Slade tried to rise but Sublette and Fitzpatrick held him back.

"Slade," Sublette warned quietly. "Settle down afore ye get hurt."

"Warm up, Mr. Yates," Smith said. "When you're ready you can give your account."

Will nodded and collapsed before a fire. He painfully stretched his feet toward the flames and vigorously rubbed them. The shivering slowly subsided. Someone handed him a chunk of mountain goat meat stuck on a ramrod. He grabbed the ramrod and bit savagely into the meat. As he chewed he imagined Slade's eyes boring into his back and he began to shiver again. He turned and sure enough, Slade stared unblinking at him. Slade laughed shrilly. "Judgment day, Yates!"

"Captain Smith," Will called out. "I'm ready."

"Mr. Sublette," Smith asked as he rose and walked toward Will. "Would you kindly escort over Mr. Slade?"

Slade was seated next to Will. All the men gathered around wrapped in their robes. More cottonwood branches were dumped on the fire and it flared brightly. Smith held out his Bible. "Gentlemen, your right hands." Will and Slade stretched their fingers and touched the Bible. "Do you swear to tell the whole truth and nothing but the truth, as God be your witness?"

"I do," Will said. An image flashed of he and Judy at the altar and he suddenly felt like weeping. Slade snickered.

"Sure."

"Mr. Slade," Smith said, "your explanation once more. "

Slade launched into a long rambling story which he frequently broke by pointing a grimy finger at Will and hurling curses. Will's sorrow turned to anger and then rage. He stared fiercely at Slade, occasionally muttering, "He's lying."

"Well, Mr. Slade," Smith said quietly when Slade had finished. "That's quite a story."

"Son of a bitch's crazy," Slade added. "He oughta..."

"That's enough, Mr. Slade," Smith interrupted forcefully. "We've heard your side." He turned to Will. "Mr. Yates?"

Will's voice trembled with stress and exhaustion. "Slade's completely right, except for one detail. Everything he said I did, he did. No one saw what happened. It's one man's word against another. We've all been together for months now. You've seen him bully the greenhorns and stomp that boy on the island. Who do you believe?" He scanned the surrounding faces, briefly trying to lock eyes with each man. Most nodded or smiled; a few looked away or scowled.

"Well, gentlemen," Smith said, "you've heard their stories. Now we must decide on who's telling the truth. All in favor of Mr. Slade's version." One man, Curt Greeley, shot up his hand up defiantly, then hastily dropped it when he saw Slade's lack of support. Smith nodded. "Those in favor of Mr. Yates."

Eleven hands were raised. "Abstentions?" Greeley and two other men raised their hands. "The group rules against Mr. Slade," Smith intoned gravely. Slade cursed savagely. Smith waited until Slade had quieted into a glare. Smith sighed deeply. "And now we must decide what to do."

"Exile," Sublette said forcefully and others echoed the call.

"Send Slade out there alone," shouted Greeley, "and he'll die. It's Yates should go."

"That's what we'll decide now," Smith responded. "All in favor of exile?" Three hands were quickly raised, two others more slowly. "Opposed?" Eight hands were eventually raised. "Abstentions?"

Fitzpatrick shook his head wearily as he lifted his hand. "I din know what's best, lads," he admitted.

Smith's face was a mask. "You've decided against exile, gentlemen. What now?" The men debated loudly for some time. A majority finally decided to award Will one of Slade's traps and six pelts. Slade snarled as he tossed the trap and pelts at his feet. "One way or 'nother, Yates, yer a dead man fer what ye done!"

It was far up the Wind River where the valley was a mere half-

dozen rolling miles wide that they finally found the Crow. Sublette and
Will were stalking a small buffalo herd when they spotted a half-dozen
Indians cantering toward them. They cocked their rifles and held their
hands high.

"Hope they's jus' happy ta see us," Sublette said nervously as the
Crow charged up yelping and striking their horses with elk horn quirts.

Will nodded grimly. "No arrows in their bows."

The Crow surged around talking gaily, laughing, and hugging
them. "Not sure who gives the most ticklish receptions," Sublette joked
as he patted the back of a warrior who warmly embraced him, "the Rees
or the Crows."

"Rose must be one helluva diplomat," Will said with a chuckle.

"Got the feeling anybody'd get 'long with the Crow. They's a lot
different than them sourpuss Cheyenne."

"Dress different, too," Will observed. He admired the elaborate-
colored quillwork on their buckskin shirts and leggings, and their long
black hair. Their war shields were painted with the owner's visions or
medicine animals. One warrior had a rattlesnake skin quiver and a
mountain sheep horn bow backed with sinew. Another used a mountain
lion pelt for his pony's blanket.

The youngest Crow rode back to his village to announce the white
men's arrival while everyone else rode to the trapper's camp. On the
way Will's good humor died when he noticed his skinning knife was
missing. He scanned the faces of the Crow but their mirth revealed
nothing. "You missing anything, Bill?" he asked warily.

"Huh?" Sublette's grin faded as he glanced down at himself.
"Some son of a bitch lifted my powder horn!" he said angrily. As if they
understood, the Crow sharply eyed Sublette and Will and shifted their
bows and spears.

"Easy, Bill," Will cautioned. "This might not be the best time…"

Sublette forced a smile. He opened his mouth wide and laughed
heartily. He poked a Crow riding alongside him in his ribs and laughed
again. Puzzled, the Crow smiled and poked him back. Soon everyone
was laughing and poking each other. Then they kicked their ponies into
a gallop and raced down the valley.

They rode over a rise and stared down at the camp along a creek.
Only a few men were visible, scraping pelts or hauling wood. The rest
had disappeared at dawn into the mountains to work their traplines.
Sublette fired his rifle and they cantered down the slope. Cradling
rifles, the men gathered around. "They're friendly," Will warned, "but
hang on to your fixin's or they'll steal ye blind." The trappers plied the

Crow with buffalo stew and restrained them from foraging through their supplies and belongings.

The other trappers trickled in that day and evening, but it took another day before everyone had recovered their traps set high in the surrounding mountain streams. They rode west late that afternoon, camped, and then reached the village around noon the next day.

The whole Crow village surged out to greet them. Everyone was shouting and laughing and pushing. Children and dogs dodged yelping through the crowd.

The men were tall and strongly built. They swung their long hair as they strutted forward. Although shells dangled from nearly all their ears, only a few had tattoos, usually a small sign of their medicine animal, etched on their cheeks with powdered charcoal of red willow and pine. The women wore ankle-length dresses trimmed with ermine or covered with elk teeth. Pendants of rounded buffalo bone dangled from their ears. Circles were tattooed on their foreheads, dots on their noses, and lines etched from their chins to their lips.

At the crowd's head were Rose and a warrior carrying under his arm a parfleche into which his hair extended. Rose pointed to the warrior as Smith and his men rode up and dismounted. "Cap'in, this here's Long Hair, head chief of the mountain Crow." Rose spoke rapidly to Long Hair who smiled briefly and enthusiastically shook hands with Smith.

"Kahe!" the chief exclaimed loudly then motioned Smith to follow him. The Crow pressed in on the trappers as they all strode into the village. The men were uneasy and irritated by the din and confusion and attempts by some Crow to rifle their packs. Other Crow grabbed the trapper's arms and enticed them to enter their lodges.

"Git along with them Crow, boys," Rose called out cheerfully. "Jus' wanna bed ye down, partic'ly them gals!"

Smith sighed. "That's right, men. Go ahead. We'll assemble later." The men dispersed among teepees, carried away by small groups of laughing Crow.

Will struggled to keep up with Smith and Clyman. He tore free of the hands groping to drag him away and repeatedly signed that he was a chief. They reached a huge lodge in the village center. Long Hair gestured to some women who took the reins from the trappers and staked out their ponies nearby. The men stooped into the teepee and sat in a circle around the fire. Smith started to unpack his pipe but Long Hair spoke sharply and pointed to moccasins hanging from one of the poles. One of the Crow chiefs leapt up and snatched them down. Rose explained.

"Damn near broke etiquette there, Cap'in! Crow don't smoke with moccasins dangling. Ain't respectful."

Smith stroked his beard. "I'll remember." He performed the pipe ceremony, lit the bowl, puffed three times, and passed the pipe to Long Hair who solemnly repeated the ritual then handed the pipe to a chief on his left. They sat in silence as the pipe slowly completed the circle. The trappers stared astonished as a squaw slowly extracted the chief's hair from the parfleche under his arm. The hair seemed endless and, when it was finally free of the parfleche, the squaw gently spread it in a half-circle behind the chief and combed it with porcupine quills.

"Half agin as tall as me," Rose noted proudly. "He ain't named Long Hair fer nothin'."

"Does it have religious significance, Mr. Rose?"

Rose shrugged. "Vanity mostly, ah reckon. Crows're the vainest cocks that ever walked the roost and each tries ta outdo the others."

Long Hair began speaking in a high-pitched, musical voice. "Welcome, my brothers," Rose translated. "Our lodges are forever open to you…" Will felt his grip on the words loosening. He had not felt so warm and secure in months, and it made him drowsy. How he longed to stretch out on a buffalo robe and nap. He pinched himself and glanced at Smith and Clyman. They were alert and absorbed in the chief's talk. How do they do it? he wondered. Why can't I keep up with them? Some 'chief' I am, he thought contemptuously.

The conference seemed to drag on for hours, with Will barely retaining consciousness. It finally ended and he struggled to his feet. Rose sidled up and slapped him on the back. "Follow me, Yates," he leered. "Ah owe ye one from ye almost gittin' kilt in that Ree village without gittin' laid first. Ye stay in my lodge and ye kin enjoy hymeneal pleasures day and night with barely a chance a' gittin' yer scalp lifted."

Like many of the others, Will distrusted Rose but was not sure why. Anyway he was too tired to protest. "Thanks, Rose. But I'll need to rest up some before I take on any Crow girls."

They crouched out of the lodge into the bright, cold afternoon. "Rest up?" Rose cackled and ran his fingers through his long gray hair. "Hell, boy, thar's no rest where yer goin'. Those gals'll ride ye in relays all year long. Shoshone jus' raised my brother-in-law's hair and I gotta keep his two fillies satisfied, 'long with my wife. Ta tell ye the truth, though I'm still strong as an ox an' kin out lay any man alive, I ain't no young'un. Need 'nother man in my lodge to hunt an' keep my women happy. Sumthin 'bout ye, Yates." Rose crinkled his brow and rubbed his chin. "Ain't quite sure what. But fer some reason ah reckon ah kin trust ye."

"The ironies of life," Will mumbled. He untied his two ponies. "Lead on, Rose. I'll see what I can do."

Once they reached Rose's lodge, Will staked his ponies, dragged in his pack, and then plopped down before the fire. Two squaws stared at him. He nodded and warmed his hands over the flames.

Rose pointed toward the plump women dying porcupine quills in a buffalo stomach over the fire. "That gal there's my wife, Stone Otter," he said proudly. "And that one there," he jerked a thumb toward a short, slender girl sewing a hunting shirt, "is my wife's sister, Sky Wanderer." Another squaw pushed through the flap and dragged in a robe full of cottonwood branches. "An this here's Raven Speaks. She's my brother-in-law's first wife, no relation to the two sisters there. Well, Yates, my wife's mine," he said forcefully. "But we kin share the other gals."

"Thank you, Rose, but I've gotta get some sleep first." Rose waved off the remark as he spoke quickly to Raven Speaks. She replied strongly and then stared down at her sewing. Then he spoke to Sky Wanderer who, lips tight, emphatically shook her head no. "Ah afeared that," Rose said sadly. "Yates?"

"Yeah?"

"Hate ta say it but...yer gonna hafta bathe an' shave first."

"Now?"

"Well, son, ahm 'fraid so. Crows're right particular 'bout cleanliness. No gal'll lay ye, ifin ye don't."

"How clean do I have to get?"

"All over and clean-shaven. Hair, too. Partic'ly the hair."

"Where?"

"Down by the stream.

"It's freezing and the sun's 'bout to go down. Anyway, I don't have any soap."

Rose handed him a parfleche. "Ashes."

"Can't this wait till morning?"

"Well, Yates, ifin it whar jus' us ah'd be jus' as foul smellin' an bearded as ye. But ah gotta live with these gals, an cleanliness be parta the price."

Will grimaced angrily, grabbed the bag, and stooped through the flap. Shaking his head, he headed toward the river.

"Just wanna get some sleep," he mumbled. He reached the bank and peered down into the river. Naked men cavorted in the frigid waters. When they noticed him shivering above them they taunted him for living in his filthy body and buckskins. Will turned heel and ran back to Rose's teepee. "Rose," he exclaimed as he burst through the opening, "I can't do it now. I just can't."

Rose looked disgusted. "Goddamn it, Yates. Ah took ye fer a better man than that."

"I'm feeling poorly." He unrolled his buffalo robe.

"No squaw'll touch ye."

"It don't matter. I'm a married man."

Rose looked incredulous. "What's that hafta do with anything?"

"Promised my wife I'd be faithful."

"What? Why'd ye do a fool thing like that?"

Will shook his head sadly. "I ain't quite sure."

"Well, why the hell didn't ye tell me? Ah'd asked Clyman instead." Someone scratched at the flap.

"That you in thar, Rose," Sublette's voice asked hesitantly. Rose's face brightened.

"Sublette! Come on in, boy!"

Sublette stooped into the lodge. He chuckled. "Captain Smith sent me round ta larn if any man had not been completely impoverished by the Crow."

"Wagh!" Rose replied in disgust. "Don't mind the Crow. Why ain't ye shaved an' washed yet?"

"Huh?" Sublette scratched an armpit. "Why, Rose, you're worse than the Crows."

Rose threw up his hands and shook his head. "Ye boys're never gitting laid. The Crow'll know ye as nothin' more 'en cowardly wimmen. Hell, ah already led a war party aginst the Shoshone." Will and Sublette's eyes widened. Rose pointed to three scalps dangling from a spear. "Bashed out the brains a' those sons a bitches with a tomahawk. Other Crazy Dogs took seven scalps and forty ponies. Shoshone kilt my brother-in-law, Nettle Fish." He jerked a thumb toward Stone Otter and Raven Speaks. "That's why those gals is missing fingers an' they's hair's short. Then a snowstorm hit us comin' over the pass. All the ponies died. Lucky ta make it back."

Rose sucked air deep within lungs and held it. Then he let it out with a long sigh. He looked sharply at Will and Sublette. "An' ta think ah was gonna get ye boys inta the Crazy Dogs. Sometimes ah git some queersome notions."

"What's the Crazy Dogs?" Will asked nervously.

"It's a club. Word for club's 'a lodge with driftwood.' Band's divided into a dozen heaps of driftwood. Each's got its own particulars of dress an' speech an' magic bundles. They's Lumpwoods an' Foxes an' Muddy Mouths an' Little Dogs an' Ravens an' such. I'm a Crazy Dog." He grabbed a short stick covered with deerskin. There was a rattle of hoofs at one end. He shook it and the hoofs clattered hollowly. "Crazy Dogs is supposed ta walk right up ta the enemy an' count coup or drag off brothers that's fallen an' such."

He pointed to a bear skin belt hanging from a lodgepole. "In battle, ye pin that belt in the ground an' don't budge an' inch and fight like hell till some son of a bitch's done ripped yer scalp or 'nother Crazy Dog unpins ye. That's what ah done when ah kilt those three Shoshone. Nettle Fish was kilt tryin' ta unpin me." Rose stared into the fire. "He was a good man," he added quietly. "I'm a great warrior 'mong the Crow!" Rose said loudly, pushing away his sorrow. "That's how ah got my wimmen. Hell, the greater the warrior the more wimmen ye kin git. Wimmen flock round a great warrior or horse thief and they's husbands don't mind 'cause the wives gain power from the warrior's seed and then pass it on ta the husbands. Why a great warrior'll have two or three different wimmen nightly and a few more 'cross the day if it take his fancy."

Rose chuckled at his memories. "Crow's is mighty generous. Boys in the same club'll jus' pass they's wives around like they was sharing a pipe. Ifin a man had a woman once he kin have 'er any time he pleased. An' when a man buys the oldest girl fer a wife, he gits first dibs on her sisters when they come of age. 'Nother fine custom the Crow has is 'bi'arusace' where at night the boys'll creep up to the tent of their sweethearts an' lift the cover an' reach in an' try to touch coup on the girl's privates. Or some boys'll steal a man's wife an' use 'er as they please till they tire a' 'er. Passing a gal on the prairie's how they call it. An' it's a sign a' character fer the cuckold ta act indifferent the whole time, even when they drag 'er outta his lodge afore his nose. Course the husband'd never touch the woman again after that. Leave 'er belongings outside the lodge and dust his hands a' 'er."

Rose smiled. "Fact is though, some these boys'll git a little jealous. Seen one cut off his wife's ear an' 'nother shove his woman's face inta dog shit an' make 'er eat it." He chuckled again. "Yup, at times those boys kin be touchy 'bout they's wimmen."

"Do the women ever get jealous?" Will asked.

"Welp, sometimes a man's wives'll fight over who gits ta comb his hair or carry his war shield but ginerally they don't mind a man takin' other wimmen. Shows he's a strong man and warrior," Rose winked.

"Watch this," he whispered.

As Sky Wanderer rose to close the smokehole flap Rose leapt up behind her and pulled up her dress. She squealed, struggled then grabbed Rose hard by his crotch. He gasped and they both broke free. They looked at each other and laughed loudly. Rose dropped back down and explained, "Gals're jus' toys to play with."

"Anybody ever steal your wife?" Will asked.

Rose's face hardened. "Thar'd be hell ta pay." Then he shrugged. "Course I wouldn't mind much ifin ah'd 'ad 'er fer a while. The Crow sez that sooner or later living with one woman's like living with a dead thing, like feedin' off one buffalo when they's more ta hunt all 'round. Ain't hard ta rid yerself of a dead woman. Jus' call 'er lazy or cranky an' cast 'er out. 'I married you, I'm through, go yer way!' is all the man has ta say." He gazed fondly at Stone Otter. "Be a while fore ah sez that ta my women. That little gal sure knows how ta love."

Suddenly Rose noticed Will and Sublette staring at him across the fire. He scowled back. "Ye boys're gonna hafta change yer ways ifin ye wanna ride with the Crow!"

Flames flickered between two lines of men. Rose and two of his Crazy Dog brothers were on one side; Will, Sublette, and Fitzpatrick on the other. Behind Rose, another Crazy Dog beat a drum and sang. A trap lay on a blanket beside the fire. The teepee wall began to glow.

Will rubbed the stubble on his chin.

"Sun's above the valley," he mumbled.

"Jus' one more round 'n it'll be all over, Yates," Rose gloated. "Then ye boys kin git some shut eye." He pinched an elk tooth between his fingers and held it high. "Ain't feelin' lucky this time. Wash it fer me, will ye, Yates?"

"I'll wash it for my own luck," Will replied testily. He grabbed the tooth and angrily rubbed it between his palms. "Damn it, Rose, you've near cleaned me out." He jabbed a finger at the trap. "That's all I've got left."

"Least ye've got something, Will," Fitzpatrick said glumly.

"Come on, Yates," Sublette urged, "this is the only chance we got left ta recover our fortunes. Hex that bone fer the Crazy Dogs."

Will's cheeks reddened. "You were the one who swore you could beat 'em at their own game, Sublette. And now we've near lost everything we worked for all these months, everything we own." His voice hardened. "I don't know why the hell I let you talk me into this." Will and Sublette glared at each other.

"Well, git ready ta lose the rest," Rose replied haughtily as he snatched back the tooth. "Ready?"

"No! I'm out. The hell with all of you!" Will grabbed his trap and started to rise.

"Hold on, Yates!" Sublette shouted and yanked him down. "Stakes is mine much as yours. We done shook on it." The drumming and singing stopped. Will brandished the trap.

"Back off, Sublette. This is all your doing."

A knife flashed, its point an inch from Will's throat. "Sublette's right, Yates," Rose sneered. "Now let go that trap." Will stared hatefully into Rose's eyes.

"Tell ye lads what," Fitzpatrick blurted. "Rose, why not let Will work off his debt. I reckon he owes us each a trap if he backs out now. That's a lotta pelts and it'll take awhile. But that way we're all better off."

"Now hold on, Fitz!" Will exclaimed.

"Nothin' till Yates drops it," Rose warned. He moved the knife a half-inch closer.

"You…" bastard, Will wanted to shout. He struggled to calm himself. "So let's talk," he said and dropped the trap.

Rose smiled and slowly withdrew his knife. "Gotta parlez with my brethren." He and the Crows laughed and gestured as they spoke. They concluded their parlez with emphatic "Hahs!" Rose warned. "You know the rules, Yates. Once a bet's on the table it don't leave till it's won."

"Then play, damn it," Will ordered. He glanced at Sublette and Fitzpatrick who nodded back.

The drumming and singing began. Rose displayed the tooth. Quickly he seemed to hand it onto to the Crazy Dog next to him who passed it on. Will and the others tried to follow the tooth's path as it was passed back and forth. But they never so much as glimpsed the tooth after Rose first passed it, if he even did that. The drumming and singing stopped abruptly. Rose and his brothers sat motionless and grinned at their rivals who glared back.

"Prairie Winds got it," asserted Sublette, pointing to the middle man. "Yup," he chuckled, "I'd bet Yates's last trap that's where it is." He gave Will a playful shove.

"May be the truth, Bill," Fitzpatrick said, "Coulda sworn I caught a peek of it with the last drum beat. Will? Whadya think lad? It's yer call."

Will stared into Rose's eyes and slowly reached toward his tightly knotted right fist.

"Been there from the start," he said softly.

Rose uncurled his hand, revealing the tooth. "Yer lucky day, Yates," he said scornfully. He grabbed a trap from the pile behind him and tossed it before Will.

"Now I'm out," Will said as he snatched the trap then dropped it heavily in Sublette's lap. He put his own trap over near his rifle and pouch, wrapped a robe tightly around himself, and headed toward the flap.

"Good luck," he called to his companions. He hurriedly pushed outside and butted heads with someone entering. Sky Wanderer yelped and tumbled into the snow, scattering a robeful of branches. Following closely behind, Stone Otter and Raven Speaks giggled.

"I'm sorry," Will said as he bent down to help up Sky Wanderer and brush snow off her. Rubbing her head, she rose unsteadily to her feet.

Rose poked his head out of the flap. "Yates, ye sure have a way with wimmen," he said as he laughed again. "By the way, jus' how'd ye know ah palmed it?"

Will shrugged. "Guessed." He resisted the temptation to explain that he knew Rose's obsession to win would lead him to hold the tooth.

"Well, now, Yates," he said, placing his hand on his chest. "Out of ma black heart's goodness, seeing ye beat me fair and square in the last round, and you finally washed and shaved as I requested, ah grant ye Sky Wanderer for tonight and as many as nights as ye desire." He spoke rapidly to Sky Wanderer then disappeared in the teepee. Sky Wanderer looked up from the wood she was gathering back into her robe. She smiled sweetly at him while the other women giggled.

Will sighed, then laughed heartily as he crunched through the snow around her and headed toward the river.

Beneath heavy buffalo robes, Will pressed as much of his flesh as possible into Sky Wanderer as they heaved silently at each other. He felt like he was swimming in air and time. Finally, she arched her back and began to shudder. He thrust harder and lost control. She squeezed him tightly, moaned, then slowly relaxed. Breathing hard, they lay tangled in each other. He savored her musky scent and the tingles pulsing through his body. If only Judy was like this, he thought sadly. A wind gusted around the teepee then twirled away. He pulled the robes more tightly around them. Soon be a year since I left her. He recalled her continuously rocking before the fire or rubbing her hands. An image flashed of himself and Judy lying stiffly in bed at her folk's farm. I can't go back to that!

Rose began to snore loudly then sputtered into silence as Stone Otter jabbed an elbow into him. Sky Wanderer giggled softly. Will gently pulled free and lay beside her. He longed to see Sky Wanderer, tell her how wonderful she was. He slid a finger down her cheek and across her lips which stretched into a smile. He imagined them in their own lodge, with a roaring fire and dozens of robes. Nothing to do but couple and slumber the winter away. And in the spring? His smile faded. Rose is staying. But I'm not. I don't love this girl. No choice but to head on with Smith.

Little Antelope appeared before him, holding a cradleboard and smiling slyly. He stiffened as he imagined her in his arms now. No woman had gripped him with so much desire since Sharon. He watched himself riding into her camp with a dozen ponies he had stolen from— the Crow! He almost laughed aloud. Now that's justice! Yellow Wolf would smile with delight and embrace him. My son, he would declare, and then present Little Antelope to him. What would she be like beneath the robes? Passionate? Definitely a virgin, unlike Sky Wanderer.

Suddenly an image seized him of Sky Wanderer heavy with child. He pulled slightly away from her. She'd promised him it wasn't her time, but could he trust her? All these girls want white babies. Panic struck him. The party would soon be heading over the pass. I may never know if I got her pregnant! What'll happen to my baby! He imagined Rose raising it. Oh, God!

Sky Wanderer pulled his face to hers and sucked his lips. He kissed her mechanically and then more passionately. What am I worried about, he reasoned as he pulled his fingers through her shoulder-length hair. Chances are I won't leave her with child anyway. She reached beneath his legs and gently stroked him. Too late now anyway. Why not? Suddenly, the stub of her little finger scraped his head, sparking a chill through him. He shriveled in her hand.

They packed up and left a week later, trudging west up the steep slopes through drifts that soon reached high as a man's waist, then higher. They took turns stomping a path through the snow, crawling forward no more than a mile daily. There was neither game nor forage. The ponies died one by one as the snowpack and cold deepened. The men grew emaciated and mutinous. Smith finally acceded to a vote, and he was the only man who voted against going back.

Days later they stumbled into the Crow camp, and spent several days gorging themselves on buffalo and elk and hovering over the campfires. Long Hair sculpted a map of sand mountains and valleys on a robe and traced a route for them where the snows were rarely more than ankle deep. Once again the whole Crow village gathered to weep and bid them farewell as the trappers mounted their ponies and rode off down the valley. To the relief of all in Smith's party, Slade and Greeley were among five who decided to stay with the Crow. "I'll be out there stalkin' ye, Yates," Slade hollered as Will kicked his pony into a canter. "An' someday I'll catch up, when ye least 'spect it!"

It took nearly a week of hard riding before they skirted the eastern end of the Wind River Mountains and headed south then west across a wide, wind-swept plain. There were no buffalo, the creek beds were dry, and the gales blew away their sage fires. They retreated up the Sweetwater River canyon and camped for weeks in an aspen grove, feasting off an occasional mountain goat or mule deer. Rested and fattened, they were just about to ride west when a snowstorm trapped them for days and killed half their horses. Once the sky cleared, they cached most of their goods and tramped off across the plain toward the western horizon. A few days later they crossed a low ridge and cheered when someone remarked that the gullies all ran toward the Pacific.

They cheered again a week later when they reached the Green River. Smith split the party in two, taking Will, Sublette, and four other men with him south and sending Fitzpatrick, Clyman, and the other two men north.

Smith and his men trapped their way down the Green and then up Black's Fork to the Uinta mountain range where they spent the spring. The beaver seemed as thick as the wildflowers which blazed everywhere. By the time the beaver began shedding their winter coats, the men had trapped a pack or more each. In early June, they hiked east toward their Sweetwater cache for a planned rendezvous with Fitzpatrick's party. When they arrived, Fitzpatrick and his men were drying the powder and goods they had just raised from the cache. Smith gathered his men for council.

"Gentlemen," Smith raised his chin and cast his eyes at the men gathered around him. "I've decided to send Mr. Fitzpatrick and two other men with our fur by bullboat down the Sweetwater and Platte rivers to Fort Atkinson. Mr. Clyman has been gone a week in that direction and may never return. Those who follow may suffer the same fate." Smith rubbed the thick purple scars across his forehead. "Any direction can bear or postpone the inevitable. All life is a series of gambles tempered by skill, luck, and faith." The men stared stoically up at him. "I will lead the rest of us to trap and explore the Columbia River basin." The men murmured in surprise. Sublette whistled. "British country!" he exclaimed.

"Our country," Smith rejoined. "And at this very moment a rich country that is being stripped of its beaver by British interlopers. We will be the first Americans to rightfully enter those distant parts of United States Territory since the Astorians in 1813."

"Who's going back with Fitz, Captain?" Will asked meekly. He had dreaded this moment. Duty demanded he return to Judy.

"Are there any volunteers?" Two men shot up their hands. "Any others? Mr. Yates? You've mentioned a need to return to your sick wife. This is your opportunity."

Will grimaced. "I suppose," he said quietly.

Smith nodded and broke a twig into three pieces, two of which were even. He held them in his fist. "Gentlemen?"

Will and the other two each pulled a twig and raised it high. Will held the short twig. The two men clapped each other excitedly. "Homeward bound!" one shouted.

Smith smiled briefly. "I welcome your further companionship, Mr. Yates."

Will nodded and repeatedly wondered, I tried, didn't I?

Ten

1824–1825

They rode back across South Pass and down the Big Sandy to the Green then slowly trapped their way north. Where the Green began to hook eastward, they veered northwest and spent the waning summer and early fall wading streams across the rugged Yellowstone plateau to the Snake River. Beaver were never so abundant. The nights were cool and sometimes rainy. They had seen no other humans since they turned their backs on Fitzpatrick and his companions on the Sweetwater. Every night they took turns guarding their ponies but no one tried to steal them.

These were mountains of Will's dreams, the most magical he had wandered since he galloped out of the Rio Grande Valley three winters before. He basked in the dry heat and clear air, distant or towering jagged peaks, silent twisting canyons, endless forests, crystalline, rippling streams, herds of half-tame elk and buffalo, soaring hawks and eagles, howling wolves at night, glimpses of grizzlies or moose crashing off through brush, velvet ashes of old Indian campfires, otherworldly figures painted or scratched on boulders and canyon faces.

High, fluffy clouds drifted the azure sky. Aspen groves glowed amber on the canyon walls. Will carefully led his pony around boulders and fallen lodgepoles. The pony's hoofs clattered over loose rocks along the riverbank. He paused occasionally to inspect faded deer droppings and tracks. He had been hunting since early morning and the sun now hung low in the west. Game and beaver had thinned and Indian sign thickened the farther they descended the river from the mountains.

Where the canyon broadened onto the Snake River plains, Will tied his pony to some sage and scrambled atop a boulder to gaze at the vista. The distant Snake River slashed gray and green across the tawny plains. Far northwest a wall of snow-capped mountains scraped the eternal blue. A bitter longing surged through Will, a longing for something he did not understand. "Amazing Grace" sang in his mind and he felt like crying. He raised his face to the sun and soaked in its warmth. The rays melted him. He set his rifle aside, stretched out on the smooth rock face, and drifted away as a magpie chattered nearby...

A moccasined foot prodded him. Will jerked awake and stared up in horror at an Indian pointing a pistol down at his forehead. He was dressed in a dirty hunting shirt, his head was shaved into a long gray scalp lock, and deep wrinkles crisscrossed his face. A half-dozen other Indians grinned at Will over the boulder top. "Don't...don't shoot," Will pleaded.

The Indian laughed. "If I was rattler, I woulda bit ye." He uncocked his pistol and offered his hand. "Tivanitagon. Whites call me Old Pierre."

"Jesus," Will gasped. He trembled as he took the old man's hand, "You scared the hell out of me. I feared you was Blackfoot. Shoshone?"

His face contorted in anger. "No Shoshone! Iroquois."

"I'm sorry...Iroquois?" He frowned as he rose to his feet. "What're you doing out here?"

"Trapping," he said simply. "You Hudson Bay?"

"Well, I uh..."

Old Pierre's eyes widened. "American?"

"Uh, well, yes," he admitted nervously.

The Indian flung his arms around him and pulled him tight. "Very good! Very good! Where ye brothers?"

"Up the canyon a ways," Will said as he disengaged himself. "You ain't mad at us being out here?"

Old Pierre seemed puzzled. "Mad? I happy! Very happy! Ye join us 'gainst Shoshone. Very bad, very bad! Shoshone steal our horses and traps and we steal back and kill chief and run, but Shoshone follow and we kill more but they steal horses again. We no horses, little powder, balls. Must join Ross and his men many sleeps north. Shoshone between us. Ye alone, we alone, Shoshone kill us all. Together they afraid to fight. Take us yer chief."

Still trembling slightly, Will slowly climbed down the boulder and untied his pony. "We're heading that way. Maybe we can dodge 'em."

Old Pierre leapt down beside Will and ran his callused palm down the pony's neck. "Ye wanna sell horse? Give ye many beaver."

"Maybe," Will replied. "Let's see what Captain Smith says."

Shadows and chill air welled up from the valley as the sun dropped behind the mountains. Smith, his men, and the Iroquois strode through a long meadow toward distant campfires where men rose and held their rifles ready. A Union Jack hung limply from a lodgepole. A large, stocky man with a ruddy face and wavy auburn hair strolled out from the camp and stared at them suspiciously.

Old Pierre nudged Smith and pointed. "Ross."

Smith extended his hand and Ross grasped it. "Mr. Ross, I'm Captain Jedediah Smith of the Ashley-Henry Fur Company."

"Captain Smith," Ross stated warily. "What brings you to the Salmon River Valley?"

"Beaver."

"Well, of course," Ross replied. "Why else would you be here? If we are to compete, we may as well compete amicably. Your men are welcome to spread their blankets in our camp."

Smith nodded. "Thank you, Mr. Ross." He turned to his six followers. "Gentlemen, you can set up here."

Ross bore his eyes into the Iroquois. "And speaking of beaver, Old Pierre, how many packs have you taken?"

Old Pierre looked embarrassed. "Shoshone very bad. Many. They take horses. We kill three." He brandished a scalp and grinned. "Chief's scalp," he said proudly.

"Old Pierre," Ross said wearily. "Before you stalked angrily away in mid-summer, I warned you not to cause trouble with the tribes, particularly the Shoshone."

"They steal me!" Old Pierre replied heatedly. "I no steal them!"

Ross held up a hand.

"All right, fair enough. Now where are your pelts?"

"We very poor. Dangerous. Very dangerous. No powder. Captain Smith our brother. Protect, trade us." The Iroquois patted his pony. "Forty pelts for horse." He pulled a spyglass from a parfleche. "Thirty-five. See enemy far away! Very good! Very good! Powder, balls, pistol for my men—thirty."

Ross's eyes narrowed. "Have you and your men any pelts left?" he said, trying to check the frustration in his voice. Old Pierre shook his head no.

"We trap more before waters freeze."

"Mr. Smith, may I ask how many furs your men have taken?"

"Over nine hundred in a cache well behind us."

"Including what you've taken, er, traded from this simple man?"

"Yes."

"Nine hundred," Ross said thoughtfully, then beamed. "May we buy them from you?"

"At what price, Mr. Ross?"

"Standard Hudson Bay price. Fifty pounds sterling for one hundred pounds beaver." Smith smiled.

"That makes seventy-five cents a pound, Mr. Ross. We can get as much as six dollars in St. Louis."

Ross laughed. "St. Louis? Why, that's fifteen hundred miles away. Surely it would make much more sense to sell out to us and re-equip your party."

"The American mountain price for beaver is three dollars a pound. Perhaps your men would like to sell to me."

The words hit Ross hard. "No, that's impossible!" he sputtered. "These men are honor- and contract-bound to sell all of their catch to the Hudson Bay Company. What Old Pierre did was illegal." He glared at the Iroquois who looked away. "These eastern Indians are more trouble than they're worth." Ross sighed heavily. "Captain Smith, I implore you. I sense you are a man of high character and intelligence, and can be trusted fully. Please do not repeat your offer before my men. It could cause the most severe disruption."

Smith nodded. "We have many important matters to discuss, Mr. Ross. My men and I will need a winter camp. May we accompany you to yours?"

"Well, I...don't know," Ross replied hastily. "Flathead Post's far north and the snows are deep and..."

"I'm sure my men will be happy to partake of British hospitality.

And, after all, your camp is undoubtedly well within American territory."

"As you surely know, Captain Smith, the boundaries in this part of the world are a matter of dispute. According to the 1818 treaty, Great Britain and America are both entitled to exploit the Columbia Basin."

Smith nodded. "As I see it, Mr. Ross, our only alternative would be to make a generous offer for your men's fur and services," he paused and then emphasized, "and allow them the liberty to choose. Liberty, Mr. Ross, as you surely know, is very dear to Americans."

Ross grimaced, then extended his hand. "Captain Smith, you drive a hard bargain. Let us dismiss the idea of engaging in a bidding war with my men over fur prices and you are welcome to join us for the winter."

Smith took his hand. "I'm sure it will be an eventful winter."

It took six weeks to trap their way down the Salmon and over the Bitteroot Mountains into the long, winding valleys that led to Flathead Post on Clark's Fork. A party of Nez Percé joined them, and their march and camps roiled with the noise of children squeals and women gossip. Blackfeet shadowed them for weeks and one night rode off with a dozen of Ross's horses.

Will joined Smith, Ross, and a score of other volunteers who rode hard after the Blackfeet and finally tracked them to a tiny meadow late the following day. There were only five Blackfeet, all exhausted and huddled around a small campfire while the horses grazed nearby. The trappers silently slipped through the spruce around the meadow. At a signal from Ross, they sprang up and trained their rifles on the Blackfeet while one of the men called out in their tongue that, if they surrendered, they would not be harmed. The Blackfeet dropped their bows and trade guns and glared fiercely as the trappers cautiously approached.

Heart pounding, Will stared curiously at the Blackfeet. They were large and muscular and their sweaty faces were smeared with vermilion. He had heard endless tales of the Blackfeet's stealth and brutality from the time Lewis and Clark returned almost twenty years before. The Blackfeet made life hell for every trapping party that had ventured into their country, and had murdered and mutilated nearly a hundred trappers over the years. He wondered how many scalps these warriors had ripped, and what emotions now surged through them—regret, hatred, fear? Unarmed, Ross walked up and solemnly shook hands with each, and then questioned them through his interpreter.

"Let's sink our hatchets into their thieving skulls!" someone called out and others echoed the cry.

Ross held up a hand to quiet them. "Gentlemen," he said firmly, "think! We gain nothing by killing them, and much by releasing them to tell their people of our magnanimity. The Blackfeet annually fetch hundreds of beaver packs to our posts. If word of a heedless killing of their brethren reached their villages, we would not only lose that trade, but we would be most fortunate to escape with our lives."

The mumbling stopped. As the Blackfeet gaped, the men rounded up the horses and disappeared into the forest.

Ross seemed to half-smile the last week of trudging to Flathead Post. True, Old Pierre's incompetence and Smith's Yankee shrewdness meant they had lost a pack of beaver and allowed a rival into their camp. But his men had trapped nearly fifty packs of beaver over the year, and to top it off, Ross had recovered the horses without bloodshed. Sir George Simpson, who directed the Hudson Bay Company's vast operations from Fort Vancouver on the Columbia, would undoubtedly be greatly pleased as soon as Ross's full report and huge catch reached him. Ross prided himself on his verbose prose.

A promotion was inevitable. Ross was mentally composing his report as they rode the switchbacks down beside Thompson Falls. Just below, in a tight group along the river, were the dozen cabins of Flathead Post, and in the broad valley beyond over a hundred teepees and wood shelters and thousands of horses. Whooping and firing guns, a melange of trappers and hundreds of Flathead, Pend d'Oreilles, Kutanai, Nez Percé, and Spokane surged out to welcome the returning party. Someone touched off the brass three-pounder pointing down the valley. BOOM!!! Grinning broadly, a short, swarthy bear of a man pushed out from the crowd. He carried a brown envelope in his hand. Will and Smith, riding beside Ross, heard him mutter, "Ogden, that murderous blackguard."

"Alexander, old friend," Ogden shouted. His eyes swept the several hundred heavily laden horses strung out across the meadow. "Looks like you've made quite a haul!"

"A fair year's work, Skene," replied Ross, trying to sound modest. "To what do we owe this visit from distant Spokane House?" Ross said as he dismounted and they shook hands. "Oh, forgive my manners," he said, gesturing. "These gentlemen are Mr. Smith and Mr. Yates of the Ashley-Henry Fur Company. Four more of their men are farther back."

Ogden's smile faded. He shook with them. "Work for idle hands, my friend," Ogden said heartily as he handed Ross the envelope.

"That's what brings me."

Ross nervously tore open the envelope. "What!" he exclaimed. "You're to replace me!"

"That's right, Alex. I'll be leading out the next Snake River brigade in little more than a month. Seems Governor Simpson believes you need a rest."

"Rest! My devotion to the Hudson Bay Company is tireless and constant. Surely…"

Ogden threw an arm around Ross. "Alex, let the business drop for now. Time to celebrate! I've a small keg in my, er…your cabin tapped and just waiting for two old friends to swap war stories. You lads," he nodded to Smith and Will, "are welcome to join us."

"It'd be a pleasure, Mr. Ogden," Smith replied, tenderly stroking one of the thick white scars on his face. "And congratulations on your promotion. Mr. Ross has proven to be a fine gentleman and host. I am certain I can expect no less from you." Ogden carefully eyed Smith.

"Well, my American friend, we'll just see about that."

With each gust of wind, clouds of fine snow and chill shot through the log hut's chinks, but the dozen men crowded in a circle did not notice. All eyes were on the chessboard illuminated by two tallow candles. Hands pressed lightly at his temples, Ross stared down at the board. A smile crept over his face. He picked up his queen and set it down loudly before Sublette's king, then locked his eyes into his opponent's.

"Checkmate!" he exclaimed triumphantly.

Sublette frowned, then tried to smile away the defeat. "That didn't last long."

"Certainly not. You know little of the game. Now then, I believe you owe me five pelts."

"Yourn tomorrow. I wanna watch ye skin the next victim."

"I'm so sorry, Captain Smith has yet to return from his scout with Ogden to Flathead Lake. Now there's a worthy rival." Ross glanced around the spectators. "Do any of you other rubes play chess?" he inquired.

"Some," Will replied quietly. He recalled the long nights over a board with Jameson.

"Mr. Yates. You surprise me. And here I thought you were merely Mr. Smith's largely quiet and faithful companion. So different from your boisterous friend Mr. Sublette. Any good?"

Will shrugged. "I know how the pieces move."

"Well, enough to stake some furs?"

Will hesitated. Ross played as well as Jameson, maybe better. The old lawyer beat me two games of three, and also held his liquor better, he reasoned. But Jameson usually only began winning after their third or fourth glass of brandy. I'll play clearheaded tonight, he promised himself. "How much were you figuring?"

"A pack?"

"I lost more than that at hand with the Crow," he said, chuckling.

"Hand is a game of luck. Chess one of intelligence and skill. Are your brains as poor as your luck?"

"I wonder sometimes," Will said, smiling.

"Why not venture half a pack?" Ross sniffed. "Should you lose it, you or your comrades will undoubtedly discover some way to again fleece my Iroquois."

"Go ahead, Will," Sublette bellowed, then gulped again from a jug Ross had handed him before their game. "Whip his ass!"

Will grimaced. "Bill, it was listening to you that got me near wiped out last time." Sublette laughed. "I'll take your wager, Mr. Ross."

"Well, gentlemen," Ross announced to his men silently watching, "you are about to witness yet another British victory." Most of the men chuckled but a few smiled. Ross snatched up two pawns, held them briefly behind his back, then extended his fists. Will pointed to his right hand. Ross uncurled it. "Black," he declared. "I've already the advantage."

Will had realized shortly after meeting Ross on the Salmon that a deep arrogance lay just below his courtesy. Ogden's humiliation of Ross had stripped away his benevolent surface and the arrogance had been oozing out every since. He was determined to humble him. "You had the advantage at New Orleans, Mr. Ross, and played it poorly," he stated quietly. Some of the Hudson Bay men mumbled angrily.

Ross reared back. "What! How dare you bring that up? Such insolence. We'd have destroyed you American upstarts if you hadn't cowered behind your trenches. And what would you know of the affair anyway? I suppose you were there."

"I was not much more than a boy then," Will replied pensively. "And I've seen a good deal of the world since." He paused, then looked Ross in the eye.

"Few Americans like the British, Mr. Ross. They're considered arrogant, rude, possessive." The trappers muttered curses and threats. Ross's eyes widened and his lips pursed. Sublette squirmed nervously. He opened his mouth to caution Will then held his tongue. "I was reared on those hatreds, and shared them myself when the British army encamped before New Orleans." He glanced around at the trappers and said with compassion, "But when I watched those brave British soldiers march across that soggy field and die for no purpose, I felt nothing but sorrow and pity for them." The Hudson Bay men and Sublette relaxed slightly.

"Those men died for king, country, and honor," Ross stated proudly.

"It's not the British people that rile me, Mr. Ross," he nodded to the trappers. "Most of those few I've met are good and honest men." He paused for effect. "It's the British tyrants I despise. The lords and generals and merchants who plunder what little wealth the people scrape from the earth then press them into uniform and send them to be slaughtered like pigs at the earth's far ends. People like yourself, Mr. Ross." Some of the men grinned and poked each other.

"What!" Ross exclaimed. "You popinjay!"

"What'd you call me?" Will demanded merrily.

"You heard me," Ross pointed to the board. "Enough now of your prattle. Set up your side and prepare to be destroyed." Will complied. Ross pushed his king's pawn two squares forward. Will followed by pushing his queen's pawn to the center.

"A standard and unimaginative opening," Ross stated dryly as he moved a knight to cover his threatened pawn. "Forgive my earlier harsh words," he said as he snatched the jug from Sublette. "To honorable men everywhere." He tipped the jug briefly to his lips then handed it to Will who shook his head no. Ross sneered. "As you wish. Your move." Will pushed his queen's pawn across to Ross's side of the board. Ross frowned. "Aggressive, aren't we?" He blocked it with a pawn. Will pushed his knight's pawn forward, forming a half-diamond of three pawns. Ross tisked. "I've rarely seen such reckless play."

"Reckless?" Will asked quietly. "I'm about to capture the center." Ross frowned and studied the board a long time before he moved a pawn. Will pushed a bishop to complete the diamond. "Mr. Ross," he announced, "the center is mine."

Ross glared back. "We'll see who gloats in the end."

Will smiled and said nothing. He played his standard game, pushing out his other pieces so that they all supported each other and freed his king to castle at either side. Meanwhile Ross tried to develop an attack but cursed and sputtered as he continually found himself hemmed in. They traded pieces with neither taking the advantage or making a mistake.

"Trying to refight the battle of New Orleans?" Ross demanded huffily. "Or is it Bunker Hill? You hope for me to destroy myself against your defense which I've never before seen. You play unconventionally. Once I understand your stratagem, I will destroy you."

"My strategy is inspired by that of one of your countrymen."

"Oh, and who is that?"

"The Duke of Wellington."

Ross reddened. The men burst out laughing. "Ah hope it ain't yer Waterloo, Captain," one of them shouted.

"We're a long way from Flanders' fields," Ross replied dryly and moved a castle. "I'll send this young pup packing before long."

"Be hard to do without your queen," Will said quietly as he forked the white king and queen with his knight. "Check."

"What!" Ross grunted in disgust. "Balls!"

Will could not help smiling. "Your move, Mr. Ross."

"You...you distracted me with your prattle! It's not sporting!"

"Not sporting? Perhaps you had in mind the wages you pay your men."

"You've got that right, lad," someone muttered, then lowered his head as Ross glared angrily at him. His composure shot, Ross's mistakes multiplied and Will picked off his pieces one by one until only the king remained.

"Mate in one move, Mr. Ross," Will stated coolly.

Ross pushed bitterly away from the table. "I'll have my revenge one way or another, Yates. You just wait."

Will sighed. "I expected as much, Mr. Ross. But you'll have to go to the end of the line. No matter how far I wander, I can't seem to shake people like you."

They departed in late December, the day after a snowfall, and the hoofs of their heavily laden ponies crunched loudly as they slowly retraced their way up the Clark's Fork and Bitteroot Valleys. Though it seemed madness to try crossing the Rockies in mid-winter, Ogden had resolved to be in the Snake River Valley when the streams unfroze and the beaver re-emerged with their fur thick and silky, and damned anything that blocked his way.

Troubles and mishaps plagued the brigade. In the Big Hole Valley, Blackfeet ran off a couple dozen horses and the pursuit never caught up with them. On the Lemhi Pass, a squaw "accidentally" murdered her Iroquois husband when he yanked toward him a rifle whose trigger she had hooked with her finger. Horses began to drop dead from the high snows and sparse forage. Worst of all, snows bound them twenty days in the Salmon River Valley. For subsistence, they wiped out the valley's small buffalo herd. They trapped beaver by digging down into the snow until they reached the dens in the frozen ponds then chopped through with their hatchets and bashed in the heads of the frenzied animals.

But they mostly cowered in crude log shelters, buried under huge snow drifts and pummeled by below-zero temperatures. Their faces and bodies grew emaciated. They became stir-crazy and brittle. Fights broke out over trifles. Some called for retreating to Flathead Post or despaired of surviving until spring.

Normally dispensing an endless series of pranks and ribald jokes, Ogden got edgy, mean. He huddled for days at a time with his Nez Percé wife in their small teepee, sending her out to gather wood and dung for their fire, and hollering orders and curses out the flap to his men.

One day Will tramped through the icy paths with Smith and Sublette to Ogden's. "What do you want?" Ogden demanded when they appeared at his teepee.

"A word if you please, Mr. Ogden," Smith replied.

"To bid me farewell, Smith? You've just about outworn your welcome."

"That may well be, Mr. Ogden. But I'd hoped that when we leave we do so on good terms."

Ogden waved them in and barked in Nez Percé to his wife. She quickly ladled out buffalo stew into wooden bowls from a kettle over the fire, and handed one to each man. "I don't know whether to try the pass or not," he declared bitterly. "We'll end up losing most of our horses, but I've got to get to the Snake River for spring trapping. But without horses, we'll never get our packs to market." He scowled for a moment and then hoarsely shouted, "Goddamn it!"

"We face the same dilemma, Mr. Ogden."

Ignoring Smith's comment, Ogden sneered. "That bastard Ross may end up trapping more packs than me, despite the fact that Simpson thought him nothing more than an empty-headed windbag. Simpson read me some of Ross's reports." He hooted. "Son of a bitch fancied himself the Shakespeare of the Rockies."

Ogden squinted at the Americans as if noticing them for the first time. "That bastard Ross brought back fifty packs and the local tribes traded another eleven at the winter fair. But once I get out of this valley we'll take even more than Ross. I've a small army," he boasted, "the largest Hudson Bay brigade ever, eleven engagés, forty-six free trappers, over 250 horses and 350 traps. Hell, with thirty squaws and as many children, we're a traveling village. Once over the pass, we'll trap ever' last beaver from the Snake Valley and every stream that feeds it. That'll keep you Americans away from the Oregon Territory," Ogden said haughtily. "You lads may as well enjoy the Snake River country now, 'cause my instructions are to keep trapping it till there's nothing left. 'Make a fur desert of it,' Simpson ordered me, and that I'll do." He laughed harshly.

"Fur desert!" Will exclaimed and glared at Ogden.

"That's right, Yates. First come first served. And what're you gonna do 'bout it?"

Will's hands tightened into fists.

"You've no right, you bas..."

"Mr. Yates," Smith warned sharply as he squeezed his shoulder. "My men and I will be more than happy to leave for more hospitable climes, Mr. Ogden," Smith stated calmly, "but we'll need some supplies—powder, lead, tobacco, and a half-dozen horses."

Ogden squinted at Will.

"What'd ye start ta call me, Yates?" Will glared back.

"Forgive Mr. Yates," he shot Will an irritated glance. "We're all feeling tense. Now, then, Mr. Ogden, about those supplies."

"You and your men, Smith, are an arrow in my ass. Don't want you with me. Don't want you head of me. Don't know what ta do." Ogden cocked his head back. "I'd like ta drop you off the end of the earth."

"The sooner we're provisioned the sooner we'll disappear."

Ogden bit his lip angrily. "All right, goddamn it! Mountain prices. Ours, not yours, Smith. Take it or leave it."

"Very well."

"Now that you've scraped your bowls clean, get out. My clerk Kittson'll make the trade." The Americans rose to leave. "Oh, and Yates?" Ogden asked with mock politeness. Will turned. "Anytime ye wanna lock horns, just let me know."

Will began trembling with fear and anger. "America'll take this land all the way to the Pacific," he blurted, "by war if necessary."

Ogden sneered. "If that ever happens, Yates, you'll inhabit a desert."

"Someday our positions will be reversed," Will's voice quavered. "So, Ogden, you best mind your manners."

Ogden leapt to his feet and charged. Will threw up his fists. Smith and Sublette jumped forward and shoved Ogden back. "Enough!" Smith ordered. "This is no way for either of you to behave. Mr. Yates, out!" Will quickly slipped out the flap and stood shivering outside.

Ogden struggled to transform his scowl into a smile, but fury blazed from his eyes. "You bes' keep that pup of yourn on a short leash, Smith," he warned. "Or I'll kill 'im."

Smith pushed out of the teepee and stalked away. Sublette followed, whispering as he slipped past. "Ye nearly sparked a powder keg in there, Will. Gotta guard where ye play with fire," Will trailed behind them.

When they were out of earshot of Ogden's teepee, Smith turned. "Mr. Yates, I'm very disappointed in you." Will glanced away. "I look to you for leadership, not the sort of hotheadedness you displayed before Ogden. You jeopardized our very survival. What if Ogden refused to sell? Simply exiled us from his camp? What then would have been our fate?" Smith strode away. Sublette briefly laid a hand on Will's shoulder, started to say something, then quickly walked after Smith. Will dully watched them disappear.

It took nearly a week to struggle over the pass and down into the Snake River Valley. Two dozen feet of snow lay on the saddle. Day after day, panting harshly in the thin air, breath steaming, they tramped the snow firm step by frozen step, cursed and pulled the ponies by their horsehair halters, dragged up inch by inch the packs of traps and gewgaws and forage.

The ponies slipped and stumbled up the trail, one after another collapsing, their shriveled bellies heaving. Some eventually lay still, and the men carved the flesh from their bones and wolfed it down raw and bloody. Occasionally they paused to scatter cottonwood bark before their ponies, and glance back at the receding valley. Suspiciously, they eyed each cloud front that threatened to engulf them, trembled as the flakes tumbled down and drifted higher all around. Their gaunt bodies reeked with sweat and smoke and excrement, their hair long and matted, faces charcoaled to reflect the glare, buckskins blackened and tattered. At night, silent with exhaustion, they crouched around a fire, slowly feeding fir boughs into its flames and chewing dried salmon.

Finally atop the saddle, nearly blinded by the sunlight they yelped triumphantly or wept and gazed across the jumble of icy peaks and distant valleys and deepest eternal blue sky. The snowpack lightened on the southern slopes, and they wallowed downward faster and more confidently. Sublette shot a mountain goat; they laughed and bandied lies as they roasted chunks of it on ramrod tips over a crackling fire. The ponies hoofed out snow to the trampled grass below. The forests thickened and the valley broadened. Streams trickled out from the ice. A woodpecker drummed amidst the damp ponderosa. They strode along paths trod by small herds of buffalo and elk, and feasted off the steaks at night. Each morning they dragged in their traps from the gushing streams and usually found a sleek beaver between the jaws.

The valley spread into the Snake River plains whose lava beds and stunted grass were patched with soggy snow and paintbrush and lupine. They trekked across to the Snake River and slowly trapped upstream. Only a dozen ponies had survived the snow drifts then razor sharp lava beds; their ribs slowly faded as they grazed the lush spring grasses. The April days were warm and nights rarely below freezing. The men's spirits turned boisterous and mocking.

One afternoon they stared resentfully as Ogden's caravan plodded across the plain toward them. Ogden galloped out to meet them. He jumped down from his horse and pumped Smith's hand. "Mr. Smith! Glad to see you boys are still sporting your topknots!"

Smith smiled faintly. "Is there any reason why we shouldn't be, Mr. Ogden?"

"Dozen of my boys on scout ran into a Blackfoot war party. Savages scattered into the trees, but they've been trailing us for the last few days, aiming to run off our horses and lift the hair of any stragglers."

"We've seen no fresh sign."

"You've been lucky."

"Your disposition seems considerably lifted from when we parted. I recall your wish to push us off the end of the earth."

With a grin, Ogden explained, "Oh, that. I was just funning ye. No hard feelings? Had things on me mind."

"Not at all. We were happy to tramp that trail over the pass for you."

"We were happy to let you do so, if not to allow ye to enjoy the first shot at the beaver this side."

"We'd certainly be happy to provide you with some pelts—in return for some powder and shot."

"Done." He stuck two fingers in his mouth and whistled to the caravan a hundred yards away. "Kittson! Send 'em downstream to that cottonwood grove and set up! And bring over some powder and shot! Here's trading!"

At sunrise next morning, a half-dozen of Ogden's party cantered past yelling taunts to the Americans lolling around a campfire. Sublette grunted. "British bastards're headed upstream trying ta squeeze us out!" Smith's men cursed bitterly, then wandered out to their traplines.

An hour later Will was tying a pelt onto a willow hoop when faint gunshots and hollering echoed from upstream. He grabbed his rifle and stared at the horizon. The Hudson Bay trappers and two riderless ponies galloped back down along the river. "Blackfeet!" a man yelled. "Run for it."

Sublette sprinted just behind them. A couple hundred yards away, screaming and shaking weapons, five Blackfeet charged on ponies.

"Come on, Bill!" Will shouted. He trembled as he lunged for his pony tethered nearby. The pony reared, yanking the lariat from his hands. "Goddamn it!" he wailed as the pony crashed off through the sage.

"Cover me, Will!" Sublette gasped as he tore through brush and leapt over cottonwood logs.

Will spun and trained his rifle at the charging Blackfeet. Sublette threw his rifle to his shoulder and fired. A pony dropped hard, throwing a warrior over its head. Sublette quickly began to reload.

"Don't fire till I'm ready!" he shouted. Will squinted down his sights at a barrel-chested Blackfoot brandishing a musket. The Blackfoot kicked his pony toward the thrown man who was struggling to his feet, and dragged him up behind him. "Shoot!" Sublette ordered. Will squeezed the trigger and his rifle boomed and belched smoke. When the smoke cleared another pony thrashed on the ground. Will frenziedly reloaded. The riderless men hopped up behind other warriors. The Blackfeet reined in their ponies and shouted at each other. Two warriors with muskets fired. The balls whizzed past. Sublette finished loading and leveled his rifle. Ker-boom! A Blackfoot lurched back and dropped his lance. The Indians yanked their ponies around and galloped away, two supporting the wounded man.

"Shit, that was close!" Sublette exclaimed.

Will nodded as he rammed the charge home. "Let's git!" Hoofs drummed the ground behind them. They twisted around and pointed their rifles. Ogden, Smith, and a dozen other trappers galloped toward them, leading three ponies.

"How many?" Ogden demanded as Will and Sublette mounted the offered ponies.

"Five."

"Kill any?"

Sublette grinned and pointed to the thrashing dying ponies. "Two horses."

"We've a man missing. Let's go."

The trappers kicked their ponies into a gallop. The Blackfeet had disappeared. Their pony tracks led upstream. "Bastards stole all our traps," a Hudson Bay man complained.

"Where was Benoit?" Ogden asked quietly.

"Up there near those two cottonwood," the man replied and spat tobacco juice. "Antoine always hankered to be the furthest," he added sadly.

They found Benoit's nude body between the two trees. A musket ball had smashed in his forehead, splattering brains. Blood seeped from a score of knife gouges across his body. He had been scalped and his penis and testicles hacked off and stuffed in his mouth.

"If we'd reached the Snake a day later," Ogden said malevolently, "that might've been one of your boys, Smith."

"We'd be happy to retake the lead," replied Smith. But his tone implied otherwise.

The two parties leapfrogged each other up the Snake to its junction with the Blackfoot River where the Americans raised their nine pack cache. Hoping to shake Ogden, Smith led his men south down the Blackfoot but the Hudson Bay men swarmed over the valley trying to trap every last beaver. Many times the Americans and Hudson Bay men squared off over a beaver pond or a jeer but someone with a cooler head always shoved them apart.

Smith had intended to struggle over the divide to the Bear River Valley but the pass was so steep and clogged with snow that they reluctantly turned back, still beset by Ogden's trappers. They reached the Pontneuf River and trapped their way up it and over the low pass to Bear Valley.

All along the American's luck held. Blackfeet ran off twenty of Ogden's horses on the Pontneuf. Occasionally a few trappers would gallop into camp, their ponies lathering and wheezing, just ahead of a Blackfeet war party. The Indians would wheel their ponies and disappear in sight of the camp. Many of Ogden's party neared a breaking point and grumbled about turning back. With Ogden's men scattered all around, Smith's remained secure though their beaver yield diminished.

On the Bear they stumbled upon signs that other whites had passed earlier that spring. Among the numerous pony hoof and moccasin tracks, there were enough boot and horseshoe tracks to make it a certainty. They fell in with the same Shoshone band that had robbed Old Pierre's party last autumn and traveled uneasily together for several days. The Shoshone incessantly carped for handouts, while the trappers guarded their horses and equipment from their nimble hands. One night the band packed up quietly and disappeared, taking two of Ogden's horses with them.

In late May, they met Étienne Provost's party of a score of free trappers, mostly American but with French, Mexicans, Utes, and even a Russian, who had come up from Taos. Smith's men whooped in joy as Provost passed on word that Ashley was on the Green River with a large party and had called for a rendezvous on Henry's Fork in July.

Among Provost's men were several Hudson Bay deserters. Tension rose when Ogden appeared and implored the deserters to make good on their debts. But they cursed him and sent him blustering back to the British camp. The two American parties lounged around a huge campfire. Provost had an American flag tied to a lodgepole. The cheer turned to anger as they recounted tales of British perfidy.

"Tell 'em what happened to you, Étienne," someone demanded.

Provost was a rarity in the mountains—someone with ample body fat. His body jiggled beneath his buckskins as he angrily shook his fists. "Was the British that stirred the Shoshone 'gainst us last fall," he boomed. "Murdered three of my men. I escaped by a hair's width." He wagged a finger. "Mark my words. British keep up their shenanigans and war'll break out. Just a matter a' time. Simple as that. Got nothing more to say." The men nodded or cursed then stared moodily into the flames.

A slow burn had crept through Will with each story. For months he, like the others, had struggled in the Hudson Bay Company's shadow, subject to constant taunts and extortions. Now was the chance for vengeance. He rose and stood quietly before them for a moment as he tried to briefly lock eyes with them all. "Talk's easy. We're free men," he said proudly. "We wander and trap where we will. But those British," he jabbed a thumb toward Ogden's camp, "would take away our livelihood and freedom itself. My friends and I have endured British insults and depredations since last fall. They are on American territory now. Ogden aims to turn our land into a 'fur desert.' We can't let him get away with it. We oughta…"

Johnson Gardner leapt up beside him. Tall and angular with curly chestnut hair, Gardner was known for his short fuse and hatred of bullies. "This man speaks the truth," he shouted. "Let's drive those British bastards back to Canada. Captain Provost predicted war between we Americans and the British. I say the time is now."

Smith stood and raised his hands. "Gentlemen, I implore you not to act hastily. A confrontation that spills blood could truly set off a war in which no one wins…"

Gardner cut him off. "Time's a-wastin'!" he hollered as he grabbed the American flag and marched off toward Ogden's camp. "Let's teach those English sons a bitches what happens when they try to steal our land and liberty!" The men broke into a loud cheer and, brandishing rifles, surged after him.

Smith grabbed Will as he joined their ranks.

"Mr. Yates, are you prepared to accept responsibility for any loss of life?"

Will strained against Smith's hand.

"I'm sorry, Captain. It's the British that've brought us to this." Smith released him.

"I'm very disappointed in you, Mr. Yates."

The words struck him hard and he turned his head in shame. "I'm sorry," he mumbled and ran off after the others.

As the Americans approached them, Ogden's men watched nervously and the women hurried the children away. Ogden slipped away to his lodge. "Break your chains!" the Americans shouted. "Join us! Ashley'll pay you fair wages!"

Old Pierre and his Iroquois and some of the French Canadians hurrahed joyfully and followed Gardner.

"Where's Ogden?" Gardner shouted. Old Pierre pointed to his teepee. "Come on, boys. Let's roust that bastard!" The men swarmed around his lodge while Gardner lifted the flap and shouted inside, "Ogden, you bullying, cowardly son of a bitch! Crawl outta that hole lika man!"

"Make way and I will!" boomed Ogden from within. Gardner stepped back and Ogden gingerly poked out his head. "What's all this infernal ruckus about?"

Gardner shook his fist in Ogden's face. "You're trespassing on American territory without a license to trade or trap. Your intentions to ruin our lands are well known. You're a criminal and remain at your peril. Get out now while you can!"

Ogden trembled and his face reddened. He stared up at Old Pierre, standing with arms folded beside Gardner. "Do you mean to betray me?" he demanded of the Iroquois.

"We long hate ta serve the British," Old Pierre replied. "Want to join Americans but till now no chance. Now we go. Nothing you speak can stop us!"

Gardner bent down and shouted into Ogden's face. "You've exploited these men long enough, treating them as slaves, selling them goods at high prices and giving them nothing for their skins and sacrifices." Ogden stared back defiantly.

Old Pierre called to his men. They stalked off to fetch their belongings to the American camp. The other men dispersed laughing and jeering. Will lingered to stare silently at Ogden.

"What more do you want, Yates?" Ogden snapped as he crawled out of the lodge and stood. "You and your countrymen have stripped me of most of my men and beaver and horses. There's little left."

"Do you recall me telling you to mind your manners because someday our positions would be reversed?"

"What of it?"

"And do you recall telling me that anytime I'd like to lock horns, you were ready, and if Smith didn't rein me in, you'd kill me? Young pup, you called me."

Ogden squinted. "Indeed I do."

Will took a deep breath.

"I'm ready to lock horns."

Ogden tightened his fists and glared up at Will. "Within the past three years I've killed two men with my bare hands, Yates, men far bigger and stronger than you. Men who figured they could whip me. They were wrong. You prepared to die? Or maybe I'll just rip out your eyes and that insolent tongue a' yourn."

Will nodded and tensed for the charge. He struggled to control his trembling.

Ogden snorted. "You're bluffing, Yates. You don't wanna die and you know bloody well that I won't rip you apart 'cause ifin I do your bullyboys'll charge in here and destroy me and my camp."

"We've a score to settle."

Ogden laughed and gestured toward the American camp. "I'd say the score's well in your favor." His face hardened. "But if you insist, then throw the first punch."

The fire slowly drained from Will. He imagined Ogden's huge hands pummeling and gouging. "This is crazy," he finally admitted. "I've behaved…" He extended his hand, but Ogden refused to take it.

"Just as I thought, Yates. You're yellow."

Will shook his head. "Maybe so. I'm not sure I know what I am. I was hotter than a hornet and ready to die fighting and now I'm not. If there's anything worth killing or dying for, this ain't it." Ogden frowned and crouched into his lodge. "Wait," Will cried. Ogden stared at him from the entrance. "So many've tried to hurt me or my loved ones over the years." Tears filled his eyes. "Calculating men. Mad men. Cold, arrogant men. My own father." His voice faltered. "Anger burns deep within me and nothing I do can drown it. I try to keep low and not let others trample me. But no matter how far I wander, there's no escape. Times I wanna fight back. I fantasize about torturing, even killing, my tormentors. I'm sorry. Please try to understand."

Ogden snickered and dropped the flap in Will's face.

Ogden rousted his party early the next morning and ordered them to round up their traps and horses and break camp. As they did so, Gardener, Will, and a score of other Americans and former Hudson Bay trappers stalked among them catcalling and exhorting others to defect. Toward noon, Ogden led the remnants of his party down the valley, but not before a half-dozen other trappers refused to accompany him. All told in just two days, over twenty-three trappers with their horses, squaws, equipment, and over seven hundred pelts joined the Americans.

For two leisurely weeks, the Smith-Provost brigade trekked up Bear River to the Unita Mountains and then east across its foothills to Henry's Fork. When they spotted the smoke of Ashley's campfires, the trappers joyfully fired their rifles skyward and kicked their laden ponies into a lumbering canter. Ashley's men gathered around, whooping and slapping backs.

The Smith-Provost brigade was the last to show. Parties had been trickling in the previous week until roughly one-hundred and twenty men, and a score of wives and children had gathered on Henry's Fork. Ashley had picked a fine spot for rendezvous. The waters flowed crystalline. Groves of willow and cottonwood supplied shelter and fuel. The ponies fattened in the lush meadows. A small buffalo herd trampled the valley while elk ranged the foothills. Ashley had refused to open his trade packs until the last party arrived so in the meantime the men spun yarns, wrestled, foot- and horse-raced, target shot, fished, gambled, swapped, bedded the looser squaws, hunted, and just lazed.

Trading began early the next morning. Eager trappers hauled over their packs and lined up before Ashley who sat on a stump counting and grading each man's pelts, and figuring the credit.

The sun burned down high overhead when Will dragged up his three bales of one hundred sixty-three beaver pelts, and a dozen otter. Ashley cut each bundle's bindings and began sorting the plews. Will stood by nervously. He had done well despite losing his autumn's hunt to Rose. But this was all he had to show for nearly two years in the mountains.

"Hundred twenty-three pounds of first-rate," Ashley announced. "At three dollars each, that's three hundred and sixty-nine dollars. And as for these forty-eight pounds of second-rate, at two dollars each that's ninety-six dollars." He paused for effect. "For a grand total, Mr. Yates, of…"

"Four hundred and seventeen dollars as I figure it," Will interrupted.

"Exactly so." Ashley dipped his quill in an ink-well and squabbled in his ledger. "If you'll sign here."

Will beamed and proudly scrawled his name. "Thank you, General." With mountain prices for gunpowder, lead, traps, blankets, calico, kettles, ribbons, bells, beads, brass earrings, awls, tobacco, and other supplies anywhere from fifty to four hundred percent higher than in St. Louis, he was determined to save as much of his credit as possible. He also resisted joining the hand, three-card monte, and other gambles that most of the trappers played incessantly, nor did he buy the charms of any of the Indian girls for the handful of trinkets they demanded. Will instead laughed away the afternoon with Clyman, Fitzpatrick, and other friends he had feared he would never see again.

Near sunset after all the trading was done, Ashley gathered in his teepee Smith, Clyman, Fitzpatrick, Sublette, Will and several other actual or promising trapping leaders.

"Gentlemen," he declared, "as you know, Mr. Henry retired from the business last year. I'm very pleased to announce that, in his place, I've formed a partnership with Captain Smith." The men congratulated the scarred, austere mountain man who nodded and allowed himself a faint smile.

"Each year I will convey a pack train to the mountains to a previously designated point where we will rendezvous as we have this summer for trade, and I will then carry back our furs to St. Louis. Captain Smith meanwhile will be in charge of dispatching our trapping and exploring parties to the far reaches of these Rocky Mountains and the Great Basin beyond." He paused and smiled cryptically. "Perhaps someday we can even reach the beaver streams of California."

Will thrilled at the words. California had first nestled in his mind nearly two decades before when one of Lisa's trappers had suggested Uncle Jake may well have sprouted wings and flown there. To Will, from what he could glean from the words of old sailors and tattered

maps, California was a near mythical land like those Odysseus wandered through, the continent's far western edge, of rugged golden
mountains that towered above an indigo sea, an occasional mission or
presidio hugging the coast, sun dappled during the day and blanketed
at night with warm fog; and somewhere far east beyond the coastal
range lay a vast green valley filled with beaver and elk and wild horses,
and beyond that a jagged wall of snowy mountains that even the
Mexicans had seen only from the distance.

"…You men stand out as individuals of the temperament, perseverance, and skills vital for leadership of our trapping brigades in these
lands as hostile and forbidding as they are bountiful and sublime in
beauty. Captain Smith will be returning with me to St. Louis to help
organize next year's expedition." Ashley gloated. "We'll be carrying
with us 8,829 pounds of beaver, in addition to Captain Smith's forty
packs cached on the Sweetwater. In St. Louis, our enterprise will have
earned nearly fifty thousand dollars!" Ashley scanned each of his
partisan's eyes. "I look to the most resourceful among you as potential
future partners. You, too, can share in the vast wealth we will garner
from these mountain streams in the coming years. I'll soon divide the
men among you and dispatch you for the autumn hunt. However, if any
of you have wearied of the mountains and desire to return to the
settlements, please inform me by dawn tomorrow. The choice is yours,
gentlemen."

Will wandered along the river grappling with his choices. Over
two years in the wilderness with no word sent to or received from his
loved ones. Each day his frail mother waned closer to death, if she had
not passed on already. And Sarah may well have married herself off by
now, or even dropped a child or two. And what of poor, mad Judy? Will
cursed his fate of being saddled with her. But it happened, and now I'm
roped with her till death. And as for my life's work—law or trapping?
Either could bring me riches or ignominy, he reasoned, but only one
could kill me. He sat on a boulder watching the last streaks of crimson
in the sky slowly gray.

"Mr. Yates," Smith called from behind him.

Startled, Will whirled. "You got the drop on me, Captain."

"I hesitated to disturb you. You seemed deep in thought."

"Matter a fact…I was trying to sort things out."

"I am sorry. I'll call on you another time." He started to turn.

"No, please stay," he urged. "Something eating you, Captain?"

"In fact…" he hesitated. "To my regret, it seems our companionship has soured the last few months."

Will looked away.

"Yeah, I've pondered that some myself."

Smith nodded. "I miss our long talks. You've the makings of a fine philosopher and theologian. Often you've challenged me with your probing questions and perspectives. Although your intentions may have been otherwise, overall you've helped me deepen rather than abandon my faith. And," he added with a smile, "you play a fine game of chess."

"Thank you, Captain," he replied softly, "that means a lot."

"You understand my position on the confrontation with Mr. Odgen." Will nodded. "For both practical and moral reasons there was no need to antagonize Mr. Ogden or his men. We may well need to take shelter or sustenance from the Hudson Bay Company again."

"Yeah, I understand. In hindsight I agree with you and mostly regret my actions. It's just...I had to fight back. Fight something. And Ogden'd been riding us for weeks."

"Everyone felt the same. Not everyone joined in the march on Ogden's camp." A meteor streaked across the western sky. "Did you see that?"

"I love watching shooting stars," Will said, smiling.

"What did you think of General Ashley's request for you to become a leader and possible future partner?"

"I don't know if I've got what it takes. You yourself said as much on the Bear River."

"Even the greatest of leaders makes mistakes. General Ashley did not invite Mr. Gardener to our council. He did invite you. He and I see promise in you."

"Really?" Will demanded, astonished. "I'm not sure I can live up to your expectations."

"They're only hopes." Smith gently patted his shoulder. "A man can always push a little beyond his last limit. Anyway, please do consider staying on. The enterprise needs every available good man. And I," he added, "need a friend." Smith turned and silently strolled away. Eyes blinking, Will stared after him.

He gazed at the sky most of the night, repeatedly mulling his choices, and still debated them at daybreak as he marched toward Ashley's teepee. Ashley and Smith were talking quietly before a small fire but clamped shut their mouths as Will approached. He dismissed the feeling they were talking about him.

"Morning," he mumbled and they returned his greeting. "General

Ashley," he said meekly.

Ashley raised an eyebrow. "Your decision, Mr. Yates?"

Will hesitated. "I'm going home."

Ashley's party of nearly fifty men rode off on July second, pulling their pack-laden ponies behind them. Accompanying them was a near grown grizzly whose mother had been killed the previous year by George Crogan, who pitied the wailing creature and began feeding it. The grizzly ambled alongside Crogan and curled up beside him at night. With his long, tangled, black hair and beard, ample girth, and refusal to bathe, Crogan became the butt of jokes over which was the real griz. Smith stoically tolerated the grizzly's presence, but, like most of the men, gave it a wide birth. He warned Crogan that the grizzly would be shot at its first sign of viciousness. The men speculated over how Smith endured camping with a grizzly when he had once been torn apart by one. Smith never let on, but his lined and scarred face seemed ever more grave and thoughtful.

They trekked up the Big Sandy and across South Pass to the Sweetwater where they raised Smith's cache. From there they tramped down the Popo Agie toward the Bighorn River. While camped on the Popo Agie, sixty Blackfeet appeared from nowhere and charged the hobbled ponies, yelling hideously to spook them. Frantic, the ponies snapped their rawhide hobbles and bolted.

Will joined the twenty men of the pursuit but they never caught up. Instead, Ashley had to send a volunteer by horseback back to the Sweetwater to borrow horses from another party. A week later one moonless night in the Wind River Valley, Crow slipped through the guards and tried to run off the horses. A trapper spotted the shadows flitting through the dark and fired. The Crow sprinted away leaving one gutshot and groaning warrior behind. He died at dawn.

Despite these frustrating delays, they reached the Bighorn by early August. They slaughtered enough buffalo to construct bullboats, then Ashley sent half the men with the horses into the mountains for another year of trapping, assuming they lived that long. Will embarked with Ashley, Smith, and the others down the Bighorn in the ponderous bullboats.

In mid-August they reached the Yellowstone and were astonished to view eight keelboats anchored in the river and four hundred and fifty soldiers camped along shore. General Henry Atkinson and Indian Agent Benjamin O'Fallon had led the expedition up the Missouri to smoke the pipe and spread presents among the tribes. Atkinson gladly agreed to squeeze Ashley, his men, and packs onto his keelboats for their return trip. Delighted by the grizzly's clownish demeanor, Atkinson ordered the bow of his flagship, the *Mink*, cleared, and the bear chained safely beyond his swipe of the lead polers of starboard or port.

For the next six weeks, Will lolled in the sun's warmth atop the *Mink* and watched the Missouri's barren shores slide behind him, while at night he stretched out on the hard earth and pondered the constellations and moon adrift across eternity. All along his mind whirled with memories and images.

With no current responsibilities or fears, he slipped into a deep relaxation that he had never before experienced in the mountains or the settlements, marred only by the realization that it would eventually end. I'm returning a hero of sorts, he frequently reminded himself to hearten his faith, with nearly three-hundred and fifty dollars in credit and a lifetime of adventures crammed into just two and a half years. What a fine time to die!

Eleven

1825–27

The Mississippi slid beneath them faster and faster as the sun-burned rivermen dug their poles into the muck and pushed ahead. The deck of each keelboat was packed with trappers in greasy, tattered buckskins and young soldiers in faded blue woolens who stood on tiptoes, rested hands on each others shoulders, and strained to spot St. Louis.

Will bobbed his head to grab a view through the men crowded before him. Gusts of wind chilled his face. A bright and distant sun shimmered down from a cobalt sky on clumps of trees burning golden and crimson, on cabins and whitewashed houses nestled amidst fields of trampled cornstalks and wheat stubble, on the brown, swirling Mississippi waters. He glanced back at the seven keelboats strung out up the river, relieved again at his luck to be in the lead, the *Mink*, with

Atkinson, Ashley and Smith. He faced downstream and imagined himself stealing like a spook into his family's home and astonishing his mother and Sarah with, "I'm home!" before engulfing them in bear hugs.

"Thar she is!" someone shouted and the men broke into deafening cheers.

"Whole town's turned out," Will said excitedly as he peered at the tiny black crowd packed before the toy-like warehouses, homes, and steeples atop the bluffs. A cannon boomed and echoed across the Mississippi. "How'd they know?"

"Rider got through from Franklin," Smith noted with satisfaction.

The *Mink* was poled slowly to a berth along the rotting wharves where a score of flatboats, keelboats, and a couple steamboats were tied. The crowd roared with delight at the sight of loved ones and Crogan and his grizzly staring back at them from the bow. The trappers and soldiers shoved each other aside to scramble ashore and up the steep banks, and the townspeople surged down to meet them. Gripping his rifle and pack tightly, Will jumped on a nearby flatboat and scanned the milling crowd for familiar faces. "No one!" he said aloud with a sinking heart. He leapt onto the wharf and pushed through the throng of people weeping and laughing joyfully as they embraced men long feared dead.

Suddenly someone wrapped callused hands around his neck and laughed triumphantly. "Got the drop on ye, boy!" Jess boomed as he pushed Will away. Will spun.

"Jessie!" he cried.

"Glad ta see yer still kickin', compañero!" Their faces split with wide grins, they pummeled each other with handshakes and shoulder slaps. Jess shoved a jug into Will's gut.

"Hah!" Will tipped back the jug, swallowed, and shivered as the whiskey burned its way down. "Now that's real whiskey," he shouted as he handed the jug back. "I got some tales to tell!"

Sarah broke through the crowd and threw herself into his arms. "Oh, I missed you, Will!"

He pulled her tight, first ecstatic then tense. "How's Mama?" he demanded.

"The same," she replied. "She's waiting for you at home."

"Judy?"

"I told her you were coming."

"Is she all right?"

Sarah frowned. "Not worse. Once we were such good friends," she said sadly. "But no longer."

Will grimaced. "Come on! Let's go home!"

They climbed up the steep bank and dodged through the crowded, dusty streets. Red-faced men were already chugging deep from jugs and hollering war whoops.

"All hell's broke loose," Jess noted admiringly and gulped deep from the jug.

"I'll join in soon as I see my ma." Will grabbed his sister and pulled her tight. "It's all like a dream," he exclaimed in wonder.

"Rip many scalps?" Jess asked.

Will shook his head. "Nope. Kilt a horse."

Sarah gasped. "Will! How could you?"

"There was a Blackfoot atop it," Will replied defensively. "Ain't a bad limp," he observed.

"Kin still whip yer ass running!" Will chuckled and shoved Jess.

"We've got something to tell you, Will," Sarah said demurely.

Jess's face puckered up like he ate something sour. "Maybe later, Sarah."

"What?" Will demanded.

"We're married," she said excitedly.

Will stopped abruptly and stared gape-mouthed at them. "What!"

Jess shrugged. "Sarah ain't funning ye."

"Well, ahh..." Will extended his hand weakly and Jess took it. "Now that's something. You took me by surprise. Well, Jessie, better you than someone else."

"Thanks," Jess replied shortly.

"We got a lot more to celebrate than I figured," Will exclaimed, forcing a smile and trying to sound happy. He threw an arm around Jess. "Makes us brethren!" Jess grinned slightly. "Sarah, are you..."

Sarah blushed and looked away. "Not yet."

"Never thought anyone could rope Jess," Will said in wonder.

"Me neither," Jess said sadly. They eyed each other curiously.

"There's Mama!" Sarah shouted and grabbed Will by the hand. "Come on," she urged, dragging him forward.

Jenny stood on the porch of their two-story frame house. Both his mother and the house looked smaller and more cramped than he remembered.

"Oh, my son," Jenny cried and beckoned him forward. Will set down his rifle and pack and hugged his mother tight. "You'll always be my little boy! No matter what! Even when you run off to God knows where. I've worried every day since you left."

"I missed you, Mama," he said gently.

Jenny wiped tears from her cheeks then looked him up and down. She shook her head in disgust. "How could you walk through town in those filthy rags? I tried so hard to teach you right."

Will bit back his annoyance. "You haven't changed a bit, Ma," he said stiffly. "It ain't...it's not easy finding new clothes in the Rockies. I shaved and cut my hair and washed this morning. That was the best I could do."

"Well, come inside," she ordered. "I've laid out some clean clothes on your bed. You go up to your room and change. Soon as you're proper we'll eat. You must be famished." She turned to Jess and Sarah. "And you two, finish your chores."

Will slinked upstairs to his old room that he had built onto the house after returning from New Orleans. It was all exactly as he left it. He browsed his books of history, Bryon, and Scott, occasionally pulling out a volume and quickly leafing through it. He fingered his collection of arrowheads, fossils, feathers, and bones. A collage of memories spun through his brain. His boyhood seemed decades ago, a set of barely connected dreams, and this room a museum of someone else's life. None of it made sense.

"Will!" his mother called from the bottom of the steps. "Dinner's on the table!"

"Coming," he hollered. Some homecoming, he thought morosely. Feel like a boy who's been caught playing hooky. The aroma of a melange of foods coming from the kitchen assuaged his irritation. He quickly stripped off his buckskins and pulled on his old linen clothes. He had lost weight and the clothes hung loosely on him. The stiff leather shoes chaffed his feet. He kicked them off and yanked on his tattered moccasins.

Later, seated around the table, they traded platters laden with heaps of ham, hominy, black-eyed peas, sweet potatoes, and carrots. "I sure missed your cooking, Ma," he admitted as he began stuffing his mouth. Jenny beamed and everyone began jabbering.

A wagon squeaked to a halt outside. Will cocked his head expectantly. Someone clumped onto the porch and banged loudly at the door.

"I'll grab it," Will said, jumping up abruptly. He yanked open the door to find Seth staring down at him and twisting a straw hat in his beefy hands.

"We shouldn't a' had ta come to you, boy," Seth growled. Will tried to peek around his bulk. He stood aside. "There she is, ifin ye want her," he added wearily. Judy stood awkwardly beside the wagon. Will stepped past Seth and across the yard to stiffly cup her hands in his. She seemed shorter and plumper; she blinked her eyes incessantly and trembled. Neither knew what to say and they got more flustered when Seth came to tower over them.

"You look well," Will finally blurted. Judy nodded yes then no but said nothing. "I've gotta rest up some. May I call on you tomorrow?"

Seth harrumphed in disgust. "Ye oughta…"

"No, Daddy!" Judy cried. "We'll both need time." She stared at Will's moccasins. "That's how I feel," she said, pointing down at them then twirled and clambered onto the wagon. Seth pulled himself up beside her. He whistled and hollered to his two mules and slowly turned the wagon in the road. Will waved forlornly as the wagon squeaked away.

He returned and toyed silently with his food until Jess passed the jug and started telling risqué jokes. Will started chuckling and soon they were all swapping stories and gossip. They reached a lull in late afternoon about the time Will and Jess had drained most of the jug.

"I gotta git some shut-eye," Will mumbled. "Couldn't sleep a wink all last night thinking 'bout homecoming and all that awaited me."

"Shut-eye!" Jess boomed. "And miss the wing-ding of the year, if not the century! That's ain't the Will I used ta know."

"Jess!" Jenny said sharply. "He needs and will receive his rest. Will, you go up to bed this instant. You must be bright-eyed and minded when you meet with Mr. Jameson tomorrow. Your future lies in the law. Savagery has no place in this city, and especially not in this home."

Will frowned back at her. "Well, now, I ain't that sleepy after all. Just need some cold water in my face." He struggled to his feet. "Come on, Jess, let's head to Le Barras."

"Will," Jenny commanded, "here you've been home no more than a few hours and you intend to revert to your wild ways? You're not a boy anymore. You're a man and should behave with decorum."

"But, Mrs. Yates," Jess protested mockingly, "ye say yer want Will to practice law before the bar. Well, now, that's exactly where we intend to be all this evening and into the early morning hours." Will snickered.

"Jess Baucus," Sarah admonished, "we'd better have one of our talks."

Jess squirmed uneasily. "Not now, sweetie," he mumbled.

"You give my brother a few hours at least before you boys run off. And, meanwhile, we'll take a long walk."

Will laughed. "Whoa, Jessie, sounds serious. I'll wait on you two love-birds. Take your time." He slipped upstairs to his room. He tried reading the titles to his books but they were all blurred. Sleep dragged him down. He collapsed into bed. The room spun crazily for awhile, and then darkness.

The sun was just setting when Jess jostled him awake. "Git yer ass outta bed. Time's a-wasting! We're young, the night's young, and adventure awaits us."

"'Nother hour or two," Will muttered.

"Nothing doing. Drinking's already started at the Le Barras. If we don't hurry, those other trappers and soldiers'll drink this town dry. Come on!" He rabbit punched Will's shoulder.

"Yowl." He rubbed his shoulder and sat up. "All right, goddamn it. Hold yer horses."

Jess grinned. "The ladies is awaiting our descent to warn us against all the evils we'll embark on tonight. Let's sneak out the old way. Fer old time's sake."

Will snickered. "Good thinking." They tiptoed to the window, slowly opened it, and climbed out onto the porch roof. "Ready?" Will whispered. Jess nodded. They jumped and hit the ground with thuds.

Jenny's voice shot out through the dark. "Couldn't you two have mustered the decency to wish Sarah and me goodnight?"

They struggled to their feet and stood before Jenny silhouetted on the porch. "Sorry, Mama," Will said quietly then went up and lightly pecked her cheek. "We were feeling spirited. We meant no harm."

"You never do!" Jenny turned abruptly and went inside.

"Maybe we oughta…" Will began.

"She'll git over it. Come on!" Jess urged.

They strode through the quiet streets toward the tumult wafting from the waterfront. The Hotel Le Barras overlooked the Mississippi. Ashley had rented the entire establishment for the night. All around Le Barras, men were gathered in groups before stores and in alleys, passing jugs and bottles. A few men snored drunkenly in the dust.

Crogan and his grizzly sat on Le Barras's porch. A knot of men pressed around them, teasing and poking the grizzly. "He'll tear ye ta ribbons, ye keep that up," Crogan occasionally warned. Will and Jess watched, fascinated for awhile, then, when nothing happened, pushed into the hotel.

The lobby was packed with drunken, red-faced men, wildly shouting and gesturing. Smith circulated among them, addressing one small group after another. Spotting Will and Jess, he slipped through the crowd toward them.

"Gentlemen," Smith began, "a word?"

"Whadya call us?" Jess replied in mock anger.

"Gentlemen?" Smith repeated, confused.

"Take it back, Captain," Jess warned. "No man calls us that and lives."

Smith smiled. "A thousand pardons, Mr. Baucus." Jess nodded in satisfaction. "Mr. Yates, the last time we talked, you still seemed adamantly opposed to returning to the mountains at this time. However, perhaps Mr. Baucus would be interested."

"Yer bet, Captain! When ye leaving?"

"Soon as I gather enough supplies, men, and horses. No later than four weeks at most. We're recruiting only free trappers this time. No more engagés. You can stay or go as you please and we'll buy your furs at standard American mountain prices. However, there's safety in numbers, as you know, and if you stay with our brigade, you'll be expected to handle your fair share of sentry and wood gathering duties."

"Sign me up, Captain. I've laid up too long in this town and've been chomping at the bit ever since I got back." Will eyed Jess angrily but said nothing.

"Your leg's completely healed?"

"Good as gold. Slight limp, but it's strong as ever."

Smith extended his hand. "Your father owns a blacksmith shop, if I'm not mistaken."

Jess smiled in wonder. "You've got a helluva memory, Captain. I don't believe we spoke more than a few times and that almost two and a half years ago."

"We all have our attributes, Mr. Baucus. I'm confident you're the sort of man who can reap a small fortune in the mountains, with cheer and perseverance." Smith rubbed a thick white scar on his forehead. "Well, gentle...er, Mr. Yates, Mr. Baucus, I'll stop by your shop tomorrow. I'll require your services to repair our worn equipment." Smith slipped away and was soon talking with another group of men.

"You're just gonna run off and leave Sarah?" Will demanded heatedly.

"That's right. Just like you did Judy. What's the difference?"

"Judy's touched and Sarah's my sister."

"I don't see any goddamned difference at all. They're both wimmen and we're men."

"Why'd you marry her?"

"Seemed like a good idea at the time. After all, I was always sweet on her and she nursed me back to health when I come back and I was so crippled at first I feared I could never head west agin."

"Now that you can, you're up and leaving her."

"Yer jus' jealous 'cause I'm leaving and yer back stuck with Judy with no future, no fun, and no adventure. That ain't no life ta lead."

Softening, he admitted, "Maybe you're right."

"Rest up, Will, then head west with me!" he urged.

He thought for a moment. "We'll see," he finally said. "Let's get drunk." They pushed their way to the bar.

Will hesitated before the little office on the town's edge. The windows and doors were curtained and there was no sound within. He glanced around furtively. A half-dozen little boys were noisily playing crack the whip in a yard across the street. A tight-lipped housewife plodded down the street balancing water buckets from a yoke across her shoulders. A pig rooting in the gutters paused to devour a dead rat, the sight of which made him gag. He turned away and sucked air deeply into his lungs. His head pounded harshly and, swearing off alcohol for the hundredth time that morning, he massaged his temples until it subsided. He faced the office, breathed deeply, and rapped sharply on the window.

"Who is it?" came Jameson's weak voice from within.

Will ignored him and rapped again, more lightly this time. Someone shuffled to the door and opened it a crack. "William!" Jameson exclaimed joyfully, and pulled open the door. "Come in, my boy!" Will stepped into the dark room past Jameson, who quickly shut the door behind him. "Forgive the darkness, my boy. I was merely resting." Jameson smelled of whiskey and sweat. He partially drew the curtain so that a thin stream of light fell into the room's center. "Make yourself at home, William," he said, waving toward a frayed seat. Will took it while Jameson plopped heavily into a huge stuffed chair. He placed his fingertips together and gazed through them at Will. "I heard of the Ashley party's return yesterday and so hoped and prayed that you would be among them. I wasn't feeling quite up to venturing out amongst that crowd to welcome you home. My apologies."

"Have you been sick, Mr. Jameson?"

"Sick?" Jameson asked rhetorically with a smile. "In a manner of speaking, I've always been sick." He chuckled. "Over time my sickness simply eats deeper away at me. With each year I look back at an ever-lengthening and largely unfulfilled life. There is only one cure for my ailment." He glanced at a dueling pistol lying near a half-empty whiskey bottle on the table between them. "Forgive my manners. Whiskey?"

"No thanks," Will muttered, "after last night, it'll be a while before I can touch the stuff again."

Jameson nodded, splashed some whiskey into a glass, and eagerly brought it to his quivering lips. Even in the dim light, Jameson's florid, jowly face, snow-white hair, and immense girth seemed overpowering. As always, Will felt like he was in the presence of an especially dissipated nobleman.

"You seem the better for your adventures, William. Your lean, almost gaunt, body and face radiate an immense inner vitality. Pity your hair is thinning some in front."

Will frowned. "Can't help that. It's been thinning slowly for years."

Jameson peered closely at him. "Hmmm. And beneath that vital glow you've aged. The sun and wind have not been kind to your face. I don't suppose you've been eating properly."

"I've lived," he replied shortly.

Jameson stroked his triple-chin. "The ravages of time," he said sadly. "Have you returned to resume your apprenticeship?"

"If you're willing to take me back. I had less than a year left when I headed up the Missouri."

"Of course, my boy, of course," he said happily. "I've dreamt of the renewal of our professional and personal relationship. Tell me, William, how was your homecoming?"

Will glanced toward the window. The blue sky beyond the house across the street looked so inviting, like a deep canyon pool on a sweltering day. "My ma and Sarah are fine. She married my friend Jess, did you hear?"

Jameson smiled. "As you may recall, William, there is very little gossip that swirls through the eddies of St. Louis and the circuit without me hearing of it. Eavesdropping on the affairs and foibles of others is one of the few pleasures life has granted me." He paused. "And Judith?"

Will sighed. "I'm heading there next. Seth brought Judy by briefly yesterday. Doesn't seem like anything's changed."

"Life with Judith is a constant strain, an immense and intolerable burden, is it not?" Jameson demanded. Will nodded. "If so, William, why not divorce her?"

His eyes widened. "Can I do that?"

"You most certainly can."

"How?"

"Petition the legislature. Grounds of insanity. Incompatibility. Lack of marital affection. Won't leave her parents' home. Whatever. The legislature ponders a dozen petitions a year and grants two or three divorces. Perhaps someday Missouri will allow divorce through the courts like some of the states back East. But I see no reason why the legislature should not grant you your freedom."

"That'd kill Judy."

Jameson shrugged. "You won't know until you ask her. If you put it delicately and rationally, she might just go along." He held up a fat finger. "Fear not, dear boy. I have perhaps the solution to your fears. Rather than divorce her, convince her to divorce you." He went over to his desk and rummaged through a pile of newspaper clippings. "Here it is," he noted with satisfaction. He slipped on his glasses and held the clipping close to his eyes. "Well, William, ponder the advertisement of one Reuben Warson of Howard in the *Missouri Intelligencer* on June 14, 1824 in which he advised his wife thus: 'When you readest this, suppress thy sobs, sue out a divorce, and set thy cap for another and more happy swain, while I roam through the world sipping honey from the bitter or sweet flowers that chance may strew in my path.'"

With a chuckle, Will replied, "My hopes exactly. I just don't think Judy'll go along." Suddenly he grew more serious. "She's fragile enough. I don't wanna destroy her. But I've gotta be free of her."

"Exactly."

"And what about me? Being divorced, could I get into politics?"

"That's the sensitive issue. I know of no one in public office in this state who has severed his marital vows. However, your hero, Andrew Jackson, married a divorced woman, and many expect him to be our president in the next election. You might work on Judy now but delay your petition until after you've received your law license."

Will frowned. "Could destroy both our reputations and futures."

"I don't know that Judith's future is all that bright with or without you. Yours, however, is much brighter without being saddled with her. And as for the reputation of either of you, well, most people who are familiar with you two are aware of Judith's condition. Under the circumstances, a divorce is certainly understandable."

"Wish I'd thought of that before I left. I could have become a brigade leader and maybe even one of Ashley's partners."

"What!" Jameson looked alarmed. "You mean you'd head right back to that howling wilderness if you were free of Judith? I thought she was what kept you away."

Will raised his hands to calm Jameson. "Don't worry, Mr. Jameson, I aim to stay in St. Louis until I receive my license and maybe a good deal longer after that. I just don't know. Each time I return to St. Louis, it seems more cramped, stifling. I get so restless here." He smiled happily to himself. "I love it out there," he gestured westward. "I can't begin to convey the eternal beauty and thrills and spiritual depths I experience in those far away mountains and canyons." The smile vanished. "But being married to Judy has held me back from completely immersing myself in all that. Once that tie's broken, there's no telling what kind of life I'll lead."

"But what is the point of obtaining a law license and then disappearing into the wilderness with it?" he said, exasperated.

"Ease of mind, Mr. Jameson. Whether I ever practice or not, at least I'll have accomplished something that my family and society demand of me, something respectable. Then I can choose freely what to do with my life. And who knows, I may eventually tire of my wanderings and adventures and find someplace to settle down, some place no one knows of my past, of my divorce. Then I can hang my shingle. With luck, someday find a beautiful woman who ain't touched who loves me. Raise a family. But that's years, maybe decades off. 'Til then I aim to enjoy as much of the world as possible."

"Well, now, if I am simply cutting your tether for you to fly away," he remarked bitterly, "I wished I had never mentioned the possibility of divorce."

"I won't leave anytime soon."

"Whatever," Jameson said grumpily. "Perhaps Judith won't go along after all."

"I'll go see her about it now."

Will strode hard the three miles out of town to the Morgan farm, trying to burn off some of his anxiety while debating what to say. Seth and his three sons were stacking hay in a distant field. They spotted him but did not return his wave. As before, when he entered the yard, their hound bounded toward him barking and wagging its tail. "Wish the Morgans would be as happy to see me as you, fella," he told him as he bent to scratch behind its ears.

He walked slowly toward the porch. Betty opened the door and stared at him. "Welcome back, Will," she said quietly as he stepped past her into the hall. "She's in the parlor." She started toward the entrance.

"Mrs. Morgan, would you mind...?"

Betty hesitated, nodded, then turned and hurried away toward the kitchen. Will poked his head into the parlor. Judy stared at him from her rocking chair near the fire. She had a linen shirt with a half-sewn patch on it in her lap. "Please sit down, Will." He sat on a hard bench near the window. He searched for words but found nothing.

"I really missed you, Will," she said as tears rolled down her round cheeks. "If you are back from the mountains for good, I think I am ready to start over again. I still get sad sometimes, but not as much as before. I really think things'll work out this time." Her words stunned him. It was not what he expected her to say. "Are you going to work for Mr. Jameson?"

"Yes, I talked to him earlier today."

"Oh, that's wonderful! Once you get your license and start taking clients, we can afford to get a small place of our own. I think I'm ready to leave my parents, Will. I started reading that book of Byron's poetry you gave me a long time ago, *Don Juan*. I can see why you like him. It's not always easy reading. I'd like it a lot better if you could read it to me before we go to bed at night, like you used to. Remember? You'd like that, wouldn't you, Will?"

He stared out the window. She suddenly grew frantic. "You want everything to be better, don't you? Do you still love me?"

He turned to face her. "Well, ahh…"

"You really don't love me anymore," she cried, "if you ever did! You came to leave me forever, didn't you?" Judy burst into tears and buried her face in the shirt.

He went over to her and gently patted her shoulder. "Of course I love you and want things to work out," he said hesitantly. "I didn't think you'd want me back." Her sobs deepened.

He heard a creak and looked up. Seth and Betty glared at him from the doorway. They were like the cork in a bottle and Will felt trapped and suffocated inside. I've gotta get out of here, he thought desperately. He bent over and whispered into her hair. "Don't worry, Judy. We can make things better. I'll be back tomorrow and we can talk some more." Then he tiptoed away across the room.

"Where do ye think yer going?" Seth demanded.

"I'll drop by little by little till she's used to me again."

Seth stared down at him for several moments. "All right," he finally said, and stepped aside. "Just make sure you come regular and next time bring the silver you made in the mountains. You owe us a lot."

As soon as he stepped outside, Will sucked the breath deep into his lungs. A string of geese flew overhead honking their way south. Wish

I could sprout wings and join you, he thought morosely.

Mulling a dozen problems and possibilities, he ambled back into town. The streets were deserted except for groups of armed men who peered over fences and down alleyways. One hollered out to Will. "Grab yer iron, mister! That griz's rampaging! Done kilt his master!" Will froze. Once again he faced the horror a couple years before of that grizzly crashing through the brush and scattering the other men and horses and he firing and the ball furrowing the grizzly's skull and no more than stinging him and the crazed grizzly charging and he running terrified and tripping and Smith standing between them and the click of Smith's hammer on damp powder and the grizzly tackling Smith and seizing his head in its jaws and bone crunching and…

"Don't stand there like an idiot!" the man yelled, then ran off to search with the others.

Will sprinted for home through the checkerboard streets. Panting, he turned into the road leading past his home a hundred yards away. He turned and glanced down the road toward town. Like a nightmare, the grizzly lumbered toward him, pursued by Smith and Jess. Smith stopped, leveled his rifle, and fired. The ball struck the grizzly in its fat rump and, enraged, it charged Will, who dashed for his home. Jenny and Sarah were sitting on the porch. "Get inside!" he yelled hoarsely. "And get my rifle!" They stared dumbly at him. Suddenly Sarah pointed to the grizzly charging behind him.

They shrieked and fled inside. Will's lungs felt near bursting. His body dragged like lead. He ran up to the porch just as Jenny opened the door wide and thrust his rifle in his outstretched hand. "Hurry!" she screamed. "Get inside! It's right behind you!"

He spun, cocked, and aimed his rifle in one motion. The grizzly reared and swung a huge arm toward the rifle. He shoved his rifle toward the grizzly's gaping mouth and pulled the trigger. BOOM! The ball smashed through the grizzly's teeth and into its brain, destroying it instantly. Before the smoke cleared the grizzly dropped heavily and lay still. Will's knees buckled beneath him and he slumped to the porch. Jenny cried, "He killed it," and she and Sarah ventured out, then clung together, sobbing. Smith and Jess ran up panting and stared down at the grizzly.

"That was…mighty cool…shooting, Will," Jess gasped between breaths. Will began trembling violently. Brandishing rifles, other men ran into the yard and gathered around the bear.

After Smith regained his breath, he said, "Mr. Yates, we've got to stop hunting grizzlies like this." Will nodded and smiled faintly. "You can take the beast from the wilderness," Smith observed, "but not the wilderness from the beast."

Will struggled to control his trembling. Finally he replied, "Didn't you once tell me the beast lies within us all?"

Smith smiled and said nothing.

Jameson opened the door wide and bowed. "Am I to be honored by a visit from the great bear-hunter himself?" Will grinned and stepped inside. "Why, William, your spectacular performance three days past is the talk of all St. Louis." Jameson reached for the half-empty decanter resting on the table and filled two glasses. To Will's relief, the pistol was nowhere in sight. Jameson handed a glass to him and raised his own high. "To courage—the courage of conviction and action, of which you are more than amply endowed." They swallowed their whiskey and Jameson promptly refilled their glasses.

"Facing that bear was nothing compared to running the gauntlet at Judy's."

"Quite so, William. I've been eagerly awaiting the results of that epic journey to the Morgan homestead."

"I chickened out, Mr. Jameson. Just couldn't do it."

"Well," Jameson said softly. "So be it." He sat down abruptly.

"The thought of being free of Judy sent me soaring out to the Morgan's and I was determined to gently ask her about a divorce." He swallowed a mouthful of whiskey. "But she spoke of slowly healing and getting a house of our own."

"And?"

"Nothing's settled. I made her cry. She suspects I wanna leave her. I told her I'd keep visiting more and more. That's how I left it."

Jameson rested his huge head against the stuffed chair's back and closed his eyes. "Perhaps it's best to set the notion of divorce aside for now." They fell silent. A grandfather clock ticked loudly in the corner. "The autumn circuit ended shortly before your return and we've no clients," Jameson suddenly said wearily.

"Don't worry, Mr. Jameson. I won't be idle. I'll study the books all day and into the night."

"Of course you will, William. Your knowledge of the law is already as deep as it is broad. But you must polish perhaps the most important weapon that a lawyer can wield."

"What's that?"

"The power to gently or brutally manipulate a jury's emotions and reason until they would agree to virtually anything asked of them."

Will grimaced. "I've seen enough cases decided on style rather than substance."

"Exactly. And in addition, you'll need some income. You could, of course, clerk your mother's store and do chores for your father-in-law. Or," he paused dramatically, "you could employ that nimble mind of yours for the good of society, all the while honing your skills of persuasion."

"Shall I run for governor?" Will asked facetiously.

Jameson chuckled. "Not quite yet. Did you ever consider becoming this district's teacher?"

"Teacher? What happened to that ol' son of a bitch Pringle?" He bitterly recalled Pringle's bullying and swats.

"Mr. Pringle has departed for less acrimonious climes. It seems one of his students, a certain George Wilkins, did not take kindly to a paddling." Jameson chuckled. "As I heard it, Wilkins yanked the paddle from the good teacher's hands, pushed him over a bench, and began vigorously applying it to Mr. Pringle's backside."

Will laughed in delight. "Wish I could've seen that. I spent a lot of my childhood day-dreaming of doing just that."

Jameson smiled indulgently. "The subscribers asked me to take Mr. Pringle's place. But the thought of being around little boys my son's age when he died..." Tears welled in his eyes. He dabbed them with a handkerchief. "I told them I would try to find a suitable replacement. And here you are. Now then, if you're agreed, let's visit the families and inform them their children have a new teacher."

"I wouldn't know the first thing about teaching."

"Nonsense, William. Just liberally mix rote memorization and the rod."

"I can't do that," he declared heatedly. "I hated it. I don't aim to be a hypocrite."

"The position is open, William. You can step into Pringle's shoes, if you think you'll fit. Or you can tailor your own. It's your choice."

It took several days to visit all the homes sending children to the school. He had felt so awkward greeting the parents and nodding to their children. He had been particularly nervous before meeting George Wilkins. While Jameson chatted amiably with Mrs. Wilkins, Will and George stared suspiciously at each. George was a stout farmboy with unruly flaxen hair and plump red cheeks. He towered over Will. "Licked the last teacher that done tried paddling me. You gonna try the same?"

Will cleared his throat and looked Wilkins in the eye. "George," he replied softly, "I've spent years with hard men and held my own with them. But that aside, I suffered under Pringle myself. That son of a bitch whipped my ass many a time."

"Really? Why didn't ya thrash 'im good?"

Will shrugged then smiled. "Suppose most of the time I deserved it. Tell you what, George. Sometime I'll tell you about a few pranks we pulled on the ol' geezer. Just between you and me, all right?"

"Ya bet!" George said eagerly.

"You just gotta promise one thing."

George eyed him suspiciously. "What's that?"

"You can't pull them on me."

George chuckled. "All right."

"You seem like a nice boy. Hardworking, earnest, smart. You can be a leader to the other children. Let's work together, cooperate, George. Then there'll be no trouble for any of us." George nodded noncommittally. Jameson and Will bid them goodbye and continued their round.

"That wasn't too bad," Will admitted to Jameson.

"You seem to have won over Mr. Wilkins with your deft diplomacy," Jameson tisked. "And all that fretting for naught. You'll make a fine teacher, William, if you're not too permissive."

Will tossed and drifted all night wondering what and how to teach the next morning. Thirty-seven children from five to fourteen, probably all despising both school and him. Rote and the paddle, he thought contemptuously, there's gotta be a better way. "Byron!" he suddenly said aloud and laughed. I'll get them so interested in Byron's adventure tales that they'll beg to be taught how to read. He drifted off to sleep just as the sky began to lighten.

Stomach churning, Will clutched *Childe Harold* to his chest and slipped into the schoolroom. The din dropped momentarily as the children stared at him, then they began chattering and laughing loudly. Stepping behind the lectern, he gently placed his book and hands onto its scarred wood and glanced around the room from one grinning face to the next. He slightly opened his mouth fish-like several times but said nothing. A spitwad whizzed past his ear.

He raised his hands high as if in surrender. "May I have your attention, please!" He slipped around the lectern and strolled to the front row. "Quiet," he ordered, and tried recalling their names. A few children squirmed into silence. He cocked an eyebrow and pointed toward the noisy crowd surrounding George in the corner from where the spitwad was launched. "You boys there, settle down." George elbowed and shoved several of his companions and the commotion finally ceased. The children stared back at him expectantly.

George raised his hand. "Hear tell ya seen the Rockies, Mr. Yates. Be it true?"

"Well, yes, I did."

"Did ya kill any Injuns?" he demanded eagerly.

"I was too busy trying not to get killed myself," Will replied.

"Tell us some stories!" he shouted and others took up the cry. Will smiled and motioned them into silence.

"All right, all right! I'll tell a few and then we'll begin our lessons."

"And no stretchers," the big farmboy ordered. "Just tell it like it is."

Will scratched his temple and nodded. He smiled broadly as inspiration seized him. He picked up a slate and chalk. "I'll draw a map so you'll understand where I've wandered." He briefly concentrated to recall the details of the 1820 map of North America hanging in Jameson's office, then began to carefully sketch its major oceans, rivers, and mountain ranges, naming each in turn. Then he asked if any of them were reared in another town. A half-dozen hands shot up. He pointed to a little girl with chestnut pigtails and buckteeth sitting in the front row. "Umm...isn't your name Amy?" he asked. She smiled back at him and nodded.

"Where are you from, Amy?"

"Cincinnati," she replied. He stared at her curiously.

"I was born there, too," he said quietly as a swarm of memories buzzed through his mind. He brushed them away and dotted the slate where Cincinnati would be. "What do you remember about it?"

"Hey," George interrupted. "We wanna hear your stories!" Will's smile disappeared.

"Well, George. This being our first day, I want to make sure we all get to know each other proper. I'll tell you some tales, but first you've got to understand the settings in which they took place. And before that, I have to begin to know all of you. How's that suit you, George?"

He shrugged. "Suits me fine."

Will turned back to Amy. With her and the other children, he gently drew out their stories, while interspersing scraps of history, geography, and his own experiences. Then, holding the slate high, he traced his routes across the crude map—down the Mississippi to New Orleans, across the plains to Santa Fe, up the Missouri and into the Rockies.

"When ya headin' West agin, Mr. Yates?" George demanded. Will smiled slightly.

"Time'll tell," he replied.

Trembling, Judy gripped the pot's handle with thick pads and slowly tried to lift it from the hook. Somewhere she heard screams which echoed steadily louder. The bloody, stillborn child appeared before her, its bottom smacked repeatedly by a midwife. "No!" she cried and dropped the pot. It crashed into the burning logs. The lip popped off and stew bubbled over the flames. She jumped back and crashed into the table, knocking to the floor a half-dozen eggs.

Jenny shuffled into the kitchen. "Judy! What in the Lord's name are you doing?" Judy stared at her wild-eyed as if she had never seen her before. She pushed past and ran through the house and upstairs to Sarah's room, slamming the door behind her. Jenny retrieved the pot from the fire, frowning at how little stew remained inside. Then she bent painfully down and began wiping up the crushed eggs with a towel. Someone opened the front door and walked through the house whistling "Yankee Doodle."

"Will!" Jenny called irritably, "is that you?"

"Yup," he admitted happily as he strolled into the kitchen then stopped to stare. "What happened?" He stooped beside Jenny. "Let me help you, Ma," he said as he set his schoolbooks aside.

"Judy," she replied indignantly. "Again. That girl ruins as much as she fixes. It's like having a child. I should be a grandmother, not a mother. I've about reached my rope's end."

"Well, there's nothing I can do about Judy or your delayed grandmotherhood," he said coldly.

"It's been two weeks since she moved in and it seems like two years. When are you two going to move into your own place?"

"As I've tried repeatedly to explain to you, Mother, there are no houses available for the handful of silver I have left after paying off the store's debts. Prices have shot sky-high with all the newcomers settling here or passing through."

"Well, build a place of your own. Sarah's coming home in two days and has been dreading having to share her room with Judy. As you know, she often returns in tears at all the filth and vulgarity she must endure in that Baucus household."

Will grinned. "Jess talked of fixing you up with his old man."

"Oh, my Lord!" Jenny's wrinkled lips pursed tightly. "The very thought. That Jess is as no-good as his father. What Sarah sees in that demon in disguise I've no idea."

"She loves him and he's my best friend."

"I tried to teach you both better."

"Maybe that's part of it."

"Maybe you should join your 'best friend' in going upriver and send Judy back to her parents so I can enjoy my daughter's return in peace."

Will glared at her in disbelief. "What? After all your sermons about what's proper and what the neighbors think? I thought you wanted me to get my law shingle and settle down."

"Oh, I don't know what to do or think anymore. This home's been in a tumult ever since your return."

"Well, if that's the way you want it, Mother," he said as he rose.

"Just go comfort your wife and move her into your room. And after you're done, fetch some more wood and water. And some more eggs if there's any left in the henhouse. Supper'll be a little late tonight."

Thick gray clouds pressed low and damp over the earth on that dreary All Saints' Eve. With Smith at their head, seventy men and twice as many heavily burdened mules and horses plodded west through the muddy streets. Whooping and firing guns, hundreds of spectators lined their route to the town's edge.

Jess bent from his horse to hug Sarah a last time. "Be back 'fore ya know it."

"I'll pray for you, Jess," she said quietly.

"Don't worry 'bout me, sweetie. I've more lives than a cat and I'll return a rich man." Sarah blinked back tears and nodded. Jess punched Will's shoulder. "Keep yer powder dry and pecker hard," he admonished.

With a smirk, Will replied, "Couldn't you get the captain to delay till after we'd celebrated Devil's night?"

Jess shook his head sadly. "Been a while since we pulled some good pranks. 'Member the time we knocked over near every privy in St. Louis?"

"Least all the wooden privies. We gotta figure a way to topple the brick ones."

Sarah frowned. "Do you boys ever think of anything but hell-raising?"

"Yer right, Sarah," Jess replied. "Forgive my foolishness. I done forgot the most important business of all."

"What?" Sarah asked eagerly.

"Trying ta talk this fool brother a' yourn ta grab his fixin's and join us." Sarah looked away sadly. "Come on, Will! It ain't too late!"

"Wish I could, Jessie," he replied mournfully.

"Shoulda hogtied ya and slung ya over my pony."

"Sleep with one eye open 'cause I'll get the drop on you out there when you least 'spect it."

"I hear ya talkin'. Time ta act. Saddle up and let's ride."

Will smacked Jess's pony on its rump. It broke into a trot. Jess jerked back in the saddle then regained his balance. "See ya in hell, if not sooner, Will!" he shouted joyfully over his shoulder as he kicked his pony into a canter to catch up with the brigade. "You, too, Sarah!" he hollered as he disappeared around a corner.

Will slipped an arm around Sarah's shoulder. "He'll be back, Sarah." She leaned against him and sighed.

"I'm almost afraid he will." He looked at her curiously but feared asking what she meant.

Night after night they lay stiffly on either side of the feather bed, staring at the ceiling until seized by troubled sleep. They had lost far more than a baby and Judy's ability to conceive. Thick, hard scar tissue filled their wounds and numbed their feelings. They said little to one another. When they did speak their words invariably had a bitter edge.

His once-fierce craving for her was long dead. More alarming to Will, everything about her filled him with deep loathing—her incessant hand washing and eye twitches, the fingernails chewed to the quick, the once voluptuous body turned to fat, the voice brimming with hysteria. Judy sensed his disgust, much as he tried to suppress it, and her neurosis deepened all the more.

The strain dragged him steadily downward. Dark blotched the skin beneath his eyes. His muscles atrophied. He grew surly and snapped at the slightest imagined affront. The antics of his students that once amused him, now set off rages in which he threatened the switch. His law books were piled unopened on his book shelf. When Jameson snagged a client, Will listlessly helped prepare the case and attended the hearings; sometimes he just skipped them. When Jameson remonstrated him, he would reply: "Let 'im hang, for all I care. There's no justice in this world."

Time slowed until it seemed to stop. Each day was like the previous—empty of all but constant tension and desperation. Entire months and seasons disappeared from his life with nothing joyful to carry with him. His mind spun constantly with memories of vistas, adventures, and characters from the Rockies. He welcomed even past drudgeries and terrors into his mind. Anything seemed better than his present plight. He fantasized about finding and winning the hearts of Sharon or Little Antelope. But his longing knew no release.

The late August sun blazed fire hot and steamy from a cloudless sky. Sweat seeped from every pore in Will's body. As they hurried to the courthouse, he longed to rip off his woolen suit and stiff leather shoes and dash for the Mississippi. He had snatched only an hour or two of sleep that night and his mind and body dragged heavily.

As he puffed heavily along, Jameson glanced at him. "Cheer up, William. You look as though you were heading to your execution."

"Maybe I am," he grunted.

Jameson patted his shoulder. "Fortitude, my boy. Within a couple hours it will be done."

They stomped up the courthouse steps and into the large entrance hall with its huge chandelier hanging from the ceiling and print of Washington and map of North America on the walls. "Now then," Jameson mumbled to himself. "I believe they told me the back committee room. Yes, that's right. Upstairs, William." They ascended the curving oak staircase and then continued down a long door-lined corridor until they reached the end.

Jameson raised his hand to knock but Will grabbed it. "Wait."

"We're already late, William. It wouldn't do to keep them waiting further."

Will inhaled deeply. "All right."

Jameson knocked. Someone within ordered them to enter. Five of St. Louis's leading citizens—Alexander McNair, Rufus Easton, Samuel Hammond, John Lucas and David Barton—sat behind a long walnut table. Two empty chairs faced them. The chairman, McNair, beckoned them forward. Like the other committee members, McNair's life was composed of a long list of honors, duties, and sources of wealth— lawyer, former judge, sheriff, public school trustee, inspector general of the Missouri militia, U.S. marshall, and currently the land office register. All along he speculated in virtually any promising enter- prise—lead, cattle, furs, land, merchandise, steamboats—and had amassed a huge fortune. As the eldest of the five in age and years in St. Louis, he presided.

Jameson and Will walked over and stood before the chairs. "Gentlemen," Jameson intoned cheerfully, "Mr. William Yates needs no introduction to your esteemed ranks. A resident of our fine city since 1804, Mr. Yates has ever since been an outstanding and enterprising young man in all regards. You are all aware of his epic journeys to the Rocky Mountains' far ends. You've watched him accompany me to this courthouse on innumerable occasions. You've traded stories with him on our circuit. Unfortunately, you can only imagine the brilliant, but alas unheralded, research and arguments he has prepared for my clients. Mr. Yates has now completed his required two years apprenticeship. He stands before you to be examined for entrance to the Missouri bar association."

The men nodded and smiled. "We extend our most cordial welcome to our intrepid bear-killer," McNair intoned and the others laughed. "Please be seated."

"Yes, indeed," Jameson replied, "Mr. Yates is a man of steeled courage and fortitude, a great frontiersman." Jameson bent to Will's ear and whispered, "They're in your pocket."

"We'll see."

For hours they grilled him on the intricacies of arbitration, *Marbury v. Madison*, attainders, natural law, the constitution, state's rights, Blackstone, the Code Napoleon, petitions, slander, Coke, *McCulloch v. Maryland*, reapportionment, contracts, due process, slavery, the Alien and Sedition Act, judicial review, liability, the Magna Carta, torts, the Bill of Rights, trusts, bankruptcy, appeals, inheritance, the *American Law Journal*, litigation, the Northwest Ordinance, and poor laws, all along posing dozens of hypothetical questions. Each member tried to outdo the others in encompassing even the simplest questions in the most verbose and obtuse manner possible. Will occasionally had to tactfully ask for clarification.

At first, his mind numbed under the verbal barrages, and the arrogance and hypocrisy those men and the whole legal system represented to him. His responses were stumbling, inarticulate. Easton, perhaps remembering his former association with Will's father, would bail him out by offering a key phrase or argument. But Will's heart and mind were clearly elsewhere, and he made poor use of Easton's hints. With a sodden handkerchief, he continually wiped away the sweat dribbling down his face.

I'm losing, he suddenly realized, and the thought disgusted him. Don't let these bastards with their endless sophistries and conceits beat you down, he scolded himself. A fierce determination to win surged through him. He focused and began to systematically pull from his mind's corners scraps of information and forge them into arguments. His voice grew animated as his words flowed smoothly from one link of reasoning to the next. The committee members straightened in their chairs, listened attentively, and even began pruning their own discourses to extract more from him.

Finally McNair glanced at his pocketwatch. "My word, gentlemen. We've been at it nearly five hours." The others expressed surprise. McNair looked to his right and left. "Any more questions?" They shook their heads no. "Well, then, Mr. Yates, Mr. Jameson. If you would please wait down the hall until we call you."

Jameson slapped Will on the back and grasped his hand as soon as they closed the door behind them. "Lovely, William. A bit slow at first, but then you sprinted like a racehorse. You've got it hands down."

"At this point, I couldn't care less."

"William!" Jameson admonished.

They loitered at the top of the staircase. Will stared at the map on the wall below, tracing with his mind routes west.

"Gentlemen," McNair's voice called from down the hall, "You may return. We've reached a verdict."

They strolled to the room and stood before the committee once more. The gentlemen rose. McNair smiled broadly. "Mr. Yates, we have unanimously decided that you will make an outstanding lawyer and heartily welcome you into our ranks." Each man uttered his own brief congratulatory remarks as he took Will's hand.

McNair motioned them to a sideboard where a bottle of port and glasses rested. "A toast to my friends," he said after filling the glasses and raising his own. "To William Yates and an undoubtedly great future."

"Here! Here!" the others exclaimed and tipped back their glasses.

"Well, Mr. Yates, have any prospective first clients?" McNair asked.

"Matter of fact I do, sir."

"Oh, and do we know your potential client's circumstances?"

"You know the client, and perhaps his plight," Will hesitated. He glanced at Jameson who stared curiously back. "I will represent myself in a petition for divorce before the legislature." The men gasped.

Then McNair laughed loudly. "Mr. Yates, you're a man of humor as well as knowledge." Everyone chuckled. Will smiled weakly and, saying nothing, extended his empty glass toward McNair.

• • •

Sleet crackled against the windows. The office quivered with each wind blast. Oblivious to the storm, Will dipped his quill then scratched rapidly across the paper.

There was a knock on the door. Startled, he tipped over the inkwell with his left hand. The ink spilled across his poem.

"Damn it!" He tried mopping up the ink with a handkerchief but it just smeared. Someone knocked louder. "Hold your horses," he shouted angrily. He pushed back his chair, strode toward the door, and yanked it open.

A woman shivered outside beneath a parasol. Encased in layers of black clothing, her body looked bulky. Will peered at her face and his body chilled. Botticelli's Venus! he thought excitedly, recalling a favorite engraving from one of Jameson's art books.

The scowl disappeared from his face. "Please come in," he urged. He took her shawl and parasol, and waved her toward the fire. "Did you arise from a clamshell?"

Her brow crinkled in bewilderment. "Pardon me, sir?" Then she laughed. "Oh, because I'm all wet?"

In Will's mind, her voice sounded like a nightingale's. "You remind me...I saw you...well, ah...what can I do for you, miss...?"

"Mrs. Laura Tipton."

"I've never seen you before. Not in St. Louis," he said in wonder as he accepted her coat and placed it on a chair. She had a tiny waist, and large breasts and hips. She took off her bonnet. Her chestnut hair was piled high in a bun. He felt himself stir as he imagined pulling out the pins that bound her hair and watching it cascade down her back. "Do you live here?"

She giggled. "First you say you've seen me and then you say you haven't."

"True," he admitted in confusion.

"It's hardly surprising that we've never met before...Mr. Jameson?"

"No, I'm..."

"Oh, my apologies. That's right. I was told to expect an elderly gentleman. You must be his partner, Mr. Yates."

"Yes. And you must be..." He wanted to say something gallant but his mind clouded as he gazed at her. She waited politely. He grabbed a chair and placed it before the fire. "Please be seated and warm yourself."

She smiled and sat down. "Thank you. I'm feeling warm already."

"Can I get you some br...brandy?" he asked and looked away.

"No, thank you. I rarely drink."

"Oh, me neither...or too...I mean, sometimes I do, too, but only in moderation."

"Of course, Mr. Yates."

"What brings you to me? I mean here. To our office. In St. Louis."

"I arrived yesterday by coach from Vandalia, Illinois." She shivered. "Oh, it was a horrid trip. The mud was sometimes high as the coach's hubs and the horses strained and the driver kept whipping them. And I was so frightened crossing the Mississippi by ferry. The waters were so fast and flooded the shores."

"Well, you're safe now."

She smiled into his eyes. "I'm staying at the Le Barras Hotel. The proprietor recommended Mr. Jameson to help me with my troubles. I'm so sorry to disturb you but..." She glanced at the desk. "Oh, you've had a spill."

"It was nothing."

"I hope it wasn't an important document."

"Well, actually it was...a poem." Her eyes widened.

"You write poetry?"

"Well, ahh, now and again," he said apologetically. "I'm no good."

"How charming. I'm sure you're a wonderful poet. I love poetry."

"You do?" he replied eagerly.

"Most certainly."

"Who do you like?"

"I adore William Cullen Bryant. Are you acquainted with him?"

"Yes, of course. Well, I haven't read his work. But I've heard of him. I'd love to read his poetry."

"English poets are the fashion but I've never read anyone who can express such depths of emotion and spirituality and eternal questions as Mr. Bryant. And you, Mr. Yates?"

"Well, ah, my favorite is Byron."

She blushed. "He had such a wicked life."

"Well, yes, he did live life to the fullest."

She extended her hands to the crackling fire. "So I've heard."

He restrained himself from bending over and kissing her cheek. He slipped behind Jameson's stuffed chair to hide his arousal, meanwhile trying to recall tedious Blackstone passages to dampen it. "Was there something I could help you with, Mrs. Tipton?"

She looked up at him. "Yes, my husband...We—my son and I— got word last month that he had died. A horse fell on him."

"Oh, you're that Mrs. Tipton." Will recalled the story. Drunk as a skunk, Tipton was crushed trying to jump his horse over a rail fence. And there had been rumors about him getting a local girl pregnant. "That was a tragedy. I'm so sorry."

Tears rolled down Mrs. Tipton's face. She dabbed at them with her finger. "I seem to have lost my..."

"Oh, allow me." Will snatched his handkerchief off the table. "Here. Whoops! Forgive me," he exclaimed, as they stared at the ink stained cloth. "My stupidity. Sometimes my mind just wanders and I'm not all here. I mean I am and I'm not."

She burst into laughter. "Mr. Yates, your humor is worth a dozen handkerchiefs."

"Well, I ahh...I just...your husband was buying up land across the state, wasn't he?"

"Yes, that's one reason I'm here. I need help settling the estate. And finding a place to live. My little boy and I spent so little time with him during his life. I've decided to move to St. Louis so I can tend his grave. And give my son new horizons. He is bullied horridly in Vandalia. As soon as I dispose of all that property and buy a place here, I'll send for Jonathan and our possessions. I'm told you're also the schoolmaster."

"Yes. I've closed the school this week because Mr. Jameson's home with a severe cold and I have to hold down the fort here alone. So fear not. I can and will take care of everything."

"I'm confident that you will. I place myself fully in your capable hands." Will smiled and moved back behind Jameson's chair.

He slept little that night. Tossing restlessly beside Judy, he fantasized endlessly about running off with Mrs. Tipton for a life of poetry, adventure, and passionate coupling. Laura, he whispered. Her name rolled sensuously off his tongue. I'm in love, he admitted happily.

Early the next morning, after wolfing down coffee and biscuits, he tiptoed through the muddy streets to the Le Barras Hotel. To his surprise she awaited him in the lobby. He flared inwardly at the half-dozen other men seated or lounging nearby who shot subtle glances her way. One man, however, burly and tall with a walrus mustache and thick auburn hair, leaned against a wall and openly ogled her. She pretended not to notice.

"Mrs. Tipton," he exclaimed and he approached her. "I'm early and didn't expect you for some time."

Her black gown and petticoats beneath rustled as she rose and smiled up at him. "Oh, Mr. Yates! You've no idea of the worries in my mind. I just couldn't sleep."

"Neither could I. The land office should just be opening. Shall we?" He offered an elbow and she gently took it. As they stepped outside, he glanced disdainfully at the loiterer who leered contemptuously back at him. As they strolled down the street, they chattered nervously of poetry, life in St. Louis, and Jonathan. He greeted passersby with nods or a hearty "Good morning." This is all a dream, he thought, dazzled.

Before the land office door she gripped his arm tightly. "Oh, Mr. Yates," she cooed, "I hope I'm doing the right thing. Everything has been so sudden."

"Of course you are, Mrs. Tipton. In a few days, we'll have found a buyer for your vast lands and a house for you and Jonathan."

They entered and quietly shut the door behind them. McNair hastily yanked his feet off his desk and struggled to stand. "Will! How very good to see you."

"Good morning, Mr. McNair, I mean, Alexander."

McNair raised a thick gray eyebrow and gave a short bow. "And whom do I have the honor of meeting?"

"This is Mrs. Tipton. The widow of Mr. Ben Tipton who met with that unfortunate death from his horse last month."

"Oh, Mrs. Tipton," McNair stumbled briefly as he approached to seize her hands in his. "My deepest condolences."

Mrs. Tipton suppressed a sob. "Thank you." Tears rolled slowly down her cheeks. The men quickly drew and presented handkerchiefs. When she took McNair's, Will sparked with jealously.

"I had the pleasure of sharing many a glass or two of whiskey with Ben. He was a lively one! Those times he spoke of you—which were, of course, virtually constant—I somehow pictured someone less...you are so lovely and serene."

She blushed. "Thank you," she murmured.

He looked at her strangely. "I don't know how he could...well, please be seated," McNair said, guiding her to a chair. "Now what can I do for you?"

With her melodic voice, broken for brief intervals as she dabbed at her eyes and struggled to compose herself, Mrs. Tipton explained her seven years of marriage to Ben, his long absences as he speculated in land around the region, the isolation and unhappiness she and her son experienced in Vandalia, and their desire to begin anew in St. Louis.

Tears welled in the eyes of Will and McNair as they gazed at her light green eyes, plump lips, and soft oval face.

At her story's conclusion, McNair grabbed Will's handkerchief and trumpeted his nose into it. "My dear good woman," he said fervently as he handed the handkerchief back to an aghast Will, "please rest assured that I will do all in my power to expedite your desires as quickly and efficiently as possible." He rose, hurried over to the bookcases lining the walls, and began to extract ledgers and papers. An elderly gentleman entered. "I'm sorry, Mr. Gleason," McNair said irritably, "we're closed this morning." He shooed the bewildered man out the door, hung a closed sign on the outside knob, and drew the curtains. "Now then, where was I?" he asked as he pulled a wisp of gray hair from his forehead. "Just a few more moments, Mrs. Tipton," he promised her with a wink. It took another hour to assemble all of the deeds, and draw up and sign documents transferring ownership to Mrs. Tipton.

"What a relief," Mrs. Tipton declared. "I was so afraid that somehow the deeds would be lost or stolen by someone. There are so many unscrupulous scoundrels in this world," she said heatedly.

"Indeed there are, Mrs. Tipton," McNair agreed. "But rest assured that you are in the most capable and honest hands in St. Louis."

Will smiled cynically as he recalled all the stories of "fees" and foreclosures McNair managed to extract from the unwary, illiterate, and poor farmers.

Mrs. Tipton sighed. "Now all I have to do is find a buyer."

"That's already taken care of, Mrs. Tipton," McNair exclaimed gallantly. "I will buy your property."

She squealed in delight and grasped his arm. "Oh, Mr. McNair, you are truly a wonderful man!" McNair beamed.

"I was planning to buy some," Will interjected. "To help Mrs. Tipton."

"That won't be necessary," McNair replied testily. "Besides, you're a poor, struggling lawyer and need to save every penny to support yourself and your wife. You do remember your wife, don't you, William?" McNair and Will glared at each other.

"Mr. Yates," Mrs. Tipton remonstrated softly, "that's a lovely offer. I wasn't aware that you were married. Please do save your money. Speculations of all kinds can be dangerous, particularly those involving land. That's why I want to sell off my property and live the rest of my life on a modest but secure income. And perhaps someday to remarry." She glanced coquettishly at the two men. "Young Jonathan needs a strong father to raise him properly. I struggle, but I really do need a man in my home."

"Don't worry, Mrs. Tipton," McNair assured her. "Every man in the country will soon be a suitor at your door." She lowered her eyes modestly. And I'll be the first in line, Will fiercely promised himself.

The land's value amounted to nearly eleven thousand dollars, of which McNair scraped up twelve hundred in cash and signed away the rest in credit, minus a thousand dollars for a recently vacated house on Elm Street that he sold her. To McNair's irritation, Mrs. Tipton had insisted that the cash and credits be deposited with her attorney. With the deeds signed, Will carried the heavy money bag to his office and locked it in the small safe.

"It'll be safe there, Mrs. Tipton," he said as he replaced the key behind the loose brick in the chimney near the ceiling.

Fatigued, they dined at a nearby boarding house. Throughout their meal, they spoke awkwardly as diners eavesdropped all around them. Will related some of his travels and, in whispers, the sorrows he shared with Judy. Mrs. Tipton listened attentively, often interjecting, "You poor dear."

Finally escaping the crowded boarding house, they returned in relief to the law office. Will quickly drew the curtains. Then he shoveled some coals from the tinder box and coaxed a flame in the fireplace. He lit candles and set them in the candelabra.

"Dear Mr. Yates," Mrs. Tipton declared as she settled onto the settee, "I can't thank you enough for all of your help."

Will smiled shyly. "It was nothing."

"I believe now I'll accept your former offer of a glass of brandy. I…we have much to celebrate." She extracted a slim volume from her purse. "Mr. Bryant's poems."

"I'd be honored if you could read your favorite, Mrs. Tipton," he said eagerly. He poured two glasses from the decanter. Handing her a glass, he sat beside her.

"I love them all, but after hearing of all your tragedies and wilderness adventures, here's one you may particularly enjoy. It's entitled "Inscription for the Entrance to a Wood.""

> *'Stranger, if thou hast learned a truth which needs*
> *No school of long experience, that the world*
> *Is full of guilt and misery, and has seen*
> *Enough of all its sorrows, crimes, and cares,*
> *To tire thee of it, enter this wild wood*
> *And view the haunts of Nature…'"*

She read on, her voice murmuring like a gentle stream. Occasionally she would glance up, meet Will's gaze, and smile briefly. Mesmerized by her beauty and his longings, Will's mind and stomach churned with passion.

" '...Like one that loves thee nor will let thee pass
Ungreeted, and shall give its light embrace.' "

She closed the book and looked up into his eyes.

"My thoughts exactly," he whispered, and bent to kiss her. She raised the book between their lips. "No, Mr. Yates," she softly protested, "you're a married man."

"Married legally, not spiritually, or passionately."

"Many's the man who's said the same to me."

"I...I love you, Laura. You're the woman of my dreams. I can't live without you."

"You can and you must," she declared firmly. "I'm just widowed and will bear the burden of grief for sometime. And I have a little boy to care for."

"I'll divorce Judy. I've been planning to do so for over a year now. Then we can marry. We can move somewhere far away where no one will know of our respective pasts. Please!" he implored, "say yes!"

"I'd better go now. Please escort me to the hotel."

"Oh, Mrs. Tipton. Laura. Please forgive my ardor. I love you so."

"I understand, Mr..." she smiled. "Will. I've not rejected your offer, but need time to think. My head and heart are spinning. I'm certainly not unattracted to you. But for now, I must be let alone." With her hand gripping his arm, they strolled back to the hotel, both deep in thought.

"May I call on you tomorrow?" he asked at the lobby doors. She hesitated.

"The next day. In the afternoon. I'll be ready then."

"As you wish. Is one o'clock all right?"

"Yes. I'll eagerly await your visit. But please, under no circumstances, disturb me until then."

"I promise." She turned to enter and he touched her arm. She looked up into his eyes. "Laura," he whispered fiercely, "how I long to kiss you and hold you in my arms. I know we'd be perfect for each other. Trust me."

She smiled and touched his waist. "Take this," she murmured, pressing Bryant's *Poems* into his hand. "I wrote something inside. Forgive me." She smiled beguilingly, turned, and entered the lobby. As the door opened and closed in his face, he glimpsed and saw within the leering man he had seen that morning. Dread surged through Will. He wanted to hurry after her and warn her, protect her against him, and other evil forces he sensed. He restrained himself. My chances of taking her are hanging by a thread, he reasoned. Any more pressure on her might push her from me forever.

He opened the book to its first page. "To Will, and the eternal mingling of our spirits. Yours, Laura." The words melted his foreboding. As he strode back to his office, his mind danced with fantasies of carrying off Laura to a distant hideaway for endless coupling and poetry. He stopped abruptly as he suddenly wondered why she asked him to forgive her. Then that stranger's mocking face burned dread once again into his mind.

The tall case clock in the corner ticked loudly as Governor Frederick Bates studied the papers Will had just thrust into his tiny hands. Bates's pointed Adam's apple bobbed as he swallowed nervously. The clock struck four.

The governor looked up and frowned. "Mr. Yates, have you taken leave of your senses?"

"Smartest thing I've ever done," he replied.

"Probably the most asinine thing you've ever done. You may be jeopardizing your career!" Bates rubbed his wrinkled, spotted forehead. "Many of us are trapped in marriages that are less than ideal," he said sympathetically. "But we endure. Society expects that of us. If we, the leaders, those most gifted and affluent, are allowed to sever our sacred marital ties, then we cannot prevent the common man from doing likewise. All of society might well crumble."

"The legislature annually granted several divorces. Why not mine?"

"True. But in gaining their freedom, those men lose the most important thing a man can possess—status!"

"That's never meant much to me. I've seen first-hand how an obsession with status, with what the neighbors think, is like a poison that slowly eats a person away till they're nothing but bitter and mean."

"Status holds our society together. The pursuit of status is the source of progress."

"Maybe."

"Act not in haste, Mr. Yates. You're young. I'm told you've a promising future, not merely as a lawyer, but as one of Missouri's leaders. But not any enterprising man can sit in this chair or even in the legislature. You must be respected. You must follow the social rules publicly if not privately. There are ways around an unhappy marriage."

"Thank you, Governor. I deeply appreciate your concern. I'm many things but I try not to be a hypocrite. I won't sneak around behind

Judy's back. I wrote up this petition over a year ago and have debated what to do with it ever since. I finally decided this afternoon. I aim to be free."

Bates dipped his pen and signed the petition. "As you wish," he said wearily. "With this signature there's no turning back. Your petition will appear in a couple weeks. But mark my words," he wagged a finger, "you're making a big mistake."

"I'll take my chances," he said confidently, but inside he felt like he'd just thrown himself off a cliff.

Will joyfully daydreamed away most of the next day, envisioning scores of passionate scenes with Laura and reading and rereading the volume of Bryant's *Poems* she had left in his office. Bryant's feelings toward nature and life and death are mine, he marveled, and Laura's. Far away he heard a steamboat's shrill whistle. Fate brought us together and will carry us united through life to our graves.

The door burst open and McNair charged in followed by a dowdy woman bearing a scowl as heavy as her body. "Where is she?" McNair shouted.

Will leapt to his feet. "You mean Mrs. Tipton?" he asked. McNair pointed to the woman.

"This is Mrs. Tipton!" Will blinked in confusion. "And where's my money? Open the safe, you idiot!"

Will pried off the loose brick and grabbed the key. He hurried over to the safe, thrust in the key, and yanked open the heavy door then gasped. McNair shoved him aside. The safe was empty. McNair began trembling violently.

"Yates, you'll pay for this!"

"You're really Mrs. Tipton?" Will asked the woman meekly.

"Sure as you're standing there," she growled, "and I've got the papers to prove it."

"We've got to find her before she gets away!" McNair cried. "To the Le Barras!" He scurried out the door and down the street followed by Will and the woman. They burst into the hotel lobby and hurried to the desk. "Where is that impostor?" McNair yelled.

The clerk's head tilted back haughtily. "To which impostor among our esteemed guests are you referring?"

"Mrs. Tipton!"

"Mrs. Tipton should now be on the steamboat which just left for Pittsburgh."

"Was she alone?" Will asked anxiously.

"A handsome gentleman, who was also booked on the steamboat, gallantly offered to accompany her."

Will's heart plunged. He gripped the desk tightly. "Huge mustache, auburn hair, shit-eating leer?" The clerk nodded.

"When's the next steamboat for Pittsburgh?" McNair demanded.

"Next week at the earliest."

McNair slumped against the desk. "I don't believe it," he said weakly. "I've lost all."

"So have I," Will muttered, and thought of Jameson's loaded pistol lying in a sideboard drawer.

Muffled voices rose and fell beyond the double oak doors. Jameson and Will stood nervously with a crowd of other petitioners and defendants in the courthouse lobby. Chilled rain fell outside the steamed windows.

"How's Judith taking it?" Jameson asked quietly.

"Best as could be expected," Will replied in wonder. "She was so lucid and calm when I first explained the petition to her last week. She just asked me to take her home. Haven't talked to her since, but her lawyer says Judy's fatalistic about the whole business."

Jameson pursed his lips. "Mr. Morgan insisted on representation," he stated aloud to himself.

"Am I gonna win?" Will asked irritably as he fingered Bryant's *Poems* within a waistcoat pocket.

"Possibly," Jameson replied, "there could be some pitfalls." Will arched an eyebrow. "The legislature could simply grant you a divorce from bed and board. You would live separately while you would retain control of both your properties. You would have to support her indefinitely and would be responsible for her debts and extravagances. Neither of you would be allowed to remarry."

"That's not fair!" He glared at Judy's lawyer whispering with Seth across the lobby.

"That's a possibility. And whether or not it occurs, the legislature will undoubtedly require you to give her a going away gift. Alimony, it is called."

"I don't mind paying ransom for my freedom. I was planning to do that anyway."

Jameson nodded. "Very good. Our legislators will look favorably upon that intention although they may raise the price. Are you still determined to pursue your narrow line of reasoning?"

"That's right," Will replied fiercely. "I'll never mention her being touched or withdrawing her affections. I want to limit any humiliation she suffers. Who knows, maybe some other fella'll court her someday despite the divorce."

Jameson sighed. "I fear the worst. A winning argument should be based on hard facts, not abstractions."

The double doors opened and several petitioners filed out muttering curses. A clerk appeared and intoned loudly, "The legislature calls forth the petitioner William Yates and the defendant's lawyer, Mr. Amos Callenbach!"

Jameson patted Will's shoulder. "Good luck, my boy," he said sadly, then walked away toward the staircase to the gallery.

Will and Callenbach walked stiffly into the chamber. The doors shut loudly behind them. Most of the several score of legislators twisted in their seats and stared at them curiously; some, like McNair, malevolently. Governor Bates presided from a platform before the chamber. He slammed down his gavel. "Mr. Yates, come forward and read your petition!"

Will approached the platform, nodded to Bates, and turned to face the legislature. He trembled slightly as his eyes darted around the crowd.

"'Life, liberty, and the pursuit of happiness," he intoned. "The most sacred values for which America stands...or falls." He took a deep breath. "Individuals come together to form a government and yes, a marriage. Is the state of holy matrimony all that different from the state that governs men? Both are entered into by a social contract. When a state fails to secure the life, liberty, or happiness of the governed, the people have the right to sever those ties and form another. If governments can dissolve because of the loss of liberty or happiness or common interest, why not then a marriage which has suffered the same?

"I, William Yates, hereby petition the Missouri legislature for divorce from Judith Yates, née Judith Morgan. Neither of us are happy; neither of us are free; and that lack of liberty and happiness threatens to cut short our very lives. We are prisoners of torturing forces beyond our control, beyond our anticipation when we first became bound in marriage. Allow us to sever those bounds. Restore to us both our sacred liberty and happiness which is as dear to us and to all Americans as life itself."

He paused for breath. Slow down your delivery, he warned himself.

"Across the nations, state legislatures are recognizing that there are higher truths and needs than those uttered during a wedding. Indeed, in most of New England the legislatures have granted to the courts the power to dissolve unhappy marriages.

"Between us there is no violence or drunkenness or infidelity or shiftlessness or dissipation or," he paused and glanced at Judy's lawyer, "or idiocy or impotency. But we suffer from a deep and unforeseen incompatibility, exacerbated by my long forays into the wilderness.

"We have no children to raise with the support of both parents. Indeed, it was the loss of our child, and the deep trauma and mourning that has enveloped both of us that has resulted in our estrangement. Time has not healed those forever hemorrhaging wounds of spirit. Seeing, being with each other only serves as a constant reminder of what we have lost, what we can never regain, and thus deepens those wounds, that pain. What you have are two broken hearts that can never be mended. Our mutual affection and nuptial happiness is forever alienated.

"Noble legislators, grant this petition for divorce and restore to two individuals their sacred rights. Thank you."

The governor rapped his gavel. "Mr. Yates, you may retire to the rear. Mr. Callenbach come forward."

Callenbach was a tall, reedy man with an angular face and piercing gray eyes. "Thank you, Governor and legislators. My words will be brief because I believe my arguments are unassailable. My client, Mrs. Judith Yates, pleas for the court to reject the petitioner's arguments. This marriage reveals no valid legal justification for divorce." He rattled off a long list. "The law does not recognize the loss of liberty and happiness as grounds for divorce. Mr. Yates's points are moot.

"However, if the legislature wished to ignore existing law and sever this relationship, my client requests that it grant a bed and board divorce with neither party able to remarry and Mr. Yates responsible for financially supporting Mrs. Yates until death comes to either of them. Thank you."

The legislature buzzed loudly with the unexpected tack in his argument. The governor slammed down his gavel. "Order!" he bellowed. "The parties are to retire to await the Missouri State Legislature's verdict!" Will and Jameson retreated to a lobby corner.

"God, I pray it's not a bed and board decision," Will said as he gripped his hands.

Jameson nodded and handed him a flask. "Essentially, that's your current state of affairs. An official pronouncement to that effect won't change much." They stood silently a long time, each lost in his own swirling fears.

The doors suddenly opened. The clerk ordered the *Yates v. Yates* parties to reenter the chamber. Will and Callenbach marched inside and stood before the podium.

Bates cleared his throat. "The legislature has decided as follows: That the petition for divorce by Mr. William Yates from Mrs. Judith Yates shall not be granted on the following grounds. The law states clearly that divorce may be granted only upon clear evidence of adultery, cruelty, just cause of bodily fear, abandonment and willful desertion, impotency, idiocy, bigamy and any other cause for which marriage is annulled by ecclesiastical law.

"By a solid majority, we conclude that none of those criteria are present. While we sympathize deeply with the current unhappiness of the couple, we do believe that time will heal their wounds, and the marriage will emerge all the stronger. We urge Mr. and Mrs. Yates to redouble their efforts at reconciliation and are confident that eventually happiness will be once again restored to their marriage.

"During our debate, many, including myself, expressed our concern at the growing trend in our nation which emphasizes romantic love and happiness, rather than duty and social responsibility, as the central concerns of marriage. We urge you to concentrate on the latter in your efforts toward reconciliation. Unrealistic expectations about abstract notions of romantic happiness are a plague which is destroying all too many marriages and with them, the fabric of American society. True happiness comes from the husband and wife fulfilling their separate but integrated marital responsibilities.

"And," he paused, "in addition, Mr. Yates will pay the court costs of twenty dollars." He pounded his gavel. "I hereby declare the petition of Mr. William Yates against Mrs. William Yates rejected." He pointed the gavel at the clerk. "Next petition."

Will glared at the governor, then spun and marched outside. "Well," he declared heatedly as Jameson rejoined him in the lobby. "Reckon the only option I have left is willful desertion. I'm heading West."

Jameson gasped. "William, reconsider. I believe the governor's right."

Will ignored him and pushed his way through the crowd and into the cold rain. He slopped through the streets to the law office where he had stayed since he had submitted the petition.

"Damn them all," he yelled as he slammed the door behind him.

Laura drifted into his mind, beckoning seductively. "How could she?" he said softly. He drew Bryant's *Poems* from his pocket and tore through its pages to "A Forest Hymn." He scanned down it to a favorite passage and read aloud in a trembling voice:

> "'There have been holy men who hid themselves
> Deep in the woody wilderness, and gave
> Their lives to thought and prayer, till they outlived
> The generation born with them, nor seemed
> Less aged than the hoary trees and rocks...'"

He gently closed the book and smiled. "That's my salvation."

Twelve

1827–1829

Atop a sway-backed horse, Will led seven heavily laden mules down the muddy trace toward Franklin. Dogwoods and laurel bloomed amidst the wet, dormant forests. The glades smelled of wild onions and clover. Towhees and warblers twittered among the branches. Low, racing gray clouds spread light rains in their wake. Eyes shut, he breathed deep the forest scents and turned his face to the mist. "Freedom," he murmured triumphantly. He pushed his fingers beneath a saddlebag flap, toyed with Bryant's *Poems*, and daydreamed of Laura.

Suddenly, images from the week before his departure shoved aside those of Laura. Judy had been strangely detached when he rode over to the Morgan's and announced that he was heading to Santa Fe. Seth, however, had appeared in the doorway and angrily warned, "You'll pay for this." Although the grand jury had absolved him of complicity in the Tipton fraud, McNair still blamed Will for his own folly. "You'll never practice law in this town again," he had warned.

Many other lawyers and prominent citizens now refused to greet him in the streets; some muttered "scoundrel!" under their breaths as they passed. Even his mother had rejected him. "How could you?" she demanded bitterly when he first told her of the petition. Her disgust deepened with the legislative and grand jury hearings. "You've ruined everything," were her last words to him after he pecked her cheek before riding west from St. Louis.

"To hell with them all," Will said fiercely. "There's no turning back." He struggled to expel the anger from his mind by seizing memories of himself and Jess riding this same road a half-dozen years earlier. Where're ya drifting now, Jessie? he wondered. An image appeared of Jess's bones bleached and scattered across some unnamed forest. "Wish you were with me, compañero," he said aloud, and suddenly panged with loneliness.

He turned in the saddle and eyed his mules. Twenty-five silver dollars each and not a balky one in the lot, he noted with satisfaction. His mules were packed with fifty pounds each of cornmeal and bacon, small sacks of coffee, sugar, and salt, an iron skillet, kettle, and coffee pot, oil cloth, his worn buffalo robe, capote, bars of lead, small gunpowder kegs, six beaver traps, a Spanish grammar, dictionary, and his rifle. And that was just to serve his own needs. For the Santa Fe market he had sacks full of hammers, petticoats, tobacco, calicoes, chisels, paints, beads, axes, saws, butcher knives, and small whiskey kegs. If the Mexicans don't buy, the trappers will, he reasoned.

A week of steady plodding from St. Louis brought him to Franklin, where he scoured the taverns and wagon camps looking for a party just about to set off. He soon found one—eleven men, a hound, and three oxen-drawn wagons. Newly arrived from Ohio, none of them had ever been West before and they heartily welcomed the experience and rifle Will brought with him.

They crossed the Missouri at the Arrow Rock ferry, and pushed onward through prairie and scattered woods for four days to the ruins of Fort Osage. For nearly twenty years, the fort had marked the Missouri frontier—civilization's last outpost. But the frontier had crept steadily westward and President Adams had ordered the fort abandoned and its troops deployed elsewhere. Will wandered its rotting buildings and deserted parade ground, recalling the mingled thrill and fear that gripped him when he and the others in Becknell's party rode out from its gates toward the southwest.

It was a few more days from there to the newly rising town of Independence where the din of hammer on nail, boards smacking together, and drunken laughter and quarrels was incessant. There they joined five experienced Santa Fe traders leading two mule-drawn wagons.

The wagons rattled and squeaked and jingled west along the rutted trail through the rolling tall grass prairie of bluestem and wildflowers and scattered oak groves. The tall grasses and hills slowly subsided over the next two weeks until, by the time he reached the Arkansas River's Great Bend, the flat, hard earth sprouted nothing but stunted buffalo grass and prickly pear. The Arkansas was nearly a half-mile wide and dotted with sandy islands and a bottom pitted with quicksand. The trail hugged the river's low north bank and cut across countless gullies. The few cottonwood and ash groves had mostly been chopped or sawed down for wood and only stumps remained. Chilly winds gusted and died. Nearly every day the caravan encountered small buffalo herds whose cows they killed for meat. They stretched the hides over the wagon tops to dry.

Toward each sunset, they pulled their wagons into a circle and corralled the oxen within. They staked the horses and mules nearby on thirty foot lariats. Before turning in, they beat the grasses for rattlesnakes and pummeled any they found with stones and rifle butts. Throughout the night, they took turns on guard and watched the Milky Way blaze and listened to coyotes yipping and the wind moaning.

It took most of a day to cross the Arkansas, even after they scouted for the shallowest and most solid ford. They took each wagon across separately, doubling its oxen or mule team and whipping and cursing the beasts until they reached dry land. From there it was two hard, waterless days south to the Cimmaron River's dry bed. They followed the Cimmaron for days, having to dig holes nearly two feet deep into it before they struck muddy water. The oxen's hoofs cracked and bled, and their pace slowed to a painful limp. The men tried "shoeing" them with buffalo-skin moccasins, but they quickly wore through. The dry air shrank and split the wagon wheels. The wooden wedges they drove between the loose iron bands soon jostled free and had to be pounded in again.

After leaving the Cimmaron and striking across the plains Will grew more anxious knowing that Rabbit Ear Mountain was just ahead. When he spotted the two humped mountain on the horizon, he tied his mule string onto a wagon and announced, "I killed a man there. I'll meet you in its shadow tomorrow." Then he cantered away. It felt good to ride hard unencumbered by his mules or the wagon train. But he approached the mountain with deepening dread of the ghosts or war party that might be skulking there. He reached the mountain just before sunset and rode cautiously up the dry streambed, searching for the campsite and grave he, Jess, and Joe had fled from so long ago.

His mind whirled with memories of Hank wheezing on the ground with the arrow through his throat and that stocky Comanche he shot, whose brains and shattered skull spilled out when he tried to scalp him. He found the cottonwood grove in which they had spread their blankets and the rocks that had once covered Hank. But, shortly after they had fled, the Comanche had pried off the rocks and dragged out Hank's cold body and mutilated it. No bones remained, nor any sign at all of the mayhem that had occurred there.

There was no sound. Will nervously scanned the surrounding terrain, debating whether to spend the night at this haunted site or far out on the plains. The crimson was fading from the low drifting clouds and the earth was darkening. "Gotta face the spirits," he finally concluded aloud.

He unsaddled his horse and staked it, then unrolled his buffalo robe. With his back against a cottonwood, he munched jerky, sipped warm water from his canteen, and watched the stars appear one by one and then in clusters in the black above.

He awoke just as a gray band widened above the eastern horizon. He had slept soundly, escaping the claw of any lingering ghosts or nightmares. As he watched the sunrise, he felt strengthened in ways he could not explain.

He lounged most of that morning until he spotted the caravan plodding toward him, and rode out to meet it. The men were relieved to see he was still alive, and together they pushed on westward until the sun dropped low before their eyes once again.

Toward dusk five days later, they circled their wagons near several high hills known as Wagon Mound. With a half-dozen other men, Will was pounding stakes into the ground outside the enclosure when a score of Comanche galloped toward them, waving blankets and screaming. The mules and horses brayed and kicked at the end of the lariats. Some yanked loose and ran off. Will and the men sprinted toward the wagons while the men within scrambled for rifles and pistols. Arrows thudded into the earth and canvas. The men cursed and shouted. The hound yelped frenziedly. Shots exploded.

Puffs of smoke drifted away. Seconds later the Comanche were galloping away out of rifleshot, driving a dozen mules and horses before them. Although his mules were safe, Will's horse was among those stolen. He urged the men to pursue the Comanche and recapture their stock, but no one dared. He bitterly cursed the "porkeaters" for their cowardice and the Comanche for their "thieving, murdering ways." Vexed as much by his taunts as the Comanche raid, everyone just ignored him. Will settled into a bilious silence. They herded the remaining stock inside the wagon circle and doubled the guard.

Hair-triggered after the raid, a few days later they almost shot down a half-dozen Mexicans riding east onto the plains to hunt buffalo. The caballeros were clad with leather jackets and trousers, broad sombreros shaded their swarthy faces, spurs jingled from their boot heels, and they carried lances and bows. One man prodded an ox pulling a carreta in which to pile the skins and dried meat. The two parties nodded as they passed and soon disappeared from each other's sight.

For days they followed the flank of the Sangre de Christo Mountains and then turned up into the meandering Pecos Canyon. With whiskey and songs, they celebrated their safe arrival at the village of San Miguel del Vado, New Mexico's easternmost frontier town. The traders competed with each other to sell wares to the few inhabitants. But the peasants had already spent what little money they had on previous caravans. Disappointed, the traders cracked their whips and urged their wagons on up the canyon.

A couple of days later they traversed the pass and descended through the piñon and juniper into the broad Rio Grande Valley. On Santa Fe's outskirts they rumbled through fields in which peasants hoed rows of wheat, beans, or corn, or dug irrigation ditches to nearby streams. They rolled into the plaza bound by the low adobe governor's palace, barracks, customs house, and homes of the most prominent citizens. Crowds hemmed in the traders, straining to peer into the wagons. Trying to pilfer what they could, urchins slipped around the wagons and mules. To keep the crowd at bay and for their own amusement, the wagoners cracked their whips merrily, each trying to outdo the others.

The alcade soon strolled out from the governor's palace and motioned the traders to gather around him. He bowed slightly, then politely demanded a tariff of five hundred silver pesos for each wagon, no matter what its contents' value. The traders gasped and protested but the alcade was adamant.

As Will debated slipping off with his mules, a couple of the men who had traded in Santa Fe before haggled with the governor in their broken Spanish. Will sidled up to a lean, baldheaded trader named Grierson and asked, "Let me throw in with you and we can split the fee." Grierson nodded. They dragged the packs off Will's mules and shoved them into Grierson's already overloaded wagon.

After an hour of negotiations between the patient alcade and increasingly exasperated Americans, they agreed on a four hundred and fifty dollar fee, payable either when each trader sold out or left town.

While some men led off the stock to water and graze them, others began hawking their wares from the backs of their wagons. Knots of Spanish and Indians gathered around each wagon, but there were few buyers and even the best prices taken were barely double the costs.

Toward late afternoon, Will wearied of the fruitless bartering and wandered off through the narrow streets. Worrying about how he would be received, he strolled out to the edge of town to the home where he had recovered from his illness. The father and uncle sat on the doorstep and peered suspiciously at him as he approached. Suddenly the father said something to his brother. They both rose and smiled. Will shook hands and spoke with them in his broken Spanish. He handed them a canteen full of whiskey and they laughed merrily as they sipped from it and then invited him to honor them once again by resting in their home. He eagerly agreed and hurried off to retrieve his mules and goods while the wife cooked dinner. Grierson huffed and cursed him when he announced that the partnership was dissolved. "We've but replaced one set of possibilities with new and maybe better ones," Will happily responded as he rode off. "Good luck to ya."

He stayed with the family nearly a month. Since all three daughters, including Jess's sweetheart, Luísa, had married, the father, uncle, and mother particularly relished Will's cheerful company. One day, Will asked the father how much he owed for room and board. "*Lo que gusta*," the father replied simply. Will smiled, charmed by the "whatever you care to give" attitude. He pressed ten pesos into the peasant's callused palm and they spoke no more of it.

A few days after his arrival, Will negotiated a deal with the alcade in which he received a trade license for one hundred silver pesos, and managed to sell enough goods over the next few weeks to pay it off. Rather than squat in the dusty main square all day, he simply lounged around the home and bartered with Mexicans who had heard of his wares.

Over those weeks, a half-dozen more caravans creaked into the main square while the earlier ones headed back to Independence. Each new group sold fewer goods for less silver or furs than its predecessors, and after paying off the Mexican officials and gambling away more money on cards, drink, and women, most barely broke even or actually lost.

Every day Will wandered the streets, reveling in Santa Fe's sensuality. The sky was the deepest turquoise. Piñon smoke sweetened the air. Goats, pigs, and chickens foraged the hard earth streets. Blood dark bunches of chiles and onions dangled from the adobe houses. Bells gonged hollowly from the crumbling churches.

The people charmed and beguiled him. From the raggedest peasant to the governor, the Mexicans exuded politeness and gentle manners. They bowed, tipped their hats, kissed their hands in salute to each other, touched cheeks, wrapped hands around each other's waists, and spoke in low, animated voices. With the shanks of their spurs three to five inches long, and the rowels a half-dozen inches in diameter, the caballeros chinked loudly down the streets or trotted by on horseback. Their leather jackets, pants, and sombreros were festooned with bright ribbons and cords. Silver disks studded their saddles; some bits were made of pure silver. Before doorways, young women gossiped and giggled and puffed thin cigars and eyed passing men. The woman wore thin white blouses and dark skirts to their ankles and wrapped their heads in red rebozos. Silver bracelets covered their wrists and rings their fingers.

But the well-to-do were few and the poor many. The peasants shuffled barefoot through the dusty streets. They wore dull, threadbare cotton shirts and knee britches tied to their waist with bright red sashes. Their bodies were lean and hard; dirt darkened their hands and feet. Wrapped in multicolored wool blankets, the Pueblos sat stoically in the squares before rows of pottery or blankets or wooden santos. They quietly watched the passers-by or chuckled softly at shared stories.

There was a fandango every week or so in which everyone from miles around would dress their best and drift into Santa Fe to join the celebrations. Wine and brandy from the vineyards of El Paso flowed freely. Music poured from small strolling bands that usually included guitar, French horn, drum, fiddle players, and several male singers. With cigars dangling from their lips, men and women crowded the squares to whirl to the music. In fast dances they drummed their feet into the ground and turned in slow circles. Will liked best the valise despacio, where partners clung to each other and glided to the mournful dirge. The Mexicans gambled incessantly, especially at fandangos. At crude tables and chairs on the plazas, they squinted at greasy cards under the bright sun or by candlelight. Money, wares, and horses traded hands at cock fights, mustang races, and bull baits. Women gambled, too, cheerfully placing heirloom jewelry and rebozos for bets.

The most popular game was to bury a greased cock in the ground up to its neck. Caballeros took turns kicking their mustangs into a gallop and trying to snatch off the cock's head as they thundered past. When someone succeeded, he galloped toward a group of ladies to present the mangled head to his heart's desire while everyone spurred their ponies after him trying to wrest away the head for themselves and their sweethearts. Elbows and spurs jabbed, mustangs crashed into each other, men screamed in pain or triumph, and usually the cock's head itself was ripped to mush.

The most daring game of all was bull jumping. A bull was loosened on a field and one by one the men galloped after it, jumped off on the beast's back, and tried to wrest it to the ground. The bulls crushed men's legs and ribs and with their long, curved horns gored bellies. But the men kept riding after the beast until one lucky and skilled man toppled the exhausted bull to its knees.

Will grew restless as the weeks passed. For days at a time, he rode out to explore the surrounding plains and canyons. But he longed for more distant vistas on the horizon and what lay beyond. He lingered in Santa Fe, though, since more than half of his goods remained unsold and the trapping season was several months away. Then one day he woke up and suddenly said, "Taos!"

Whistling some Spanish tune, he packed his mules, bid farewell to his hosts, and rode north along the Rio Grande. For the first two days, the trail was level and cut through huge sheep and cattle ranches. On the third day, the trail rose in ever higher switchbacks above the river's canyon. Toward late afternoon, Will crossed over the pass and stared out at one of the most beautiful vistas he had ever beheld. The Sangre de Christo rose steeply from a sage plain which gently sloped down to the narrow canyon a dozen miles away. Beyond the river, far away to the west, lower mountains undulated against the azure sky. The Rio Grande Valley narrowed north to the horizon, hinting at marvels beyond. In the Sangre de Christo's shadow lay scattered several score adobe buildings, corrals, and fields around a twin towered church.

While his mules browsed nearby, he gazed out for hours as the sun dropped steadily and then disappeared. Coyotes began yipping far off. Nearby, an owl hooted then fell silent. After staking his mules, he unrolled his robe and stretched upon it. The earth disappeared in darkness and more and more stars glittered above.

"I've come home," he murmured as he drifted off to sleep.

He rode into town at daybreak. Roosters crowed. Peasants shuffled out to the fields. Pigs rooted in the dust. Women gossiped before a well and took turns drawing water from it.

On the church steps, a man rose and stared suspiciously at Will. He was tall and wiry hard. His face was a web of wrinkles and deep smallpox holes and framed by scraggly carrot-colored hair and beard streaked with gray. He had small, ice-blue eyes and a long beaked nose that seemed to touch his chin. His shoulders were pinched and his back hunched. Will tried not to stare back.

"Heeya!" the man squealed. "Whadya packing thar, boy?"

"Hardware."

"Saw?"

Will nodded.

"Nails?"

"Twenty pounds' worth."

The man grinned. "Ya done come ta near the right place, boy." He sauntered over and ran his hand gently down the neck of the mule Will was riding. He whispered something into the mule's ear then pulled himself up behind Will and wrapped his arms around him. "Time's a-wastin', boy. Le's git."

"Where to?" Will replied, feeling uneasy but not knowing how to get rid of the old man.

He gestured north. "Head fer the fixed star. Toward my birthplace. My daddy was the north star and my mama a thunderstorm. They mingled and dropped me to earth for purposes I've yet to discover."

"Now wait a minute, mister. I don't even know you."

"Ya ain't heard tell a' Old Bill?"

Will admitted that he hadn't. Old Bill shook his head in disgust. "Greenhorns!" he said bitterly and spat.

"I ain't no greenhorn," Will replied angrily, then related his wanderings.

"Heeya," Old Bill said testily. "Ya'll do then. Now le's ride. Gotta still a few miles north a need a' the hardware ya's packin'. An' don't worry that thimble-sized noggin a' yourn, boy. We got silver and pelt ta pay fer it."

"All right then," Will said quietly and kicked his mule into a trot and yanked the lariat binding the lead mule to the others.

All the way to the distillery, Old Bill cackled and spoke incessantly in a high-pitched grating whine, one minute playing the camp jester, another relating his hazings of tenderfeet in past trapping expeditions, and then pontificating on Plato's *Republic* and reciting patches of Cicero's better known orations. "Sounds like you've had a busy life," Will remarked wearily.

"Heeya, boy, in ma time I done packed furs, preached the Bible, cohabited amongst the Osage fer near a decade, interpreted, guided, run off from a couple wives and several children, larned a half-dozen Injun tongues, and tramped near ever' stream and mountain valley in the Rockies." He paused and took a deep breath. "But all that's nothing but a wisp a' smoke. I'm the avatar of the elk and grizzly spirits. I swear it. Ya know what an avatar be?"

"Reincarnation and personification of something," Will replied over his shoulder.

"Heeya," Old Bill replied irritably. "I do believe we gotta know-it-all here."

"No reason ta get riled, Old Bill. More I know about you, more I'll appreciate you."

Old Bill lapsed into silence as he pondered Will's statement. Finally he nodded and vigorously scratched an armpit. "True. True. Ya'll do, boy, ya'll do," he observed.

They topped a rise and looked down into a shallow valley with cottonwood and aspen stumps scattered along a creek. "Thar," he pointed to several half-built wooden and abode buildings around which a dozen ragged trappers, women, and naked children sprawled. "Arroyo Hondo. Home aways from home fer me and other pilgrims."

They rode down and dismounted. Old Bill disappeared into one of the buildings while the other trappers gathered around asking questions and fingering Will's goods as he unloaded them. When Will mentioned he had trapped the northern Rockies, one of the trappers limped up to him and asked, "Why, you might know my brother, Bill Sublette."

Will eyed the man. He did resemble Sublette, though his face was flushed and he was taller and wider. "Bill and I are good friends."

"Still kickin'?"

"Far's I know. Ain't seen him for a couple years. He's a pistol." The man grinned. "He's a powderkeg."

"What happened to your leg?"

"Apache arrow on the Gila. Been troubling me ever since." He bent down to rub it then rose and extended his hand. "Name's Milt," he said. Will introduced himself. Milt turned to the others and announced.

"Boys! Welcome Will Yates to our camp." The men nodded and smiled. Someone offered him a jug. He raised it to his lips and gulped deeply, then grinned back at them.

"Thank you. Glad ta be here."

Will sold off most of his goods for furs and silver and stored his possessions in a dank cellar beneath the distillery. He helped the others mold adobe bricks and raise roofs, and the labor cleansed him. He wandered the surrounding mountains, hunting and exploring, and idled away days in Taos, either alone or with other trappers. Occasionally he would ride several miles south of town to the little church of San Francisco de Asis where he would sit quietly for hours within its thick, whitewashed adobe walls. Now and then outside a donkey would bray or playing children laugh. But the sounds seemed from another world. Sometimes he could hear his own heartbeat in the stillness.

The brightly colored wooden santo on the altar intrigued him. A huge, elongated Jesus hung from the cross flanked by a diminutive Joseph and Mary. Blood dripped from his thorn crown and spear wound. His head was slightly bowed and his sad eyes gazed down at his parents. A different vision greeted the devout as they turned to leave the church. Near the entrance on a cracked and fading retablo was painted a smiling Madonna and child surrounded by adoring angels floating in the heavens. Will would ponder possible meanings of those two icons in ways the priests never intended nor even imagined. But inevitably when he felt his mind hovered near something infinite, the huge wooden doors would creak open behind him and other worshippers would shuffle in, breaking the spell. He would nod ruefully to them and be off.

A mile west of town lay Taos pueblo. The Tiwa allowed whites only within the church and graveyard on the pueblo's outskirts or on the main plaza. On the plaza's north side rose a huge adobe building four or five stories high like a layer cake and composed of a maze of tiny interconnected rooms. Smaller multifamily adobes framed the plaza. Scattered throughout the pueblo were a dozen beehive kivas from which thrust tall ladders that reached toward heaven. Will gazed at the kivas wondering what strange mysteries were performed deep within. Once he wandered to the plaza's far edge and stared down a narrow alley toward a kiva just as naked men emerged into the sunlight as if they were newborn. Startled to see him, the Tiwas angrily gestured and cursed in Spanish. Chastised, he hurried away.

One day as he sat with his back against the church in town a column of trappers mounted on mules and horses snaked down the trail from Santa Fe. As they reached the sage they kicked their animals into a gallop and charged, firing rifles and hollering joyfully. Clattering into the main square, they milled around as the inhabitants gathered to greet old friends and pass jugs of aguardiente.

Will recognized one of the men. "Sylvestre Pratte," he said aloud. Pratte was an acquaintance from St. Louis with whom he had occasionally conversed in taverns. He shared the same age and height as Will, but was slender and dark featured. His father, Bernard, headed the French Fur Company that had traded up the Missouri and, in 1825, dispatched his son with a large party down the Santa Fe trail to garner Southwestern furs. Sylvestre's luck had been poor.

Although Bernard had tried to nurture his son into leadership, most dismissed Sylvestre as a bumbling trader and trapper who would never be anything else. Indecisive and mild-mannered, he had trouble commanding his men's respect and many deserted. Then in 1826, Papagos had wiped out one of his trapping brigades on the Gila River and the following year the governor had confiscated all his own party's furs for trapping without a license. That much was mountain lore. Word, however, had not yet reached New Mexico that old man Pratte, disgusted with the losses and mounting debts, had cut off all credit to his son's ventures that summer of 1827.

Will waited until the men had dispersed with their mules and packs then followed Pratte. He slipped up behind him and tapped him on the shoulder. Pratte whirled.

"Welcome to Taos, Sylvestre. 'Member me?"

Pratte's mouth opened in surprise. Finally he said. "Dirty Cock Tavern."

"That's right."

"You rode with Becknell back in '21." Will nodded. "Remember everything 'bout you but your name."

"Yates. Will Yates."

Pratte grimaced and slapped his side. "Doggone it. That's right. Was on the tip of my tongue. You gonna join us?"

"Maybe. Where you heading? Gila?"

"Gila's trapped out. We're headed up the Rio Grande through the Rockies to the Green."

"Kinda wanted to wander to the Southwest."

"We'll head back that way in a season or two."

"When ya leaving?"

"Few weeks."

Will nodded. "I'll sign on."

"Wages is two hundred dollars for the duration. Shouldn't be more'n year."

"What!" Will replied incredulously. "That's slave wages. I'm a free trapper. Buy my furs at mountain prices."

"Can't do it. Either you're an engagé or you don't come."

"I spent two years in the Green River country. Ponder it, Sylvestre. Anyone else in your party know that country like me?"

Pratte squinted at him. "Could hire you as a guide. Three hundred dollars."

"Either mountain prices or no deal."

Pratte glanced around furtively. Everyone was unsaddling horses or checking equipment or trading stories. They were all out of earshot. "All right, goddamn it," Pratte growled. He thrust out a hand and Will shook it. "But don't tell no one," he warned.

"All right," he responded, reckoning he could trust Pratte a lot more if the handshake had accompanied a written contract.

Within an hour almost everyone in Taos was drunk, and either dancing to the fast music of guitars and drums or sprawled on the ground passing tales and jugs. Suddenly, a stout man with a high forehead and thinning brown hair gave a chilling war whoop and danced across the plaza with three long, black scalps fluttering atop a pole. Seven other scalps festooned his grease slickened hunting shirt. Other trappers and Mexicans fell in behind him. Shrieking madly, the procession snaked around the square to the beat of the drums.

Pratte nudged Will. "Watch out for that one," he said quietly.

"Who is he?"

"Tom Smith." Pratte went on to explain that Smith, a voracious eater and drinker, sweated profusely even in the depths of winter. He salted his incessant jokes and stories with good-hearted curses, and pulled pranks that usually humiliated or physically hurt his victims. Deafening war whoops exploded from his lungs at the unlikeliest moments, startling all around. "And Smith grins his way through every Injun fight, shooting and gouging. Seems ta love killing Injuns. Ripped them scalps on the Colorado. Mohave."

"Ever kill any white men?"

"Rumor has it. Wouldn't turn my back on him."

Will sighed. "Sounds like good advice."

In early August, Pratte led thirty-six men north up the Rio Grande.

Most were French, but there were a dozen Americans, some Mexicans, and the odd Irish, English, or Scot. For a week they rode steadily through the ever widening valley. Then, where the Rio Grande cut sharply west, they struck north across a vast, arid plain which gradually narrowed between the Sangre de Christo to the east and an unnamed western mountain range. They skirted huge sand dunes and cursed the alkaline water and lack of game. They and their horses grew scrawny and listless. The men's tempers flared. Fights broke out over nothing.

They trapped the first beaver in streams running down the mountains at the valley's end. Elk and mule deer appeared and became plentiful. Although they lost several horses in the days of struggle over the 9,000-foot pass, they rejoiced in the thick spruce forests and clear waters. They descended to the Arkansas valley and trapped their way up it, taking a dozen beaver packs. The Rockies hemmed them in all around, the peaks jagged and snow-capped. Grizzly were numerous and several men just escaped being mauled. The pass out of the Arkansas valley was over 11,000 feet but the horses and mules had acclimated and fattened in the lush meadows and they crossed over without any losses. What Indian sign they had stumbled across was old and though the men posted guards at night no one tried to run off the stock. The forested, rugged plateau between the Arkansas and Colorado rivers was filled with virgin beaver streams which they spent a week plundering. By late September the aspen burned amber and the first snow flurries whitened their blankets. Pratte was determined to winter on the Green, so they pushed on to the North Platte's headwaters.

The discontent of most men had disappeared once they had reached the high Rockies. In the month since, each man had taken nearly a pack of pelts and they fattened on elk steaks and beaver tails. Yet to Pratte's irritation, most ignored his orders and instead pointedly followed the advice of his clerk.

Ceran St. Vrain was of medium height and build, had a finely chiseled face and black, wavy hair, and exuded a deep dignity and reserve which even the unruliest of trappers respected. He listened carefully to the others in council and then, when he rendered his judgment, did so with a quiet but decisive authority. He was untiring in helping others pack the mules or repair equipment or just listen to their travails. He seemed everything Pratte was not.

Frustrated and jealous at St. Vrain's popularity, but afraid to attack him directly, Pratte tried to assert his manhood by badgering Old Bill for wandering off and not discharging camp duties. When Old Bill snorted in contempt, Pratte noisily fired him and ordered him to leave camp. Old Bill warned he would hex Pratte if he didn't mind his manners. Pratte dismissed him as a "camp idiot," then stalked angrily away. Undaunted, Old Bill continued to go and come as he pleased, though he occasionally squealed that the gods would strike Pratte dead for his hubris.

One day Will was trailing an elk through the forest when he heard high-pitched chanting ahead. He slipped through the ponderosa, careful not to snap any branches. His heart pounded and breath drew quicker. He peered into a clearing in which someone hunched over a small fire. "Heeya," Old Bill's voice screeched. "Who be thar?"

Will announced himself then walked into the meadow. Old Bill pointed his rifle at Will's gut. Will froze. "Don't shoot, Old Bill, it's me, Yates," he said nervously. "What're you doing?"

Old Bill grunted and lowered his rifle. "Ain't yourn time yet. Ya ain't the one I'm fixin' ta put under. Not yet at least. Now git the hell outta here 'fore ya ruin ma medicine." On a blanket before the fire were a dried owl heart, an array of herbs, and a small lizard with its lips sewn shut.

Will felt hypnotized. "What're ya doing?" he repeated quietly.

Old Bill stared into his eyes.

"Be ya the one? My disciple?"

"I...I don't know."

"I've the powers a' the universe under my wings," Old Bill intoned shrilly. "I kin rub out any man livin' and raise the dead. I kin read the future and past and hearts of all."

Startled, Will replied, "I'd like those powers. Will you teach me?"

Old Bill squinted into his eyes.

"Naw," he said at last. "I've penetrated yourn worthless soul. Ya ain't the one. Not yet least ways. Yer growing within yer shell. Either ya'll break free or it'll smother ya."

He snorted and then warned, "An ifin ya tell anyone what ya seen, I'll gut ya alive. Ya hear?" Will nodded fearfully. "Now git while yar still breathin'." Will turned and scrambled into the trees. "Ya'll see my powers in a day 'er two," Old Bill called out behind him and cackled merrily.

The next evening the men were scattered around fires in a wild-flower filled meadow. The sun had set behind the mountains. The clouds were turning rose and lavender. Shadows darkened across the valley. Will lounged at a fire with Pratte, St. Vrain, Milt, and Smith.

Milt was retelling his tale of stealing back a pack of pelts the alcade had confiscated when someone excitedly shouted, "*Regardez le chien!*"

Old Bill cackled loudly from another fire. Everyone looked up and glanced nervously around. Staring straight ahead and mouth foaming, a huge black dog trotted through camp. Most men stared mesmerized at the dog. Others fled shouting, "*Diable!*" The dog approached Pratte who rose and faced it. Will and the others jumped to their feet and scrambled off.

"Run for it, Sylvestre," Will warned.

But Pratte just stared down at the beast. "This is the end, boys," he said weakly. The dog bared its fangs and growled. Pratte stepped back. Suddenly the dog lunged and sank its teeth deep into his leg. Pratte screamed, cursed, and slammed his fist into the dog's head but it would not let go. He seized the dog's head in his hands and dug his thumbs into its eyes. The dog howled and jerked free. Pratte kicked it in the throat and it scurried away whining.

Old Bill wobbled, rather than aimed, his rifle at the dog and squeezed when he felt right. The .50-calibre ball shattered the dog's head. "The Lord giveth and the Lord taketh away," Old Bill trilled as the gunsmoke cleared.

The men gathered around Pratte who had dropped to the ground moaning and tearing at the deep wounds in his leg. "The poison's in me," he gasped, "get it out." With Will and Milt holding down Pratte's arms and legs, St. Vrain cut away the pants and poured whiskey on the wound. Pratte screamed.

"Don't let Sylvestre bite or scratch you," St. Vrain warned. "That dog was rabid. In fact, we'd best tie him down." They bound Pratte's wrists and ankles and staked him to the earth.

"Don't let me die, boys," Pratte pleaded. "Not out here. Take me home." St. Vrain tipped a water gourd into Pratte's mouth and he gulped it down.

"We'll just have to wait, Sylvestre. Maybe the poison didn't hold." Pratte wailed and cursed and tugged at the rawhide bonds all night.

The trappers moved to the meadow's far end where they built up a circle of fires and cowered within, fearing other rabid beasts lay in wait just beyond the fire's glare. They tried to drown Pratte's rantings with jokes and stories. St. Vrain and Will kept vigil beside Pratte, trying to soothe his torments with water and calm words. Will trembled with guilt and fear. Like the others, he had fled when the dog approached. I could've killed that dog before it got Pratte, but I was yellow, he rebuked himself. He puzzled over whether Old Bill really conjured up that mad dog. He dared not reveal his suspicion to St. Vrain for fear Old Bill would fiendishly murder him, too. Will resolved to shoot Old Bill if he hexed anyone else.

Pratte died just as the sky began to lighten. They dug a shallow grave and buried him beside where he died. Old Bill led them in the Lord's Prayer.

After they finished, Smith demanded, "Who's gonna pay our wages?"

"I'll take responsibility," St. Vrain replied quietly.

"Reckon that makes ya cap'in," Milt pointed out. "Rest ya boys agreed?" They nodded. "Looks unanimous ta me, Ceran."

St. Vrain glanced at the worried faces surrounding him. "So be it. Let's head to the Green."

For eight days, they trapped their way down the Platte Valley until it broadened into high plains. All along, snow deepened on the high mountain ranges on either side and drifted across the meadows. Fierce winds stripped away the golden aspen and cottonwood leaves and froze the streams until the men had to hack through the ice with hatchets before they could set their traps. They followed buffalo trails through the snow and feasted off the cows. They stripped the bark off cottonwood trees and fed it to their starving horses.

When they reached the point where the western mountain range dwindled to frozen plains, they struggled for three days across it to the Muddy River Valley which, to their relief, was snow-free. They camped there several days to trap, revive their stock, and butcher a small buffalo herd that they had cornered in a nearby canyon. After trapping off all the beaver, the men spent their days scraping hides and drying meat.

Will was cutting and hanging strips of meat on a cross-pole when St. Vrain stepped beside him. "This country look familiar, Yates?" he asked.

Will shook his head wearily. "Never been here before. All I know is the Green's due west of here. How far I don't know."

St. Vrain nodded. "There's shelter and game along this river. I'm tempted to follow it south till it reaches the Green."

"No telling how long that'll take or where it'll lead. As Ashley tells it, the Green leaves the grasslands and enters a long, meandering canyon that eventually emerges in desert and mountain void of beaver, game, and forage. We're over the divide so I'm sure this river feeds the Green but I fear it'll lead us down to that desert country," St. Vrain gestured westward. "Mighty bleak that way. Little water. We'll lose horses. Don't wanna be caught out there in a blizzard."

"True. Maybe we could trap our way south till the beaver play out, winter in some canyon, then head on to the Green next spring. We're bound to run into trappers out there who'll know where rendezvous'll be."

"I was thinking of skipping rendezvous altogether and taking our pelts down the Platte and Missouri to St. Louis."

Will lifted an eyebrow. "Home?" he said quietly.

"That's right."

"Wasn't expecting that. Have mixed feelings about it."

"Many of us do," St. Vrain said, thoughtfully. "Appreciate it if you could keep my words to yourself. It's only a possibility." Will nodded.

"By the way, Captain, there's been something I've been meaning to ask you."

"Yes?"

"Perhaps Sylvestre mentioned to you a deal we shook on when I joined the expedition?"

"Nope."

"We agreed that I accompany the party as a free trapper and sell out my pelts at mountain prices."

He shook his head. "Pratte mentioned nothing to me and there's nothing in the account books about it."

Will winced in disappointment. "I was hoping he had. He told me to keep quiet about it."

St. Vrain arched an eyebrow.

"This expedition's composed solely of engagés."

"Not solely. Not according to our deal."

With a sigh, St. Vrain admitted, "Yates, you place me in a very difficult position. I know nothing of what you speak. The account book does record Sylvestre as owing you four hundred ninety-three dollars, some for mules and sundries he purchased from you and the rest that he borrowed from you in Taos."

"That's right."

"And you'd receive an additional two hundred dollars upon the completion of our expedition."

"I've nearly a pack and a half of furs. That's nearly five hundred dollars at Santa Fe prices and seven hundred fifty dollars back in St. Louis. And if I take as many in the spring hunt, I'll have double those values."

St. Vrain grimaced. "This enterprise is deeply in debt. Sylvestre owes creditors like yourself thousands of dollars. Even if we can return safely with our furs, I won't have enough to pay off the men and creditors. Try to understand. You don't have any written record of your alleged transaction with Sylvestre. Maybe you're telling the truth. Maybe not. I've no way of knowing." He hesitated.

Rifle in hand and grinning wildly, Smith ambled up. "Ceran, I've got a funny feeling."

St. Vrain held up a hand. "Just a minute, Tom. Yates, I've no recourse but to reject your claim."

Will was about to remonstrate when the sounds of thundering hoofs and war whoops filled the air. Startled, they looked up to watch a score of mounted Indians riding down on the herd. The trappers dashed back to camp or took shelter behind cottonwood trees.

"Killin' time!" Smith hooted and shoved Will. "Fetch yer iron, Yates!" Screeching at the top of his lungs, Smith charged the Indians. Will snatched up his rifle and ran after Smith. Most of the Indians galloped around the herd which broke into a frenzied run toward the horizon. Five warriors veered toward Smith and Will, screaming taunts and brandishing bows and clubs. An arrow whizzed past Will's head. He dropped to his knee, aimed, and fired. When the smoke drifted away, a pony lay still on the ground with its rider struggling to pull himself free. Smith fired and the ball smashed in a warrior's face and he dropped heavily. Two of the Indians jerked their ponies around and kicked them into a gallop beyond rifle shot with the other raiders and captured stock. But one warrior ducked behind his pony and charged Will and Smith who were hastily trying to reload. The pony reared before them. The Indian pointed the musket at Will's jaw. Laughing crazily, Smith dropped his rifle, pulled his skinning knife, and lunged at the warrior who fired down at Smith instead. The bullet struck Smith in the ankle, shattering both bones and knocking him over. Will dashed toward the warrior and swung his rifle butt toward the Indian's face. The warrior dodged and the butt glanced off his shoulder. Milt ran up and fired point blank into the warrior's chest. The Indian dropped heavily to the ground. The pony cantered away. Will reloaded. Other men ran up. Milt yanked his knife, sawed off the Indian's scalp and waved it crazily. "Whoa thar, Thomas!" he shouted merrily. "I'm one up on ya this time!"

"That one yonder with his head blown off's mine, Milton!" Smith roared and struggled to his feet. Waving his skinning knife, he tried to stumble toward the other dead warrior but his exposed bones stuck in the soft earth. Smith screamed as much in rage as pain.

Milt chuckled. "Whatever ya say, Thomas!" He dashed over to the other Indian who had pulled himself free of his dead pony and, dragging his smashed leg, now crawled toward his lance a dozen feet away. Milt hovered triumphantly over the Indian and laughed harshly. The Indian stared up at him and began chanting his death song. Milt yanked his knife and swiped toward the warrior's throat, cleaving it open. Blood spurted and the Indian dropped back dead. Milt bent down, sliced off the Indian's scalp, and war whooped triumphantly. "Two to yer one, Thomas!" he yelled.

"Goddamn it, Milton," Smith gasped. Will and St. Vrain helped Smith pull his bones from the mud and tried to force him down. "Haul me thar," he ordered, pointing to the unscalped Indian.

"Your foot's near shot away," St. Vrain replied quietly.

"I don't give a damn," Smith shouted. "I want that scalp!"

St. Vrain shrugged. "All right." He and Will dragged Smith over to the dead warrior. Blood streamed from Smith's shattered foot as he ripped off the Indian's scalp. Smith laughed hoarsely. "Look ta be Arapaho. Ain't scalped an Arapaho before." He winced and fell back. "Goddamn that hurts!" The men hovered around staring down at Smith. "Looks like my dancing days are over, boys," he said cheerfully. The men chuckled uneasily.

St. Vrain bent over the splintered bone and muscle and blood steaming into the cold. "I don't know what the hell to do," he muttered.

Excruciating pain gripped Smith. "Well, don't just stand there like an idiot, Ceran," Smith shouted. "Cut it off!"

St. Vrain grimaced. "I don't know. We don't have a saw..."

"Goddamn the pain!" Smith bellowed. He gritted his teeth. "Then use...my skinning knife." St. Vrain took the knife but hesitated as he stared down at Smith's mangled ankle.

"Let me do it," Smith ordered. St. Vrain handed him the knife. Gasping and cursing, Smith sawed at his flesh and chopped at the shattered bones. He weakened and fell back heavily. "Gotta rest," he muttered.

Milt reached down and grabbed the knife. "I'll finish it for ya, Tom," he said grimly. He severed the last tendons and bone fragments. "Gimmee something to bandage it," he ordered. Someone handed him a dirty shirt.

Milt torn it into strips and tightly bound the stump. The shirt was soon blood soaked.

"My foot," Smith gasped. "Gimmee it." Milt handed it to him. Whimpering softly, Smith peeled off the moccasin and hugged the filth- and blood-covered foot to his chest.

"Son of a bitch'll be lucky ta last the night," Milt remarked.

The next morning, Smith joked lewdly with the men gathered nervously around him as he wolfed down sizzling strips of buffalo hump. Finally stuffed, he belched loudly and patted his potbelly. "Dessert time, Milton," he called out cheerfully.

Milt nodded grimly. He brandished the Arapaho's lance. "Sure ya want it from this?"

Smith chuckled gleefully. "Kain't think of a finer memento to carry me the rest a' my days."

Milt chopped off the lance's butt and lay it beside Smith's bandaged stump. "Reckon that's the right size," he said quietly. "Ready, Tom?" Smith grinned fiendishly and nodded. He gripped a rawhide strip between his hands, shoved it between his teeth, and bit down hard. Will and St. Vrain seized Smith's shoulders and biceps.

"This is gonna hurt," Milt warned.

"I know that goddamn it, Milton," Smith mumbled through the rawhide. "Jus' do it!"

As Smith winced and cursed, Milt ripped away the encrusted bandage. Then he pried apart the bleeding skin folds of Smith's stump and pushed the lance butt inside. The rawhide in Smith's teeth muffled his screams.

Some of the spectators turned away gagging. With sinew for thread and a bone needle, Milt tightly sewed up the torn skin then wrapped the stump with strips of calico. Finished, he sat back wearily. His hands began to shake. "Best I can do, Tom." Gasping and moaning, Smith nodded feverishly. From that day, his sobriquet was "Peg-leg."

The Arapahos had stolen all their stock except a dozen mules so the trappers had to cache their furs and most of their goods. A week later, with Peg-leg slung in a litter between two mules, they trudged off along the Muddy River. They found a Ute village in a cottonwood grove at the Muddy's juncture with the Little Snake. The chiefs welcomed the exhausted men and invited them to spend the winter.

It was the coldest winter any of them had ever endured. Even within the smoke-filled teepees, water froze in gourds and the trappers shivered constantly. Although there was little snow, the rivers froze near solid. Each day, the numbing cold killed more ponies from the Ute herd. Wrapped in several buffalo robes, the women would hack the ponies apart and carry back the meat to their lodges.

Morose and lethargic, the men huddled away the endless days and nights within their robes. The only one who seemed to enjoy himself was Peg-leg. To their surprise, Peg-leg not only survived but was soon humping compliant squaws for handfuls of beads.

The spring was late, and when it came the snowmelt was unleashed in mighty floods that forced the Utes and trappers to move to higher ground. Only six mules survived the winter. Having expended all the fofarraw they had brought with them for shelter, meat, and sex, the trappers had nothing left but the cached goods to trade the Utes for ponies. But with their herd decimated, the Utes were reluctant to trade, and even then could spare ponies only at exorbitant prices. St. Vrain finally managed to bargain for enough ponies so that there was one for every two men. The trappers and a score of Utes then traveled up the Muddy River to raise the cache and complete the trade. But when they dug down into the earth, they found that water had seeped in and ruined most of their furs and goods. The trappers salvaged only enough goods for five ponies. Bitter and homesick, the men agreed with St. Vrain's suggestion to trap their way back to and down the Platte and then finally on to St. Louis.

But the trapping was poor that season since many beavers had drowned within their lodges. And when they reached the Platte they found tracks of a huge war party just a day ahead of them downriver. Short of powder and lead, no one wanted a fight so they turned tail and fled. With the central Rocky Mountain passes buried under twenty or so feet of snow, they first headed east onto the high plains and then followed the Rockies' front range south.

When they reached the Cucharas River, they followed it up into and over the Sangre de Christo, and lost only three ponies as they struggled over the snowpack into Rio Grande Valley. From there it was an easy trek south to Taos. With tattered buckskins hanging from their lean bodies, they shuffled into Taos in late May. They had cached their sixteen beaver packs north of town so when the alcade inspected them, he found only eleven pelts hidden away. Haughtily accusing them of breaking the law, the alcade not only confiscated the pelts but all the party's traps. St. Vrain had to journey on to Santa Fe to plead his case. Most of the French trappers accompanied him.

While St. Vrain was in Santa Fe, Will and the other Americans resumed their dissipated life around the Arroyo Hondo still. They loafed away the days drinking and passing women between them, occasionally riding out to shoot a deer or, with their wild stompings, bluster, and war whoops, boisterously take over a Taos fandango. Through it all, Will felt the restlessness and longing swell again within him which pilgrimages to San Francisco de Asis did not quell.

Five weeks later, St. Vrain rode into Arroyo Hondo. He called the trappers together and related all the frustration and finaglings he had encountered in Santa Fe. For week after week, Governor Armijo had delayed seeing him until St. Vrain had scraped up enough coin to pass under the table. The governor then ruled that St. Vrain had violated the law forbidding foreigners to trap beaver and ordered the pelts sold at auction. The traps, however, were returned. Meanwhile, St. Vrain had managed to have the packs smuggled down and sold to some American traders in return for badly needed equipment with which he partially paid off the trappers with him. Altogether St. Vrain, on behalf of the French Fur Company, still owed his trappers and creditors over four thousand dollars.

"So where's our cut?" Peg-leg demanded.

St. Vrain grimaced. "My friends," he said quietly, "I owe you much and can deliver little, but a promise to eventually pay you in full with interest." He pointed to his pack mules. "I've brought you some powder, shot, and traps."

"That's not fair," Will shouted and others piped in.

St. Vrain held his hands high as if in surrender. "Couldn't agree more," he finally said when the men settled down. "Put yourself in my place. Upon Sylvestre's death, you asked me to lead you and I reluctantly agreed, even though as clerk, I knew I was taking over a financially bankrupt enterprise. I didn't run up the debts, Sylvestre did. Then, beyond the control of any of us were the adverse forces of nature and savage which destroyed or stole our livelihood." The men nodded sympathetically. "I'm sorry," he added weakly. "I did the best I could."

The men drifted off to drink away their disappointment. St. Vrain sidled up to Will. "Yates," he said quietly, "I need to speak with you."

Will felt his stomach twist as he imagined St. Vrain brought tragic news of his family. "What is it?" he asked cautiously.

"I didn't mention this before the others because you're the only one affected here." He hesitated.

"Well?" Will demanded, irritably.

"In Santa Fe, I got a letter from Bernard Pratte dated June 9 of last year, in which he stated he would not be responsible for any debts incurred by his son after that date."

"What!" Will cried. "You mean that son of a bitch won't pay back the money and goods I lent to Sylvestre?"

St. Vrain nodded somberly. "I'm afraid so."

Will gripped St. Vrain by his shoulders. "First, you tell me my free trapping handshake with Sylvestre's no good, and now this?" St. Vrain reached for the pistol in his belt.

"Settle down, Yates," he ordered, "none of this is my doing." Will struggled to control his fury.

"I've lost everything," he blurted and dropped his fists.

With his hand on the pistol butt, St. Vrain said, "I'm heading to Sonora with some other traders. I'll make you a full partner and credit you goods which you can sell for several times the price. Deal?"

"You want me to be in debt to you?" Will replied sarcastically.

"Do you have any other options?" St. Vrain asked softly.

"I'll ponder it." Will turned and strode off down the arroyo toward the Rio Grande.

Mulling all his life's defeats, Will spent the afternoon sitting on the canyon's edge watching the river run past far below. As the sun dropped below the distant mountains he wept bitterly. Finally purged, an idea slipped into his mind. "California," he said aloud and laughed happily.

He wandered back up the arroyo. Sucking at a jug, Peg-leg sat before a campfire before the buildings. His face glowed in the half-light.

"Where you been catting 'round, Yates?" he called out to him as he entered the firelight.

"River."

Peg-leg passed him the bottle. "Set a spell," he said gravely. "Tell me what ya seen."

Will smiled and sat cross-legged before the fire. "You're awful tranquil tonight, Peg-leg. What's eating you?" Peg-leg shrugged. "Mighty quiet 'round here. Where is everyone?"

"With St. Vrain into Taos," he replied as he tapped a stick on the hard ground. "Talk a' stirring up a fandango."

"When a fandango's brewing, you usually lead the charge into the midst of it. What's holding you back tonight?"

Peg-leg tossed his stick into the fire. "Reckon I got…what's that word ya taught me. Melan…"

"Melancholy?" Will replied with a smile.

"That's right."

"St. Vrain's bad news?"

Peg-leg nodded. "That's part of it. And Milt heading back to St. Louis last week. Rest is life in general."

"I was feeling that myself earlier," he replied.

Gazing into the flames, they lapsed into a long silence. Peg-leg occasionally rubbed the pain in his stump. Finally Will said, "I got an idea on the river." Peg-leg continued to stare moodily into the fire. "You ever hanker for setting foot," Will smiled at Peg-leg, "or stump, in California?"

Peg-leg's face broke into a wide grin. "Yates," he chuckled, "you're not half the nigger I think you are."

Although they quickly rounded up Old Bill and two Frenchmen— Jules Ducet and François Turcotte—everyone else feared setting off that far alone with such little equipment and few men. "Corral 'bout a dozen more and I'll join," was a common response. Those committed to the expedition shrugged off the failure to recruit more. Their plan was to reach California in time for the fall trapping season, winter in one of the coastal towns where they would sell their pelts to a sea-captain, then return to the mountains for spring trapping. Although they were free trappers, they agreed to stick together and share duties and hardships until then. After that, *"quién sabe?"*

They set out in mid-July in high spirits, traveling briefly down the Rio Grande to where the Chama River flowed into it and then up that gently meandering stream to the small town of Albiqui which marked New Mexico's northwest frontier. They tarried there a few days, trading for supplies and bedding the looser gals.

They were lounging around the plaza trading tales when chanting broke out from within a small adobe chapel adjoining the church. Suddenly the chapel's weather-beaten wooden doors opened and a half-dozen penitents shuffled out into the bright sunlight. Their long, hooded brown robes were pulled down to their corded waists. The last penitent pulled a small cart within which a wooden skeleton aimed a bow and arrow. Chanting solemnly, they marched slowly around the plaza and slashed at their naked backs with whips and thorn branches until they were raw and bloody. The townspeople gathered and stared quietly.

"La Muerte," an old women mumbled and crossed herself as the death cart rattled past. Thus purged of their sins, the penitents shuffled painfully back into the church. The doors closed behind them and the chants echoed within. The crowd solemnly dispersed. The trappers stared in astonishment.

"Injun's ain't the only savages in this world," Ducet observed with a smile. He was a lanky man with tangled black hair and a mole on his chin. Unlike Turcotte, Ducet spoke fluent frontier English.

"Heeya!" Old Bill hooted. "Savages ye say, Ducet? They's whipping themselves into ecstasies that makes all the liquor and musky scents a' wimmen nothing more 'n a shadow in comparison."

"Ecstasy, hell!" Peg-leg snorted. "Whadya talking 'bout, Bill, ya ol' fool. I'll tell ya 'bout whippings and they's nothing ta do with ecstasy. Hell's all that whippings bring. When I was a boy near ever' body whipped me. Preacher. Schoolmaster. My pap whipped me day and night jus' fer the fun a' it. Ol' man once whipped me so bad I laid up a week licking ma wounds. No, sir, I don't take to it. Had ta run west when I crushed the schoolmaster's nuts with a dogwood poker the son of a bitch tried ta whip me with."

"That what makes you so ornery, Peg-leg?" Will asked.

"I was born ornery," Peg-leg replied. "And I'll die that way, too."

"Wagh!" Old Bill bellowed in disgust. He rose and hurried away.

"Where the hell ya headin'?" Ducet called after him.

"Ute country," Old Bill replied. "Where a man kin cleanse himself of the sins that cling to him in his wanderings like so many cockleburs. But gnat-brained wonders like yerselves jus' don't savvy such truths. 'Sides," he added, "I fancy one of the squaws." The others blinked at each other and scrambled after him.

"Is he really leaving us?" Will whispered to Ducet.

"Hard ta say," Ducet whispered back. "We gotta ride together for a week or so anyway 'fore we get west a' the mountains and Old Bill can ride north. Maybe we kin change his thinking. Doubt it though. That son of a bitch is 'bout as hardheaded as they come."

Back at their camp outside of town, they quickly saddled their horses, and packed their mules. For a week they trekked up between the rose and salmon-colored serpentine walls and mesas of the Chama Canyon. Eventually it broadened into a high valley covered with ponderosas and meadows blazing with purple lupines, yellow buckwheats, red paintbrush, and Blue Beard's tongues. The men tarried a few days in the valley, feasting off elk and a plump black bear while the horses fattened off the belly-high grasses. The cold streams were full of beaver but their pelts were summer-thin and the men did not bother setting their traps. They slowly picked their way through the thick forests up to and over the high pass into the San Juan Valley. A week's journey on the San Juan led them down through Douglas fir and blue spruce into a narrow canyon with high piñon-covered walls which finally lowered and spread into buttes and weirdly twisted hoodoos. Here and there they poked through the crumbling stone ruins of walled towns with mazes of small rooms filled with pottery shards and arrowheads. Fearing ghosts, they dared not spend the night and pushed on long before sunset. The San Juan finally descended into desert across which were scattered huge rust-colored mesas. The river dwindled into a small stream whose banks yielded few grasses or game.

They had lingered a few days at the San Juan's juncture with the McElmo River to recruit their horses and mules. The sun had just set, leaving the air still and oven-hot. Turcotte broiled a jack rabbit over a small fire while the others sat around cross-legged hungrily watching the sizzling flesh.

"Heeya Turcotte!" Old Bill squealed. "Keep rounding that hare! Yer burning its backside!"

Turcotte looked up angrily. Though diminutive he had rock-hard muscles and was quick with a knife. "Enough! Ef you don' like it, you cook eet," he blurted in a thick French accent. Then he rose and stalked away.

"Frog-eatin' moron's touchy as a rattlesnake," Old Bill remarked as he twisted the spit. "Ifin he don't cook he don't eat."

"That go fer the rest of us?" Ducet asked as he strolled away a dozen feet and urinated.

Old Bill squinted at him. "Should go to he who cooks and he who kills. Young Yates and me's the only hunters amongst ye. No more'n bite or two a' this rabbit fer us two anyways."

Peg-leg eyed Old Bill warily and put his hand gently on a pistol lying beside him. "Williams, ya ol' coot," he said in a low, menacing growl, "ya jus' may be the first man who died over a rabbit." Old Bill glared back at Peg-leg.

"Now hold on, boys," Will interjected as he reached over and grabbed the spit from Old Bill's hands. "I shot it and I'll divide it fair amongst us."

"Four ways, Will," Ducet said cheerfully as he walked back to the fire. "Turcotte's done disappeared."

Old Bill grabbed his rifle, rose to a crouch, and peered into the twilight. "Felt something stirring," he muttered to himself. "Pushed it aways like a pesky sqeeter. Gotta listen to ma voices. Kain't let imbeciles distract me."

"Near-sighted little son of a bitch prob'ly tripped an' broke his weasel-neck," Peg-leg said contemptuously as he raised the pistol and glanced around nervously. Will dropped the rabbit and scrambled for his rifle. Ducet kicked sand on the flames and reached for his. The four men crouched in a circle.

"Ifin it's Injuns," Ducet remarked, "they's Navaho. This be their country."

"Should we call out for Turcotte?" Will asked.

"Ta hell with Turcotte," Peg-leg snorted. "Fetch in the stock, Yates!"

"Me?" Will asked. "Why me?"

"'Cause I'm a goddamned gimp on a' count a' you and Old Bill and Ducet're better shots than you, that's why! Now git out there and fetch the stock."

"Whadya mean, you're a gimp 'cause a' me?" Will replied angrily. "If I hadn't charged out against those Arapaho with you, that warrior'd have killed you."

"I shoulda let the thieving Injun bastard kill ya rather than act like a target fer him. Jus' round up the stalk ya yellow shit-eater afore I gut ya alive!"

Will glared at Peg-leg. "I'll fetch my own mules first," he replied.

He grabbed his powder horn, shot pouch, and possibles bag, then stooped and slipped through the sage brush. There was little light left. He could see the dark shapes of the hobbled mules and horses scattered a hundred or so yards in all directions. "How the hell am I gonna round up all that stock?" he mumbled irritably, "let alone pick out mine first." A mule brayed nosily far away. A shot exploded from camp then another. A man screamed in agony.

War whoops erupted all around. Mules and horses crashed away as Navaho tried to seize them. Will flattened on the ground and squirmed through the sage. Brush crackled nearby as dark, naked figures rushed past toward camp. A shot exploded. One of the dark figures grunted and fell heavily. The others disappeared into the sage. Arrows twanged. "Look out!" Ducet yelled. A pistol shot.

Two crouched figures slipped through the brush toward Will. One held a huge war club and the other a bow and arrows. They halted abruptly and seemed to stare toward where he lay hidden. Will raised his rifle and squinted down the barrel toward the one with the bow. He gently tugged the trigger. Kerboom! Will jumped to his feet and charged through the gunsmoke toward where the two men had been. One thrashed and groaned on the ground. The other sprinted away. Will glanced back toward camp and saw three dark figures running toward him. Terrified, he turned and fled, reloading as he ran. An arrow whizzed by him then another.

Two shots exploded. Someone groaned behind him. He turned abruptly and aimed his rifle but the three had disappeared. The brush crackled nearby. He sprinted away. A small arroyo appeared before him. He jumped into it and dashed up its twisting course toward a distant butte. Gasping for breath he finally collapsed. Silence. A shot banged and Peg-leg cursed far away.

Will finally caught his breath, although his heart still raced. He poked his head above the arroyo and peered through the dark. Stars were brightening across the sky. Black mesas and buttes etched the horizons.

The two meandering riverbeds gleamed. But the dark had swallowed any humans or animals. He debated what to do. He'd likely be killed by either Indians or his comrades if he tried to slip into camp. If he stayed put, he risked being discovered and killed either that night or more probably after sunrise. He turned and quietly picked his way farther up the arroyo until it disappeared at the butte's sandstone base. There he scanned again the silent valley and horizons. Bats flittered above. A cool breeze sprang up and died. The crescent moon rose. Calm filled him. He struck off in a long arc toward the tributary, carefully threading the sage and rocks. A rattlesnake clattered before him and he jumped back.

"Goddamn it," he hissed. Heart pounding, he detoured around the rattlesnake's lair and pushed on. He reached the tributary a good mile up from its mouth at the San Juan and crouched on its bank listening. His throat was parched and aching. He longed for the water trickling somewhere in the riverbed but feared exposing himself against the glistening sands and rocks. Trembling slightly from exhaustion, he retreated a hundred yards, cut a large fan of sage, and returned to the river bank. Slowly he crept across the dry wash, trying to stay on rocks and wiping clean any tracks he left behind. He finally reached the trickle, threw himself down, and gulped deeply. It tasted warm and alkaline, but it renewed him. He rested there, drinking and listening a long time. His greasy buckskins clung to his sweating body. He resisted the urge to tear them off and roll in the warm waters before him. He lay on his back and stared up at the Milky Way blazing above. The hard-bitten faces of his compañeros swirled through his mind. They're still alive or I'd have heard triumphant war cries, he reasoned. But he could not figure out a safe way to rejoin them. Strangely, he felt secure, more so than if he were back in camp.

Content, revived, he stepped across the stream which was nowhere more than ankle-deep. He brushed and tiptoed his way to the far bank and disappeared into the sage. A low hill appeared before him covered with boulders and cedar. Prodding his way with his rifle butt, he slipped carefully through the rocks. He found a sandy spot surrounded by huge sandstone cliffs and lay down exhausted.

He awoke at first light and opened his eyes to see a Gila monster staring at him a few feet from his face. He gasped and jumped back. The Gila monster blinked and whipped his slender tongue but did not move. Will poked it with his rifle barrel and it scuttled away. His stomach gnawed with hunger and his throat felt as dry and gritty as sand. He crept through the rocks until he reached a point where he could peer out without being seen. There was no movement or sound. The sun burned down from a cloudless sky. Heat waves rose from the desert. He could not see the river but knew it was only a few hundred yards away, and he craved its warm waters. He shook his powder horn. About two-thirds full, he reckoned.

Twenty-five or thirty shots if he was careful. He counted the lead balls. Seventeen. He tried to figure how far it was to California. A month? Maybe two? Was it all desert like this? He tried to imagine the camp scene. Turcotte probably dead. How many of the others? The horses and mules were undoubtedly all run off. We can never make it to California this route, he concluded. If the Navaho or some other tribe don't kill us the desert will. Seventeen shots—one shot a day and I can make it back to Taos, he realized happily. Safer to trek back alone rather than try to rejoin his friends. Friends? It seemed a funny word to describe the four men he had accompanied until last evening. They all had hair-triggered tempers, monstrously domineering egos, and deeply ingrained cruelty. They enjoyed watching men, even companions, die agonized deaths. They thrilled at actually punching a knife between a man's ribs or bashing in his skull with a rifle butt. They tolerated each other only for the reduced danger numbers brought, but would cast off the weak and wounded as easily as Peg-leg had chopped off his own foot.

Am I like them, he wondered in horror. He weighed out his weaknesses and concluded that he wasn't that bad. The more I stay with them though, the more I'll become like them. He felt no guilt at choosing to abandon those wretched men, if in fact any of them still lived.

He dozed away the day, dreaming mostly of the water trickling so seductively nearby. What little urine he passed was dark brown. Toward dusk, as he slipped through the boulders toward the sage a rattlesnake slowly emerged from a crevice then lifted its triangular head and flicked its tongue toward him. Sensing him, the rattlesnake coiled and buzzed angrily. Trembling, Will picked up a rock and flung it at the serpent's head. The rock bashed in a dozen of its delicate vertebrae and the rattlesnake twisted in agony. Will slowly lowered his rifle butt toward the rattlesnake which lunged weakly and grazed the stock which its fangs. He trapped the rattlesnake's head beneath the rifle butt and crushed it. Then, continuing to press down his rifle, he yanked his knife and chopped the still convulsing rattlesnake in two, several inches below its head. He skinned the body and sat on a rock slicing away small strips of bloody flesh and pushing it in his mouth. He chewed the meat carefully, trying not to gag it back up.

By the time he finished, it was dark. He crept out through the sage toward the river and crouched again on its bank, listening intensely. The waters flowed just beyond him in the dark. Crickets chirped. Far off a coyote yipped briefly. There was no sound downstream. Will brushed and tiptoed his way to the stream, dropped heavily to his belly, and guzzled the tepid waters. Bloated, he slipped back to the sage and walked up its bank.

He hiked all night, occasionally returning to the stream to drink or rest on a rock and watch the stars until he revived. As the eastern sky lightened he trekked into an arroyo, curled up between some boulders, and slumbered away the morning. Around noon he crawled out and walked down to where the arroyo spread into the river valley. He studied the horizons and everything in between but saw no movement other than a vulture circling high above. After drinking to his fill at the river, he scoured both banks for tracks but found only deer sign, the most recent not more than a day old.

He followed the scat and faint tracks upstream and then into a side canyon where the sign was more numerous. He spent the rest of the day beneath some junipers at the canyon's mouth. Around dusk, two does wandered down the canyon, pausing briefly to scan the surroundings or bend their mouths toward grasses. Will hesitated as he aimed down his barrel at one of the does. His empty stomach ached and mouth watered at the thought of venison. But he feared his shot would attract any war party that happened to be nearby. Finally he squeezed the trigger. The shot's explosion startled him.

He quickly reloaded then ran to the dead deer. Straight shot to the heart, he noted in satisfaction. As he skinned and butchered it, he chewed strips of meat and glanced nervously out into the valley. He hung the strips on the juniper to dry. Then he staked out the skin, scraped it clean, and rubbed it with mashed brains and urine. He rested the rest of that night and the following day in the canyon, and then that evening set off up the valley. Although the skin was far from cured he fashioned it into a crude bag and filled it with the dried meat.

For the next several days he hiked east along the river until it turned north into the foothills of the San Juan mountains. He continued east, hiking up and over the pine-clad plateaus and mountains that split one valley from the next. Although there was no sign of humans, deer, antelope, elk, and grizzly were plentiful. Will had never been alone so far from civilization before and he reveled in his solitude. He was stripped to the basics and wandered unencumbered by foul-tempered trappers or balky pack animals. He risked a shot every other day and managed to kill each time he squeezed the trigger.

He rolled up in an elk skin at night and fashioned moccasins and a shirt from other skins he had stretched and scraped. Although the summer days were hot, he never lacked for water or shade in the foothills. He lolled away afternoons on streambanks, pulling out one trout after another and roasted them on sticks over a bed of coals. He poked through Anasazi ruins and pondered the meaning of petroglyphs on canyon walls.

At times loneliness did strike him. His eyes teared when he thought of his mother and Sarah so far away, anguishing that they knew nothing of his fate, nor he of theirs. Sometimes he would look back through his life and see nothing but blunders and bitterly revile his stupidity. And then there were other times when he was seized by a powerful longing to dissolve himself into atoms and blanket the world with his presence and be everywhere and know everything at once—like God. But mostly, he wandered and stalked and gazed the wild country in something near bliss.

He ambled into Taos over six weeks after the Navaho attack. A dozen trappers were packing animals in the plaza while other trappers and Mexicans looked on. To Will's surprise, Ducet was among them. He slipped up behind Ducet and tapped him on the shoulder as he was tightening a saddle cinch on his pony. Ducet whirled around then stared gape-mouthed at Will, who grinned back at him.

"Figured you'd gone under, Ducet."

"Yates, you son of a bitch," Ducet replied excitedly, "where the hell ya bin?"

After quickly relating his adventures, Will learned that, miraculously, all four men had survived the attack. While Turcotte was stalking off, he spotted the Navaho creeping up on the camp. He dropped to his belly and wiggled back through the brush. During the attack, the trappers killed at least a half-dozen Navaho. Later that night, Turcotte had even managed to slip out again and steal back three ponies from the Navaho camp. The Navaho slipped away before morning. Old Bill had wandered north toward Ute country while the other three returned to Taos.

"So where's Peg-leg and Turcotte now?"

"Back at Arroyo Hondo. Peg-leg wants no part of this party." Ducet pointed toward a tall, powerfully-built man conferring with several other men before an adobe. "You know Ewing Young?"

"So that's Young. Heard plenty of him but never crossed trails. He's been leading parties through the Gila country since '22. Peg-leg hates Young with a passion."

"That's right. You coming?"

With a grimace, Will admitted, "Not much choice. I've nothing to show for over a year out here. Maybe my luck's ready to change."

He slapped Ducet's shoulder and walked over toward Young. He stood quietly by while Young finished giving orders to the other men. When they scattered to perform their duties, Will extended his hand. "Ewing Young?"

"That's right," Young responded as he shook hands.

"I'd like to sign on."

Like most others who trapped the Southwest, Young had lost entire season's trappings to Mexican officials and was determined to shake them this time. He spread word that they were heading to the Green River and led his men north along the Rio Grande for several days. Satisfied that no one trailed them, they angled southwest across the San Juan Mountains, crossed the Chama Valley, well above Albiqui, then struggled over the San Pedro Mountains and into the rugged desert beyond.

Water was scarce. Thunderclouds drifted across the sky trailing fans of rain that evaporated before they hit the ground. Mirages gleamed just ahead. With picks and shovels, the trappers dug into the drywashes, but rarely hit anything more than stone and hard earth. The ponies began dropping dead one by one.

After five days they struck the Chaco River and followed its trickle northwest for a day. They entered a canyon filled with the largest stone ruins any of them had ever seen. The most impressive was built in a huge half-circle of plazas, rooms, kivas, and towering walls. While their animals' hoofs echoed eerily off the stone walls, the men rode through in awed silence. Superstitious, they feared waking the dead who had built a once-flourishing civilization. They finally pitched camp beyond the last ruins and rested there for several days while their horses munched their fill of the valley grasses.

They rode south toward distant mountains and, several days later, reached the Puerco River Canyon, slicing across the foothills. They followed the river west until the mountains played out in mesas, then rode south again for a couple days across a rolling plain to Zuñi pueblo. The Zuñi were the first humans the trappers had seen since leaving Taos, and swarmed around the ragged trappers as they rode wearily into the plaza. Young parleyed with the chiefs, presenting them with knives and awls. The Zuñi feasted the trappers with corn, pumpkins, squash, and venison. The trappers traded gewgaws for blankets and the favors of women.

From Zuñi, the trappers continued south toward a tiny, jagged line on the horizon which gradually rose into a vast mountain range. Slowly they trapped their way across the mountains, rejoicing in its crystal waters and grassy meadows and tall ponderosas and bountiful game and frosty nights. Apache began to shadow them after they crossed over the mountains into the headwaters of the Salt River. They sometimes caught glimpses of Apache scrambling away over the ridges and stumbled across still warm campfire ashes and butchered deer. Young doubled the guard at night and the men trapped in pairs during the day. They grew increasingly uneasy as they descended farther into the Salt River Canyon. The serpentine walls grew higher and more narrow and the sun did not warm the canyon floor until long after dawn.

The men rarely questioned Young's decisions, mostly because they were usually the best under the circumstances but also because he could back them up with a powerful body. Young was long-limbed and slightly stooped; his chest and shoulders were all hard muscle and bone. His face was screwed up in the sour expression of someone in steady pain. To placate the acids eating away his stomach, he constantly rubbed his belly, nibbled at venison, and sipped water from a gourd canteen. At times he would explode in a barrage of oaths when a mule got loose or he found someone asleep on guard duty. But mostly Young silently mulled his discomfort and the strain of leading a fourteen-man trapping brigade which he had equipped out of his own pocket.

It was a couple hours before dawn when Will tiptoed through the blanket-clad bodies scattered across the ground. Only Young was awake, staring moodily into the flames of a small campfire. A pony nickered. Squinting through the half-dark, Will finally found Ducet and prodded him with his foot. "All right," Ducet mumbled as he groped for his rifle.

Will felt uneasy but was not sure why. He sensed something out there beyond the staked out pack animals and three guards slowly circling camp. He walked over to the fire. Young nodded to him as he crouched to warm his hands at the flames.

"Don't you ever sleep, Captain?" he asked. Young shrugged. "Mighty quiet tonight," Will commented.

To Will's surprise, Young chuckled. "'Cept for all the snoring. Some of those boys kin wake the dead."

"I've been accused of that myself."

"Something on yer mind, Yates?"

He hesitated. "I don't know."

Young peered around into the dark beyond the campfire. "Be glad when we're outta this canyon. Hate being hemmed in. Injuns pestered us ever' trip I took Southwest. Apache. Papago. Mohave. Kilt a heap, but it don't seem ta shake 'em. Injuns up north as pesky as the ones down here?"

"Seem to be troublesome near everywhere."

"One a' these trips I'm heading to California."

"Always dreamt of heading there myself," Will said sadly. "Tried earlier this summer."

"Heard 'bout that," Young replied sourly. "Sorry the Navaho didn't put that son of a bitch Smith under."

"They almost put us all under."

A mule started braying and then others. Cocking their rifles, Will and Young half-rose and stared into the dark. Some of the men stirred and instinctively reached for their rifles. Will kicked apart the fire. One of the guards screamed. A rifle shot exploded from another guard.

"Apache!" Young hollered. "Save the mules!" Arrows whizzed past and thudded into camp. Groans and curses filled the dark. The Apache screeched war cries and taunts. The trappers shot at flitting shadows and sounds. The ponies and mules screamed and reared against the lariats.

Will crouched behind a boulder and half-aimed his rifle, but there was nothing to shoot. Something slammed into his left shoulder and hurled him to the ground. He gasped for breath and pulled at the arrow with both hands, but it would not budge. An arrow skipped off the hard earth beside him.

Shots exploded sporadically. A war cry erupted behind the boulder and a shadow appeared above it. Someone shot at the shadow and it disappeared. With blood streaming from his shoulder, Will crawled toward a cottonwood behind which three other trappers cowered. One of them whimpered and called out for God to save him.

"My rifle," Will muttered and then passed out.

Someone jerked on the arrow in his shoulder and Will screamed. There was harsh laughter and Ducet said, "That woke the bastard."

"Ya hear me, Yates?" Young said softly. Will squinted up at him in the dawn light. He nodded.

"Kin ya move?"

Will tried to sit up but the dull pain in his shoulder became excruciating. He gasped and moaned and fell back heavily.

"Hold 'im down, boys," Young ordered and rough hands pinned his legs and arms. "This is gonna hurt, Yates," he warned and then tugged steadily on the arrow. Will screamed as the arrowhead tore through muscle and blood vessels. The shaft broke off in Young's hands. "Goddamn it," he growled. "Head's hung up behind a rib. Hand me your skinning knife!" Young prodded the wound with the knife then began digging. Each knife twist burned pain throughout Will's body. Someone stuck some leather in his mouth to muffle his screams. He bit down hard and bucked against the iron hands and knees that restrained him. "Got it!" Young said in triumph and dangled a bloody arrowhead before Will's blinking eyes. "Ya'll be good as new afore ya know it, Yates!" Young promised as Will slipped back into unconsciousness.

He awoke a long time later, weak and starved, his mouth bone-dry. "Water," he gasped.

"Yates's awake," Ducet yelled and lowered a water gourd to Will's mouth. He sucked eagerly at it then choked. Each heave unleashed vicious pain. He moaned and cursed.

Young hovered over him and shook his head. "Boy, yer a mess. Blood's soaked through yer bandage." Then he added impatiently, "Ya ready ta ride, Yates?"

"Where?" he mumbled.

"Taos," Young replied bitterly. "Apaches is swarming the canyon. Three men dead and four wounded nearly as bad as you. Run off half our mules. Stole most of the traps in the stream. Helluva trapping season."

"Can't move," Will gasped.

"Then we'll hafta move ya. Can't leave ya ta those savages. Ain't proper mountain etiquette." Young glanced around the camp. The men crouched tensely and scanned the surrounding canyon walls. "Fetch yer belongings and let's ride!" Young hollered. "Time's a-wasting!" Young and Ducet helped Will onto a horse.

"He'll make a pretty target," Ducet commented.

"Well, Ducet," Young replied. "Ya kin make sure he don' fall off."

Ducet chuckled. "Least I'll have a fine shield on one side."

Young deployed the five best shots in a circle a hundred feet around himself and the four other healthy men who led the mules and wounded. They retreated slowly up the canyon. Occasionally they would glimpse an Apache disappearing into the piñon or a side canyon as they stayed beyond rifle shot.

Day after endless day, they trekked up the Salt River, over the mountains, and finally onto the arid plains. Will slumped over the mule's neck and slipped feverishly in and out of consciousness. His wound festered and burned beneath his dirty bandage. He sipped water and chewed venison, but often puked it back up. At times, tears streamed down his cheeks and he bit his lip hard to keep from crying out.

Nearly two weeks after the attack, they rode back into Zuñi pueblo. Ducet and Young dragged Will into a room and left him there. A woman appeared to float around him, clucking softly and spooning water into his mouth. Her hair was rolled and pinned in large buns on the sides of her head and she wore a long cotton dress painted with red swirls.

Young pushed past her and piled Will's rifle, blanket roll, and a score of beaver pelts in the corner. He crouched beside him. "Yates, we're pushing on. Maybe we kin still trap some of the upper Rio Grande before the snow flies and streams freeze. Took back the pony and traps I fronted ya. Ya ain't gonna need 'em. I wrestled with deducting pelts 'gainst yer expenses." He sighed. "Yer a good man, Yates. Ya kin keep all the pelts ya trapped. Ya may jus' survive after all. The chief's council said they'd look after ya till either ya get well or...well, good luck." Young turned quickly and disappeared out the door.

"Wait," Will called after him. Tears trickled down his face and he sobbed quietly. The woman knelt beside him and unwrapped the bandage around his shoulder until she reached the layer where the blood and pus had crusted thick between the cloth and skin. She yanked it and the deep scab tore free. Will gasped as the wound burned like it was scorched with a red hot poker. The woman pressed the bandage against the wound to staunch the blood.

Someone shook a turtleshell rattle at the door and she quickly fled from the room, taking the bandage with her. Will moaned and squinted through the half-light. A grizzly appeared before him. "No!" he yelled, then struggled to calm himself when he realized it was a shaman. The grizzly chanted and rhythmically shook its rattle. Red feathers adorned its paws and head. A necklace of turquoise and white shell draped its chest. It wore a white cotton skirt and tall moccasins adorned with yellow-dyed porcupine quills. The grizzly chanted louder and shuffled slowly toward Will. Human fingers spread beneath its paws and pulled six blue prayer sticks from a slit in its fur and waved them over Will's body, limbs, and head. It placed one at either side and at his feet and above his head, slid one beneath him, and finally lay one on his chest. The grizzly's chants and songs droned on for hours.

Weird mobiles of colors and shapes and faces and landscapes slipped through Will's mind as he drifted in and out of something between sleep and waking. Suddenly he looked down at himself from high above and felt an infinite peace and longed to drift upward through the adobe ceiling and disappear in the sky.

He watched the grizzly bend its shaggy head toward his chest, and recalled in horror the Sioux grizzly shaman ripping out that Ree warrior's heart before the Arikara village years before. "No," his mind screamed and then he flashed down into his head and fluttered his eyes open as the grizzly jaws tickled his shoulder. "No!" he shouted again and tried to crawl away but collapsed in agony. The grizzly sucked nosily at a reed pointed toward his wound, then turned its head and spat out a mouthful of bloody mucus. It continued sucking and spitting as Will squinted up at it. Finally the grizzly growled deeply and spat a Spanish doubloon into its paw.

Will stared at the doubloon and his pain drained away. The grizzly extracted a small gourd from beneath its fur and poured a thick salve over the wound, then gently rubbed it in with its callused human fingers. Will gasped as the salve burned briefly then felt cool. The grizzly reached within itself once again, placed something in Will's right hand, and closed it tight. Then the grizzly chanted and rattled as it shuffled out the door.

Will raised his hand and opened it before his eyes to reveal a small stone mountain lion fetish with its long tail bent over its back and a yellow macaw feather tied behind its head. He smiled and drifted off to sleep.

He gradually strengthened over the next weeks. The wound drained and filled with a thick, jagged scab that eventually crumbled into an ugly purple scar. He held down the gruel and later mutton.

Assisted by the woman, he painfully began to sit up and then rise wobbly to his feet. Although he tried to speak with her in sign or Spanish, the woman never replied. After bringing his bowls of food she always sprinkled a pinch of cornmeal on a stone shrine on the west wall then hurried away.

Finally one day Will summoned enough strength to struggle to his feet and shuffle out into the plaza. The sunshine dazzled him. He leaned blinking against an adobe wall as blanket-clad Zuñi gathered around. He signed to them but they just stared back. The wind gusted a bitter cold and he turned to retreat to his room. Out of the corner of his eye he saw a heavyset child push through the crowd.

"Wait!" the child cried shrilly.

Will twisted and stared down in astonishment at a hunchbacked dwarf who grinned up at him. He had a huge beaked nose and protruding ears and a potbelly. He was missing some teeth. He carried a small staff.

The dwarf giggled and said, "Pleased to meet you, you son of a bitch."

Amazed, Will asked, "Are you real?"

"Real?" the hunchback asked. "That word I trouble understand."

"You're Zuñi?"

"Real Zuñi!" the man giggled merrily.

"Where'd you learn English?"

"Pete Reed. He trapper like you. He stay winter like you. He teach me many things."

"Why didn't I see you when we passed through a month or more back?"

"Holy trip. I travel to Salt Lake two sleeps south. No eat. No drink. Pray day and night. Make salt. Dream." The dwarf grinned at him. "Chiefs say I your guide. What name?"

"Will," he said and offered his hand. The dwarf giggled as he placed his tiny hand in his. "What's yours?"

The dwarf giggled. "I no can tell. Lose medicine. Pete Reed call me Little Dwarf Bastard."

Will smiled. "Well," he replied, "how about if I just call you Little Friend? Or just Friend? It's nicer."

The dwarf thumped his chest. "Friend. Good." He giggled again.

Although he eventually strengthened enough to travel, Will decided to winter at Zuñi. It would take at least a week of cold, lonely trekking to reach Santa Fe, and anyway all the trapping parties had long since departed from there and Taos. To survive there he would have to run up debts to some slick trader for supplies. Here at Zuñi he was fed and sheltered without being asked for anything tangible in return. Friend explained that as a warrior wounded fighting their enemy the Apache, Will honored the Zuñi with his presence. Though they honored him, they also feared his power. So they kept their distance. All except Friend, whose medicine the people also feared.

But Will mostly stayed because he was entranced by Zuñi's beauty and mystery. Each day he climbed to the highest roof of the pueblo and gazed across the horizons while Friend told Zuñi myths and gossip. Twin buttes rose to the north and to the east flat-topped Corn Mountain towered a thousand feet above the plain. Cholla and sage covered plains stretched away to the south and west, broken by smaller mesas and buttes. Like other pueblos, Zuñi was surrounded by peach or-chards, wheat, corn, and bean fields, and herds of cattle, sheep, burros, and horses. The pueblo was composed of six groups of multilayered adobe buildings, each with its own kiva. Here and there a bedraggled bald eagle was tied to a perch atop a roof. A church crumbled away at the pueblo's edge. The Franciscan priest had returned to Santa Fe several years earlier in despair that the Zuñi would never accept Catholicism.

One frosty dawn, Friend pushed open the door and woke Will from a deep slumber. "Come watch sun," he ordered with a giggle. "Very important." Wordlessly, Will pulled on his moccasins and wrapped himself in several blankets. He had gotten used to Friend's appearances at odd hours and his disappearances sometimes for days, and followed his orders without question. He had not been able to make friends with anyone else at Zuñi. The people stared at him curiously and often seemed to look through him as if he were not there.

They climbed the series of ladders to the highest roof and then sat huddled at the edge waiting for the sunrise. As the Zuñi did every morning, they emerged from doors and stood facing the sun. They chanted softly and sprinkled cornmeal. Women raised newborn babies into the rays.

Friend nudged Will and nodded toward an ancient Zuñi on an adjacent roof. "That man watch sun and stars and moon," he whispered. "Tell people when ceremony come. Much power."

"Do Zuñi worship the sun?"

"Tek'ohannanne," the dwarf smiled. "Life and sunlight the same Zuñi word." The dwarf wrinkled his brow as he did each time he was about to tell a story. "Many gods. Sun god of all. He bring people to earth. People once soft like sala..." he frowned in concentration. "Sala...What that word you teach?"

"Salamander."

"Like salamander. Have tails. Trapped four layers below deep in earth. Sun feel sad for people. Sun tell Twin War Gods, morning and evening stars, to free people. Twin War Gods led people to earth. That beginning of time. Sun finish people. Cut tail. Make bodies hard. Then Sun send people find earth's heart. People travel four years. Look everywhere in circle. After four years they come here." He spread his arms wide as if to embrace the horizons. "This is Itiwana! Zuñi town name mean Itiwana—center, heart of universe."

Will nodded solemnly. "What happens when people die?"

"Every living thing have four lives. After die four times go back four layers deep in earth below."

"Then what?"

The dwarf shrugged. "Maybe stay down there. Good people maybe come back. Maybe become Kachina. Don't know."

"How many lives have you lived?"

"Four." Friend giggled.

"I'm sorry," Will said sadly, imagining Friend dead forever.

"No worry!" the dwarf replied and stamped his staff on the roof. "People never die. Never live. Past, present, future. All are one."

Will's brow crinkled in confusion. "How can that be?"

Friend laughed shrilly. "You think time and things separate. Begin here and end there," he said gesturing with his staff. He emphatically shook his head no. "Not true. Time and things one. Seem different but same. Someday you understand!"

Will shook his head wearily as he struggled to make sense of Friend's words. He wanted to ask questions and debate Friend's beliefs, but restrained himself, fearing that in doing so, he might hurt the dwarf's feelings.

Suddenly in the plaza below ten men appeared clad only in black cotton skirts and wearing pink cloth masks with protruding circles for a mouth and eyes and knobs on their heads. Through the growing crowd of spectators, they dodged, whimpering and squealing, somersaulting and leaping, tweaking women's breasts, throwing pots of water on each other, and mocking the priests. One raised his open mouth to an upheld arrow and slowly lowered the arrow into his throat until only the feathers remained.

"Who are they?" Will asked in astonishment.

"Koyemshi!" Friend giggled happily. "Mudheads! Brother sister make body together. Very bad. Become Mudheads."

One of the Koyemshi noticed Will perched above. He pointed up at him, squealed, then began climbing up after him. Several other Koyemshi followed.

"Oh, terrible," the dwarf said, then jumped up and scurried to the roof's far edge. "Much danger. Don't let touch. Koyemshi much power. Kill."

Heart pounding, Will leapt to his feet. "There's no place to go," he shouted. As a Koyemshi climbed the ladder to the roof, Will seized it and pushed it away. The Koyemshi toppled to the ground with the ladder on top of him. The crowd laughed and shouted. The first Koyemshi was joined by three others. Together they set the ladder against the wall and tried climbing. Will twisted the ladder and knocked it over. The crowd roared in delight. Now all ten Koyemshi gathered on the floor below Will and raised the ladder again. One after another of the Koyemshi clambered up it.

Will tried to push the ladder away but the Koyemshi at its base held it tight. Trembling with fear, he locked his fists and slowly backed away as the Koyemshi climbed onto the roof and squealed and gestured toward him. It was like a nightmare where monsters chased him and he tried to run but his legs dragged like he was running through water and the monsters were soon breathing down his neck and cornered him in a canyon with no escape. Will retreated to the roof's edge where the dwarf cowered. He glanced over at the two-story drop. "Damn it!" he yelled. The Koyemshi advanced toward him. Will's face twisted in rage. He grabbed the dwarf's short staff and sliced the frigid air with it as he stomped toward them. "Come on you bastards, I'll kick all your asses!" he roared. The Koyemshi scurried back squealing.

"Pautiwa!" someone shouted in the plaza and others took up the cry. The Koyemshi stared down. Then erupted with a chorus of high pitched whimperings and leapt.

Will rushed to the roof's edge and stared down. A huge figure strode through the crowded plaza as the Zuñi backed quickly away from him. He wore a mask with a black scalp on its crown into which were braided macaw and eagle feathers. His turquoise-colored face had black slits for eyes and a mouth, and huge ears. His body was encased in a white cotton shirt, skirt, and leggings, all fringed with fox skin and painted patterns of green and black. A blue sash wrapped his waist. He wore a dozen necklaces of turquoise and shell. In his right hand he shook a stick covered with bluebird feathers and in his left hand power wands for each head priest of the six kivas, and a dozen prayer sticks.

"What the hell is going on?" Will shouted as Friend appeared by his side.

The dwarf giggled shrilly. "Ah, Pautiwa save us!" he said excitedly. "Pautiwa save everyone. Come to hear Zuñi's prayers. See his big ears? Come to bring back corn maidens so they can plant in spring. Pautiwa very kind, beautiful, wise. Greatest Kachina."

"Why's all this happening today?"

"Before I start to tell you. Today beginning of Itiwana. Most important time. Same name as Zuñi village. Itiwana mean center of place and center of time. Time when sun travel most south. If sun no come back food no grow. Pautiwa one of Shalako Kachina that travel between high gods and people. Take message. Make good, bad things happen. Later today come Salimobia warrior Kachina. Together Shalako and Salimobia come when sun far to south. Try to bring back sun. Four days Kachina and people pray. Poetry. Sing. Dance. Zuñi give food to Kachina. Young girls give bodies. Make sun return north so we can live another year."

Over the next several days, Will watched a parade of other grotesque and brightly-colored Kachinas wander the plazas and narrow alleys to perform rituals and delight and awe the people. He crouched in the crowded square kivas of each clan as its priests recited epic poems that took hours to conclude. The dwarf explained as best he could the meanings and stories behind the esoteric rites and Kachina. It was all like a prolonged, bizarre dream, at the end of which Will felt both renewed and empty.

Throughout the rest of the winter, Friend often expressed his fear that Will would someday leave. Will had to reassure him that he would stay at Zuñi until the people began once again to till the hard earth and scatter seed. Then it would be time to move on. Meanwhile, he spent days wandering the surrounding countryside on foot, exploring its canyons and arroyos whose walls were often covered by mysterious petroglyphs. In some places he felt surrounded and pervaded by powerful, unseen forces. At those times, he would scatter cornmeal in the six directions, place his mountain lion fetish between his hands, and pray fervently to whatever gods might be present. Most days though, he wrapped himself in blankets and perched for hours atop the pueblo, surveying the earth's ends and pondering the kaleidoscope of thoughts, memories, and images that spun through his mind. He tried to make sense of his life and the world, and somehow marry the two. But answers to the question "Where from?" were always easier than those to "Where next?"

Thirteen

1829–1831

The Council gave him two ponies and its blessing for his journey. Most of the pueblo turned out to stare silently at his back as he rode off. Friend wept openly and made him promise to return. "I lonely here," the dwarf blurted through his sniffles.

Will's emotions churned as he headed east from Zuñi. Gratitude, for the nearly half-year of Zuñi hospitality and Friend's guidance, meshed with regret that he had only stirred the surface of a world he could never truly know. A deep longing to trek alone to unknown horizons and immerse himself in secluded magic places jockeyed with an urge to drink and dance himself into a frenzy with flirtatious señoritas at fandangos. Pangs of homesickness for his mother and Sarah and, yes, even Judy, seesawed with an eagerness to trade stories and tramp wilderness with boisterous and dangerous fellow trappers.

But that day and for years after, he found himself puzzling over Friend's words the morning of his departure. "I have many magic secrets to teach you," he whispered with giggles. "Now you too here and there and here again. No good for magic secrets. You come back and be here only. I show you other worlds. You eat magic cactus. Make you fly inside," he tapped Will's chest, "and through sky over world." He gestured above. "You be everywhere same time. Talk to gods." He frowned and shook his head. "But I no tell you before now. You not ready. Mind broken. Make mind one. Come back."

It was an easy week's ride along the trail from Zuñi to Santa Fe. Springs were abundant at the foot of the mesas. The days were warm and nights cool. The desert blazed with the blossoms of cholla, wild buckwheat, phacelias, milkweed, primrose, locoweed, purslane, mullein, corydalis, and dozens of other stiff, prickly plants. He camped a night at Inscription Rock where petroglyphs and the chiseled names of Spanish conquistadors mingled at the bottom of a huge sandstone cliff. The only discomfort arose when he reached the Rio Grande which flowed wide and frigid. He led his ponies across, with a staff poking the riverbottom for quicksand and once was almost swept away by the powerful current.

As he neared Santa Fe, he grew more excited. A melange of Santa Fe images swirled through his mind of fandangos and penitents, cockfights and sticky-fingered officials, sunlit plazas and the cool, silent interior of churches, hundreds of Keres, Tiwa, and Tano wrapped in blankets and squatting before rows of pottery and dark adobes where fry bread baked in beehive ovens and plump women chopped onions and ground meal on metates. But Santa Fe was also the terminus of a thousand-mile tenuous link with St. Louis. At times he was tempted to just keep riding until he could embrace his mother and Sarah once again. But he wondered whether St. Louis or even his family's house was still his home. "Home's wherever you stretch your blanket," he would reassure himself. Anyway, he could not go home an even greater failure than when he left.

He rode into the central plaza which was filled with a dozen wagons surrounded by Americans, Mexicans, and Indians haggling over goods. He glanced eagerly around for familiar faces but saw none. He dismounted and led his ponies up to the nearest American who was nosily hawking in broken Spanish a frying pan to a Mexican housewife. The woman finally shook her head no and pushed away through the crowd.

"Goddamn it!" the man exclaimed. "Selling's slow!" He turned to

Will and held out the pan. "You wanna buy it, Mister?" The man was lean and clean-shaven. His pants were held up by red suspenders. He wore a slouch hat.

"You shoulda told her she could use it to whack her husband when he stumbled home drunk at night," Will replied with a grin.

The man laughed. "That's not a bad sell. I hafta..." His smile widened as he looked beyond him. "Don't look now but..."

Will started to turn when powerful hands gripped his neck and someone jumped on his back and together they fell heavily to the ground.

"Ha!" Jess's voice shouted triumphantly. "Got the drop on ya, boy!" Jess leapt to his feet. Will jumped up and they grinned at each other in amazement. "Where the hell ya bin? I feared ya'd gone under long ago!"

"Nearly so more than once?" Will replied with a laugh. "What about you? What're you doing here?"

"Jus' come across from Independence with these boys," he jerked a thumb toward the man and the other wagons. "Will Yates, meet Bob Teppit." Will shook hands with Teppit, who still brandished the frying pan in his left hand.

"Have you been back to St. Louis?" Will asked eagerly.

The grin faded from Jess's face. "Let's walk some," he said and started off through the crowd.

"What happened?" Will urged as he caught up with him. "My mother. Sarah. Are they all right?"

Jess turned abruptly. "Your mama..."

"Dead?" Will asked quietly. He felt his heart tighten.

"Got the shakes. Bedridden. Eats no more than a bird and pukes up most of that. Sarah's taking care of her. Didn't look good when I left two months ago. Doctor said she probably wouldn't last long."

"I gotta get home."

"Maybe too late."

"They need me." He frowned. "Why aren't you with them?"

Jess looked away nervously. "Needed the money. Me and Bob threw in together. Lotta those goods is from yer mama's store. Times ain't good in St. Louis and for yer mama's business they's real bad."

"So you're heading back when you dump these goods?"

Jess nodded. "It'll be awhile. Business is even worse here. Market's flooded."

"I'll see you in St. Louis."

"You won't make it alone. Comanches raided us twice on the way.

Killed a man. Run off half our stock."

"I ain't taking the main trail. I'll head north on the trail to Taos and then over the Sangre de Christo and north again till I reach the Arkansas and then follow it down till I reach the Santa Fe trail and home."

Jess's grin returned. "Never bin that way afore. Maybe I'll ride with ya after all. Bob kin take care of things."

"Can you trust him?"

Jess shrugged. "More than most."

The urgency with which they set out dissolved into hilarity as they caught up on each other's adventures in the almost three years since they had last been together. They tarried briefly at Taos where Young was equipping a forty-man party for the Gila and, he swore, eventually California. Will was only briefly tempted to throw in with Young again. Jess took nearly half a day relating the pros and cons of St. Louis versus California, and seemed to favor the latter.

Will finally blurted in irritation, "Your wife and my sister Sarah oughta come first."

"How often did Judy come first?"

"Goddamn it, Jess, you know that's different!"

"All right, all right," he said in irritation, then shook his head sadly. "Why the hell'd I ever git hitched?"

"Least I had an excuse."

Jess glared at him. Then he softened.

"Yeah, that's true." He rose to his feet and started toward their ponies. "Let's ride."

As they rode out of Taos and up into the Sangre de Christo, they were soon reminiscing about all the misadventures and pranks they had shared in St. Louis over the years and recalled with pride their trip down to New Orleans and back.

The snow was deep in the passes and it took over a week to struggle over the mountains. But they set their traps into the numbing streams and managed to haul out a score of beaver. They made good time once they re-emerged onto the plains and rode north along the Rocky Mountains' front range. Five days later they were on the Arkansas River, which was nearly a mile wide in places and flowing hard with snowmelt. About mid-stream where they had to swim, the current tore away Will's pack pony which carried his thirty-three pelts, blanket roll, and equipment. To Jess's surprise, Will did not explode in anger at the loss as he might have in the past. Instead he explained that, considering all that had happened to him over the years, he had expected to return to St. Louis with little more than the clothes on his back, if that.

Toward late afternoon several days down the Arkansas, they rode over a ridge and, to their horror, stared down at a huge Indian village whose teepees and pony herds were scattered along a valley filled with ancient cottonwood trees and thick grasses. The trappers were spotted as soon as they appeared on the ridgeline. People rose from their hide-scraping and arrow-straightening and stared. Warriors hopped on ponies and rode hard toward them.

"Too late now," Will said nervously. "If we run they'll chase us down and murder us. If we ride down to meet them, we might just have a chance."

Jess nodded and kicked his pony forward. "Too far north to be Comanche, but even if they're Cheyenne or Arapaho, there might be trouble."

With their right arms held high, they rode down the slope. A score of warriors cantered up and surrounded them. They shook their spears and bows and spoke menacingly. Trying not to show any fear, Will signed that they were friends and wanted to speak with the chief. The warriors escorted them to the village, where the people pressed in close and jeered them. They pushed their way to a teepee in the village center.

"Yellow Wolf," Will exclaimed as he scanned the symbols painted on the teepee and then the powerful old man who stood before it with arms crossed. "They're Cheyenne."

Smiling, he dismounted and walked up to the Yellow Wolf. "Father," he signed, "please welcome me. I have traveled many years since we last met on the Powder River. I am happy to be with my father again."

Yellow Wolf smiled in recognition. He beckoned Will, Jess, and the other head men to enter his teepee. They sat in a circle and passed a pipe. An old squaw shoveled buffalo stew into wooden bowls and set them before Will and Jess. Will signed a brief account of his adventures in the nearly six years since they had first met. When he explained he was returning to his home far to the east to visit his dying mother, the chiefs grunted in approval. All along Will hoped that Little Antelope would enter the lodge. But she did not appear and he knew he would break etiquette if he asked about her. With Will and Jess nodding or grunting sympathetically, Yellow Wolf and the chiefs spoke long of their band's history and their individual coups and losses. The light outside gradually dissolved into darkness. Finally the council broke up and the chiefs disappeared to their own lodges.

Someone pulled aside the flap and crouched inside. Will turned and his heart fluttered. Little Antelope! She was as beautiful as he remembered. His eyes devoured her slender, curved body, thin face with high cheekbones, huge brown eyes, and thick black hair to her backside. He smiled openly at her. A slight smile tugged at her lips as she looked at the ground and sat down behind him. Will glanced back at Yellow Wolf, who grinned at him.

"You promised to bring many ponies the next time you visited," he signed and spoke in Cheyenne simultaneously. "I saw only three, and two were your brother's."

Will laughed. "With my people, there is a saying." He paused to wonder how to translate "The third time's the charm." He smiled and signed, "Magic comes with the third try. This is only my second visit to my father. On my next visit I'll bring many ponies."

"Sure ya know what yer gittin' inta?" Jess said with a chuckle.

"All I know is Little Antelope's the prettiest girl in the mountains and I wanna bed her for as many nights as possible." Jess glanced back at her and laughed.

"I see what ya mean."

"When is your third visit?" Yellow Wolf asked.

Will frowned. "It rests on my mother's health."

Yellow Wolf nodded gravely and said something to Little Antelope, who refilled their bowls. "Strengthen yourself for your long journey."

Will got little sleep that night with Little Antelope lying just on the other side of the pitch-dark teepee. He fantasized about coupling endlessly with her in a lodge all their own. He drifted off at dawn just as the village stirred to life. Jess prodded him awake. After more buffalo stew and puffing a pipe with Yellow Wolf, they saddled up outside and trotted away. Will was tempted to press his fetish into Little Antelope's hands at some point but he never had the chance. As they rode off, he turned in his saddle and stared back at her. Their eyes met briefly before she cast hers toward the ground. He sensed her eyes were as full of desire as his.

They reached the Santa Fe trail four days later and saw no Indians and few buffalo as they followed its ruts on to Independence. The monotony of the endless flat lands was broken only an occasional wagon train plodding toward New Mexico. A couple more weeks and they rode through tall grass prairie and not long after that through thick, steaming forests broken here and there by farms and hamlets.

Nearly eight weeks after leaving Santa Fe they clattered into the muddy streets of St. Louis. Will's stomach churned. "Sure wish I was invisible," he commented.

Jess grinned. "You sure raised some hell here afore ya last left."

"Just hope I don't see anyone I know."

"Folks' memories fade."

"I'm branded for life in this town."

"Ya got nothing ta be shamed of. Ya've trapped and fought your way across the plains and up and down the Rockies. Hold yer head high. Ta hell with those rich city snobs."

Will squinted at Jess then nodded. "Getting mighty crowded," he said, trying to change the subject. Once on St. Louis's outskirts, the Yates home was now in the city's heart and increasingly hemmed in by dozens of other houses and businesses to which the family had sold off lots.

"Too much competition," Jess remarked, glancing around at the general stores, bootmakers, saddlemakers, gunshops, and blacksmiths lining the west road. "Like the New Mexico trade. Harder 'en hell to git anywhere first anymore. Ain't like back in '21 when we was the first to Santa Fe. Those days is gone forever."

"Once could horserace down this pike," Will replied as they reined their ponies around wagons and carriages creaking down the road.

"There's your place," Jess said, urging his ponies into a trot. They dismounted in the yard and tied their ponies to the rail. As they clumped onto the porch, Sarah burst out the door and flung herself into their arms and kissed them both repeatedly.

"I can't believe you're back!" she marveled.

"How's Mama?" Will asked guardedly.

"Come up and see her," Sarah replied, grabbing Will and Jess by the hand and pulling them inside.

"You head on up, Will," Jess said with a wink as he yanked Sarah into the parlor. Will nodded and tiptoed upstairs, wondering how his mother would receive him. He knocked gently at her bedroom door.

"Come in," Jenny's voice called weakly. "Is that you, Willie?" He pushed open the door and stood smiling wanly. "Well, don't just stand there," she ordered. "Come hug me." He crossed the room and lightly kissed her. She wrapped her frail arms around him and drew him tight. "My prodigal son returns," she murmured.

He pulled away and gazed down at her wrinkled face and iron-gray hair. "You've lost some weight, Mama."

She pursed her lips and glared up at him. "How long are you staying?" she demanded.

He shrugged. "I'm not sure."

"So did you make your fortune?"

Will sighed and crossed his arms. "Pocketed a fortune in memories and experiences."

She sniffed. "But you're flat broke, aren't you?"

"Lost everything to white and red thieves."

"You're just like your father," she said bitterly and turned her face toward the window. "Chasing rainbows."

"I'm not like him," he fiercely replied.

"That's true. At least your father aspired to become someone. You've thrown everything away and alienated everyone who could have helped you."

"I've heard it all before. Is that all you have to tell me after I've been gone over two years?"

She brushed away the tears welling in her eyes. "You must be famished. Have Sarah fix you something. I just can't do it myself anymore."

Fearing the reaction if he appeared unexpected at the Morgan farm, Will had Jess deliver a letter to Judy, requesting a meeting. Judy said she would receive him early the following day. He spent a sleepless night worrying over what he should say to Judy and how she would react.

Early the next morning, Will and Jess rode to the cemetery north of town. While Jess grazed the ponies outside, Will wandered through the maze of weathered tombstones until he stood before the graves of his father and daughter. He burst into tears and dropped to his knees between the grassy mounds. His body shook in waves of sobs until it was finally still. He prayed for forgiveness to both graves, then gently patted Catherine Elizabeth's mound, trying to envision the little body within slowly crumbling to dust. He rose wearily and slowly wandered back to the road.

They walked their ponies out to the Morgan's, all along quietly debating just what Will's duties were and how he should fulfill them. They had not reached any conclusions by the time they rode up to the Morgan's porch.

Betty ushered Will into the parlor while Jess went into the kitchen to distract Seth with stories. Judy rocked by the fireplace. "I'm so glad you're safe, Will," she said quickly as he walked over and sat in a chair beside her. She gripped her hands and glanced nervously all around the room, everywhere except at him.

"You look fine, Judy." She reminded him of a plump little bird in a cage with a cat in the room. "How're you feeling?"

"Same I guess. Highs and lows. I've made lots of quilts. See my latest?" she said, gesturing toward the diamond pattern on a nearby quilting frame.

"It's beautiful," he said sincerely. "You really are talented, Judy." He struggled to keep his voice from quivering. He felt a tear gathering in his eye and he brushed it away. They sat in silence broken only by the sound of Judy's incessant rocking. Finally Will asked, "What do you want to do?"

Judy twirled a strand of her hair between her fingers. "It's always been up to you." She began to weep.

He patted her shoulder. "It hasn't been up to either of us. Our lives are ravished by forces beyond our control."

"It's not fair," she blurted between sobs.

"My mother's sick. It's best we don't live there. We have no money for our own place. I'll have to move back here. It's our only choice." Judy cried bitterly. She pushed away his hand and yanked at her hair. He debated whether to try again to comfort her, sit quietly beside her, or just leave. Finally, her sobs lessened.

"All right," she said as she wiped her face with a handkerchief. "We'll try again. But you have to promise me something."

"What's that?" he asked warily.

"That you'll give up the mountains forever." To his horror, he heard himself agree to her terms.

Will did not immediately move in with the Morgans. He rode out to St. Charles that afternoon to find Jameson on the circuit. Jameson was overjoyed to see him, whom he repeatedly called "my boy." Will was appalled by Jameson's appearance. He was fatter than ever. His face and hands had a yellow cast. He perspired profusely and winded easily. Will took Jameson's place on the circuit, sending a letter back with him to Judy, promising he would return eventually.

He spent the rest of the summer riding the circuit from one village to the next through central Missouri, defending chicken thieves and tax evaders, wife beaters and swindlers, and losing as many cases as he won. By early autumn, he returned to his partnership with Jameson in St. Louis. On both the circuit and in St. Louis, he abstained from politics, flamboyance, and the occasional offered bribe. He calmly defended his clients, countered the prosecutor's arguments, and shrugged off both victories and defeats. He had soon captured the grudging respect of most of the judges, prosecutors, and lawyers he encountered.

He went home to the Morgan's every night, sometimes tipsy after drinking with Jameson in their office or with Jess at the Dirty Cock. Judy had seemed to improve some over the past years. Neither her withdrawals in stony silence nor her explosions of manic energy were as frequent or deep as before. She still cried easily at the least provocation, but allowed Will to clumsily embrace her until she quieted. Seth and Betty were cold at first, but gradually thawed until they spoke to Will with civility if not animation.

Judy's sister and three brothers had married and moved away, so that removed a large source of tension. Although his desire for Judy had died completely, he brushed off the offers of quick tumbles with the whores in the Dirty Cock and other taverns. As a drizzly winter descended on St. Louis, he increasingly welcomed his warm bed, crackling fires in the parlor, and Betty's cooking.

The calm in the Morgan homestead and his law practice was unsettling. He often feared he was trapped in an iron cage of routine and obligation with no key for escape. He daydreamed constantly of all the wonders he had experienced in the West's far corners, with visions of Little Antelope increasingly prominent.

Will's anxieties deepened after Bill Sublette straggled into St. Louis in February 1830 and immediately began organizing supplies and men for that summer's rendezvous. Will spent many a drunken evening with Sublette, Jess, and others at the Dirty Cock, trading stories and plans for the future. Sublette, along with Jedediah Smith and David Jackson, had bought out Ashley's fur company in 1826, and the partners had since earned a small fortune in the trade. Smith had trekked twice to California, surviving massacres of most of his men by first Mohaves and later Umpquas, and stumbled into the 1829 rendezvous at Pierre's Hole. Sublette hinted that he and his partners might sell out their enterprise at rendezvous and withdraw from the northern Rockies, and he pumped Will for information on the Southwest trade. Will silently damned himself for not heading back to the mountains with Smith back in October 1825. Today he might be a wealthy partner in the company rather than the struggling lawyer he was.

In mid-April, Jess headed west with Sublette, eighty other men, and ten wagons hauling over eight thousand dollars' worth of trade goods. Sublette and Jess had urged Will to join them, but he reluctantly refused, citing his promise to Judy.

After waving off Jess and Sublette, Will plunged into a deep despair. He only vaguely heard people speak to him, then would answer in monosyllables if at all. Riding the circuit and into the lives of the dregs of society once fascinated him. Now he was too emotionally numbed to enjoy it or anything else. In court, his indifference allowed several innocent men to be fined or thrown in jail for crimes they did not commit. His reputation suffered, and his clients dwindled. Alone in the law office, he would frequently toy with Jameson's pistol, debating whether or not to place it against his temple and pull the trigger. Although the weeks and months and seasons passed, time stood still for him.

The wind shook the office and blew sparks into the room from the blazing fire. Wrapped in a blanket, Will sat with his feet propped up on a stool and gazed into the crackling flames before him. A half-glass of whiskey and Bryant's *Poems* lay on the table beside him.

Someone rapped at the door. Will barely heard it. Whoever it was rapped again more insistently.

"It's open," Will called hoarsely.

The door flew open and a tall, emaciated man with a long straw-colored beard and hair and scarred face stepped inside. He pushed the door shut and turned toward him. "It's been a long time, Mr. Yates," he said quietly.

Will looked up astonished. "Captain Smith!" He rose and shook Smith's hand. "I heard you were back in town."

Smith brushed some snow from his capote and stretched his hands toward the fire. "The longer I spent in the mountains, the less I missed the comforts of civilization. And having returned, I am so easily seduced by them."

"Have you retired from the mountains?" Will asked, motioning Smith to a seat.

"I've wrestled with my future in the three months since I returned in October," Smith replied as he sat down. "We did quite well in the mountains. Enough for my partners and I not to have to work another day in our lives."

"Over eighty-thousand dollars split three ways," Will said in awe.

Smith nodded. "I've taken care of my father and brothers and drawn a new will. But as for me, I still haven't decided. I'm here to renew our friendship and ask your advice. What would you do in my circumstances?"

"I never thought you spent all those years in the mountains just for the riches you might take out of them."

"I didn't. My pursuit of wealth was always secondary to wandering the land. My material needs are simple. Yet, I've allowed myself to be talked into buying a large house on Federal Avenue along with two Negro slaves."

"You once agreed with me that slavery was wrong."

Smith sighed. "I remember."

"Now that you can afford slaves, you've changed your mind?"

"I'll allow them to buy their freedom. I fear my wealth has as much imprisoned as liberated me."

"You know what the Bible says about the chances of a rich man getting into heaven," Will said with a smile.

Smith smiled back. "And you often told me the Bible can be interpreted in many different ways."

"You did agree with me on that."

"Indeed I did."

"But tonight you wish to discuss something other than theology."

"I'm thinking of entering the Santa Fe trade. If I go I'll need someone who knows the land and peoples. Mr. Sublette and Mr. Baucus tell me you've spent some years there. I was always deeply impressed with your abilities, Mr. Yates. Mr. Baucus tells me of your unhappiness and troubles here in St. Louis. Would you like to accompany me to the Southwest, as a guide and friend?"

"I would if I could," he replied wistfully. "I promised my wife I'd give up the mountains."

"So I've heard. I recall your deep concern for your wife and the dilemma you faced over being true to yourself and to her."

"Would you talk to her?" he asked eagerly. "I've spoken to her of you and our adventures together. Maybe you could get through to her."

A deep chuckle welled from Smith. "I've no real experience negotiating with women, Mr. Yates. But if you think it could help..."

"It couldn't hurt. Tomorrow?" After some hesitation, Smith agreed. Will smiled impishly and leaned toward Smith. "And now that you're here, I've been meaning to ask you about California."

Florid-faced and sweating, Seth beamed at Smith throughout the meal and plied him with questions about the saving grace of Jesus and keeping God's word in a wilderness of savages and evil men. Seth's awe of Smith, though, did not restrain him from cutting him off, often in mid-sentence, to deliver rambling answers to his own questions.

As Seth stuffed more ham into his mouth, Smith seized the chance to tell Betty how delicious it all was. Then Smith helped himself to more yams. Betty giggled happily.

"That's certain," Will exclaimed patting his potbelly. "You can see what all this homecooking's done to me the last couple of years."

Seth reached across the table and gripped Will's flabby arm. "The boy's gone soft with all that lawyering," he noted with disgust. "Should make an honest living with a plow. Ain't that right, Captain Smith?"

"We all have to find our own niche in the world, Mr. Morgan," Smith replied. "Even if it takes a lifetime."

"You've certainly found yours, Captain," Seth said fawningly. "You're a rich man!"

Smith blushed and looked over at Will. "Mr. Yates may have told you that I've asked him to accompany me to Santa Fe and beyond. He's an expert mountaineer."

"Of course, he is, Captain," Seth rejoined as he poured himself another mug of whiskey, "of course! Why I've often nudged him to be more enterprising. Treat 'im like my own son. Just one of the family."

"I'm so sorry Judy couldn't join us," Betty whispered, glancing across the hall toward the parlor. "She means no offense."

"I understand completely, Mrs. Morgan," Smith replied gravely. "It must be so hard on her when Mr. Yates is away."

"We'll work on 'er, Captain," Seth declared emphatically. He jerked a fat thumb toward Will. "That boy's heading back to the mountains, whether he and Judy like it or not!"

Smith slowly ran a finger over his lips. "We all have to do what's right," he said quietly. "Sometimes the distinction's blurred between right and wrong." He turned to Will and sighed. "Maybe I should encourage you to take care of your wife rather than...After talking with your friends, I feared you were wasting away here and would be better off in the mountains. Your life is filled with dilemmas, Mr. Yates."

"Ah, don't worry about all that, Captain," Seth asserted, and sliced himself another large wedge of peach pie. "The boy's heading to the mountains and that's final."

Smith nodded and pushed back from the table. "As I mentioned earlier, I have to meet with my partners Mr. Sublette and Mr. Jackson this afternoon about our proposed Santa Fe trade." Smith thanked them all profusely and politely refused the Morgan's demands that he stay longer. On the way out, Smith poked his head into the parlor. "I hope you soon feel better, Mrs. Yates," he said gently.

Judy refused to acknowledge Smith's presence, if she was even aware of it. She rocked maniacally. Her hands trembled violently in her lap. A log burned through in the fireplace and fell, scattering coals on the hearth toward her feet.

"Judy," Will said quietly, "I'll walk Captain Smith to the road. Then I'll be right back to visit with you."

"Me, too," Seth said eagerly, as they put on their coats and stepped outside while Betty hurried away to clear the table.

Smith mounted his horse tied out front. "'Fraid I'm late for my meeting," he said as he reached down to hastily shake hands with Will and Seth.

"It was a pleasure, Mr. Morgan. Do thank Mrs. Morgan again for the delicious meal." Seth assured Smith that it was their pleasure and made him promise to visit anytime. Smith then kicked his horse into a canter and disappeared down the road.

Seth slapped Will on the back. "Son," he exclaimed, "now there's a man worth leaving home with. A man of God and rich to boot." He winked at him. "We'll see what we can do to change Judy's thinking."

Judy and then Betty began screaming hysterically within the house. "Help!" Betty screeched repeatedly. Will sprinted toward the house followed by Morgan. Through the parlor window he saw someone engulfed in flames, dancing madly within. "God, no!" he cried. "Judy!" He flung open the front door and charged into the parlor. Flames blazed from Judy's dress and hair and she screamed in agony and jumped around the room jerking her arms, legs, and head as if to fling off the fire. Betty screamed helplessly nearby. Will tackled Judy and tried to smother her torched body with his. The flames scorched his hands and face and set his clothes smoldering. Judy screamed and struggled beneath him. He smoothed her burning hair with his hands. The flames burned his hands and singed his eyebrows and hair.

Morgan puffed into the room and flung a tub of dishwater on them. Then he yanked the quilt off the trundle and wrapped it around them. The fire had charred or blistered most of her body and her face beyond recognition, and reduced her once-thick blonde hair to blackened stubble. While she moaned and cried endlessly, they ripped off her clothes, whose fragments had fused with her flesh, and doused her repeatedly with water. Then they carried her in a sheet up to their bedroom. Will ran to the barn, stuffed a bridle in a horse's mouth, and galloped into town. It took hours to frantically track a doctor and he did not arrive at the Morgan's until that evening. The doctor could do little for her but apply a salve to her wounds and administer a huge dose of opium. "After childbirth," the doctor said wearily as he clumped down the stairs, "fire's the leading cause of death for women."

Will kept a constant vigil beside Judy, spooning water, opium, and hominy between her blistered lips, and emptying her chamber pot.

Within a day her burns oozed with pus. She drifted in and out of consciousness. When awake she mostly ranted and screamed in agony. But there were rare moments when she was suddenly lucid and whispered haltingly to Will with a mind he had not heard for nearly a decade. In some ways those moments were the most painful of all for him as she apologized for the suffering her dementia had inflicted on him. "Go back to the mountains, Will," she moaned. "You'll be happy there."

Judy lingered in agony for a week before she died. The last words she gasped to Will were, "Tend our baby's grave."

Oven-like heat enveloped Will and Smith and sucked them dry. Dripping with sweat, they stared out from beneath their broad-brim hats to a maze of eroded buttes and arroyos blasted by a relentless sun. The horizons glimmered within heat waves. They saw no living thing other than patches of withered prickly pear and thin grasses protruding from an earth baked cement-hard; heard no sound but the clatter of horse hoofs over the lava rocks.

The shallow gorge they trekked broke into two twisting branches. They dismounted and crouched in the shade beneath a rock outcropping and debated what to do.

"Seem to go in opposite directions," Will remarked.

Smith nodded. "We'll hafta split up." He grimaced. "I'd be surprised if we found a spring either way."

"I'm beat. Must've ridden a half-dozen miles from the Cimmaron. Never seen the Cimmaron so dry. Used to hit water after digging a couple feet. But everywhere the men dug along the riverbed they hit nothing but bedrock. We haven't had anything to drink since about this time yesterday."

"Let's rest here awhile," Smith said, yanking off his hat and wiping his brow with a grimy red handkerchief. "We'll find water. It was as bad as this back in '28. After struggling over the snowpacked Sierras, I set off across the desert with a couple men. Always found some seep but all our mules died. Nearly a month to reach rendezvous. Hell itself couldn't have been hotter."

"Don't worry, Captain," Will said with a grin. "As I've told you before, that's the closest to hell you'll ever get." He tossed a pebble into the harsh sunlight. "Wish I could say the same for myself."

Smith smiled. "Just what could send you to the netherworld? Aside from your pagan beliefs."

Will grimaced and wiped away a tear. "I saw those coals tumble toward Judy's feet," he finally blurted. "But I didn't say anything. My mind was elsewhere. I fear deep-down I foresaw what would happen and looked the other way."

Smith lay a hand on his shoulder. "I saw the coals spill, too," he said quietly. "Coals roll out of fires all the time. I didn't think anything of it. They seemed far from her feet. I figured they would soon burn themselves out. She must've moved closer to the fire and the coals fired her dress. We couldn't have foreseen that. We had other things to worry about. There's no reason why you should feel guilty."

"Over the years I sometimes wished she were dead," Will admitted. "I got my wish."

"It was all a tragic coincidence," Smith said, tugging at his beard. "It's been four months since the fire. You've got to let go."

Will picked up another stone and tossed it. "I killed a Comanche farther down the Santa Fe trail and maybe a Navaho on the San Juan. They were both trying to murder me. Yet I still feel guilty. Those savages hound me in my dreams and when I turn to fight I can't kill them. I tear them apart with my hands but some mass of flesh and crazed spirit still struggles with me till I wake. Now I have nightmares over Judy. I watch her explode in flames and do nothing."

"I've heard your moans at night."

"If there's a hell, it's guilt for all the horrible things I've done and failed to do."

"Then we all live in hell. At least partly. But there's more to life than that. There's salvation on earth, too. Love. Friendship. Happiness. Those fleeting immersions in the eternal spirit. You've told me you've experienced all that."

Will sighed. "At times. In some ways, Judy's death freed me. In other ways, it's just another bar in my cage. I wonder if I'll ever be truly happy. I'm happy when I wander the earth. Though on days like today, when it's hot as blazes and I'm dry as a bone, I'm not so sure. But it's a melancholy happiness. It's not complete."

Smith nodded. "Same for me. What's missing for you?"

"The thought that it'll all end someday before I see and do all I desire. That's part of it. But I'm also searching for a dream woman with whom I can share my life. A woman as beautiful of spirit as body. A woman who loves me as deeply as I love her."

"You're not going to find her out here."

"That's my life's central dilemma. But I might have a solution." Will told Smith about Little Antelope and his plan to marry her and wander the West together.

"That just may be your answer," Smith said, smiling. He glanced at the fork. "You rested up? Longer we set, the dryer we get. We've gotta find water for those men back at camp. I'll take the right fork and you the left. We'll circle and meet back at on the Cimmaron."

A pang of dread surged through Will. "Maybe we should stick together," he suggested quietly.

Smith lifted an eyebrow. "You sense something?"

"I don't know. Just a feeling. Remember the feeling you had before that grizzly appeared."

"Seen no sign of grizzlies nor Indians. It's like we're the last life on earth."

"Just a strange feeling."

"Maybe just the heat and lack of water. But if you'd feel better, we could stick together."

"No, that's all right," Will said, mounting his horse. "The odds are twice as good finding water if we split up."

They rode up to the fork and paused to squint into each other's eyes. "Will," Smith said. "Don't worry. I'll see you back at camp." Will powerfully shook hands with Smith, but choked when he tried to say goodbye. He nodded and reined his horse up the gorge. He never called me by my given name before, Will marveled. Wish I called him Jedediah.

When he turned to look back at the fork, Smith was gone.

Toward sunset, Will rode into the deserted campsite. Tracks led up the dry riverbed. Can't be too far ahead, he reasoned. They must have found water.

Suddenly, the dread welled up within him again. He scanned the surrounding mesas and plains but saw no one. Sucking nervously at the pebbles in his mouth, he kicked his weary horse into a walk up the Cimmaron.

When he reached the mouth of the sandy gorge that he had rode up with Smith that morning, he discovered in horror the tracks from at least a score of unshod ponies leading down from it and mingling with those of the wagon train. He cocked his rifle and peered ahead into the dusk. There was no telling if the Indians had joined or were following the wagons. A mile later the pony tracks veered north of the Cimmaron and into low hills beyond. Lights flickered far up the riverbed. He kicked his pony toward them.

"Who the hell's that!" someone hollered as he neared the camp.

"Don't shoot," Will yelled back. "It's me, Yates!"

"Come on in," the voice replied. He rode past some of the hundred or so horses and mules hobbled around the dozen wagons in a circle beside the riverbed. He saw the silhouettes of men patrolling beyond the stock. Within the wagon circle the men sprawled listlessly around campfires.

"Water?" someone asked as he dismounted in their midst.

"Not a drop," he answered.

Sublette and Fitzpatrick rose and ambled over. "Where's Smith?" Sublette asked.

"Split up," Will replied simply. "See those Indians tailing you?"

"Indians!" Fitzpatrick exclaimed excitedly. "Where?"

"North. In those hills."

"I'll double the guard," Sublette said darkly. He called out orders for the second watch to join the first then turned to Will. "We hit water," he said, gesturing toward the riverbed. "Ain't much left now."

"I'll walk you down, Will," Fitzpatrick said cheerfully.

Will nodded wearily and guided his horse to the center of the wide mudhole trampled with countless hoof and foot prints and fouled with dung. As his horse bent to drink, he placed his handkerchief over the muddy water and sucked eagerly at the warm liquid. His stomach felt queasy and his head ached. While he bloated himself, Fitzpatrick hobbled his horse.

"Not quite like old times," he said as Will rose from the mud.

Will smiled.

"You mean your Irish accent isn't as strong as when I first met you?"

Fitzpatrick grinned. "Wish it were just that. You, me, Bill, the captain. We've changed."

"How so?"

He shrugged. "The mountains've aged us. We're stronger than before, but more solemn." He chuckled. "We've all become like Captain Smith."

"True. But the most important change I see," he said morosely, "is that you three are rich and famous and I'm a nobody."

"Will!" Fitzpatrick remonstrated. "You've had some bad breaks and faced some tough decisions. You've survived where lesser men'd gone under or just given up. Your time'll come."

"I don't know," he said, shaking his head. "I'm sure glad we could all be together a last time." He stared down the sun-cracked Cimarron and worried about Smith. "That was lucky, us meeting you in Lexington on your way back from the mountains. If you hadn't been late, you'd be heading to rendezvous with the supplies rather than chasing us to Santa Fe."

"Fate's a funny thing." Fitzpatrick scanned the horizons. "Comanche trailing us. The captain not in yet. Never know what'll happen next."

"You aren't sore 'cause Bill didn't release the goods to you so you could return to the mountains?"

"Deal's a deal even between friends," he stated strongly. "I promised to be back in St. Louis by April first and, if I didn't, Bill was free to sell them elsewhere. It's my fault I have to follow him to Santa Fe to buy any leftovers. I just feel bad for the boys gathering right now at rendezvous. They're gonna be mighty disappointed."

"I miss the northern Rockies."

"Still got your heart set on pursuing Little Antelope? That little gal probably run off with some buck long ago and dropped a load of young'uns since."

"I'll take my chances. I promised to guide the captain in his Southwest ventures." He grimaced. "But if that doesn't work out, I might as well guide you on your way north from Santa Fe at least as far as the Arkansas."

"Finding Yellow Wolf's village'll be like finding a needle in a haystack."

"Not that bad. With a drought this severe, the Cheyenne and the buffalo'll stick close to water. Unlikely they'll stray far from the Arkansas."

"And if Little Antelope's no longer available, you'll rejoin us?"

"Yup, I'll catch up." Will replied and smiled deeply. "Just like old times."

He slept little that night. Nightmares yanked him awake and he would burrow in the darkness a long time before exhaustion dragged him down again.

Smith had still not shown up the next morning. Sublette ordered the men to break camp.

"Hold on, Bill," Will protested. "What about the captain?"

"I got responsibility for the lives of eighty men. We drunk that hole dry and the stock's dropping dead one by one. We gotta find more water or we'll lose everything."

"Let me lead a search party."

"Listen, Yates," Sublette replied angrily. "We can't split up if there's a war party stalking us."

"Smith was your partner and friend."

"That's right, goddamn it! And either he's dead, or holed-up someplace, or following us. And there's not a damn thing I can do about any of those possibilities."

With sun burning down mercilessly from a cloudless sky, they trudged upstream another ten miles. When a horse died, they drained the blood into canteens and passed them around and carved off strips of meat and chewed them raw. They saw no sight nor sign of Indians. They finally found a waterhole and camped beside it.

Once it got dark, Will bid goodbye to Sublette and Fitzpatrick.

"Where the hell ya going?" Sublette demanded.

"To look for Smith."

"You may end up sharing his fate."

"I'll take my chances."

"Suit yourself," he said in disgust and stalked off.

Fitzpatrick sighed and warmly shook Will's hand. "Would join you," he said sadly, "if I didn't have obligations…"

"I'm the only one of us without ties. I may just take a short scout and be back within a few hours. I may return to the arroyo where the captain and I parted." He grinned. "Or I may just head north to Little Antelope. If so, take care of my horses and traps and other fixings. I just gotta cut loose and do something."

Fitzpatrick nodded. "I understand, Will. Good luck ta ya."

Will slipped out of camp and through the sparse saltbrush alongside the riverbed. There was no moon. Countless stars glistened. The baked earth gradually cooled. The distant buttes and mesas were dark shadows against the night sky. He wondered why he had left the camp's safety to retrace his journey. Sublette was right. Smith was probably dead and if the Indians still trailed the wagon train, they would murder anyone who strayed from it. But he had to find out for himself.

He had hiked about a mile when he heard a pony nicker somewhere north of the river. He crouched and strained to see and listen through the darkness. There was a low hill a hundred yards away. Shadows moved at its base. He crawled silently toward the hill until he could make out scattered horses grazing and Indians bunched nearby speaking softly. He listened to their guttural voices a long time. Suddenly they drew silent and rose. Will's heart pounded. Did they spot him? Were they about to charge? He raised his rifle and prepared to sprint away. Instead, one shadow flitted up the hillside while the others filed silently away to the west and were quickly shallowed by darkness.

Will debated slipping back toward the riverbed then running up it until could take word to camp. But he worried the Indians would see or hear him and chase him down. A pony whinnied softly. Will smiled. There's the dowry for Little Antelope's hand, he realized in excitement. But how do I steal them?

The mustangs did not seem tied or even hobbled. Probably had lariats tied to their necks so the Indians could easily seize and pull them close before mounting. All I need to do is hop atop one and gallop through the herd and the rest would follow. And the guard? Probably a boy barely in his teens so busy staring toward the wagon train that he wouldn't see me slip up to the herd. Even if he saw me, I could spook the ponies and escape in the darkness and confusion. Circle far to the south and then run in to camp at daybreak.

Will trembled slightly with fear and excitement as he slowly crawled toward the ponies wondering how they would react to his smell. He stopped occasionally to peer at the shadow atop the hill. It had not seemed to move but he had no idea which direction it was facing. He got within a dozen feet of a pony and it turned to stare at him in the dark. He wanted to speak softly to it, gently reassure it. But he knew the guard would hear him. He crawled forward a few feet. The pony turned and walked away, trailing a lariat behind it. Will rose to his feet and tiptoed after the pony.

A few feet separated him from the lariat's end. Other ponies stood staring at him or slowly walked off. He glanced up at the hilltop. The shadow was creeping down its face toward him. Heart racing, Will pointed his rifle toward the shadow and placed his thumb on the hammer to cock it back. The pony he was trailing halted and turned its head toward the hill. The shadow disappeared behind some rocks. Will stepped forward, grabbed the lariat, and coiled it as he slowly pulled himself along toward the pony. He expected the pony to lash out its hoofs or gallop off. But instead the pony turned its head and nickered. Will patted its flank and slid his hand along its backbone to its mane.

A rock clattered from the hillside. The pony tensed. Will gripped his fingers around the coiled lariat and a hunk of mane. A bow twanged on the hillside and an arrow whizzed past his head. He leapt upon the pony's back. The pony dodged sideways, bucked, then broke into a gallop through the pony herd. Will dug his knees into the pony's flanks and struggled to stay on and hold his rifle tight. The other mustangs galloped all around him, their hoofs thundering on the hard earth. The herd galloped for several miles before it slowed to a walk.

Will twisted and scanned the dark. No sounds or flitting shadows. He felt like war whooping. Instead, he searched the sky for the north star and reined his pony toward it. The other mustangs followed. "Little Antelope," he said aloud. "You'll soon be mine."

Fourteen

1831–1832

Will trotted and walked his herd northwest all night. Within hours of stealing the mustangs, his adrenaline burned off and exhaustion slowly dragged him down. His backside chaffed against the mustang's backbone and every muscle throbbed. He battled to stay awake by singing but that only irritated his parched throat. Half-waking dreams drifted through his mind. Though he struggled to envision Little Antelope, she was continually pushed aside by squabbles with old friends and enemies, ancient and recent defeats and aspirations, and Judy's gruesome death. Mostly he dreamt of gulping deeply the mountain waters of the Rockies far beyond the western horizon.

As the eastern sky grayed, he rode up to the banks of a dry streambed. The mustangs were stumbling and blowing. He almost collapsed when he dismounted. With his legs trembling violently, he

448

held onto his pony while it snatched at bunches of grass. He counted the other mustangs as they grazed. Twenty-three! Can buy a harem with those ponies, he thought and chuckled.

He scanned the rolling, arid landscape. Several cottonwoods poked above a bend far downstream. He led his pony down the steep slope into the streambed. Suddenly the mustangs scented water and broke into a gallop, including Will's pony, which yanked the lariat out of his hands and charged away. Will stood there staring after them, thanking the gods that he was not trampled in the stampede. He ambled painfully toward the grove and found the mustangs bending their necks along a dozen feet of shallow muddy water. Setting down his rifle, he stumbled toward the pool, threw himself between the hoofs of two ponies, and drank deeply.

Will raised his head and glanced around. Most of the ponies were already munching grass. The half-dozen cottonwoods huddled together would provide shelter from the blazing sun throughout the day. He rose and studied the tracks in the dried mud—plenty of deer and some antelope and horse hoofs. And a few moccasin tracks! Although they looked weeks old he nervously scanned the arroyo again anyway. Shale banks rose an eroded hundred feet on either side. The Comanche would know this waterhole and could trap him here like a rat in a barrel. He was not sure if he had run off all the ponies or not. If not, the guard might have retrieved a pony or two. The Comanches could be tracking him right now. He figured he'd got at least an hour jump on any organized pursuit and had ridden a score of miles during the night. Odds are they'll never catch up, he reasoned. He tied his pony to a cottonwood log in a grassy clearing, then stretched out behind a tree and plunged into sleep.

He slept hours and awoke with his stomach gnawing with hunger. The sun was high overhead. The mustangs were scattered up and down the arroyo. He stretched painfully. His body felt like every part had been beaten with war clubs. Walking stiffly over to the dung splattered stream, he dropped to his belly and drank deeply.

A rock clattered down the shale cliff. Two ponies grazing nearby trotted off. Will jerked up his head and searched the rim. Nothing but cobalt sky beyond. A horsefly buzzed past. Silence. Heart pounding, he pushed himself to his feet and cocked his rifle. The mustangs grazed up and down the arroyo. He walked over to his pony, untied it, and slipped onto its back. He winced at the pain in his backside, swearing he would sell his soul for a saddle. He walked his pony down the dry bed, driving the other ponies before him. The ponies up the arroyo followed.

He pushed the herd all that day, halting briefly at waterholes and grassy bottoms. Toward dusk he reached a broad streambed with water trickling down its center which meandered northeast across eroded plains. Mountains etched the horizon far to the south. I've been here before, he thought excitedly. This is the Purgatoire River that I'd ridden up with Becknell a decade ago!

Another two days of hard riding and he reached the Arkansas, then turned west and trotted for days along its sandy banks. Huge buffalo herds shuffled along the river and the flat plains on either side to the horizons but he did not risk a shot that could spook his ponies. He lived off rattlesnake meat and once grilled a rabbit he knocked over with a rock. His mustang herd steadily diminished. On the Purgatoire, one pony went lame and several others wandered off. With so much grass and water on the Arkansas, the ponies scattered at night and he had trouble rounding them up each morning. A week after running them off, he had only fourteen left.

All along he wondered how he would ever find Yellow Wolf's camp. It was early June and the Cheyenne would have long before dismantled their lodges, packed all their belongings on travois, and wandered across the plains behind buffalo herds. But with all the buffalo along the Arkansas, chances were the Cheyenne were not far off.

Finally one morning, he spotted a dozen teepees ahead and boldly rode toward them. Probably Cheyenne, he reasoned, but even if they're Arapaho, etiquette wouldn't permit murdering a guest in their own home. Someone spotted him and shouted. Older men, women, and naked children swarmed around and stared suspiciously at him as he rode in trailed by his ponies. He figured the younger men must be chasing buffalo. To his relief he recognized the markings on their teepees as Cheyenne.

"I come in peace, Father," he signed to the chief who pushed through the crowd. "I've ridden eight sleeps since I stole these horses from the Comanche."

The old man's left arm was withered. In his right hand he carried a tall coup stick curved at the top from which a score of eagle feathers dangled. He nodded in approval.

"I look for my father, Yellow Wolf," Will said as he dismounted.

"I know," the chief signed. "I saw you two springs ago when you visited our camp at Big Timbers. Yellow Wolf and the people are now many sleeps north of here. They journey to renew the Sacred Arrows at Bear Butte."

Bear Butte, Will marveled, that's in the Black Hills! "Why do you not join him, Father?"

"We await the return of our sons who have journeyed far east to take Osage scalps and ponies."

"I must fulfill my promise to Yellow Wolf to bring him many ponies. I will give a horse to any man who guides me to him."

The chief called a council. The head men and Will smoked the pipe. While the Cheyenne debated his offer, Will accepted bowl after bowl of buffalo stew. After an hour or so, the head men hammered out a consensus. They could not spare any men. However, the chief's son, Laughing Owl, would guide him if he gave one pony to the chief and another to the boy. Will agreed and thanked them.

Will and Laughing Owl rode north shortly thereafter, each carrying a parfleche packed with buffalo jerky. The second morning after they set out they hit a broad trail of travois and hoof tracks. "Yellow Wolf," the boy stated, and Will wondered how he could be so sure. Day after day, they followed the trail north across the rolling plains.

His body now hardened and lean, Will luxuriated in his pony's rhythmic drumming on the hard earth, the dry baking heat, the prickly pear blooming amidst the stunted grasses, the yellow buttercups and sunflowers carpeting the creek bottoms, the jagged purple wall of the Rockies far on the western horizon, and the immensity of sky caressed by drifting clouds and clusters of sparkling stars at night. The vividness of Judy's agonizing death and his guilt slowly faded. He mourned also Smith's disappearance and succeeded in emotionally packing it away with Uncle Jake's.

Nearly two weeks later as they splashed across the North Platte River, Laughing Owl announced that Yellow Wolf's people were just ahead. Will carefully shaved and washed his body and clothes in the river. Then they rode on.

They reached the village at sunset and herded the ponies through the camp toward Yellow Wolf's lodge. Cheyenne gathered all around him, laughing and pointing. Yellow Wolf emerged from his lodge and stood with arms crossed watching Will approach. A slight smile tugged at his lips and his eyes sparkled. He greeted Will as he dismounted before him. "You bring many horses," he signed. "Do you wish to become Cheyenne?" The people crowded around, gawking and chattering.

"Yes," Will replied. "I wish to become Cheyenne by becoming Yellow Wolf's son, by marrying Yellow Wolf's daughter, Little Antelope."

The old chief's smile broadened. "Many men have staked horses before my lodge but had them returned the next morning. You bring more than any of those men. But do you think you bring enough horses to become my son and take my daughter?"

"That is my deepest hope. But if I need more, I will go steal more from the Comanche."

"I must smoke and discuss your offer with my male relatives and examine your horses. Your answer will come tomorrow. You may stay in my brother Lame Bull's lodge until then." He gestured toward a tall, lean man whose body was covered with scars. He had a broad face contorted in a perpetually sour expression.

"Thank you, Yellow Wolf," Will said. He shook hands with Laughing Owl, who then disappeared with his pony to a relative's lodge. Then he followed Lame Bull as he pushed away through the crowd. Within his teepee, Lame Bull ushered him into the place of honor across from the opening. He then crouched out to return to Yellow Wolf's lodge. His three wives brought Will bowls of buffalo stew.

The enormity of what he was doing suddenly struck him like lightning and he panicked. This is crazy! For a decade I moaned about my loss of freedom and now that I'm free again, I am throwing it all away! I locked myself into love for a girl I briefly spoke with ten years before. Sure she's gorgeous, he conceded, but her grip on my heart has more to do with the primal forces she symbolizes than who she really is. She's a complete stranger! He wondered why Little Antelope wasn't married yet. Yellow Wolf claimed that her suitors had not brought enough horses. But was there something wrong with her? Or was she so exalted that no warrior had yet proved worthy of her hand? He poked his head out of the teepee flap. Only a few Cheyenne still talked together or strolled through camp. The evening star shone brightly in the purpling Western sky. Was it too late to call off the whole thing? Could I slip away without being caught? He debated which was crazier, staying or fleeing.

Lame Bull returned late that night but revealed nothing of what had transpired in the council. Tomorrow you will know, he said simply and fell into an impenetrable silence.

Will slept little that night. At dawn, he slipped out and down to the creek where he bathed and shaved. People were dismantling their teepees and loading them on travois. A few families had already set off north. As he strolled back to his lodge, he half-hoped to find his ponies tied out front and his marriage offer rejected. Instead, Lame Bull stood waiting before his teepee. "Come," he signed, and they walked rapidly through the disappearing village.

They stooped into Yellow's Wolf's lodge. The old chief and Little Antelope sat across from the opening while his wives, adult and young children, and relatives were squeezed in a circle. Yellow Wolf motioned Will over. He took a deep breath, stepped around the fire, and sat beside him. He glanced at Little Antelope. She was dressed in a white buckskin dress covered with elk teeth. Her long black hair had been combed into a luster. She stared demurely down at her hands in her lap. He felt himself fill with desire.

Chanting a prayer, Yellow Wolf offered his pipe toward the six directions. Then he pulled a burning stick from the fire and lowered it onto his pipe bowl. He sucked noisily at the stem and exhaled a mouthful of smoke toward heaven. He handed the pipe to Will who managed not to choke as he puffed deeply, then passed it on to the next male. Silence filled the teepee. The din outside of people shouting, dogs barking, and lodgepoles clunking together seemed to recede as well. Smoke drifted heavily upward. After the pipe's fourth circle among the men, Yellow Wolf placed it back in a parfleche.

He rested a hand briefly on Will's shoulder then began to sign and speak. "This man has traveled across distant plains and mountains and deserts. He has fought many enemies and survived. He has stolen many ponies from the Comanche. He is still young but is wise beyond his years. He offers twelve ponies for my daughter's hand. I give him my daughter and make him my son." The relatives grunted in approval and spoke merrily.

Little Antelope cupped her hand in Will's and led him out outside. He blinked in the bright sunlight. Only a few teepees remained and those were rapidly being dismantled. A broad stream of hundreds of Cheyenne and ponies dragging heavily laden travois stretched to the north. Followed by Yellow Wolf and the relatives, Little Antelope led Will to a nearby teepee around which were staked a half-dozen ponies. Once inside, she pegged shut the flap behind them. Beyond the relatives loudly joked and spoke. Some children tried to peek under the teepee cover but it was staked down too tightly.

Passion surged through Will. He gently embraced Little Antelope and led her to a pile of buffalo robes. He softly ran his fingers across her cheeks and neck and bent down to lightly kiss her lips. She hesitated and then wrapped her thin arms around his back and kissed him. He pulled her tight and sucked at her lips and ran his fingers down her curved, slender body. They stood there entwined, sucking softly at each other's mouths a long time, while the clamor outside died.

Will slowly pulled off her dress and gazed down at her small outthrust breasts and erect nipples. He lowered his mouth to her breasts and sucked. He pulled off his clothes and rubbed his naked body against hers. The hot teepee and their passion beaded their bodies with perspiration. He lowered her slowly onto a buffalo robe, wetted his fingertips with his mouth, and gently stroked the cleave between her legs. Her body tensed and she pulled him tight against her. She moaned and gasped softly. Gently she cupped her small hand around his hard penis and drew it toward her. Although her vagina was soft and wet, he could only get two fingers inside her and feared hurting her with his erection. But she guided his penis head into her opening and slowly thrust against it, until it disappeared within her. He rubbed his loins against hers and she moaned louder and arched her body and dug her fingers into his back. She began to shudder and he thrust harder and faster. She cried out and he released himself with a gasp.

They coupled and dozed and snuggled the rest of that day and throughout the night. Occasionally, Will would emerge from the teepee to urinate and marvel at the vast, silent emptiness that stretched to all horizons. All around him, crows picked at offal, grasses lay trampled, breezes scattered campfire ashes; dung whitened. The earth seemed to have swallowed up Yellow Wolf's band, leaving nothing but scattered debris behind.

At dawn, they dismantled their lodge, packed their ponies, and followed the trail north. Will was both relieved and disappointed to rejoin the band late the next day. He had dreaded the sudden raid of a Crow or Pawnee war party that might have lurked in the band's wake. But he rued the loss of privacy as they raised their lodge beside Yellow Wolf's.

The obligations of being a Cheyenne were many. Will and Little Antelope, of course, had no time for intimacy as they spent their days among the rest of the band, leading their ponies across the rolling plains. During the evening, they had to entertain relatives who visited their lodge. Will could be friendly to all of his relatives except his mother-in-law. Custom would not allow him to speak directly to her or be alone with her, and he always had to wear his hat in her presence. Every few days, he would have to tear himself away from Little Antelope and hunt buffalo with other men of Yellow Wolf's former warrior society, the Coyote. And he spent many a night crowded in a lodge with other Coyote Society men, singing and drumming and dancing. Although Will tried to be generous and friendly, most of the young warriors treated him brusquely. He wondered which, if any among them, had courted Little Antelope, and imagined their smoldering jealousy.

To Will, Little Antelope was the most desirable woman he had ever seen in the mountains. Whenever they were alone, he caressed and stroked her constantly. When others were around and he could not hold her, his eyes furtively stalked her every move. She blushed when she noticed his stare and he would grin and look away. He thrilled at her every glance and the soft touch of her fingertips on his face and the sway of her lithe body strolling or bending. She spoke in a rushed high voice full of mirth. She slept with her lips slightly parted and her hands between her thighs. She would lock her eyes on something—a grasshopper, a colt, a hawk soaring above—and become oblivious to all else around her. And she was his, he triumphed!

Yellow Wolf was the only relative whose visits he did not resent. The old man cheerfully told stories and asked questions about Will's wanderings. Since he had first met Yellow Wolf a decade earlier, he had been amazed by his tolerance toward him and other whites. One evening Will asked Yellow Wolf if he sometimes regretted having a white son.

Yellow Wolf seemed puzzled by the question. "The Cheyenne want new blood. Our people have men and women who were born Sioux, Arapaho, Kiowa, Arikara, and Comanche. You are the first American to be join the Hair Rope people. I hope many others come and join us."

"But, Father, my skin and face are different. Your grandchildren may look like me. It does not matter?"

The old man shook his head slowly. "No. If my grandchildren speak my tongue and see the world through my eyes, their skin and bones and blood do not matter. That is the Cheyenne way."

About two weeks after Will had first joined the Cheyenne, they reached the plains east of the Black Hills. Memories surged of his trek across the plains and over the Black Hills with Smith and the others back in '23. The paths I've trodden since, he smiled in wonder, through both landscapes and people!

He was riding beside Yellow Wolf and started to tell him of his first journey through the Black Hills when the chief cut him short.

"My son," he announced. "Tomorrow we join the Cheyenne circle at Bear Butte to renew the Sacred Arrows. There are many things you must understand."

Will nodded. "What are the Sacred Arrows?" he asked.

"Sweet Medicine brought Sacred Arrows to the People. He was the greatest Cheyenne. He lived when my grandfather was a young boy, when the Cheyenne were weak and few and living around these Black Hills and raided often by our enemies. One day an old woman found Sweet Medicine in the forest. He was a baby and no one knew where he came from and she raised him as her son. One day Sweet Medicine disappeared within Bear Butte which is hollow inside like a teepee. Within were all the great wise spirits of the universe and the greatest of all, Maiyun. Maiyun and the other spirits taught Sweet Medicine many things for the people."

"So Maiyun is the strongest god?"

"No, Maiyun is the most powerful son of the great spirit which unites and pervades all, Heammawihio."

Will smiled. "The white people have similar beliefs. They call Heammawihio God and Maiyun Jesus."

Yellow Wolf struggled with the words. "G-God...Je..."

"Jesus. God and Jesus."

"God and Jesus," the chief repeated with a smile.

"God sent Jesus to earth to clean the people of evil and many people followed him."

"What gifts did Je-Jesus bring?"

"Only one. Love your neighbor like yourself."

The chief nodded. "Jesus was very wise. That is the Cheyenne way. I'm glad the white people also believe in loving their neighbors as themselves. Where is Jesus now?"

"Some bad people killed Jesus and he went back to heaven. What did Maiyun give Sweet Medicine?"

"Maiyun gave Sweet Medicine the same message as Jesus. But he also gave Sweet Medicine four Sacred Arrows, clothed him in a red painted buffalo robe with horns and hoofs, then sent him out to the people who were starving and weak and poor. Sweet Medicine brought food, medicine, and horses to the people and showed them how to do the Sun Dance and organized each band into the five warrior societies. He gave us the Council of Forty-four Chiefs whose members come from each band and look after all the Cheyenne people. Each council chief must resign from his warrior society and set aside his coup stick and war bonnet and take up the pipe and wear a single eagle feather. I am a council chief.

"Most important of Sweet Medicine's gifts were the Sacred

Arrows, two of which are to kill buffalo and the other two to kill our enemies. If the priests point the arrows against our enemy they will become confused and afraid and we will defeat them easily. If the priests point the arrows toward the buffalo we will slaughter as many as we need."

"You said the Sacred Arrows must be renewed?"

"Yes," Yellow Wolf replied solemnly. "We unite to renew or purify the arrows for many reasons. Anyone who wants to do a great thing can pledge their renewal. Success in war. The healing of a loved one. To encourage a vision. But the most common reason is when one Cheyenne murders another the sacred arrows are defiled with blood and that blood must be cleansed. That is why we gather now. Someone in the Sutaio band murdered another and the chiefs sent runners to all the other bands to gather and cleanse the Sacred Arrows."

Yellow Wolf paused and gazed across at the Black Hills undulating across the western horizon. "My son, you will see powerful and secret medicine over the next few days. You must never reveal anything you do or see to any foreigners."

"My father, I promise," Will stated, and he meant it.

Later that day, they spotted Bear Butte pushing into the sky far away to the north. They pushed on eagerly and set up camp at dusk. At dawn, they dismantled their lodges, dressed in their finest clothing, ornaments, and weapons, and painted their horses. With Yellow Wolf at their head, the people formed into a column and walked or rode forward, singing songs of happiness on their way into their place on the south side of the camp circle.

Cheyenne from other bands surged out to joyfully greet them. Yellow Wolf's people then busied themselves erecting their lodges and preparing cooking fires. The Cheyenne mingled and gossiped and told funny stories. As his people raised their lodges, Yellow Wolf stood proudly surveying the great Cheyenne camp. The circle of bands was open several hundred yards wide on the east toward the sunrise. Each teepee also faced east.

Will stepped beside him. "You look very happy, Father," he remarked.

Yellow Wolf smiled deeply. "I am always happy when the Cheyenne are one!" he replied. "Our Cheyenne camp circle is one big lodge. Each band is a lodgepole and the people the skin." Yellow Wolf pointed to each band around the circle, "the Eaters to the northeast, the Bashful to the north, the Grasshoppers to the northwest, the Sutaio or Adopted

Ones on the west opposite the lodge opening, Scabies to the southwest, and the Aorta to the southeast. He smiled and spread his arms wide as if to embrace his own village. "And here on the south are our people, the Hair Rope."

"What are those teepees in the center?"

"Those are the Offering and Sacred Arrow Keeper lodges. They will be joined by the Sacred Arrow Lodge."

"Is this all the Cheyenne?" Will had counted around three hundred lodges, and with about eight or nine people in each, there could be more than twenty-five hundred people and twice as many ponies present.

"Some of the newer bands are missing: the Fox, the Pipestem, the Bare-legged, the Narrow Noses. But those are smaller bands, of not more than one hundred lodges altogether. Maybe they will come later. But the four ancient bands are here."

"How are new bands born?"

"Many ways," Yellow Wolf said with a shrug. "Some people like one hunting ground and other people another so they separate. Or there is a conflict and one group moves away. Sometimes small bands join together when they lose many from war or sickness. Bands are born and grow and die like people."

"Where were the Cheyenne people born?"

"Where we were born no one remembers. But long ago, the Cheyenne were only four bands and they lived apart far to the northeast in a land of forests and many streams and lakes. One band, the Sutaio, did not even speak the Cheyenne tongue, but we adopted them as brothers. At that time we were few and had only stone arrows and lances and no horses. Our enemies to the east, the Cree and Assiniboines and Chippewa and Sioux, got muskets from the French and attacked us and drove us onto the plains where we got horses and lived in earth villages along the Big Muddy. But our enemies kept coming and we traveled to these Black Hills and lived in its shadow and hunted buffalo and raised buffalo-skin lodges and grew tobacco and corn in the valleys and traded with our friends, the Hidatsa and Mandan and Arikara on the Big Muddy. That was the time of Sweet Medicine and it was our happiest time. But later, when I was a boy, Sioux bands crossed the Big Muddy and for two generations tried to push us away from the Black Hills. We fought many battles until recently the Cheyenne and Sioux chiefs met in a council and agreed to share the Black Hills."

"Will you move back to the Black Hills now that there is peace between the Cheyenne and Sioux?"

Yellow Wolf sighed and shook his head no. "I love the Black Hills but I love peace more. The Crow and Assiniboine and Pawnee still raid this land. The Hair Rope people will remain far to the south along the Arkansas. The buffalo are as many as up here but the winters are not as cold and our enemies fewer." He paused in thought then added, "Now the Arkansas is a happy and peaceful land for our people. But my sleep is disturbed by dreams that someday powerful enemies will come whose numbers are as many as the stars above and they will hunt down the Cheyenne and buffalo until both are wiped from the earth."

Will glanced away nervously. "What do the enemies look like?" he asked quietly.

"They look like you," Yellow Wolf replied, and walked away.

The Sacred Arrow Renewal Ceremony lasted four days. Only men could participate in its rituals. The women were secluded in their lodges and were not permitted to emerge for any reason. As a Cheyenne man, Will was able to witness nearly everything.

On the first day, each man brought a present for Maiyun and piled it before the Offering Lodge. Then, in the afternoon, men gathered long poles for the Sacred Arrow Lodge, to which the three bravest and purest warriors contributed their teepee covers. The Sacred Arrow Lodge was huge, twice the size of a regular teepee. Priests laid sage around the Sacred Arrow Lodge to purify it.

The next day, the pledger's body was painted red and wrapped only in a buffalo robe. He led the three virtuous warriors toward the Sacred Arrow Keeper's Lodge. They advanced and retreated before the lodge four times before entering. Within, the pledger, warriors, and priests prayed and chanted. Carrying the arrow bundle, the pledger emerged, followed by the others and they slowly shuffled toward the Renewal Lodge, halting four times before they reached it and entered. Within the head priest ceremoniously opened the bundle on an altar. Then all retired.

On the third day, a man from every band offered a willow stick before the altar in the Renewal lodge. A priest purified each stick with smoldering sage incense before laying it with the rest.

Finally, on the fourth day, the Arrows were set on a tall pole under the sun. Every Cheyenne male from the most ancient to the newest born walked or was assisted past the Arrow pole. The priests and sacred warriors then dismantled the Sacred Arrow Lodge and set it up over the Sacred Arrow pole and the new lodge was called Sweet Medicine's Lodge. The Sacred Arrows were wrapped within their fox bundle and carried away to the Sacred Arrow Keeper Lodge. That night, the head chief and all the medicine men entered the Sweet Medicine Lodge and sang and prophesied about the future of the Cheyenne. Just before dawn, they emerged and went to a sweat lodge to purify themselves.

On the morning of the fifth day, all the Cheyenne emerged joyfully from their teepees to celebrate their lives and the world renewed.

The Cheyenne circle remained a beehive of motion and noise for several more weeks. The Pipestem band straggled into camp a few days after the Sacred Renewal ceremony ended and they were received with songs and laughter. Men from different bands traded goods and stories or rode up into the Black Hills to hunt elk. The women gossiped and sewed and scraped hides, or wandered the arroyos to dig for wild turnips and prickly pear or pick chokecherries and thistles or gather dried dung. Men pulled their sweethearts up behind them on their horses and they fondled and giggled to each other as they rode away to secluded ravines. Camp criers strolled among the teepees announcing council meetings and decisions. Young teenage boys wandered up to the hills to pray and fast for a vision that would reveal their adult name and future. Hemaneh, or transvestites, bedecked themselves in their finest clothes and ornaments and sashayed through camp mincing and beckoning to leering men. Children raced and shouted and fought. Dozens of mangy curs snarled and sniffed about. In closed lodges, priests chanted over the sick and dying. At night, here and there, five elders would gather and purify a lodge by burning sweetgrass and sage and chanting prayers. People would crowd into the lodge and the elders would take turns telling segments of Cheyenne legends.

The Cheyenne ceremonies and stories and fellowship fascinated Will. Since the grammar of Cheyenne and sign language were similar, people would speak to him as they signed, and he gradually acquired a proficiency in the language. He and Yellow Wolf shared many long talks about their lives.

But Will grew restless as the weeks passed. The constant visiting and noise and confusion wore him down. It seemed like someone was always scratching at their teepee flap to be invited in and fed and entertained. He longed to be alone with Little Antelope, to recapture the magic and passion of their first time together. And increasingly, he just longed to be alone.

Finally the Council of Forty-four agreed that the bands should disperse in search of fresh grass and buffalo. The bands dismantled their teepees and disappeared over the horizons. Yellow Wolf's band headed south for the Arkansas. Will planned to journey from the

Arkansas on down to Taos and sign on a trapping party, and debated endlessly whether to take Little Antelope along.

Indian wives were relatively scarce in American trapping parties, particularly those of the Southwest where those few men with women kept them in Santa Fe or Taos. He could leave her in Arroyo Hondo but feared she would become despondent away from him and her own people. But the dangers and crudity she would be exposed to on a trapping expedition would be much worse. Still, the half-year of winter in the mountains would be warmed with her by his side at night and eased considerably as she scraped pelts during the day while he checked his trapline or hunted.

But he explained none of this to Little Antelope. No use fretting her unnecessarily, he reasoned. Who knows what choices the future'll bring?

He was forced to decide sooner than he expected. After the band crossed the North Platte in late August scouts rode in with word of a large party of whites camped just ahead. Will hopped on his pony and rode with other warriors toward the camp. When the whites spotted the score of Indians trotting toward them, they grabbed their rifles and stood tensely. Will told the Cheyenne to wait while he cantered ahead waving his hat. He reined in his pony in a cloud of dust before the trappers.

"Will Yates!" someone shouted with a slight Irish accent. "Last I heard, the Comanches killed you!"

"Fitz!" Will said excitedly. "You're a sight for sore eyes." He jumped down and shook hands with Fitzpatrick. His smile vanished. "Captain Smith?"

Fitzpatrick looked away. "Never rejoined us. Later in Santa Fe we met some Mexicans, who had traded with the Comanche. Got the captain's rifle and pistols. Seems the Comanche surrounded him at a waterhole. He killed the chief before they put him under."

"Least he went down fighting," Will said sadly. "He survived so much—three massacres, grizzly attack, damn near dying countless times of starvation, frostbite, or thirst. Then to be killed out after he'd struck it rich. Just ain't right."

"Figured the Comanches rubbed you out, too. How the hell'd ya escape?"

"It's a long story." He glanced at the trappers still standing edgy around their camp and gestured their way. "Looks like you did some fair recruiting in New Mexico."

"Forty-two men, over a hundred pack and riding animals, and a year's worth of supplies for the Rocky Mountain Fur Company," he said proudly. "Now all we have to do is find the other trapping brigades. They'll be on the fall hunt already." He pointed to the Indians who sat on their ponies nearby and remarked, "Look to be Cheyenne."

Will grinned. "Some of them are my relations."

Fitzpatrick slapped his side and laughed. "So ya finally did marry that little girl you mooned over when we first come to the mountains together?"

"Yup," he replied proudly.

"Welp. I've got your two horses, traps, and fixings. Ya gonna accompany us to rendezvous?"

Will hesitated. "Believe I will. Just gotta speak with my wife."

Little Antelope wailed when Will told her he was joining Fitzpatrick. He awkwardly tried to soothe her but her unbridled cries frustrated him. After an hour, she dried her tears and begged to join him. He quickly agreed.

The trappers and Cheyenne camped a night together on the North Platte, then separated early the next morning. Yellow Wolf was saddened by the departure of his favorite daughter and new son. "I knew you would leave someday," he admitted. "But not so soon."

"We'll return," Will promised, but he knew it might be years before they saw each other again, if that.

After moping for several days, Little Antelope resigned herself to the separation from her family. She became increasingly fascinated by the other trappers and their ways, and plied Will with endless questions. He was pleased that she had adjusted so quickly and welcomed her lithe body alongside his. But the leers and ribald comments of the trappers flared him with jealousy, and he warned Little Antelope to avoid the more violent or sex-crazed men.

For over two weeks the party plodded along the North Platte. The monotonous plains stretching to the horizons were gradually transformed into long red sandstone escarpments and distant purple mountain ranges. A couple days after the Platte arched south, the trappers reached the Sweetwater and tramped up it past such landmarks as Independence Rock and Hell's Gate.

Several days west on the Sweetwater they met Henry Fraeb's party of twenty-three trappers. Fraeb was one of the five partners, which included Fitzpatrick, Milton Sublette, Jim Bridger, and Baptiste Gervais, that had bought out the company of Smith, Bill Sublette, and Dave

Jackson at the 1830 rendezvous the previous year, and renamed it the Rocky Mountain Fur Company. Fraeb was short, stocky, and bandy-legged. He had a round red face and fringe of graying hair. He seemed near bursting with nervous energy and spoke rapidly with a thick German accent punctuated by obscenities.

"Where da hell ya bin?" Fraeb shouted as he cantered up to Fitzpatrick. "It's September. Rendezvous's done! Everybody's gone back to mountains! We fear ya dead! Kilt! Then we ask Crow medicine man and he pray and pray and say ya not dead but on wrong trail. So I come to meet ya."

Fitzpatrick explained all that had happened, then ordered the supply-laden mules handed over to Fraeb's brigade. The two parties set up camp and the men mingled and shared stories over a small cask of rum Fitzpatrick tapped.

Fraeb's wife, Running Calf, was Crow. Despite the animosity between their tribes, she and Little Antelope quickly struck up a friendship. They raised their teepees alongside each other and chattered away for hours in sign.

Will took out the ink and paper from his saddle bag, climbed up to the rimrock, and wrote a long letter to his mother and Sarah. He related all of his experiences except the most important—that he'd married a Cheyenne girl. His mother would never forgive him for marrying someone whose race she believed were nothing more than savages. He wondered if Sarah could ever accept Little Antelope. Perhaps in time. Homesickness gripped him as he wrote. He stayed the rest of the afternoon and through the sunset, ruminating on his life. Finally, he ambled down through the dusk and joined Fraeb and Fitzpatrick by a fire as they drew up next year's supply list. Then the three swapped tales far into the night.

The next morning, Fitzpatrick had the dozen or so men who wanted to return to the settlements saddled shortly after daybreak. As Fitzpatrick rode off, he reached down and grabbed Will's hand. "See ya at Pierre's Hole next July," he said. Will smiled up at him and nodded.

Fitzpatrick called back to Fraeb, "Take care of my amigo here, Henry. We go back a fair ways." Fraeb nodded and everyone stared as Fitzpatrick and his men disappeared down the Sweetwater.

Fraeb led his party swiftly across South Pass and on to the Green, then headed north through the broad sagebrush and hill-covered valley. The Green was largely trapped out as was the rugged plateau over to the Snake River and Jackson Hole. But the trapping picked up as they slowly followed the river north past the Grand Tetons and far down onto the broad Snake River Valley. They left the river and headed west across the valley's black lava fields and sagebrush until they reached Birch River, then followed it deep into the mountains. It was early November by the time they crossed over the snow-covered pass to the Lemhi River and trapped down it to the Salmon.

Parts of their route were the same that Will had followed with Smith back in 1824, and vivid memories of that journey continually swirled through his mind. But his knowledge of the country also nearly brought him to blows with Fraeb's guide, Antoine Godin, when Will would correct his directions.

Godin buzzed with nervous energy that flared quickly into anger. He was lean and swarthy. He sported a long, wispy mustache that dropped to his jaw and a small birthmark on one cheek. His father was French and his mother Iroquois. Godin frequently boasted of his pledge to avenge himself against the Blackfeet who killed his father two winters previous.

The tension between Will and Godin went beyond disputes over the best route. Behind his back, Godin would leer at Little Antelope and smack his lips and sign for her to slip off with him. Little Antelope would pretend to ignore him or, if he persisted, would retreat into their teepee. But before she disappeared, she would cast Godin a quick, beguiling smile.

One day on the Big Wood River, Will trod happily into camp with three beaver pelts and his five traps slung over his shoulder. There was frost in the autumn air. The cloudless sky was the deepest blue. The amber leaves of the aspens on the mountainsides and cottonwoods along the river rustled with the wind and blazed in the bright sunshine. He stirred at the thought of entwining with Little Antelope that night under their thick buffalo robes, of slowly pulling up her elk skin dress and putting himself deep inside her. Before their lodge on the camp's edge, he saw Little Antelope and Running Calf pounding and rolling chokecherries and deer fat into pemmican balls. Godin suddenly appeared before them and gyrated his loins before Little Antelope. Running Calf giggled and put her hand over her mouth.

Little Antelope turned her head, but suddenly laughed and glanced back at Godin. Will's happiness transformed into rage. He dropped his traps and pelts and strode toward Godin. Little Antelope noticed him coming and gasped. Godin turned to see what she stared at. When he saw Will charging him, his leer disappeared and he hurried away. Will broke into a run and Godin turned to meet him with a skinning knife in his hand. Will stopped abruptly a few feet away. They glared fiercely at each other.

"Got a problem, Yates?" Godin smirked. As he stared coldly into Godin's eyes, Will debated whether to charge or pull his own knife. A dozen trappers gathered around egging them to fight. "Yeah, Yates," Godin taunted. "Here's your chance. I'll gut ya alive."

"Godin," Will said quietly. "If I ever see ya bothering my wife again," he paused. "I'll kill you." Then he turned and walked back toward Little Antelope who waited anxiously beside their lodge.

"We'll see who'll kill who," Godin hooted.

On the juncture of the Lemhi and Salmon, they met Jim Bridger and Milt Sublette's brigade of over seventy men and a dozen wives and children. Small bands of Flathead and Nez Percé camped nearby. Several days of wild Saturnalia followed, as whiskey kegs were drained, supplies replenished, and the charms of many a squaw bought.

Milt Sublette was happy to see his old fellow Taos trapper Will, and the two spent many an evening reminiscing. Through Milt, Will struck up a friendship with "Old Gabe" Bridger. Although a half-dozen years younger than Will, Bridger had also headed up the Missouri in 1822, but with Henry rather than Ashley. So the two men had never before spoken although they remembered each other from the first rendezvous. Bridger was tall and slightly stooped. He wore his thick brown hair to his shoulders, which sloped noticeably. He had small gray eyes, thin lips, a broad nose, large ears, drawn cheeks, and an expression of mild surprise at everything around him. He loved telling long rambling stories, which he shamelessly embellished. It was Jedediah Smith who had hung on Bridger the sobriquet, "Old Gabe." The Biblical angel Gabriel had the duty of revealing truths and orders from God to earthly mortals. Bridger's ability to thread wilderness, often alone, for weeks to carry a message from one trapping party to another had made him the personification of Gabriel in Smith's eyes. That "Old Gabe" was a full partner despite his relative youth and inability to read and write was a nagging reminder to Will of his own lost opportunities.

After having guzzled down the whiskey and recovered from blinding hangovers, the men dispersed to the surrounding streams for a few more weeks of trapping before ice locked away the beaver deep within their lodges. Around Christmas, the trappers and Indians trekked up the Lemhi to where it widened into Horse Prairie which had relatively light snowfalls and abundant grass for the horses. But it was also in the shadow of Lemhi pass leading over the Bitteroot mountains into Blackfoot country. Throughout the winter, Blackfoot war parties lurked in the mountains and slipped down through the canyons in a series of raids that ran off a score of horses and killed five trappers.

As if the Blackfoot were not trouble enough, the American Fur Company was elbowing its way from its Missouri River trading posts into the heart of the Rockies to snatch away the Rocky Mountain Fur Company monopoly. Andrew Drips's party of forty men had shadowed that of Sublette, Bridger, and later Fraeb all that fall and into the winter.

One night Will asked Milt how serious the American Fur Company threat was. Milt exploded in a tirade while rubbing his bad leg, "Those bastards've cut a deal with the Blackfoot and supplied those red niggers with powder and ball to attack us. Got a trading post at the mouth of the Marías on the Missouri called Fort McKenzie where they trade with the Blackfeet. They've another'n called Fort Union at the mouth of the Yellowstone to trade with the Assiniboine and anothern called Fort Cass where the Bighorn flows into the Yellowstone to capture the Crow trade. Pretty soon they'll be building posts in the heart of the Rockies. They're slowly trying to squeeze us outta the mountains."

"It ain't that bad, Milt," Bridger interrupted. "Drips," he pointed down the valley toward the rival camp, "and Vanderburgh and Fontenelle bin leading parties into the Rockies the last two years dogging our trapping parties. But they's river boys, they ain't mountain men. Took us years ta learn the skills and every twist and tumble on these mountains. They kin follow us all they wants. But with our boys leading, the American Fur parties jus' git the leftover beaver and grass fer they's horses." Old Gabe cackled. "And the Blackfeet don't have no truce with the American Fur Company in the mountains. The Blackfeet's killing off those river boys with the same powder and ball the American Fur Company 'riginally sold 'em. Put under a half-dozen of Drip's men just this season."

"I don't know," Fraeb reflected. "It war bad 'nuff when we was competing with jus' the Hudson Bay Company. I don' know if we'll survive 'gainst the American Fur Company. They's driving down the prices a' goods and raising the price a' wages. They kin undersell us 'cause Astor's company's spread over the whole continent and sells furs to Europe and China. We're just one small partnership in the mountains. We gotta sell our furs to and buy our trade goods from others."

"Ah, come on, Fraeb," Bridger replied. "Only 'vantage they's got is more and cheaper trade goods." He chuckled. "We'll survive. One way or 'nother we'll survive." Then he added pensively, "Or die trying."

To Will's relief, Godin had avoided Little Antelope since the tense stand-off, and after arriving at the winter camp, had shacked up with a Flathead girl. But months of associating with Running Calf and living in a licentious and rowdy trapping camp had transformed Little Antelope from a demure maiden into an increasingly assertive woman. She continually begged Will for more bells, ribbons, brass bangles, vermilion, red cloth, capotes, beads, rings, garters, mirrors, and other gewgaws with which to bedeck herself, and better ponies upon which to ride proudly around camp.

With Will trapping and Little Antelope scraping, he had expected his pelts to pile high in their teepee. Instead, he found himself trading one pelt for Little Antelope's fofarrah for every two pelts he brought in. When he would refuse her demand for some shiny gewgaw, she would flirt openly with other trappers and remark haughtily that she should find a man who treated her better. Will would inevitably give in, but his resentment at her spendthrift ways rankled deeply. And, like most Indians, she could not handle alcohol.

He had first shared a cup of watered-down whiskey with her on the Sweetwater. But she quickly grew drunk and belligerent, and Will swore he'd never let her drink again. At the winter rendezvous, Running Calf stole a pint of whiskey and sneaked it away to Little Antelope's lodge, where they quickly gulped it down. Will returned to his lodge to find both of them passed out in puddles of vomit. Later after she awoke to a throbbing hangover, Little Antelope promised never again to touch firewater.

"Henry," Will had once blurted to Fraeb, "you've gotta rein in Running Calf. She's teaching Little Antelope plenty bad ways of drinking and flirting. I fear my wife'll run off with someone else. It's gotten so I can't let her out of my sight without dreading she'll do something awful behind my back."

"What kin I do?" Fraeb replied wearily, with a shrug. "Running Calf's Crow. Spreading her legs fer a handful a' trinkets is in her blood."

"Little Antelope's Cheyenne. She ain't Crow and I don't want her to become one."

"Then swing a lodgepole against her backside like any self-respecting husband would," Fraeb said angrily. "Beat her back inta the meek creature ya married. Ya've got only yerself ta blame fer her mischief."

But the thought of striking Little Antelope for any reason revolted Will. Instead, he tried to blow off his frustration with horse races and hunting trips. Little Antelope also grew bitter when she compared her husband's generosity with that of other husbands, including Fraeb. And as both their frustrations and resentments deepened, their desire for each other cooled. Those rare times they did couple, they did so either perfunctorily, or thrust and pulled angrily at each other, until they finally lay back in exhaustion.

For the spring trapping, they got the jump on Drip's party and straggled over Lemhi Pass and into the Beaverhead Valley. Yet, they did not enjoy the streams to themselves. Blackfoot haunted the forests and murdered several trappers. The men worked their traplines in groups of a half-dozen or more, in which two or three would constantly scan the trees and hills for the glimpse of a painted face or naked torso. Despite the constant danger as they slowly trapped their way up the valley, they dragged hundreds of thick-furred beavers from the icy streams.

When the beaver began to shed their winter coats in late May, the trappers and their Indian allies headed south over the Bitteroots into the Snake River Valley then up the Teton River to Pierre's Hole, where they awaited Sublette's supply caravan. Pierre's Hole was a long narrow valley, hemmed in on the east by the three snow-capped Grand Tetons and the west and south by lower mountain ranges. The flat valley was a dozen miles wide. Through its center flowed the Teton River, which eventually reached the Snake forty meandering miles away. Groves of cottonwoods and willows lined the Teton and the dozens of streams feeding into it from the surrounding mountains.

Scattered across the valley's center were the ragged collection of teepees, tents, and log lean-tos of the Rocky Mountain Fur Company and the lodges of Flathead and Nez Percé, and smaller groups of Shoshone and Bannock. Within a week, first Andrew Drips and then Henry Vanderburgh led American Fur Company brigades into the valley and set up camp a mile downriver of the Rocky Mountain Fur Company. Fourteen men of the small Gantt-Blackwell Fur Company under Alexander Sinclair's leadership arrived a few days later. Other small groups of free trappers dribbled in. Baptiste Gervais's party rode in one evening to swell the Rocky Mountain Fur Company encampment. Almost three thousand ponies and mules grazed the thick valley grasses.

The two rival companies anxiously awaited which of their supply caravans would arrive first to rendezvous. Bill Sublette was hurrying overland from St. Louis up the Platte and Green River route. The American Fur Company's supplier, Lucien Fontenelle, had shipped his goods up the Missouri and Yellowstone rivers by keelboat and then transferred his goods to horses for the overland route from Fort Cass. The winner would capture the entire year's catch of the Indians and free trappers. While the American Fur Company could afford to lose, the Rocky Mountain Fur Company would be bankrupted if Fontenelle arrived before Sublette.

Finally, on July 8, a long column of over eighty mounted men leading several hundred heavily-laden pack animals rode into sight from the south. They fired their rifles in a ragged popping volley and screamed war whoops as they raced their horses toward camp. "Sublette!" the Rocky Mountain men cheered and surged out to greet the caravan.

Shouting happily, Bill Sublette jumped off his horse and grabbed his brother Milt in a bear hug, then shook hands and boisterously greeted Will, Bridger, Fraeb, and Gervais.

"Welcome back from the dead, Will!" Sublette exclaimed as he clamped his hand and slapped him on the back. "Goddamn, it's great to be back in the mountains!" he shouted, glancing around at his friends.

"Whiskey?" Old Gabe whispered to Bill.

"Four hundred fifty gallons," Bill chuckled. "Got Superintendent Clark to issue a whiskey license for my riverboat men."

"Riverboat men!" Will laughed. "Since when do trappers fording rivers make them riverboat men?"

"Whenever the great William Clark designates them so." Bill winked. "Of course, a slight contribution to his favorite charity—himself—helped him decide the issue." Everyone laughed.

"Welp, don't jus' stand there, Bill," Old Gabe replied. "Tap a keg and let's git ta drinking!"

Bill ordered some subordinates to bring over the mules bearing the whiskey kegs. Then he glanced around. "Where's Fitz?"

"I was gonna ask you the same," Will said.

Bill looked worried. "He rode out from the Sweetwater to bring word of our coming." He turned and scanned the mountains he had just crossed. "Should've been here long before."

"He'll show," Bridger asserted. "Ol' Fitz is just on the wrong trail agin like he was last year!" The men laughed uneasily.

"That's right," Sublette replied as he tapped a small keg at his feet. "Maybe he done what Will done last year and stopped off fer a Cheyenne wife!" The men guffawed and nudged each other.

They spent the afternoon loafing around the camp, getting progressively drunker, and catching up on mountain and back East gossip. The sun was low in the west when they spotted two men on a horse trotting through the campsite.

"Tom!" Will shouted, and the men struggled drunkenly to their feet. Fitzpatrick rode behind one of Sinclair's trappers named George Nidever. He was haggard, filthy, scratched, bruised, and barefoot; his buckskins in tatters. And to the astonishment of all, Fitzpatrick's hair had turned white! The men gathered around pumping him with questions as he wearily dropped off the horse.

"Ran into him while I was hunting up the valley," Nidever explained. "Man's been through hell."

They helped Fitzpatrick into a teepee and crowded around him. He sat bent and slurped buffalo stew broth slowly between his teeth. After he had eaten and rested some, he explained briefly that he had run into a Blackfeet war party on South Pass. They chased him into a box canyon and he had to abandon his horses and scramble up the rimrock and then hide in a crevice while they searched for hours. After dark he slipped out and accidentally stumbled into their camp and they hunted him again until he finally escaped. Then while crossing the Green River he lost his powder horn and rifle which he had perched on a makeshift raft. He had mostly subsisted on berries but once gnawed raw meat from a buffalo carcass.

When he finished his tale, Bridger delicately mentioned that his appearance had changed some since they'd last seen him. Fitzpatrick asked how and someone handed him a mirror. When he saw his whitened hair, tears streamed down his eyes.

While they were comforting Fitzpatrick, someone with a high-pitched Eastern voice called at the teepee flap.

"Wyeth," Bill Sublette muttered with a frown. "Coming, Mr. Wyeth," he said aloud, then smiled. "Will," he whispered, "you're an educated man. Got a man I'd like ya ta meet. Fact is, I'd sure 'ppreciate it if ya could get 'im off my back fer a while, while I parlez with my partners."

"Sure," Will replied, and they slipped outside. Wyeth was gawky and reed-thin and moved in jerky motions. Lambchop sideburns framed his gaunt face. Bushy eyebrows hovered over his deep-set brown eyes. He had a long, thin nose with tiny nostrils from which hairs protruded.

"Will," Sublette said. "Meet Nathaniel Wyeth of Boston. Ice-maker, hotel-keeper, and now fur company head, and above all, man of vision." Will and Wyeth shook hands. "And Will here is not only a master trapper, but one of St. Louis's leading lawyers. Mr. Wyeth, here, has great plans for the mountains. Why don't you explain 'em ta Will here, Mr. Wyeth."

"By all means!" Wyeth said excitedly. "Integration! What does integration mean to you?" Will started to say something but Wyeth cut him off. "Global integration of a trade and production process! Fur, salmon, ice, tobacco! And that's just the start!" When he spoke his eyebrows undulated and his large hands gestured erratically. Words tumbled from his mouth in short bursts, broken by rapid suckings of air. "Vessels sometimes take a year or more to sail from Boston to the Columbia. The expenses in insurance, wages, supplies, and so on are exorbitant. The key is to make the voyage pay both ways. If ships take out trade goods and bring back dried salmon and furs, we can make an enormous profit! A barrel of salmon will fetch fourteen dollars. A thousand barrels fourteen thousand dollars! We engage the Indians of the lower Columbia to supply our salmon. At this very instant the brig *Sultana* is sailing somewhere between Boston and the Columbia. My plan is invincible."

"John Jacob Astor tried the same plan back before the 1812 War," Will replied. "What makes you think you'll succeed where Astor failed?"

"War with Britain and an unfortunate shipwreck caused Mr. Astor's bold enterprise to fail."

"You mentioned tobacco?"

"Ah, yes, Mr. Yates. I will plant a colony of settlers in the Oregon Territory which will raise tobacco and other crops to sell to the rest of the world."

"Yes, siree, Will," Sublette grinned and winked. "Mr. Wyeth here is truly a man of vision. Why, he equipped his men's muskets with bayonets and had special bright green uniforms and plumed hats made for them, and if they was ever feeling low, even taught a boy to play the bugle to raise morale. And he invented a wagon that can also be used as a boat."

"Not all of the details have worked out as I intended," Wyeth admitted ruefully. "Mr. Sublette encouraged me to leave my bugles, bayonets, and uniforms behind in Independence. I only got half of what I paid for my wagon-boats. 'Amphibiums,' some derisively labeled them."

"I'll leave you two learned men to discuss the wisdom of the ages alone," Sublette said with a sardonic grin and he ducked back into the teepee.

"Most of my inventions have been much more successful. Take, for example, my horse-drawn ice-cutter. It grates the ice surface in uniform squares which can be broken apart with cutting bars. That simple invention has reduced the cost of ice from thirty cents to ten cents a ton and made ice a leading Boston export and revitalized Boston's trade with the West Indies and Far East. My ventures here in the mountains and Oregon will be no less successful." He stared down his nose at Will. "Mr. Yates," he said with a professorial air. "Master trapper and prominent lawyer. A most unusual combination of talents." He paused for effect. "Mr. Yates, I've an important proposition to make you." Will blinked. "My enterprise could most certainly use a skilled lawyer and guide. How would you like to sign on, at say, five percent of the gross?"

"Well, ahh, I'd hafta think about it," he replied. The offer was tempting but he feared getting tangled with a greenhorn.

"Seven percent," Wyeth said seductively.

"We'll see. If you'll please excuse me, Mr. Wyeth, I must attend some duties."

"Yes, yes! By all means, Mr. Yates," Wyeth said loudly as Will shook hands and hurried away. "A man of politeness, learning, and responsibility. Just the man I'm looking for."

Once the kegs were tapped, three hundred trappers and over a thousand Indians wildly debauched away a week or so of days and nights. War whoops, drumming, fast-picking fiddle and guitar music, laughter, barking dogs, and gunshots echoed across the valley. Boisterous crowds gathered around scalp dances, horse and foot races, wrestling matches, shooting contests, hatchet tosses, tall tale sessions, hellfire and damnation sermons, and eye-gouging brawls. Squaws dressed up in their finery and paraded through camp trolling for husbands. Trappers lured away girls for quick tumbles in the woods then pressed bolts of red cloth or beads in their eager hands and thought of them no more. With a toss of the dice or turn of greasy cards, men gambled away a year or two of trapping wealth and even their women.

Trappers gobbled down flat bread baked with Missouri wheat and sweetened with Louisiana sugar, puffed clouds of Kentucky tobacco from clay pipes, guzzled African coffee to sober up.

Will and Fitzpatrick sat on a small hill relishing the orgy swirling across the plain before them.

"This rendezvous's a helluva lot wilder than that first one back in '25," Will remarked.

"Each one's wilder than the previous," Fitzpatrick replied. "More trappers and Indians gather and the suppliers bring in more goods and whiskey."

"You've been paying six dollars a plew to free trappers. That's almost double what you'll get for pelts in St. Louis. I know you gotta buy out free trappers like myself and the Indians and get American Fur Company men to switch sides. But won't you end up bankrupt?"

"No choice but to offer top dollar for pelts," Fitzpatrick replied. "We get it all back when we sell them trade goods. Prices of our goods is five hundred percent higher than what we paid for 'em from Bill, who gouged us prices four hundred percent higher than what he paid for the same goods in St. Louis."

"Thought so. You're selling goods at prices two thousand times what my family's store charges in St. Louis."

Fitzpatrick winked. "Sometimes fer more than that. Drunk Indian'll sell a year's worth of trapping for a pint of watered-down whiskey. We bought over three hundred of those spotted Nez Percé horses, Appaloosas, for not more than ten dollars a piece."

"Indians live for the moment and I'm getting that way, too."

"Enjoy it while ya kin, Will," Fitzpatrick remarked somberly. "These days won't last much longer."

"What, with all the competition?"

"That in part," he shredded a sage branch. "We're trapping out the streams. Beaver's getting scarce."

"Won't that raise prices? We'll get more for less."

"Maybe for a while. Higher the prices, the faster we'll trap 'em. Someday there might not be any left."

"That just might be."

"But demand'll dry up afore the supply. In St. Louis, I heard there's machinery now that kin make felt much cheaper than stripping it from beaver plews. And some says felt hats're losing fashion. Eastern gentlemen's switching ta hats of Chinese silk." He stared at the Tetons glimmering in the distance. "Yup," he said sadly. "Someday rendezvous and wandering the Rockies'll be no more than a memory."

"We boast of being the freest men alive," Will said thoughtfully, "but our livelihoods depend on the whims of fashion and inventiveness of tinkerers on the other side of the earth."

"Not sure what I'll do if beaver play out." Fitzpatrick shrugged. "Reckon some kinda trading. Ain't fit fer much else. Least ya gotta profession ta fall back on."

"Look there," Will said, his voice brimming with fear. They watched a group of trappers circle another one passed out in the grass. One trapper poured a small kettle of whiskey over the sleeping man and another touched him with a firebrand. The whiskey burst into flames and the man awakened screaming. The men roared with laughter as the man danced away trying to beat out the flames with his hands.

"That's sickening," Will said bitterly, recalling Judy's gruesome death. "I ain't watching anymore." He rose and turned away.

"Yeah," Fitzpatrick agreed as he stretched and followed. "Sometimes the boys get a little out of control. Let's head down to the Nez Percé camp."

As they descended the hill, Bill Sublette's voice boomed behind them, "Hold up, boys!" he shouted. They turned and watched Sublette march up to them. He held an envelope in his hand. Sublette nodded as he stepped before them. "Will, almost forgot to give you this," he said handing over the letter. "Your sister gave it to me," he said as Will opened it. He placed a hand on Will's shoulder. "You might wanna read it somewhere private," he added gravely.

Will's heart pounded. "My mother?" he asked.

Sublette nodded. Fitzpatrick mumbled his sympathy. Then his two friends left him.

With tears fogging his eyes, Will crossed the plain to a bluff overlooking the valley. He sat on a rock and watched thunderheads miles high billow across the sky, listened to distant laughter and shouting and horses whinnying from the encampment along the river. Finally calm, he broke the seal and opened the letter.

"Dearest Will, Tragically, our dear mother has died of yellow fever. She didn't suffer much. Many of her last words, prayers, and thoughts were of you. I hope you are well. This is just a quick note to hand to Mr. Sublette as he leaves this morning. Jess returned safely last autumn and we're going to have a baby! Yes, in six months you'll be an uncle! Please be careful. Love, as always, Sarah."

Will hugged his knees and broke into sobs. He crouched there, balled up, a long time until the tears ran dry and he heaved no more. He lifted his eyes to the sky. A high blanket of gray clouds now covered the earth and a chill wind gusted. Dusk darkened the world.

He gazed out over the valley and the ant-like people scurrying across the plain and among the tiny teepees. Scores of campfires flickered. Little Antelope was somewhere down there. He regretted that he hadn't spent much time with her since rendezvous began. I've gotta make things better between us, he promised himself. Tom's right. Everything'll end someday—the beaver trade, my wanderings, life itself. Might as well live day to day as fully as possible. If Little Antelope wants ta be the gaudiest squaw in the mountains, so be it.

He rose and ambled down onto the plain and into the camp. He dodged out of the way of a half-dozen Indians and trappers racing past on horseback. Stepped over drunks passed out in the grass. Nodded to acquaintances staggering past with huge grins on their faces. He paused to squint over the shoulders of four trappers playing euchre over the still body of a fifth with a dislocated neck covered with purple bruises.

"Looks dead," Will remarked.

"Oh, I've seen ol' Jim here more lively," one trapper cracked and the others burst into laughter. They all had long matted hair and scraggly beards. "Ah'll take three," he said, slapping down some cards on the man's chest. He took the cards and glanced at them. "Raise ya two," he said and pushed a couple of deer vertebrae into a large pile on the man's stomach.

He squinted up at Will. "Fact is, ol' Jim here's 'bout as dead as ya kin get. Ah jumped his ass and snapped the son of a bitch's neck when he dealt himself one from the bottom." The man giggled. "Yup, ol' Jim's done cheated his last hand." The men howled with laughter.

"Ain't he gonna smell?" Will asked disdainfully.

"No more'n when he was kicking," the trapper remarked and his companions roared.

Will grimaced and slipped away. He shrugged off the men's cruelty and tried thinking how nice it would be to curl up wordlessly with Little Antelope and just hold her tight. His teepee came into view at the river's edge in the brush and trees a hundred yards from the main camp.

Their four horses were staked nearby. Elk meat dried from cottonwood racks and the hide was stretched on a willow loop nearby. He had expected to see Little Antelope sewing buckskins or mashing pemmican or fetching firewood. But there was no one in sight and the teepee neither smoked nor glowed from a fire within. He stopped to pet his horses. As he mumbled words of endearment, he heard a male's harsh whisper and then a female's inside the teepee. His knees went wobbly and the bottom seemed to drop out of his stomach.

"Who's in there?" he demanded shakily. "Little Antelope?" As if in a nightmare, he jerked his skinning knife, hurried to the teepee flap, and fumbled with the bone fasteners. As he ripped open the flap, he heard the blackened buffalo skin at the teepee's rear tear. He burst into the dusky teepee. Little Antelope crouched away, holding a buffalo robe over her naked body and two hairy male legs squirmed through a rip in the back.

"Goddamn it!" Will screamed and dove for the legs just as they disappeared and their owner tore away through the brush. Little Antelope threw herself on Will and shouted, "No!" He elbowed her gut hard and slashed at her with the knife. The blade gashed her upturned arm and she leapt back, cowering, trembling, and babbling in Cheyenne. Will pushed through the rip and jumped to his feet outside. Quivering with rage, he listened as the brush crackled nosily far down the bank. But he saw no one.

He crawled back into the teepee and asked in Cheyenne who the man was. Little Antelope wailed and begged forgiveness. Her breath stunk of whiskey and her words were slurred. Through the dark he saw black liquid streaming from her arm. He touched it and she winced. He groped around for something with which to bind it and found a calico dress he had just bought her.

As he ripped it, a cruel sense of justice surged through him. He tightly bound her arm then asked, "Godin?" She stared at her lap and said nothing. "You are my wife no more!" he said in Cheyenne. She burst into sobs and clung to him, but he pushed her away. He waved his finger in her face. "I will never touch nor speak to you again," he said enraged, knowing his words would devastate her. "In my eyes, you are dead!" She curled up under a buffalo robe and whimpered. He quickly pulled together his equipment and loaded it on two of the ponies. Then he led them away toward the main trapper camp. He walked as if in a trance. Why? he kept demanding but nothing made sense. He turned and stared back at the teepee through the twilight. Should I forgive her? he wondered. Do I throw away everything in an instant? But he realized he could never trust her or feel the same about her after her infidelity. Now I truly am free, he realized, and stumbled away.

Will slinked through the camp feeling as if the word cuckold was branded on his forehead, that everyone already knew and derided and howled at him behind his back. He appeared at the teepee circle of the partners and quietly explained what had happened. All agreed that he was right to abandon her although Milt was dumfounded he hadn't slashed off her nose-tip before he left, Indian fashion. They invited him to spread his blankets in their midst and tried to cheer him with mugs of whiskey and funny stories.

Milt slapped Will on the back and said, "Yates, life's full a' choices and I'm handing ya one. In a few days, we're heading southeast across the desert to the Humbolt River country then north back to the Snake and Salmon. Wyeth's gonna accompany us as far as the Snake where he'll head on west to Oregon."

"Oregon," Will said quietly, and recalled the superlatives with which those who had journeyed there spoke of the territory.

"So join us, Yates," Milt snorted. "Ya kin keep on trapping with us like a real man or follow Wyeth ta Oregon and be a fishmonger. It's yer choice."

Will wanted to ask if Godin was coming, but did not want to advertise his suspicions and jealousy. "I'm with ya," he finally said, imagining himself standing on some sandy windswept shore of the Pacific Ocean gazing west into eternity.

Two passes led out of the valley's south end. One climbed east over the mountains to Jackson Hole. The other angled southwest across the low rugged mountains to the Snake River Valley. Meadows, small clear streams, and small groves of willow and cottonwood covered the upper valley.

With Milt, Fraeb, and Will at their head, over one hundred trappers, a few wives and children, and several hundred Flathead and Nez Percé straggled in a long, ragged column south up the valley toward the southwest pass. As they reached the meadows sloping up toward the pass, Will spotted riders descending into the valley from the Jackson Hole pass a half-mile away. He squinted at them. "Look!" he said, pointing.

"Who the hell'd that be?" Milt said. He pulled a spyglass out of his saddleback and peered through it. "Ain't white. Injuns. But they's carrying a Union Jack flag. And they's got travois and women and children and dogs."

"Crow?" Fraeb asked.

Milt shook his head. "Can't tell. We'll know soon enough. They's heading this way."

"Could be the Gros Ventre that shot up Bill's camp on the Green on his way to rendezvous," Will remarked.

Milt nodded. He turned and bellowed back at the column to get ready for a fight. The Indians and trappers rode cautiously toward each other and halted several hundred yards apart. A chief rode out from the band. He wore a scarlet blanket and held high a long pipe whose stem was festooned with strips of bright cloth and feathers. He trotted his pony to within thirty yards of the trappers and beckoned.

"His pipe bowl looks ta be green soapstone not red pipestone," Milt remarked. "That makes 'em either Blackfoot or Gros Ventre."

"Seems to want peace," Will replied. "They wouldn't risk a fight with their women and children beside them. Let's parlez with them."

"Kain't trust those Blackfoot savages farther than ya kin shit," Fraeb observed.

Antoine Godin and a Flathead rode up. Will began to boil with rage. He had never heard who had cuckolded him, but knew it had to be Godin. He struggled to quell the urge to step in front of Godin, shove his rifle in the bastard's face, and squeeze the trigger.

"Blackfoot?" Godin demanded. His eyes blazed and mouth scowled with hatred.

"That or Gros Ventre," Milt replied nervously.

"May be the same Blackfoot bastards that kilt my pa couple years back," Godin said fiercely. "Come on," he urged. Before anyone could stop them, Godin and the Flathead cantered out to the Gros Ventre chief.

"Killing time," Milt observed and checked the pan of his rifle. Godin and the Flathead rode along either side of the chief who continued to hold his pipe high. Godin seized the chief's wrist.

"Shoot," he hollered, and the Flathead shoved the muzzle of his rifle into the chief's ribs and squeezed the trigger. The shot exploded through the chief and hurled him off from his pony, which raced away. The Gros Ventre howled in anger and horror at the murder. The women and children fled into a cottonwood grove around which the Teton River flowed in a horseshoe, while the warriors brandished their weapons and war shields, screamed taunts at the whites, and fired their muskets and bows. Amidst a ragged volley of shots and arrows, Godin reached down and yanked off the chief's robe. Then, waving it triumphantly, he and the Flathead galloped back to the trappers.

"What the hell ya do that fer?" Fraeb yelled as Godin rode past. Shots exploded from both the trappers and Gros Ventre, and then both sides retreated to cover.

"What'll we do?" Fraeb demanded.

"Sit tight till we got reinforcements," Milt replied, then dispatched someone to carry word of the fight back to rendezvous. He peered at the cottonwood grove through his spyglass. "They's throwing up breast-works," he observed. "Logs, blankets, digging holes. We'd be crazy ta charge 'em."

Wyeth rode up and bitterly denounced Godin's treacherous murder. "That pipe was just a trick," Fraeb explained, defending Godin to Wyeth. "Kain't trust Blackfeet or Gros Ventre. Best ta kill 'em on sight."

For a couple of hours, both sides kept up a desultory long-range fire that hit no one. Finally, Bill Sublette rode up with a score of men. "Why haven't you wiped out those niggers yet, Milt?" he demanded. Milt shrugged.

"Take a look, Bill. They's holed up in that grove."

"Those're prob'ly the same bastards," Bill shouted, "that dogged me fer a week and shot up my camp and chased Fitz all over hell an' back! Let's wipe those niggers off the face of the earth!"

"How ya gonna do that?" Milt asked quietly. His face frowned with worry.

"Charge 'em." Bill glanced around. "Who's coming with us 'gainst those red niggers?" he called to Milt's men.

Will drew a deep breath. "I'm with you, Bill," he said. Soon about sixty trappers and Indians were gathered around Bill, including Fitzpatrick, Sinclair, Fraeb, and Wyeth. Milt's leg was troubling him so he opted out of the fight. Godin had disappeared. Bill and Fitzpatrick made verbal wills to each other. Bill glanced at Will. "Ya wanna tell us yer will?"

"Got nothing left ta lose except my life," he replied. "That's why I'm joining."

Bill nodded. "All right, boys," he shouted. "Let's go." He trotted toward the grove followed by the others. The Gros Ventre fired a ragged volley. Bullets and arrows whizzed all around. A ball shattered a trapper's knee and left him screaming and thrashing the ground. The other men flopped on their bellies and crawled forward. Occasionally a trapper or Indian fired at the grove. But there were no clear targets. The men scattered, most of the trappers continued to inch forward directly toward the grove or made for the low banks of the stream, while the Flatheads and Nez Percé tried to slip around the Gros Ventre position. Behind them, other trappers kept firing over their heads. The Gros Ventre ululated and fired arrows and musket balls that kicked up dust all around. Wounded horses in the grove screamed and galloped away across the valley.

Will alternately crouched and dashed forward until he dropped behind a cottonwood at the grove's edge. His heart raced and he gasped in short breaths. A cold chill shook him as he realized he was the first into the grove. He stuck his flop hat beyond the tree and several bullets and arrows whizzed past or thudded into the bark. One bullet clipped the hat's brim.

He glanced behind him. A score of trappers squirmed or dashed toward the grove. An arrow thudded into one stout trapper's stomach as he rose and flung him back on the ground where he thrashed and moaned. Sublette sprinted forward and dove behind a nearby log. He shouted behind him, "Come on, goddamned ya!"

Fitzpatrick, Wyeth, and other trappers slipped behind trees on either side. Missing several toes, Sinclair could only crouch and hobble slowly toward them. He had almost reached cover when a musket ball tore through his chest and into his lung. "Help," he gurgled.

The trappers glanced at each other. "Somebody carry him off," Bill shouted.

"I'll do it," Fitzpatrick replied. "Just keep their heads down!"

"Pin down those bastards!" Sublette hollered as he poked his rifle over the log and fired. Will and the other men popped up, fired off a quick shot, then dropped back down. Fitzpatrick sprinted back to Sinclair's side, helped him to his feet, and then dragged him off beyond rifle shot. Wyeth rose from behind a nearby log and scurried off after him. A half-dozen other trappers fled toward the rear. One trapper, his face flushed and movements dulled with liquor, gave a fierce war cry and stumbled toward the Gros Ventre breastwork.

As he scrambled atop it, two bullets smashed into his face and almost tore off his head. He toppled back heavily.

"We gotta git in closer," Sublette yelled, then ran forward and jumped behind another log. Will took a deep breath, charged, and dropped down beside Sublette. "This is some fight!" Bill shouted. The Gros Ventre sang their death songs.

"Biggest since the Rees," Will yelled back. He pushed his rifle under the log and sighted down it. Painted faces and bodies flitted behind buffalo robes and blankets stretched between trees and piled logs and brush.

Rifle barrels and arrows pointed briefly toward the trappers, then there was an explosion or twang and they disappeared. Yellow smoke drifted through the trees. He aimed his rifle toward a gap between two red blankets. A face and half a body appeared and an arrow whizzed. Will squeezed the trigger and his rifle roared. When the smoke cleared a body lay slumped between the blankets. A spasm of blood lust surged through Will and he screamed obscenities at the Gros Ventre. He groped for his ramrod then realized in horror that he had left it behind his last tree. "Goddamn it!" he shouted.

"What's wrong?" Sublette demanded as he piled up sticks and tinder.

"Lost my ramrod," he replied fiercely.

Sublette thrust his ramrod toward him. "Use mine!" Will quickly reloaded and handed back the ramrod. "Burn the niggers out!" Sublette shouted. "Fire the woods!" Sublette groped in his possible sack and extracted flint and steel. He rose slightly and began striking sparks. A bullet tore into his shoulder and he fell back to the ground. Will crawled beside him. "Bind me up," Sublette ordered.

Will ripped off Sublette's linen shirt and examined the gaping wound from which blood throbbed. "Didn't go through," he observed tersely, then tightly wrapped Bill's shoulder with the shirt. "I gotta get you out of here."

Sublette's half-closed eyes opened and he nodded. "Don't leave my rifle," he muttered.

A trapper moaned and cursed nearby and then limped away. "Keep firing," Will shouted. "Sublette's hit and I gotta take him back." Several shots exploded from the trappers. He dragged Sublette to his feet and pushed his rifle in his hand. Two arrows hissed past. Sublette leaned heavily against Will as they crouched and hurried out of the grove and across the meadow. Will suddenly realized he had left his own rifle behind. Milt, Fitzpatrick, and other trappers and Indians rose from the high grass and greeted Will and Bill as they stumbled among them. Will gently eased Bill to the grass. "Forget to duck?" Milt chuckled as he hovered over his brother.

"Yates saved my ass," Bill murmured.

"Well, thank him," Milt replied and glanced around. "Hey, where ya heading, Yates?" he called to Will who pushed away through the crowd.

"Left my rifle," he replied over his shoulder. The men laughed merrily. Will turned in anger. "Why don't you join me!" he demanded, shaming them into silence. He faced the grove. Before him, trappers were fleeing or crawling away. From across the creek, Flatheads and Nez Percé retreated, carrying off wounded and dead. Will charged forward.

A trapper fled past him shouting, "They's massacring the others back at rendezvous!" Fraeb and a half-dozen other trappers ran past.

"Henry!" Will shouted as he grabbed Fraeb's arm. "What's happening!"

"The Gros Ventre sez a bigger war party's attacking rendezvous!" Fraeb yanked free. "We gotta save the others!" he cried and ran off.

Will stood alone in the meadow. He stared, unbelieving, as the hundred or so trappers and Indian allies mounted up and galloped back down the valley. He turned toward the grove. The Gros Ventre warriors shouted taunts and dodged through the trees. Women and children and old men emerged from beyond the grove and led travois toward Jackson pass. Some limped or slumped on horseback.

Somewhere in that grove was his rifle. "Yup," he mumbled sardonically. "Just like the Ree fight." Will raised his hand toward the Gros Ventre and briefly waved it. Then he turned and ambled away.

Thick, mottled clouds blanketed the sky, making it look like the inside of a brain. Cold, moist winds gusted and died. Hugging his knees, Will sat on a rock overlooking the valley. He had been there for hours trying to make sense of things and just remembering. He watched Fitzpatrick stroll out of camp and up the hillside.

"Ya all right?" Fitzpatrick asked somberly as he sat down beside him.

Will shrugged. "Reckon." He brushed away a tear filling his eye. Fitz was a true friend.

Fitzpatrick laid a hand briefly on his shoulder. "I know how much ya loved Little Antelope. I'm really sorry about how things turned out."

Will turned and looked Fitzpatrick in the eye. "Thanks, Tom," he said quietly. "I'll get over it. Ain't just that though. It's a lotta things. A lifetime of things."

"We all got burdens to bear. They pile up like driftwood." Fitzpatrick sucked in his breath and scanned the valley. "Life ain't as burdensome out here though," he added with a smile.

"That what keeps you out here?"

He chuckled. "That's one of them." He ran this fingers through his whitened hair. "A man's got no past in the mountains. Least not much of one. You are what you are. That's it."

"Past makes a man who he is. He can't escape it. A man with no past is dead."

"True. But that's nobody's bother but his own. And there's no point wallowing in it."

"I suppose," Will said morosely.

"Ya heading west with Milt and Fraeb?"

"I dunno." He bit his lip. "I dunno what ta do about anything. Whole life's a shambles."

Fitzpatrick nodded. "Milt and Fraeb could use you. And you never know. Those boys may say ta hell with the Snake River country and head straight on to California."

"California," Will repeated and the word sang through his mind like a poem. Campfire tales of California's golden coasts and mountains whirled and echoed within. A smile spread across his face. "That's where I'm heading, Tom." He laughed triumphantly. "To the ends of the earth! California!"